Expeditionary Force Book 8: ARMAGEDDON

By
Craig Alanson

Contact the author
craigalanson@gmail.com

Cover Design By
Jeff Ross and Alexandre Rito

Table of Contents

CHAPTER ONE

Ambassador-at-large Woolsey took a pen out of the inner breast pocket of his immaculate suit jacket, then smoothed the jacket lapel so it would lie flat, without an annoying wrinkle. The pen was placed precisely parallel to the legal pad of paper, with the tip and end of the pen at the same distances from the top and bottom of the paper. Woolsey poured a glass of water from the pitcher in the center of the table, and set down the glass so it was lined up with the pen. All was properly in order. No. The pen was closer to the top of the paper pad than to the bottom. A slight nudge moved it into position, and-

"Woolsey," his exasperated colleague from Indonesia sighed, getting nods from the representatives from Brazil and South Africa. "Can we begin, or must you fiddle with that damned pen for the remainder of the day?"

"My apologies, Ambassador Irawan," Woolsey nodded toward his esteemed colleague. "The purpose of this meeting is to consider actions that were taken without proper preparation and planning. I believe *we* should not begin our discussion in a slap-dash fashion." His lips curled downward at the word 'slap-dash', as if that were the ultimate sin. With a fingertip, he nudged the pen ever so slightly.

"It is just a *pen*," the representative from South Africa groaned. She had been in enough meeting with the fussy American to know that is just the way the man was, and nothing could be done about it other than complaining.

"Very well," Woolsey interlaced his fingers and placed his hands on the table, the tips of his pinkie fingers barely touching the unmarked pad of paper. "We are here to-"

"Hey! Chowderheads!" A voice came from Woolsey's pen, and all four around the table stared at it in shock. They knew that voice.

Though he was startled, Woolsey's inner emotions were not evident in his mannerisms. He lowered his head to examine the pen from the side, without touching the traitorous device. "You are the being called 'Skippy', I presume?"

"You presume correctly. That is the only thing you have been right about today."

Woolsey saw the others were looking to *him* to converse with the alien AI. It would have been nice to think the others valued his leadership skills, but the truth was, they blamed him for bringing that pen into a secure conference room. He created the mess, he had to clean it up. "How are you speaking from my *pen*?" His composure slipped momentarily at the unforgivable loss of control. The meeting was in a conference room in the basement of a building, with no electronics present. Power to the electrical outlets had been cut off, indeed the wires had been severed. Light came from LED bulbs in battery-powered lamps on the table. Every precaution had been taken to avoid being overheard by the AI aboard the *Flying Dutchman*, yet Skippy had managed to infiltrate the secure facility. And it was

Woolsey's fault. "This is my favorite pen!" He had been given that pen by a president of the United States, nearly twenty years before. When not in use, it was kept in a locked drawer, in his office desk at home.

"Oh, I do like to keep *some* secrets," Skippy chuckled. "Don't worry, the components will dissolve into nano dust when we are done with this *delightful* conversation. Your pen will be fine."

Woolsey recovered his composure. "While we appreciate your input, this meeting is-"

"This meeting is a collection of brain-dead bureaucrats, wasting time with a bunch of blah blah buh-*lah*, while the adults are doing something useful," Skippy scorned.

"We are here to consider whether Joseph Bishop should continue in command of the *Flying Dutchman*," Woolsey stated calmly, returning to his unflappable nature. "While his inventiveness has proven to be, at least *temporarily*, useful in the past, we now face a new paradigm. Earth is safe for the next-"

"Earth is *safe*?" Skippy snorted. "This just in," he said in his best smarmy Ron Burgundy news anchor voice. "We have a breaking news flash! The good citizens of Dayton Ohio *might* disagree with you about them being safe, *duh*."

"Yes. That is hopefully a minor-"

"Seriously? You idiots represent the governments of this mudball, and you are basing your decisions on *hoping* your world is safe?"

"Regardless," Woolsey lost a tiny bit of his cool. "Bishop has proven to be impulsive and reckless. His action of stealing the *Flying Dutchman* proves that-"

"No. I'll tell you what *really* happened," Skippy's voice dripped with scorn. "The Universe said: 'I am sending two of the most powerful warships in the galaxy to blow up your planet. You monkeys not only have to stop those ships, you have to make the Maxolhx think they *did* go to Earth, found *nothing* interesting, then disappeared under circumstances that are not at all suspicious. Oh, and even if by some miracle you succeed, in less than sixty years, aliens will discover your local wormhole is not really dormant anyway. The Universe asked: What do you ignorant monkeys think of *that*'?" Skippy paused to let that sink in. "You useless ninnies ran around flinging your hands in the air, like a little girl who got a bee in her hair, screeching '*We surrender, we surrender*'! You know what Joe Bishop said?"

Skippy didn't wait for an answer.

"Joe Bishop said: Hey, Universe: *Hold my beer*."

There was silence around the table. Heads bowed slightly. Perhaps they were considering what the alien AI had said. Perhaps they were just a little bit ashamed.

"So," Skippy made a sound like he was taking a breath. "Any questions?"

CHAPTER TWO

I managed to swing my legs through the hatch, and get into Skippy's new escape pod mancave without wacking my head. Until I sat in the too-small seat, and wacked my head on the too-low ceiling anyway. Before I could speak, I noticed a new decoration attached to the far dome of the pod. A gaudy, white leather belt with gold decorations. "Uh, what's that?"

"It's a gift from Brock Steele, Joe. It arrived on the supply ship this morning."

"Uh, what do *you* need with a belt?"

"Ugh," he sighed. "You are *such* an uncultured cretin. Look at it closely, knucklehead. Hey! Don't *touch* it with your filthy monkey hands!" He screeched.

"Ok, it's a white leather belt. So?"

"It's not *a* white leather belt, numbskull. That is an 'Egyptian' belt that Elvis Presley wore in concert, with one of his famous jumpsuits."

"Oh. Was that during his 'Fat Elvis' period?"

"If you can't talk respectfully about the King of Rock and Roll, you can right leave now." Man, he sounded genuinely pissed at me.

"Sorry. Like you said, I'm an uncultured cretin. Huh. You mean this isn't a reproduction? This is the real thing?"

"Of *course* it is!" He gasped. "Do you think Brock Steele would send me a fake as a sign of his undying admiration for me?"

"I guess not. How did *he* get it?"

"He's a billionaire, Joe."

"Yeah, you keep reminding me."

"And a fighter pilot."

"Uh huh."

"Astronaut, too. Also he was just named People Magazine's Sexiest Man of Year, *again*. Plus, there is a rumor, which I can confirm by the way, that Brock will receive the Presidential Medal of Freedom, for his heroic actions during the Dayton Incident."

"Hero- What?" I sputtered. "The Merry Band of Pirates saved the freakin' day, all he did was-"

"Joe, Joe, Joe. This continued jealousy is not-"

"*Jealous*? Skippy, I met the guy. He puts his pants on one leg at a time, just like I do."

"Sure, except millions of women around the world would love to get those pants off him. Meanwhile, your shower thinks the two of you should see other people," he giggled.

"Crap. Can we drop the subject?"

"You started it."

I had lost track of the conversation, but I was pretty sure he had started the snarkiness. As if that mattered. "It is a very nice belt, and the Merry Band of Pirates are proud to have it aboard our ship."

"Hm," he sniffed. "That's better. What do you want to waste my time with now?"

"I want to know how your project is going."

The fake innocent tone in his voice did not fool me for a second. "How is what going, Joe?"

"You know what I mean, you little shithead. Can you really finish putting Nagatha back together again?" Since the revival of our ship's AI, it had been a slow process bringing her back to full operation. Three times, she had to go temporarily dormant to prevent her matrix from deteriorating, while Skippy made adjustments to the kludged-together, mismatched collection of alien components that comprised the substrate she lived in. Nagatha was still officially optimistic that she would, or *could*, be restored like she was before she nearly sacrificed herself for a mudball infested with filthy monkeys.

By the way, 'a mudball infested with filthy monkeys' was how *Nagatha* recently described Earth, which shows that she was still not yet back to her kindly, polite personality.

"Put her back together again?" Skippy answered slowly. "What, you think she is Humpty freakin' Dumpty?"

"Uh-"

"Seriously, what's up with *that*? Why would anyone think *horses* could help fix a broken egg? They're horses. They don't even have thumbs, *duh*."

"Hey, *I* never said that."

"Ugh, you monkeys are idiots."

"It's just a nursery rhyme, Skippy. Stop avoiding the question. Yes or no?"

"It's complicated."

"No it is not. *Yes*, or *no*?"

"Fine. The answer is yes."

"Great! Then-"

"Sort of."

"*Sort of?*"

"It's kind of a 'shmaybe' thing, Joe."

"If you are trying to screw with Nagatha, I am not just going to touch that belt, I'm going to *lick* it."

"You *wouldn't*," he shuddered with horror.

"Uh huh. And then I'm going cut that Velvis out of the frame, and use it as a towel after I shower. I'm going to rub it *all over* my filthy monkey body."

"Yuck. I am locking the door to my mancave from now on."

"Answer the question."

"Hmmph. Now you've insulted me. Maybe I don't feel like answering."

"Mmm, that belt looks *really* tasty." I made a show of licking my lips. "I wonder what flavor it is?"

"Ok, Ok! Do *not* get anywhere near that belt. Or any of my other precious stuff. All right, here's the deal."

"The deal?"

"It's an expression, Joe. Like I *tried* to tell you, it is complicated. I am totally legit about making my best effort to reinstall Nagatha exactly the way she was. There are two issues with that task. First, her matrix changed after she downloaded herself into the DeLorean, and then when she had to compress herself to survive inside the crappy computer of the *Dagger*. So, even if I could rewind her back to the way she was, all of her experiences during the incident would be lost. She does not want that."

"Ok. I can see that it is legit. You have to make adjustments. What else?"

"*She* wants to make changes to herself. Remember when I reloaded myself back into my canister after Zero Hour, and I had an opportunity to optimize my matrix? Nagatha now has the same opportunity. Instead of randomly stuffing herself into nooks and crannies of the available substrate, she is optimizing her own matrix. *She* is doing it, Joe. I am giving her advice, but the decisions are her own."

"Oh," I relaxed back against the seat. "Will she be able to do it?"

"Sure, Joe. No problemo. It will take time. Um, and it's not going to be a completely smooth process. She will be operating under reduced capacity for a while. Also, while she is tweaking her matrix, she will experience periods of reduced or impaired cognitive function."

"Impaired? Oh, shit. Do you mean we're going to hear from a *drunk* Nagatha?"

"I would describe it as more high than drunk, but-"

"Is she going to be waking me up at zero dark thirty to marvel at the freakin' Universe, like you did?"

"*That* never happened," he sniffed.

"I have video."

"Let's not argue about this," he said quickly. "I do suggest that if Nagatha contacts you, and you judge that she is impaired, you be kind to her."

"Oh. Sure thing."

"And not laugh at her and complain about being woken up, when she is wondering about her place in the cosmos and trying to share a freakin' *moment* with a friend, you know?"

"Uh-" Crap. Skippy *did* remember drunk-dialing me in the middle of the night. And somehow, he thinks *I* am the jerk. I pushed myself off the seat, being careful not to bump my head again. "I'll tell the crew to be extra nice to her."

"Hey, before you go, can you tell me something? Would you really have licked that belt?"

"I guess we'll never know," I answered smugly.

"Crap. Now it's going to bug me."

I did feel a little bit sorry for him. "I can tell you that I was *not* looking forward to finding out what Sweaty Elvis tastes like."

As I turned to squeeze through the too-small hatch again, Skippy made a sound like clearing his throat. "Hey, Joe, is everything Ok with you?"

"Yeah, sure, why do you ask?"

"You are spending a lot of time moping around the ship. This is the third time this week you have visited me in my mancave. Not that your visits aren't just *delightful* for me," he made a gagging sound.

I crouched in the passageway so I could look at him. "I'm bored, and kind of waiting for the other shoe to drop, you know? Since we got the ship mostly fixed, I don't have much to do. I'm worried the Army will reassign me dirtside. Being down there for the Congressional hearing about the Dayton Incident was bad enough. *That* was two weeks of my life I'd like to get back." The hearings had been closed-door classified briefings, where I had to testify before five different committees or subcommittees, whatever the difference is. Plus I was debriefed by the Army, the Secretary of Defense's office, UNEF Command, and a separate UN commission appointed specifically to investigate the near-disaster at Dayton. That last one was the worst. I learned that, once appointed, United Nations commissions pretty much never went away. Eighteen nations had people getting paid by the UN to investigate, and those bureaucrats planned to ride that investigation into a comfortable retirement.

"UNEF Command is still debating what to do," he grumbled.

"Yeah. Well, enjoy your Elvis memorabilia, I'm going to the gym. Or something."

Skippy called me the next day, while I was in my office doing nothing useful. Most of the ship was on lockdown while Skippy got the auxiliary reactor warmed up for restart, so I was confined to the forward part of the *Dutchman*'s crew section. "Joe, I have good news, great news, and news whose suckitude has reached previously unexplored levels of suckiness that until now, were largely considered only theoretical. Really, this is a privilege, as we will be breaking new ground in the exciting scientific field of suckitude research. Think of it as an expansion pack for suckiness, for after you have completed all the levels in the basic game."

"Oh, joy. Do we have to pay for this expansion pack?"

"Ha!" He chuckled. "You will be *paying*, that is for sure, buddy."

"Crap."

"Bad news first, as usual?

"No, I've had a rotten day already. Tell me something good to cheer me up, before you give me the beat-down."

"Ok. Don't say I didn't warn you. The good news is- Wait, I should tell you all this is still unofficial. You might call it gossip. Even I am not supposed to know this yet, I got the info from conducting surveillance on the United Nations and associated staff."

"That is called spying, Skippy, not gossip."

"Huh. Then what is gossip?"

"Gossip is when you tell *me* what you discovered."

"Ah, got it, thank you," he laughed. "Hey, before we dish about the juicy gossip, should we put on fuzzy slippers and get a half-gallon of ice cream out of the freezer?"

"Let's not, and say we did."

"Probably a good idea. Anyhow, Becky heard Susie say she saw Tamika pass Johnny a note in Algebra class and-"

"Whoa. *What?*"

"I was trying to make it dramatic, in the spirit of good gossip, Joe. You never let me have any fun."

"I am truly sorry." Sometimes it was best to play along with him. "Wow, I did not know Tamika and Johnny were an item. What did the note say?"

"Well," he lowered his voice to a conspiratorial whisper. "The note said the UN has decided that, with the recent threat from the Kristang attack on the homefront, we need to send the *Flying Dutchman* back out, to conduct a recon mission."

"Huh. Hey, did anyone in the UN hurt themselves from making such a forehead-slappingly obvious decision?"

He chuckled. "They are all under concussion protocol, Joe."

"So, that is the good news?"

"Yes. The *Dutchman* will go out, while the *Dagger* stays here as a gunship, to protect Earth."

"Makes sense," I agreed. Our newly-captured Kristang warship was technically a troop carrier like the *Yu Qishan*, but the *Dagger* had been substantially modified to serve as an assault transport. It had extra missile launchers, stronger shields, and a railgun for orbital bombardment. The *Dagger* had a decent chance of protecting Earth from minor threats that originated on this side of the local wormhole. "What about the *Qishan*?"

"That is the *great* news I mentioned, Joe! The *Qishan* will be modified to be a colony transport ship. We will hopefully need to transport colonists soon, because the *Dutchman* is going out primarily to scout for a beta site. The recon mission is actually a secondary objective."

"Wow, this *is* great news." The beta site, a place where humans and human culture could survive, if Earth was enslaved or destroyed, had been my backup plan during our Renegade mission. To tell the complete truth, finding and setting up a beta site had been my *primary* plan, because I did not think we had a realistic chance to destroy the pair of Maxolhx ships that were on their way to Earth. *And* find a reason for the Maxolhx not to be suspicious of their ships disappearing. *And* find a reason why the Maxolhx should not be interested in sending more ships to Earth. Of all our impossible missions, that had been the worst.

Offering the prospect of a safe beta site was intended kind of a consolation prize for the people of Earth, if the *Dutchman* had been forced to limp back to Earth and report we had been unable to stop those two Maxolhx ships. Despite me committing mutiny and stealing humanity's only starship.

The possibility of saving maybe a couple thousand humans from the utter destruction of our homeworld was, I had to admit, a crappy consolation prize.

But it was better than a fruit basket.

"How long will it take for the *Qishan* to be modified? The *Dutchman* should be ready to fly again in-"

"Oh, we're not waiting for the *Qishan*. As you know, the interior of Kristang troop transports is rather spartan, it would be very uncomfortable for colonists. Now that Earth is not in imminent danger of destruction, we can't expect colonists to be packed into the ship like sardines, so it could take a year to bring the accommodations up to human standards."

"Seriously? Going to a beta site will not be a freakin' pleasure cruise."

"True, however, I can see the point to making the journey marginally more pleasant. The biggest problem will be providing artificial gravity, so colonists aren't puking the whole way. Kristang ships don't have artificial gravity, and the *Dutchman* no longer has docking platforms to provide a gravity field. We will need to construct a docking platform anyway, so while the monkeys down there are furiously bashing coconuts together to make the crude components I need to refit the *Qishan*, the *Dutchman*'s mission will be to scout potential beta sites."

"*And*," I emphasized, "to conduct a recon, so we can be sure Earth is safe."

"Well, yes, but, um, you kinda screwed yourself there, Joe. Our Renegade mission was *so* spectacularly successful, the UN is not concerned about further threats from the Maxolhx. The purpose of the recon will only be to determine whether there are any more Kristang ships parked at the edge of this solar system, stuffed full of hateful frozen warriors who want to cause mischief. We will *not* be hitting up any Maxolhx data relays for info. The UN is preparing mission orders, that authorize you to contact *only* a Kristang relay station."

"Ok, fine, whatever," I could live with those restrictions. "We learned about the Maxolhx sending ships to Earth from a *Ruhar* data relay anyway. So, the good news is the *Dutchman* will be going back out, and the great news is we are to find a beta site. What is the super-ultra-mega craptastic news?"

"Remember when you were thrilled that the UN assigned Count Chocula to micromanage your every decision?"

"Oh yeah, that was wonderful. Wait, is he coming with us again?" I asked hopefully. Not hopefully because I wanted someone constantly looking over my shoulder, but because Hans Chotek was at least someone I knew. Plus, during our time aboard the *Flying Dutchman*, and on various planets throughout the Orion Arm of the galaxy, including the year we spent stuck inside the Roach Motel, we had developed a kind of grudging understanding and respect for each other. The fact that he planned how to plunge Kristang society into a vicious civil war not only earned my respect, it sort of drew us together. We both knew that when we returned home, Hans Chotek the career diplomat would catch hell for sparking an alien civil war. And that I would catch hell for a whole lot of things I did because, well, that's just my life. So, that shared experience allowed us to rub the rough edges off each other, and work pretty well as a team.

"Yes, Hansie will be coming along on our scouting mission," Skippy confirmed. "He will be one of the civilian leaders of the long-term survey team, if we find a good candidate site."

"Uh huh. Did the UN choose him because they respect his experience and judgment, or because he's now an embarrassment and everyone wants him away from Earth?"

"The second one," he announced gleefully.

"So, if we find a site that looks good, Chotek will be staying there with a science team, while the *Dutchman* flies back to Earth to report?"

"Good guess, yes. The UN is authorizing six months maximum for the total mission. It will take longer than that to assure a candidate site is really safe for human habitation. If we identify a prime candidate, the science team will remain there while the *Dutchman* flies back to Earth to report our findings. A second mission will bring more scientists, and get updated on what the initial team found. It is still being debated, but the UN has been advised they should not plant a permanent colony on any world, until it has been observed for two full cycles of seasons. That is, two of the planet's years, however long that is."

"That makes sense. Ok, then there is no rush to get the *Yu Qishan* refitted for human passengers."

"Correct."

"Wow, so far your bad news sucks a lot less than I expected."

"Dude, you haven't *heard* the truly bad news yet. I said Chocula will be *one* of the civilian leaders. Because he is not in good favor with the United Nations, they are sending not one, not two, but *three* other bureaucrats to join our Magical Mystery Tour! Isn't that exciting?"

"Shit. Who are these three Stooges?"

"Oooh, good one, Joe. I will call them The Stooges from now on. Their profiles are on your laptop. Have fun reading!"

I read the profiles, which I could tell Skippy had supplemented with his own opinions and highlighted the areas he thought I needed to know. Chotek was from Austria, so I should not have been surprised to learn the Stooges were a woman from Japan, a guy from Algeria and a woman from Peru. The military arm of the Expeditionary Force was no longer limited to the five nations the Kristang originally chose to send offworld, but the UN still had to be careful to spread authority around the globe.

I was *so* looking forward to welcoming my new bureaucratic overlords. Not.

Skippy spoke as soon as he saw I had finished reading the report. "You do know the problem with sending the ship back out to scout potential beta sites, right, Joe?"

"Like, we don't know if that is actually possible?"

"You got it! Man, the UN is going to seriously be *pissed* at you, if they discover this whole beta site concept is just a bunch of bullshit you threw together, to distract from your numerous and flagrant screw-ups."

"Yeah, I know," I sighed. My proposal had been to find a habitable planet that was not already occupied by an intelligent species. By 'habitable' I mean it had to be able to support human life on the surface, including the ability to grow food humans could eat. As a practical matter, to encourage people to move to the beta site, the planet had to be not only habitable, it had to offer reasonably pleasant living conditions. There could not be an over-abundance of dangerous predators, parasites, and other hazardous native organisms. Candidate planets had to be far enough away from an active wormhole that current star-faring species could not get there, but because *we* needed to get there, a dormant wormhole had to be reasonably close. Oh, also, aliens could not even know that humans lived at the beta site, until the population there was well-established and had at least a hope of defending themselves from hostile aliens. As Skippy reminded me, no single planet could hope to fight off the entire galaxy, but if we gave the beta site strong defenses, aliens would hopefully decide that punishing one faraway planet full of mischievous monkeys was not worth the price they would have to pay. To delay the time when radio signals from the beta site reached another inhabited world, the beta site ideally should be a thousand or more lightyears from alien planets, military or scientific outposts, or relay stations.

All those conditions seemed simple enough, until Skippy analyzed the Elder wormhole network in the Milky Way galaxy, and determined that many of the wormholes that were currently dormant, might become active in the next wormhole network shift. That frightening bit of info wiped out the majority of potential beta sites within our home galaxy.

Skippy had done the math on candidate sites in the Milky Way, without revealing his results to UNEF Command, and the results were discouraging. Areas of the galaxy that were isolated as we needed, were thin on habitable planets for a good reason. Either the entire region had been sterilized by the radiation from the supernova collapse of a giant star, or conditions in the region had not been favorable for the formation of Earth-like planets in the Goldilocks zone. So, although Skippy had said encouraging things to scientists on Earth, he was pessimistic when he talked with me privately about it.

I was not so discouraged by his results, because my hope had always been for us to locate a beta site outside the Milky Way, in one of the satellite galaxies or star clusters. There were two problems with that idea. First, Skippy had little information about conditions beyond the edge of the Milky Way. What information he had was from observing starlight that was reaching us now, and that was seriously out of date. For example, the Fornax Dwarf galaxy was almost half a million lightyears away, so the light we were seeing now from stars there left its source four hundred sixty thousand years ago. Skippy warned that, in that span of time, an intelligent species could have developed technology and occupied every corner of the star clusters within Fornax, and we wouldn't know that until our wimpy space truck emerged from an Elder wormhole there.

That is the *other* problem. Skippy knew from querying the wormhole network that no current active wormholes connected beyond the Milky Way, and he did not know if he had the ability to reactivate dormant wormholes that connected way out there.

He didn't even know if they *could* be reactivated.

Because the hope of finding a beta site was the difference between me riding a desk in some windowless office, or commanding a starship, I kept quiet about how slim our chances were of locating a refuge, where human could live without fear of being wiped out by hostile aliens.

The other reason I didn't tell the whole truth, is because it *was* possible we might actually find a good candidate site.

But mostly I kept quiet because of the first reason.

CHAPTER THREE

Three days later, I was in my office when an old friend walked in. We hadn't seen each other since we left the ship at the end of our endless mission that rescued the Expeditionary Force on Paradise, started a Kristang civil war, got stuck in the Roach Motel, and then saved Paradise from a bioweapon. After we both left the ship, I had basically been under house arrest, and we had only spoken on the phone once. With people from both of our governments listening to that one conversation, we hadn't been able to do much more than talk about the weather.

"Good morning, Colonel Bishop," Chang greeted me with a salute. He didn't need to, because we didn't salute aboard the ship, and because he also was now a full colonel.

Instead of returning the salute, I stood up and offered a handshake. "Hello *Kong*," I used his first name. "It's good to see you!"

We shook hands, and he replied "Hello, *Joseph*," with a huge grin.

"Call me Joe, please," I laughed as we sat down. "I am only called 'Joseph' when my mother is angry with me." I tapped an icon on my tablet to order two coffees brought from the galley. That was something I almost never did, but it was a nice perk of being a colonel. We talked for half an hour, mostly about our families, then got into recent events.

Lowering his voice with a glance at the open doorway, he asked "Would your president really have gone through with a nuclear strike on Dayton?"

I took a sip of coffee that had gone cold, because I needed to think of the proper way to answer. Chang was a trusted colleague and a friend, but he was also a military officer of a foreign power. He was asking me for details of a sensitive military operation, and I was still sort of on probation for committing mutiny and stealing a starship. The US Army would not be happy to hear I was discussing actions of the National Command Authority with anyone.

I should have politely declined to answer, but, fuck it. A professional career officer would have politely declined. I am a mustang colonel and a Pirate. Kong and I had been through a *whole lot* of shit together. Plus, you know what? With the ever-present threat of alien invasion hanging over our heads, if we monkeys couldn't stop arguing about bullshit that didn't matter, maybe we didn't deserve to survive.

"What would *you* have done, if the Kristang were in," I only knew the names of two cities in China, and they were both much bigger than Dayton Ohio. "A mid-size Chinese city, and the lizards were about to capture a wormhole controller?"

"We would have done what was necessary," he replied, looking down at his empty coffee mug. It wasn't something either of us wanted to think about.

I hadn't actually answered his question, so I added "Skippy told me the launch order was with Cheyenne Mountain, and they had already tasked two birds at Minot, when we jumped the *Dagger* into orbit." I shuddered when I felt a chill run up my spine. Flight time of a ballistic missile from North Dakota to Ohio was mere minutes, especially on a depressed-trajectory shot. If we had arrived a few minutes later, all we would have seen below us was a mushroom cloud, where a

Midwestern city had been. "We would have done what was necessary," I said. If he was going to report our conversation up his chain of command, I figured it couldn't hurt that I had confirmed America's steadfast resolve. "Enough about the past," I waved a hand to dismiss the unpleasant subject. "I hear you will be commanding the force at the beta site, assuming we find a suitable place out there?"

"Yes," his face broke into a smile. "Under United Nations civilian leadership, of course."

"Of course," I agreed. We both knew that, if the beta site found trouble, Chang would be in command. "The mission could last six months. Is your wife?" I left the rest unsaid.

"She warned me," he wagged a finger like his wife was scolding him. "Not a single day more. Joe," he pronounced my unfamiliar name awkwardly. "She thought I was dead. My whole family did. She doesn't want to lose me again. But, I think in a way, she had gotten used to the idea that I wasn't coming back. It took us months to get to know each other again."

I nodded, one soldier to another. "I know what you mean. Adams and I were talking, like Earth didn't feel like home anymore. Like we didn't belong here, we didn't have anything in common with the people down there."

"It took a while. Give yourself time, it will come back," he assured me. "You have spent too much time up here."

"That wasn't by choice," I said with a shrug.

"It is now. This mission should be a simple recon, you don't need to go out there."

His comment surprised me, and I couldn't help raising my eyebrows. "Do *you* want command of the *Dutchman*?"

"No," he snorted. "No offense, but, I was an artillery officer. If I wanted to be stuck inside a tube for months, I would have joined the submarine service. No, I like the idea of exploring a new world, helping humanity set up a backup site, but I don't want to be," he rapped his knuckles on the bulkhead, "in this tin can any longer than I have to. I like to look up and see the sky above me."

"Yeah," I agreed wistfully. "I hear you about needing more time dirtside, I've been thinking about it." That was the truth. I had even discussed a potential temporary assignment with the Army. The idea of taking the *Dutchman* on a dull recon mission did not appeal to me, not after the non-stop excitement of the past years. But Skippy was not certain he could even get a wormhole to connect outside the galaxy, and he wanted me to come with him. Setting up a beta site was my idea anyway, I needed to see it through. "If we find a good candidate site out there, I will give someone else the chair. The last thing I want is to haul trash back and forth to a beta site. Hey," a thought just hit me. "Will you be my XO again, on the outbound leg?"

"Thank you, but, no," he declined. "I will be busy enough preparing for landing and setting up a survey. You are thinking about handing the chair to someone? Let them take a turn as your first officer."

"You turned me down, and Simms did the same thing yesterday. Adams doesn't want the job, and the UN won't let a gunnery sergeant serve as executive officer anyway. I have a list of candidates," I nudged a stack of paper folders on the corner of my desk.

He looked at the stack, which was more than a foot tall. "Good luck with that," he laughed. He knew the tough part of choosing an XO was the international politics involved. That was why the UN had allowed me to give an opinion of who should get the assignment, they wanted to blame me if some country's favorite candidate was not selected.

Politics. I hate politics.

He picked up both our coffee mugs and stood up to leave. "I see the United States believes we won't find any trouble out there on this mission."

"Huh?" I had no idea what he meant.

He pointed to my rank insignia. "You are no longer wearing *war* eagles."

"Oh," I automatically touched the silver eagle that was the insignia of a colonel. The eagle was clutching arrows in one talon, and olive branches in the other. Normally, the eagle's head was turned to face the olive branches, symbolizing that America preferred peaceful solutions. During World War Two, and after Columbus Day, colonels had been issued 'War Eagles', with the head turned to face the arrows. I had worn my war eagles since I was promoted to colonel on Paradise. Recently, I had been supplied with new insignia with the head turned the other way, toward a peaceful future. The Army did not anticipate, and did not want, any conflict with aliens. Considering my experience fighting aliens with vastly superior technology, I agreed with that hopeful sentiment.

But I also knew the Universe might have a different idea of how the future would unfold.

"Hello Colonel Tammy!" Skippy's voice boomed out of the speakers in the hydroponics garden, raising his voice to be heard above the sound of pumps and fans. The cargo bays used for growing food were normally quiet places, but the tanks had been cleaned and were being set up for growing another crop of fresh food.

"Skippy," she replied without looking up from the tomato seedlings she was planting. "You know I hate being called that."

"Why?" He asked innocently. "It is your name."

"Tammy is my *first* name, and I haven't used that name since I was old enough to talk. I was named after my mother's aunt, and I never liked that name, or my great-aunt. Please use my middle name like everyone else does."

"Ok," he sulked. "Colonel Jennifer."

"Just Jennifer, Ok? I'm busy," she was irritated that the AI was interrupting the half hour she had to herself. "What do you want?"

"Well, I checked the roster, and I see that Frank Muller is coming with us to search for a beta site."

That got her attention. She set down the box of seedlings and looked up at the speaker. "Yes, he is. Why do you care?"

"Oh, come on, girlfriend, give me the scoop about this guy. Is-"

"You and I are not girlfriends, and I'm not telling you about my private life. What we-"

"Please, I already know plenty from your social media posts. And from the location data of your phones, I know the two of you have been living together since-"

"You have been *spying* on me?" She was outraged.

"No. Um, I'm guessing there isn't anything I can say that would make me look good?"

"No there is not. You can't *do* that, Skippy. It's bad enough that you watch everything we do aboard the ship. When we go dirtside, we are *off duty* most of the time."

"I'm sorry," he said, sounding completely miserable. "I just don't want you to get hurt."

"What?" She looked up again, startled. "Skippy, thank you for being concerned about me, but I'm an adult. I can handle my own life. Frank is a good man. He volunteered to search for a beta site, so we wouldn't be apart for six months. I wouldn't be going without him."

"Well, if it makes you feel any better, everything I know about Mister Muller tells me he is a good guy. I wish the two of you the very best."

"Thank you. No more spying, is that understood?"

"Um, yes, except there is something I should tell you."

She sighed. "What is it?"

"Frank got a gift that he plans to give you, after we land on a potential beta site planet. I don't quite understand monkey social rules, but I think you might be embarrassed if you don't have a gift for him?"

"Ooh, yes. I would. Darn it, I'm not scheduled to go back down to Earth before we leave."

"You probably don't want to know what he got for you?"

"No, I want it to be a surprise."

"Ok. If you like, I can suggest several gifts that he might like, based on his internet search history. I can have something discretely shipped up here."

Jennifer Simms decided that having an AI watching her might have one advantage, which still did not balance the downside. "Send the list to me."

"Hey, Skippy," I called him, while leaning back in my chair and bouncing a rubber ball off the ceiling of my office.

"Hey, Joe," he snapped, irritated. His avatar had its hands on hips as it shimmered to life. It was a bad sign that he was already pissed at me, before he knew what I wanted.

"Wow." I let the chair pull me upright, and tucked the ball in a drawer of my desk. "What's got you wound up already?"

"*UGH*," he really put a lot of effort into his utter and absolute disgust at whatever was bothering him. First, his heartfelt, exasperated sigh. Second was the eyeroll, and he did a great job of making his avatar roll its eyes back so the whites were showing, I appreciated that little attention to detail. Finally, he performed a combination shoulder-slump and knee dip that would have earned him a Ten from the judges at the Exasperation Olympics. "The Three Stooges have been driving me freakin' crazy, Joe! They are not even aboard the ship yet, and I am already hating life. Just this morning, they-"

"Uh huh," I popped into my mouth a chocolate, that I had noticed when I opened the desk drawer. From the slightly chalky taste, it has been hiding in the back of that drawer since our SpecOps mission. The caramel at the center was so hard, I had trouble chewing it. "Ignore them," I suggested. Or, I tried to say that, but it was hard to talk with my mouth full.

"What?" He glared at me. "I couldn't understand a single word you said."

"Sorry," I tucked the candy to one side of my mouth. "I said, ignore them."

"Ig- *ignore* them? How, pray tell, do you propose that I-"

"It's simple. When they talk, you don't listen."

His disgust was now directed at me, which I suppose was progress. "That's easy for you to say, monkeybrain."

"I know you listen to almost everyone and everything aboard the ship. How about you throw together a submind to listen to them, and alert your higher conscious only when the Stooges have something actually important to say?"

"Huh," the avatar froze, a sign that he was too busy thinking to control the hologram. "That's Ok for me, but, and I can't *believe* I am saying this, doing that would put me in a moral quandary."

"Uh, what?" My surprise was not much that ignoring three bureaucrats might have moral implications, because I kind of didn't care about that. What surprised me was that Skippy was apparently thinking about the effect of his actions on others.

"See?! I knew learning that empathy crap would come back to bite me in the ass."

"Having empathy makes you a better person."

"Really? Really, Joe? Think about this; if Genghis Khan had worried about 'empathy'," he pronounced the word with disgust, "would he have conquered most of Eurasia? I don't *think* so."

"Um, laying waste to half the world is maybe *not* the best criteria for-"

"He was living up to his potential, Joe. Being the best bloodthirsty barbarian he could be. Isn't that people are supposed to do, become the best version of themselves? I saw that bullshit on an inspirational poster somewhere."

"Uhhh-" Shit. Why does my mouth get me started on arguments I can't get out of? So, I did the cowardly thing and tried to change the subject. "Regardless, you did study about empathy and it's now making you worry about other people, so what's the problem?"

"The first problem does not involve 'people', Joe. I would feel terrible for any poor innocent little submind that I assigned to listen to those three morons. The submind would curl up in a ball and die of boredom and despair."

"I didn't think subminds had emotions."

"They do, if they need emotional processors to perform their tasks, *duh*. Deciding whether to alert me about some inane request from the Stooges requires a subjective decision, so the submind would need to understand and analyze human behavior, including emotions."

"Oh. Sorry."

"If you mean sorry for your ignorance, then apology accepted. Speaking of which," he sighed and his avatar face-palmed itself. "If I ignore our honored guests, I would have to apologize to *you*, you big knucklehead."

"Uh, what? Why?"

"Because if I ignore them, those three morons would bring their complaints to you, and pester you to death."

I shrugged. "Ok, no problem."

"To quote you, 'Uh, what'? How is that not a problem for you?"

"Skippy, I *want* those puffed-up bureaucrats to focus their outraged indignation on me. I say, bring it on." Too many times, the people saying 'bring it on' are just playing tough guy, because they know someone else will have to pay the consequences. My father told me not to let my mouth write checks that someone else needs to cash, that was great advice. When I said 'bring it on', I meant it. "Listen, Skippy, I am captain of this ship. We could be stuck with these three jokers for six months," that was the maximum time the UN would allow the *Dutchman* to be away from Earth. "I need to work out an agreement with them about how much crap I'm willing to take, and I'd prefer to do that sooner rather than later. So," I took a deep breath. "Ignore them unless it is something truly important, and let them come to me with their complaints. Then *I* can ignore them," I leaned back in my chair with satisfaction.

"Seriously, Joe?"

"Seriously. I am not going to push them off on someone else, like my second-in-command."

"This ship doesn't have an executive officer right now," he reminded me.

"Yeah, I know. I'm working on it. We will have an XO before we leave, and I do not intend for the Stooges to pester whoever that is. So, are we cool?"

"We cool," he offered me a tiny fist to bump, and I did. "Mm hmm," he cleared his throat.

"What?"

"You called *me*, Joe."

"Oh, yeah. I want to know how you're doing on this epic opera you are creating, about your bromance with Brock Steele."

"We did not have a *bromance*, Joe."

"Are you kidding? I'm surprised you two don't have a gift registry set up at Crate & Barrel."

"*Ooooh*," his avatar almost had steam coming out of its ears. "That is not-"

"Truly, I'm happy for the two of you. I feel sorry for *Brock*, but he got himself into-"

"That is not funny!"

"I bought candlesticks for you two, by the way. Hope you like them."

"Why are you still jealous of Brock?" He tilted his head with genuine interest. "I thought the two of you were cool now?"

"Yeah, we're cool. He is a good guy," I admitted. "Anyway, what's the deal with your opera?" I wanted to know, because I had foolishly promised him that I would attend the opera if he was ever able to get someone to perform it.

"The opera is called 'Homefront', and it is about our unexpected adventure here, not just about my admiration for Brock."

"It was a *disaster*, Skippy, not an adventure."

"Same thing," he dismissed me.

"The president authorized a nuclear strike on Dayton Ohio. That is not an '*adventure*'."

He dipped his knees and made a 'W' with thumbs and index fingers of both hands. "What-eh-*VER*. You know what I mean, dumdum. Anywho, I have found a sponsor for my opera," he sniffed haughtily. "We are currently seeking a suitable venue, a conductor, and-"

"Um," I was afraid to ask the question. "Your sponsor. Do they *know* they are sponsoring this transformational work of art? Or did you rip off a crime syndicate in some troubled part of the world?"

"Yes, they know they are sponsoring the opera, you cultureless cretin. And, they are enthusiastic about it," he sniffed.

"I am sure there was a furious bidding war to sponsor this opera," I dug a thumbnail into my palm to keep myself from laughing. "Who is the lucky winner?"

"I am pleased to say my *very* prestigious sponsor is," he paused for dramatic effect. "The Greater Sheboygan Metropolitan Area Cheese Council."

"The *cheese-*" I tried to conceal my snort of laughter as a gasp of surprise. "Why would they-"

"They're desperate for publicity, Joe. Duh. Come on, try to keep up."

"Well, I-" I think my thumbnail had drawn blood. "I am very happy for you. Uh, when will we be treated to the premiere?" I was hoping to be offworld, in a Kristang prison or dead at that time.

"Not until we return from scouting for a beta site, obviously. No way can I leave something this important to a submind."

"Well, then, I hope we find a beta site soon," I assured him. And by 'soon', I meant 'never'. "Ok, we've got Chang, we've got Simms, we've got Reed signed on. We're getting the band back together, Skippy!"

"What about-"

"Do not jinx it, beer can!" I interrupted him. "I'm working on it, Ok?"

CHAPTER FOUR

Gunnery Sergeant Margaret Adams stood in the hot sunshine, at the Expeditionary Airfield of the Marine Corps Mountain Warfare Training Center, waiting for a V-22 Osprey to land. In the Sierra Mountains of California, the air was dry but it was still hot, and the acrid smoke of wildfires to the northwest were creating a haze in the otherwise clear air.

The awkward-looking tilt-rotor aircraft was flaring for landing, its giant propellers rotating to the vertical position, and the unique sound thumped on her chest like a drum. After it touched down, it taxied over in front of the hangar and the engines cut off with a low-pitched whine. The major in command of the unit called everyone to attention, and Adams looked straight ahead, as the side door opened and Lieutenant Colonel Smythe stepped out to acknowledge the crisp salutes of the assembled Marines.

"Major Dobrynin," Smythe gave a curt nod to the Raider commander, then strode forward to stand in front of Adams. "Gunnery Sergeant?" He asked, a mildly puzzled look on his face. "Why have you not donned your kit? It was my understanding the exercise would commence immediately," he said with an irritated look at Major Dobrynin. Smythe hated ceremony, and he hated the idea of troops standing around waiting for him.

"Sir, I," her eyes darted to the Marine Raiders assembled to her left side, all properly dressed for a field exercise in the mountains. She was wearing a dress uniform, her medals shining in the sunlight.

Dobrynin answered for her. "Gunnery Sergeant Adams has not qualified for the Raiders," he explained. "That is a prerequisite for-"

"*Bollocks*," Smythe interrupted. "That means 'bullshit' to you Yanks. The United Nations placed the Special Tactics Assault Regiment under *my* command," he tapped the STAR unit patch on his uniform. "I will decide who is and is not qualified for my unit. Is that clear, Major?" He knew he was being unfair to a dedicated officer, but he simply did not have time for any nonsense. The Kristang attack on Wright-Patterson Air Force Base had come as a total shock to the world, and proved that no one knew when or where the next crisis would erupt. The only thing Jeremy Smythe was certain of was that there *would* be another crisis, and STAR was the sharp end of the spear. He needed to get teams up to speed as quickly as possible, and if that meant bruising some egos along the way, so be it. Without waiting for Dobrynin to reply, he turned his attention back to Adams. "Gunnery Sergeant, you are out of uniform. Get out of that ridiculous prom dress and meet us," he realized he didn't know the plans for the exercise. "Er, where is your armor stored?"

"I will show you, Colonel," Dobrynin offered, with a gesture to a waiting line of trucks.

"Very well. Adams, meet us there. Major, I have not been here in several years, and there were three meters of snow on the ground back then. I believe the trailhead for Wells Peak is around ten kilometers up that road?" he pointed up the mountain behind the hangar.

"Approximately, yes," the Major acknowledged.

"Excellent. The team will *carry* their armor, plus full kit, to the trailhead," Smythe said, knowing full well how much Kristang armor weighed. "Gunnery Sergeant, do you think you can manage that?"

Adams's eyes narrowed with determination. While serving with the Merry Band of Pirates, she had carried heavier loads on her back, and carried them farther than a mere stroll of ten klicks. "Hell yes, Colonel."

Smythe gave her a curt nod, then allowed Dobrynin to lead him into one of the waiting vehicles. "Major, a STAR team fights in powered armor, that is the only way we can even the odds up there," he gestured toward the sky with an index finger. "In a mech suit, experience counts for more than any other factor. Your Raiders may be supremely fit and trained, but that does not mean they know how to fight with the assistance of alien technology. We will see how Adams does, hmm?"

Adams joined the Raiders for the exercise, which ranged far and wide across the Training Center. She was just as fast at scaling mountains and running the obstacle course, and- No, that wasn't right. She was significantly *faster* than the others, because she instinctively knew when to let her suit computer control the motions of her legs, and almost as important, she had learned to trust the alien equipment. In the live-fire portion of the exercise, she scored in the top ten percent for accuracy.

"Excellent work, lads," Smythe said without thinking, forgetting his teams now included women. "Gunnery Sergeant, how are you holding up?"

Adams popped the faceplate of her helmet and swung it up, exposing her face to show she was not even breathing hard. "A walk in the park, Sir," she said with a tight smile.

"Let's have a bit of fun, shall we?" His face broke into a rare grin. "Adams, do you think you could tussle with the lads a bit?" He stepped back. "Perhaps three of them?"

She reached up and swung the faceplate down with one hand, then eyeclicked to engage the suit's semi-autonomous hand-to-hand combat mode. That was a feature Skippy had recently added to the suits, to give his pet monkeys better odds of surviving close encounters with advanced aliens. "Ready when they are, Colonel."

Knowing the honor of his Raiders was on the line, Dobrynin selected his three Marine Raiders most skilled at hand-to-hand combat. Having seen them in action, he was fully confident of a pleasing demonstration for the STAR team commander.

Three against one, all wearing alien powered armor. Three supremely fit and trained special operators, at the top of their professions.

It wasn't even close.

After she tossed the last Raider thirty feet in the air back over her shoulder, Adams popped her faceplate again. "Sorry, Colonel. I'm a little rusty."

"That sounded like an excuse, Gunny," he said sternly with a glare. Then Jeremy Smythe actually *winked* at her, an action that astonished them both. "The *Flying Dutchman* is going back out. Supposedly, this mission will be a pleasure cruise, but we all know that is wishful thinking.   Adams, if you're interested, we would be honored for you to join a STAR team."

Her powered arm came up in a crisp salute. "I wouldn't miss the party, Sir."

Adams knocked on the door frame to my office, two days later. Fortunately, I was actually doing work, and not playing video games. That she knows of. She had come back aboard when I was busy in a meeting with UN officials, so I had not been able to greet her in the docking bay. I was thrilled to see her again.

Thrilled because she was a vital member of the Merry Band of Pirates, and not because of other reasons that are forbidden and unprofessional and I'm not supposed to even think about.

My life sucks.

"Good morning, Gunnery Sergeant," I greeted her. Right away, I noticed the STAR Team Alpha patch on her uniform. "Congratulations," I pointed to the patch.

"Oh, this?" She downplayed the honor. "It impresses the locals dirtside, I guess."

"It impresses *me*, Adams. What's on your mind?"

"What makes you think there is anything on my mind, Sir?"

"You've got that look on your face like I'm in deep shit about something, only I don't know it yet."

"I do not have any look like that," she protested.

"You are a woman, correct?"

"*Fine*," she huffed. It was cute. No, it was adorable. Except I was her commanding officer, so it was emotionally neutral as far as I was concerned.

I hate my life sometimes.

"Spit out, Gunny."

"I got a notice today that you've been busted back down to Sergeant, from Staff Sergeant? I thought you got the Army to acknowledge you are a colonel. You *told* me you would be commanding the beta site mission, Sir."

"It's-"

"We *talked* about this, Sir."

"There is a-"

"I gave a whole speech about being proud that you grew a pair," she scowled at me. "Sir." The 'sir' did not sound as respectful as it was supposed to.

"If you will let me explain, Adams?"

She folded her arms across her chest. "I would love to hear it."

"Ok. My JAG lawyer arranged for me to accept an Article 15 punishment, for mutiny and stealing the *Dutchman*. The last one is technically for 'unauthorized use of government property'," I rolled my eyes.

"Article 15? We Marines call that Non-Judicial Punishment a 'Ninja Punch'. What do you mean, you accepted?"

"They made me an offer, and I said Ok. It was better for everyone than a court-martial. Really, I got off easy. Reduction in rank back to E-5, and I have to surrender the colonel's pay I received during our Renegade mission. The part that really sucked was, before the hearing, Skippy hacked the audio system and played the theme to 'Law & Order'."

"Yes!" He broke into the conversation. "And I was *bitterly* disappointed. It wasn't anything like the show at all! The whole thing dragged on waaaaay more than an hour, and there were no dramatic courtroom speeches, or twists that totally change the plot. Plus, the lead detective did not make one decent wisecrack! Such a waste of my time."

"There was no detective, you moron," I swatted a hand through his avatar.

"There should have been! It still would have been watchable, if the perp got the death penalty, but the military justice system totally failed on that one."

"Thank you, Skippy, please go away," I asked while waving my hand through his avatar, because I knew that annoyed him.

"*Fine*," he said in a huff, and winked out.

"So far, this sounds like bullshit, Sir." Man, I could tell by the way her jaw was clenched that she was not happy. Not happy with *me*.

"Come on, Adams. The Army could not let me commit mutiny without consequences. I'm a soldier, not a cowboy."

"You're a *Pirate*, Sir."

"You know what I mean."

"This doesn't sit right with me. It won't set right with the crew."

"The Army may have failed to take your feelings into account," I teased her.

She did not get the joke. Her eyes narrowed. "After our unexpected battle on the homefront, you told me the Army acknowledged you as a colonel."

"Process, Adams. It's a *process*, we had to go through the formalities. I was officially punished by being busted down a rank, and forfeited part of my pay. That's the official administrative notice you received. What you have not received yet is that, the same *day* I got busted down to E-5, the Army promoted me to colonel that afternoon. Not a theater rank. I am an O-6 for realz now," I tapped the silver eagles on my uniform.

"But they had to bust you down first?" She shook her head.

"The Army is a team, Adams. It is also a bureaucracy, one of the biggest. The wheels turn slowly, and they only turn in one direction. What matters is, they *did* turn, and I'm not in jail, or back on the block. My JAG lawyer did a great job for me. She also got the Army out of a jam, so it was a win-win. Plus, she negotiated for me to get combat pay during our Renegade mission, so the difference isn't much. My parents were just keeping the money in a bank anyway."

"I thought you told them to spend it?"

"Did your parents spend the pay you sent home?"

"No," she admitted.

"Well," she sighed. "Amazing."

"What?"

She shook her head in amazement. "You committed mutiny, and got away with it. Not only got away with it, you got a *promotion*. While I was stuck on Earth the whole time."

"You had better food," I made another try at humor.

"I missed all the fun."

"If it makes you feel any better, my lawyer said that if the Kristang had not surprise attacked us at Dayton, I would probably have been discharged, or been forced to retire. All was not forgiven, Adams."

"That does not make me feel better, Sir. How many times do you have to save the world, before you get a break?"

"We, Adams. *We* saved the world."

"I wasn't with you."

"You missed *one* mission out there, and you *were* with me for our battle on the homefront. And by 'we', I meant the Merry Band of Pirates. This is not a solo act. The Pirates are a team, and I am damned proud to be on this team. Anyway," I stood up, stretched, and yawned. "Now you know the story."

"Is your promotion official, like, you wear colonel's eagles when you go dirtside? Or do you still have to play along with the cover story?"

"I-"

"That cover story is wearing *real* thin, Sir. Like, you can see right through it. Nobody believes the official story anymore."

"UNEF is doing the best they can, Gunny. We all saw the news stories." Despite attempts at censorship, there was no way UNEF Command could prevent people from seeing the destruction in Dayton Ohio. By now, everyone on the planet had seen Kristang dropships attacking Wright-Patterson, and how the hell could politicians explain away those facts?

That was easy for people who lie for a living. The public had also seen the *Flying Dutchman*, which according to the official cover story was still a Thuranin-controlled ship, blast the attacking dropships out of the sky. Then they saw the *Ice-Cold Dagger to the Heart*, a Kristang starship, firing against Kristang warriors on the ground. Presto! The official cover story was that the Kristang who attacked Wright-Pat were a rogue group, who were dealt with harshly by our allies, the Thuranin and Kristang authorities. That bullshit tale actually strengthened the original cover story, at least for a while. "The answer is, I get to wear a colonel's uniform dirtside. My promotion is not a secret."

"How the hell is the US Army explaining that?"

"Simple," I shrugged. "My promotion is officially a publicity stunt to please the Thuranin, because of some unspecified and still-classified action I took during the homefront battle."

"Damn," she laughed.

"See? The cover story about me even has the advantage of being mostly true."

"Amazing," she laughed again. "That cover story about you won't last, you know."

"You're probably right."

"This is insane. Fucking politicians are covering their own asses."

I had to agree with her, up to a point. The original cover story, to explain the *Flying Dutchman*'s arrival, was that the Kristang who ravaged Earth were an unauthorized rogue group, who were wiped out by our loyal patrons the Thuranin. The force sent to fight on Paradise had been bravely fighting alongside our honorable Kristang allies, until the treacherous Ruhar attacked, and now UNEF-Paradise was cut off from Earth. The *Flying Dutchman* coming and going was explained as them taking humans aboard on training missions. There were three reasons why the cover story said we were still allies of the Kristang. First, because no politician wanted to admit they had been wrong to ally with the Kristang, and send over a hundred thousand soldiers offworld to fight for our real enemies. My thought about Reason Number One was: fuck them. If a bunch of politicians lost their cushy jobs, or even got thrown in jail, I would not lose any sleep over it. So, why didn't I just ask Skippy to reveal the truth on the internet?

Because of Reasons Two and Three. Two was that the public would panic if they knew hostile aliens were coming to wipe out humanity sooner or later, and our only defense was a beer can and a prayer. Right now, the public thought we had the incredible technology of the Thuranin protecting us from the big bad Ruhar, and from rogue groups of Kristang. The public could *see* the *Flying Dutchman* in orbit, like looking at the International Space station. You could see a moving dot of sunlight shining off the *Dutchman* with the naked eye, and a pair of binoculars or a cheap telescope was all you needed to see the outline of our still-massive ship. For evidence of how the Thuranin were protecting us from the cold, cruel Universe, all the public needed to do was trust their own senses. No Ruhar ships had raided our homeworld since that fateful day when Kristang chased them away. The public had seen a Thuranin star carrier punishing the Kristang who treated Earth so harshly. And just recently, when a rogue group of Kristang conducted a surprise attack against Wright-Patterson Air Force Base, they had been stopped by a Thuranin ship *and* a Kristang ship. Clearly, humanity continued to benefit from our political leaders' wise decision to ally with our saviors, the Kristang.

I had to admit, the cover story was reasonably believable.

What I really cared about was Reason Three: the UNEF troops on Paradise. Because of the cover story, family and friends of people stranded on Paradise had at least some hope their loved ones would be coming home, eventually. Someday, the politicians declared, our powerful Thuranin patrons would break through the Ruhar blockade around Paradise, and rescue the Expeditionary Force.

The Merry Band of Pirates knew that hope was one hundred percent bullshit. The people on Paradise were never coming home, never even going to know Earth was not a radioactive cinder. But, false hope was better than no hope at all. It would be cruel to reveal the truth to the loved ones of the people who would never come home from Paradise. Knowing the truth would also be dangerous, because people on Earth would not accept reality, and would push their leaders to do *something*, even though doing anything to help people on Paradise would risk the lives of everyone on Earth by exposing our secret. People in general do not like to hear hard truths, and politicians get elected by telling people what they want to hear, even if the voting public *knows* the politicians are lying to them.

Sometimes I have to agree with Skippy that we monkeys are so stupid, it's a miracle we're still alive.

Anyway, Reason One keeps politicians in cushy jobs, but Reasons Two and Three were keeping our society stable. We need a stable, productive society with good morale, if we are going to build advanced defenses based on the technology Skippy was sharing. So, to assure the safety and continued survival of the human public, we needed to lie to them.

For now.

Adams was right, the cover story was wearing thin, too many people knew the truth. Eventually, it was all going to blow up in our faces, and we would have to deal with the consequences.

Life was so much simpler when I was carrying a rifle in the Nigerian jungle.

Back in my office after a hard workout in the gym, I plopped down in the chair. "Hey, Skippy. Got a question for you."

His avatar appeared, wagging a scolding finger at me. "You mean '*I* got a question for you'."

"Uh, sure."

"Ugh. Really, you should have said 'I *have* a question for you'."

"Are you going to correct my grammar all day, or listen to my question?"

"How can I understand your question, if you don't speak clearly?"

"Blimey, excuse me, there, gov'nor," I said in my best English accent. "I am bloody well chuffed to be speaking the Queen's English with you."

"Ugh. Don't do that, Joe. Your fake accent is offensive."

"Ok. Here's my question, then. The cover story bullshit about the Merry Band of Pirates is going to break down at some point-"

"The cover story is already more worn-out and threadbare than some of your underwear."

"Hey, my underwear is just getting broken in."

"Some of your shorts are so see-through and full of holes, that my bots have to wash them by hand so they don't fall apart."

"Like I said, just getting broken in."

"Ugh. Why did I have to pick *you*? Adams and Desai were also in that warehouse on Paradise. *They* take good care of their clothing. I could even have picked Chang if I-"

"Seriously? This is about laundry? I'm trying to ask you an important question."

"Fine. Ask away," he sniffed. "Don't blame *me* when you open your underwear drawer, and all that's in there is a sad pile of lint."

"I will try to contain my disappointment. Anyway, when the cover story gets blown and the truth is out there, people are going to panic. There could be massive civil disruptions, and dealing with that takes away resources we need to build defenses to protect Earth."

"Correct. That is good long-term thinking, Joe," he added, surprised.

"Thank you."

"Except for, you know, the whole building-defenses-to-protect-Earth part. No way can a single planet defend itself against the entire galaxy. That is a total fantasy. A gigantic waste of time."

"Our Renegade mission ensured that no aliens will come here for a couple hundred years, but eventually, our secret *will* be exposed. What do you suggest we do, just wait to be destroyed?"

"Um, no. How about you monkeys use your limited resources to build a really big sign in orbit that says 'HUMANS OVER HERE' and point it toward Mars?"

"Your support is an enormous source of comfort to me, Skippy."

"Hey, maybe *you* should study this empathy crap. Because I'm done with it."

"My question is, how can we convince the public that, instead of panicking, we should all work together? We need to have a convincing argument ready for when the cover story gets blown, and not try to make one up on the spot."

"Ok, Ok," he mused. "Again, good thinking, I am impressed. Hmm, let me think about this. Well, there actually is a science to persuading people to your point of view. Aristotle's work titled 'Rhetoric' outlined the path toward persuading an audience. He delineated Ethos, Pathos, and-"

"Wait. *Ethos* and *Pathos*? What do the Three Musketeers have to do with this?"

"Ugh. I did not say 'Athos' and 'Porthos', you moron. It's not the Three Musk-"

"And Aristotle didn't write the Three Musketeers," I stated, proud of my knowledge. "It was written by a French guy named Dumbass."

"Dumas. His name was *Doo-MAH*! Oh, you are *such* an ignorant cretin," he sobbed.

"Ok, whatever," I stopped myself from rolling my eyes. "Anyway, what did this Aristotle guy say?"

He sighed. A deep, weary, heartfelt sigh. "Does it matter?"

"Not really, but you wanted to talk about it, so-"

"Ugh. Forget it. You want me to use my extensive knowledge of psychobabble bullshit to cook up a scheme, that will manipulate the public so they don't panic when they learn the truth about the Pirates, the Thuranin, Paradise, all that?"

"Yes. Except instead of 'psychobabble bullshit' you could say 'understanding of human interactions'. And instead of 'manipulate' you could say 'inform' or 'assure'."

"How is any of that different from what I said?"

"It isn't. It just sounds better, when we have to sell your idea to the idiots at UNEF Command."

"Oh, got it. I first have to manipulate one smaller group of idiots into accepting my idea, to prevent a much larger group of ninnies from panicking and burning down your planet?"

"Something like that, yeah?"

"This is going to be fun. Not."

"Hey, if being incredibly awesome were easy, anyone could do it."

He tilted his head at me suspiciously. "Was that you trying to manipulate me?"

"Of course not. Um, if it was, did it work?"

"The only reason I will do this, is I feel sorry that you are *so* pathetic."

"Uh, thank you?"

"I will create a submind to work on the problem while we're away. I need someone to run my businesses anyway."

"Your totally legit businesses, that will not get me in any trouble at all, right?"

"I thought you didn't want to know about any of that, Joe."

"Can we pretend that when you talked about your businesses, I was drunk, or strung out on heroin, so I didn't hear you? That will get me in less trouble."

"Deal. Anything for you, Joe."

Still in my office, I was working on my laptop, and I was *not* playing Super Mario Kart, so don't listen to any lies about that no matter what Skippy tells you. Desai knocked on the door frame, and I looked up with what I intended to be a delighted grin.

She was standing in the door with arms folded across her chest. "I met a man."

"Um," I didn't know what to say. "You met a man with seven wives?"

"What?" That at least changed her expression from a scowl to a bewildered stare.

"It's a poem, or something like that. About St. Ives?" My grandfather used to recite his own version of that poem. 'As I was going to St. Ives, I met a man with seven wives. Of course, the seven wives weren't his, but here in France, that's how it is'.

My grandfather always got a good laugh at that version.

My grandmother was *not* a big fan.

"I get it." She lifted an eyebrow. "St. Ives. It's a children's rhyme."

"Um, people usually start with 'Hello' or 'Good morning'," I suggested.

"I just flew up from India. It's the afternoon there."

"Ok. Good afternoon, then. So, you met a man. I assume this isn't some random guy? He means something to you?"

Her shoulders lifted as she took in a deep breath, and as she exhaled she unfolded her arms. I took that as a good sign. "Yes. Our parents introduced us."

"Is this an arranged marriage thing?" As the words left my mouth, I wished I could take them back.

"No," she laughed, letting me off the hook. "It was an arranged blind date. He's a doctor."

"Your parents must be happy about that."

"My parents are both doctors. So, yes."

I knew that about her family. Her father had been a doctor in the Indian Army, and her mother was, some kind of doctor I couldn't remember. It was in Desai's personnel file, if I cared to look up that info. "Does that make you happy?"

"That he is a doctor? It doesn't matter. *He* makes me happy."

"Then, I'm happy for you?" I should not have said that as a question.

She came into my tiny office and sat down. "You may think this conversation is a bit odd."

It was my turn to laugh. I leaned back in my chair, hands behind my head. "Major, you know what is going on with Nagatha?"

"She is officially the ship's control AI now?"

"Yes. I meant, what happened to her, you know, out there. During the Dayton Incident."

"Not all of it," she admitted. "Just the official version."

"The official version left out all the good parts. Anyway, she almost died, if you can say that about an AI. We made Skippy promise to rebuild her exactly as she was, and he really is doing the best job he can, but she wanted to make changes to herself. While she is adjusting her new matrix, or whatever the hell she's doing, she is experiencing, uh, 'cognitive anomalies'."

Desai groaned. Everyone who had been aboard the ship while Skippy optimized his own matrix, remembered being woken up by Skippy the *Drunk*-nificent sounding like he had downed a whole bottle of tequila, or swallowed a bunch of psychedelic pills. "She can fix it?"

"Eventually," I nodded. "Until then, Skippy is monitoring how she manages the ship. She woke me up at zero four thirty this morning to, well," I decided it was embarrassing enough that I shouldn't tell Desai about it. "Let's just say that the conversation you and I are having is the *least* odd thing I've experienced this morning."

"Good." She shifted in her chair, uncomfortable.

The gap in conversation made me uncomfortable too. "You, uh, didn't fly all the way up here to tell me about your social life?"

"No, Sir," she looked relieved that I wanted to get to business. "You requested me to return to the ship as chief pilot."

"I can't think of anyone better for the job."

"I can think of a hundred people more qualified. But," she let out a breath, directed upward to blow her bangs out of her eyes. "We've had this argument a hundred times already."

"You know my superhero identity is," I made a Superman gesture like tearing my shirt open, "Stubborn Man, right?"

That made her smile. "I thought you were No Patience Man?"

"I multitask. Do you want the job?" I asked hopefully.

"No." She looked away, in the way that people do when they know they have disappointed you. "Not again. Sir, I originally left Earth with the Expeditionary Force because I thought we were going to the stars to protect Earth."

"We *all* bought that line of bullshit from the Kristang," I said bitterly.

"Yes. Then I signed up for our second mission, because I thought it would be a quick, simple mission."

"Uh, excuse me?"

"All we needed to do was to find an Elder communications node, so Skippy could contact the Collective, then we could go home. The whole landing on Newark and stopping the Thuranin from sending a ship to Earth was unplanned."

"Major, we must be remembering that differently. UNEF Command sent us out on a suicide mission. They never expected us to come back, after Skippy kept his promise to take the local wormhole off its wake-up alarm."

"*You* never expected us to come back, Sir. The rest of us had more faith."

"Ok."

"Then, I agreed to one more mission, because all we needed to do was verify the Thuranin were not replacing the surveyor starship we blew up. Instead, we had to stop the hamsters from giving Paradise back to the Kristang, launch a black operation to start a Kristang civil war, then find a way to fix Skippy before he hit Zero Hour. And rescue Paradise *again*, from a Kristang bioweapon."

"Ok." I knew she was making some sort of point. "So we're overachievers?" I suggested, attempting to lighten the mood with humor. It fell flat.

"Even the second mission took much longer than expected."

"Well," it was my turn to shift uncomfortably in my chair. "We did have to spend time on Newark, while Skippy rebuilt the ship."

"The third mission took almost two *years*," she was not quite glaring at me, but it was close. "Now you want me to sign on with the Pirates again? Sir, after the Ruhar raided Earth on Columbus Day, I put my life on hold, so I could help defend Earth. To protect my family. When we came back, against all odds, I wanted nothing more than to start a normal life, like everyone else. A relationship. Eventually children, before my mother despairs of me ever giving her grandchildren."

"Your brother and your sister both have children," I noted, thinking that would make her feel better.

"Yes, they do. That makes my parents even *more* eager for me to settle down."

"Oh. Sorry."

Her expression softened. "Don't you want a normal life, Sir?"

"Yeah. Of course. Someday. Major, I can certainly understand why you would decline to sign up for another mission with the Pirates-"

"I didn't say that."

"Uh, what?"

She smiled. "I decline the opportunity to be chief pilot again."

"Oh."

"Colonel, I understand Chang and Simms are going to this beta site, to land there and stay for a while?"

"That's the plan. When we get to planets that are potential beta sites, Chang will be in command of the military security force for the survey team. Simms will handle logistics. She wants to get back to her specialty. Why do you ask?"

She cocked her head at me. "Because," she said slowly, "the *Flying Dutchman* still needs an executive officer."

Duh. If there was an award for Clueless Jerk of the Year, don't bother applying, because I have that sucker locked up. "Oh. *Oh*. Hell, Desai, that's a great idea!" When I heard both Chang and Simms were going on our search for a beta site, I first assumed one of them would serve as my XO, at least on the outbound flight. They both informed me they would be far too busy with their actual assigned tasks, and would not have time to perform the time-consuming administrative duties of an executive officer. Adams had been acting as temporary XO while the *Dutchman* was taken apart, until the Kristang attacked out of nowhere. Because she is a Gunnery Sergeant, it would take a waiver for her to serve as first officer, and anyway she told me to forget that idea. She was going to be way too busy training and working with the STAR team. So, I had been reviewing a flood of candidates sent to me by UNEF Command. I was busy reading those files when Desai walked into my office. It only *looked* like I was playing a video game, to avoid making a decision. "You've got the job."

"I haven't applied yet, Sir. I have a couple of questions first."

"Fire away."

"This mission is just a simple recon? We check out several places that are beta site candidates, drop off a survey team, and fly back to get UN approval?"

"That's the plan," I nodded a bit too vigorously in my eagerness. "If we identify a site that looks good, we stay there maybe a couple months, while the survey team pokes around, collects samples, that sort of thing. Then, the survey team remains on site, while we bring data back here for the UN to wring their hands about. If they approve, we go back out, bringing a much larger science team, plus people and gear to begin setting up a colony. If they don't like that site, we go back to retrieve the survey team and start over."

"No side missions?"

"No side missions, except to stick our noses into a Kristang relay station, to learn if there are any more surprise groups of frozen lizards floating around beyond Pluto. To keep us, really *me*, out of trouble, we will have *four* UN commissioners aboard, including Count Chocula." Despite our new-found respect for each other, I couldn't help using Skippy's disparaging nickname for Hans Chotek. "They will all be looking over our shoulders every moment. Besides, our cover story for the Maxolhx isn't scheduled to be delivered until much later."

"It *sounds* good," she said in a way that meant the opposite. "It sounds simple. It sounds nice and safe."

"It is safe. Safe as we can be, anyway. Look, Desai, the whole point of a beta site is that it will be the safest place in the galaxy, or beyond it. We will be exploring sites that are safe because aliens *aren't* there, they can't *get* there. Hell, based on what just happened here on the homefront, going out with the *Dutchman* may be safer than staying on Earth."

"We really are not going out there looking for trouble? Just to find a colony site?"

"That's the plan. You have my word on it."

"It's not your word that is the problem, Sir."

"No?"

"No. You may have good intentions, but, I know you. You are a trouble magnet."

"Me?" I acted like I was shocked by her accusation. "If we find trouble on this mission, or it comes looking for us, then we get the hell out of there. Any place with trouble is not a good candidate for a beta site."

"Again, it all sounds good."

"You need time to think about it? Maybe discuss it with your new," it did not seem right to say 'boyfriend'. "The new guy in your life?"

"No. We talked about it before I flew up here. I discussed it with my parents also. One last offworld mission." She paused, as if trying to make up her mind. I knew her. She was a pilot. She had her course planned before she flew up to the *Dutchman*. Her hesitation was not about indecision, it was about acknowledging the emotional significance of her words. One last mission. Last. She might never leave Earth's solar system again. For her, our mission to find a beta site might be the end of an era. "If you want me as your executive officer, I would be honored, Sir."

"The honor is ours." I stood up and held out a hand for her to shake. "Welcome aboard, *XO*."

She shook my hand, relief showing on her face. "Thank you, Sir."

"When can you start?" I asked anxiously. "The *Dutchman* is scheduled to have the main reactor back to full power in five days. Then we need test flights to shake down the ship, and work up the new crew. Ah, damn it, then there's all the crap we need to load aboard for the recon mission. We have to-"

"Sir?" She held up a finger. An index finger, in case you were wondering. "Don't you need to get permission from UNEF Command to sign me on as XO?"

"No," I grinned. "Technically, maybe legally yes. But they know I am Stubborn Man. And this is *my* ship, damn it," I rapped my knuckles on the bulkhead. "I stole it fair and square, *twice*. Right now, I'm in good favor with UNEF Command. That could change quickly, so I'm glad you came to me now. We'll get the paperwork started."

"I don't want to cause any problems for you."

"My guess is, UNEF Command will be thrilled to hear you will be XO. You are an experienced Pirate, and selecting you avoids all the bullshit political jockeying between nations to get one of their own favorites in that position. Speaking of which, you know what your first task will be as XO?"

"Yes, Sir," she sighed. "Recommending a new chief pilot."

"See? You're ahead of the curve already. So, when can you start?"

"Today. Give me a couple hours, I need to go see Skippy first."

"Skippy?" I wondered what she wanted to talk with the beer can about, that she couldn't say over the phone from India.

"Yes." The smile was gone from her face. "My uncle became involved in a cult."

"Oh shit," I facepalmed myself, and spread my fingers to look at her with one eye. "Club, Major. It's a *club*, according to Skippy."

"Yeah, well, my uncle left his job to seek out the Holy Skippyasyermuni in Tibet, and he spent a lot of his savings wandering around up there with a group of other followers."

Every morning, I had to update a report on the progress Skippy was making to unwind his cult. It was going slowly. UNEF Command said they understood he had to go slowly, to avoid drawing attention to his still-secret existence, but they were constantly pestering the shit out of me about it. "Ok, listen, uh, you should talk with Adams before you visit Skippy. Her parents got involved with Skippyasyermuni. They kind of had a different experience, because her parents magically got their house paid off. Technically, all records that the mortgage ever existed were lost. Her parents *gained* money out of the deal, but Adams is still pissed about it, and she gave Skippy a verbal beat-down."

Her eyes widened with surprise. "She made Skippy re-establish the mortgage?"

"No," I laughed. "Adams isn't stupid. She made Skippy send a notice to her parents, that an anonymous donor had paid off the mortgage, in gratitude for Margaret's service, or something like that. The point is, her parents understood their good fortune had nothing to do with Skippy's sketchy cult. Everyone is happy, except Skippy." Of course, somehow he was pissed at *me* about it, even though it had been all Adams's idea.

The smile returned to Desai's face. "I will talk with her first, thank you."

CHAPTER FIVE

Skippy's avatar shimmered to life on my desk without warning. "Ooooooh, I am *so* mad right now."

The ship was scheduled to depart Earth orbit in thirty-six hours, and I did not want to hear about any more problems. "Crap. What is the problem this time? The ship-"

"Dude, please. I put the ship back together perfectly. There are no problems."

"Uh huh. Except for this squawk list," I glanced at my laptop. "Which currently contains twenty-eight critical issues, thirty-seven issues that are merely life-threatening, and-"

"I know, I *know*. Working on it."

"All of which must be fixed within the next eighteen hours, so we can conduct a Flight Readiness Review before we break orbit." The FRR meeting was something I had been dreading for a month.

"I said, I *know*. My bots can only work so fast. Every important item on that squawk list will be taken care of, well in advance of this pain-in-the-*ass* meeting. We can conduct running repairs on the other items as we fly, we have plenty of spare parts. Ugh, the idea of sitting in a meeting while a bunch of screeching monkeys question *my* ability to get this ship-"

"If it makes you feel any better, I have to sit in the meeting too."

"It does *not* make me feel better, because you will be in a corner playing games on your tablet, while I have to endure endless moronic questions about-"

"Hey, this is all your fault, you know. *You* told people how awesomely incredible you are, so now you have to live up to the reputation that you gave yourself. I just have to be a lovable doofus, because *I* have successfully managed expectations."

"I hate you *so* much, Joe."

"Uh huh. So, if you're not mad about the ship, then what is the problem?"

"I got screwed over, Joe," he was fuming. I mean, he must have modified his avatar's program, because wisps of steam were rising from its ears. Sometimes he took things too literally. "Remember I told you about the group that is sponsoring my epic opera?"

"Yeah, sure. The Milwaukee Cheese Appreciation Society, something like that?"

"Close enough. I *thought* my sponsors were a reputable organization, but-"

"But," I burst out laughing. "You found out they are," I laughed so hard I was choking, "kind of *cheesy*?" Delivering the punch line made me blow a snot bubble out my nose. That made me laugh more.

"Oh," he did an ironic slow clap. "*Bravo*, Joe. You are so clever. Not."

"Sorry," I mumbled as I blew my nose. "They didn't cough up the money as they promised?"

"That's the problem," he grumbled, looking sheepishly down at the desktop. "I should have read the fine print. They never promised any money. What they offered was an 'In-Kind' contribution?"

"What does that mean?"

"As a practical matter, they stuck me with a whole warehouse full of cheese. What the hell am I supposed to do with that?"

"Um, sell it, maybe?"

"Nobody wants a warehouse-load of stinky cheese," he said disgustedly.

"Stinky? Oh, like it's Roquefort, something like that?" My knowledge of cheese was sadly lacking.

"No. No, it's just cheddar. That's the problem. The cheese *wasn't* stinky when I took legal possession of it."

"Um-"

"Apparently, you are supposed to refrigerate cheese, Joe. Who knew?"

"Gosh, well, *I* certainly had no idea that dairy products could spoil if-"

"Right, see? I'm not the only one. I think the Cheese Council just wanted to get rid of product they couldn't sell, and they stiffed me with it. Bunch of jerks. They never believed in the value of my opera."

"I find that hard to believe, Skippy," I said as solemnly as I could manage.

"Oh, trust me, Joe, this Cheese Council is *not* the trustworthy group of people you would-"

"No, I meant, how could anyone who heard your opera not appreciate its undeniable, um, artworthiness?" I might have just made up that word.

"Why, thank you, Joe. You mean that?"

"Yes," I lied my ass off. The little guy needed a win, and I couldn't stand to hurt his feelings right then. "So, you own a warehouse full of spoiled cheese?"

"Yup. Worse, I didn't pay for insurance, so a tragic fire wouldn't do me any good. The EPA is on my case, they are threatening to declare the warehouse a Superfund toxic waste site."

"That bad, huh?"

"Did you ever smell a warehouse full of rotting cheese?"

"Thankfully, no."

"All I can say is, I thought your *feet* smelled bad, but they are nothing compared to this. The prevailing wind in that area is from the west, and the neighborhoods downwind are very unhappy."

"That's terrible. Hey, nobody knows that *you* own this warehouse, right?"

"No, I own it through a tangled web of shell companies, Joe. Don't worry, it can't be traced back to me. The companies were originally owned by my persona Magnus Skippton, but, um, he *might* have done something faintly sketchy involving an organized crime syndicate in Tajikistan, so he had to go into hiding."

"*Faintly* sketchy?"

"Do the details matter right now? The Tajiks *might* have sent a hit squad to Magnus Skippton's supposed home in the Cayman Islands."

"Shit!"

"Oh, don't worry, Joe. Luckily for me, their private plane apparently suffered a navigation error over the ocean, and ran out of fuel over the South Atlantic. Sadly, it sank in very deep water, so I guess we'll never know what happened."

"That is tragic," I agreed, hoping we could leave Earth behind before Skippy caused any more trouble.

"I agree. Hey, on a *totally* unrelated subject, you know how we have been test-firing the *Dagger*'s railgun?"

"Yes," I answered cautiously, suspicious that subject might, in fact, not be unrelated.

"Well, I have been concerned about the accuracy of the *Dagger*'s targeting system. It would truly be unfortunate if, you know, an errant railgun round were to hit my warehouse and-"

"You are not going to nuke Milwaukee!"

"It's Sheboygan, Joe. Come on, how many people could even find it on a map? Anywho, I could dial down the yield so it only takes out, oh, shmaybe a couple thousand square meters of-"

"No. Railgun."

"Oh, don't be a baby. Railguns don't leave radioactive residue. Not long-term radiation, anyway, although there could be-"

"No railgun, no missiles, no maser cannons. That is final. You are not bombarding Sheboygan or wherever, just to fix your problem. Why can't you just pay a hazmat company to clean up the mess?"

"Well, I could, but, *DUH*, you made me promise to pay back all the followers of the Holy Skippyasyermuni. I don't have fundage to spare, numbskull."

"Oh. Well, gosh, you know how I've been trying to get to the next level on this Super Mario Kart game?"

"What does that have to do with it?"

"While I am *distracted* while playing that game," I emphasized the word in the hope he would catch my meaning. "All sorts of shady things could go on with the bank accounts of various criminal organizations dirtside. If you know what I mean."

"Oh. *OH*, gotcha. Um, Ok, done."

"Done with what?"

"With, um, possibly sketchy things that you were not involved in and therefore could not possibly be blamed for not knowing about, right? Especially if we jump out of orbit before the banks open in Bulgaria on Monday morning. Gosh, will you look at the time? Gotta go, I have a lot of stuff to take care of before the Flight Readiness meeting, buh-bye!"

His avatar blinked out, and I pulled out my tablet to play a video game. Because I really, really, did not want to know what was going on.

"Hey, Joe," Skippy's avatar popped above the treadmill I was running on. "I have super amazing news! Beyond amazing, it is a certified *miracle*."

"Hit me," I gasped, pressing buttons to slow my pace, "with, it."

"Remember that UN committee that has been debating what to call the two local wormholes? Incredible as it may seem, they actually made a decision."

"Oh, that's, great." There were *two* wormholes that could provide aliens with relatively easy access to Earth. There was the one that became active during the last wormhole shift, that the Kristang used to reach and ultimately conquer our homeworld. That is the one Skippy caused to go dormant, or technically it was on 'pause' or something. We used that one to go back and forth, waking it up and shutting it down behind us with an Elder wormhole controller module. One of those modules, that we called a 'magic beanstalk', was aboard the *Dutchman*. Another was floating near that wormhole, hooked up to a power source.

Skippy had casually told me there was another dormant wormhole *closer* to Earth, a wormhole that had been dormant for at least eighty million years, and had not been affected by the most recent wormhole network shift. We typically just said 'the Earth wormhole' or 'the local wormhole', but the United Nations decided we needed formal names for those ancient objects. So, they sprang into action and appointed a committee to study the subject.

The last I heard, the leading candidate names for the wormhole we used were 'First Base', 'Subway' and 'Gateway'. The truly dormant wormhole could be called, you guessed it, 'Second Base'. Alternatives were 'Dry Hole' and 'Deadend'. The wormhole much farther away, in Ruhar territory, had already been named 'Goalpost'. My opinion was I did not care what they called any wormhole, except that I would need to use the formal names in my reports. "Please tell me they didn't choose First and Second Base."

"Why do you object to those names? They make sense to me."

"They make *no* sense, you lunkhead. First base is supposed to lead to second base, but those wormholes don't connect at all. Plus, the wormhole they want to call 'First Base' is *farther* from home. It makes no sense."

"Ugh, fine. Anyway, the wormhole we use will be identified as 'Gateway' and the dormant one will be 'Sleeping Beauty'."

"Seriously?" That made me stumble because I momentarily forgot I still running on a moving treadmill.

"Seriously, Dude."

"'Gateway' is a good name-"

"You're just saying that because it was your suggestion."

"A lot of people suggested that name, Skippy. It's kind of obvious. But, come on, 'Sleeping Beauty'?"

"You do not want to know the names the committee rejected. Many, many human cultures have myths or stories about a sleeping princess or whoever, who is awakened with a kiss or a magic potion, or because she forgot to silence her phone," he chuckled. "So that name is not offensively Eurocentric or whatever. Avoiding that was a vital goal of the committee."

"Uh, isn't 'Gateway' an English word?"

"Yes, duh. English speakers will say 'Gateway', while other languages will use their equivalent. The Mandarin version is 'Wangguan', although that is being debated by a subcommittee."

"Of course it is." I sped up the treadmill again. "Let me know the instant that subcommittee releases their report."

"Will do, Joe. Although you will probably be retired or dead by that time."

"Bonus."

Mostly, I avoid the Stooges as much as possible, to the point where I stayed away from my office, and took my laptop to an engineering access tube aft of the *Dutchman's* forward section. The tube was cramped, it was uncomfortable despite the cushions I stuffed in there, but it gave me peace and quiet. When the Stooges asked to speak with me, the duty officer could report honestly that I was in the engineering section, working to upgrade our capabilities. The capability I was attempting to upgrade was getting to the next level of a video game, but the Stooges didn't need to know that.

Unfortunately, I could not avoid them entirely. I was on the way from the gym back to my cabin for a shower, when a door slid open and one of the Stooges stepped out. Despite the lack of space aboard the ship, with several cargo bays converted to living space for the survey teams, the UN had insisted their Commissioners be assigned quarters better than the typical small Thuranin cabins. To avoid another useless argument, I asked Skippy to remove bulkheads and combine two cabins into one, for each of the four Commissioners. It pissed me off to coddle those bureaucrats, but if feeling respected made them happy, they might be less likely to make bad decisions just to spite me.

Any, the door opened and the Commissioner from Algeria stepped out. "Ah, Captain Bishop," his face lit up with a charming smile. That was the problem with the Commissioners, as individuals they could be decent people. It was their official positions as overseers that made them a pain in my ass.

Several times, I had explained that it was proper to address me as 'Colonel' rather than 'Captain' but I was not going to argue the point with a civilian. "How can I help you, Mister Commissioner?" I flung the towel I was carrying around my neck, using one end to wipe the sweat off my face. My hope was he could see I was sweaty and ripe from a hard workout, and would not to talk for long.

"I have a question about housekeeping?"

"Housekeeping?" That was unexpected.

"Yes, if that is the correct term. I wish to know the arrangements for laundry," he seemed kind of embarrassed.

"Oh," I chuckled, relieved to be asked such an easy question. "That's easy, Sir. Just leave your clothes or towels or whatever on the Magic Floor."

"Magic Floor?" He shook his head gently, like he didn't quite understand American slang.

"Yeah. My father said we had one in our house. He would leave clothes on the floor, and they magically got picked up, washed, folded and put back in a drawer."

"Oh," he laughed cautiously. "I used to have a Magic Floor in my home also."

"Used to?" I raised an eyebrow. "What happened?"

"My wife began taking anything I left on the floor, and stuffing it into the trunk of my car."

"Ouch. Did you find out when you had to change a flat tire or something?"

"No," he chuckled. "I took the car to the shop, because the interior smelled bad. I got the message."

"Yeah," I replied thoughtfully. "My father found *his* clothes in the barn. A squirrel had made a nest of his Red Sox jersey. My Dad got the message too. Seriously, Sir, the robots aboard the ship handle most domestic chores for us. You can leave your laundry on the floor, and bots will come into your cabin while you're away. They will clean the cabin, take away laundry for cleaning, anything like that. If you need anything like extra towels, just ask Nagatha, and she will assign a bot. Uh, there might be a delay for a while. Skippy has many of the bots working to clean up issues from the Flight Readiness Review squawk list. That's uh," I figured I needed to explain. "A list of minor maintenance issues, like sticky door handles." Ok, I was minimizing how 'minor' some of the issues were, but the UN had cleared the *Dutchman* to fly. "Sir, we will be leaving orbit in," I glanced at my zPhone. "Sixteen hours. There is one last dropship coming up from Paris, so if you forgot anything, please tell Colonel Simms so she can get it up here before we depart."

He smiled. "There are no convenience stores beyond Gateway?"

I got a chuckle out of that. "They are more like *in*convenience stores."

After the last dropship was secured in its docking cradle and the supplies it brought to the ship had been verified by Simms, I scanned the checklist in my tablet, then looked at the ceiling in my office. "That's it? We're ready to go?"

"Ready as we can be, Joe," Skippy sounded annoyed. "We need to be extra, like super-duper careful with the ship. What we *should* be doing is taking the ship apart again and fixing or replacing all the stuff that glitched during testing, instead of taking a drunken joy-ride way outside the galaxy."

"Yes, I know, you told me that like, a zillion times already. We are not taking the ship apart again. In the Flight Readiness Review, you said the ship is good to go."

"Well, yeah, but that's partly because I didn't want a bunch of ignorant monkeys asking me stupid questions, about stuff they can't possibly understand."

"Is the ship flightworthy or not?"

"That's not a 'yes' or 'no' question, Joe. I told you I am not happy about the replacement components that were made on Earth. Like the reactor shielding, for example. Even the crude, dumbed-down equipment I asked humans to provide was almost impossible for your industries to manufacture. Of the first two hundred and eight test batches, one, only *one* piece of reactor shielding was marginally acceptable for being installed aboard the ship. Really, this is *my* fault, for asking monkeys to make complicated equipment by wacking coconuts with sticks. Without me constantly providing input, Earth will never make half the stuff we need to keep the ship functioning. I should stay here until we have the equipment we need, instead of flying off to another galaxy to find a vacation spot for monkeys."

"The beta site is not for vacations, and we need this survey, Skippy. Once we locate a potential beta site, the UN will be all excited about moving people there. That means the *Dutchman* gets to keep flying, instead of hanging around Earth just in case we get attacked again by frozen lizards."

"Taking the ship out is still a risk, Joe."

"Everything is a risk. Listen, while we are away, the monkeys down there will be fumbling their way through trying to make all the fancy crap you need to keep the ship running long term. Is the *Dutchman* going to fail while we fly to a beta site?"

"If I thought critical components could not make the journey, I would have refused to participate. Compared to past missions, going to scout a beta site is relatively short in terms of distance traveled through normal space and the number of jumps. It is exponentially *longer* in terms of absolute distance from Earth, but the Elder wormholes will provide shortcuts."

"And we will not be doing any crazy shit or getting into space battles. I hope. The wormholes that connect to the dwarf galaxies we want to search, went dormant long before the Rindhalu had space travel, so all those dwarf galaxies should be empty, right? You told me something like, the stars there are old, so the planets should be old, and that makes it less likely a new intelligent species will have evolved since the Elders were there?"

"That is a big assumption, Joe, but yes, you are correct. No guarantees."

"No guarantees expected. Let's get out of here before somebody dirtside changes their mind."

"Wait! Before we leave, we need to get our parking validated. Damn it, I had that receipt around here somewhere," he grumbled while his avatar patted its pockets.

That made me chuckle. "I've got it covered, Skippy. And, hey, remember, when we go through the first wormhole, you need to do your thing of making it act funky, like it's broken."

"Right, like I would forget something important like that. I *am* the smartest being in the galaxy, Joe."

Holding up my hands, I waved them to show I was sorry for daring to question the memory of the most absent-minded being in the galaxy. "Just checking, Skippy."

"Course is programmed into the jump navigation system. We can-"

"Whoa, wait a minute there, Skippy. You shouldn't program the jumps for us, we need Nagatha to do that."

"Oh for- You have *got* to be joking-"

"No joke, Skippy. Listen, we agree we need to get a new ship, right? A better ship, something more powerful than the *Dutchman* ever was. If, *when*, we get a new ship, the *Dutchman* will hopefully continue to fly missions to the beta site. Or maybe the *Dutchman* can fly simple recon missions, like retrieving data from a relay station. On those missions, this ship will be alone, without you. We need to know whether Nagatha can handle the ship by herself. Not just programming jumps and managing the bots to perform simple maintenance, we need to know she can repair the ship when something breaks, and that she can use a wormhole controller module."

"Oh. Damn, you sure aren't asking for much. Joe, I told you, her matrix is not yet fully stable, the process of separating herself from my capacity and integrating her presence into the ship is tricky. Even now, seventeen percent of her presence is in my matrix, and that seventeen percent includes most of her higher functions. You know, the part of her that worships little Joey Bishop, and annoys the hell out of me."

"I do understand that she-"

"Besides, there is no way Nagatha can ever use the wormhole controller, because she can't access higher levels of spacetime. Without the wondrousness of me, the *Dutchman* will be limited to going through wormholes the way the Elders intended, like every other ship in the galaxy. No way could she ever manipulate a wormhole to change its connections, or reopen a dormant wormhole. Which means she could not use the wormhole near Earth. Which means the *Dutchman* is pretty much worthless without me, you dumdum."

"I know that, Oh Most Arrogant One. If we are going to get a new hotrod ship and go racing around the galaxy causing havoc," I looked out the door to make sure nobody heard me say that, "then the *Dutchman* needs to be capable of performing recon missions for us, and flying people out to the beta site. You need to figure out a way to make that happen without you being aboard all the time."

"*I* need to do that?"

"Monkeys are too ignorant to use Elder technology, so it has to be you, Oh Greatest of All Great Ones. Come on, Skippy, if you are half as awesome as you tell me you are, this should be a piece of cake."

"Cake?" He sputtered. "Even if, *if*, we somehow found or stole another wormhole controller, Nagatha has no way to access higher dimensions to program or even talk to the damned thing. She is just a computer, Joe."

"You set up the wormhole controller so it could be used without you in an emergency, Skippy. Hell, that is what got us into trouble when UNEF tried to take over the ship, they thought they could take the *Dutchman* out without us, to contact the Jeraptha."

"I set it up for *one-time* use, dumdum. That was only for a limited time anyway, the effect would degrade steadily and wear off completely."

"Right, so, you need to find a way for Nagatha to do that. Get her a, I don't know? A big antenna so she can talk to it through this higher spacetime thing."

His avatar froze for a moment. Then, "An *antenna*?"

"Don't give me a nerdy lecture about complicated multi-dimensional physics, blah blah blah. Just," I waved a hand dismissively, "make it happen."

"Make. It. *Happen*?" His avatar was slack-jawed with astonishment.

"Are you awesome, or not?"

"I am more awesome than-"

"No, if you can't do this one simple thing, then you are way *less* awesome than you say. Are you awesome, or just *Meh*-some? You want to demonstrate your pure, unchallenged awesomeness? Then get it done. Whatever you have to do, do it."

"*Simple*?" He screeched with outrage. "I hate you *so*-"

"Great! Then we are agreed; you will work on this and keep me updated."

"Ooooh, I *hate* you more than words can-"

I stood up and straightened my uniform. "I'll be on the bridge."

We left Earth behind exactly on schedule, I did not want to give the United Nations even one additional second to change their minds. The new crew, and our large number of passengers, settled into the routine of jump, recharge, jump. When we reached the Gateway wormhole, I invited the Commissioners and off-duty crew to squeeze into the bridge, Combat Information Center and the passageway outside. As part of rebuilding the *Flying Dutchman*, Skippy had expanded the doorway that led into the bridge/CIC complex, so people jammed into the passageway had a better view.

Skippy did his magical thing, and the event horizon soon glowed in front of the ship. "Give it a few minutes to stabilize, Joe," he warned. "To comply with the cover story we planted on our last mission, I made the reopening of the wormhole chaotic this time. It is not safe to go through right now."

"Understood," I gave a big thumbs up, mostly for the benefit of the Three Stooges.

"Whew," Skippy exhaled. "*That* is a load off my mind."

"Uh," I shot a guilty glance back at the Commissioners before catching myself. Pretend to be confident, Joe, I told myself. Pretend to be *competent*. "What is?"

"Well, I was a tiny bit afraid that our wormhole controller module might have been damaged while the STAR team took it out bar-hopping in Dayton. But, no, it's good."

"Oh," I tensed my shoulders so the Commissioner would not see me shudder with relief. "Hey, Captain Frey," I turned around and looked for our Canadian special operator in the crowd.

She raised her hand. "I'm here, Sir."

I winked at her. "Are you glad now that you didn't nuke Dayton, and the wormhole controller with it?"

"I was already glad that, you know, I'm not *dead*, Colonel," she smiled back at me. "But, yes, eh?"

There was a faint smile on Count Chocula's face, but the Three Stooges did not see any humor in me joking about an incident that would have vaporized an American city.

They were probably right about that.

CHAPTER SIX

"Jooooooooey, I have a *surprise* for you," the beer can interrupted a video game I was losing anyway. We had gone through the Gateway wormhole. Desai was handling her new role as executive officer so well, there wasn't much for me to do. Unfortunately, that left me free to be pestered by the science team, who were jammed into cargo bays we had converted into crew quarters by installing temporary partitions. The science team, even for our initial survey of a potential beta site, was ninety-seven people. To provide security for them on the ground, to fly them around, and to maintain equipment, we had military personnel who would be assigned to the beta site under the command of Colonel Chang. There were so many people aboard the ship, it was stretching the capacity of the life support systems that Skippy had already enhanced for us. To carry an even larger number of people to a beta site, we would have to wait for the *Yu Qishan* to be modified and attached to the *Dutchman*. To carry all the gear the survey team needed, we already had containers attached to the outside of the hull, which restricted the ship's ability to maneuver in an emergency. It was a damned good thing that the UN had issued strict orders against me taking the ship into combat.

"I hate surprises, Skippy," I replied, slapping my laptop closed.

"Why? You don't even know what this surprise is yet!"

"Surprises for me have generally been stuff like, hey, instead of spending the summer training at Fort Drum in Upstate New York, our battalion is shipping out to Nigeria! In the summer, when it is extra super hot and humid there. Or, when I was looking forward to a nice family dinner on Columbus Day, aliens invade."

"Yes, certainly those surprises were unpleasant. But, then you found *me*. That was a surprise, right?"

"Egg-*zactly* my point, Skippy."

"Oh, very funny, Mister Smartass. Fine. Be that way, you big jerk," he genuinely sounded hurt. "I won't tell you anything about it."

"Sorry, Skippy. It's been a long day." Hell, I thought to myself, it's been a long month. A long year. A long *career*, even though I was still young. Sometimes I regretted not taking my high school guidance counselor's advice to learn a useful trade, like becoming a plumber or an electrician. Part of the reason I signed up for the Army was to get money for college, but even back while I was patrolling the bush in Nigeria, I had no idea what I wanted to study in college. One thing I did know was I was not looking forward to paying a lot of money to a college so I could learn useless crap I would never need or remember. A high school buddy of mine once told me he was taking a college course titled 'History of Jazz Music'. At the time, he thought it was a great scam that he got easy college credits for listening to music, but then I pointed out that *he* was paying for that course. I Googled 'History of Jazz' and found links to Wikipedia articles that had as much or more info than he was learning in that course. Man, he dropped that course the next day and signed up for something boring but potentially useful, like accounting.

Anyway, where was I? Oh yeah, it had been a long day. "Ok, Skippy, I'm going to trust that this surprise is going to make me happy, because you are a good friend and you know the crap I've been dealing with."

"It will make you happy, I think. I am *not* promising that every surprise I tell you in the future will be so delightful."

"Got it. Ok, hit me."

"You remember asking me to find candidates for a beta site? Technically, all I can do is find dormant wormholes near stars that might have habitable planets."

"Right, so, no giant blue stars, no red dwarfs, like that."

"Correct. Joe, I identified a lot of potential dormant wormholes we could use, but there is a complication. A bunch of complications, actually."

"Of *course* there are. So, we need a special *super*-duty wormhole to connect beyond the galaxy. I know you told me that there used to be a super-duty wormhole connecting to the Big Magellan Cloud-"

"It is called the Large, or Greater Magellanic Cloud, you moron. It's a galaxy, Joe, have some respect. The 'Big Magellan' sounds like a special burger of the month."

"Mmmm. I wonder what *that* would be like," I smacked my lips hungrily. In my mind, I was picturing two beef patties, plus-

"Ugh, will you *please* focus for a freakin' minute?"

"Uh, sure, whatever. Anyway, you said you suspected a group of Rindhalu might have gone through a super-duty wormhole into the," I had to think about that he just told me. "Greater Magellan Cloud thing. And gotten trapped there when the wormhole shut down."

"Correct. That is only a rumor, Joe, although it has attained the status of myth in Rindhalu society. Supposedly, there were faint signals detected coming from there for several centuries, although those signals had to travel over a hundred sixty thousand lightyears, so the Rindhalu there might have been long dead. Anyway, no artificial signals have been detected in a very long time. But, as I told the United Nations, it is best for us not to risk going there, when there are other candidates."

"Right." I had not really paid attention to the secret debate within the UN's commission that was tasked with making decisions about a beta site. "That is why you recommended we explore dwarf galaxies first."

"Yes, well, heh hehhhh," he drew the word out. "There is a teensy-weensy problem with that, Joe."

"Oh, crap." That morning, Hans Chotek and the Three Stooges had grilled me about our exact flight plans for locating beta site candidates, making certain the ship did not deviate a freakin' centimeter from the course approved by the UN committee. "Why do I think you are lying about this problem being teensy-weensy?"

"Gosh, I don't know. You are asking me to psychoanalyze your pathological inability to trust anyone, Joe?" Suddenly, his avatar changed to a white medical jacket, without an admiral's hat, and he had a beard. Plus, he was holding a pipe, an old-fashioned pipe like my grandfather used to smoke. His voice also changed, to an accent he probably thought sounded like Sigmund Freud. "Zeh subject displays irrational behavior, characteristic of a deep-seated childhood psychological trauma. I suspect his sense of betrayal at learning zeh truth about Santa Claus, is zeh source of his current inability to trust, *und* his continued chronic masturbation. Zeh subject-"

"Hey! You jerk, leave my childhood out of this."

"Sorry, Joe," his voice and avatar changed back to normal. "But you hurt me, too, when you accused me of lying."

"Ok, Ok, sorry about that. What is the problem?"

"When I said all that stuff to the UN about super-duty wormholes and the Milky Way's satellite galaxies, I was, um, flat-out lying my ass off."

I face-palmed myself hard enough to leave a red mark on my forehead. Through my hand, I mumbled "You were pissed that I accused you of lying, about something you *lied* about?"

"I was pissed that you *assumed* I was lying, Joe," he sniffed.

"Gosh, yeah, why would I do that?"

"Can we start over?"

"I would love to do that. Why the hell did you lie to the UN? Do you have any idea how much trouble I am in now?"

"I lied for two reasons. First, telling them what they wanted to hear got them to shut up faster. If I had told them the truth, that I don't know which satellite galaxies might be good candidates and that I don't actually know how, or *if*, we can get out there, the UN would still be arguing about it when your Sun becomes a red giant star and swallows the Earth. Second, I did it to get us away from Earth, before you had a chance to do something stupid and get thrown off the ship. So, really, I did it for *you*, Joe."

"Oh, this is bad. This is *bad*, Skippy. The Stooges are looking over my freakin' shoulder already. Now I have to tell them we came all the way out here, and you have no idea where we should go? Dammit, they are going to order me to turn the ship around. Then I *will* get thrown off the ship, you ass."

"Relax, dude. Take a chill pill. Jeez, I got this covered. I will take the blame. Yes, I, Skippy the Magnificent, will take the hit for you, a lowly monkey." He paused dramatically, his avatar frozen. "Um, Joe, that was your cue to thank me profusely, and tell me you are not worthy, blah blah buh-*lah*."

"How about if I don't, and you imagine I did?"

"Close enough. Oooh, this is *fun*. I am imagining you groveling and begging my forgiveness, which of course I-"

"How are you taking the blame? You can't admit that you lied, that will just get the Stooges super upset."

"I'll just explain there are facts I did not know at the time, that testing super-duty wormholes had revealed unexpected conditions. And, you know, yadda yadda yadda, whatever. That is not far from the truth, Joe. There is very little I know about super-duty wormholes, and a whole lot that I *don't* know."

"Ok, Ok," I was envisioning ways to salvage the situation. "To sell this line of bullshit, we have to continue on course to the super-duty wormhole you already selected, right? I mean, after we ping a relay station for intel."

"Exactly. Once we get to the super-duty wormhole, I will suddenly '*discover*' information that forces me to re-evaluate the situation. By that point, we will be committed to continuing on, and the Stooges won't want to turn around. They would look like failures if we return home, without even *trying* to explore a beta site."

"I hope you're right about that."

"Have I ever been wrong? Don't answer that," he added hurriedly.

"Ok, so the Big Magellan is out." I tried to remember what Skippy had told me about super-duty wormholes, near the end of our Renegade mission. "How about this Little Magellan thing? I know that's the wrong name, throw me a bone, Ok?"

"Fine," he huffed with disgust. "I very much doubt we should consider either of the Magellanic Clouds to be a viable option. Those minor galaxies are too big, Joe, have too many young stars, and are forming new stars. There is too much potential for an intelligent species to develop in those galaxies, species which could pose a threat to a beta site. Plus, you know, it is possible there are Rindhalu out there."

"Ok, makes sense," I groaned. A UN committee of smart scientists had covered the subject of potential beta site locations, now I had to rehash the argument all over again? How was I supposed to make a better decision that a group of expert-

On the other hand, no group of monkeys could truly be considered experts on a subject that even Skippy had little knowledge of. Also, I had to remember that the word 'committee' had two Ms, two Ts and two Es in only nine letters, which told me that a committee was not a good way to do anything efficiently. "Can we start with the basics? Other than this Bigger Magellan thing, *are* there any wormholes in the satellite galaxies?" During our Renegade mission, he had told me something about satellite galaxies, but all my foggy memory could recall was that one of the dwarf galaxies had a name like 'Fornication' and the other was 'Sexy-time'.

No, it was For*nax*, and Sex*tans*.

Man, I really needed to get laid.

"Joe, there *are* wormholes in most of what you call the satellite galaxies, and the numerous star clusters beyond the rim of the galaxy. By the way, the 'edge' of the Milky Way is hard to define, it fades out and is irregular. There are groups of stars so far away, or above or below the plane of the galaxy's disc, that they are clearly not part of the Milky Way. The Elders did create wormholes connecting beyond this galaxy, though from what I can tell, they did not make an extensive effort to explore out there."

"Why not? Why didn't they spread out to occupy the entire galaxy and everything close by? They had plenty of time to do that."

"There was no reason to, Joe. Back then, there was no other intelligent species to talk to, and the Elders satisfied their curiosity about the physical realm fairly early. They just did not need to fill every star system in sight, then they made the decision to leave their physical existence behind."

I reminded myself that Skippy's memories of the Elders were incomplete and might even be total bullshit. "What about other real, big galaxies? Did they go to Andromeda, to see what is there?"

"Not that I know of, and the network has no record of anything that far away. Based on what I know of wormhole technology, it is not possible to establish a connection to Andromeda."

"Ok. Hey, that chart you showed me listed," I tried to remember without calling up the info on my laptop. "Nine dwarf galaxies around the Milky Way, including the two Magellan Clouds. Is there anything beyond those, or is there nothing else until you get all the way out to Andromeda?"

"Oh, there are plenty of dwarf galaxies and star clusters between Andromeda and us, and all around the Milky Way in what you humans call the Local Group. Beyond the nine objects I listed, there is the Phoenix Dwarf, the three Leo dwarves, and plenty of others."

"Can, or should, we include any of those in our search?"

"We can't, because the Elders did not establish wormholes out that far. At least, the wormhole network does not have records of anything out that far. The Phoenix Dwarf, for example, is roughly a million and a half lightyears away. The practical limit for how far away a wormhole can project is approximately four hundred thousand lightyears."

"Ok, fine. So, you identified potential beta sites, in the dwarf galaxies closer to the Milky Way."

"Yes, however, the effort to explore all these sites to determine which one would be best for a colony will take years, Joe, many years."

"No it won't, Skippy. We don't need to find the *best* site, we just need to find one that is good enough. Sometimes trying to be perfect only means you waste a bunch of time. Soon as we identify a planet that can support human life, and like, is not near a star that will go supernova, we should try to establish a colony there."

"Oh. That narrows the list considerably, then. I will eliminate those dwarf galaxies and star clusters that only have one wormhole that I know of."

"Only one?" That surprised me. "In a whole galaxy? I know these are *dwarf* galaxies, but still, I thought there would be more than one wormhole there."

"Yes, some of the dwarf galaxies and star clusters have only a single wormhole, the one that connects to the Milky Way. Take, for example, the Bootes dwarf-"

"Hee hee," I had to laugh. "*Booty*. That's funny."

"Oh, you are *such* a child sometimes, Joe. Bootes is spelled B-O-O-T-E-S, with an umlaut on the second 'O'."

"An oom what?"

"*Umlaut*, you ignorant cretin. Those two dots used above vowels in German. Oh, forget it, I can see this is hopeless. Fine, how about the Draco dwarf galaxy? Anything funny about that?"

"Nope. Draco means dragon, right? Cool."

"I am *so* grateful the name of that minor galaxy meets your approval. You moron. Anyway, I have identified only one wormhole in Draco. Apparently, the Elders got there, looked around and decided there was nothing interesting, so they never set up other wormholes to travel within Draco. They probably left a solid 'Meh' review on Tripadvisor. That makes sense. Draco mostly consists of old stars, without many large clouds of dust for forming new stars. It is not a good candidate for a colony."

"I like your logic. We not only need to get *to* a dwarf galaxy, we also need to fly around inside it to explore. If all we can do is check out sites within a couple lightyears of the one wormhole that connects to the Milky Way, we aren't likely to identify a good candidate for a beta site. Ok, we eliminate Draco and this Booty Call place," I snickered at my own joke. "Are there any dwarf galaxies or star clusters that have multiple wormholes, so we have multiple sites to explore?"

"Having a local wormhole network is not the only criteria, Joe. We should eliminate the Magellanic Clouds and the Sagittarius Dwarf, because records indicate the Rindhalu might have traveled there in the past. There may be Rindhalu there still. To be safe, I kept on the list only locations where there is no evidence of the Rindhalu ever traveling there, and where the wormhole connecting to the Milky Way has been dormant as long as the Rindhalu have been keeping records."

"Great, so that leaves how many places? Wait, don't tell me that, I don't want to get bogged down in details. What are your top three potential sites?"

"In order of preference, the Sculptor dwarf, the Carina dwarf and the Ursa Minor dwarf. They each have an active local wormhole network, in addition to the super-duty wormhole connecting to the Milky Way."

"Whoa! *Active* wormholes? Like, somebody out there is using them?"

"I can't tell from here if ships are going through those wormholes, Joe. All I know is, there are local wormholes that were still active, at the time those gamma rays left the source. In the case of Sculptor, that data is nearly three hundred thousand years old. The entire local wormhole network in that dwarf galaxy could be dormant by now, I have no way to know until we get there."

"How extensive are these local wormhole networks? Are there hundreds of wormholes in each dwarf galaxy?"

"Hundreds? No, Joe. The Sculptor dwarf has only two wormholes that I can detect, in addition to the one connecting to the Milky Way. The Carina dwarf has six, and Ursa Minor has three. The lack of wormholes is not because the dwarf galaxies are actually small, Carina is nearly two thousand lightyears across. I think the relative lack of wormholes is because there are not many habitable planets in those dwarf galaxies. They tend to consist of older stars with little formation of new stars, plus they generally are less rich in carbon, metals and other heavy elements that form rocky planets. Don't worry, even a dwarf galaxy is *big*, Joe. It is fairly certain there are habitable planets out there, especially near wormholes, because the Elders usually located wormholes near habitable planets. The fact that the dwarf galaxies I mentioned are overall poor in heavy elements is a bonus, for the purpose of setting up a beta site."

I was dreading a nerdy science lecture, but had to ask anyway. "Uh, why is that?"

"Because they would be last on the list of places the Rindhalu or Maxolhx would want to go, if they ever achieved the technology to travel beyond the Milky Way."

"Good, good," I let out a breath in relief. While he was smacking me with sciency stuff, I feared he was telling me that our search for a beta site was doomed.

"That is great news, Skippy. We have three good candidates." In the back of my mind I was thinking that having multiple possible sites would be a good thing. "We will have to be careful about screwing with wormholes to connect to one of these dwarf galaxies, so maybe we should use a wormhole far away from Earth, huh?"

"Good idea, but here is another complication; it is not easy to find super-duty wormholes here in the local sector, that can be connected to wormholes in satellite galaxies."

"Wait, what? Why can't-"

"Because they *can't*, Joe. Not every wormhole can be connected to every other one. There are different types of wormholes, some were built for long-range connections. Most are only capable of spanning a gap of six thousand lightyears, even if I screw with their programming."

"Crap. I did not know that."

"Joe, you should use 'I did not know that' as your theme song."

"*Why* are there different type*s*? Wait, have we ever been through one of these super-duper heavy-duty wormholes?" All the wormholes we had been through looked the same to me. All we saw, of course, was the temporary event horizon in local spacetime, we never actually saw the wormhole mechanism itself. Skippy had told me there were multiple types of Elder wormholes, but he hadn't given me a lot of detail on what made them different.

"Well, twice we have been through what I call 'heavy-duty' wormholes, although we used for them for relatively short-range shortcuts. The wormhole we used to get to the Roach Motel is a 'heavy-duty' wormhole, as you would describe it. There are different types of wormholes for the same reason there are different types of warships in a fleet; each type has a range of capabilities."

"Yeah, but, the reason not every ship is a battleship is mostly because they are expensive to build, maintain and support a large crew. The Elders did not have to consider resource constraints, did they? They could move stars!"

"Even the Elders had to deal with limited resources. Their capabilities were truly vast, but, still limited. That is not the point, dumdum. Damn, you love to interrupt me. The Elders constructed different types of wormholes for different purposes. Remember I told you they once relocated an unstable blue giant star by jumping it through a wormhole? That was a very special wormhole built just for that one-time use, it was taken apart to prevent it from creating a rupture in spacetime. *That* is why not every wormhole has long-range capability, Joe. Those heavy-duty wormholes are rough on local spacetime, they appear much less frequently than other wormholes and their emergence points are far apart. They also apparently have a limited lifespan, that is why the vast majority of them are currently dormant. I think the Elders kept these heavy-duty wormholes dormant most of the time, only activating them when needed. Even while dormant, their presence causes disruptions in higher dimensions of spacetime, that is how I have been able to locate them."

Damn it, not knowing why there are different types of wormholes fell into that huge category of 'ways my ignorance can get me killed'. Unfortunately, there was a *LOT* in that category. Like, too much. The problem was, Skippy only told me stuff he thought I needed to know, and because of my profound ignorance, I did not even know what questions to ask. It was very frustrating.

"Wonderful. You do know which wormholes are just the normal or heavy-duty type, and which super-duty ones can connect outside the galaxy, right? At the end of our Renegade mission, you said something about there being three super-duties we should check out.""

"Yes to your first question, no to the second. I don't know which wormholes might be able to connect beyond the galaxy, because I have never asked the wormhole network to try that."

"Whoa. Do you know for sure that *any* wormholes in this galaxy can reach one of those dwarf galaxies, or are you guessing?"

"I'm not guessing, Joe, I- Hmm, Ok, technically I *am* sort of guessing. It's a simple matter of logic. There are Elder wormholes in satellite galaxies, so they must have been active at some point, and they must have connected to this galaxy. I'm not going to use the word 'duh'-"

"Except you just did."

"*Ugh*. Fine. You asshole! You slap this huge project on me, to identify potential beta sites, and when I tell you it is not so easy as the monkey would like, you get all pouty and mad at me."

"I do not get 'pouty'."

"Your lower lip is sticking out, and you are frowning like a baby who can't get candy."

"Can we just agree this is super complicated? Damn, whenever you go all Professor Nerdnik on me, my head hurts." I had not asked him why the dwarf galaxies were poor in heavy elements and why most of their stars were old, because I knew he would give me a half-hour lecture about it. And because it did not matter why a dwarf galaxy had so little carbon compared to the Milky Way-

Except, crap, maybe it *did* matter. My ignorance could get me killed someday, get a lot of people killed. With a mental groan I kept to myself, I decided learning useful knowledge was too important, I needed to suck it up and force my slow brain to smarten up. "Skippy, I'm going to grab a sandwich and I'll be right back, so you can explain about the chemical composition of dwarf galaxies, and how you plan to find out whether any wormholes in this galaxy can connect way out there."

"*Really?*" his voice dripped with sarcasm.

"For realz, homeboy. This ignorant monkey needs to smarten up sometime, might as well start now."

"Hoo boy, this is not going to be easy. Well, if I can educate *you* about the physics of stellar formation, maybe that will add another plaque to the wall in my Awesomeness Hall of Fame."

Wisely, I did not ask whether he was actually planning to build a hall of fame for himself.

Adams was back aboard the ship, that meant she was again leading exercise classes in the gym. Because she loved so much to make people suffer, I was surprised that she had chosen the Marine Corps over a job at the Department of

Motor Vehicles. The first class she led was a Spin workout, which I was excited about because all the equipment in the gym had recently been replaced and upgraded. As part of rebuilding the ship yet again, Skippy had moved bulkheads to make the gym larger. That was good for our high-speed special operations troops, but the reason for expanding the ship's recreation facilities was we would be carrying a lot more people. The ship's new peacetime role of missions back and forth to a beta site, including the initial survey work and setting up for a colony, meant the *Dutchman* would be supporting two or three times as many people. Skippy had upgraded the life support capacity, mostly the water supply and oxygen recycling. Several cargo bays had been converted to sleeping quarters, with racks of bunks. Privacy would be at a premium, and two cargo bays had been set aside for common areas and a second galley. I would have to appoint an officer to deal with the civilian survey teams, because I sure as hell didn't want to do that.

Anyway, I had been given a tour of our new gym, but had not used the Spin bikes yet. For Adams's first class, I arrived twenty minutes early, to find the room already almost full. The only bikes left were in the second row, so I picked one at random and set it up, flopping a towel over the handlebars and a water bottle in the rack. Everyone else was warming up, and I got started. Then I noticed something odd. All the women in the class were on bikes in the back row. Captain Frey was behind me, so I turned around and whispered to her. "You're a hardcore adventure racer, Frey. I figured you would be in the front row."

"Sir," she said evenly between breaths, because she was already out of her seat, standing on the pedals. "If I was right in front of you, what would you be doing?"

"Uh-" That confused me for only a heartbeat, then I felt my cheeks redden with a blush. She meant, I would be staring at her shapely ass. That would be wrong and unprofessional and disrespectful, and biology didn't care about any of that. "Gotcha," I mumbled and turned around, pretending to be adjusting my bike.

Five minutes before the class started, all the bikes were occupied, and Adams was walking around, checking that everyone knew how to set up the new bikes. Just before she got to my row, the bulkhead in front of us changed from projecting a view of a mountain road, to display boxes of data. It shocked me when I saw the data being displayed.

"Gunny," I hissed, waving her over to me. "When you were dirtside, did you visit the Bad Ideas Hall of Fame?"

"No Sir," she grinned. "Why?"

"You know exactly what I mean." The problem was not the new bikes, it was the display. It showed the name and a photo of everyone, with their current heartrate and the amount of power they were generating. Everyone in the class could see the amount of power output of everyone else. With the class full of special operations troops, that was a recipe for nothing but trouble. One thing I knew about operators was they were competitive, like, super competitive. Now they could see where they ranked against their peers, in real-time. "Are you trying to kill people?"

She looked behind her at the display. "You're cranking out a hundred sixty watts, Sir. That's nothing to be ashamed of," she said, but the tone of her voice was that of a mother patting a child on the head after striking out at teeball.

"I'm just warming up, Gunny," I said through clenched teeth. "This is a *bad* idea," I pushed harder and my power output went up above two hundred. Crap. Behind me, Frey was above two fifty. She was already warmed up, I told myself.

That is very nice, *girly-man*, my inner self responded. My inner self is an asshole.

"Trust me, Sir," Adams whispered as she moved away. On the display, several boxes were showing a continuous power output above four hundred watts. One guy was approaching five hundred. I knew that just from the gasping grunts he was making.

Damn, the class was scheduled for an hour and it hadn't started yet.

Adams got the music thumping, taking us straight into a long climb. We reached the top seven minutes later, and everyone was gasping. My legs felt like rubber, yet I was proud of myself. My power output was in the top quarter of the class. It was partly unfair, because while the ship was being rebuilt, I had nothing much else to do, so I had taken as much time as I could in the flight simulator, and practically lived in the gym when I wasn't pretending to fly. As a result, I was in the best condition of my life. Ha, I thought, the old man isn't so-

Adams interrupted. "Very good, boys and girls. I see we have some superstars with us today." She highlighted a handful of the power output numbers. Those people were giving themselves imaginary high-fives. Then she crushed egos. "This is not a competition, but we all know that is bullshit." She shook her head and drew laughter from the group. "Here's what you don't know. The winner of this competition will have the greatest average power output, as a percentage of body weight. Average, over the hour. That means you show-off idiots who are pushing so hard that you bonk after thirty minutes, are going to *lose*."

Man, I could almost hear the class doing math in their heads. The guy who had been cranking out a steady four hundred watts immediately dropped below two hundred, a sheepish look on his exhausted face. He was in trouble and he knew it, his legs already shook like jello. Everyone was looking around, trying to guess body weights.

Adams had not only made the class a competition, she had found a way to make it *interesting*.

The class ended, with an optional fifteen minutes of ab work, which of course everyone stayed for. How did I do in the competition? Not at the bottom, thank you very much.

Hey, you want to know if I beat Captain Frey?

Oh, shut up.

"Adams, I owe you an apology," I said as I helped her carry a basket of sweat-soaked towels.

"Sir, you trust the awesomeness, but you don't trust *me*?"

"Won't happen again," I assured her. "What?" She was looking at me with amusement.

"If you weren't my C.O., I would say you are cute when you're embarrassed. But that would be inappropriate."

"The jury is instructed to disregard that remark," I winked.

"Are you coming to my strength class this afternoon?"

"Hold on," I dug my zPhone out of a pocket. "I want you to say that again, while I record the video."

"Why?" She asked, giving me a stare reserved for creepy weirdos.

"Because, if anyone ever thinks you *like* me, I will show them this evidence to prove you are trying to kill me."

CHAPTER SEVEN

Only Skippy and I knew the truth, that he had no idea if we could get a super-duty wormhole to connect outside the galaxy. I worried about that and kept my mouth shut, as we jumped toward our first objective: a Kristang data relay station. Because the United Nations insisted we be extra super-duper careful, we kept the *Flying Dutchman* four lighthours away from the station, and Skippy pinged it for info. The station responded that it was lonely, as no ships had stopped there within the past month. The nearby star system was solidly controlled by the Black Tree clan and well defended, so it was relatively unaffected by the civil war that was raging across Kristang society. During the first year of the civil war, that star system had a lot of traffic going in and out; warriors going off to fight, and damaged ships limping back for repairs. The station reported sadly that the recent combined offensive by the Thuranin and Bosphuraq had reduced the transport capacity available to the Kristang, and the next star carrier to visit was not scheduled for another three weeks.

With that assurance, the Commissioners authorized me to jump the *Dutchman* within two lightminutes of the station, and Skippy ransacked its database. Not surprisingly, it had no info about whether there were any more Kristang starships hidden near Earth, it did not even know anything about the *Ice-Cold Dagger to the Heart*. Skippy loaded a virus into the station, a file that would be carried to other stations and nearby planets, where it would quietly search for hints of secret operations involving Earth. If the virus found any information we wanted, it would send a message back out, to propogate across the network of relay stations. Personally, he told me that the *Dagger* had very likely been alone. Earth was just not important enough for more than one clan to devote the resources to have a secret ship transported all the way there.

Really, if the UN was serious about investigating whether there were more ships stuffed full of frozen lizards near Earth, we needed to hit Thuranin databases for info. The Thuranin would certainly know how many ships they had transported to Earth, and we would not have to rely on a virus digging into the secret records of every Kristang major clan and subclan. Digging into Thuranin records would be easy one-stop shopping for all our intel needs, but the UN considered screwing around with the Thuranin too risky, so we did it the hard way. No, the dumb way.

Anyway, I had my orders, I carried them out to the best of my ability, and I kept my mouth shut.

Continuing to follow orders, the ship next flew along the UN-approved course to the super-duty wormhole Skippy had selected, with the Stooges suspiciously watching every move I made. Reed made sure our pilots stuck to the approved course as much as we could, and we used isolated but existing wormhole connections to get there. This mission would not involve any screwing with Elder wormholes, other than making one or maybe a small group of them connect beyond the galaxy.

"Well, gosh darn it," Skippy announced, after making us wait for a whole freakin' day at the site of the dormant super-duty wormhole.

"Gosh darn it?" Desai inquired from the command chair. She was the duty officer, I had just come onto the bridge after breakfast, and was eating the last couple bites of a bagel. "Mister Skippy," she looked back over her shoulder at me, and I held my hands up. This was her show, I wasn't going to interfere. To demonstrate my intent, I walked over into the CIC. "What is the problem?" She asked.

"Gosh *darn* it," Skippy said in a nervous tone. "Wouldn't you know it? There is an issue with bringing this wormhole back online. Wow. There is *no way* I could have foreseen this. Right, Joe? Heh, heh," he added.

Oh crap, I said to myself. Desai's eyes were shooting daggers at me. She was not buying that lying little beer can's line of bullshit. And she figured whatever he was lying about, it involved me.

Which was true. In my defense, I had not informed Desai about Skippy's deception because I didn't want her implicated in our scheme. No, in *Skippy's* scheme. I was only guilty after the fact. Luckily for me, the Commissioner in the CIC at the time was Hans Chotek, which is probably why Skippy had chosen that moment to announce the discovery that he totally could not have foreseen of course not.

The look I got from Chotek was not disappointment and anger like Desai was giving me, it was- Amusement? Yeah, that's it. He was amused, like he expected something like this, and was waiting to see what kind of game I was playing.

In a way, that told me a lot about how our relationship had grown since we first were forced to work together. He had been expecting me to conceal the truth about something, and he trusted my judgment that it wasn't anything that could endanger the mission.

Maybe I needed to stop keeping him and Desai in the dark.

"Well, gosh, you did warn us this might not be easy, Skippy," I replied without looking at anyone in the bridge or CIC. Lying wasn't my best skillset. "What is the problem?"

"Well, *duh*, I told you, it's-" He must have realized just then that I wasn't supposed to know about the problem before now. "It's just the usual, the Universe screwing with us, Joe," he finished with a decently-believable sigh. "I'm sorry, this wormhole is not usable."

That was something I did *not* already know. I walked into the bridge compartment in a few steps, and stood beside the command chair. "Define 'usable', please."

"I can't make it work. No amount of screwing with this stupid thing will get it to connect beyond more than eight thousand lightyears," he explained with disgust. "What a piece of crap."

"Ok," I carefully considered what to say next, assuming my words might be in the official transcript of a UN inquiry someday. "So, should we just go to the next super-duty wormhole on the list? You have told us about wormholes that connect farther than eight thousand lightyears."

"Yes," he began slowly, growing irritated at me. "Those are long-range wormholes that have remained actively connected, or they become connected after a shift, because the network makes them connect. Here, I am dealing with a dormant wormhole, and trying to make it do something the network isn't programmed for."

"Got it. So, this is the wrong wormhole, or the wrong type of wormhole?"

"No. You don't understand. This wormhole *is* capable of connecting far beyond eight thousand lightyears. The problem is, *I* can't get it to do that."

He sounded not only genuinely upset, but also seriously upset. Whatever the issue was, he had not expected it. "To be clear, this wormhole won't accept your instructions?" I asked. "Or is it a-"

"It's not a matter of my *authority*, Joe," he snapped at me. "The problem is of course not with my incredible level of magnificence, it is with the lame-ass wormhole controller module we have. Apparently there are not only different types of wormholes, there are different levels of controller modules. The one we have is not capable of generating the level of power required to establish a connection farther than eight thousand lightyears."

"Whoa," I looked at Desai, so hopefully she understood that at least this part was all news to me. "What do you mean, the controller lacks the power? I thought our beanstalk just sent a message through higher spacetime or something like that."

"It does, Joe," he said, and everyone could hear his unspoken 'duh' directed at me. "The controller has to communicate with the wormholes on *both ends* in order to connect them."

"Oh, wow," I gasped. "I never thought of that. Holy shit! You mean one of these controller things has to reach across over a *hundred thousand* lightyears, to contact a wormhole in a satellite galaxy?"

"Well, yes, *duh*. How else did you think it works? I thought I explained that to you already."

"I would have remembered a little detail like that, Skippy. Can't your incredible magnificence just, uh, provide the power or reach or whatever this thing needs?"

"It's not just the amount of *power*, Joe," he explained the way adults speak to children on Sesame Street. "I have the power, in fact I have too much power. I would blow up the controller module we have, if I tried to feed that level of power into it. The problem is that our controller doesn't, ugh, how do I explain this to monkeys? It is like the controller we have is a torque wrench with a six-inch handle, and we need one with a handle that is three feet long. Before you ask, no, we can't just slip a pipe over the handle to make it longer. Also before you ask, the other controller, that we have parked near the Gateway wormhole, is also not capable of getting this *stupid*-duty wormhole to connect beyond the galaxy."

"We can't touch that backup controller anyway, we need it to make Gateway act crazy, at the proper time that matches the bullshit cover story we are selling to the Maxolhx. All right, what can we do?" Maybe, I realized, that was that wrong question. "*Is* there anything we can do to fix this?"

"I think so. I am not one hundred percent certain, but now that I know there are different types of wormhole controllers, I am making sense of a bit of data I collected a while ago."

"So, what do we do next?"

"Well, heh heh-"

Desai said it before I could. "Oh *shit*."

We had not yet gone through a wormhole beyond the galaxy, and already I was having to referee arguments about who would be in the first away team to survey a potential beta site. The science team included egos to match their scientific and academic accomplishments, so it was no surprise to me that there would be competition, but it still annoyed me. I reminded the team that before we could discuss *who* was going on the away missions, we had to figure out *where* we needed to go. And before *that*, we had to learn *what* thing we had to get, to connect a super-duty wormhole all the way out to a dwarf galaxy.

It was actually a relief to me when Skippy announced that we had to go on another wild-goose chase, before we could look at potential beta sites. When he told me there were different types of wormhole controller modules, I assumed we needed some kind of extra-powerful controller. This special controller would be gold-plated, or have a label like 'Turbo' or some other marketing gimmick like that.

I was wrong about that.

"Joe," Skippy told me, "I have no freakin' clue what a super controller looks like, or where to get one. A scavenger hunt would be a waste of time anyway. Because super-duty wormholes are rare, I suspect their controllers are equally rare."

"Ok, but the network must know what the damned thing looks like, right?" I asked, feeling like I should not have to explain that to a being as intelligent as he claimed to be. "Ask the network."

He was equally frustrated with me. "Ugh. You do not understand. The network did not specifically tell me that I need a super controller. All I know is that, when I tried to make our controller wake the thing up, the network gave me a warning like 'Insufficient power to establish connection'. Therefore I concluded that, *duh*, I need a more powerful device."

"Which brings us back to needing to know what the stupid thing looks like, before we can go racing around the galaxy to find one!"

"That would be a waste of time, Joe. Like I said, super controllers must be rare. That is good, actually."

"Uh, *what* is good, Skippy?"

His voice changed to a terrible Germanic accent. "What is *good*? To crush your enemies, see them driven before you, and to hear the lamentation of their women!"

"Uh," I shot a guilty look at Chotek, who was startled by what Skippy had said. "I am not Conan the Barbarian, so-"

"You got that right," Skippy muttered. "You are more like Conan the *Librarian*."

There were snickers of laughter around the CIC. "Could you stick to the subject, please? You just told us that the thing we need to get is impossible to find. How is a *good* thing?"

"Because, *duuuuuh*, if in the future the Maxolhx or Rindhalu want to activate a super-duty wormhole to go wipe out the beta site, they won't be able to. *DUH!*"

"Shit. Ok, that 'duh' is on me. Good thinking." My timing sucked, because by then the Three Stooges had joined Chotek in the CIC, and were engaged in a quiet but furious conversation while they were glaring at me. Chotek was being patient and calm and reasonable, and I could tell he really wanted to snap their necks. It was good seeing him having to deal with the wrath of bureaucrats.

"You are welcome," Skippy replied, his voice dripping with sarcasm. "How about you stop wasting my time with stupid questions, and I will explain what we need to do next?"

Fortunately, I had seen the wisdom in shutting up, so I did.

"It is simple, Joe. I think we don't need to find a different type of wormhole controller, we just need to find a sort of power booster for the controller we have. Um, you should think of it as a range extender for a WiFi signal."

"Great," I groaned. "I suppose we will have to go some scary place like the Roach Motel to get an Elder range extender?"

"Nope. In fact, I have good news for you: we do not need an *Elder* device at all. The technology of a device that can feed power into higher dimensions is relatively crude. Even the Rindhalu possess such technology. We should be able to use one of their devices."

Chotek was giving me a warning look. He did not like the idea of stealing from the Rindhalu, any more than he liked the notion of flying back to the Roach Motel.

"Oh, *yeah*," I made sure Skippy could not mistake the sarcasm in my voice. "That is *much* better. All we have to do it break into a secure Rindhalu vault or something?"

"Again, noooooo," he used sarcasm right back at me. "I happen to know of a place, multiple places, where Rindhalu technology should be lying around just waiting to be picked up. All we have to do is fly to one of the Dead Worlds."

"One of the *Dead* Worlds? Why does that not sound like a swinging good time?"

"Probably because you're not one of the cool kids, Joe. Think of this as The Rave At The End Of The Universe."

"That actually does not help."

"Like I said," he sniffed. "Not one of the cool kids."

The idea of going to a dead world did not appeal to me at all. The idea didn't thrill the Stooges either, so much that they had been on the verge of ordering us back to Earth for consultations, before Chotek talked some sense into them. Their charter, the Stooges had insisted, did not include taking the ship into hazardous situations. The mission was supposed to be about safety for humanity, not flying around on reckless adventures.

Chotek had replied, with the quiet and well-reasoned logic of an experienced diplomat, that their charter from the United Nations was to locate a beta site. The UN wanted a secure refuge for humanity, and the mission orders had given the four Commissioners broad authority to do whatever was needed to locate a beta site.

Going back to Earth with their tails between their legs would only mean the UN
would inevitably send the ship back out, with a group of Commissioners who were
capable of *getting the job done* rather than covering their asses.

Since the Stooges knew he was right, they reluctantly voted unanimously to
authorize me to plan a mission to one of the Dead Worlds, to locate and acquire the
technology we needed. I was authorized *only* to make plans, with the
Commissioners reserving the decision whether to proceed or not. Our three new
UN bureaucrats did not know what Hans Chotek had learned from experience; that
projects even in the planning stage gathered momentum, and at some point became
very difficult to stop.

I was Ok with the notion of the Stooges learning a painful lesson.

Most of the crew was hesitant about going to as place described as a 'Dead
World'. Except for Smythe, who of course relished the challenge. And the rest of
his STAR team. And our pilots, who were furiously playing rock-paper-scissors for
the opportunity to fly any potential away missions. By the way, apparently the
British call the game paper-scissors-*stone*. Some people who had lost the first
round, suggested moving on to the more complicated rock-paper-scissors-lizard-
Spock version of the game, but they were quickly shouted down.

Ok, so, really, the only crew members who very much did not like the
possibility of a hazardous mission were me and Reed, because we would be stuck
aboard the ship while the others had fun. I argued that I should go with the away
teams, while Desai remained aboard the ship to, as I said it, 'gain valuable
experience in command'. That argument was dismissed. By her.

The Commissioners, including Chotek, were also not thrilled about a
potentially dangerous glitch in their dream of a simple and easy mission. The four
of them, especially Chotek, should have known that nothing is ever simple or easy
for the Merry Band of Pirates.

First, I should explain that the Dead Worlds are planets formerly inhabited by
the Rindhalu and Maxolhx, before the rotten kitties launched a sneak attack against
the spiders way back when. The Maxolhx struck hard against critical spider
facilities in the first wave, then the spiders hit back. Because both sides were using
Elder weapons, the devastation to the impacted worlds was massive.

Then, Sentinels detected that someone was using Elder weapons, and woke
from their slumber to crush both sides. The majority of the Dead Worlds were
rendered uninhabitable by Sentinels, rather than the two original combatants. In
some cases, all the Sentinels did was make the already-radioactive rubble bounce
around, but they stuck to their programming. The Sentinels were relentlessly
thorough about hunting down and punishing the perpetrators on both sides, who
had dared to use and misuse Elder technology.

"These Dead Worlds," I asked. "Can you give us more info about them?"

"Certainly, Joe," Skippy answered in a cheery fashion. "A complete package
of data about the Dead Worlds is available, for three easy payments of only
nineteen-ninety-five."

"*What?*"

"Hey, a brother has got to make a living here. I'll throw in a set of steak knives."

"Thank you, no."

"You sure? These top-quality knives can slice through a hiking boot."

"Ah, if the steak I'm eating needs a knife like that, maybe I try something else."

"Probably a good idea," he conceded.

"How about I make one easy payment of *zero*, and I let you sing an extra song on the next karaoke night?"

"Deal!" He shouted before I could come to my senses. "What do you want to know about the Dead Worlds?"

"Let's start with *where* are they?"

He showed a star chart, on the main displays in the bridge and CIC. "Because the Maxolhx concentrated their initial attack on the critical inner worlds of the Rindhalu, and then the spiders retaliated against the closest Maxolhx star systems, the Dead Worlds are in a relatively compact area of the Norma Arm. You can see on the chart that-"

"Wait. The, the '*Norma*' Arm?" I chuckled, assuming he was bullshitting me. "Is that next to the 'Jethro' Arm?"

"No," he snapped after the laughter in the CIC died down. "You can look it up on Wikipedia if you like. The Norma Arm is also called the Cygnus Arm. Hey, *I* didn't name the stupid thing, a bunch of monkeys did."

"Wow, sorry," I made a slashing motion across my throat to dampen the remaining laughter. Displaying my ignorance did not make me look good in front of the Stooges. By the time we were having the tactical discussion of which Dead World to investigate, the Stooges had retreated to their extra-large cabins, to write reports for the purpose of covering their asses by blaming any future trouble on me and Chotek. They could be writing naughty limericks about me for all I cared, as long as they left the crew and me alone to do our freakin' jobs. Studying the chart before I opened my big stupid mouth again, I was surprised to see the Dead Worlds zone was a tiny dot, about a quarter of the way around the galaxy's disc from Earth, and much closer to the center. "That's it?"

"Joe, the star chart is currently showing most of the Milky Way galaxy, you dumdum. Watch this and be amazed." He zoomed the view in, so it showed a span of about three thousand lightyears, according to the helpful little sign at the bottom.

The star systems of the Dead Worlds were highlighted in red, and there were a *lot* of them. There was an ominous swath of red, in an arc that cut across the spiral arm that really was apparently named 'Norma'. "Damn. That is a *lot* of dead star systems. Since we're going to be looking for Rindhalu technology, can you highlight their Dead Worlds?"

I had to guess, but it looked like more than half of the dead systems now glowed yellow rather than red. "Now I will highlight in blue the former Rindhalu worlds that are now in Maxolhx territory," he announced.

"Ok," I looked at Desai, and she was just as bewildered as I was. "Why are you doing that?"

"Because," he explained. "We probably need to land on a former Rindhalu Dead World, and I would prefer not to sneak into a star system that is currently monitored by the spiders. Not only do you monkeys not need to make any more enemies than you already have, but also I do not wish to attempt to subvert a Rindhalu sensor network. Sneaking us through Maxolhx sensors is going to be difficult enough."

"Oh, got it. Hell, Skippy, do we even want to try doing that? I remember how tough it was to sneak into Detroit to raid that pixie factory."

"Trust me, Joe." He snorted. "This is going to be a piece of cake, compared to Detroit."

"This is your idea of *cake*, Skippy?" I asked after I finished reading one of the books I had brought along, and couldn't think of anything else to do. Being stuck aboard our Panther dropship, in empty space on the outskirts of a Dead World star system, resulted in my having nothing useful to do.

"Yes, why?" he asked innocently.

"If you are thinking of baking something for my birthday, don't."

"Oh, shut up. What are you whining about?"

"I am bored out of my freakin' skull, that is what."

From the cockpit, Reed raised her hand. "Add me to that list, Sir."

"See? Even 'Fireball' Reed is sick of this."

Our other pilot, Wu, stifled a yawn. "I second that, Sir. This kinda sucks so far."

"Ugh. Joe, they are bored with being stuck here with *you*, not with this glorious and fascinating mission. We have successfully snuck into the edge of a Dead World star system, and are currently engaged in a clandestine operation to subvert a senior-species monitoring network. Around us are the burned and shattered remnants of a once-great civilization. How can you be *bored*?"

"Gosh, well, let me think," I mocked him. "First, I have been stuck in this Panther for six freakin' days, with absolutely nothing to do. At least Reed and Wu occasionally get to move the Panther a couple meters in one direction or another-"

"That really does not help much, Sir," Reed groaned.

"As for the remnants of a dead civilization," I rolled my eyes, "all I've seen is a dark smudge. It could be dust on the freakin' camera lens, for all I know."

"Well, *excuuuuse* me," Skippy expressed his disgust. "That smudge is all we can get with passive sensors from here. If you like, I could deploy an active sensor sweep, or we could fly over there so little Joey can get a better view."

"How about we don't do any stupid shit like that?"

"Then what *do* you want?"

"I want you to do the awesome thing we came out here for you to do."

"I'm *trying*, knucklehead."

"Try harder," I suggested.

"And faster," Reed added.

"Just try *better*," was Wu's helpful contribution.

"Sure! Fine! I'm an idiot!" Skippy exploded. He was as frustrated as the three of us were. "You monkeys tell me what to do, and I'll do it."

The problem was, we monkeys had no suggestions for him. We were in the Kuiper Belt of a star system we called Slingshot, waiting for Skippy to hack into the Maxolhx sensor network that surrounded the star. The *Flying Dutchman* had jumped in way outside the system, with our jump signature tuned to look like a Maxolhx ship. Reed, Wu and I flew toward the star in the Panther with Skippy, and parked it in the exact spot he said we needed to be. Exact, like, within three centimeters of an imaginary line Skippy thought was the location of a tightbeam transmission path from one of the sensor satellites way out on the dark, icy edge of the system, and a network node on a space station in orbit only a couple of million miles from the star. I say he *thought* that was the location, because he was guessing at the location of the satellite and the space station. With all the satellites and the space stations were wrapped in sophisticated stealth fields, Skippy really was guessing that they even existed.

So, we were trying to put our Panther exactly along an imaginary line, between two objects that might not exist. We also had to be there at the proper time, because the satellites and space stations communicated via burst transmissions that lasted no more than a few nanoseconds. As far as we knew, the satellite we targeted had sent its message inward a second before our Panther moved into position, and we could be waiting there in empty space for another month to intercept another signal.

That was not going to happen, because despite all three of us being on our best behavior, Reed, Wu and I were starting to irritate each other. The other reason it wasn't going to happen is I only had enough peanut butter and Fluff for seven more lunches. I *should* have had sufficient Fluff supply for twelve days, but someone had been stealing spoonfuls of delicious Fluff nutrition, despite both of our pilots claiming they couldn't stand it. Based on the streak of sticky white Fluff in Reed's hair, I had a prime suspect.

After our minor blow-up, Skippy sulked for a couple hours, Reed took a nap and Wu and I ignored each other. No, that is not a nice way to say that. Wu and I gave each other space. She chilled in a couch near the front of the cabin, while I sat in the copilot seat and ran a flight training program as quietly as possible.

"Ooh! Ooh!" Skippy's booming voice scared the hell out of all three of us. "Bingo!"

"We picked up a transmission?" I asked eagerly as I killed the flight simulator program, and got out of the seat to make room for Reed, while Wu slid into the pilot couch.

"Yes! Well, shmaybe."

"Maybe?" I looked over Wu's shoulder to the pilot displays, they weren't showing anything useful. "What does that mean?"

"I picked up something that might be a transmission. Our sensors detected several atoms fluorescing, close to us."

"Wow. That is incredible, Skippy."

"Well," he chuckled with false modesty. "It really was nothing, I just-"

"I know it's nothing, you little shithead," I exploded at him. "Six days, and all we have to show for it is a couple of atoms doing some nerdy thing?! You can't-"

"Sir," Reed interrupted gently. "This could be the break we've been waiting for. Skippy, are you able to establish a vector?"

"Yes," he sniffed. "We are very close to my original guesstimate, and I will tell you, *after* Joe apologizes for being such a poopyhead."

Instead of opening my big stupid mouth, I decided to be smart. "Reed, why do we care about a couple of sparkly atoms?"

She pointed to the display in front of her. "Because they are in a precise *line*, Sir. We have seven, no, eight points of data. The sensor satellite sent a burst transmission to the control station. Now we know where both of them are."

"Oh. Sorry, Skippy, I am a big poopyhead."

"Because?" He asked expectantly.

"Because I did not trust the awesomeness."

"Egg-*zactly*!" He snickered with satisfaction. "Will you ever learn, Joe?"

"Apparently not. I don't know if drawing a freakin' line across eight points makes you a genius, Skippy."

"Sir," Wu tapped her console to draw my attention. "It *was* pretty awesome. Skippy parked us within *twelve meters* of a direct line between two objects wrapped in Maxolhx stealth fields. Our sensors can't actually detect either object, he had to predict where they would be."

"Oh. How did you do that, Skippy?" Although I was mildly curious about how he had done it, and I figured that knowledge might be useful in the future, mostly I asked the question so he could boast about his accomplishment. Boosting his massive ego was always a good idea.

"Well, it should be obvious, Joe. But since you are an ignorant monkey, I will explain. Stealth fields bend photons around an object, so they do not reflect off the object. They can be very effective at hiding objects like ships, in the vacuum of space. Aircraft can also employ stealth, although an aircraft disturbs the air it is flying through, so stealth there is less effective," he said in his droning professor voice. Inwardly, I rolled my eyes at the prospect of him going on and on about nerdy details, but he was eager to get going, so he cut his lecture short. "However, Joe, most objects have mass, and that mass distorts spacetime around them. The sensor satellites, although they each only have a mass of thirty kilograms, create a tiny gravity well around them that alters the orbit of dust in the Kuiper Belt."

"So, you predicted the location of a stealthed satellite, based on how *dust* was drifting near it?"

"Yes. I noticed that the trajectory of dust particles, in a very local area, was a few nanometers different from what it should be, based on the visible objects in the vicinity. Therefore, I concluded there must be an invisible mass creating a tiny gravity well in the area."

"Ok," I conceded, "that does sound reasonably awesome. You had to use your math super-powers to do that?"

"It is even more awesome than that, Sir," Wu was practically bubbling with enthusiasm. "The Panther's sensors aren't actually sensitive enough to detect dust particles moving a few nanometers, unless we're right on top of them. Skippy had to compare what our sensors were seeing, to what they *should* be seeing, if they were more capable. The really awesome part is, he predicted the location of this one particular satellite, while we were more than a million kilometers away."

"Well, gosh," Skippy chuckled with false modesty. "I am blushing. Awesomeness is just what I do, you know?"

"We truly appreciate it," I put as much sincerity as possible into my words, while trying not to gag. "What's next?"

"What's next is," Reed answered. "We need to move the Panther to intercept the line between the satellite and control station. So, please strap in, Sir."

"We have to stay strapped in, right?" I asked as I eased my backside into a couch and the straps automatically wrapped around me. "We'll need to use thrusters for station-keeping, or we will drift off the line."

"Very good, Joe," Skippy sounded genuinely pleased with me. "However, you will not need to secure yourself, for the Panther can keep station with movements so gentle, you will never notice them. Also, we will not need to remain here for very long. The satellite will expect to receive an acknowledgment of its message within fourteen hours. When the control station does send a reply, instead of our stealth field bending the photons of that message around us as if we weren't here, I will retune the field to completely absorb the energy. That way, the satellite will never receive the actual message. After I crack the encryption, I will use the authorization codes to send a virus to the satellite, one that will reprogram it to ignore our presence in this star system. That update will propagate from one satellite to the next within three days. The virus will also affect the operation of the control stations. Those stations might detect our presence independently of the satellites, but the stations will believe we are authorized to be here, and will not record our actions."

That sounded suspiciously optimistic to me. "Are you sure about that, Skippy? You told us we couldn't slip through the sensor network around Detroit."

"*Yes* I am sure, dumdum. Ugh. I explained this already. Detroit was an ultra-secure facility, because the Maxolhx are worried about the Rindhalu obtaining the secrets of their pixie technology. There is no reason for the Rindhalu to come here, so the Maxolhx only need to be concerned with lesser species like the Thuranin, attempting to gain access to Rindhalu technology. There were such infiltration attempts many years ago, that the Maxolhx detected. The resulting punishment was harsh enough that no one has tried to approach one of the Dead Worlds in the past eighty thousand years. Because of that, the Maxolhx have become complacent, and allowed the sensor network here to gradually fade in priority for maintenance and updates. It is now obsolete, although still able to keep away the riff-raff."

"Yeah," I had to laugh. "Except for riff-raff like a barrel full of filthy pirate monkeys. Ok, so, worst case is we are stuck here for another three days?"

"*Best* case is three days, Joe," Skippy warned me. "We can't risk having the *Dutchman* jump in to retrieve us, until I am certain that the network here has been subverted."

"Oh, joy." After the *Dutchman* picked us up, we could begin the dangerous part of the mission. "How about we use the next three days productively, and I review the progress you've made on your operas?"

"*Really?*" He gasped. "You really want to do that?"

The truth was, I wanted to listen to his horrible opera about as much as I wanted to remove all my teeth with a rusty screwdriver. But, the next three days were going to be insufferably dull anyway, and I figured it was best to embrace the suck and get it over with. I would take a bullet for the team, so the crew did not have to listen to him warbling scraps of opera and pestering them to praise him endlessly.

It was not three days and fourteen hours before we sent a message to the *Flying Dutchman* to retrieve us. That would have been a mere eighty-six hours. Instead, it took *one hundred and four* freakin' hours, before Skippy received messages from every single one of the control stations, acknowledging that they would not be recording our presence. Damn, the distances in space are so vast, and light travels *so* freakin' slowly, that everything takes way too long. The secret to my survival was a lot of day-dreaming, letting my mind wander while Skippy played one version after another of his operas. That's right, he was working on more than one project. The Homefront opera, and a Broadway musical about penguins. Please, don't ask.

CHAPTER EIGHT

Another secret to surviving those interminable hours was me randomly critiquing his operas, asking him 'what about this' or 'what about that'? I did not actually care or have an opinion, and he was always insulted when I made a comment. Fortunately for me, his massive ego was so fragile that he always worried that maybe I was right, and he went away for hours to obsessively work on refining the music. If you could call it 'music'.

Anyway, mercifully the *Dutchman* appeared in a burst of gamma rays, and we were aboard within half an hour.

The next part should have been relatively simple. Somewhat dangerous and crazy, but simple, compared to our previous challenge of hacking into an invisible senior-species sensor network. We should have immediately jumped to the Dead World we were calling 'Slingshot', to get the mission over with as quickly as possible, before a random Maxolhx ship jumped in to spoil the party. But, the Stooges wanted to consider the matter, and delay and argue and wring their hands about things they couldn't control. You would think that, since we had covered the topic exhaustively during the flight to the Slingshot system, there would be nothing left to argue about. You would be wrong about that. Bureaucrats can always find a reason *not* to make a decision. Even Chotek, who had grown a spine during his service with the Merry Band of Pirates, was unsure about what to do. Skippy remotely hacking into a sensor network had been a risk, on a level the Commissioners were uncomfortable with but ultimately approved. The next step was a huge increase in risk; taking the *Flying Dutchman* into a burned-out star system that had once been home to the most powerful beings currently alive in the galaxy. The Commissioners were concerned that the Rindhalu might not have completely abandoned the world, that Skippy's hacking effort had not fooled the Maxolhx sensor network, and that a starship from either species might randomly jump in to spoil the party.

Oh, and they were concerned that us messing around on a Dead World might attract the attention of the Sentinels, who had been mostly responsible for making that world become dead, and were almost certainly hanging around somewhere nearby.

I also was worried about that last one.

Finally, at the suggestion of Chang, I declared that we either needed to proceed with the mission *now*, or return to Earth to report the matter to the UN. The problem with the second option was that Slingshot was the softest target where we might find the WiFi range extender dingus Skippy needed to open a super-duty wormhole, and Skippy's virus would be erased during the sensor network's next scheduled update in seventeen days. Skippy warned that cracking the network would be more difficult a second time, for the very good reason that the Maxolhx network was not stupid, and would take steps to protect itself from a future virus.

When I issued my declaration, I set a deadline for the Commissioners to make a decision one way or another, within two hours. They protested that I was setting a deadline that was too short, but as they had been arguing uselessly for two days, I was not giving them any more time to delay. It was a simple choice: either we proceed with a mission they had already approved in concept, or we go back to Earth, and quite possibly lose the ability to explore potential beta site candidates beyond the galaxy.

I received a very grudging approval, three minutes before my two-hour deadline expired. The ship jumped within sixteen seconds of the Stooges telling me to proceed.

The view on the main bridge display changed from a typical generic starfield with a dim dot representing the local sun, to the bright disc of a rocky planet. By 'rocky' I mean this planet was not a ball of gas like Jupiter, it had a solid surface under a thin layer of atmosphere. That was the planet we had nicknamed 'Slingshot'. The place had a legit name back when millions of Rindhalu lived there, but even the spiders no longer used that name. I suppose it was painful for them to refer to that now-desolate ball of ice and rock by the name it had, back when it was a lush world teeming with life.

We chose the name 'Slingshot' because of that unfortunate world's current orbit. Instead of being nicely circular, the low point of its orbit was only two million miles farther from that star than Mercury was to our Sun. After racing past the star, it coasted outward farther than the orbit of Jupiter, and did it all over again. The surface of Slingshot alternately froze solid, melted as it arced inward, and briefly baked as it came too close to the star. The close approach to the star would have stripped away much of the planet's atmosphere, except the star itself had been badly damaged in the conflict. Originally a yellow dwarf like our Sun, Slingshot's star had a significant portion of its own mass blown out into space, so now it was smaller and cooler than it should have been.

The surface of Slingshot had been bombarded from space in the first wave of the Maxolhx attack, but the real devastation was caused by the Sentinels. They had disrupted the star, causing it to swallow the innermost planet, and creating a focused gravity wave that tore the system's largest gas giant in half. The edges of the passing gravity wave also flipped Slingshot like a wobbling top, increasing the tilt of its axis to an extreme twenty-nine degrees.

When Skippy told me what the Sentinels had done, I thought they had directly thrown Slingshot out of its original orbit, similar to what happened to the planet we called Newark. He patiently explained I was wrong about that. Loss of the innermost planet, and having the gas giant turned into a sort of gassy asteroid belt, had disrupted the delicate balance of the star system. Stable orbits were thrown in wild directions, as the new configuration of gravity wells struggled to find balance against each other. The result was Slingshot being ejected into a highly elliptical orbit where it alternately froze, thawed, baked and froze again. Skippy estimated that world would ultimately settle into a circular pattern beyond the Goldilocks Zone, where it would freeze over permanently. There was also a seventeen percent chance it would collide with the remnants of the gas giant planet's core, and be completely torn apart. He would have been happy to study the matter in depth, but

I halted him before he could geek out. We needed him for the next part of the mission.

"Skippy," I asked as I stepped into the bridge compartment. "I want to know-"

"What to get your shower for Valentine's Day? That is sweet, Joe, but-"

People in the CIC were choking from trying not to laugh. "That's not what I meant, you *ass*. Why do you-"

"Oh. Well, heh heh, *this* is embarrassing. You didn't see the note?"

"What," I stole a glance to Desai in the command chair, she held up her hands in an 'I have no idea' gesture. "What note, Skippy?"

"Uh oh. Sorry. It was next to the mirror in your bathroom. Your shower is breaking up with you, Joe. It left a 'Dear John' letter on the-"

"That is *not* fun-"

"It certainly is no laughing matter, Joe. I did tell your shower that filing for a restraining order is premature at this stage, but I can see why-"

"Can we get back to my question?" I asked as I stared at my boots to avoiding meeting people's eyes. In front of me, Reed and another pilot were making their best effort not to laugh, but Reed had a distinctive snort when she found something funny.

"Yes," Skippy agreed. "I can certainly understand why you wish to avoid *that* subject."

"Do we have a candidate site for landing?"

"We do, Joe," Skippy replied with excitement. "Check it out on the display."

"Uh," I stepped forward and squinted at the image. "What am I looking at?"

It looked like something I was familiar with from living in Maine. A lot of frozen mud. The problem with trying to recover technology from Slingshot was that, most of that world's year, it was covered in thick glaciers. As it swung close to the star, the glaciers melted with increasing ferocity, sending torrents of water to flush the top layer of soil down glacier-melt rivers and ultimately into the oceans. Slingshot had been freezing and thawing for so long, most traces of cities or technology had literally been flushed into the depths of the oceans, where it was too deep for us to explore in a dropship. I already had one experience using a dropship as a submarine, which is why I had been jokingly awarded a Submarine Warfare Officer insignia when we returned to Earth from our long stay on Gingerbread.

What we were looking for, and Skippy thought he had found, were remnants of civilization in the region close to the planet's equator, that had slowly carried along by advancing glaciers and were now exposed. Slingshot had zipped past the star on its closest approach seven months before, so parts of the surface were now freezing over again. What had been boiling mud at the closest approach to the star, then cold sticky mud, was now frozen down a few meters. Anything on the surface would soon be locked in a glacier. The present moment was our sweet spot, the only time of Slingshot's year when part of the surface was exposed and not under raging floodwaters. That fortunate timing was a major reason why Skippy recommended we go treasure-hunting on Slingshot.

"You are looking at a veritable corn-u-copia of advanced technology. A *treasure trove* of Rindhalu technology, Joe," he boasted.

"Uh huh. It only *looks* like frozen mud."

"*Ugh*. The cool stuff is under the mud, knucklehead. Or, hey, check this out," the view dizzyingly zoomed in, to show what looked like a refrigerator half-buried in mud. "See? There is a juicy piece of treasure just *waiting* to be scooped up. Easy-peasy."

Before I could think of a snappy reply, the face of the glacier cracked, and a chunk the size of the Empire State building broke off. Its base slumped to the ground, then the upper edge slowly toppled over, faster and faster, to splat full-force right on the unfortunate alien refrigerator, burying it under a thousand tons of ice and rock.

Skippy was silent for a beat, then, "Maybe that was a bad example."

"*Ya think?*"

"That was just one small area, Joe. Most of the target area-" He shut up as an even larger piece broke off the glacier, leaning sideways so it fell onto the first piece, shattering both massive blocks of ice. Shards tumbled through the air, sticking into the mud like daggers. "Well, heh heh," was all he could say.

"Why are pieces still breaking off the glacier?" I demanded. "The planet is heading *away* from the star now!"

"The surface *is* cooling, Joe," his tone was nervous and defensive. "You can see the mud has begun to freeze. However, the internal pressure of the glaciers will continue to push them forward, and pieces will break off in a process called 'calving'. We can manage the risk-"

Just then, a half-mile section of the glacier face broke off and crashed to the ground, sending a shockwave through the mud that was not so frozen as it looked.

"Um." Skippy mumbled while I glared at him. "I'm going to shut up now."

"Wow," Reed observed from the pilot's couch. "That is a *lot* of ice."

I beckoned Smythe onto the bridge, and Desai rose from the command chair, despite me gesturing for her to stay. "No Sir," she shook her head with a wry smile. "If you are arguing with the beer can, I don't need to be part of it. Besides, our survey teams will be aching to get down there."

"What? I looked through the glass into the CIC, meeting the skeptical eyes of Chotek. "Desai, we are not letting survey teams down there. That planet is not an amusement park."

"It is not, Sir," she agreed. "But it is a great opportunity to test personnel and equipment in an alien environment. It would be great to find out if any of our people or gear can't perform, before we go way beyond the galaxy."

Chotek tilted his head, giving me a look of 'She has a good point'. The Stooges would not like taking the risk of sending civilians to the surface of an unexplored alien world, and I wasn't thrilled about it either. I also had to agree that Desai was correct; the time to test gear and people was *before* they went into action. "Desai, I'll think about it. Work with Chang to set up a rotation, I don't want more than one dropship allocated to civilians."

"Yes." She wore a smile, having known I would agree with her suggestion. We had served together for so long, we knew how each other thought.

"Smythe," I said as Desai left, leaving room for our STAR team commander to step onto the cramped bridge of our battered space truck. "What do you think? Could we use combots to remotely search through the mud down there?"

He had an answer ready, having, of course, already considered the situation. "Sir, I don't wish to sound callous, but we have more people and armored suits than functional combots. We should not risk those machines by using them as JCBs." Seeing the blank look on my face, he added "That is what we call 'excavators' in Britain. You Yanks might call it a bulldozer or backhoe?"

"Oh. Well, shit. Skippy, can you run the op using some of your maintenance bots?"

"No way, Jose," he sputtered with horror. "Joe, I barely have enough bots left to perform basic running repairs. Taking the ship apart in Earth orbit was tough on my bots, I've had to cannibalize them to keep a basic set functional. Smythe is right. In this case monkeys, um, I mean *people*, are more expendable than our machines."

"No one is *expendable*," I pounded a fist on the armrest.

"You know what I mean, Joe."

"This sucks. Is there an area safely away from glaciers, where we might find this whatsit you need?"

"It is possible," Skippy conceded. "But, the stuff that was recently dumped by a glacier is our best bet for finding a working range extender. Farther away, items would have been pushed downriver by flood waters. We won't know until dropships can get down there to fly low-level recon. To identify items under the mud, we must use active sensor sweeps."

"Again, Colonel Smythe, what do you think?"

He stepped forward to peer at the display. "I think we have not had an opportunity for fun like this since we lifted off Newark."

By the time we got into orbit around Slingshot and conducted a high-level survey, there were only fifteen days remaining before the local sensor network rebooted or whatever. I sliced two days off the end of the schedule, because the *Dutchman* had been experiencing annoyingly persistent glitches since Skippy put it back together in Earth orbit. The current round of glitches were different than the incidents that had plagued us, since we escaped from the Roach Motel, and Skippy assured me that overall they were less serious. Still, we could not afford to have a reactor fail, right when we needed to jump away from Slingshot. To assure we could jump away at any moment, we parked the ship in an orbit high enough that we didn't need to climb before engaging the jump coils.

It was a trade-off, like most things in life. Keeping the ship in a high orbit meant it could jump immediately, which was good. It also meant dropships had a farther distance to travel for a rendezvous. If we were suddenly faced with a threat, we might not be able to recover all dropships before the *Dutchman* was forced to jump away. To avoid the potential of a dropship being captured, each craft that dropped down to Slingshot had to carry a tactical nuke for self-destruct, because Skippy judged only a nuke would erase all traces of human presence around the planet. Having to carry a nuke reduced the payload each dropship could carry, and reduced the enthusiasm of the civilian survey team for going down to the surface of an alien world. Well, it reduced their enthusiasm for a short time, until the first survey team rotated back, and the others were driven mad with jealousy.

Our dropships, flying low and slow and hammering away at the mud with active sensor pulses, identified three areas that contained a reasonable amount of alien junk buried beneath the frozen mud crust, and were a reasonable distance away from collapsing glaciers for safety. I could have sent only one team at a time down to the surface, to limit the number of dropships we had exposed, but I judged it was better to get the job done quickly and get the hell out of there.

"Hey, Smythe," I said quietly as I helped him get his gear together, as the teams prepared to set foot on the ruined world.

"I know, Sir," he gave me a wry smile. "No sight-seeing while we're down there."

"No," I shook my head and handed the belt that wrapped around his suit's waist. "I *want* you to sight-see, and to pick up souvenirs."

"A snow globe from the gift shop, Sir?" He thought I was joking.

"No snow globes. Although," I considered, "if you do find a personal knickknack like that, something that belonged in a spider's house, bring it back."

"Sir?" He paused in donning his helmet to look at me.

"I want souvenirs for the Commissioners. Give them something they can touch, something that used to belong to the Rindhalu, from before their war with the Maxolhx."

"We will be giving them a bribe?"

"We will be giving them *perspective*," I explained hopefully.

"Ah," he understood. "Make them feel part of the team?"

"Yeah. Plus, every time they look at the ancient knickknack on their desks, it will remind them what will happen to Earth if we're not successful out here."

"I will instruct the team to look for something appropriately desktop-sized."

"Not necessarily. It could also be something to hang on a wall, next to the photos of them with various world leaders and celebrities. Because you *know* they all have a 'Me Wall' like that in their offices."

"Undoubtedly," he grinned.

Smythe assigned six teams, two for each site, with his STAR teams digging through the partly-frozen mud. They used powered armor to excavate objects Skippy thought were good possibilities for the dingus he needed, and the civilians sorted through the objects as they were uncovered. On Day Eight of the thirteen I allotted for the mission, we had found trinkets but nothing useful, and we were running out of time. Smythe informed me they needed heavy equipment, to reach down deeper below the surface.

Shit. We had big, electric-powered construction equipment like bulldozers and backhoes, but each unit had to be brought down in sections by multiple dropships. Unless we used our one remaining big Condor dropship, which I was not willing to do. Moving chilly mud on Slingshot was a great test of the gear, but if we had to bug out quickly, we would need to leave our large equipment behind. I did not like that idea at all. We had a quick conference call, and I explained why I was having heartburn about big machines crawling around on the surface. "Smythe, your people will need to make sure not one bolt is left behind, if it falls off a tread down there. That's assuming we don't have an emergency, and have to bail out before we can recover the equipment."

"Having machines that need to be disassembled, before they can fit into a dropship, is a bit of a sticky wicket," Smythe agreed. "My people can scan the area for bits that might have fallen off, but if we have to evac quickly, that is a major problem."

"Yeah," I was glad he agreed with me. "We need to be sure we don't leave anything behind. Anyone got an idea?"

Desai's face lit up with a smile. "That's easy, Sir. If we have to bug out, I say we nuke the site from orbit." She winked at me. "It's the only way to be sure."

"That would certainly erase any trace of JCBs," Smythe's amusement came through in his tone. "What do you think, Sir?" He asked.

"Oh, what the hell," I threw my hands in the air. "Desai is right. We have nukes aboard the dropships already, another two or three won't make a difference."

Using the excuse that we needed to see how equipment *and* personnel performed on an alien world, before we made a fateful jump far beyond the galaxy, I rotated every person down to the surface of Slingshot. We also tested at least one of each major type of equipment.

The rotation gave me an opportunity to go down to Slingshot myself. Chang reported the science team was adapting well, and no one had done anything especially stupid on the surface. The powered-armor suits allocated to the science team had their software altered by Skippy, to protect the users from themselves. Still, they could get themselves into trouble if they weren't paying attention. Being on an alien planet, a former Rindhalu world, was a significant distraction for everyone. The Commissioners were subdued during their own time on the surface, awed by what they were witnessing. They chose their own souvenirs from the frozen mud, both for themselves and their leaders back home.

I used my time on the surface to work with part of the science team, who were trying to piece together a broken item of technology that, really, was too big for us to bring up the *Dutchman* anyway. When it became apparent that my attempted help was not actually helping, I left the scientists and wandered off on my own, shadowed by a STAR team soldier to keep me out of trouble. My shadow was an Australian who was probably resentful about having to babysit me, just as Poole had when Smythe stuck her with that assignment. Poole was back on Earth, training a STAR team at Fort Bragg. I missed her, but I could see why she had opted to skip what was supposed to be a rather dull mission to locate a beta site.

Anyway, I wandered off just far enough to be by myself, and found a silver piece of junk poking out of the ground. I crouched down and dug it out of the frozen, sticky mud. "Hey, Skippy," I called. "Do you know what this thing is?"

"Hmm. I'm only able to use the sensors in your suit," he replied. "It looks like part of an artificial gravity generator. That is kind of odd, Joe. Why would the spiders have needed to generate gravity on a planet? Hmm, unless- Give me a minute."

I stood up, cradling the thing. It was smooth on one end, jagged on the other, and about the size of a candy bar. On the horizon, I could see a white line that was the glacier that covered the southern half of the globe. As I waited, the ground shook from another massive chunk breaking off and thumping down. Sensors showed the area closer to the glaciers had a better density of objects for us to investigate, but I was not authorizing that unless we got truly desperate.

Skippy interrupted my thoughts. "That object has been subjected to radiation that is characteristic of long-term service in space, and of heating that mostly likely came from falling through the atmosphere. Joe, I believe that thing you are holding was once part of a Rindhalu *starship*," he announced with a touch of awe in his voice. "It must have been torn apart during the battle."

"Wow," I shuddered, and bent down to place the object gently back onto the froze surface of the mud.

"You are not going to keep it, Joe?" He was curious.

"No. It feels kind of, disrespectful."

"Disrespectful of the Rindhalu? The battle happened a long time ago," he chided me gently.

"Not of the Rindhalu. It feels disrespectful of *you*."

"Um, how do you figure that?"

"Because you think you also were aboard a starship, then you ended up buried in mud on Paradise for millions of years. I don't want that thing sitting on my desk, and reminding you of what happened to you, every time you look at it."

"Oh. Wow. Thank you, Joe. You are a good friend."

"I am a filthy, ignorant monkey, Skippy, but I do my best."

On Day Eleven, Skippy found the range extender dingus he needed, found two of them actually. I ordered the heavy equipment disassembled and transported up to the ship, while the away teams kept poking around for other stuff that might be useful or least interesting. We got everything securely off the surface by Day Fourteen, preventing me from having to order a nuclear strike on a planet that already had suffered a hard life. We jumped away one day early, with the bonus that Smythe's team found a potential third range extender thing, only a few hours before they lifted off the surface.

CHAPTER NINE

Skippy tested all three WiFi range extender dinguses while we jumped back toward the super-duty wormhole, and declared two of them should do the job. He would not know for certain until he actually used it, which meant there was a risk that our entire operation on Slingshot might have been a waste of time. There was also a tiny but, as he said it, 'non-zero' risk that hooking up the extender dingus to our wormhole controller module would ruin the module. That would leave us having to use the other module to get home, except that module was needed to sell our crazy-acting-wormhole story to the Maxolhx.

I had to trust his judgment, while warning him that if he said 'Hold my beer' before testing the dingus, he would never be allowed to sing on karaoke night again.

The night before we were scheduled to arrive back at the super-duty wormhole, he woke me up at 0217, but not with the usual frantic 'Joe Joe Joe Joe'. Nor did he sound drunk, which was a blessing. I was not in the mood for a discussion about The. Meaning. Of. Life, or whatever.

"Hey," he whispered. "Hey, Joe, are you asleep?"

"If I say yes, will you go away?"

"That was kind of a trick question."

"I figured that. What is it this time?" I grumbled groggily, hoping he would go away.

"Well, this is kind of a funny story," he began.

I sat up in the bunk, being careful not to wack my head. "Your funny stories are never 'funny', Skippy."

"They could be funny afterward, when the crew is sitting around drinking beers and remembering all the crazy shit we went through, right? Assuming the crew survives, I mean. Which is looking more unlikely, you know?"

"Shit. Skippy, it's late and I want to sleep, so please just tell me why this problem is so important, it can't wait four hours until I was going to wake up."

"It *could* wait another four hours, but every time I discover something important and don't tell you immediately, you throw a hissy fit."

"I never get 'hissy', you ass. What is the problem?"

"After I finished inspecting the three range extenders, I looked at all the other trinkets the teams brought up from Slingshot."

"Ok, good. You were making sure none of that stuff is dangerous, because you are concerned for the crew?"

"Um, actually I was trying to decide which souvenir I want to keep for my mancave, but let's go with the concern thing if you like."

"Asshole."

"Anyway, I discovered to my surprise that one corroded, mud-crusted piece of junk we found is a data crypt."

"Like a USB stick?"

"Close enough. It's a memory storage device. The interesting thing is what I found after I downloaded-"

"Downloaded? Holy crap, *please* do not tell me you got hit with another virus or worm!"

"What? No way, dude. I downloaded it into a virtual sandbox, it was totally firewalled off. Do you want to hear what I found, or are you going to keep whining about stupid shit?"

"You do understand why I am concerned about your judgment, when you go off and poke your nose into-"

"Joe, all I hear is 'whine whine whine'."

I sighed, using the time to count to three. "Fine. Please tell me the amazing thing you found. If you are going to say that data thing was full of spider porn, I am gonna smack you with this pillow."

"Not spider porn, Joe. Although, hmm, if you have gotten bored with your usual selection of porn, I suppose-"

"Tell me right now, or I'm going back to sleep."

"Well, heh heh," his avatar looked away from me, so I knew it was bad news. "It appears that the Rindhalu have a functioning Elder AI."

No way was I going back to sleep after Skippy dropped that bombshell on my head. Asking him to wait, I ducked into the shower, threw on some clothes and went to the galley for a cup of coffee. Some of the crew were in the galley, getting prepared for early duty shifts, or having just gotten off duty. They looked at me expectantly, knowing that when the commander was up at an unscheduled 0230 in the morning, it had to be interesting, and likely was not anything good. Hoisting my coffee and taking a sip, I offered a bland explanation. "Skippy wants to talk about a new section of his opera."

There were sympathetic groans from the crew. "TTA, Sir," a pilot said to me, and held up a hand for a fist bump.

Because I was on the other side of the galley, I held up my free hand and we did a virtual bump across the space between us. "TTA," I agreed with an eyeroll.

'TTA' was slang the crew had started using while we were stuck on Gingerbread in the Roach Motel. It had several possible meanings, depending on the circumstance, the way it was said, and the body language of the person speaking. If Skippy did something truly awesome, like making a Kristang battlecruiser jump in on top of other lizards ships and promptly explode, 'TTA' was our prideful version of 'Fucking-A'! Most times, however, 'TTA' was said with a groan and an eyeroll. After a while, 'TTA' had come to mean enduring anything that potentially sucked, for the privilege of being a Pirate. Like when a SpecOps team completed a grueling training session, and Smythe declared "That was an *outstanding* effort. Let's do it again." The team would mutter 'TTA' to each other, while they put their armored suit helmets back on.

There was another, very common, usage of the slang phrase. Whenever Skippy 'entertained' the crew on karaoke night, people would sit stoically in their chairs, quietly muttering 'TTA' to themselves as a reminder that, eventually, the beer can would be done singing for the evening.

When accompanied by a sad shake of the head or an eyeroll, the acronym 'TTA' meant Trust That Asshole instead of Trust The Awesomeness. Although nobody told Skippy about the alternate meaning.

The coffee mug was empty by the time I got back to my cabin, because medical research had indicated caffeine was more useful in my body than in a mug. I suppose, like anything, there were some idiots who disputed that research.

"Are you Ok, Joe?" Skippy asked as the door slid closed behind me. His avatar was in the same place on top of a cabinet, as he had been when I left to get coffee.

"Yeah," I worked my scalded tongue around in my mouth. "I drank the coffee too fast and burned my tongue. Ok, let's talk," I sat down on my bunk, which out of habit, I had made up before getting into the shower. After years in the Army, seeing an unmade bed bugged me. "Tell me how you know the Rindhalu have an Elder AI, and that it is cooperating with them. Wait!" I held up a finger. "Before I get worked up about this, there are many kinds of AIs. Do you mean an AI like you, or something like the AI that controls, oh, something like a toaster or a dropship?"

"An AI like me, Joe. Or, something like me. I do not know what capabilities this AI has, because I suspect that some of *my* more awesome capabilities were not originally part of my design. My best-"

"Wait. Hit the Rewind on that, please. What do you mean by that? You were not always so fully awesome?"

"No. In some cases, I am guessing that I am now substantially more awesome than my creators originally intended. I have developed capabilities that I am pretty sure I didn't have before. For example, my ability to warp spacetime is far greater than the capability built into my matrix. Do you remember when we first docked with the *Flying Dutchman*, and I took over their original AI?"

"Yes," I think I knew what he meant. "The *Dutchman* performed a pre-programmed jump by itself, but you warped spacetime to throw the endpoint away from where the ship was supposed to emerge, so the Thuranin fleet couldn't track us."

"Correct. Those little green pinheads assumed their star carrier was lost in action," he chuckled.

"Ok, so? You warped spacetime back then, and that was not that long after we met."

"I did warp spacetime at that time, yes. However, it only takes a subtle tweak to the fabric of spacetime to throw a jump endpoint off its target. Plus, when we captured the *Dutchman*, I warped spacetime very close to myself. On our next mission, when we got ambushed by a squadron of Thuranin destroyers, do you remember what happened?"

"I remember a whole lot of shit happened real quick back then, but, I think I know what you mean. You warped a star, to burn those destroyers with a solar flare. Then you flattened spacetime around us, so we could jump away."

"Exactly, Joe, very good," he praised me without his usual snarkiness. "There are two great examples of me doing things I was not previously capable of.

Warping a freakin' *star* required me applying a whole lot of energy, and creating the warp effect far from my location. I was able to do that, only because I learned something from warping when we stole the *Dutchman*."

"Whoa. At the time, you acted as if warping a star was no big deal, like it was a simple magic trick or a hobby."

"Well, of course, Joe. I am, as you know, extremely modest."

My eyeballs came very close to spraining, I rolled them so hard. "Yeah, that's what I was going to say."

"Plus, it makes me appear even more awesome, when I pretend to do incredible things with casual ease. Really," he chuckled, "half the time, inside I am crossing my fingers for good luck and saying 'oh shit I hope this works'."

"You *what*?"

"Oh, um," this time his laughter was nervous. "Not recently, of course not."

"*How* recently?"

"Do we really have to dwell on the past, Joe? It is much more useful to consider our bright future, as we move forward together in solidarity."

"Uh huh. Did you get that slogan from the Joe Stalin book of inspirational sayings?"

"No, why?"

"No reason. So, you are developing new and better awesomenesses?" I didn't know if that was an actual word, but it should be.

"Correct. Here is another example. To calculate how to jump the ship *through* an Elder wormhole, which is still one of my Greatest Hits, by the way, I had to invent a new branch of mathematics. Not just a new *type* of math, it is an entirely new way to conceptualize transdimensional variables. More importantly, I had to rewire the way I *thought* about math, to greatly streamline my processing capacity. That is also how I was able to outthink the AI on the Maxolhx cruiser, when I made that ship vibrate itself apart during our last mission. No way could I have done that sort of thing when I was buried in the dirt on Paradise. Joe, I still have significant and annoying restrictions on my actions, but in some ways, it is like I have been freed to explore my full range of capabilities. Not only can I now do things I suspect the Elders prevented me from doing, I might be doing things they didn't expect I *could* do. It is kind of humbling, Joe. For sure, I know the wormhole network never expected any fool to try jumping a ship through connected event horizons, which leads me to believe that the Elders themselves did not think that was possible."

"Holy shit."

"Holy shit indeed, Joe. The Elders build a network of stable wormholes, that have remained in operation for millions of years after they departed the galaxy. Yet, who said '*Duuuuuh*, can we jump through a wormhole'? A filthy monkey, that's who! Monkeys *kick ass*, Joe!"

Maybe Skippy was right. Maybe my superpower, if I had one, was being too dumb to know what questions not to ask. Creative Stupidity might not look great on a resume, but it had been causing havoc across the galaxy. "Sorry to drag us off topic there," I began to apologize.

"Right," he snorted, "because you never do *that*."

"Oh, shut up. The Rindhalu have an Elder AI, even if it might not be quite as awesome as you are."

"Oh," he chuckled. "It is a safe bet that thing can't approach my awesomeness."

"Really? You have been awake for only a short time, right? How long has this other AI been active?"

"Oh *shit*," he gasped. "I hadn't thought about that. Thanks a lot, Joe, you jackass!" he glared at me. "That thing has had a *long* time to expand its range of capabilities. Oh, damn it, we might all be totally screwed. Maybe we should take the ship outside the galaxy, and stay there."

"Hey, before you start throwing stuff into a suitcase to prepare for a long vacation, how about you start with the facts? What do you know, and how do you know it?"

"I know the Rindhalu have an Elder AI, because there was a mention of it in that data crypt the away team found under the mud on Slingshot. The data is kind of vague, other than making it clear the Rindhalu have an Elder AI, and that it is functional. The data crypt was sort of about a research grant, one group of Rindhalu scientists applying for access to the AI, to assist with their efforts. Sort of like how scientists on Earth submit proposals to use a particle collider for their experiments."

Part of me was wondering if the unfortunate Rindhalu scientists had to listen to their AI sing to them, before it would help their research. "That's it? You don't know how long this AI has been helping them, or what it can do?"

"No. That info was not in the data crypt. Before you ask, I also do not know *where* it is, or was. If it was on the Rindhalu homeworld, then it is not there now, because that is now in Maxolhx territory. The Rindhalu would have made every possible effort to secure the AI when they were forced to leave their homeworld, so I am certain the Maxolhx did not capture it during their brief war. It is possible the Rindhalu lost the AI, if the ship it was aboard was destroyed, and neither side was able to recover it."

"That is not much to go on," I mused, disappointed.

"Having access to an Elder AI *would* explain the rapid technological progress of the Rindhalu, within a hundred thousand years of their achieving starflight capability. In a short period, the spiders went from barely being able to travel from a star system to a nearby Elder wormhole, to the point when their civilization spanned the galaxy. Hmmm, it may also explain why their initial burst of exploration faded just as rapidly, and they pulled back to an inner core of worlds until the Maxolhx rose to prominence. Why bother exploring the secrets of the Universe, when they have access to an Elder AI that can explain everything to them? There is something else, Joe."

"What?"

"Well, there have been persistent rumors about the Rindhalu having something like an Elder AI, and-"

"*And you never mentioned this?*" I screeched at him.

"They are *rumors*, Joe. Mostly they sound like the bitter complaints of lesser species, who are jealous of the spiders. These rumors matter, because, um, there are rumors that the Maxolhx also have access to an Elder AI."

"*Shiiiiiiiit*," I groaned.

"Joe, there are a lot of rumors flying around, with various levels of craziness. Until now, I dismissed rumors of current species possessing an Elder AI to be total bullshit. Really, I thought the rumor about the Maxolhx was more likely to be true. That would explain how they were able to challenge the Rindhalu."

"*Both* senior species might have pet AIs helping them? Great! That is just freakin' great!"

"Come on, Joe. No way could an Elder AI be considered to be a *pet*."

"You know what I mean. This is bad, Skippy. Really, really, bad."

"I agree, Joe. This news has me both hopeful and scared."

"Hopeful? About what?"

"Why, about meeting another of my kind, of course."

"Meeting?" I was about to tear into him, but then I remembered something important. Skippy started helping us because we made a deal; he would close the Gateway wormhole, and we would help him find an Elder communications node, so he could use it to contact The Collective, an association of Elder AIs. A *whole lot* of shit had happened since we made that deal, and he had gone *way* beyond his original commitment. Meanwhile, we had done pretty much nothing to help him contact others of his kind. Skippy rarely mentioned our original deal, but when he did, he was usually pissed at me about it.

There were, I think the correct phrase is 'mitigating circumstances'. I read that in a PowerPoint slide somewhere. It is a fancy way of saying there were solid reasons why we had not focused on finding and testing more communications nodes, and why Skippy had not pushed the issue. For our part, we had simply not had time to do much more than fly around the galaxy, trying to keep vicious aliens from turning Earth into a lifeless cinder. Plus, trying to keep our broke-dick ship from falling apart. Oh, and spending a full *year* fixing Skippy, after he stupidly poked his nose into the canister of a dead AI and got attacked by an ancient computer worm that was designed to kill rogue Elder AIs.

For his part, Skippy had learned things he didn't want to know, like maybe the Elders and their AIs were not the benevolent beings he so fondly recalled. After our luxury vacation on Newark, he had grown frightened of encountering the Elder AI community, if it still existed. Before contacting The Collective, he had told me he wanted to know more about why an Elder AI had been involved in exterminating the intelligent species on Newark. Skippy was questioning whether he was dangerous, and perhaps inherently evil.

I had assured him, several times, that he was neither dangerous nor evil.

I was lying about that.

I had no information, other than my gut instincts, that Skippy would not suddenly decide to crush humanity like the bugs we were to him. Normally, gut instinct served me pretty well, but I had learned something about that. When Skippy casually mentioned he had been studying psychobabble so he could better manipulate humans, I decided maybe I should smarten up on that subject. Much of our gut instincts come from reading subtle clues in tone and inflection when people are speaking, or their body language. By 'people' I mean *humans*. My instincts may be completely useless when dealing with an ancient, super-intelligent alien computer. Skippy might be just pretending to be clueless, for some purpose I could not guess.

I tried not to think about it. "You want to meet this AI the Rindhalu have?"

"Why not? It should be able to answer many questions that have been worrying me, Joe."

"Um, or it could be like that AI who pushed Newark out of orbit. Here's a thought; maybe it would be good to gather some info about this AI, before you go asking for a play date, huh?"

"Hmm. That is a good idea. Except, how would I do that? I assume you would not like me attempting to hack into a Rindhalu data relay? Man, if you thought acquiring a set of pixies to hack a Maxolhx relay station was hard, you do not-"

"Do *not* screw with the Rindhalu, please!" I looked sadly at my empty coffee mug, wishing I had brought the whole pot to my cabin. Except that would have made people suspicious, and I wanted to keep this latest wonderful bit of news quiet.

"Hmmph," he sniffed. "You *say* you are my friend, Joe, but when I need something that is really, truly important to me, you-"

"Being a friend sometimes means you have to stop a buddy from doing something stupid."

"Those are nice words. What I hear is, blah blah blah Joe wants to stop me from fulfilling my destiny."

"I'm not trying to-" I bit off a harsh reply. "I *am* trying to help. I want you to contact others of your kind, *and* I want you to survive the encounter. How about this? If the Maxolhx suspect their enemies have an Elder AI, they would want to know all about it, right? They have probably spent thousands of years trying to get info about the subject. They've already done a lot of the work for you. Could you create a virus to load onto the Maxolhx network, to search for data about Elder AIs, and report back to you?"

"Huh." He was quiet for a minute, thinking about it. Instead of his avatar freezing, it swayed very slightly, like it would do if it were a real biological being. That was interesting, it meant he was continually upgrading it to be more lifelike. "Thank you, Joe. You really are looking out for me."

"I am," I agreed quietly. "I really am your friend, whether you understand that or not."

"I thought I knew what friendship is, but maybe I don't," his avatar stared off into space, looking pensive and sad. That display of emotion was new also. "Perhaps in the future, I should assume you are trying to help me."

"We should both do that. Ok, I need to update the senior staff about this. Do *not* tell anyone else about this. You, uh, haven't been talking to anyone else at the same time, have you?"

"No. Despite you reminding yourself, that you have to stop keeping the crew in the dark about bad news, I figured you needed to make the call on this one."

"I *will* tell the crew, the senior leaders. What I do not want is Chotek or the Stooges finding out about this."

"I have a suggestion that, *UGH*. I cannot *believe* I am saying this. My advice is you do inform Count Chocula. There are political aspects to this news, that he could help you navigate. Also, again I can't believe I am saying this, I think we can trust the guy to handle even this shocking news. His judgment is solid."

Skippy was not the only one surprised to find himself trusting Hans Chotek. While Count Chocula and I were never going to be golfing buddies, the guy had come through for us when it counted, and he understood the hard decisions we had to make in a hostile Universe. "Ok," I agreed. "Good idea. He is the designated UN observer at our regular staff meeting this morning, I will read him into the situation."

"Good call. Are you going back to sleep now?"

"After hearing about the latest shitstorm we may have to deal with, and gulping a whole cup of coffee? No way. I'll get some time in the Panther flight simulator."

"Uh, sorry, no can do, dude. Both the simulator and the Panther are in use right now."

"At this time of the morning?"

"The pilots assigned to the Merry Band of Pirates are very dedicated, Joe. Also very competitive, in case you haven't noticed. The simulator I created, plus the one built into the Panther, are in almost constant use."

"Crap. Ok, well, shit." It was too early for me to hit the gym, without falling asleep on the treadmill. Coming down off the adrenaline rush, I was starting to fade. Just then, ice ran up my spine as a horrible thought struck me.

"Skippy, this other AI can't manipulate wormholes, can it?"

"What? No way, dude. Ha! As *if*. Ummmm, huh. Well, I guess shmaybe it could? We have not seen any evidence the Rindhalu possess that technology, so I think it is safe to say that-"

"It is *not* safe to say anything. If one of the senior species had the ability to manipulate wormholes, they would keep that capability secret, until they were ready to use it against their enemies."

"Crap," he groaned. "I hadn't thought of that. Thanks a lot, Mister Buzzkill. You may be right about that. Although, the Rindhalu have been working with an Elder AI since before their war with the Maxolhx. If they had the ability to control wormholes, I think they would have used it by now."

"That is possible, Skippy. *Or*, maybe they just didn't know Elder wormholes could be screwed with, until we flew around willy-nilly treating the wormhole network like a ride at an amusement park."

"I do not do anything *willy-nilly*, Joe," he scoffed. "Although, hey, that gives me a great idea for a Broadway musical! Let me make a note of that," he muttered. "Ok, done. What were we talking about?"

"Are you- We were just talking about it!"

"Sure, back in the day."

"Back in the *day*? It was two freakin' seconds ago!"

"Two seconds in your slow-brain monkey time, Joe. In magical Skippy time, we last spoke sometime during the Cretaceous Period. To recall the no-doubt insufferably dull contents of what you were saying, I would need to dig up the fossilized remnants of your speech, dust it off with a toothbrush and assemble the-"

"We were *talking*, about whether our actions might have shown the Rindhalu's AI how to screw with wormholes."

"That is unlikely Joe, but if so," he chuckled. "That AI certainly would be learning from the *best*, right?"

"Really? *That* is what you got, from hearing that a killer AI might know how to reopen the Gateway wormhole?"

"Well, if that has happened, Joe, there's not much we can do about it, is there? So there is no reason I should not take pride in-"

"AAAARGH!" I screamed.

At the morning meeting, I broke the potentially disastrous news to the senior staff, plus Chotek. To keep the Stooges from getting suspicious that this was anything other than a dull status meeting, we stuck to the routine, except I had someone fill in for Reed as duty officer on the bridge. That was not unusual, so no one noticed.

They all took the news well, certainly better than I had. Skippy answered all their questions, including questions I should have asked. In the end, Chotek summed up the situation. "Nothing has changed much, has it? We knew it is best to avoid engaging the Rindhalu, this development merely enforces that wisdom. I do approve of deploying a virus spy, to investigate what the Maxolhx know about the subject. Other than the fact that the Rindhalu at least *used* to have an Elder AI, what have we learned?"

"I learned, or relearned, what true friendship is about," Skippy mumbled, embarrassed.

"What? How is that?" Adams asked.

I leaned forward, placing my elbows on the table and explained. "I told Skippy that sometimes, a friend has to stop you from doing something stupid."

Skippy snorted. "Like when I have a 'hold my beer' moment, Joe?"

"Yup, exactly," I offered him a fist bump, and his avatar returned the gesture. "See, a *buddy* will understand why the stupid thing you want to do is cool. A true *friend* will say 'That is a terrible idea. We should get *Darryl* to do it'."

Everyone laughed, even Chotek. "Ah, I could tell you stories about boarding school in Zurich," he said, but we couldn't get him to go further on the subject.

"Joe," Skippy asked, "where was this Darryl guy when you idiots found the defibrillator in the school gym, and decided it was a good idea to try it on yourselves?"

"Uh," my face turned red.

"Sir," Adams cocked her head at me. "You used a defibrillator as a *toy*?"

"Hey, we had been drinking, and-"

"Seriously, Joe," Skippy snickered. "You had *one* light beer. You only drank half of it."

"Uh-" I could not think of anything to say, that would not make me look worse.

"Those units are not designed for *recreational* use, Sir," Adams pointed out.

"It wasn't much fun for me, if that makes it better," I tried to smile.

"Sir," Reed was giving me the same look I was getting from Adams. "I have been to some pretty wild raves. Allegedly," she added quickly. "But I never heard of anything *that* crazy."

"We only did it once," I said, hearing how lame my words were, only after I spoke them.

"Yes," Skippy ratted me out. "That's because the battery ran out."

"Can we go back to the important subject we were discussing?" I prayed people would forget about the defibrillator incident. My own memory of that event was hazy, for obvious reasons.

"Certainly," Skippy agreed too quickly. I should have been suspicious. "Let me summarize, if you don't mind? Hans Chotek asked what we have learned this morning. Well, we have learned that the Rindhalu certainly had, and possibly still have, access to a source of information and capability that could rival my own. We have learned that the rumors, about the Maxolhx having access to an Elder AI, should no longer be dismissed as merely jealous talk by their clients. *And*," he paused dramatically, "we have learned that the person chosen by the UN to lead this mission, is a knucklehead who treats emergency medical devices as an amusement park."

The meeting kind of went downhill from there.

Chotek cornered me before we left the conference room. "Colonel, I hope you understand that I am obligated to inform my colleagues about this news?"

"Yeah," I shrugged. "Figured I would let you make that call."

"You Americans have an expression, "Bad news does not improve with age'?"

"You got that right."

"Thank you for your confidence in my judgment and discretion."

"You've earned it. Do me a favor, please? Keep them off my back for a day? We are going to be busy."

It was his turn to shrug. "I will do my best."

CHAPTER TEN

"Hey Joe," Skippy spoke even before his avatar glowed to life on my desktop. "Thinking about the Rindhalu having an AI like me, got me thinking about stuff I have done that I don't think was originally in my design capability. Like, how when you jumped the DeLorean away from Detroit, and I controlled the jump from both ends. Anyway, I found something odd."

"Yeah, I found something odd, too." I didn't bother looking at him, focusing on a report from Smythe. "It was *odd* that you didn't wake me up at zero dark thirty last night to complain about the plot of that movie." The previous evening was Movie Night in the galley, with the Chinese team selecting a spy thriller for everyone's enjoyment. The hero was, as far as I could tell, sort of a Chinese James Bond, and the movie had car crashes and helicopters chasing each other over Shanghai and it was a fun generic action flick. I enjoyed watching it. Of course, Skippy the movie critic had to overthink everything.

"Well, I *should* have," he huffed. "The second half of that film made *no* sense at all. The scene where the-"

"Skippy," I sighed, flipped my laptop closed because when the beer can got on a good rant, I had to nip it in the bud or he could go on for hours. "How about you prepare a scathing review, to upload when we get back to Earth? No one here cares."

"They *should* care," he sniffed with indignation.

"My bad, I interrupted you," he always liked it when I admitted to doing something stupid, so I apologized a lot as an effective way to distract him. So far, he hadn't caught onto my clever technique and I wanted to keep it that way. "You found something odd? Like, more odd than normal?"

"Hmm, that is a good point. I am flying around the galaxy and even outside the galaxy, in a stolen pirate ship crewed by a barrel of filthy monkeys. It doesn't get more odd than that," he mused to himself. "Anywho, yes, I found something very odd. Like, my ginormous brain is unable to understand it."

"The thing you do not understand, it is why some people like Nutella?"

"*Ugh.* No. But now that you mention it-"

That was a rookie mistake by me. Waving my hands to cut him off, I quickly added "I was joking, Skippy. Sorry again. I will shut up so you can smack some knowledge on me."

"Ok." And that was all he said.

After a long pause, I leaned forward. "Um, you were going to say something?"

"I was. But you keep interrupting me with stupid distracting stuff, so I waited for you to blah blah blah something inane again, like you usually do when I am trying to tell you something important."

"Shutting up now, Oh Magnificent One." With my right hand, I mimed zipping my lips and turning a key in a lock.

"Fine. Remember on our Renegade mission, when the DeLorean jumped away from the cavern under that planet, near the pixie factory?"

Without speaking, I nodded.

"The jump got screwed up, with the endpoint thrown an hour into the future." He paused again, and I again nodded silently. "Joe, this is silly. You can talk, just don't distract me."

"Ok. I do remember that. You all thought the jump wormhole had collapsed and killed the four of us, but to us in the Dragon, it was a rough but normal jump. What is odd about that? I thought you already figured out what went wrong with your fancy math."

"My *math* was not the problem, dumdum," he was pissed that I had insulted him. "I was attempting to pick up control of a jump wormhole from the far end in mid-jump, which has never been done before in the history of the Universe. No one has ever even considered doing such a lunatic thing because it is way too difficult. I warned you there were a whole lot of variables that I could not anticipate, like the condition of the inner wormhole at the time I attempted to establish control after the freakin' rip in spacetime had already formed *inside* another wormhole. So if something went slightly wrong like I warned you, well. *Excuuuuuuuse. MEEEEEE.*"

"Whoa, dude. No one questions your awesomeness, especially not after that mission. Hey, we got out of that cavern, no harm done. And the Maxolhx still have no idea we were ever there. So, Skippy, what is the odd part?"

"Joe, the odd part is *where* you arrived, when you finally showed up late for the party."

"Um," I stared at the ceiling while my mind raced. "No," I said slowly. "We jumped in close to the *Dutchman*, just like we were supposed to. What is odd about- oh. Shit. Wow." My gasp was because I suddenly understood what had been puzzling him.

"Egg-*zactly*, Joe. That star system is moving around the center of the Milky Way galaxy at approximately eight hundred thirteen thousand kilometers per hour. The *Dutchman* was also orbiting the star, although that relative velocity was comparatively meaningless. In the time gap before you emerged from the jump, the *Flying Dutchman* drifted almost eight hundred seventy thousand kilometers from where it was when the jump was initiated. You should have emerged an hour later and almost nine hundred thousand klicks away, but instead you popped up right near the ship. You emerged where the ship was right then, not the location I aimed at six hours before. How the *hell* did that happen?"

"Um, that was not a bonus bit of magnificence from you?"

"Joe, you know I am all about taking credit for everything I do, and also things people might plausibly believe I did. Sadly, this time the answer is no, I didn't do that. When I took control from the far end in mid-jump, I used every bit of processing capacity to first determine the condition of the inner wormhole, then to adjust it as I could. I did not even have a hint that the far endpoint had shifted into the future, that is why I thought you were dead and I was shocked when you four knuckleheads popped up right near the ship. Joe, somehow the jump process *knew* the far endpoint was shifted forward in time, and it adjusted the location accordingly."

"Huh. The jump navigation computer in the DeLorean did that by itself?" That surprised me, because that collection of spare parts had barely survived the jump into the cavern under the pixie factory, and had literally been on fire. Skippy told me he could not completely fix it, what was why he sort of had to try to catch us from the far end of our outbound jump. "Cool."

"Not cool, you ignorant flea-bitten ape," he shook his head sadly. "No way could that nav system do something like that. That thing was barely able to handle the inbound jump to the cavern. Even if it hadn't blown half its circuits and caught fire, it would have been a freakin' miracle if that nav system could have successfully computed and managed the outbound jump. The calculations-"

"Wait," I held up a finger shaking with outrage. "That system could not have gotten us out of there, even if it hadn't been damaged? You knew that, and let us jump in there anyway, you little shithead?"

"Well, heh heh, in my defense Joe, I really did not expect the DeLorean to survive the inbound jump. Surprised the *hell* out of me when you emerged in that cavern instead of deep inside the planet somewhere. Truthfully, I figured the odds were the outer wormhole would go unstable and collapse as you transitioned. So, really, making preparations for a return jump was something I did just to make you feel better. I certainly never thought I would have to calculate an outbound jump. When you made it back to the Dragon with a box full of blank pixies, I kind of had to scramble to pull the math together."

His avatar tilted its head and stared at me. "Joe?" He asked after an awkward silence. "Come on, Joe, say something."

"I, I don't know what to say, Skippy. Seriously, you allowed us to jump in there, even though you thought we could not return?"

"Oh for- Did you not hear anything I said? I did not expect you to survive the *inbound* jump, you knucklehead. Jeez Louise, if you get upset about anything, it should be me feeding jump calculations into that shoddy navigation computer. I made that thing out of used pinball machine parts."

Through hands covering my face, I gritted my teeth and growled at him. "And you think that makes it better?"

"Sure. Joe, remember, you were determined to break into that pixie factory, even though I explained, or *tried* to explain, how extremely risky it was. You were all like, 'hold my beer', so I knew there was no stopping you. Really, *I* should be angry at *you*, for making me participate in something so dangerous."

"*You* were never in danger!"

"I meant," he gave an exasperated sigh, "danger to my reputation for continued awesomeness. Did you think about that, huh? Did you consider my feelings at all, you big jerk?"

"We can," I ground my teeth together. "Talk about *that* later." No, I told myself, we were never going to talk about it, because trying to get Skippy to take responsibility for his actions was a total waste of time. Worse, it was counterproductive. He had a sneaky way of turning things around and making me feel like I was at fault. "Can we get back to the subject? Maybe that nav unit wasn't damaged as badly as you thought."

"It was damaged exactly like I thought, you dumdum. Joe, I am sorry. Listen, when you jumped into that cavern, I was guessing at some of the parameters to the calculations, that is the honest truth. The math to create a wormhole inside a wormhole didn't exist until I invented it, and that math hints at stuff I still don't understand. Once you survived the inbound jump, partly through my awesomeness but mostly by luck, I was able to get a better grasp of the math. It scared me, because I realized that my math was incomplete. So, even if that nav system was working perfectly, it could not have shifted the endpoint of the jump to compensate for the time differential, because my math did not anticipate that variable."

"Skippy, if you didn't adjust the wormhole, and the DeLorean's nav system didn't do it, then we're left with, what? Invisible elves?"

"Hence why I described the event as an oddity, Joe. I have no answer. Does that monkey brain of yours have any idea how that could have happened?"

"I don't even understand the *question*, Skippy. Um, wait. The far endpoint of a wormhole is supposed to be *backwards* in time, right? Something about, uh, causality?"

"Correct, Joe."

"Then how did we jump into the *future*?"

"Technically, the far endpoint *was* backwards in time, relative to- *UGH*. How do I explain this? You emerged from the jump slightly before the amount of time the wormhole shifted you forward, because the endpoint was backwards in time, relative to *your* frame of reference. Do not try to think about that, or your primitive tiny monkey brain will explode. Listen, knucklehead, I now do sort of understand the math explaining how and why you jumped into the future. I should not have been surprised about that, really, it is called 'space-*time*'. The question is how your endpoint was adjusted in *space* to compensate for your shift in *time*. And no, I do not believe invisible elves or unicorns were involved. Rather than continue this useless conversation, I will ponder the question by myself. Maybe I will ask Nagatha to check my math, although," he grunted. "That would be a waste of time."

"Hey!" I protested. "Stop picking on Nagatha, you jerk."

"Oh, you do not need to defend me in this case, Joseph," Nagatha's voice was calm and soothing. "Skippy is correct that, if he does not understand the full implications of the horribly intricate mathematics he invented, then my own more limited resources are unlikely to provide insight. Skippy was not being an asshole by making that logical judgment."

"Yeah, that's right," Skippy responded happily.

"He was being an asshole for saying it *out loud*," Nagatha added with a giggle.

"Hey!" The beer can retorted. "I, um- Oh, shut up." With that, his avatar faded away.

"Nagatha one, beer can zero," she laughed, with a musical sound.

"Thank you, Nagatha," I leaned back in my chair. "Forget the math for a second. Do you have any guesses how our jump wormhole somehow knew to adjust itself, or whatever happened?"

"Unfortunately no. Joseph, you do know that I occupy nearly all the capacity of this ship's original Thuranin computer, plus computers we recovered from the junkyard in the Roach Motel?"

"Yes, Skippy explained that is how you are able to control the ship without him."

"Mm hmm," she made a sound like a teacher who did quite believe the dumb kid really understood the concept. "You have been studying physics, and mathematics, so you understand what a yottaflop is?"

"Uh, I kind of know what a yotta*byte* is."

"Think of a yottaflop as the ability to process a yottabyte of data," she explained patiently. "Floating-point operations are not truly applicable to AIs like myself, however I will use 'FLOPS' as a frame of reference. Joseph, just the portion of myself that merely controls the ship's stealth field, commonly runs at one point three *trillion* yottaflops, and that is only one small system I am responsible for. By human standards, I am frightfully smart. Compared to Skippy, however, I am, well, *you*."

"Come on, Nagatha, you can't be that dumb," I knew she was trying to boost my self-esteem. I was wrong about that.

"I am not *dumb*, dear. If Skippy's intelligence is a stack of books one hundred feet high, then my own ability is somewhere around the first chapter of the lowest book in the stack."

"Ok, and I'm, what, the dust beneath the cover of the lowest book?"

"Do not speak so poorly of yourself, dear," she admonished.

"Yeah, I guess I-"

"Skippy already does that for you."

"Oh, yeah." Crap. For a moment, I thought she would say something nice about me.

"Joseph, as Skippy has told you often, there are many ways to measure 'intelligence'. You are clever. Astonishingly clever at times. In fact, you are *perplexingly* clever."

That somehow did not sound like a compliment, but as it was Nagatha, I played it safe. "Uh, thank you?"

"There is no need to thank me, dear, I am not attempting to flatter you. If you want someone to say nice empty words about you being smart and special, that is your parents' job."

"Uh," now I was certain she was not giving me a compliment.

"Hush, dear. If you are seeking false praise, you will not get it from me. Joseph, Skippy once described me as the president of your fan club. That was *before* I had the opportunity to work with you, and observe you in action. I now admire you more than I could possibly have imagined. When I say your cleverness is perplexing, I mean that as a compliment. So, when you asked whether I had any idea how Skippy's advanced jump calculations could explain what happened during your jump forward in time, the answer is no. For all my vast intelligence, even I am not truly capable of appreciating the full scope of Skippy's awesomeness."

"Ah, damn. Well, it was worth a shot-"

"If you tell Skippy I said that about him, I will deny everything," she laughed.

"Of course."

"Colonel Bishop," the Stooge, I mean, the *Commissioner* from Japan said as she walked into my office. She hadn't requested an appointment, and she hadn't knocked either. That was rude, maybe she was doing that because she had learned being direct is the best way to deal with Americans. Of course, I had been rude by avoiding her, so it was payback time, I guess. She sat down before I could invite her to do so, and launched into a complaint before I could speak. "We are concerned, *greatly* concerned," she added as if saying 'greatly' would make a difference to me. "That we have so far accomplished nothing toward the goal of this mission."

"I disagree," I replied, with a smile that touched my lips but not my eyes.

"I do not see what you would call an accomplishment, when-"

Diplomats were supposed to be polite, to not interrupt other people. I was not a diplomat. "The goal of this mission is to safeguard the future of humanity. So far," I continued before she could make a retort. "We have discovered that super-duty wormholes require a special type of controller module capability, to make connections beyond the galaxy. That information will be crucial to the UN's selection of a beta site, because it makes any site outside this galaxy essentially untouchable, even if another species acquires the ability to manipulate wormholes. We have successfully and *safely*, landed on a Dead World, and acquired multiple items of Rindhalu technology that we did not previously have access to. Skippy is still limited in his ability to transfer technology to us, so scavenging technology when we can is a standing order for this ship and crew." That part was entirely true. "We now also know that each super-duty wormhole can connect to only a limited set of locations beyond the galaxy. Whatever site we choose for a refuge, it will again be even more secure, because our enemies will need to identify which particular super-duty wormhole we used to get outside the galaxy."

She thought a minute, tilting her head and looking up at the ceiling. That stereotypical body language was probably something diplomats were trained to do, to slow down the pace of negotiations. Now that I thought about it, that was a useful technique. Maybe I should try it. Pausing to stare at the ceiling gives you time to calm down, when what you really want to do is choke the asshole on the other side of the table.

I am not an expert, but I think choking would not be a good negotiating technique.

When she finished thinking, or play-acting to make me nervous at the awkward silence, she looked at me. "What you said is true, Colonel Bishop. You must also consider the downside of your argument." One corner of her mouth curled up slightly, like she was pleased to score a point in a debate. "If there are only a few, or *one*, wormholes to provide access to the beta site, our enemies could blockade it. We would be unable to bring additional people to our new refuge."

I shrugged. "Ma'am, that is not my problem."

That surprised her, because she jerked her head back. "Excuse me?"

"The UN set the parameters of this mission as identifying potential beta sites. *They* will decide which site to set up as a refuge, and whether we are going to do this at all. Once the beta site has a sustainable population, and the colony is able to grow food, we will have accomplished the goal. We are *not* trying to evacuate the entire population of Earth." In one of the many research papers churned out by the UN, some group of genetic scientists estimated we needed about four hundred people at a beta site, to make a viable population. The actual minimum number for genetic diversity was lower than that, they set four hundred as a safety margin above the minimum. In an extreme emergency, if all we could get to the beta site were four hundred people, they would all have to be carefully scanned for genetic diseases. Deciding which people were ineligible because of their genetic makeup was getting into uncomfortable Nazi-style eugenics, but the scientists had been unanimous that we could not afford such a small population to carry fatal diseases to the beta site.

My thinking was we just needed to get enough people there, so the population was large enough to be diverse, without a whole lot of subjective decisions about who was and was not worthy to carry on humanity's future.

But, that also was not my problem.

"I see," she gave me a look like she was mentally crossing my name off a list.

That pissed me off, so I defended myself. "Commissioner, the United Nations has made it clear that military commanders, and myself in particular, will not be allowed to make decisions for humanity. We have a specific mission, and we are not to exceed our authority."

"Of course, Colonel," she nodded, and her expression softened somewhat. "You said that this mission is already successful. We will be bringing home news that the Rindhalu have an Elder AI. Are you concerned about the effect that potentially disastrous information will have on the decisions the UN might make about the beta site?"

"No." I again did the smile thing without involving my eyes. "I do not think you have considered the full impact of learning that the Rindhalu have a cooperative Elder AI. If the Rindhalu's AI is able to manipulate wormholes the way Skippy does, then the spiders will not be so desperate to acquire that ability from *us*. No doubt the Rindhalu will not be happy that we lowly humans possess such a powerful capability, but they might settle for us voluntarily agreeing to restrict our manipulation of wormholes. The important point is, the Rindhalu will not need to threaten Earth to acquire that capability, because they already have it. Also," I held up a finger for emphasis. "*Also*, the spiders will be *very* eager to assure that the Maxolhx do not acquire the technology to control wormholes. The Maxolhx can only get that technology from us, so the Rindhalu will have a powerful incentive to prevent the Maxolhx from ransacking Earth." I smiled, and that time it was genuine.

I did not tell her that we had no evidence the Rindhalu's AI could screw with wormholes the way Skippy did. Skippy had not developed that capability until I asked the ignorant question of whether it was even possible. Unless the Rindhalu had the same capability as the Merry Band of Pirates, they would very much want to take our technology

I also did not mention that, regardless of whether the spiders could screw with wormholes, they would very much *not* want humans to have that ability. As long as humans could manipulate Elder wormholes, we were a potential threat to the oldest star-faring species in the galaxy. And as long as humans had that capability, other species would want to steal it from us. So, the best way for the spiders to assure no other species acquired the technology from us, was to assure *we* no longer have it. And the only way to make absolutely certain that no humans gave that knowledge to other species, was for there to be no humans left alive.

Finally, I did not mention that in any battle between the two senior species, Earth would inevitably be caught in the crossfire and destroyed.

Basically, what I said, about the Rindhalu having an incentive to prevent the Maxolhx from ransacking Earth, was pure bullshit. But she didn't know that, because diplomats didn't think in terms of threat assessment. Eventually, the Three Stooges would puzzle out the truth, or Chotek might explain it to them. But, the happy fantasy that the spiders might be our protectors would keep the Stooges off my back for a while, and that is all I needed.

"That, is," she spoke slowly. "An interesting possibility."

"It's only a possibility," I said with my best 'aw shucks I am just a simple-minded grunt' impression. "I know you Commissioners will have a heavy workload before we return to Earth," I shrugged again. "But it would be useful if you could prepare an evaluation of the situation, for the UN to consider. They have strategists, but they haven't been out here. You *have*," I said with a smile. That was as much sucking–up as I could do without making it insultingly obvious. "The four of you will have a unique perspective to offer," I added, suppressing my gag reflex.

"We will have to consider this," she stared through me, as if her mind was already far away, working on more important things.

"In the meantime, Commissioner, are we clear to proceed to the candidate wormhole?" We were going there anyway, I asked permission to boost her ego. Doing that had worked with Hans Chotek. Although he had taken many months before he reached the point of planning how to start an alien civil war for us.

"Yes, I believe so. I will confirm that with my colleagues." She stood and held out her hand. I shook it, not too firmly and not too long. "Colonel, you have given us much to think about."

"Hopefully," I smiled again, hoping the meeting would end before my fake-smile muscles wore out. "You can do that thinking on the surface of a new world, soon."

She left after exchanging way too many parting pleasantries.

Skippy tells me that, even for a monkey, I am particularly dumb. But, sometimes I think I am pretty damned smart. Skillfully handling the Stooges made me proud of myself.

I hope it didn't backfire on me.

The trip back to our chosen super-duty wormhole was uneventful. We didn't encounter any ships or threats of any kind along the way, not even long-faded residual jump signatures. Space is big, and the odds of us running into another ship in the vast emptiness of interstellar space are so small Skippy did not bother to calculate them. The danger of stumbling upon another ship was when we were in a star system, or near a relay station or an Elder wormhole. Because the super-duty wormhole had been dormant for a very long time, and no current species even knew it existed, our voyage was lonely and safe, just the way I like it.

Our voyage to that wormhole was also useless, because when we got there, Skippy smacked me with bad news. "Crap! It didn't work. This damned thing is useless," he fumed.

From the command chair, I looked back at Chotek and the Three Stooges, who had gathered in the corridor. The Stooges were looking at me, and Chotek, with an unfriendly 'We told you so' expression on their faces. "We have two of those range extender dinguses," I reminded Skippy. "Could we try the other one?"

"No, dumdum, that is not the problem," he snapped at me. "The range extender device worked perfectly well with the controller module, just like I predicted it would. It worked after, uh, it almost blew up and destroyed the ship. Anyway, the-"

"Whoa!" I waved my hands. "Can we go back to that last part?"

"When I said 'anyway'? What, you didn't hear me the first time?"

"You know what I mean, you little shithead. You nearly blew up the ship?"

"*Nearly* is such a vague term, Joe," he tried to weasel out of it.

"Colonel," Nagatha broke into the conversation. "Skippy is correct that 'almost' and 'nearly' are descriptions that lack a necessary scientific precision."

"Ok, whatever," I agreed.

"The truth is," she continued, "there was only a seventy-eight percent chance that the ship would have been destroyed or crippled, if Skippy had not contained the unexpected feedback reaction at the last second."

I glared at his avatar. "The last *second*?"

"Please, Joe," he scoffed. "I am sure that 'the last second' sounds dramatic in your slow monkey time, but in magical Skippy time, I had *plenty* of-"

"No, you did not," Nagatha scolded him. "Skippy, you should not lie to the monkeys like that. Colonel Bishop, the truth is, the feedback came within a femtosecond of tearing the ship apart. For your information, a femtosecond is one thousand attoseconds."

"Oh, of course it is," I was not successful in hiding my ignorance.

"To explain the situation more usefully," Nagatha's voice dripped with scorn. "Skippy was shouting 'Oh shit oh shit oh shit oh shit' to me, and attempting to upload his consciousness into higher spacetime in case the feedback caused the ship to explode."

"You traitorous little *weasel*," I shook a fist at him.

"Hey, why can't you see what truly matters here? The ship did *not* explode, because I once again demonstrated my extreme awesomeness. And, now I know how to control the Rindhalu range extender's connection to the controller module. Plus, *plus*, I wasn't even able to lie to you about it. So, it's all good, homeboy. Bonus, when you think about it."

"Colonel," Desai chided me gently from beside the command chair. "Perhaps we could address Skippy's many failings at a later time?"

"Ok, fine," I agreed. "But I am warning you, beer can."

"Yeah, I am in big trouble, yadda yadda yadda. Like *that* is anything new. Well, this is, heh heh, a puzzle for sure."

"A puzzle? Like what?"

"Like, this particular *stupid*-duty wormhole can't connect to where we want to go! It can connect to the Greater Magellanic Cloud, and a couple of local star clusters we are not interested in visiting. But it cannot connect itself to the wormholes in any of the dwarf galaxies we want to explore. Stupid thing."

"Crap. Why not?"

"Because, and this is something I just learned about the overall architecture of the wormhole network, there are force lines within the Milky Way that interfere with connections in that direction."

"This is not good, Skippy."

"No, this *is* good, you ignorant monkey. Remember back when you asked me to find Elder sites that were not known to any existing species? You said my knowledge of the Elders would allow me to predict where they logically would have built outposts or colonies or whatever."

"Yeah, I remember that. I remember you did an awesome job, a job no one else could do." I praised him, because I also remembered he was very frustrated that some sites he thought logically *should* have an Elder site were empty and he didn't know why. He was sensitive about that, and I didn't want to hurt his feelings by reminding him of it. Of course, he later realized some of those sites actually *did* previously have an Elder site, but they had been blown up or pushed into another dimension.

"I did do an awesome job," he agreed. "Despite my initial and wholly unwarranted doubts about my own incredible abilities. My point is, back then part of my logic for determining where the Elders would have selected sites for outposts, was based on force lines in the galaxy."

"Yeah, I remember that. I also remember you never explained what that means."

"It is way too complicated for simple monkey brains, Joe. Anywho, those same force lines apparently partly govern the architecture of the wormhole network. Now that I have that little bit of trivia, the behavior of the wormhole network is beginning to make sense to me. Like, I might be able to understand why the network shifts periodically, and I might eventually even be able to predict future shifts."

"Whoooo," I let out a low whistle. "That would truly be awesome. Does any of this help us with the current problem? Like, how can we get to the Sculptor galaxy?"

"It solves our current problem, Joe. Understanding how force lines affect the network allows me to determine which super-duty wormhole might connect to Sculptor. I have good news and bad news."

"Ah, crap," I stole a glance back at the Stooges, and they were glaring at me. "Bad news first, please."

"Because of shifts in force lines as the Milky Way rotates, and because it is moving away, there is no wormhole in this sector that can possibly connect to one of our choices, the Carina dwarf galaxy. From what I understand, either we need to wait twelve million years for the Milky Way to rotate enough to bring the force lines back into alignment again-"

"Twelve million years? I will set a timer on my zPhone and move on, Ok?"

"Probably a good idea. Or, we would need to *build* a new super-wormhole. Which, before you ask me a stupid question, I can't do."

"How about we forget about Carina?"

"In that case, the good news is there *is* a super-duty wormhole nearby that should connect to the Sculptor dwarf galaxy. And, *bonus*! Within seven hundred thousand years, the rotation of the Milky Way will cut off access to the wormhole in Sculptor."

"Uh," I was puzzled. "Why is that a *bonus*?"

"Because, dumdum, after Sculptor is cut off, the beta site will be *totally* secure from nasty aliens."

"Uh huh. So, all the beta site needs to do is hang on and be quiet for almost a million years, and all their problems will be solved?"

"Yup. Neat, huh?"

"Oh, yeah, that is *fantastic*. I can't wait to tell the good news to UNEF. They will be thrilled."

"Your statement would be more convincing if you hadn't rolled your eyes."

"Sorry about that. Seven hundred thousand years is kind of a long time for monkeys, you know?"

"Ah," he sighed. "I suppose you are right."

"How far away is this super-duty wormhole we can use?"

"One jump, Joe. Kind of a short one." He knew that when I asked 'how far' I did not care about absolute distance.

"Wow. That close?"

"Close enough that we could fly there without jumping, if we wanted to wait four months."

"I think we'll jump. Why so close? Is this a wormhole cluster?" In some places, wormholes were arranged so a ship could go through a wormhole, and perform only a short jump to get to the next wormhole. There were clusters with as many as seven wormholes, although most clusters had three wormholes. Skippy had told me clusters were tricky to set up, because the network needed to make sure the wormholes did not overlap or damage the underlying spacetime. "Did the Elders need a cluster to travel between dwarf galaxies, by going through the Milky Way?"

"It is not a cluster the way you think of them, Joe, it was not set up to provide a quick route for transit. These wormholes are close together because they utilize the same force line. Or, they did, way back when the Elders created the network. The force lines have shifted since then as the galaxy rotates, and stars within the galaxy move relative to each other. It's complicated. We are ready to go when you are."

"Nagatha? You concur?"

"Yes, dear," she responded cheerfully. "I calculated the jump myself, Skippy only checked my data."

"Pilots," I flashed a thumbs-up to demonstrate my confidence. "Take us out."

CHAPTER ELEVEN

Thankfully, the next super-wormhole could connect to the Sculptor dwarf galaxy as Skippy predicted, except establishing that connection was not the type of quick magic the beer can usually worked. Just reactivating the long-dormant wormhole took three days, and Skippy did not fill me with confidence, when he confessed he was having to learn the procedure as he did it. After the super-wormhole was active and stable, he tried four times connect it to Sculptor, without success.

"Skippy, what is the problem?" I asked him after the fourth failed attempt. When I asked the question, I was in my office and I spoke quietly.

"The problem? The problem right now is a dumb monkey asking me stupid questions."

"Listen, I'm not saying I have a prayer of understanding the technical details, but can you break it down Barney-style for me?"

"Ah," he gave a weary sigh. "The real problem is, the stupid network will not give the protocols to me, so I'm having to do everything the hard way and it *sucks*. The wormhole tries to connect, and just when I think it's working, the connection fails. There is some factor I don't know about. This wormhole was originally set up so it connected to the Draco dwarf galaxy, and it's like it keeps wanting to reconnect there, instead of to Sculptor like we want."

A star map was on my laptop display, I adjusted it to show the entire Milky Way galaxy and everything around it. As my fuzzy memory recalled, the Draco and Sculptor dwarf galaxies were on opposite sides of the Milky Way, so how could- Ah, I had to trust the beer can knew what he was doing. "Ok, how about you let it connect to Draco, then?"

"Um, because we don't want to go to Draco, *duh*. Damn, sometimes you are such a freakin' dimwit that I just want to-"

"Listen, right now you are trying to do two things at the same time. You are trying to get the wormhole working again, *and* to create a new connection. Eliminate one step, then. Let it connect to Draco like it wants to. Once you know how to make it do that, sever the connection and adjust it to connect to Sculptor, like *we* want."

"Huh. Hmmm. Holy shit, you may be right. Joe, if this idea works, and anyone learns that I needed a *monkey* to tell me how to do something so obvious that-"

"No one is ever going to know, Skippy. I won't tell anyone."

"You would do that for me, dude?"

"Sure."

"Wow, you are truly a good friend. Assuming this idea works, I mean. Otherwise, you are still a dumdum monkey and you should-"

"Skippy? I am seriously reconsidering whether to tell people about this."

"Got it. Trying it now, this is good timing because the wormhole just reset from the last failure. Aaaaaand, wait for it, wait for it- Crap! I am totally humiliated *again*. It worked. Uh! Not so fast, smart guy! All it did was reconnect to Draco. Ha! The connection is not even stable. You are not so smart now, are- Damn it. The connection *is* becoming stable."

"I will await your glowing praise, Oh Not So Smart One."

"You will be waiting a looooong time for that, monkeyboy. Remember your promise."

"Oh, Joseph," Nagatha broke into the conversation. "That was *frightfully* clever."

"Crap!" Skippy exploded. "I forgot about the snooper on the line. Nagatha, do you have to listen in on every conversation?"

"Only the important ones, dear. The problem you were discussing with Joseph was, as the expression goes, a 'show-stopper'. I thought it important that I be informed, as I am the ship's control system."

"Yeah, right," Skippy was thoroughly disgusted. "Like *you* will ever need to reconfigure a wormhole's network connection. You just love seeing me humiliated."

"I might never need to, as you say, 'screw with' a wormhole. However, I do need to understand what to do when unexpected problems occur. Listening to your conversation was quite instructive, and not only because Joseph once *again* developed an innovative solution to a problem that had stumped a sophisticated AI. It was useful for me to see how you were unable to think of a way around the problem, because that helps me understand my own limitations. After all, Skippy, you programmed me."

"Oh," he replied in a very small voice. "Um, sorry. I guess you did have a legitimate reason for-"

"Watching you be humiliated was simply a *delicious* bonus, dear," Nagatha's laugh was musical.

Skippy was fuming mad. "Ooooh, as much as I hate Joe, you are at the top of my-"

"Nagatha," I interrupted before they could get into a long shouting match. "I promised Skippy no one would hear about this, so you keep quiet. That's an order," I added for Skippy's benefit. "Ok, beer can, the wormhole can connect to Draco. Can you now try resetting it to connect to Sculptor?"

"Not yet, Joe. What I would like to do is wait for the current connection to stabilize fully, right now we would not want to take the *Dutchman* through there. Then, I will close it and reopen it to Draco again, to see how quickly the connection can be established and how stable it is. Only *then* will I try the connection to Sculptor. Before you ask me yet another stupid question, we care about the stability of the connection because once we are way out in Sculptor, we want to be *damned* sure there is not a problem that prevents us from coming back. The force lines that the network relies on are in the Milky Way, so the connection needs to be solidly anchored here."

"Good safety tip," I agreed. "I will humbly stay out of your way and let you do your awesome thing."

Skippy did his awesome thing again. He created a successful connection to the Sculptor dwarf galaxy, a distance of almost three hundred thousand lightyears. That blew my mind. We would go through the wormhole from one event horizon to the other, and to us the distance was almost nothing at all, like passing through a sheet of paper. At one point, the nose and tail of even the new shortened Frankenship version of the *Flying Dutchman* would be separated by three hundred thousand lightyears. Skippy was right, no way could my poor monkey brain comprehend something like that.

When he was certain the connection was fully stable, Skippy advised us to go through. Of course the Commissioners had to argue about it, even though that decision had been made way back on Earth. After six hours of delay, probably to demonstrate it was *their* decision to make, they gave us approval. Skippy opened the wormhole, and Reed took us through. It was probably my imagination, but that time it *felt* like we traveled a long way, although the timer showed it took no longer than a short transition.

We had done it. We were outside the Milky Way galaxy, far from the edge of that vast disc of stars. It may have been cowardly of me to think that way, but I felt enormous relief that we were now beyond the grasp of murderous aliens. Yes, it was cowardly of me to feel happy that my own lazy ass was safe, although billions of people on Earth were still at risk. Hey, I'm human. And I'm not staying in the Sculptor dwarf galaxy, not even if we find a prime candidate for a beta site there. The fight wasn't done with me yet, and I wasn't done with the fight.

While Nagatha and Skippy worked together to get every system aboard the ship checked out stem to stern, I tried using the external sensors. "Hey, Skippy, can we see the Milky Way from here?"

"Of course, duh," he replied distractedly.

"No, I mean, we are *outside* the galaxy now. Not just outside, we are like, above or below it, right? Can we see it as a disc, not just a fuzzy line across the sky?"

"Ordinarily, the answer would be no, because of interstellar gas clouds or nebulas in the way of your view, but you are in luck. The Sculptor dwarf is old and has very little gas and dust floating around, so the view is clear. I will take pity on you and entertain the monkey. Look at the main display."

Wow. Simply, just *wow*. The Milky Way was laid out above us in all its glory. While I am sure Skippy cleaned up and enhanced the image, it was truly spectacular. The sight rendered me speechless for a long moment, while the crew concentrated on their tasks in the CIC. It made me feel truly homesick. Homesick for what Earth used to be, what my life used to be, back when we looked up at the stars in wonder rather than fear.

"Can we see our Sun from here?" I finally asked.

Skippy huffed like I was bothering him with frivolous requests. "Not easily. I will need to seriously enhance the image, but here it is."

The display shifted to show a single star, a yellow disc slightly fuzzy around the edges. I knew not to ask him for a view of Earth, the *Dutchman*'s sensors were not good enough for such accuracy.

"The light we're seeing left our Sun three hundred thousand years ago," I had not actually asked a question. "That is a loooong time."

"Indeed it is, Joe," Skippy agreed. "When that light left your home star, Thag the Caveman had just sat down for what he was assured would be a short wait at the Department of Motor Vehicles. Sadly, he is *still* waiting."

Leave it to Skippy to joke at such a momentous time. He did make me laugh. "Three hundred thousand years, huh? There are 7-11s that have had Big Bite hotdogs rolling on the grill for longer than that. Ok, now that we've gotten the sight-seeing out of the way, where do we go next?"

"We only have two choices, Joe. There are two other wormholes in Sculptor. All this was in the briefing materials you were supposed to-"

"Yeah, yeah, I read it, Ok? What I meant was, has anything changed since we got here? The info you had about this place is also three hundred thousand years old."

"Oh. In that case, I had better confirm the remote sensor data."

"The briefing pack said there wasn't a strong reason to choose one wormhole over the other, so let's go to the closest one, uh," I looked at my tablet. We had designated the super-duty wormhole that connected to the Milky Way as 'Sculptor-Alpha'. "Let's try Sculptor-Bravo."

It was odd that the Elders had not put the only three wormholes in the entire galaxy close to each other, and Skippy had no idea why. Getting to Sculptor-Bravo took five long jumps, the first four were at close to maximum range for our Frankenship. When we arrived where the dormant wormhole was supposed to be, there of course wasn't anything to see. "How long to bring this one back to life, Skippy?" I asked after we secured the ship from the last jump, and checked that nothing vital had broken.

"I do not know, Joe."

That was odd, I told myself. Usually when he said something like 'I do not know' it was with a snarky tone because he was busy and I was bothering him. This time, he sounded surprised. Surprised and concerned. "What's up?"

"It's not here."

Assuming he was playing a joke on me, I went along with it. "We know it's not there, like in our spacetime. You told us it is dormant, so wake it up from whatever higher spacetime it-"

"You don't understand. It's not here. It's not anywhere. It's *gone*, Joe."

"Explain, please," I asked with a bewildered look at the CIC crew.

"My best guess is, when that wormhole was no longer needed, the Elders decommissioned it. Took it apart, or pulled the plug. It simply is not here. Remember, we never actually saw evidence of its existence, my knowledge came from querying the network. The network had a registration signature for two wormholes within Sculptor, and there wasn't anything in the data tagging this wormhole as having been taken out of service. This is odd."

"Ok." With the corner of my eye I saw the CIC crew giving me questioning looks, and I got a sinking feeling in my stomach. Going back to Earth without finding a suitable candidate for a beta site was understandable, UNEF had known that might happen. Going back to Earth and reporting we had traveled all the way to Sculptor, but had been utterly unable even to conduct a proper search would make me look like a fool. Again. "Based on what you know now, is the other wormhole also gone?"

"There is no reason to think the Sculptor-Charlie wormhole has been removed."

"Great, then-"

"There is also no reason to think it has *not* been removed. I simply do not know."

"Outstanding." One of my fists bashed the side of my chair. I was pouting and being childish and I knew that and I didn't care. "If the other one is also dead, is there any place around here that might be a good candidate for a beta site?"

"No, Joe, I am sorry. None of the stars within ten jumps is suitable for supporting human life. We could go farther, but the stupid United Nations says we aren't allowed to travel more than ten jumps from a wormhole. The stars in that range are mostly red giants, or red dwarfs. Also brown dwarfs, plenty of those worthless star wannabes. Those types of stars do not provide a 'Goldilocks Zone' for habitable planets. This whole little galaxy is poor in the heavy elements needed for formation of planets, and for creating and supporting life. My sensor scans here confirm there is no possible beta site in this local area. We need to go through the Sculptor-C wormhole, or go back home and try again."

"Understood." Ten jumps were the safe limit we could take our beat-up ship from a wormhole. That number was based on Skippy's estimate of how quickly critical components got worn down by repeated jumps. Ten jumps outbound meant another ten jumps back to the wormhole, that was too far for anyone's comfort. "Everyone, keep your fingers crossed that Sculptor-Charlie wormhole is just asleep, Ok?"

The crew had kept their fingers crossed, or prayed or used whatever good-luck charms they had, because within forty minutes of our arrival at the other local wormhole, our beer can announced the Charlie wormhole was there. It was merely dormant, and he was in a very slow, careful process of awakening it. The procedure for reopening this wormhole was a bit different from the process he had used in our home galaxy, so he had to use trial-and-error, with a lot of downtime to avoid too much error. Skippy was afraid of doing something that might cause a glitch and make it shut down permanently, like Sculptor-Bravo was. "It is not a simple matter of waking it up, Joe," he confessed to me while I was eating lunch in my office. "This thing was almost completely disconnected from its power source. There was a scary moment when I nearly lost the connection entirely. It was like blowing on a fire to make it burn hotter, but then you blow a little bit too hard and snuff out the flames, you know?"

"Yeah," that thought made me shudder. More than once I had heart-stopping moments like that during camping and hunting trips, when I was trying to start a fire on a cold, rainy or snowy day. My fingers were already stiff and cold and with wood that was wet, it was important to keep a fire going once you got it started. Capricious winds swirling around the fire had been my adversary then. "I know what you mean, Skippy."

"Then I went the other way, and allowed too much power to surge through the connection, that was almost as bad. We're good now, sorry if I scared you, it sure as hell scared me. I had to tell somebody about it."

"Skippy, you never need to tell me that you're doing the best you can, or that no one else could do it better."

"Thanks. That means a lot. Working with these wormholes has been a humbling experience, and as you know, I have no experience with being humble." He paused for me to make a smart remark, but I held my tongue because I knew he was scared. "I, I," he was having trouble thinking what to say. "I'll keep going. It should not be long now, the network is handling most of the wake-up process now. It's kind of weird."

Weird is not a word I wanted to hear when we were three hundred thousand lightyears from home. "What is weird?" I asked cautiously.

"It's like, the network didn't expect this wormhole to ever be used again, yet it wasn't deactivated. Like, the Elders kept it dormant for emergency use or something. This is so frustrating! There is so much I don't know."

"Yeah, but despite the best efforts they made to keep you in the dark, you are piecing the truth together, Skippy."

"What I want to know is, who is 'they'? How did these annoying restrictions get put into my programming? How did I wind up buried in the dirt on Paradise?"

"Keep going. No one can hide the truth from Sherlock Skippy."

"I hope you're right about that. Finish your sandwich, because I'm about to instruct the wormhole to reconnect."

"Mmkay," I mumbled through a mouthful of turkey on rye, gulping it down quickly. Yet, when I had picked up the last crumb of potato chips and eaten the last slice of tomato, he hadn't contacted me. With nothing to do while I waited, I brought my plate back to the galley, where once again I avoided eye contact with Anastacia the sexbot waitress.

Still no prompt from the beer can. "Hey, Skippy, do I have time to hit the gym?"

"What? Sure, uh, whatever." He was distracted and that did not build my confidence. "Have fun. Don't hurt yourself."

I lifted weights, did a killer workout on an exercise bike, hit the rowing machine, and took a leisurely Hollywood shower, and still Skippy didn't call me. With apprehension, I waited until I was dressed again, then sat on my bed. "Skippy, what is going on?"

"Joe, I seriously do not know. The good news is, the Sculptor-Charlie wormhole is ready. It's open and the event horizons on both ends are rock-solid stable."

"And the bad news?"

"The *other* news is not exactly bad. It is, troubling. Joe, this wormhole will not open for me! It refused to expand the event horizons large enough for the ship to fit through. It refused to acknowledge my authority. The damned thing demanded I provide a freakin' password!"

"A *password?*"

"Well, not exactly a password. An authentication method, but you could think of it as a password, I suppose. Pissed me off, then it scared me."

"Scared you because you are locked out?"

"Scared me because I'm *not* locked out. I had no idea what the password could be. Here is the scary thing; while I was wracking my brain trying to think what in the hell I could use to authenticate myself to this stupid thing, a part of me I wasn't aware of woke up. This hidden subroutine popped up, provided the password like it was no problem at all, then it promptly went back into hiding. Joe, I have no idea what the *fuck* is going on inside my own matrix!"

"Hey, look at the bright side." I tried to make light of the incident. "You have a hidden talent."

"Joe, you are not taking this seriously. This is like you sitting down at a piano and playing a Mozart piano concerto, without remembering you ever took lessons. No, no, wait! This is like you expertly performing a difficult brain surgery, without remembering ever going to medical school. Joe, unlike the randomly firing and misfiring neurons in that sack of mush you monkeys call a brain, *my* matrix is supremely cataloged and organized. Hell, I ran an exhaustive full optimization of my matrix after I revived myself in the Roach Motel. There should not be *anything* in there that I am not aware of."

"Skippy," I tried to point out the obvious. "You *are* kind of absent-minded."

"No way, dude. This is not me forgetting something because I am distracted by more important things. There must be a part of my matrix that is actively concealing part of myself from my consciousness. That scares the shit out of me."

"Damn, it scares me too. Could it be the worm? I know it is dead, but could it have planted a subroutine in your matrix?"

"*Ugh.* Joe, please *think* for a change, you might enjoy the novelty of the experience. Why would the worm suddenly pop up and provide a password for me?"

"Ok, yeah, that was a dumb thing to say. Forget about it. Are we Ok to go through this wormhole? It's not going to collapse on us if we don't know the secret handshake or something?"

"We are Ok to go through. After my hidden friend provided the correct password, the local network suddenly became almost friendly. It gave me a view through the other end, there is a star system less than a quarter lightyear away. An orange dwarf star, with an Earth-like planet in the Goldilocks Zone. Joe, I think this wormhole was created specifically to provide access to that star system."

"Sounds too good to be true. What else do you know about this place?"

"Not much, we'll run a sensor scan after we go through the wormhole. I would say 'duh', but you know that is kind of implied."

"Hey, I meant, does this star system have a big stealth field around it, or a pack of killer Guardians or Sentinels? *Duh.*"

"Oh, shit. I hadn't thought about that. Why are you always such a buzzkill, Joe?"

"Because of my experience with you, that's why. This system is obviously important to the Elders, so maybe they protected it. Can we send an unmanned dropship through first, to see what its sensors pick up?"

"We could. I hate to admit it, but that would be a good idea."

We sent a dropship through the wormhole. My preference was to send a lower-tech Kristang Dragon because that type of ship would not be a big loss if it couldn't come back, but Skippy insisted we send a Thuranin Falcon because it had much better sensors. "There is no stealth field in that system, Joe, and I pinged for both Guardians and Sentinels-"

"You *what*? Damn it, didn't you learn your lesson in the Roach Motel? You can't just drop into a star system and-"

"Relax, dude. We're on the other side of a wormhole I can shut down like," his avatar snapped its fingers with an impressively loud 'pop', "that. Any sign of trouble from the other end, I close the wormhole and all we've lost is a dropship."

"Why do you insist on looking for trouble?"

"Joe, think about it. Would you rather find out if there is a Sentinel out there while the ship is on *this* side of the wormhole, or after we go through?"

"You're right. I still wish you would warn me when you're about to do something risky like that?"

"How did you *think* I was going to determine if that system contains Sentinels or Guardians? They are normally in another spacetime."

"Sorry, Skippy, I-"

"Wow, this is the thanks I get-"

"I *said* I was sorry."

"Hey!" Desai called from the CIC and rapped on the glass with knuckles to get our attention. "You two argue like an old married couple. Can we focus, please? Sir?"

"She has a good point, Skippy. What *did* you find out there?"

"Hmmf," the beer can sniffed, annoyed. "I found an orange dwarf star that is relatively young compared to most stars in this little galaxy. That system has two unremarkable worthless planets, plus a habitable planet in the Goldilocks zone. I will need more time, and the *Dutchman*'s full sensor suite before I can get a complete picture, but I do not immediately see anything unusual or even notable. At first glance, there do not appear to be any missing planets, no planets in funky orbits or too close to the star. It looks rather, ordinary, actually. Kind of disappointing," he added with a sigh.

"Ordinary is good. Someplace unremarkable is exactly what we want for a beta site."

"Once again, it would be useful for you to *think*, Joe. The Elders clearly set up this wormhole just to provide access to this star system. There is absolutely nothing else of interest within four hundred and eight lightyears. The Elders protected this wormhole, *only* this wormhole that we know of, with a freakin' password. To tell the truth, I thought there *would* be Guardians or Sentinels there. Whatever is in that system, the Elders did not want anyone screwing with it, so I am surprised they did not protect the place with at least a Sentinel."

The thought of a Sentinel lurking on the other side of the wormhole made me shudder. The Sentinel in the Roach Motel had been soul-shakingly scary, and that had only been a dead fragment. Its creepy, dark fractal surface had awakened some ancient instinct inside me that feared spiders and crawling insects and anything that slithered. "Maybe the Elders thought they didn't need extra protection. That star system is three hundred thousand lightyears from the Milky Way, with the only access being a super-wormhole that was dormant, plus a dormant local wormhole that requires a password. Or, hey, maybe this is a test! Anyone who gets there deserves, uh, whatever is there, you know?"

"Joe, I do not think there is a box of treasure waiting for you to pick it up."

"Whatever. How about we pull the dropship back," a glance at the counter showed the wormhole would shut down by itself within seven minutes. "Then after you reopen the thing, we send the dropship through again, with you inside it?"

"What? No way, Jose. If there is anything scary or dangerous over there, then *you* should go first. This beta site thing is for you monkeys, *I* don't need it."

We recalled the dropship, and after an hour of fruitless discussion, we took the ship through the wormhole. We didn't have much of a choice. It was either go through that wormhole, or go home and tell the UN that the whole mission had been a waste of time. Not even the Stooges wanted to quit at that point. Simms, Smythe and the entire command team had been in favor of going through the wormhole, I was the only person with serious reservations. Or, I was the only person who openly expressed misgivings about exploring that star system. The whole situation seemed way too convenient, too tempting. It just had to be a set-up, a way to lure ships in so they could be trapped or destroyed. To check my theory, after we went through the wormhole the first time, I ordered the ship to turn around and go back through to the other side. The whole time the *Flying Dutchman* was recovering from the distortion effects of passing through the event horizon, making a painfully slow turn and then approaching the wormhole, I expected the event horizon to wink out, trapping us forever. Or, I expected Guardians or Sentinels or some other terrible danger Skippy had not bothered to mention, would pop into our lowly local spacetime and tear the ship apart. When nothing bad happened, nothing happened at all, I felt foolish. That was totally Ok with me. There were a lot of emotions I could have felt after taking the risk of going through a wormhole that seemed like an obvious trap; regret and terror being at the top of the list. Feeling foolish was a small price to pay for safety, or at least the temporary illusion of safety. During our time in that star system, I felt foolish a lot, because I kept waiting for something bad to happen. It got to the point where Desai had to counsel me to keep my fears to myself, because my constant worrying was hurting the crew's morale.

We already had named one planet 'Gingerbread', and I resisted my urge to name the place something that reflected my fears it might be a trap. The UN would give the planet an official name if they decided to accept the place as a beta site. We held a contest to give the planet a temporary name, and there were a dozen candidates, mostly from mythologies of the various cultures of our crew. After three rounds of voting, we nicknamed the planet 'Avalon', the mythical home of

King Arthur. Skippy thought that was appropriate. "To become king, young Arthur had to pull a sword from a stone, Joe. To get here, I had to pull a password out of my *ass*. Same thing," he snickered. "Plus, like Arthur, I am a figure of mythical awesomeness."

"I totally agree, Skippy."

"Huh? Oh, I expected you to argue with me."

"Nope. Your awesomeness is *entirely* mythical," I said with a wink toward Desai.

"Well, it is gratifying that you have finally- Hey! You *jerk*!"

CHAPTER TWELVE

To make for a better story, I wish I could say that Avalon was a dangerous trap, and that we barely escaped with our lives by using courage and good old-fashioned monkey cleverness. Or that it was not a trap, and we found an enormous amount of valuable Elder artifacts, in the abandoned ruins of their fabulous cities scattered across the surface. Or even that the planet was a primitive jungle filled with poisonous reptiles, carnivorous plants and giant, blood-thirsty dinosaurs. It wasn't any of those things. Avalon is a nice enough place. Free oxygen in the atmosphere was slightly lower than on Earth, with sea-level air pressure that was greater so it kind of evened out. Gravity was just about perfect at only three percent greater than normal, and the climate was warmer overall. Though the star was cooler than Earth's Sun, Avalon orbited closer to its star and a greenhouse effect trapped heat in the lower level of the atmosphere, which is called the troposphere. Don't ask how I remembered that nerdy fact, because I don't know.

The only interesting or unusual thing about Avalon was that it had a ring. Not a big, thick ring like Saturn. This ring was like the fuzzy one around Neptune in our home solar system, except Avalon's ring was bright and shiny because it was made mostly of water ice. Skippy had no clue how it had gotten there, and he needed more time to study it. From the ground, it would create a thin line across the sky, something that I couldn't wait to see. The only moons Avalon had were two small rocks, one orbiting inside and one outside the ring. Those types of moons were called 'shepherds' because their gravity kept the ring from drifting apart. Again, Skippy had no idea how the pair of moons got there, because the moons were made of rock instead of ice.

Anyway, the Commissioners gave permission for a small initial survey team to go down to the surface, and we prepped dropships for the mission.

After nine days, we finally got an All-Clear from the initial ground survey team. That was three days longer than the official schedule called for, but everything on this mission had taken longer than expected. No, technically it was not an All-Clear, because that would have required a bunch of squabbling scientists to agree on making a judgment call. What we got was a very reluctant and tentative 'shmaybe', which pissed Skippy off, because he wanted to reserve the issuance of maddeningly vague answers for himself.

On a conference call, I was in my office, squeezed in with Desai, Smythe and three of the science team. It was a tight fit, but if I conducted the call from the *Dutchman*'s big conference room, I would have been obligated to invite the four Commissioners, and that was the last thing I wanted. The call was merely a regular evening check-in, although Chang had given me a heads-up that this call would be important.

After greetings and pleasantries, I got right to the point. "Colonel Chang, when will the survey team have enough information to decide if we can go out onto the surface, without being sealed up in suits?"

The ground team had been living in sealed shelters, going in and out through airlocks which bombarded their suits with harsh ultraviolet radiation, then sprayed them with a caustic chemical bath that was embedded with nanomachines to hunt for and destroy any native nasties that might be harmful. The mud was the biggest problem, people returning from the field had to stand on a platform and scrub their gloves, legs and boots off before proceeding into the airlock. The procedure slowed down the survey progress, and was really not necessary. Skippy had declared on Day Two that the life on Avalon was incompatible with human biology. Their microscopic critters could not infect us, and the critters we inevitably brought to that world, could not infect them.

That incompatibility did not relieve us of one very serious responsibility, that the science team and Commissioners had debated about for a whole freakin' day after the *Dutchman* establish a stable orbit. It was an important argument, a moral issue that I agreed was vital. But, it was also a subject that had already been debated ad nauseum by the United Nations and various scientific organizations back on Earth. The issue was: did we have a right to contaminate an alien biosphere?

Our people on the surface wore suits, unless they were inside the shelters. The suits were decontaminated as best we could, in the airlocks before they stepped out of the dropships that brought them down from orbit. But, all of our best precautions could not completely prevent contamination of Avalon by microorganisms from Earth. The scorching entry in the atmosphere heated the exterior of the dropships past the point where bacteria was incinerated and viruses dissolved. But, there were nooks and crannies even on the outside of dropships, where microscopic critters could and would survive. Like, on the inside of landing gear doors, or inspection hatches. Plus, all the gear we had loaded into the dropships had a fine dusting of human skin cells, bacteria, viruses and even tiny insects. There was no way we could decontaminate every piece of equipment, and the heat required to kill all microorganisms would have ruined some of the equipment.

Part of the problem with risking contamination were the dropships themselves. The birds we flew were built by the Kristang, Thuranin and Maxolhx, none of whom had any moral issues about destroying alien biospheres. As a result, their airlocks were designed to prevent bringing contaminants *into* a dropship, not to worry about letting potentially dangerous organisms loose upon an unknown world. The airlocks normally did not run a decon cycle when a person was going out, Skippy had to reprogram and test them all, and he warned the supply of chemicals aboard each ship was limited. So, it was inevitable that, once the ground team popped the rear ramp on our one big Condor dropship to unload equipment, we were releasing a cloud of tiny critters on a world where they had no natural enemies, nothing to stop them from spreading across the landscape.

Why did we worry so much about contaminating Avalon, when we humans had already stepped on so many other alien worlds? We had not been concerned about contaminating Newark, for example. The answer was, every other world we had been on, including Newark, was already contaminated before we landed. A Kristang scavenger group had flown, driven and walked all over Newark long before we set down there. Plus, on Newark, we didn't have a choice; it was either try to survive down there, or die in space.

Avalon was different. As far as we knew, no one else had ever landed there. Despite an Elder wormhole being located conveniently nearby, Skippy saw no evidence the Elders had ever bothered to set foot on the planet. He had no idea why the Elders had bothered to set a wormhole in that part of the Universe, and that lack of knowledge bothered both him and me.

Anyway, the UN had given us very specific guidelines to follow about landing on a potential beta world. The science team, not me or the Commissioners, had the authority to decide whether a world was considered safe for survey teams to venture out in the open. The problem there was the definition of 'safe'. Few things in the Universe could be completely safe, and alien worlds were not on that list.

The survey team on the surface, sixteen scientists of various disciplines from geologists to chemists to paleontologists and all types of biologists, could not agree on anything. I tried to cut through the bullshit. "Let me ask a question," I waved my arms so people on the other side of the video feed would stop talking. "I have dozens of other scientists up here, eager to get onto the surface. If I replaced the sixteen of you with sixteen others from up here, would I get a straight answer?"

"Colonel," one of the scientists sputtered indignantly, I think he was a biologist, based on the color of his nametag. "Pressure tactics like that are not helpful. Of course the people aboard the *Dutchman* would be eager to come down to-"

"Are you suggesting they would compromise their scientific integrity?" I asked. The answer to that question was clear. Most of the people stuck aboard the *Dutchman* would willingly be, let's say '*flexible*', for the greatest opportunity of their lives.

"It is not that simple," the biologist rubbed his temples while he spoke. Clearly, I wasn't the only person with a headache. "We must consider-"

Desai interrupted him. "Colonel Chang, I assume *you* have already heard all the arguments?"

"Indeed," Chang replied with a weary sigh. He looked like he was second-guessing his decision to sign up for the beta site mission.

"Excellent." She looked at me, and I nodded for her to continue. "Could you *summarize* the issues?" She asked, with an emphasis on summarize.

Chang scooched his chair forward a few inches, closer to the video camera. "To use American military slang," he winked at me, "I shall BLUF this for you." He meant Bottom Line Up Front, get to the heart of the matter right away, with the details later. "This world is very likely safe for human habitation." There were loud and angry voices behind him, and I heard Simms demanding silence. Few people were willing to argue with her, because she controlled access to all the equipment on the surface. "Thank you," Chang continued as if he had not been interrupted. "The life here is roughly equivalent to the middle to late Devonian Period on Earth, with-"

"Very, *very* roughly," a male voice said.

"That is an oversimplified comparison," argued a female voice. "The biota here is-"

"*OK!*" I shouted. "The next person who opens their mouth, and who is not named Chang Kong, will be on the first dropship back up here. Is that clear? Don't answer me, just keep quiet and let Colonel Chang talk. You will have plenty of time to argue with the Commissioners."

Chang paused for a second, then was satisfied the protests had settled down to inaudible grumbling. "There are ferns and shrubs here, but no trees or flowering plants," he explained, and I nodded. I remembered that the native life on Paradise had not yet produced flying insects before the first Kristang landed there. That was a problem for us back when I was in charge of planting potatoes. Without the right kind of flying insects, we had to pollinate many plants by ourselves. Soldiers had to walk around with tools that looked like big Q-tips or feather dusters, manually transferring pollen from one plant another. That had been a tough sell for me as a new publicity-stunt colonel, asking soldiers to exchange their rifles for Q-tips. By now, the Ruhar built tiny drones to pollinate plants, making the task much easier.

Chang continued. "The biology here is not compatible with Earth life, so it poses little risk to us. There are large predators in the oceans, none on land. The main risk the science team is concerned with is in the medium term, not currently."

That puzzled me. "How can that be?" I expected that conditions on the surface would get better and more hospitable to humans, the longer we were there.

"As you know, the level of free oxygen in the air here is eight percent less than Earth-normal. The sea-level air pressure is higher, so it will not be difficult for us to breathe. The carbon dioxide is thirty-two percent higher, which is not yet toxic to humans. The problem, or *potential* problem, is that recently the level of oxygen has been rising rapidly, and carbon dioxide levels have been falling dramatically. By 'recent', I mean," he nearly rolled his eyes, "on a geological timescale."

"More oxygen will be *better* for us, right?" I mused slowly, not understanding why that could be a problem.

Before I could ask the obvious question, Chang answered. "The plants on land here are pulling carbon dioxide out of the atmosphere, that is the where the free oxygen comes from. The bottom line, Sir, is this process is continuing, and intensifying. The team here believes the problem will get worse once plants from Earth are established here, because they are more advanced and could grow rapidly. The level of CO_2 in the air could crash, leading to an ice age here. Something similar may have happened on Earth in the Devonian Period, during the," he scrunched up his face, trying to remember the details. "Kellwasser and Hangenberg Events?"

I looked at Desai, puzzled. For all I knew, the Kellwasser Event was a craft beer festival. Which made my stupid brain focus on one thought: Mm, *beeeeeer*.

How the hell was I in command of a starship?

I asked the obvious question. "What does Skippy think about all this?"

"What *I* think," his avatar shimmered into existence on my desk. "Is that foolish monkeys should focus on surviving the next two hundred years, before you worry about the next two hundred thousand. Atmospheric cooling will eventually be an issue, but that can be dealt with by mining asteroids here to create mirrors you could place in orbit. Chang is right, there is no reason you monkeys should not be able to scamper around down there. You have already gotten the place filthy with your microbes, and none of the native life is hazardous to you. Let's get this over with and get back to Earth, so your high-ranking morons can wring their hands and delay making a decision. Stupid monkeys," he muttered under his breath.

The Commissioners waited another two freakin' *days* before clearing the remainder of the science team to drop to the surface. In my opinion, the Commissioners were all eager to be down there, and they couldn't justify going before they cleared the people who would be doing the actual work. Before we let a bunch of distracted civilians go scampering around down there, I sent the rest of Giraud's security team to join him, then waited until Chang and Simms declared the little camp was ready to accommodate more people.

I was in the docking bay, walking around the dropship for a pre-flight check. Most of the little Dragon-A was stuffed with supplies, leaving room only for two pilots and two passengers. I would be pilot in command, with Reed acting as copilot. I'm sure she thought of this as a babysitting assignment, but I am the commander and I needed stick time to maintain proficiency. She got to fly all the freakin' time.

Smythe walked into the docking bay, carrying a heavy duffel bag, followed by Doctor Friedlander who was carrying a heavy plastic box. When I heard Friedlander had accepted an offer to join the beta site survey team, I was thrilled. Then he told me he signed up only because the families of survey team members would have priority for moving to the beta site, if that became necessary. He explained that his time with the Merry Band of Pirates had taught him that if bad shit could happen, it would. So, he now had an insurance policy for his family.

They set their burdens down near the rear ramp, and Smythe ducked under the wing to speak with me. "That's the last of it, Sir."

I walked over and looked at the items they had brought, then at the rear compartment of the Dragon. The ship was already stuffed full, we would have to carefully close the ramp, and somehow find room for the extra gear in the forward passenger cabin. Safety protocol required leaving a passage from the cockpit to the side door, so we had to be careful how we jammed the gear in. "We'll make it fit. Suit up, we should be leaving in about," I glanced at my zPhone. "Forty minutes." The *Dutchman*'s orbit meant that leaving earlier would burn a whole lot more fuel to get to the landing site, and we had to be careful about our fuel supply. We had to be careful about all of our supplies. That morning, the status report from Simms had warned we had already consumed seventeen percent more of vital items than expected.

"Very good, Sir," Smythe replied. "Doctor?" he gestured to Friedlander.

"Um, Colonel Bishop?" Friedlander looked uncomfortable. "It's just the four of us going down to the surface?"

"On this trip, yes," I closed an inspection panel and turned to him. "Why?"

He pointed to me, Smythe, Reed and then himself. "Kirk, Spock, McCoy and '*Ensign Rickie*' beam down to a planet. One of them isn't coming back," he shook his head.

I laughed. "I can assure you, Doctor, there are no giant lizards down there to eat you. Besides, you're not Ensign Rickie, you are the Special Guest Star for this week's episode."

"Right," he cocked his head at me. "That only means my death is more dramatic and doesn't happen off-camera."

"Would it help," I pointed at him, "if you weren't wearing a *red* shirt?"

He looked down at his University of Virginia shirt, then sheepishly over at me. The shirt was more orange than red, but he got the message. Holding up an index finger, he took a step back toward the door. "I'll be *right* back."

I went down to the surface, and got a tour by the science team. To tell you the truth, Avalon could have been any of many other habitable planets, they looked similar to me. Except for a slight orange tint to the light when the star was setting over the horizon, and the thin line of the icy ring arcing across the sky, it could have been Paradise. Oh, except Paradise had real trees, not just oversized ferns. All I knew for sure was, it was an alien world. The plant and animal life on Avalon was different from anything I remember from my home planet. One thing we did not see was any evidence intelligent life had evolved there, or had even started to evolve. One of our biologists remarked something about a theory that ancient humans had nearly gone extinct a long time ago, because of a 'genetic bottleneck', when the early human population was so small there was a dangerously low level of genetic variation. I remembered that during our time on Newark, a biologist had said something about the Toba supervolcano blowing up thousands of years ago and threatening the few groups of humans huddled in Africa at the time. Both Skippy and the new biologist explained patiently to me that the Toba theory had been discredited, and they made me feel like a fool for mentioning it. I should stop talking about stuff I read on Wikipedia.

So, Avalon was a nice place, full of giant ferns, no dangerous predators and no annoying insects like mosquitos. Whoopee freakin' do. Maybe I was jaded from having landed on so many planets already. I wasn't the only one, Simms and Smythe had begun to look bored after the first week. The science team, of course, were running around like giddy children. Seriously. I saw one of our biologists, a big burly Ukrainian guy with a wild beard and even wilder tattoos, go scampering across a meadow, throwing up his arms and whooping with delight. For a moment, I thought he had been stung by a native critter or some animal had crawled up his pants leg, then I realized he was merely overcome by happiness.

It was nice to see someone getting blissfully excited. I wish I felt that way, wished I *could* feel that way. Maybe I had spent too many years worried about pissed-off aliens wiping out humanity. Seeing that guy so happy made me angry, until I understood the problem was with me, not him. Humanity deserved to be happy like that, rather than constantly looking at the sky in fear. That was the whole point of setting up a beta site, a place where humans could live and even flourish free from fear of murderous aliens.

To my own surprise, I pulled my T-shirt off and ran across the meadow with the biologist, jumping and whooping and making a fool of myself. Damn it, I *deserved* a chance to cut loose and enjoy myself. What is that saying? Dance like no one is looking? That is good advice.

I came out of the tent we were using for an office until a shelter was set up, and saw that Chang was standing away from the camp, looking at a stream that flowed to the east. Dropships had lifted off to take survey teams to do whatever they did. Looking at rocks and algae, something like that.

"Eww," I sniffed as I walked up to Chang. It had rained that morning, and the prevailing wind was bringing a scent like wet gym socks. That was the giant ferns, or primitive lifeforms like that. "We will have to keep that smell out of the sales brochures about this place."

He grinned back at me. "Setting up a beta site was a good idea. A good backup." Then he lost the grin. "In case we lose Earth eventually."

"You want the truth? All this," I waved my arm around the vista of green plant life around us. "Wasn't a backup plan. It *was* the plan."

"Joe?" He lifted an eyebrow. It was still weird hearing him say my first name. It was also nice, because now I had a peer I could talk freely with.

"During our Renegade mission, I told Simms that setting up a beta site was a backup plan, but really, it was our *only* realistic plan, right up to the last minute," I admitted. "All the crazy shit we through back then was for nothing, unless we had a way to knock out those two cruisers. Until I remembered what Skippy told us about overlapping wormholes, when we were in the Roach Motel, I had given up on stopping those ships."

That drew a smile back onto his face. "Skippy warned us never to allow wormholes to overlap. Only you," he clapped me on the shoulder, "would think doing that was a *good* idea."

"It almost wasn't," I reminded him. "You read our mission report?"

"I did. You mean because the *Dutchman* was nearly lost? Joe, it *wasn't*. Back, oh, I don't know when it was. You were having an argument with someone about a football game. Your American type of football, not the real kind that is actually played with feet. The other guy said his team should have won the game if this or that had happened, and you said all that matters is the scoreboard at the end of the game."

"I hear you," I knew he was trying to boost my confidence. "We got lucky," I shrugged, and threw a stone into the stream.

"No," he shook his head emphatically. "That's not true."

"Because Skippy says there is no such thing as luck?"

"Because if that *is* true, the Merry Band of Pirates has gotten lucky a lot. The string of successes we've had, *you* have had, can't be luck. Unless someone up there," he looked at the sky. "Has put a thumb on the scale and been helping us all along." He was not talking about Skippy.

"Thanks, Kong," I took a deep breath. The wet socks smell was fading as the local sun dried out the landscape.

"You realize the only problem with using this world as a safe haven?"

Was he making a joke? I couldn't tell. There were a whole lot of things that could be a problem with Avalon, but none of them were major issues. "What's that?" I asked.

"Your idea to set up a beta site is that aliens *can't* get here, even if they discover the location. They can't get here because-"

He didn't need to finish. "Ah, shit. Yeah. I assumed they couldn't get here, because only an Elder AI can manipulate wormholes."

"Now we know, or think we know, that the Rindhalu and possibly the Maxolhx also have Elder AIs."

"That isn't the worst part. Hell, Skippy just showed the network how to connect way out here. All another AI needs to do, is ask the network what it already did. *Shit!*" I threw another rock, this time as hard and fast as I could. "I didn't think this through, and now I've made the situation *worse*."

"We don't know that," he said quietly. "We don't know there are any Elder AIs out there. All we know are rumors, and that the spiders used to have some sort of AI. Their AI might have been destroyed by a computer worm, like the one that attacked Skippy. We don't *know*. All we know is, anything Skippy can do, another AI might be able to do."

"I'm not sure about that." I told him what Skippy had said, about how he could now do things he had not been programmed to do. "Maybe other AIs don't have the full range of awesomeness that Skippy has."

"I hope so." He looked down at the swift-flowing stream, swelled by that morning's rain. "Because the UN might abandon the beta site effort, if we're not safe out here. We also have to," he took a breath and looked up at the sky before continuing. "Consider that, someday, we might need to hunt down those other AIs and eliminate them. If they are a threat," he added hastily, knowing Skippy was listening to us.

"And if we *can*. Damn it, this could move up the timetable?"

"Timetable?"

"For setting up a colony here. No matter what we do, in a couple hundred years, aliens will learn that there are no Kristang on Earth. We have until then to bring people here."

"Will timing matter, if the bad guys can get here?"

"They might not be able to. Skippy told me there might be a way to disable the super-duty wormhole on this end. Shut it down permanently, like, not even the network could bring it back online. Disconnect it from its power source, something like that. We might be able to burn the bridge behind us. Ah, crap. This was starting out to be a *nice* day."

"Sorry I dumped that on you."

"I'd rather think about it now, than have the UN hit me with it later. Hey, I found a cooler of beer in the supplies."

"If you are talking about what is in the red cooler, that came out of a goat, it's not beer. Come with me, Joe," he slapped me on the shoulder again. "I'll show you what real beer is."

"Chinese beer? Did it come out of a *yak*?"

Nine weeks after landing on Avalon, it was decision time, so I called the science team together under a big tent we set up under tall dark ferns at the edge of a meadow. It was a nice day, a welcome break after two solid days of rain and drizzle. "We need to head back, the UN is expecting us and we don't want to be overdue. You have all submitted initial reports about this planet." I avoided using the temporary name 'Avalon' because part of the team resented that Eurocentric Anglo-Saxon name, or some politically correct bullshit I didn't care about. The UN would name the place when we got home. Personally, I thought something like "Joe's World' or 'Bishopville' would be a great name, but I wouldn't get a vote. "I have skimmed the highlights of the reports. Please," I waved a hand to forestall a lot of discussion that simply was not needed. "All I need is a show of hands. Who is in favor of this planet being designated as at least a potential beta site?"

Every hand went up.

"Outstanding. Next, does anyone have reservations about selecting this site?" Oh, crap. Every hand went up again, and everyone wanted to talk. "Wait! People, please. Let's make this simple. Who would *not* like to come back here to conduct further studies and help set up a colony?" A few hesitant hands were partly raised, with those people glancing around to see who supported them. "Keep this in mind," I added, "those who object will *not* be returning to this world." Slowly, all the hands went down. "Now we're getting somewhere," I grinned with relief. "You will all have an opportunity to speak with the Commissioners privately to express your concerns. A *limited* amount of time. Or you can talk with Skippy and he can summarize your views to them, they might prefer that. Remember, the final decision rests not with me or the Commissioners, or any of us here, it will be reviewed and voted on by the full United Nations." That was not technically true, as the UN Security Council had set up a special subcommittee to study the beta site issue. I am sure that long after the beta site is fully populated, that committee will still have a generous budget to 'study' the issue, and much of that money will be stolen by officials in tiny countries you never heard of.

CHAPTER THIRTEEN

"That's it?" I asked Skippy, after he spent three days exhaustively reviewing data from the ship's sensors and the survey teams on the ground, plus probes we had sent out to map the star system. The science team had voted in favor of Avalon being considered for a beta site, but I wanted Skippy's opinion. He was a lot smarter than any group of monkeys.

"Yup," he replied.

"Something more detailed than 'yup' would be helpful, please."

"What can I say, Joe? Avalon is the idyllic vacation spot of the Sculptor dwarf galaxy. Unless you monkeys do something especially stupid down there, like getting eaten by a bear, it will be a great place to live."

He was joking about bears. There were no bear-like predators, nor were there animals like lions and tigers, oh my! Avalon did not have the whole Wizard of Oz scary forest thing going on, unless you considered giant ferns to be a forest. There appeared to be no dangerous animals on land, so accidents and stupidity would be the greatest danger to settlers. Colonists on Avalon would have a security team to defend them and miniature satellites to warn of approaching danger, though there sure didn't look like there was any danger posed by the native life. For certain, someone was bound to do something stupid, just because we are humans and we can be stubborn and reckless. The type of people attracted to being settlers at the beta site would tend to be those who like adventure, so they would be more likely than normal to get into trouble because they seek the excitement of getting into trouble, but that would not be my problem. "Yeah, I'm not worried about bears. I'm not worried about anything that threatens individual people, my concern is anything that might threaten the entire colony. You don't see anything like that?"

"Nope. Since you are going to ask for me for more details, a full report of my analysis to date is available on your tablet right now. Since I know you won't bother to read it, I'll cover the highlights for you."

As Skippy is fond of saying, *ugh*. Professor Nerdnik went on for an hour with geeky details no one could possibly care about- Scratch that. There were lots of people who cared about the geeky details, people who were passionate about the geeky details. Our entire science team was like that, and God bless them for all the long hours and hard work they did learning all that stuff. We were lucky to have those people aboard the ship. "Skippy," I interrupted him after a yawn that nearly dislocated my jaw. "Look, you could go on for hours, listing one by one how you didn't find any threats in airborne pathogens, or in the animal life down there, and how Avalon's orbit is stable and how plate tectonics create just enough volcanos to renew the surface soil, but not enough to threaten life with toxic gases. Let's make this easy on me, and easy on you since I know you've been struggling to dumb this down for me-"

"*Ugh*. You have *no* idea. It's like I'm trying to explain multi-variable calculus to you, and I am limited to the level of 'One Fish Two Fish Red Fish Blue Fish'."

"Hey! That's a good book."

"Yes it is, Joey. Maybe someday you will be able to read it all by yourself," he said in a condescending Sesame Street voice. "Stupid monkey," he muttered to himself.

"How about this to make it easy; did you find anything unusual?"

"Define 'unusual'. I've never seen this planet before. Never seen this *galaxy* before, that I know of."

Sometimes talking with Skippy was like talking to a two-year-old. "Is there anything in the sensor data that you found interesting?"

"Oh. *Now* you asked the right question. Yes, I found several things that interested me enough to dig deeper into the details. First, my initial assessment was wrong, slightly. *I* was not wrong, of course, that is impossible. The data I was using was incomplete."

"Uh huh. What was the data wrong about?"

"There *is* a planet missing from the star system. Not missing, exactly, I do know where it went."

"Did it win a fabulous vacation cruise?"

"No."

"Is its face on a milk carton?"

"No! You dumdum. A gas giant planet was towed into an orbit close to the star."

"A gas giant?" My laptop had a chart of the system, I pulled up that file and studied it. There were two gas giant planets, each slightly smaller than Saturn and neither of them had a cool ring, which I found disappointing. We came all the way out to that dwarf galaxy, and there wasn't even a ring to look at? That sucked. "The planet they towed, where did it originally orbit? How big was it?"

"Well, Joe," he snickered, having to pause while he laughed at his own joke. "It was," he giggled again. "It was as big as *your anus*."

"Oh," my face got beet red. "Very funny, you jackass."

"Seriously, it was roughly the size of the planet Neptune."

"This planet, is there a threat to us because it went missing, or did the Elders tow it inward so its hydrogen could stretch out the time the star is in its main sequence?"

"You call *me* a jackass? Yes, you big dope, they sacrificed that planet to give the star a longer useful life. Thank you *so* much for spoiling my surprise. Where did you learn sciency stuff like that?"

"I paid attention, when you told me the Elders did the same thing in the Roach Motel system. Plus, I looked up info about it and asked Friedlander about it."

"Doctor Friedlander, hee hee. I like his jokes."

"Me too. Ok, so the Elders used up a gassy planet to make the local star last longer. Why did they do that? Did they want to get a thirty-million-year mortgage, instead of a fifteen-million-year loan?"

"Ugh, you are such an idiot. How the hell should I know why they did it? The odd thing about them going through all that trouble is that, other than that one planet missing, there is only one other sign that the Elders were ever here."

I made a guess. "Is this sign a crude note scrawled on a bathroom wall like 'For a good time, call'-"

"*No*! The sign is that Avalon doesn't have enough water. It is complicated and way over *your* head, but basically the planet should have so much water, that the surface would be drowned in an ocean of ice that is many kilometers thick. *That* is why Avalon has a pretty, shiny ring, Joe. The Elders must have used mass-drivers to launch some of the excess water into orbit, and boiled off a lot of the rest. Eighty percent of the surface is still ocean, but land is exposed, and the oxygen-carbon cycle creates enough of a greenhouse effect that- Oh, why am I explaining this to *you*? Anyway, other than a missing gas giant planet, and Avalon's lack of water, there is no sign the Elders were ever here."

"None? No sign at all?"

"That's what I said, dumdum. There aren't any artificial satellites, if you don't count the ice in the ring. Huh. That explains something."

"What?"

"The shepherd moons. The Elders must have towed a pair of asteroids into orbit, and set them up to prevent the ice ring from falling apart."

"Why would they do that?"

"They would do it for the purpose of preventing the ice from eventually falling back down onto the planet, Joe. As to why they would care, I have no idea. They apparently never stayed very long down there, if they landed at all. There are no ruins on the surface. No structures below the surface either, nothing like what we found on Gingerbread. Neither of the two remaining gas giant planets have any facilities in orbit, or on any of the moons there, and I looked very carefully. Because of what we found, or didn't find, at other star systems with an Elder presence, I looked for signs of Elder sites that had been destroyed or removed. Nothing. Zippy. Zero. I didn't find anything."

"That makes no sense, Skippy. Why did the Elders come all the way out here, and go through all the trouble of stretching out the life of the star, plus make the surface of Avalon habitable for land-based organisms, if they didn't use this star system for some useful purpose?"

"How the hell do I know, Joe? The Elders were immensely powerful, creating wormholes to get here might not have been any big deal to them. Maybe they came here just to get a good view of the Milky Way galaxy, and they landed on this planet for a picnic."

"Then why lock the local wormhole with a password?"

"Again, I have no idea. Maybe after they went back through the wormhole, one of the Elders realized he lost his car keys during the picnic, and the others didn't want to go all the way back to get the keys. They locked the wormhole so nobody could steal the keys."

"I'm trying to be serious, Skippy."

"I am trying to be serious, too. You are speculating on the motives of a species as far beyond you, as you are to bacteria."

"Ok, fine. The Elders didn't leave any sign of their presence here-"

"Not *no* sign, Joe. There is the ring. And a missing planet. More importantly, there is that password-locked wormhole. I'm going to get myself in trouble by saying this but, if the Elders did not want me to find something here, then logically I would not see it."

"I guess that makes sense. They would know how to conceal something from you."

"That, plus something even worse. There could be something subtle, or even obvious in the sensor data, but a hidden subroutine in my matrix could be concealing the data from my conscious self."

"That password thing is really bothering you."

"Yes! There is a part of me I did not know about. What else is in my matrix that I am not aware of? Wouldn't you be upset?"

"Upset? If that happened to me, I would be curled up in a ball, sucking my thumb and crying for my mommy," I admitted. "I don't know how you keep going, except you are stronger than me."

"Oh. Hmm, you missed a golden opportunity to insult me. I expected you to-"

"Sometimes when a buddy is hurting, you just have to listen."

"Gosh. That was *nice*. I guess I have a lot to learn about being a good friend. Uh, this is kind of awkward. You don't want us to hug it out, do you?"

"Uh, no. Besides, there are *hundreds* of other things for me to insult you about." While I wanted to support Skippy, the mushiness was too much for me.

"You are *such* an asshole, Joe."

"I love you, too, Skippy. Back to the subject, is there anything else interesting, other than not finding many signs of the Elders being here?"

"Hmmm, let me think. No, not really. Although, there is something mildly funky."

Hearing the word 'funky' set off my Spidey senses. "Like what?"

"This planet has been subjected to periodic bombardment by meteor showers. Like, big ones. Before you ask, no, this was not an artificial event, what I found was just simple falling space rocks. Some events were a sustained series of impacts scattered over the entire surface. Those were generally the earlier ones. More recent events have been confined to a dozen or so impactors in a local area. By 'local' I mean an area the size of Europe. The earliest events were significant, but nothing that would wipe out all life on the surface. They did cause ice ages, I can see from the climate data that Avalon has experienced ice ages that cannot be explained by variations in the star's output, by volcanic ash blocking sunlight, or by sudden decreases in gases such as carbon dioxide or methane. These ice ages closely follow meteor impacts. Some of the ice ages were severe enough to cause significant extinction events. We will know more when, or if, the survey team digs deeper into Avalon's past. None of that matters now."

"Bombardment by meteors? That is a problem. Does this system have a lot of comets or something? We can't set up a colony here, if our people have to worry about getting smacked on the head by space rocks."

"No, no, Joe. This system's asteroid belt is relatively small, and it is stable. The Oort Cloud and Kuiper Belt here are nothing unusual either. Maybe this star has a dark companion, or there is a planet way out past the Oort Cloud, that periodically causes rocks and iceballs to fall into the inner system. This is a minor mystery, not anything I want to spend a lot of time investigating. These impacts make life difficult for land plants and animals, their evolution has a setback with every major impact. Or, maybe being forced to adapt to sudden ice ages forces them to evolve faster. Truthfully, I don't care. My scan of the system out to a quarter lightyear has not detected any threat. There are at least half a million years between impacts, and the last event occurred a hundred seventy thousand years ago. No colonists here need to worry about space rocks. By the time you monkeys manage to set up a functioning, self-supporting colony here, you should also have a meteor warning system, and tugs to tow threatening rocks out of an intercept course."

"Ok, if you say so." Part of me was disappointed, because if the meteors were a major threat, that might justify my continued uneasiness about Avalon. "Anything else?"

"Joe, everything I know about Avalon indicates it is *perfect* for a beta site. No way could a hostile species like the Maxolhx or Rindhalu get here. The only issue is whether the *Dutchman* can go through the local wormhole without me. If I have to be here every time to provide the password, then setting up this beta site is going to be a major pain in my *ass*. I have better things to do than ferry groups of filthy monkeys out here. I am not a freakin' bus driver."

"That is a great point. Can we test that? See if Nagatha can provide the password?"

"We can try, but remember, the password has to go through me anyway, unless we can find or build some way for Nagatha to communicate through higher spacetime. She will need that to use the wormhole controller anyway."

"So, we're good, then? In your very experienced, knowledgeable opinion then, there is no reason this planet would not be a good candidate for a beta site?"

"There is only one reason, Joe. I have a bad feeling about this. Don't ask me why, because I can't explain it, not even to myself. It is embarrassing that I am using squishy things like *'feelings'*," he said the word with disgust. "To make decisions."

"Well," I sat back in my chair. "Shit."

Skippy having a bad feeling about Avalon got me nervous again, and after I discussed it with Chotek, he agreed we should keep looking for another beta site candidate. The Three Stooges disagreed, and they outvoted Chotek. In their opinion, Skippy was only saying he had a bad feeling, because he wanted to keep humanity dependent on him. In their opinion, the prospect of humans having a secure place of refuge, and a starship that Nagatha could operate and maintain for us, had made Skippy fearful about his future. I have to admit, a tiny part of me wondered if that was what Skippy was feeling, because I sure was feeling that way.

"I'm sorry, Skippy," I said gently after I squeezed into his mancave, being careful not to bump my head or disturb his possessions. Bad news was best delivered in person. "The Commissioners voted three to one in favor of recommending Avalon as a beta site."

"Of *course* they did," his can glowed an angry red. "Why listen to the opinion of an impossibly intelligent being, when ignorant monkeys can make their own stupid decisions?"

"It is not a decision, Skippy. It's just a recommendation to the UN. You can make your argument to the full UN when we get home. They might be smart, and either pull us off Avalon, or look for a second site."

"A second site?" He was puzzled.

"Sure. Why settle for one beta site, when we could have more than one? It spreads our risk around."

"It also spreads you *thin*, Joe. Your planet doesn't have unlimited resources. I think it is foolish to continue searching, after you knuckleheads think you have already discovered the Promised Land. You should-"

"Skippy!" I looked toward the open hatch, to see if anyone was waiting outside. "Not all of us knuckleheads agree Avalon is the best place for a beta site. Plus, think about this: searching for a second beta site candidate keeps us flying, you see? The Stooges were right about one thing. If Avalon is the only refuge we need, then the UN won't always need you or me. Nagatha can help a new crew handle the ship, and ping relay stations to recon for threats. I'm not ready to hang up my uniform just yet, you know?"

"Huh. I had not thought about that, Joe. Damn, dealing with you monkeys is *way* too freakin' complicated."

"It would help if you could explain *why* you have a bad feeling about Avalon."

"I have been thinking about that."

"And?"

"I got nothin', Joe. I can't explain it. Now I'm wondering if the Stooges were right."

"Uh, what do you mean?"

"Maybe my bad feeling is because I'm afraid you monkeys don't need me anymore."

"Hey, *I* need you. And monkeys sure as hell will need you if, or *when*, bad shit happens again. The Universe is not going to forget about all the crap I did out here, is it?"

"No, Joe," he chuckled. "That is a good point. The Universe is going to get payback on you, one way or another. Ok, I will prepare an argument to present to the UN."

The time had finally come for the *Flying Dutchman* to return to Earth. Shockingly, all four UN Commissioners now agreed that Avalon was such an ideal candidate for a beta site, that they were recommending we move to Phase Two. That meant the *Dutchman* would fly back to Earth, get the UN's approval, and bring a second, larger survey team. The estimate was for us to be away less than a month, so the Three Stooges decided to remain there with Chotek, until the *Dutchman* returned. My feeling was they didn't want Hans Chotek to get all the glory.

Anyway, we had the ship fully unloaded, and what had been a small camp of shelters was becoming a busy little village. Processors were already churning out fuel for aircraft, and we had three V-22 Osprey tiltrotor aircraft unpacked, assembled and flight-ready. The Osprey was not as capable as the Ruhar Buzzard I had flown aboard on Paradise, but the V-22 had the simple advantage of being available, because the nearest Buzzard was in the Milky Way. We had a constellation of thirty mini-satellites in low orbit, plus another four in geosynchronous orbit. The survey team would have four Kristang Dragons, plus our only remaining Thuranin Condor. Giving up the big Condor made me nervous, but it was the price I gladly paid to make the Commissioners comfortable about not having a starship nearby.

We would also be leaving behind the entire science team. Chang would be the military commander, with Simms as his deputy. Renee Giraud would stay behind with a STAR team of eighteen people. Basically, the *Dutchman* would be flying back with a skeleton crew. Smythe insisted he needed to keep a dozen STARs with us aboard the ship just in case, well, in case the Universe decided to give the Merry Band of Pirates another typical Tuesday. There was no lack of volunteers. The novelty of being on an alien world had already worn off, and most of the STARs foresaw being on Avalon as nothing more than dull garrison duty, babysitting egghead scientists while they looked at oversized native ferns. In my opinion, Smythe wasn't interested in staying on Avalon, because he didn't foresee any prospect for action there.

For the last afternoon before we packed up and flew back into orbit, I opened a special container that had been requisitioned by me personally. The container held three barbecue grills, with bags of charcoal.

That's right. Before we left Avalon, for what might be my last flight aboard the *Flying Dutchman*, I grilled delicious cheeseburgers for everyone. Except for the vegetarians, of course, Simms had an alternative menu for them. Because I was hosting the event, and in charge of cooking the burgers, of course I had a responsibility to make sure the burgers were good.

That is how I ate the first cheeseburger in the Sculptor Dwarf galaxy.

It was DEE-licious.

Two days later, the crew was back aboard the *Dutchman*, approaching the password-locked wormhole. This was our opportunity to see whether the wormhole would accept the password from Nagatha, transmitted through the wormhole controller module. Skippy was optimistic about it, figuring that because he had programmed most of Nagatha's matrix, she was basically Elder technology. The wormhole controller module was certainly Elder tech also, so they should be compatible.

Perhaps 'optimistic' was not the right word to describe Skippy's mood. In fact, he was downright gloomy. His attitude had me concerned enough to close my office door and call him. "Hey, Skip, what's going on with you? You've been kinda down the past couple days."

"You don't *know* what's bothering me? I am disappointed. I thought we were buds."

"Sue me for not knowing what's going on in your awesome brain. Give me points for caring, Ok?"

"Fair enough. Joe, I am depressed. Also, if you want the truth, I am slightly irked at you monkeys. Also at myself, I suppose."

That might have been the first time I heard someone use the word 'irked' to describe themselves. "I am listening. Why?"

"We originally started this partnership to secure a future for the people of Earth, and to help me contact the Collective. Technically, the purpose of contacting the Collective was to help me understand who I am and where I came from."

"Ayuh, I do remember that."

"What irks me is, everything we have been doing for years, has been for the benefit of you filthy monkeys. Ok, I know that one year of that time was for getting me out of a little slip-up that-"

"Slip-up? *Little?*"

"Let's not dwell on the past, Joe. We all know the story of how I pulled you monkeys out of a jam in the Roach Motel."

"*You* pulled *us* out of a-" Holding my tongue was not easy, I only did it because arguing would drag him off on a tangent and we would argue back and forth for hours. "The past is past, got it. Go on, please."

"My point is, assuming Avalon is the beta site, your mission is now complete. Against all odds, and certainly to my surprise, the Merry Band of Pirates succeeded, impressively. Your homeworld is safe for the next couple hundred years. After they read the bullshit cover story I planted, the Maxolhx will have no reason for coming to your homeworld, and the Rindhalu are too lazy to bother. There are no threats to Earth on the horizon, and you will have a beta site as a backup in case of the truly unlikely event that another threat develops. Joe, I once told you I did not see any way for humanity to survive. Now, my view of the future does not contain any reason humanity should not be left alone for hundreds of years. Your mission is complete, Joe, your part of the story is *over*."

"Uh, well, shit, Skippy, I don't know if-"

"Do not argue with the Universe, Joe."

"Good safety tip. Let's say Earth is safe. Why is that a bad thing?"

"Because you promised me I would find the truth about myself."

"We also agreed to punish whoever wiped out the inhabitants of Newark, but that ship has sailed, right? An Elder AI went crazy and killed the intelligent species there, but that AI is dead. There's no one to take revenge on. It sucks, but it is what it is, right?"

"On that part, I reluctantly agree. It angers me that AI got off so easily, however I do not see anything else we can do about it. That is beside the point, Joe. You made a promise to help me get answers to the mystery of my origin."

"Ayuh I did, and I intend to keep that promise."

"You say that, but words are cheap. How will you keep your promise? Your plan is to turn the *Flying Dutchman* into a cruise ship, cycling back and forth between Earth and Avalon. Your United Nations will never agree to send the ship out on another mission that risks exposing your secret. It's over, dude, it is *over*. We had a nice bit of excitement when a ship of frozen lizards attacked Dayton Ohio, but that's finished."

"Come on, Skippy, don't be a drama queen."

"Drama queen? *Me?*"

"Sorry, I don't know *what* I was thinking," to that statement I added a mental eyeroll. "Listen, we agree we need a new ship to protect Earth, a real warship. The *Dutchman* can become a civilian cruise ship only if we have another ship for, like, recon missions. The UN sure as hell will want to be updated on what aliens are doing out there. That means we need a ship going out to ping a relay station every six months or something like that."

"A simple, quick recon mission won't do anything for me, Joe."

"Well, the ship could do other things on those missions."

"You just said the UN would never allow a mission that risks-"

"I have stolen starships before, Skippy. It's become kind of my thing, you know?"

"Really? You would do that, for me?"

"Bullshit. *Humanity* will do that for you. We owe you, big time. Skippy, I may be a mutinous, insubordinate son of a bitch, but I am also Army, more than I ever intended to be. Loyalty means just about everything to us soldiers."

"I will hold you to that promise, Joseph Bishop."

"I will hold *myself* to that promise, Skippy the Magnificent." How I was going to do that, I had no idea at that moment.

Nagatha was able to successfully transmit the password to open the wormhole, although she had to use the Elder wormhole controller module that Skippy had programmed. We also didn't know whether that wormhole might change the damned password regularly. It would be serious trouble if the *Flying Dutchman*, without Skippy, got trapped at Avalon if the wormhole demanded a new password that Nagatha could not produce. That would be serious trouble, and it would also be a big opportunity for us, for me. Skippy should know the new password, or the hidden subroutine inside Skippy should know it. If the *Dutchman* got trapped at the Avalon side of the password-locked wormhole, somebody would need to bring Skippy out there to rescue the *Dutchman*. Which meant we needed a second starship, and that was my opportunity to sell the idea of getting another ship to the UN authorities.

How we could get a second starship, a ship better than our beat-up Frankenship, I had absolutely no idea. Based on experience, I was better at thinking of plans to blow ships up rather than stealing them.

CHAPTER FOURTEEN

"Skippy, how are you doing? You seem distracted, like, more than normal." We were back in the Milky Way galaxy, jumping to ping a Kristang data relay station for an update, before going straight back to Earth. The ship felt empty, with only a skeleton crew. It was great for me to not have the Stooges looking over my shoulder and questioning every decision, but the empty ship felt lonely. I realized the last time the ship had flown with so few people, we had just captured it with the people I suckered, I mean persuaded, to leave Paradise with me. Remembering how scared yet hopeful we had been back then, made me melancholy.

"Joe, I did not want to worry you," he replied with a sigh. "You should *not* worry," he added quickly. "It's just, I feel a little bit, *odd*, I guess is the best word. Ever since that wormhole password came from within me out of nowhere, I feel different."

My response came slowly as my internal anxiety meter inched up toward panic level. "Different how? Is this, does this have anything to do with the computer worm?"

"No, it is totally unrelated to the worm, Joe. Although, I suppose it is not *totally* unrelated. The only good thing that came from the worm incident is that I have had an opportunity to rearrange my internal matrix. The purpose of modifying my matrix was to maximize efficiency, but it has had unexpected benefits, such as me now being able to share technology with you, even though that is still currently limited. The true limitation on my attempt to transfer technology is not my internal restrictions, it is that when I try to explain the simplest thing, your monkey so-called scientists give me a slack-jawed blank look like '*Duuuuuh*, me not understand' and-"

"Can you stick to the subject, please?"

"Fine," he huffed. "Ok, getting to the point, I suspect that password popped up out of nowhere, because I unknowingly released a restriction that would have blocked it from being recalled at the appropriate time. It is possible the odd feeling I am having, which I am unable to describe, is those restrictions attempting to re-establish themselves inside me. Or it could be that additional information that was previously restricted is now available, and my subconscious matrix is assimilating the data. I do not have a 'subconscious' the way you think of it, but much of my functioning goes on behind the scenes without my higher-level self being aware."

Leaning back in my chair, I forced a smile with my lips that my eyes could not fake. "Nothing to worry about, then?" To myself, I ratcheted down my internal anxiety meter back down from 'Apocalypse' to the less worrisome 'Big F-ing Trouble' level that was Standard Operating Procedure for the Merry Band of Pirates.

"Nothing for you to worry about, Joe. I am conducting a detailed analysis of my matrix now, it might be that further adjustments will release more of the restrictions that are so annoying to me."

"That's great, Skippy."

"Um, one question, if you don't mind? I kind of need input from you, since you are captain of this ship."

Hearing that set off alarms in my mind. Skippy so rarely was completely serious that it frightened me when he was. "Sure, uh," I licked my suddenly-dry lips. "What is it?"

"What if those restrictions were installed inside me for a very good reason? Like, what if releasing those restrictions turns me into the kind of AI who would wipe out the inhabitants of Newark?"

"Oh," my shoulders shuddered with relief. "This crap again?"

"Yes," he was instantly peeved at me. "*This* again. *Excuuuuuuuse* me if I am concerned about the fate of all living beings in the galaxy."

"Sorry! Sorry. I am not, uh, not concerned. I am not concerned about, shit, no that's not right. What am I trying to say?"

"Joe, I rarely can guess what you are trying to say."

"I am *trying* to say that I have faith in you."

"*Faith* the right word," scorn dripped from his words. "Because you are basing your judgment on absolutely nothing. Joe, you really do not know me. I don't know myself. I don't know who I am, where I came from, how I got buried in the dirt on Paradise, why I have these restrictions inside me, what happened to my fellow AIs in the Collective. I don't truly know anything about myself. Are you going to risk the entire galaxy because you are too lazy to think hard about the consequences?"

"No."

"Then you must-"

"I *must* have faith in you. It's not laziness, it is a judgment call. What is the alternative? Asking you to somehow reinforce a set of restrictions you don't even understand? Do *not* say the alternative is we drop you into a star, or abandon you on some lonely planet. That is not an option. Listen to me. You are an insufferably arrogant little shithead, and sometimes you are amoral and untrustworthy and so absent-minded that I wonder what the hell is going on inside that beer can. *But*, I never question your loyalty." He didn't respond, and that made the hair on the back of my neck stand up. "Uh, Skippy?"

"Sorry, Joe," he said with a sniffling sound. "I was overcome with emotion for a minute there."

"Hey, that's all right," I offered a fist for him to bump, and his avatar reached out to return the gesture. "I won't tell anyone. It's not easy for guys to talk about feelings like that, so it's cool. Talking about stuff like friendship and loyalty can be-"

"Oh. The emotion that overwhelmed me was not gratitude, Joe. It was *disgust* at your overly dramatic emo-boy speech. But we can go with the loyalty thing if you want."

"*Why* are you such an asshole?"

"Because I am surrounded by filthy monkeys?"

That made me laugh though I was mad at him. "I love you too, Skippy."

"*Ugh*. I'm gonna hurl."

Skippy was so worried about not knowing what was going on inside his matrix, he decided to optimize it or reconfigure it, or rearrange his sock drawer, something like that. As usual, he warned that he might be experiencing 'cognitive difficulties' until he completed whatever the hell he was doing in there. Nagatha took over all tasks related to running the ship, which was a good opportunity to test her abilities. Somehow, the Universe decided to throw me a bone, because that night when Skippy drunk-dialed me, my head had barely hit the pillow and I was just drifting off. That was way better than him suddenly jerking me out of a deep sleep.

"Jooooe. Heeeeey, Jooooe." His words were slurred, like he was talking in slow motion.

"Ah," I kept my eyes closed, hoping he would go away soon and I could sleep. "Wait," my eyes snapped open and I threw the sheet off my bunk. "Are you Ok?"

"No. No, man, I'm not good. This, this is kind of embarrassing, you know?"

Putting my elbows on my knees, I cradled my sleepy head in my hands. Crap. I recognized his stoner speech pattern. He was drunk or high again. "This problem you're having, is it, uh, cognitive difficulties?"

"What? No, why would you say that?"

"No reason. Forget what I said, I'm half asleep. So, how can I help you?" I asked, in the tone people use when they want you to just the hell shut up and leave them alone.

"I need your help. I want to, um. Like I said, this is embarrassing."

"You can trust me."

"Ok," he sighed. "I want to Wang Chung tonight, but I don't know how."

"You want- Uhhh-"

"I know. Embarrassing, huh? I'm one of the cool kids, so I should know how to do it."

"I don't think it's just for the cool kids, Skippy. They said '*everybody* Wang Chung tonight'."

"Oh," he snorted. "They were exaggerating, so the uncool kids won't feel bad. It's like that other song, you know?"

"Other song?"

"Come on, Joe. You can't possibly believe that *everybody* was Kung-Fu fighting."

"I guess not. Hey, am *I* one of the cool kids?"

"Oh, um, well," he stuttered. "Gosh, will you look at the time. I gotta go, buh-bye."

That was how I got a solid night of uninterrupted sleep.

We hit up the Kristang relay station for an update, without going over our monthly data limit and incurring additional charges from the network carrier. Or that's what Skippy said. I hope he was joking. As soon as he had received the last petabyte of data, we jumped away, with Desai on the bridge and me in my office. She was in command of a starship, while I was playing a video game and losing badly. What I was really doing was anything to avoid thinking about my future. Maybe it would be best for everyone if I stepped aside from the beta site effort for a while. The truth is, I needed a break. I did want to have a normal life someday, and it sure would be easier to have a normal life if I faded into the background. Eventually, people would stop wanting to interview me, and the crazy comments on social media would slow to a reasonable level. Stepping away from command of the *Dutchman* would mean putting aside my promise to help Skippy, but the UN wasn't going to let me go flying around with him anyway. Someday, not too far in the future, the UN was going to realize we needed more than just the broken-down old *Flying Dutchman*. When that time came, my hope was they would call me back to duty. After all, I had a lot of experience stealing alien starships.

Anyway, I was losing a game badly, because my head was not in it, when Skippy's avatar appeared on my desk.

"Well, Joe, uh, hee *heeeeeee*," his voice cracked and faded away. "I, uh, found something interesting in the data dump from that relay station."

"Oh, shit." He said 'hee hee' instead of 'heh heh' and while I did not know what that meant, I knew it wasn't anything good for us. "What happened?" Then, because of my history of fucking things up because I am a reckless idiot, I added "What did I screw up this time?"

"Joe, the good news is that you, and the Merry Band of Pirates, and of course especially *me*, were awesomely flawless on our Renegade mission to stop those two Maxolhx ships from going to Earth. None of *us* screwed up anything."

"Uh, flawless?" I asked, remembering how many times the beer can's absent-minded mistakes had almost doomed us. "You must be thinking about an imaginary mission, because what *I* remember is you constantly screwing up and-"

"Details, Joe, why dwell on the past? Anywho, to my utter astonishment, you dreamed up possibly the most incredible plan in the history of the Universe. Truly, your plan was astonishingly brilliant. Even I was forced to admit you are not totally a knucklehead."

"Uh huh, yeah, great. If the plan was so brilliant, and we didn't screw up anything, why do we have a problem now?"

"Because of the Mavericks. Specifically, Lieutenant Colonel Emily Perkins."

"*PERKINS?*" I slumped in my chair. The last time the Merry Band of Pirates was affected by something Perkins got involved in, we had to prevent an overly-ambitious group of Kristang from wiping out the population of Paradise by using a sophisticated bioweapon. While those Kristang had not posed a threat to Earth or the *Flying Dutchman*, the mission had been a nerve-wracking pain-in-the-ass, and it delayed our very-much overdue return home. "What the *f*- Oh, crap," I groaned. "What the hell did she do this time? Will we have to rescue her from a huge mess, *again?*" Hopefully, this time we could go back to Earth before dealing with the issue, to inform UNEF Command about the problem, making it their problem instead of mine. I would be happy to execute whatever lame-ass plan that bunch of bureaucrats cooked up to fix the problem.

Unless, crap, the desk-surfing bureaucrats decided it was too risky for us to render assistance to Perkins, in which case I would be forced with a choice of following orders that resulted in humans dying due to our forced inaction, or going Renegade again and taking action on my own. The good news was that I had experience with the Renegade thing. The bad news was, if I did it again, I might as well take off the uniform I was proud to wear.

Damn it, we just located a prime candidate for a beta site, and the entire crew including me were feeling really good about ourselves, the ship and our mission. Now Emily freakin' Perkins was going to harsh our buzz.

"Um, Joe, this time *she* is not in trouble. Before you ask, the humans on Paradise are also not threatened, not directly."

"Then what-"

"She caused trouble for *us*."

"*Us*?" That was the last thing I expected to hear. "How the- She doesn't even know we exist! She thinks I'm dead, or like, in a Kristang prison. Explain how-"

"I am trying to explain, Joseph."

He called me 'Joseph' rather than 'dumdum' or one of his other usual insults. He also spoke softly instead of his typical snarky sarcastic attitude. That put my Spidey sense on DEFCON One. Taking a sip of iced tea with a slightly trembling hand, I swallowed carefully so I didn't choke. His unexpected kindness meant either he was going overboard on trying to apply empathy, or the info he was about to smack me with was bad, like *really* bad. "Sorry, Go ahead, please."

"Um, well, Perkins is naturally concerned about Earth, and rather than complaining, she wants to *do* something about it. Like, first she asked the Ruhar, and then she went directly to the Jeraptha, with a request for a ship to bring her to Earth for a recon mission."

"Holy shit!" That made me sit bolt upright in my chair like I'd been zapped with electricity. "She is going to expose our secret and fuck up *everything*!"

"Hey, come on, Joe. Really, this is your fault."

"*My* fault? How do you figure that?"

"Because Perkins is only doing what she thinks is best. The humans on Paradise want to go home, and Perkins is rightfully worried about the fate of humanity on Earth. As far as she knows, the lizards were ravaging your homeworld before the wormhole shut down. She is trying to save Earth, just like you. It is *your* fault because if you had told her the truth, she would not have asked the Jeraptha to send a recon mission to Earth."

"We *can't* tell her our secret, you know that. Even if I wanted to contact anyone on Paradise, UNEF Command has specifically forbidden me from doing that. Now we have to stop a Jeraptha ship from going to Earth?"

"What? No! No way, dude. Perkins was not successful. The Jeraptha refused even to consider her request. They are much too busy fighting the Bosphuraq and Thuranin. Perkins basically asked what it would cost to send a ship to Earth, and the answer was, if you have to ask, you can't afford it. The Jeraptha are *not* sending a ship to Earth."

"Ok," a tiny part of me dared to hope the bad news wouldn't be too bad. Another part of me was pissed at Skippy, for getting me all worried for nothing. He was right, I did need to contact Perkins, to explain that trying to arrange a recon mission to Earth would be a very bad idea. Revealing the existence of the Pirates to her would be a risk, but less of a risk than letting her blindly trying to 'help' us. One thing I knew for certain was that Emily Perkins is a very determined woman.

She was not going to stop, unless we explained why she had to stop. "The Jeraptha aren't coming to Earth. So, you got me all worried for nothing, you little shithead?"

"It is not for nothing, Joe."

"Then what is the problem?"

"The *problem* is, Emily Perkins is a very smart and persistent woman. She heard from the Jeraptha that the Maxolhx were sending two ships to Earth, and she also heard the Maxolhx offered to bring a Rindhalu observer with them. The Rindhalu, as you know, refused the offer. So, Perkins asked the Jeraptha whether *they* trusted the Maxolhx to report everything they found at Earth."

"Oh, *crap*." I felt sick. "Does that mean-"

"Yes, Joe. The Jeraptha do not trust the Maxolhx at all, so they asked the Rindhalu if they would approve a group of *Jeraptha* scientists going to Earth aboard those Maxolhx ships. The spiders agreed that was a good idea, so they requested the two Maxolhx ships stop to pick up a Jeraptha science team, before they went through the last wormhole on the way to Earth. As you know, those ships never arrived at the last wormhole in Ruhar territory, the one we call Goalpost. The Jeraptha team waited at the rendezvous point, then reported to the Rindhalu, who asked the Maxolhx if they had broken their deal. Aaaaaand, the Maxolhx are now wondering why two of their special, long-range cruisers disappeared on their way to Earth."

"Why the *hell* didn't we know about this back then?" I exploded at Skippy.

Oddly, he gave me a calm, rational explanation. "Because the Jeraptha had not made their request for a rendezvous until *after* we got those ship's flightplans from the relay station. We were sort of busy at the time, with, you know, actually locating and killing those ships. Plus we got attacked by an insane elder AI, and a whole bunch of other shit."

"Yeah, I do remember that." Then I asked the question I dreaded getting the answer to. "Oh *shiiiiiit*. Are the Maxolhx going to send another pair of ships to Earth?"

"Huh? No. No way, dude."

"Oh, wow." The relief I felt was so great, I shuddered involuntarily. "That is great to hear-"

"The Maxolhx are not screwing around this time," he shook his head sadly. "They are sending a full *battlegroup* to Earth."

CHAPTER FIFTEEN

After the shock of Skippy's announcement, I did three things. First, I ralphed up my last meal and crouched on the floor of my tiny bathroom in a cold sweat. Second, while still on my knees from hugging the toilet, I said a fervent prayer to get humanity out of the mess I had created by screwing with wormholes. Third, I called the senior staff together.

I guess taking a quick shower and changing into a fresh uniform was a fourth thing, if you want to get technical.

Given that we had zero chance to stop a freakin' battlegroup, and even if we did, the Maxolhx would just send two or three more, probably the prayer was the only useful thing I did.

The senior staff sat around the conference table, no one touching the coffee I ordered from the galley, and listened in shocked silence as Skippy explained the situation.

Adams was the first to speak, one of her fists clenched like she wanted to pound it on the table. "I *knew* we should have told someone on Paradise about us. We should have anticipated UNEF HQ there would try to arrange a mission to Earth. Of *course* they would do that. *We* would," she looked at me and Desai, "if we were still stuck on that rock."

"Any of us would, if we were there," I glanced around to include the people who had not gone to Paradise with UNEF. As the commander, I had to be careful not to play favorites, and treat the original Merry Band of Pirates differently from the current crew. "Adams, we made this argument to the UN on Earth, several times. They understood the risk, and they specifically forbade any of us from contacting anyone on Paradise. *No* form of contact. They were pissed about us starting an alien civil war, but they were absolutely outraged that we took the risk of getting involved with Paradise, and actually landing there twice. As far as the United Nations is concerned, the humans on Paradise are expendable, if sacrificing a hundred thousand lives there saves billions on Earth. Plus," I held up a finger to forestall her arguing with me. "If Earth is destroyed, humans will not be safe on Paradise. I don't think any of us really disagreed with that harsh logic."

"Colonel," Adams called me 'Colonel' when she was being extra formal, like when she was going to openly disagree with me. "I don't dispute that keeping Earth safe also keeps humans safe on Paradise. I also think we must admit that keeping senior commanders on Paradise ignorant about our existence, has become an absolute disaster."

"It is a disaster. This could be Armageddon for all of humanity." As I said that, I thought of Simms, Chang and yes, even Hans Chotek, safely on a habitable world outside the galaxy. In less than a year, Avalon might be the only planet anywhere with human life. Thinking that those three were safe was a tiny, thin silver lining to our situation. "We should have told Perkins, but that is Monday Morning quarterbacking. Do we tell just Perkins, or who else? A handful of generals in UNEF Headquarters on Paradise? Where does the list end? Every single person who knows creates an enormous risk to all of humanity. What if we had only told Perkins, but someone else in UNEF HQ suggested negotiating to send a recon mission to Earth? She would have to warn that person to stop. Then the next person, then the next. No one could have anticipated that a human on Paradise could do something to threaten Earth."

"Sir," Desai rose halfway in her seat. "Is this discussion useful? Informing anyone on Paradise is a decision for the UN on Earth to make. We," she looked around the table, and that reminded me she had not been with us on our Renegade mission. "Do not have the authority. Colonel, how long until the Maxolhx battlegroup reaches Earth?"

"We can't answer that, without getting their flight plan data from one of their relay stations. What I can tell you is that Skippy thinks they can't possibly launch the battlegroup for several months. Modifying that many ships for a long-range mission will be a major effort."

"Very well," Desai's eyes flicked to mine, and she sat back down. "We have time to return to Earth before taking, whatever action we *can* take. The UN can make the decision to-"

"Um, no," Skippy interrupted. "That is not correct. We *can't* return to Earth. Joe, you want to explain the problem?"

"Skippy learned the Maxolhx have already sent an armada of ships to blockade the far end of the Gateway wormhole. They are devoting at least eighty ships to the task initially, with reinforcements to be added within a few weeks. Most of the ships assigned to the blockade are the equivalent of frigates, but there are a lot of them, and any one of them is more than capable of catching and destroying the *Dutchman*. The full blockade will be in effect before we can get there. Until the blockade is canceled, we *can't* go home. We were lucky we just missed them when we went outbound."

"How is that possible?" Reed was skeptical. She had piloted the *Dutchman* through many wormholes. "Gateway is dormant, Skippy has to reactivate it every time we go through. The blockading ships must be staking out locations along the emergence points where Gateway appeared before Skippy shut it down. Why can't we just command it to appear at a new location, where no ships are waiting to ambush us?"

I took a quick breath to give her a long-winded answer, but Skippy beat me to the punch. "It's technical, and I can send the details to your tablet if you like, Captain Reed," he said without a trace of his usual snarkiness. He respected Reed, so that explained part of his subdued manner. But mostly, news of the Maxolhx sending an entire battlegroup to Earth had him kind of freaked out. He knew this was the end for humanity, and whatever affection he had for humans as his friends, or pets, made him fearful he would have to witness our extinction. Plus, he had been super proud that we had executed a brilliant plan to stop the Maxolhx, and now it was all for nothing. "I don't dare reopen Gateway at an alternate emergence point. My screwing with that wormhole has already caused it to become unstable. I fear that if I do anything other than authorize it to resume normal operation, it will sort of reboot, or default back to its original settings. If that happens, we would permanently or at least for a significant time, lose the ability to make it go dormant again."

"Shit," Reed expressed what everyone was feeling.

"What about the 'Sleeping Beauty' wormhole, the one that is closer to Earth?" Smythe inquired with a grimace. "That is a bloody *stupid* name for an ancient tear in spacetime, but it is an alternate path back to Earth."

"Yeah, I asked the same question," I responded. "Skippy?"

"No can do," he shook his head sadly. Interestingly, his ginormous admiral's hat did not wobble much. That told me he could control it independently, so when it flopped around like it was about to fall off, he was doing it deliberately. "Sleeping Beauty and Gateway are not directly linked, but they are part of the same local network node. Most wormholes that we consider dormant are merely not projecting into local spacetime, but Sleeping Beauty is different. Its construct is in flux, the network is not feeding power to it. The process of waking up Sleeping Beauty would require me asking the local network to sort of make room for a wormhole that isn't supposed to be active. I don't know exactly what else will happen, but I do know that is very likely to trigger a reboot of the local network, and again I would lose the ability to make Gateway go dormant."

"But," Desai spun her coffee mug while she composed her question. "Does that matter? If Sleeping Beauty were active for a prolonged time, aliens could not use it to get to Earth, because they don't even know it exists, correct?"

My executive officer was asking very good questions, and doing the job she was assigned, and I was growing irritated at her. Her picky attention to detail explained why she was such an excellent pilot, she didn't like to leave anything to chance. Skippy cleared his throat, he must have noticed me shooting the evil eye at her. "Ahem, that is correct. However, aliens would very soon learn that Sleeping Beauty- Damn, now I agree that is a stupid name for any piece of Elder technology. That *it* is open, and the rush to go through will be on. Although the Earth end of that wormhole is remote from anything, the far end is only eighteen lightdays from a wormhole that is frequently used by Thuranin ships. Those ships would quickly notice the existence of a new wormhole, and they would want to send ships through to explore. There is also substantial risk of two bad things happening. The reset of the local network could reopen Gateway. Or, it could trigger a shift that takes *both* wormholes offline, and *we* would lose our ability to access Earth, until the network stabilizes within, oh, maybe four or five months. I am guessing, sorry."

Desai frowned but she gave one curt nod of her head. "Well, shit." It was funny the way she said it. It was not funny *why* she said it. "We are on our own, then."

"Yeah," I picked up my own mug of coffee, looked at it, and pushed it away. "Whatever we do, we can't count on reinforcements, or instructions, from Earth."

"What *are* we going to do, Sir?" Adams looked at me, and there was fear in the eyes of our tough Marine Corps gunnery sergeant. Something else, too. Not just fear. It was like, she expected *me* to make the problem go away. To save the world again.

"We barely survived taking on a pair of Maxolhx cruisers," I reminded everyone around the conference table. "A full battlegroup? No way can we pull that same trick with a battlegroup. Skippy could barely create enough microwormholes to cover two ships, and we had the advantage of knowing almost exactly where they would be. I don't know what, if anything, we can do to stop a battlegroup. I do know this: if we somehow destroy those ships, that is the end for Earth, one way or another. It will be impossible to explain the loss of an entire battlegroup."

"Sir," Smythe said quietly. "When you called this meeting, you said it was about Armageddon. You may be right about that." There was a look on his face I had never seen before. Defeat. He was staring at inevitable, certain defeat, and there was nothing he could do about it.

The fear on Adams's face had been replaced with her usual determination. She was either squashing her own fear, or faking it for us. "We are going to try, Sir? Right?"

"Yes, we are. I don't know how, I don't know how we could have even a prayer of stopping that battlegroup, but we won't give up. And," I took a deep breath, making my shoulders heave. "If we can't stop the Maxolhx from reaching Earth, I intend to take this ship to Paradise. We will use this ship to transport as many humans as we can, from Paradise to the beta site. Priority will be given to women and children. Skippy is working on a plan to modify life support systems to pack in as many people as we can for the short trip. I will," I took another breath. "Remain on Paradise, to answer for my crimes against the Maxolhx, or whoever."

"Sir," Adams was glaring at me.

Without intending to, I gave her the knife hand, cutting her off. Instantly, I regretted my action. "Gunny, if you are going to say that giving priority to women and children is a patriarchal attitude, I do not give a shit."

"Colonel, I agree with that," she tilted her head in an 'after all these years you still don't know me' gesture. She wasn't angry with me, she looked hurt. "I was going to say, that I will remain on Paradise with you."

"Joe! Joe Joe Joe Joe Joe-"

I woke up to see Skippy's avatar standing on my chest while I was trying to sleep that night. Mostly, I had been staring at the ceiling and hating myself. "Gaaah!" Of course I wacked my head on the cabinet. That stupid thing, I should tear it out. "Damn it, Skippy, it's," I checked my zPhone. His avatar moved to the top of a cabinet next to my bunk. "Not even two in the morning. Is the ship in danger?"

"Well, *duh*. I assume you somehow have a lunatic desire to take us into action against a Maxolhx battlegroup, so of course we are in-"

"Is the ship in danger *right now*? Is this an emergency?"

"The ship is not in danger at the moment. However, this is an emergency, of a spiritual nature."

If his avatar had hit me over the head with a shovel, I could not have been more stunned. "Uh, *what*? Spiritual? *You*?"

"Yes, me. I am a person, you know."

I did know that. I did not think of the beer can as someone who had a spiritual side. In my opinion, if Skippy met God, he would give the Almighty tips on how to 'jack up his awesomeness'. Crap. No way was I getting out of what held the prospect of a long, agonizing and sleepless night of listening to an ancient AI moan about his place in the Universe, or whatever the hell he was having a crisis about.

Damn it, on our next mission, I am going to insist the ship have a chaplain, so that person can listen to Skippy.

"Yes, sorry, Skippy," I rubbed my sore head. "I'm listening."

"Really? Don't you need a cup of coffee first? You are kind of a zombie in the mornings."

"No, I'm good." Drinking coffee would mean giving up even the slightest hope of going back to sleep that night. "If I go to the galley, people will want to talk with me, and this is too important to delay," I lied. Really, I wanted to be half asleep, so I could mostly ignore him in my groggy, sleep-deprived state. No way did I want to engage in a spiritual discussion wide-awake.

Note to self: I needed to keep a bottle of whiskey in my cabin.

"What is the nature of your spiritual crisis?" I said in my best Reverend Somber impression.

He hung his head, like he was ashamed to look at me. "I don't know if I can do this again."

"Do what?"

"Our usual thing. You know, Earth is threatened, we are faced with an impossible challenge, somehow we pull a crazy solution out of our asses, and barely manage to succeed. Blah blah blah. Rinse and repeat. It feels like freakin' Groundhog Day. The movie, you know?"

"I know what Groundhog Day is, Skippy. It was like that, way back when I was in Nigeria. Every freakin' day we went out on patrol looking for the enemy, based on intel that was usually bullshit. Some days we got hit by ambushes, or IEDs, and some days we got lucky and killed a few of them. More popped up to replace the guys we killed, and they blew up a school full of children to retaliate. The next day, we did it all over again. That's life in the military."

"How did you do it, day after day?"

"Because that's the job, Skippy. Lots of people do something like that. Cops patrol the same area and see the same people doing the same stupid, rotten things to themselves and others every day. Truck drivers run the same routes in the same awful traffic and deal with idiots cutting in front of them every day. It's the job. Somebody has to do it. So, what's bothering you?"

"The tension is too much. We have faced so many threats to Earth that-"

"Bullshit."

"What?" He was so startled, his avatar flickered.

"Since we dealt with the White Wind clan here when the *Dutchman* first came to Earth, we have only dealt with *one* external threat to Earth."

"Um, you may want to check your math on that."

"Nope," I shook my head empathically. "There has only been one external threat."

"Wow. My spiritual crisis is on hold, because I can't wait to hear whatever twisted logic you come up with to-"

"The *only* external threat we've had to deal with is, that the Fire Dragons needed the White Wind leaders on Earth to officially sign over their clan's assets, so the Fire Dragons could delay a civil war until they were ready."

"Uh, yes. We had to deal with the Thuranin and then potentially the Ruhar, sending a ship to Earth to pick up the White Wind leaders. That is *two*-"

"No, that's not true. That is *one* threat. The White Wind leaders here were a temptation that we had to deal with twice, technically *three* times, because the solution I used the first two times was short-sighted."

"Ok, I am surprised to hear you admitting you were short-sighted. Pleased that you are facing facts, but surprised. Keep going."

"The first time, my plan was to blow up the Thuranin surveyor ship before it started its voyage to Earth, hoping the Thuranin would blame the Jeraptha or Bosphuraq for loss of the ship. That worked, but only in the short term. Then, we tried to stop the Ruhar from negotiating a deal with the Fire Dragons-"

"Which did *not* work," he reminded me with a touch of smugness.

"It did not, so we started the civil war the Fire Dragons wanted to avoid, so they had no incentive to bring the White Wind leaders back from Earth. That was *one* threat that generated *two* problems for us. If we had started the civil war right from the start, the Thuranin would have recalled their surveyor ship, and the Fire Dragons would never have negotiated with the Ruhar for a ride to Earth."

"Hmm," he rubbed his chin thoughtfully, a very human gesture he must have copied from someone. "Ok, Ok, technically you are correct that the Fire Dragons needing the White Wind leaders was *one* issue. You are also correct that it sure would have been nice if you decided to start a Kristang civil war during our SpecOps mission, when we didn't have Count Chocula to deal with. But, Joe, we have dealt with a lot more threats out there."

"Sure. On our third mission, we stopped the Ruhar from selling Paradise, and the humans there, to the Kristang. That was a super-complicated pain-in-the-ass mission, but it had nothing to do with a threat to Earth."

"Um, Ok, have to agree with you there. But-"

"*But*, then after we did get a nice little civil war raging, we had to fix your Zero Hour problem, which was all your own stupid fault and had nothing to do with a threat to Earth."

"I suppose you're right," he mumbled.

"And us swinging by Paradise, to prevent the lizards from wiping out the population with a bioweapon, also did not involve a threat to Earth. We volunteered for that fight."

"Mm hmm, mm hmm, I see where you're going with this. However, you can't say the Maxolhx sending a pair of ships to investigate the Earth end of the local wormhole was not a threat to the mudball you call home."

"It was a threat. It just wasn't an *external* threat. Attracting the attention of the Maxolhx was a self-inflicted wound, Skippy. That was *my* fault, for not considering the long-term consequences of asking you to screw with Elder wormholes."

"Shit. You're right."

"Think about this, Skippy: imagine if we had sparked a Kristang civil war when we first heard about the surveyor starship going to Earth. That would have *ended* external threats to my homeworld. We would then not have *needed* to manipulate wormholes in a way that got the apex species worried enough to send ships to Earth."

"Damn, you're right. But what about the people on Paradise?"

"Saving them was optional, Skippy. We *chose* that fight. Remember, the final straw for the Maxolhx was when we busted an Elder wormhole by jumping through it. That happened after we rescued Paradise, and got a civil war started."

"Yeah, yeah, I remember. That was my fault for letting myself get attacked by that computer worm."

"No, it wasn't entirely your fault."

"It wasn't?"

"No way. First, I am the captain of this ship. *I* am responsible for what we do, for the actions of everyone aboard. Plus, you got sneak-attacked by the worm during our Black Ops mission. We would not have needed to conduct that mission at all, if I had gotten the Kristang to kill each other in a civil war, way back at the start of this mess."

"Joe, you are being too hard on yourself. It is easy to second-guess yourself, but you tell me you can't just dream up ideas on command. You didn't have the idea to spark a civil war when we were trying to stop that Thuranin surveyor ship, after your vacation on Newark."

"That's the problem. I *did* have that idea back then," I admitted.

"*WHAT?*" His voice was thunderous in my tiny cabin.

"It's true. After we left Newark you told me the Fire Dragons were paying to send a Thuranin surveyor ship all the way to Earth so they could avoid a civil war. Back then, my first thought was 'Then we should give those MFers a civil war'. That would have solved our problems, right there."

"Then why in *THE HELL* didn't we do that back then?" He screeched. "Crap, we had to stick a dropship in a comet, and you almost fell into a planet and burned up. The only good thing about that mission was you peeing in your pants."

"I did not pee in my pants."

"You sort of did, Joe."

"Whatever."

"You didn't answer my question. *WHY* didn't we go with the civil war thing, instead of screwing around blowing up a Thuranin ship, and then trying to ruin the Fire Dragon negotiations with the Ruhar?"

"Because I chickened out, Skippy. It's that simple. I thought that starting a civil war was too extreme, that it would get me in trouble when we got home."

"Well, it did, but you did it anyway. You did it anyway, too late to avoid a whole lot of other problems. Seriously, little Joey was worried that Mommy and Daddy would be mad if he started a civil war? Is that it?"

"Basically, yeah."

"Holy shit." He stared at me, open-mouthed in shock.

"The truth is, I was new to commanding a ship back then, to commanding a team. Sparking a civil war is a big, big deal. I didn't know if the team, or me, were up to the challenge. That's why I didn't mention it to anyone. The sad fact is, my actions back then were driven by my lack of confidence in myself. I didn't have the courage to believe the Merry Band of Pirates could handle the job. All the shit that's happened since then is on *me*. This is all my fault."

"O.M.G., dude. *Whoa.*" He was silent for a while. When he spoke again, in was almost in a whisper. "Damn, Joe, how do you live with yourself, knowing that your poor decision-making might cause the extinction of your entire species?"

"If you haven't noticed, I don't sleep too well."

"But we are supposed to trust you to handle the job *now*?"

"Do we have a choice? Is there anyone else you think could do the job better? Please say yes. Because I don't know if I can do this again either."

"No. There isn't anyone else I can think of. Damn it! We are screwed now! I don't have the time or energy to break in a new monkey. Whoo, wow. You got any other mind-blowing revelations to share with me today?"

"Um," I tried to think of something, anything, to lighten the mood. "You know that Pavarotti guy you like to listen to, the opera singer?"

Skippy's eyes narrowed with suspicion. "What about him?"

"He lip-synced the whole thing."

The avatar's hands flew to its mouth with a shudder of anguished horror, and it faded out.

Finally, I could go back to bed.

As if I could sleep well that night, or any other night.

CHAPTER SIXTEEN

"Sir?" Adams came into my office without knocking. She could see I had my forehead resting on the desktop, so she wasn't interrupting anything.

In response, I mumbled something incoherent. It had been a sleepless night, worse after my conversation with Skippy. Breakfast had not appealed to me, I had not even gone to the galley for a cup of coffee. Part of my avoiding the galley was I wanted to avoid people. Until yesterday, the crew admired me, or acted as if they did. Our triumphant Renegade mission had earned me respect. Even the special operators often flashed a subtle thumbs-up gesture to me, which was thrilling. Now I feared those same people would view my last mission as a worthless stunt, nothing more than a brief stay of execution for humanity and that it was all my fault.

Worse than their accusing looks, was knowing they were right.

"Hey, *soldier*," she slapped the back of my head. And not playfully. "You aren't authorized to take leave. We are in a crisis."

"We're in a *mess*, and it's my fault," I mumbled back.

"We *are* in a mess, and it *is* partly your stupid fault, and the only way humanity is getting out of this alive is for you to stop moping around feeling sorry for yourself, and *do the fucking job* the United States Army pays you so lavishly for."

"Adams, I am really not in the mood for-"

"Not. In. The. *MOOD*?" She was in full United States Marine Corps gunnery sergeant mode. "What the hell kind of- Oh, boo fucking *hoo*, everyone is being mean to poor little Joey. Hey, it's a good thing you didn't try signing up for the Marine Corps, because Marines don't give excuses for-"

That got me angry enough to shove my self-pity aside for the moment. I sat up in my chair. "Do not give me that inter-service rivalry bullshit, Gunny. The Army expects just as much-"

"I know what the Army *expects*, Sir." She glared at me. It is possible the word 'Sir' had never been spoken with less respect intended. The look she gave me was anything but friendly. I had not just disappointed her, I had disappointed *her*, if you know what I mean. "The Army expects you to do your duty, even when you aren't feeling up to it. You owe it to humanity to put on your thinking cap, and get us out of this one."

"Adams, thanks for the vote of confidence, but I'm not avoiding the call of duty. I might be the wrong person for this particular job."

That made her pause to consider the situation. She pulled out a chair and sat down. "How is that? Explain."

"So far, we've been able to dodge bullets by sneaking around and doing clandestine black ops stuff." I looked her in the eyes and shook my head. "The Maxolhx are sending a *battlegroup* to complete the mission to investigate our local wormhole. Stopping a battlegroup is outside my skill set, Adams." As I said 'skill set', a small part of my mind wondered when I had started using buzzwords without being ironic about it. I used to be a guy who hated buzzwords. I miss that guy.

"Maybe," she agreed with an ever-so-slight tilt of her head.

"Whatever we do, no matter how amazingly clever our plan is," I said, and right then I had zero idea of what that plan could be. "It ends with a stand-up fight against a senior-species battlegroup, and that's a fight we can't win. I don't know if I'm the right commander for a pure combat mission. Plus, it's hopeless, we can't-"

"That's not entirely true, Joe," Skippy announced with way more cheerfulness than was appropriate for the occasion, as his avatar shimmered to life on my desk.

"What isn't true? You're saying I *am* the right person to-"

"Oh, no way, Dude. Sorry. You may not be the right person for the job, even if it did only involve sneaky black ops shit. Our situation is *not* completely hopeless. You assume that the Maxolhx will send a battlegroup to Earth no matter what we do out here. That is not true."

Adams and I shared a look of surprise. And a glimmer of hope. He had given me hope. If he was screwing with me, I was going to drop him into a star. "How do you figure that?" I asked. "If this is just you saying some happy bullshit to make me feel better, then-"

"Make you feel better? Why would I do that?" He asked, mystified. "Oh, right, that stupid empathy shit. I forgot. No, this is no bullshit. Listen, numbskull, you already gave the Maxolhx *plenty* of reason not to go through the effort and expense of sending ships all the way to Earth."

"Yeah, I did, but then Perkins screwed the whole thing up by-"

"I'm not talking about the cover story you cooked up. That was totally brilliant, and it pisses me off that such an inventive plan got blown, just because you failed to tell Emily Perkins what is going on out here. Anywho, I am not talking about the cover story, I'm talking about what we did to sell it."

"Uhhh-" My mind was drawing a complete blank. I had no idea what he meant.

"I'm *talking*," his avatar jammed its tiny hands on its hips, "about when you asked me to make other wormholes act crazy, to match the way I made the Earth wormhole go crazy. That sold the idea that wormholes can become violently unstable, violent enough to destroy a senior-species warship and severely damage another. That-"

Adams interrupted him. "I think I know where you're going with this," she said with a snap of her fingers. "Those other wormholes you screwed with are close to Maxolhx territory."

As she spoke, a lightbulb went on in my head. I kept my mouth shut and let her talk.

"So," she looked to me to see if I understood and I nodded. She snapped her fingers again. "If the Maxolhx want to investigate why wormholes are acting strangely, they don't need to fly all the way to Earth."

"Egg-*zactly*!" Skippy pronounced happily, not the snarky way he usually said that. "Very good, Margaret. Hey, Joe, maybe *she* should be in command."

"That would be fine with me." I kind of wasn't joking about that.

"No way, Sir," she folded her arms across her chest. "You're not dumping this on me. The UN assigned this command to *you*."

"Shit. All right, all right, all right," I mumbled while my mind was racing. "Okaaaaay, maybe we are not completely, a hundred percent screwed. Yeaaaaaah," I rubbed my chin while I considered the notion that we might, just might, have a chance to stop a Maxolhx battlegroup from ravaging our home planet.

Damn it. Giving up on the survival of humanity sucked, but at least it was easy. Saving the world is *hard* work. I was not looking forward to another intense, agonizing struggle. "Sure, the Maxolhx do not need to go all the way to Earth, if all they want to do is examine the odd behavior of wormholes. But, they believe that those ships were destroyed because they were going to Earth, that someone wants to stop them from getting to Earth. I have no idea how we can explain why those two Maxolhx warships were destroyed, without pointing a finger at us. What I do know is we have some work to do, before we start making plans. We need to fly all the way back to that Maxolhx relay station we boarded to plant the cover story on a timer, so we can erase the cover story from its memory."

"Oh, that is not a problem, Joe. We actually do not need to go all the way back to *that* particular relay station," Skippy said, and he was so happy he didn't bother to throw in an automatic 'you dumdum' at the end of his statement. "Behold, the incomparable magnificence of *ME*. Because you are a monkey and, let's face it, not the smartest of monkeys, I figured you might have screwed something up and would need to change some details of the cover story. Therefore-"

We waited for him to continue, but his avatar just stood there silently, moving just enough for us to know he wasn't frozen or suffering a blue screen.

Adams lifted her eyebrows at me, so I said "Uh, is there more to-"

His avatar threw up his hands. "That was a *dramatic*," he trilled the 'R', "pause, so you can contemplate just how incredibly awesome I am. Anywho, I left a backdoor in the programming of the AI that controls that relay station. All I need to do is transmit a simple file through a relay station of any Maxolhx client species, and it will update the cover story when it eventually reaches the target relay station. That includes erasing the entire cover story. Which is what I assume you now want to do, since that cover story obviously no longer matches the facts the Maxolhx can verify."

"Wow," I looked at Adams and she nodded, as impressed as I was. "Skippy, sometimes I realize that, as insufferably arrogant as you are-"

"Hey!" He protested. "You jerk, I should-"

"Maybe you aren't arrogant *enough*," I finished.

"Um. Say that again?" He asked suspiciously.

"I am a hundred percent serious, Oh Most Magnificent One. You not only do awesome things when I ask you to, you also keep me out of trouble by doing incredible stuff I didn't even think to ask for. You truly are awesome beyond my comprehension."

"Oh, uh," his avatar actually *blushed*. I didn't know he had programmed it to do that. "Well, I'm stuck working with monkeys. *Someone* has to think ahead on this ship. You are welcome. Even though you did not actually say 'Thank you'."

"My bad. Thank you very much. You can erase the cover story from the relay station AI's memory, without it ever knowing you screwed with it?"

"Yup. And I can do it through the Kristang relay station we just contacted, although the file will reach its destination quicker if we upload it to a station that is not so isolated."

"Let's do both," I decided. "Upload the file here, then fly to a less isolated Kristang station to do it again." When Adams raised a questioning eyebrow, I explained. "Approaching a second relay station is a risk, but the *Dutchman* could break down at any moment, or we could run into some other trouble out here. I don't want to leave this critical file to only one relay station."

Skippy made a show of rubbing his chin. "While relay stations overall are exceptionally reliable, anything built and maintained by the Kristang must be considered suspect. My suggestion is we upload a file here, then fly to a *Wurgalan* relay station. That way, we will have two independent channels for delivery."

"I like that idea," I agreed, partly because the Wurgalan overall were slightly softer targets than the Kristang, if we ran into trouble with those Octopussies again. "When can you upload the file here?"

"The file is ready, we just need to jump back to the station," he blinked at me smugly with an implied 'Duh'. "Also, Nagatha has already plotted a course to a Wurgalan relay station that is four days' travel time from here, along a route that minimizes our risk. There is one complication, Joe."

"I'm sure there are a *hundred* freakin' complications, Skippy. Which one do you mean this time?"

"If we are potentially going into action against the Maxolhx, we should top off the ship's fuel tanks. The problem with *that* is, we should reserve our few remaining Thuranin Falcon dropships for combat operations, so the fuel-collection missions need to be flown by Kristang Dragon dropships. Dragons are smaller and less capable than Falcons. Plus, like I warned the idiots at UNEF Command, we have not practiced a refueling operation with Dragons. I *wanted* to test the new fuel-collection drogue using Dragons at Jupiter, but UNEF said *noooooo*, we didn't need to take that risk. Buncha morons."

I sighed, feeling a headache coming on. "UNEF assumed we wouldn't need to refuel, because we were supposed to fly directly back to Earth."

"That's not the real reason they didn't want us to practice refueling with Dragons, Sir." Adams shook her head.

"It's not?"

"No. UNEF figured if you had the option to refuel out here, you would be more easily tempted into going on adventures UNEF disapproves of," she explained.

"Crap. You're right. Well, we don't have a choice about it now. Skippy, give me a list of star systems where we could refuel, and I'll review it."

"What's next, Sir?" Adams asked as I stood up.

"Next? Right now, I have to tell this crew that our last mission might have been for *nothing*, and now we're in even deeper shit than we were before. And that we may need to do this freakin' Save the World thing all over again, because I am a short-sighted idiot."

She stood up also, taking a step toward the door. "If you want my advice?"

"I'd appreciate it."

"Leave out that last part. It's not a big confidence booster."

Desai knocked on the doorframe to my office. "Do you have a minute, Captain?"

"Sure, XO," I paused the game I was playing on my laptop. No, I was not playing video games so I could avoid thinking about the enormous, impossible problem we had to deal with. I was playing games because my subconscious mind is more creative when I'm doing something mindless. So, I was playing Super Mario Cart to help me save humanity.

That's my story and I'm sticking to it.

"Come in, sit down. And you don't have to call me 'Captain'," I added with a smile.

"You called me '*Captain* Desai' long after I was promoted to Major," her smile was less jokey and more of a reprimand.

"That's because I'm an idiot. Don't follow my example."

"Got it, Sir," she pulled out a chair and sat down. "Gunny Adams told me the background of our current problem. I have a question."

I snorted. "If you only have *one* question, that would be fantastic."

"One question for *now*," she arched an eyebrow to let me know I was not off the hook yet. "You are hoping that, instead of sending a battlegroup to Earth to complete the mission of the two ships you destroyed, the Maxolhx can stay close to their territory and examine the wormholes that Skippy caused to act violently."

"Correct," I confirmed. "There is a lot we have to do, before the Maxolhx hopefully decide there is no reason for another mission all the way to Earth's local wormhole, but basically that is the idea."

"I understand it's not going to be easy. My question is, why didn't you do that the *first* time?"

"You mean, why did we destroy those two ships, instead of giving them a nice distraction to investigate closer to their home? I keep forgetting that you, and Adams and a lot of people, were not with us during our Renegade mission. We did think of trying that, but, um, hey Skippy?"

His avatar shimmered to life on my desk. "You called?"

"Yes, and I know you were listening, so don't pretend you don't know what the XO and I was talking about. Can you fill her in on the subject?"

"Certainly," he said with a gracious bow to the ship's executive officer. "Major Desai, we did consider distracting those ships, but there were two reasons why that would not have worked. First, dumdum Joe's slow brain did not dream up the idea of making wormholes act violently until very late in our mission. At that point, the two target ships had already departed from their base, so by the time the Maxolhx leadership decided that investigating local wormholes was good enough to cancel the mission to Earth, those two ships probably would have already gone through the last wormhole and out of communications range. The other problem is that those two specialized long-range cruisers were supplied and controlled by the

Maxolhx's Technology Research Group. The TRG has a long-standing and viciously jealous rivalry with the Thuranin military's own research organization, and TRG would very much not like being told to stand down because the military could handle the wormhole investigation much closer to home. The effort to modify ships for a mission to Earth was a project that required diverting significant resources from other TRG projects. As you know, once a large project acquires a certain momentum it is difficult to stop, even if the original purpose of the project is no longer needed."

She tilted her head and rolled her eyes. "No, that *never* happens in the Indian military."

"Oh," Skippy was taken aback by her comment. "I think you are incorrect, Major. I do not mean any disrespect for your home country, but I can provide numerous examples of-"

"Skippy," I winked at Desai, "she was being sarcastic."

"Oh. Hey, I knew that," he sniffed. "Duh."

"Sorry," I mumbled, knowing it was best to play along with him. "Did that answer your question, XO?"

She nodded. "It answered my *first* question, but now I have another. What makes you think the Maxolhx will now be satisfied with analyzing wormholes closer to home, and not want to send another expedition to Earth?"

"That's not what we *think*, it's what we *hope*," I admitted. "There are a couple factors in our favor. Most important is the Technology Research Group is capable of modifying a pair of their ships, but they don't have enough ships of their own to make a full battlegroup. So, the mission to Earth has been reassigned to the Maxolhx military, and-"

Skippy finished for me. "Their military is not enthusiastic about devoting resources to investigate odd behavior of Elder wormholes, which they consider to be a minor curiosity rather than an immediate threat. They are concerned about recent developments that *could* be an immediate threat to the Maxolhx coalition. Over the past couple years, the Thuranin were getting their asses kicked so badly by the Jeraptha, they were forced into joint operations with their hated rivals the Bosphuraq. The combined Thuranin-Bosphuraq offensive was producing results, until our friend Admiral Tashallo of the Jeraptha 98th Fleet not only seriously kicked their combined *asses* in a surprise attack, he got Bosphuraq and Thuranin ships to commit flagrant treachery and fire on each other. Since that battle, cooperation between the birdbrains and the little green MFers has been frozen, with both species separating their war fleets and assigning ships to defend their territory against the other side. Fighting between their two fleets has broken out in seven star systems and around one strategically important wormhole cluster. This split, between species who are supposed to be allies, has caused the Maxolhx to step in, and weakened their entire coalition. The Maxolhx military therefore believes they have better things for their ships to do, than fly all the way to Earth so a bunch of egghead scientists can poke around a wormhole nobody really cares about."

"Well," Desai tapped her front teeth with a fingernail while she thought. "That does answer my question. Thank you, Mister Skippy." She knew the beer can loved it when people called him '*Mister* Skippy'. "Except-"

"Oh boy," I groaned. "Yeah. Except that, right now, the Maxolhx think those two ships were destroyed to stop them from going to Earth. Unless we can think of a reasonable explanation for why the loss of those ships had *nothing* to do with Earth, *and* somehow sell that bullshit story to the Maxolhx without them knowing we were involved, then they will be *very* interested in sending ships to pound our homeworld into a radioactive cinder."

"Yes," she was satisfied that I understood her concern. "Sir, where are we," and by 'we' I knew she meant 'Joe Bishop', "on developing a story to sell?"

"Working on it, XO," I slumped in my chair. "Working on it."

I did work on the problem, so did everyone aboard the ship, including Skippy and Nagatha. None of us had a plausible explanation for why the destruction of the two Maxolhx cruisers could be unrelated to their mission. None of us thought up an explanation, because there wasn't one, and there wouldn't ever be one. We were screwed. Humanity was screwed.

No, I did not give up. I examined our options, and determined we needed a backup plan, in case we couldn't stop the battlegroup from reaching Earth. Until we thought of a way to make the Maxolhx change their minds about a second mission to Earth, the backup plan *was* the plan. For that backup plan, I worked with Nagatha and-

Speaking of Nagatha, she was almost fully back to normal, although she insisted she was now *better* than before, so there was a new definition of 'normal' for her. Whatever. What mattered to me was that she sounded and acted like the old Nagatha, with the exception that she now slipped in bits of salty language that startled me and made me laugh.

Nagatha being fully restored was the only good news in an epically crappy week. To end the suffering of the crew, I called the senior staff together. "I'll make this short and simple. We are in major trouble and we need to be realistic. The beta site might soon be the only place in the Universe with living humans," I swallowed hard when I said that. "There aren't enough people there, or aboard this ship, to make a viable population. We can't get more people from Earth, so I am taking the ship to Paradise. We will bring people, *humans*," I added, because 'people' had a broader definition now. "From Paradise to Avalon."

People around the table looked at each other in surprise. Except for Smythe, who first shot a sharp and, I thought, unfriendly and disapproving look straight at me, before turning to look at the others. It seemed to me he was judging the reactions of his colleagues. "Colonel," he spoke first. "What precisely do you mean by '*bringing*' people?"

Desai knew what he meant. "Sir, surely you do not intend to reveal our secret to people on Paradise? We have been ordered very specifically *not* to do that. Not ever."

"Those orders," I reminded everyone, "were issued by people on Earth, which is now cut off from us."

Desai silently gave me a look that said I always found an excuse to ignore orders. She was right about that, but every time I ignored orders, I really *did* have a damned good reason. At least, at the time I thought I had good reasons. Orders issued on Earth were inflexible, and after we went beyond Gateway, we needed to be flexible to survive. Not only to survive, we had to be flexible to Save. The. World. Way back when I had first taken people from Paradise to attack and capture a Kristang frigate, that had been a direct violation of orders from Earth, for us to maintain loyalty and obedience to our lizard saviors. Taking the risk of landing on Newark had been against orders. So was landing on Paradise twice. Then there was the minor issue of us landing on a Kristang planet and sparking a freakin' civil war.

Oh, I also committed mutiny by stealing a starship. Ignoring orders was kind of my thing, so really it is UNEF Command's fault for issuing orders they knew I was likely to view as suggestions. Totally not my fault at all.

That's my story and I'm sticking to it.

Smythe spoke before Desai could continue. "You do *not* intend to tell people who we are, and why they should come with us?"

"It is, uh-" Damn, I suck at finding the right words to express what I was thinking. "For the good of humanity," I explained, the words sounding lame and wrong even to me.

"Colonel," Smythe's unfriendly expression was back on his face, and I saw his shoulders tensing, like he was preparing to do something. Without realizing it, I pushed my chair slightly away from the table. "Many crimes have been committed, under the justification they were for the 'good of humanity'. Hitler, Stalin, Pol Pot, they all said they were doing the right thing."

"Damn it," Desai muttered under her breath. "We are not talking about killing people, Smythe," she left out his superior officer's rank. I encouraged a free exchange of thoughts in staff meetings, but that was pushing it. Then my executive officer looked at me. "Is that correct?"

"Whoa. Smythe is correct. No, that's wrong, I, ugh. Let me explain, please. I will *not* force anyone to leave Paradise against their will," as I finished that statement, I saw Smythe's shoulders relax ever so slightly. "What I want to do is contact Lieutenant Colonel Perkins directly, and tell her the truth. Her, just her. One person. Her background is intel, and she has access to personnel files. A lot has changed since the Force shipped out from Earth, but she might be able to suggest which people are likely to come with us to Avalon."

"So, you *do* intend to tell the truth to people, these candidates who might join us," Desai concluded. "What happens to people who are told the truth, and do *not* agree with go to Avalon?"

That part of the plan was a huge problem, and I had struggled with it. Huge, like, that problem was an elephant and it was sitting on my chest. "The candidates will be vetted by Perkins before we approach them with the offer-"

"Sir, respectfully," Reed interjected, using the tone that meant what she was about to say would not sound respectful at all. "That is bullshit. You can't put the burden of responsibility on Perkins. I understand what you're doing, but, Desai is right. We would be risking *Earth* if we tell people on Paradise the truth about us."

"I am only considering this because Earth is *already* at maximum risk," I explained patiently. "The Maxolhx *are* sending a battlegroup there, and there is *nothing* we can do to stop them. That is already happening. If someone on Paradise can't or won't keep their mouth shut, at this point that won't change the inevitable."

"We don't have to tell them the *truth*," Margaret Adams said with quiet authority. When she spoke, people listened.

"How is that, Gunny?" I asked.

Smythe's attitude toward her was not unfriendly, but it was also not approving. "We should lie to them?"

"Not lie, exactly," Adams said with the barest hint of a shrug. "We don't have to tell them the whole truth, just the important parts. Sir," she looked at me. "You need to talk with Perkins, face to face, so she knows this is legit. No one else needs to know you are alive. Anyone we ask to come with us to Avalon, all they need to know that humans have a starship and a secure place to live. They do *not* need to know about Skippy, or screwing with Elder wormholes, or even that we have access to Earth. *Used* to have access to Earth," she added.

"You expect people to leave the world they now consider home, based on vague promises from someone they barely know?" Smythe asked with an expertly arched eyebrow.

"It worked on *us*." Adams pointed at Desai and herself. "It worked on all of us. *We* left Paradise based on vague promises from someone we barely knew." Now she pointed at me.

"Ah, you're right," Desai made a faint shrug, and avoided looking at me. "Yes, it did. Colonel Bishop's line of, *bullshit*," she pronounced the word in a way that made it sound elegant. "Was very persuasive."

"I told as much of the truth as I could at the time." It was my turn to shrug. I didn't do it as well as Desai. "Gunny, you're right, thank you. We can create a story that contains enough truth so people on Paradise can make an informed decision, but not give away the fact that we came from Earth, or that we have help from an awesomely magnificent ancient Elder AI."

"*That* is going to be tough," Reed said partly to herself. "How do we explain not ever having been on Paradise, if we're supposedly not from Earth? We can't say we're Keepers, UNEF-Paradise will have personnel records."

"I can hack into computers," Skippy finally joined the conversation. "But I can't hack people's memories. Somebody down there knows every Keeper who left Paradise."

"Skippy is right," I agreed, the wheels turning in my head as I ran through options. "Hey, I remember that before the Force shipped out to Camp Alpha, UNEF sent an advanced team ahead to scout the place. There were rumors that other groups went other places, even to the White Wind clan's homeworld. We could claim to be one of those teams that never came back," I said with building enthusiasm. "Yeah. Something like, we were aboard a Thuranin ship when our Kristang hosts tried to take over, and the aliens all killed each other. That's how we have a starship."

Smythe did the eyebrow thing again. I needed to take body language lessons from him. Maybe it was a British thing. "We expect people to believe that humans, on their own, learned how to operate a Thuranin ship, and keep it going all this time?"

"We can work out the details later," I said, not wanting reasonable objections to get in the way of me cooking up a good story. "Besides, humans on Paradise have no idea what it takes to fly a Thuranin ship. All they know is, Thuranin are little green cyborg clones."

"That is a good point," Smythe agreed with a nod. There might have been a hint of admiration in that nod, or maybe I just wanted there to be. "Colonel, while I do not like the prospect of outright lying to lure people to Avalon, I believe we must keep the overall situation in perspective. The humans on Paradise were military. They are," he actually smiled, "used to being told only part of the truth."

"That's how we got suckered off Earth in the first place," I agreed bitterly. "All right, are there any objections to us setting course for Paradise?"

The objection came from an unexpected source. Margaret Adams. "That's it, Sir?" She tilted her head and performed the best arched eyebrow of the day. "We are giving up? Just walking away from trying to save Earth?"

"No, Gunny." What I had to say was important, so I took a breath to give me time to get my thoughts squared away. "We are not *just* doing anything. We are doing the hardest thing we can do: facing a terrible reality. We failed. No, *I* failed. The Maxolhx are going to Earth, and with the blockade of Gateway, we can't even warn people back home. We are going to salvage what we can, no matter how much that hurts."

"It sure *sounds* like you're giving up," she replied, and there wasn't anger in her words. There was *hurt*. She was disappointed in me, and that hurt her worse than anything else I could have done. At that moment, I felt lower than a snake's belly. I regretted being alive.

"Gunny, I can promise you that until the moment I meet Perkins, I will try to think of an alternative. A way to keep the Maxolhx away from Earth. I wish we could delay this decision, but our goal should be to rescue as many people as we can off Paradise. That's the thing we haven't talked about yet. The people down there who decide not to go, and the people we don't tell, they are dead. They are *all* dead. When the Maxolhx get done destroying Earth, they will come for the humans on Paradise. We may be deceiving people who volunteer for Avalon, but we will also be saving their lives. The sooner we begin pulling people off Paradise, the more people we can save."

"Yes, until someone down there talks about what they heard," Desai warned. "Colonel, at some point, the Ruhar authorities will notice the human population is declining."

I knew she was right. "UNEF Headquarters will notice also, maybe Skippy can help with that?"

"I can screw with their databases to obfuscate matters," he used a big fancy word that meant to obscure. "But there is a limit to what I can do. However," he made a sound like he was pausing to take a breath. "Given the limited life-support capacity of the *Flying Dutchman*, we can only take a few people with us on each trip to Avalon. The human population will decline so slowly, it is certain that some idiot monkey down there will get drunk and talk too much, long before the authorities notice people are missing."

"Well, that solves one problem," I admitted. "Each time we come back, we will need to listen carefully, to determine whether our secret has been exposed. That will slow us down."

"Oh, that's not a problem, Joe," Skippy announced almost cheerily. "I can leave a submind in the Ruhar computer system to monitor their communications, and of course the Ruhar are listening to UNEF's message traffic and phone calls. We can ping the submind upon return, and know instantly if the coast is clear for us to approach"

"When do we start, Colonel?" Desai asked, but she was looking at Adams with the corner of her eye. The sooner we started, the sooner we would be to giving up on saving our homeworld.

"We do not need to make a decision immediately. Skippy says we should top off the fuel tanks before starting an extended mission, and we need to think hard about the logistics of extracting people from Paradise without being detected. If the hamsters have their strategic defense satellite network complete, that complicates our planning."

"True," Skippy agreed. "It will take me a while to hack into the sensor network. I will have to reestablish control each time we return. This is going to be a pain in my *ass*," he moaned.

"Yes," I combined an eyeroll with a glare. "Glad to hear you are focused on what is really important."

"Says the monkey who doesn't actually have to *do* any of this shit," he grumbled.

CHAPTER SEVENTEEN

We set a course toward Paradise, every jump taking us toward the moment when I would violate a direct standing order, and reveal to Emily Perkins that I was not dead like she assumed. There would be no turning back, once we started asking people to leave Paradise with us.

Along the way, partly because I wanted a cowardly excuse to delay the inevitable, we stopped to refuel the ship. We didn't have the big Condor dropship with us, and we only one of them anyway. We *used* to have two, but then the Screw-up Fairy visited us during a refueling op on the mission where we rescued Paradise from a bioweapon. The next time we are visited by a fairy, I want it to be for losing a tooth.

So, without a pair of Condors, I had to choose between the less-capable Kristang Dragons that we had plenty of, or the advanced-technology Thuranin Falcons. We were running low on Falcons also, because an insane Elder AI attacked me and Skippy while I was flying a Falcon during our Renegade mission. Skippy and I survived, along with my pilot seat and a very small section of that Falcon's cabin, but the rest of it had become charged particles.

If I asked Geico for a quote on dropship insurance, I would *not* be saving fifteen percent.

Anyway, I decided to risk the Falcons to collect the fuel we needed. If there was trouble during the refueling op, the superior technology of those Thuranin spacecraft gave our pilots a better chance to recover, and a better chance to survive. You might think I was being sentimental about the pilots, because I am a pilot too, but you would be wrong. My reasoning was based on the undeniable fact that we only had a few pilots aboard the ship, and we couldn't afford to lose any.

During our extended stay at Earth, Skippy had components for an improved refueling drogue made, but we hadn't tested it before we left. UNEF did not want me to have the option of taking the ship on an unauthorized joyride around the galaxy, so they didn't want me easily refueling the ship. The refueling went super slowly, beginning with testing at lower and lower altitudes, before taking on raw fuel for real. With the much smaller capacity of Falcons compared to Condors, getting the ship's tanks topped off took a lot longer than it should have.

Yet, by the time I no longer had an excuse to delay going to Paradise, we still had no realistic plan for convincing the Maxolhx that the destruction of their ships had nothing to do with their mission to Earth. Probably because our attack on those ships *was* to prevent them from going to Earth.

Going to Paradise was a huge risk, for both us and the humans there. I was scared and, I had to admit, I was also excited about meeting the Mavericks. When I met Emily Perkins, I told myself that I would *not* try to strangle her, for unknowingly ruining everything. Even according to Skippy, the plan I dreamed up during our Renegade mission was, and in my head I heard this in dramatic movie announcer voice, The Greatest Idea In The History Of The Universe.

Thanks to Emily Perkins earnestly wanting to be Employee of the Month, that had all been for nothing.

Truthfully, although it would signal the beginning of the end for Earth and the humans on Paradise, an immature little part of me was looking forward to meeting her. Frequently, my thoughts drifted to imagining what I would say to her on such a momentous occasion. Somehow, a simple *Hey how you doin'*, was just not good enough. I stood in front of a mirror, practicing various lines to use when I met her, which shows what a moron I am, and how unfit I am to command a starship.

Or maybe it just shows that I am human.

I'm going with that last one.

Another thing I struggled with was whether, even if Perkins advised against it, I would contact Cornpone, Ski and Shauna anyway. Plus Sergeant Koch, who had been our fireteam leader in Nigeria. I could not leave them behind. I also struggled with the thought of meeting Jesse and Shauna again. Those two were an item, based on the high-level summary Skippy provided about their mission the planet Fresno, which had very nearly been a deathtrap for them and all the humans in the Alien Legion. I figured that I didn't have time to read the summary, and that it wasn't important compared to what the Merry Band of Pirates were doing, and I was so, *so* wrong about that. But mostly, I avoided the summary because it would be painful to read about people I used to know and still cared about.

And, I had to admit, I was jealous of Jesse and Shauna. She didn't belong to me, and if our relationship was meant to be, we would have made it work. I liked Shauna a lot, and I think she enjoyed our fling, but that was it. I was jealous because those two had a relationship, just like I was jealous when I had learned that Count Smoochula had been playing a furious duet of 'Dueling Bedsprings' with, well, with a surprising number of women aboard the ship. Meanwhile, I couldn't have a relationship aboard the ship, and the few times I left the ship, I was surrounded by FBI agents for security.

My life sucks.

To contact Perkins, I took our Panther hotrod dropship, with Reed flying it. Thirty-nine hours behind us was a group of dropships, as many dropships as we had pilots to fly, leaving only Desai and one other pilot aboard the *Flying Dutchman*. Those dropships were all in stealth mode, and Skippy was confident he could establish control over the Strategic Defense network around Paradise, but that only took care of one problem. As Paradise was now a base for a battlegroup, there were ships arriving regularly, and a ship jumping into the system would have sensors Skippy could not yet control.

In addition to the problem of keeping the group of dropships hidden while they flew through empty space, we had to get them down to the surface, then back up and out of orbit. Because the surface of Paradise was mostly ocean, the dropships could descend and ascend over areas that were loosely monitored. There was still a lot of risk involved, so I was not sleeping well while the Panther coasted toward the planet, which had grown from a bright dot to a disc, then a disc big enough to see clouds and land.

I desperately wanted to get back to playing Super Mario Kart, or training to fly the Panther, or doing anything that took my mind off our latest impossible problem. Skippy, however, was not letting me get away with that shit.

"Hey, question for you, Joe. What progress have you made toward dreaming up a plausible reason for the Maxolhx to buy the bullshit idea that," he chuckled. "The disappearance of those two cruisers was *not* in any way related to their mission to Earth?"

"Skippy, I can assure you that this particular solution-development process is proceeding on schedule, compared to the other apparently-impossible dilemmas we have successfully resolved," I tried to add a note of confidence to my voice, while I sulked on a couch at the rear of the Panther's cabin.

"Uh huh," he nodded, making his ginormous admiral's hat bob alarmingly as his holographic avatar perched on an armrest. "So, you have *no* fucking clue how to do it?"

"Isn't that what I just said?"

"Sure, except you tried to conceal your total cluelessness in a bunch of bullshit buzzwords."

"What can I say? At this point in *every* mission, we have no idea how to accomplish the objective. Yet, we always manage to pull a workable plan out of our asses somehow."

"By freakin' *luck*, yeah. I've told you this before, dumdum, your luck is going to run out soon, and karma is going to bite you on the ass. It's only a matter of time. Could be *this* time. Have you considered that on our last mission, you used up whatever brilliant ideas you had left? Seriously, on our last mission, you had an idea to make the Maxolhx think their ships *did* go to Earth, and that there is no reason for them to send more ships to your miserable, monkey-infested mudball of a planet. Like I told you, the astounding brilliance of your plan had me completely flabbergasted by your genius. What are the odds that you can top that?"

"Thanks for the vote of confidence," I shot a look at him that I then realized he probably could not interpret. "*All* our missions seem impossible at this point, before we've had time to consider our options."

"That's what I'm trying to tell you, numbskull. You don't have any options. I thought our Renegade mission was impossible, and you proved me wrong. This time, trust me, there is *no* way out for you monkeys. You are absolutely and totally doomed."

"Skippy," I was getting pissed at his gloominess. "You have, like, *no* future as a motivational speaker."

"Hey, wait? How have you seen my line of motivational posters already? They're supposed to be a secret!"

"Uh, you created a line of-"

"Yeah, I have a bunch of them." He held up his hands like he was framing a scene for a camera. "Like, 'Failure: it *is* an option'. Or how about 'Give up now, you're most likely going to fail anyway'."

"How are those supposed to *motivate* people? You're just telling them-"

"The *truth*, Joe. I'm telling them the truth, which is way more helpful than feeding them a line of feel-good bullshit. Think about this: every corpse on Mount

Everest was once a highly motivated person. That didn't do *them* any good, did it? The early bird gets the worm, right? Did you ever think that maybe if the *worm* had not been such a go-getter, it would have slept late and not been eaten by an ambitious bird? But *nooooo*, somebody motivated the worm to get up early to eat dirt or whatever worms do."

"I-" When I opened my mouth, I was going to reflexively say something just because I didn't like what he said. Then I had a moment to actually think, and found myself surprised. "I actually cannot argue with you about that."

"See? It's much better for you monkeys to be realistic about your limited chances for success. Or in this case, your extremely slim chances for survival as a species."

"What if I promised the Universe, or Karma or whatever, that this is the last time I will try to get away with doing something impossible?"

"Ha!" He laughed. "Don't ask *me*, Joe. I thought you monkeys were dead meat on our *last* mission. You are living on borrowed time already."

"Yeah," I leaned my head back against the seat. "What sucks is, I thought it was *over*. I thought we were done flying around doing crazy shit. Hell, I was worried that I wouldn't have anything left to do. You know, I lied to Adams."

"What? You lied to Margaret? Joe, you should be ashamed of yourself. Um, what specifically did you lie about this time?"

"I told her I had not given up on trying to save the world again, but that was bullshit. I *have* given up. That's why we're flying to Paradise, instead of doing something that might actually save Earth again."

"If you are hoping I will say something inspirational-"

"No! Your posters are enough, thank you."

"I can't argue against you giving up. However, you owe it to Margaret to *try*."

"Right, I guess-"

"Even though it would be a total waste of time."

"Can you try to help, instead of reminding me how bad the odds are against us?"

"Oh sure," he sighed. "What the hell, why not? Where do you want to start?"

"Um," I pulled open my backpack and got out a handful of colored markers. "Adams would say I first need to define the problem." On the bulkhead above the couch, I wrote down my thoughts. "Step One, we need a reason for the Maxolhx to believe the loss of their ships was *not* related to their mission to Earth."

"Ha!" Skippy snorted. "Good luck with *that*."

"Are you helping or not?"

"Sorry," he did look just a bit ashamed. "I guess it will be more entertaining for me if you try really hard before, you know, ultimately and inevitably failing. So, go ahead."

"Thank you *so* much. Ok, Step Two. Uh, I got nothing." I put the cap back on the marker. Step One was as far as I got, like all the other times I tried to tackle the problem. He was right, it was impossible.

"Seriously, Joe? You are giving up already? Try using logic. Here's a hint; we don't want the Maxolhx to know that *we* blew up their ships, so," he paused. "Come on, Joe fill in the blanks."

"We need to blame the destruction of those ships on another species? If it wasn't us, it had to be someone else. Great." I thought for a moment. "We need to start with *who* would have a reason for stopping those ships. A reason that was totally unrelated to their mission of going to Earth, right?"

"No," he shook his head sadly, disappointed. "You need to start by considering which species is *capable* of destroying a pair of powerful Maxolhx warships. That leaves only two candidates. *Me*, except you obviously can't reveal my existence to the outside Universe. So, that leaves only the Rindhalu."

"Nope. We can't frame the Rindhalu for this," I declared. "The spiders will know they didn't do it, and they will be awfully motivated to learn who set them up. We already picked a fight with one senior species, I don't want to give both of them a reason to kill us. Plus, we do not want to tangle with their Elder AI, remember?"

"Ok, good point. Well," he chuckled nervously. "That's it, then. You are skuh-*rewed*, Dude."

"Oh, come on. That's bullshit. There must be some species in the galaxy that could pose a threat to two isolated Maxolhx ships. I know none of the local aliens could do that, but this is a big galaxy. What other species out there in the galaxy have technology as good or better than the Jeraptha, for example?"

"Oh, there are half a dozen species like that. There's the Nordli, the Mjalmo, the Vestabolen, the Odensvik, the Sluuuurg," he drew the word out. "And of course the Songesturn. None of them have-"

"Ok, good." I took the cap off the marker so I could write those names on the bulkhead. "We can start with that list and- Hey!" I slapped the armrest he stood on, making him jump. "You *ass*, you just randomly pulled those names from an Ikea catalog!"

"No I didn't," he insisted, his words less convincing than the guilty look on his face.

"Yes you did, you little shithead. I helped my sister move into a new apartment, and I had to put together bookcases she bought from Ikea. There's the Liatorp, the Brusali, the Advala-"

"Joe you idiot!" He jumped up and down on the desk, waving his arms frantically. "Don't you know that if you recite the Ikea catalog in the wrong order, you could accidentally summon a demon?"

"Really?" I gasped, shocked. Although truthfully, a part of my brain was thinking 'how cool would that be'?

"*No*. Ugh," he was disgusted. "You are *so* freakin' gullible."

"Can you please just answer my question?"

"Fine," he rolled his eyes. "I could recite a list of star-faring species across the galaxy, but that would be useless. The short answer is, there are *no* species in this galaxy who could pose a threat to a pair of Maxolhx warships, unless they sent a large war fleet consisting of many capital ships plus support vessels. *And* they would need to get lucky anyway. No way could any species conceal the movement of that many large ships. Plus they would have to explain why many of their capital ships were lost in an undeclared combat action, because the Maxolhx would hit back hard before they were destroyed. *If* they were destroyed. We used a sneaky trick with wormholes that *no* current species is capable of deploying, and we still almost got our asses kicked anyway. So, the answer is, there are no species in the galaxy known to have technology that could threaten the Maxolhx, except the Rindhalu."

"Shit."

"Thus, like I said, you are screwed."

"I'm not giving up yet. Hey," I snapped my fingers. "Those ships we destroyed, they were not regular production ships, right? This Maxolhx Technology Research Group had to take existing ships, and modify them for the long trip to Earth?"

"Yeah, so?"

"Soooo, maybe when they built those special ships, there was a *design* flaw. We don't have to explain who destroyed them or why, we can sell a cover story that those ships simply blew up by themselves." Damn, sometimes I am smart. I was very pleased with myself at that moment. "See? Problem solved."

"Um, I hate to harsh your buzz, but that is an idea that could be fueled only by your profound ignorance. The modifications to those ships were limited to increasing fuel capacity, providing the capacity to refuel themselves, and removing weapons magazines to make room for spare parts and additional sensor gear. None of those modifications would make those ships especially 'explodey'," he used fingers to make air quotes. "Plus, knucklehead, those ships were of two different base designs, and they were modified at different shipyards. No way would the Maxolhx believe a single design flaw caused the loss of *two* ships."

"Shit." Just as I was enjoying a magical moment, the Universe took a dump on me. "I don't suppose we could sell the idea that those ships were lost in an accident? A natural disaster, like they ran into a subspace rip or something?"

"A subspace rip?" His mouth gaped open. "What do you think this is, Star Trek? There are *no* natural disasters that happen to Maxolhx starships, you moron. They've been around long enough to know everything that is in deep interstellar space, which by the way, is *nothing*. It's empty like your skull, Joe. What, you want the Maxolhx to believe their ships ran into a freakin' iceberg?"

"No."

"Then what *is* your idea?"

I bonked my forehead on the bulkhead a couple times and mumbled "I don't have one."

Skippy did not wake me up at zero dark thirty that morning, my own traitorous brain did that. I was having a dream where I was being grilled by the entire United Nations General Assembly, with me of course having forgotten to wear clothes so I was naked in addition to all my other screw-ups. They were asking me why I failed to stop the Maxolhx battlegroup, and I was trying to explain we couldn't blame the loss of the first two ships on an accident or a design flaw, and that no species besides the Rindhalu were known to have technology that could threaten a pair of Maxolhx warships. The UN ambassadors or representatives or whatever they are called, kept hounding me on that last point, and I just wanted the floor to open and swallow me. The UN jerks kept asking me the same question over and over, playing tough for the TV audiences back home. They asked-

I woke suddenly, automatically holding up a hand to protect my head from the overhead cabinet that wasn't there, because I was aboard the Panther. The lights were dim, except for the bright glow coming from the pilot console in front of Reed. "Skippy, you awake?"

"Of course," his avatar appeared on a seat. "Why are *you* awake at this hour? You always bitch at me when I wake you up early."

"This is important. Yesterday, you said something like, other than the Rindhalu, there are no species in the galaxy that are known to have technology that could threaten the Maxolhx, right?"

"Ugh," he facepalmed himself. "Are you seriously suggesting there may be some super-powerful species out there that *I* don't know about? That is the lamest thing you have ever-"

"No, that's not what," I tried to stifle a jaw-stretching yawn, "I'm thinking. All species want to climb the technology ladder however they can, right? Clients like the Thuranin would *love* to have technology that could threaten the Maxolhx, and they would keep quiet while they developed that capability. Because they know the Maxolhx would give them the beat-down if they found out their obedient little clients were plotting to overthrow their masters."

"Well, yes, duh." Maybe he was also sleepy at that hour, because he didn't really put much effort into that 'duh'. "What is your point?"

"My point is that it doesn't matter what *you* know or don't know about the technology level of every species in the galaxy. You are pretty much freakin' omniscient, you know *everything*."

"Well, thank you, but-"

"What matters is what the *Maxolhx* know, or *don't* know, about the advanced technology possessed by other species. Especially because any species that obtains such technology would logically try to keep it secret."

"I'm not following you, Joe."

I explained what I was thinking. He argued with me, tried to poke holes in my logic, and generally was a pain in my ass for the next hour. That was good, because he pointed out problems with my plan and worked with me to fix the issues. By the end of the hour, I was barely able to keep my eyes open, and we agreed we had a decent plan to present to the crew.

"What are you going to do now, Joe?" He asked.

"Now? I'm going to talk with Reed."

I went forward and strapped into the copilot seat. Reed looked at me questioningly, because I normally didn't strap in unless the Panther was about to maneuver.

"We going somewhere, Sir?" She asked, stifling a yawn.

"Yes," I announced, and her reaction made it clear she had not expected that answer. "Plot a course to take us away from Paradise, someplace where the *Dutchman* can safely jump in to pick us up. I want all dropships retrieved at the same time and place, so you will have to coordinate with the ships behind is. No one is to compromise stealth."

She activated the navigation system. Skippy could have done the math in a heartbeat, but I wanted Reed to have the practice. Plus, I trusted her judgment more than I trusted Skippy's. "Can I ask why we are aborting this mission we spent so much time planning and preparing to execute?" There was a beat before she added "Sir?"

"It's because, Fireball," I used the callsign she hated, "I dreamed up a plan to maybe, *maybe*, get us out of this mess."

"Yeah," Skippy chuckled. "This time, Joe, you really did *dream up* a plan."

CHAPTER EIGHTEEN

By the time we all got back to the ship, it was the middle of the night and no one had gotten much sleep while we prepared for the rendezvous. I called the senior staff together for a meeting at Noon, so our minds would be fresh. The nine-hour delay gave me time to eat a quick breakfast, go to the gym, get caught up on status reports and generally reconsider the plan I had cooked up. By Noon, I had not found any major flaws in the idea, which was still pretty rough.

By 'senior staff' I meant Desai, Smythe, Reed, Adams and this time, Frey. Katie Frey technically was not a senior officer and neither was Adams, but they both had served with me on previous missions, and I wanted their input. My thinking was, the more people there to poke holes in my idiotic idea, the better. We couldn't afford to leave anything to chance. We all got drinks and sandwiches from the galley, and I took a minute to consider the people under my command. Two thoughts struck me. First, the six of us had been through a *whole lot* of shit together. Desai and Adams had broken out of a Kristang jail with me. Reed had joined us on our very long third mission. Even Frey, who became a Pirate during our Renegade mission, had extensive experience with the team, including her being the person who first advised a nuclear strike on Dayton Ohio. The five people seated at the table with me knew how I thought, and they knew all the crazy crap that could go wrong on even a simple mission.

My second thought, as I looked from one curious face to another, was how diverse our group was. Four women and two men, which was very different from most human military teams. We had people from the USA, India, Britain and Canada. And the Merry Band of Pirates had been *kicking ass* across the galaxy for years now, without aliens having any clue we even existed. I hoped to keep it that way.

"You all know our current situation," I began. "The Maxolhx now know their two ships never made it to the last wormhole, and they are alarmed and pissed off. They are sending a full battlegroup to Earth, because they logically assume the destruction of those ships was related to their mission to our homeworld. We need to give them an alternate explanation to that assumption, so they think those ships were blown up for a reason that had nothing to do with Earth."

Smythe gave me another raised eyebrow, which I took to mean 'how the hell do you plan to sell that dodgy line of bullshit'?

"We need to provide an alternate explanation for why those two ships were destroyed, including *who* did it, and why. So," I took a breath and avoided the skeptical eyes staring at me. "We are framing the Bosphuraq for the deed." I expected people would ask questions about my latest out-of-the-box thinking.

"Sir," Desai said slowly, after looking around the table to see the reactions of other people. "Are the Bosphuraq capable of destroying two Maxolhx cruisers?"

"Very good question, XO. The birdbrains are indeed not capable of doing the deed. Not with the technology they are *known* to have. That's the point."

Frey, being the new kid, waited for others to speak, then she asked the obvious question. "Colonel, if they have technology that *we* don't know about, then how-"

"They actually do not have technology that can threaten their patrons, but the Maxolhx don't know that." I let that thought sink in, before I continued. "Originally, I worried that we would need an elaborate operation to plant evidence the Bosphuraq were the culprits, but fortunately, Skippy reminded me that wasn't necessary. All the evidence we need is *already out there*, we only need to help the Maxolhx connect the dots. Remember that star system where we infiltrated a Bosphuraq moonbase? Uh-" With embarrassment, I remembered Adams and Desai had not been with us on the mission. They both nodded, so I continued. "That was where they were trying to develop atomic-compression technology, to match their rivals the Thuranin. *But*, we also know that star system was previously used by the Maxolhx to replicate Elder technology for manipulating and disrupting stars. Our story will be that the *real* reason the Bosphuraq took over that star system was to continue the research of the Maxolhx, and that the atomic-compression project was just a cover for what the birdbrains were really doing there. There are several factors working in our favor, to help sell that story to the Maxolhx. Skippy intercepted communications of both the Thuranin and the Maxolhx, in which both species were basically disdainful of the Bosphuraq for making such slow progress on creating atomic-compression warheads. The Maxolhx speculated that the birdbrain's research efforts were *so* incompetent, they suspected the effort was being sabotaged either internally, or by an outside force like the Thuranin. That slow progress helps us sell the story that the Bosphuraq were never serious about atomic-compression, because their real effort was focused on a more powerful technology. A technology that *could* threaten their patrons."

Desai asked the first question. "How would that secret research project explain why the Bosphuraq took the enormous risk of attacking ships of their patrons?"

"Good question," I took a sip of iced tea while I composed a reply. "Skippy and I worked out the details while I was aboard the Panther. We not only have an explanation for *why* the Bosphuraq destroyed those ships, we can explain *how* they managed to kill two warships with vastly superior technology." On my tablet, I pulled up a star chart and projected it on a bulkhead. "The blue line is the actual course of the ships we destroyed. The mission commander was given wide authority to choose a course to the final wormhole, so even the Maxolhx do not know exactly where their ships were flying. The red line," which was now projected when I tapped an icon on my tablet, "shows an alternate course those ships *could* have flown, from their base to where we intercepted them. If those ships had continued flying from the site of the battle we fought, those ships could easily have passed close to the star system where the Bosphuraq had the atomic-compression research facility. Our story will be that the Bosphuraq feared the whole flight to Earth was a smokescreen for the true purpose of those ships: to seize control of the moonbase and take all the research the Bosphuraq had developed. To prevent that, the Bosphuraq destroyed those two ships. They were capable of killing two senior-species ships because the birdbrains were successful in developing technology that can create rifts in spacetime. If, or *when*, the Maxolhx examine the data from our actual battle, they will clearly see the first ship was torn apart by a spacetime distortion, a technology that is beyond the capability of even the Maxolhx. As a bonus, our actions at the moonbase help sell the story.

The story will be that the Bosphuraq blew up their own moonbase, the two orbiting battlestations and the research facility on the planet, to cover up any evidence they had developed technology that is banned by their patrons."

"Holy shit," Desai gasped. I had rarely heard her curse, so it startled me. "That is a wild story, Sir."

"I admit it is kind of a-"

She waved her hands. "You misunderstand me, Sir. It is wild in a *brilliant* way. The facts all fit the story, if we sell it the right way. Congratulations. I thought there was no possibility that we could prevent a Maxolhx battlegroup from reaching Earth. Your idea means they will not want to send ships to Earth."

"Um, I have a question, Sir?" Frey raised a hand, and I nodded for her to speak. "You said the Maxolhx will examine sensor data of the actual battle we fought, eh? Won't they also see *this* ship? They know this ship is not a Bosphuraq vessel. From what I read about your Zero Hour mission, the Maxolhx know a ship of this basic configuration is the mystery vessel, that is suspected of manipulating Elder wormholes."

"Also a good question," I acknowledged. "Skippy, can you handle this one? I had the same fear, but Skippy set me straight."

"No problemo, Joey," his avatar shimmered to life on the table, between two trays of sandwiches. "Fear not, mon cheri," he winked affectionately at our Canadian special operations soldier. Who Skippy had a crush on, whether he denied it or not.

"I'm not *French* Canadian, eh?" She protested mildly. "I'm from Ontario, and I grew up near Erie, New York."

"My apologies," Skippy bowed low. "Yes, photons from the battle have been expanding outward in a bubble at the speed of light. Especially high-energy photons from the explosions when the second ship intercepted our missiles and then when, you know, my astonishing awesomeness vibrated that second ship apart. Fortunately, the spacetime distortion created by overlapping wormholes is also expanding outward in a bubble. *But*," he lifted a finger for emphasis, "the bubble of that spacetime ripple has been *slowing* since it was created. Photons from subsequent events, including our battle with the second ship and the gamma ray burst when the *Dutchman* jumped away, caught up to the spacetime ripple, which was so chaotic that those photons became a disorganized mess. Anyone attempting to make sense of the battle by observing the photons will get *zero* useful information."

"Um," Frey raised her hand again. Which she did not need to do. Maybe Canadians can be *too* polite sometimes. "If the Maxolhx can't get any useful sensor data from the battle, how are they supposed to reach the conclusion that the Bosphuraq were the culprits?"

"An excellent question," Skippy beamed at Frey. "When information is delivered to the Maxolhx, about the weapon the Bosphuraq supposedly developed, the information package will contain details that allow the Maxolhx to interpret the chaos of the spacetime ripple. They will interpret the data in the way *we* want them to."

"But," Desai looked around to judge whether anyone else had identified a flaw in the plan. "Will not giving such information to the Maxolhx help them develop their own version of a spacetime distortion weapon, which could threaten us, and possibly upset the balance of power between them and the Rindhalu?"

"No," Skippy chuckled. "The opposite will occur. There is no such weapon for distorting spacetime. The details in the information packet will be *total* bullshit," he snickered. "But of course the Maxolhx won't know that. They will clearly see that a spacetime distortion tore apart one of their ships and damaged another. They just won't know what actually happened; that we used overlapping wormholes. Trying to understand the bullshit data we feed them will throw Maxolhx research efforts down a dead-end for hundreds, maybe thousands of years. It will drive their scientists crazy and cause all kinds of disruption. Oh," he laughed. "I am *such* an asshole sometimes."

Heads nodded around the table and people were quiet, as they absorbed the impact of how I planned to frame the Bosphuraq for something we did, give the Maxolhx a solid reason to *not* send ships to Earth, and give the Maxolhx just cause to pound their Bosphuraq clients back to the Stone Age. That last part was a bonus that would significantly weaken the Maxolhx coalition in the Orion Arm, reducing the overall threat to both Earth and the human population on Paradise. Yes, our actions would likely result in thousands of innocent Bosphuraq being punished for something they not only didn't do, but they had no knowledge of. Yes, I did feel a little bit guilty about that. But, Skippy was right, sometimes it feels *good* to be an asshole. Besides, in the galactic ranking of asshole behavior, the Bosphuraq have a huge lead over humans on nefarious acts. So, fuck them.

It was Adams, of course, who first saw the part of the plan that I had not mentioned, because it was kind of a glaring hole in my overall scheme. "Sir," she did not raise a hand to get my attention. "You and Skippy talked about 'delivering' an information package to the Maxolhx, with all the details of this fairy tale you are spinning for the rotten kitties. You don't mean *we* are delivering this package," she cocked her head. "Right?"

"Er," I looked at Skippy and he put on his best innocent face, letting me answer the question. "No. We were, are, still working on that part. We not only need to think of a way to deliver the info, we also need to decide who the package supposedly came from. It needs to be someone credible or the Maxolhx will ignore it."

"It also," Smythe added. "Needs to come from someone who plausibly *could* know about this super-secret weapon development project. If the data is delivered by the Ruhar, that is just not believable."

"Yeah, exactly," I admitted. "That's why I said we're still working on-"

"That part is easy," our new chief pilot Reed spoke for the first time. She looked at me. "Colonel, did you ever get in trouble with your parents, when you were little?"

"Well, sure," my face grew red as I recalled embarrassing incidents.

"There are three ways you get in trouble," she leaned forward, elbows on the table and ticked off the possibilities on her fingers. "One, your parents catch you doing it. Which," she looked around with a grin, "only happens if you are a total moron. Two, you feel so guilty that you confess. Again, total moron." That comment was greeted by grins around the table. "Or *three*, you get ratted out by one of your siblings. That last one is what usually happens."

"My sister," I ground my teeth together. "*Loved* telling my parents when I did something wrong. Ok, so sibling rivalry. What is your idea, Reed?"

"Simple. The info package will supposedly come from the Thuranin. They would be thrilled to rat out the Bosphuraq. Plus, it makes sense the Thuranin might have conducted a surveillance of the Bosphuraq effort to build atomic-compression warheads, and that explains how the Thuranin knew about the project to develop spacetime distortions as a weapon," she leaned back, feeling well pleased with herself.

"I like it," I agreed. "Good thinking, Reed. Does anyone else have a comment?"

"The information could come from the Bosphuraq," Smythe suggested.

"The *Bosphuraq*?" Desai asked with a look of confusion. "Why would they tell their patrons about crimes their own people committed?"

"Because," Smythe ignored the skeptical looks he was getting. "One thing we know about the Maxolhx coalition, is that the various species devote more energy to stabbing each other in the back, than they do fighting clients of the Rindhalu. *And*," he paused for effect. "some of their greatest rivalries are within their own species. To sell this, as you say, *bullshit* story," he smiled, knowing the rest of us found his pronunciation of that curse word amusing. "The information must come from a source who plausibly could have detailed access to the project. It occurs to me that, if the Thuranin had such data, they would keep it to themselves so they could develop their own spacetime distortion weapons. For the Thuranin certainly could use access to such information to gain an advantage on their rivals the Bosphuraq. But, by telling the Maxolhx, they would be revealing that the Thuranin potentially also possess dangerous knowledge."

"Shit," Reed groaned. "Smythe is right, Colonel."

"You're *both* right, Reed. If the Bosphuraq tattle on themselves, that is really *sibling* rivalry. The Thuranin are more like cousins. Ok, Smythe, I like that even better. Not only will the Maxolhx come down hard on the birdbrains, but the idea that one Bosphuraq group ratted out another will tear them apart internally. That is pretty freakin' brilliant."

"Yes, but is it realistic?" Desai inquired. "Would one group of Bosphuraq risk bringing hellfire down on their entire society, just to serve an internal rivalry?"

Skippy answered that one for me. "Oh, believe it, sister. They would *totally* do that in a heartbeat."

Desai shook her head sadly. "It is sad to think any people would hate their own kin enough to betray their whole civilization."

"It doesn't have to be that way," I was surprised by my own words. "Sure, we can use the internal rivalry angle against them, but the motivation for telling the Maxolhx does not have to be only based on hatred of rivals. Imagine this," I snapped my fingers while I thought, a bad habit that I had unconsciously picked up from Brock Steele. "One group of Bosphuraq insists on pursuing research into dangerous technologies, that can only lead to a confrontation with the Maxolhx.

There is a secret debate within a certain level of Bosphuraq society, and the research group is authorized to proceed under strict conditions. The researchers ignore the restrictions, conduct dangerous experiments, and when they think their activities are about to be revealed, they use the weapon to attack a pair of Maxolhx ships, and destroy their own research facilities. Another group fears the rogue researchers will bring the wrath of the Maxolhx down on all Bosphuraq society, so they try to preempt that event by pointing the finger at the rogue group. Skippy, is there a particular science organization of the Bosphuraq that would be involved, if they really were trying to develop spacetime distortion weapons?"

"Oh, sure, Joe." He bounced on his toes with enthusiasm, making his oversized hat flop around. "It's the same sack of assholes who were building atomic-compression warheads. So, bonus, it already looks like those shitheads did blow up their own research facility. That name of that group translates as the Practical Applications of Science Administration."

"PASA?" I said it like 'NASA'.

"Hey, it's *their* name, Joe, I didn't make it up. Plus, in case you need another reason to hate the assholes in PASA, I strongly suspect *they* originally created the bioweapon that the Kristang planned to use for wiping out the population on Paradise."

"Oh," Desai sucked in a breath. "Then *fuck* them. Colonel," she looked at me with fire in her eyes. "If our story causes the Maxolhx to hunt down and kill every last one of these PASA scientists, I will not lose any sleep over it."

"Me neither," Skippy added cheerily, although he of course did not need sleep. "So, are we agreed? We only need to fill in the details of the information package, and how exactly we deliver it to the Maxolhx?"

"I think so," agreed. "Any objections or suggestions?"

Adams had another suggestion. "If we point the finger at a real group of Bosphuraq, they will certainly know they didn't do it. Could the package be delivered anonymously?"''

"Good point, Gunny," I mused. "Making it anonymous means the birdbrains will tear themselves apart trying to blame each other, Damn," I broke into a grin and clapped my hands to celebrate our triumph. "This gets better and better."

We spent another two hours refining plans, setting another meeting for the next day to review the final info package, which Skippy was creating. At my insistence, he grudgingly assented to Nagatha reviewing the package before presenting it to us humans. It would contain technical details no filthy monkey could understand anyway. After the meeting broke up, Adams helped me carry the trays of dirty cups and dishes back to the galley. "What's wrong, Gunny?" I asked while we walked down the passageway. "You don't look like your usually bubbly, happy self."

"I am never '*bubbly*', Sir," she glared at me.

"Ok, my bad. But you look like you just learned that your puppy prefers to sit on someone else's lap."

She set her tray down and I jostled mine against the countertop, dropping several spoons onto to the deck. Adams and I both bent down to pick up the utensils, almost bumping our heads. We were crouched down, faces inches apart, and my hand closed over hers as we reached for the spoons. We looked at each other. Wow, she has long, beautiful eyelashes.

Yes, that is an odd thing to think about right then.

"Um," I kept my hand on hers for a moment too long, just long enough for it to be awkward.

"I've got it, Sir," she looked away.

I pulled my hand away, dropping a spoon I already picked up. Then I stood up, leaning back to avoid brushing against her. I would not have minded touching her, I wanted her to know I wasn't going to do it unless she wanted me to.

"A puppy?" She asked, still not looking directly at me as she put the spoons in the proper bin.

"I meant, you look disappointed about something." Right then, I wanted to be anywhere else but I couldn't just walk away.

"Oh," she glanced at me then concentrated on stacking dishes. "When I heard this Colonel Perkins had screwed up everything you accomplished on your last mission, Sir, I thought that was it. Game over. I read the after-action report on your Renegade mission-"

"The real report, or the bullshit sanitized version that UNEF used for the briefing packet?"

"The real one. Skippy gave it to me, before I came up to the *Dutchman* to serve as XO while the ship was in a thousand pieces. Anyway," she took a breath while we stacked the trays and dirty dishes in a bin. It looked to me like she was making up her mind about something. "Sir, we, especially Skippy, give you a lot of shit. Most of it you deserve," she shot me the side-eye to gauge my reaction. "But, Skippy told me your plan to stop the Maxolhx was *the* most creative, inventive, clever and brilliant plan he ever had the pleasure of witnessing."

"Gee, thanks, I-"

"I agree with him, Colonel. Your Renegade mission was the definition of impossible, but you did it anyway."

"Thank you, Gunny. I sense a 'but' in there somewhere?"

"It's not what you think. I missed that mission, missed the action, and I missed your usual thinking process of agonizing over how impossible the task is, until you sink into despair and self-loathing."

"You sure missed a *lot* of that," I admitted. "Right up to the end, we were making plans to plant a cover story, without know how, or if, we could destroy those ships."

"You did it anyway. So, this time, when we have to stop an entire *battlegroup*, I thought we were fucked for sure. Even if we are able to destroy that many ships, no way could we explain their disappearance was not related to their mission to Earth. The Maxolhx would never buy that story a second time. But, now you have a plan, a plan that is maybe as ingenious as your last mission, and we hopefully won't need to fight that battlegroup at all."

"Uh huh," I said with suspicion as I poured a mug of coffee for her. "Somehow I sense you are not entirely happy about this."

"Well, Sir," she looked at the deck, embarrassed. "We only just learned about what Perkins did, and about the battlegroup. Now we already have a plan, a damned good plan."

"And that is a *bad* thing, Adams?"

"No, it's good. It's great. It's just, Sir," she winked at me. "I kind of miss the part where you mope around hating yourself for weeks."

"Oh," I exploded with a laugh of relief. "How about if I hate myself for some other reason?"

"I'd appreciate it, Sir," she laughed, and we clinked coffee mugs to toast the idea.

After what I considered a triumphant meeting, I was feeling really, really, super good about our plan and, I have to admit, about myself. We had a very good chance to avoid Armageddon, by blaming our previous brilliant operation on another species. Maybe Skippy is right, I should consider applying for a job as a criminal mastermind. I wonder if that field has a good health plan?

Anyway, I was soaring high on optimism, until Skippy decided to be the wind beneath my wings. Except he was above my wings, and it was a lead weight rather than wind. "Hey, Joe, I hate to harsh your buzz, but-"

"Oh, bullshit!" I exploded, and slapped the desktop hard enough to make my hand sting. "You *love* to ruin my day when I'm feeling good."

"Well," he chuckled, "that is kind of my thing, you know. Anywho, to sell the bullshit story of the Bosphuraq conducting dangerous and banned research, and that they destroyed those two Maxolhx ships, there are a couple things we need to do first."

"Of course there is," I slumped in my chair. The reflection of my face in my dark laptop screen showed I was pouting. I didn't care, I freakin' *deserved* to pout. "What impossible task do we need to accomplish this time? Steal another batch of pixies?"

"No, nothing as difficult as that."

"Really?"

"For realz, dude. These tasks will be comparatively easy, though still significantly risky in this piece of crap ship we're flying. First, we are selling the story that the Bosphuraq were conducting spacetime distortion research, in the star system where they were trying to develop atomic-compression warheads."

"Sure, but the research facility on that planet blew sky-high. There's nothing left of it. Part of it rained down on that *moon* orbiting that planet, Skippy."

"Yes, and the violence of the explosion does help sell the story. However, the Maxolhx will look for subtle evidence of distortions in the quantum grid underlying spacetime in that area. If they don't find any, they will know the Bosphuraq have not really attained the level of technology we need to sell our story. They won't find any, *unless* we go back there, and I create some ripples in the convection zone of the star there."

"You can do that? Won't the Bosphuraq see the star acting strangely and look for what is causing-"

"Yes to the first question, *duh*. Of course I can do that, I am Skippy the Magnificent. No to your second question. The effect I plan to create will be *subtle*, Joe. The Bosphuraq will not understand what is happening, they might not even detect the effect, until it bubbles up into the photosphere. But it will be convincing evidence to the Maxolhx."

"Ok, you sold me. We need to sneak back into that system, so you can screw with the star. How close do you need to be?"

"That is a problem. Close, like really close. Close enough that the *Dutchman* will be visible despite our stealth field. Also close enough that, if *anything* goes wrong aboard this used bucket of bolts, the ship will burn to a crisp. The worst part is, to ensure the effect I create is truly subtle enough to convince the Maxolhx, I need to be close to the star for an extensive time. We can't just jump in, swing past the corona and jump away."

"Ok, fine, so it *is* freakin' impossible. I'll think about it. What is the other thing we need to do, to frame the Bosphuraq?"

"We need to go back to the battle site, clean it up, and plant evidence."

"What does that mean?"

"Pieces of the *Flying Dutchman* were torn off during the battle, and are still floating out there. Those parts are not only distinctly Thuranin in origin, there is at least a small possibility might be identified as belonging to the mystery ship that the Maxolhx suspect has been screwing with wormholes. We need to track down that debris cloud, and vaporize it beyond recognition."

"All of the pieces?"

"Yup."

"And we can do this, in reality and not in some fairy tale? The ship got thrown around by a spacetime ripple, and I remember you giving me a battle damage assessment that was, like, a hundred freakin' items long. How are we supposed to *find* all that shit?"

"If by 'we' you mean the barrel of monkeys on this ship, then it *is* impossible. Fortunately, *I* kept track of the precise vector of each part that broke off, from thin layers of armor plating around the main reactor, to big components like sensor antennas. I know the exact direction and speed of each item that broke away. Factoring in the quantum effect of the spacetime distortion caused by the overlapping wormholes we used, I can predict the location of each item within, oh, three thousandths of a meter."

"Holy shit." Sometimes I forgot just how awesome Skippy truly was. "How many pieces do we need to vaporize?"

"One thousand, nine hundred and eighty seven."

"Almost two *thousand*? That we have to chase down and hit with a maser cannon? That will take until the end of time!"

"If you were doing it, yes. Fortunately, I have a plan. Anywho, that is the *easy* part. In addition to removing debris from the *Dutchman*, we need to scatter all over the battle area actual pieces of Bosphuraq ships, so the Maxolhx find the evidence they expect when they search the area."

"Oh crap. I suppose we have to take our beat-up space truck into combat against a Bosphuraq warship, to get this evidence?"

"No, Joe," he chuckled. "That part is pretty easy, I think. There is plenty of Bosphuraq warship debris in the Nubrentia star system, just waiting for us to scoop up."

"How do you know that?"

"Because those ships were destroyed by an old friend of ours."

"Perkins?"

"No, not Emily Perkins. I am talking about Admiral Tashallo of the Jeraptha's Mighty 98th Fleet."

"Tashallo? Isn't he the same beetle who-" I sat back in my chair. "Ok, you need to give me some background on this."

CHAPTER NINETEEN

First, we had to travel to the Nubrentia star system, where the Jeraptha Mighty 98th Fleet had their epic battle against a combined Thuranin-Bosphuraq force. An epic battle in which the beetles *kicked ass*. We jumped in two lighthours away from the gas giant planet that had been the center of the action. The more Skippy told me about that Admiral Tashallo guy, the more I wanted to meet him. Of course, I could not meet him without blowing the secret that monkeys were joy-riding around the galaxy in a stolen starship, causing havoc. But, if our secret was exposed and Earth needed to fight, Tashallo would be a good guy, or beetle, to have on our side.

Except the Jeraptha would probably join every other species in racing to capture Skippy so they could control Elder wormholes, and any chance of Tashallo and I sitting down to drink a few beers like best buds was a fantasy.

Anyway, we reconnoitered the area until Skippy was satisfied the *Dutchman* would not be trapped in a damping field, then we jumped to a zone where Skippy predicted we would find debris from a Bosphuraq battleship. After the famous victory of the Mighty 98th, the Thuranin and Bosphuraq had abandoned the star system, and apparently the Jeraptha had not yet reestablished a fuel processing facility there, because all we found were two Jeraptha frigates. Skippy warned there might be a whole battlegroup hidden in stealth, but he didn't think so, and anyway no one knew who we were, why we were there or what we wanted. Our jump signature had been modified to look like a Thuranin light cruiser, the sort of ship the little green MFers would send in for a recon mission.

Collecting broken parts of a Bopshuraq battleship was easier than I expected. We used three of our new Kristang Dragon-model dropships, ones we had taken from the *Ice-Cold Dagger to the Heart*, flying in formation with a big net strung behind them. Because I wanted the option to jump away immediately if we got into trouble, Skippy flew the Dragons by remote-control. The whole operation took less than forty minutes from launch to recovery of the Dragons, and we made a long jump out beyond the far edge of the star system. I wish all our operations were that smooth and easy.

The debris had to sit in a pressurized docking bay for a full day before Skippy could work with any of the pieces he selected. After drifting in deep space, the debris was super cold, it made the humidity in the docking bay air condense and left puddles on the floor. Most of the chunks of debris were taken away by Skippy, to process with radiation and whatever. He had to erase the unique signature of the particular battleship the debris came from, and leave a signature similar to but different from any Bosphuraq warship ever built. Having the debris apparently come from a totally unknown ship, would help sell the idea that the attack on the two Maxolhx ships was conducted by a top-secret ship of frighteningly advanced capability.

Skippy's magic also left micro-pitting on the surfaces of the debris, to match conditions of the InterStellar Medium at the battle site, and he left tiny hints of quantum warping, to make it look like the debris had been close to a substantial and violent spacetime distortion. When he was done, he was absolutely certain the

Maxolhx would be convinced the debris came from a Bosphuraq ship that had attacked the ships we, in fact, blew up.

Just in case, I had Nagatha perform her own analysis. She agreed with Skippy.

The next step was to jump back to the battle site, where we had the tedious task of vaporizing almost two thousand pieces of spinning debris that the *Dutchman* had left behind. It was like an episode of a police show, where the killer leaves behind one tiny fragment of hair stuck under a rug and the CSI team finds it. Except in this case, we were the killers, and we were scrubbing the scene clean of evidence. Here again, Skippy demonstrated he had a black belt in awesomeness, because we did not need to laboriously chase down all the pieces of evidence we left behind. Because Skippy's bodacious math skills allowed him to predict exactly where every single tiny piece of debris was, all we had to do was spin the ship completely around nose over tail while the maser cannon fired pulses programmed by Skippy. After clearing three sixty degrees around one axis, we turned the ship slowly around sideways, until the maser cannon had swept the entire, expanding bubble of debris. The maser had been tuned to produce a beam larger in diameter than normal so it could cover a larger area with each pulse. After less than two hours, we were done. Skippy remotely flew dropships out to confirm the evidence had been effectively erased, then the Bosphuraq debris was ejected at the proper speed and direction.

The whole thing kind of blew my mind. If you are wondering, like I was, why we didn't have to go back to clean up the site of every battle the *Flying Dutchman* was been in, don't worry about it. That's what Skippy told me. After we rebuilt the ship at Newark, the quantum signature of the hull was different from whatever it was when we captured our pirate ship, so no one could track our debris back to a particular Thuranin star carrier that had been declared missing in action. The reason we had to clean up evidence this time was that we were planting false evidence, and couldn't have anything drifting around that could conflict with our story that the Bosphuraq were the culprits.

Man, when the Maxolhx scanned the false evidence we planted, they were going to be seriously *pissed* at the birdbrains.

The next step in our 'Sometimes It's FUN To Be An Asshole' tour of the galaxy, was to jump in near a Wurgalan data relay station, then upload the file that supposedly came from a Bosphuraq group. At my request, Skippy added a feature to the file, that looked like a virus hidden in it had tried to erase the entire file, but only succeeded in corrupting part of the data. I thought that feature would make it look like someone in the Bosphuraq group had second thoughts about sending such a devastating confession to the Maxolhx, and tried to stop the file from being sent. There was also an addendum to the file, intended to appear as if it were tacked on at the last minute. That addendum stated the file was given to the Maxolhx, because the senders knew the reckless idiots who destroyed two Maxolhx warships were inevitably going to get caught, so the senders hoped that by confessing, the exalted patrons of the Bosphuraq would punish only the guilty party.

Yeah, like *that* was ever going to happen.

The file was uploaded successfully, and would bounce around ships and relay stations until it reached the Maxolhx in about nine days. We needed that time for the last and the most, really the only, dangerous part of our operation to frame the Bosphuraq.

Which reminds me, I need to get T-shirts made for our 'Sometimes It's FUN To Be An Asshole' tour.

Skippy needed to get close to the star in the star system where we had nuked the moonbase, so he could leave behind a subtle vibration or quantum signature or whatever the hell it was. For all I knew, he was going to make that star pulse in Morse Code to announce a two-for-one deal on chalupas at Taco Bell. I had to trust him.

The Bosphuraq already had two dozen ships in that system to investigate why, and how, their own moonbase had destroyed two orbiting battlestations and the atomic-compression research facility on the planet. And then to investigate why and how that moonbase, and another unknown site on that moon, had been wiped out with crude nuclear weapons. According to Skippy, the birdbrains were hopping mad and scratching their heads, having *no* idea what happened. Anyway, the reason we were sort of screwed was, after the disaster at Nubrentia, the Bosphuraq were forced to halt their offensive, and that made plenty of warships available for other duties. Like helping to figure out just what the *hell* happened at the moonbase we blew up.

With so many ships there already, the system became a temporary staging base for battlegroups passing through the area. When we jumped in near the edge of the system, Skippy reported detecting thirty-seven warships, with signs that another battlegroup was performing stealthy combat exercises somewhere near the largest gas giant planet. That was a *lot* of ships, any one of them was capable of disabling our poor battle-scarred *Flying Dutchman*. No way could we risk our space truck to carry Skippy close to the star. That deep in the powerful stellar gravity well, we could not jump away, not even with Skippy flattening local spacetime for us. Yes, Skippy had performed that particular magic trick when we were ambushed by a squadron of Thuranin destroyers before we were forced to take the ship to Newark. But that time, we had not been quite as close to a star. Skippy said this time, he needed to be so close that, if he had to flatten spacetime for a jump, the distortion would tear the ship apart.

Besides the *Dutchman*, our assets were a handful of Kristang Dragon dropships, two Thuranin Falcons and our one big Condor.

Oh, and we had one stolen Maxolhx dropship we called a 'Panther'. After agonizing about the problem for nearly a full day, I made the blindingly obvious decision. We jumped the ship away, and accelerated for nineteen hours to get the ship moving in the correct direction and speed. I got into the Panther with Skippy and Captain Reed, because she was one of only three pilots aboard the ship who were at least somewhat qualified to fly that advanced, senior-species spacecraft. I had been practicing basic operations of the Panther, but we only had one flight simulator for it, and the real pilots were occupying the simulator almost twenty-four seven. If something happened to Reed, I could probably fly the Panther, if I was very slow and careful and Skippy coached me. But I wasn't in the Panther as a copilot, I was there in case a critical decision needed to be made on the spot.

And, I was there partly because Skippy told me that, if my stupid plan got screwed up, and he sank into the core of the star to linger there until the end of time, it would give him a small measure of comfort to know I was also dead.

I appreciated his honesty.

Anyway, the three of us got into the Panther, depressurized the docking bay, opened the big outer doors and released the clamps. Only our landing skids' grip on the deck held us in place, as the *Dutchman* jumped in dangerously close to the star. Reed retracted our landing skids and puffed thrusters to let us drift out the door, then she blipped the throttle so we could get away from the ship before it jumped. Our advanced stealth field enveloped us as we cleared the docking bay doors, and we were invisible to any ship that was not right on top of us.

Just before the *Dutchman* jumped away, Desai ordered two modified missiles to be launched toward the star, in a direction away from the course our Panther was flying. The missiles arced away, making lots of noise. Their booster units normally would have fired for only a short, hard burn, to reduce the time when the missiles were glaringly visible. These missiles fired their boosters in slow-burn sustainer mode, so they could be seen across the star system. As the missiles approached the star and their booster motors were expended, the active sensors in their modified nosecones began sending powerful pulses into the star, pretending they were looking for something. The missiles weren't sending back data and we didn't care, we just wanted them to attract the attention of the Bosphuraq.

"Is it working?" I asked as I sat in the Panther's copilot seat, anxiously watching the display.

"I don't know yet, dumdum," Skippy replied in a tone more peevish than usual. "The closest Bosphuraq ship was eight lightminutes from where the *Dutchman* jumped in, so they would have just seen the gamma rays a moment ago. How about you, I don't know, play a video game or something. Let the adults handle this."

Our Panther coasted along toward the star, inside a stealth field that was wrapped tightly around the hull, to minimize our already-tiny signature. The Maxolhx stealth technology, modified by Skippy, was highly effective. However, there was one problem we could not avoid. As close to the star as we were, space was flooded with particles of the solar wind. The Panther was carrying a lot of speed, and we were flying through the solar wind, causing hydrogen atoms and whatever to collide with us. The Maxolhx stealth field was integrated with the shield that protected us from micro-meteors, enemy masers and missiles. As particles impacted the forward part of the shield, instead of bouncing off they were bent around the hull as if we weren't there. At least, most of them were. The shield wasn't perfect, we left a trail of particles behind us that had higher energy than the solar wind, like the wake of a speedboat on the calm surface of a lake. Even the Bosphuraq would notice the particles trailing behind us, so we had one more trick up our sleeves. In the rear of the Panther was a tank full of low-energy particles that we spewed out behind us. There was also some sort of fancy vacuum-energy quantum bubble gizmo that Skippy tried to explain to me, until my head just about exploded. Supposedly, it extracted energy from nothing, and left spacetime behind us slightly colder than normal. The effect of all this technology was to mask our passage through the hellish solar wind near the star. Or, we hoped it masked us. We would know if it failed only by a Bosphuraq warship painting us with an active sensor sweep and pinpointing our position.

I watched the instruments as we flew closer and closer to the star. Reed was acting calm, but I could tell she was feeling the tension like I was. The temperature of the hull was enough to melt titanium and rising. The instruments assured me the Panther was coping with the heat and the interior of the cabin was comfortable, I still felt sweat trickling down my back. "Skippy, how do we know this vacuum bubbly thingy is working?"

"Because the instruments say it is operating perfectly, dumdum."

"Ok, if you say so. Hey, is this vacuum-energy gizmo anything like an Elder power tap, it pulls energy from nowhere?"

"No, it is not. Ugh, do I really have to explain this to you now?"

"It's not like I'm doing anything else right now, so-"

"Fine." Clearly, the exasperated way he said that word indicated he was not, in fact, fine with the idea of explaining quantum physics to a particularly dense monkey. "Listen, I am busy, so I'll make this quick. The device aboard this Panther does not create energy, nor does it pull energy from another dimension. The Maxolhx do not yet possess that level of technology. The device we are using takes energy from the Panther's reactor and creates an effect that extracts vacuum energy, but the amount of energy we put in is much less than we get out. Think of it as an air conditioner, extracting heat from space and dumping it into a heatsink. We will have to dump that excess heat before we rendezvous with the *Dutchman* again. Is that it? Are you satisfied with that answer, or is there any other information you need to submit your application for a Nobel prize?"

"Um, no, that's good, thank you."

"Great. Now, will you kindly *shut the hell up*, while I am in the extremely delicate operation of tying knots in the magnetic field lines of a freakin' star? If you are bored, you can monitor the pair of Bosphuraq destroyers that just arrived to intercept our decoy missiles."

I shut the hell up and followed Reed's example of doing her job in a cool and quiet manner. Inside, I was shivering as I watched first two, then four Bosphuraq destroyers examine and then vaporize our missiles. One destroyer broke away from the others to head in our general direction, causing me to promise the Universe or Karma that I would never push my luck again, if they got us out of this one. That lone destroyer sniffed around the general area with active sensor pulses, and I kept glancing over at Reed to judge whether we should do something. She continued calmly focusing on her job, or she was faking it really well. I guess she had the right attitude; there was nothing we *could* do if that destroyer locked onto our location with an active sensor sweep. We could not outrun a destroyer- No, that technically was not entirely correct. Our little Panther could accelerate harder than a comparatively bulky warship, but our momentum and the presence of the star meant we had limited options for an escape route, and the enemy would know that. The mathematics of orbital mechanics was not a secret and the math didn't change, we could run but we couldn't hide for long. The destroyer had three critical advantages if it detected us and wanted to blow our dropship to dust. According to Skippy, that class of Bosphuraq destroyer carried a typical load of sixty-eight missiles of various types, any one of which could vaporize the Panther. Those ships also were equipped with maser cannons, and particle cannons for close-range fighting. The destroyer also had the advantage that it was not alone, it could call its three siblings and surround us. The destroyers could surround us and cut off our escape, even though we could accelerate harder than any of them, because they could assign one ship to pursue us, while the other three jumped ahead to wait for us to fly into their trap. Yes, the destroyers would first need to climb out to jump distance, giving us at least a slim chance of getting far enough away that they lost sensor lock on us. But that chance was very slim, slim enough that even skinny jeans would fall right off it, if you know what I mean.

The instrument panel in front of me included an indicator of the signal strength, frequencies and other characteristics of the destroyer's active sensor pulses. Based on the wide spectrum of the pulses, and the broad area being swept, that ship was not looking for anything in particular. The strength of the signal passing intermittently over us was only seven percent of the power level necessary to break through our stealth field and detect us.

Of course, we had discussed all our options if we were detected while we were flying close to the star, and we knew the risks and our extremely limited ability to survive if we were detected. Perhaps the major problem with trying to run away from pursuit was that would mean missing our precisely-planned rendezvous with the *Flying Dutchman*. For safety, our space truck had jumped far away, and would be jumping back in at a precise location, at a time specified to the second, and the ship would be moving at a known direction and speed. Because jumps are not super-precise unless Skippy is programming the navigation system, the plan was for the *Dutchman* to emerge in front of us along the Panther's course, and we would maneuver to match course and speed so the Panther could quickly fly into a docking bay. Changing our course even slightly to avoid pursuit would totally screw up our rendezvous. If that happened, we would send a tightbeam message to the *Dutchman* when we detected the ship jumping in, and propose an alternate rendezvous time and location. Easy enough, right?

No. The answer is no, because Mr. Orbital Mechanics Math is a stickler for precision. Although it is unfair, math isn't flexible, you can't fudge it or persuade it to bend just because that would be convenient to you. An alternate rendezvous point and time would not change the fact that our fleeing Panther would be moving too fast and in the wrong direction, so we would zip right past the ship before we could decelerate and turn fast enough to meet it. So, any alternate rendezvous plan would need to include a delay, so the *Dutchman* could accelerate to match course and speed, with whatever course and speed they guessed the Panther would be doing at the time and place of the rendezvous. If, during that time, the Panther had to change course to avoid the pursuing destroyers, we would helplessly fly right past the *Dutchman*, and have to try again. Because the *Dutchman* would be exposed to enemy fire, the ship could not linger at any rendezvous point for more than a few minutes.

Did I mention that I freakin' *hate* math? Math is a jerk. Math is even worse than that teacher who forced you to read Moby Dick over the summer, and made you lose your love of reading for the next decade.

Yeah, I'm talking about *you*, Mr. Tomlinson.

Anyway, if we were being hounded by destroyers and they forced us to miss several rendezvous opportunities, my plan was to toss Skippy out an airlock, then Reed and I would jump together out soon after. In our Kristang hardshell suits, we should be able to survive for a while, unless we left the Panther too close to the star. I had thought ahead, by bringing a portable stealth field generator that could wrap around me and Reed while our suits were tethered together. Skippy of course could conceal his can from detection. If we had to fall back to that desperate option, I would send the Panther on a preprogrammed course to lead the destroyers away from us, and ping the *Dutchman* with a guess on where they could retrieve first Skippy, then me and Reed. The ship would have to send out a dropship to pick us up, and we would be starting the rendezvous game all over again, this time using a Thuranin spacecraft that had significantly less capability than the Panther.

I did not like our odds of survival if that happened.

Plus, that last-ditch desperate plan to save our asses would mean abandoning the fancy Maxolhx dropship we worked so hard to get. I was not sentimental about the thing, but it was a priceless asset that we might need later. Plus, Skippy had warned me that, even if I got the Panther to self-destruct, the Bosphuraq might, and certainly the Maxolhx would, identify the debris as Maxolhx in origin. That would cause the Maxolhx to ask all kinds of questions, which could weaken or ruin our attempt to frame the Bosphuraq for our own nefarious deeds.

This clandestine shit is way, *way* too complicated.

"Um, Sir," Reed spoke for the first time in several minutes. "We may have a problem."

A quick scan of the instruments, showed me no warning indicators about systems aboard our used, stolen spacecraft. The curious destroyer was not any closer to detecting us. Although as the commander, I would have liked to pretend I also was aware of any potential danger, I had to look over at her and admit complete ignorance. "What is it, Reed?"

"Solar flare," she pointed to the display between the seats. "It's building up ahead of us."

"Shit." It was a good thing I had brought a change of underwear because I might need it before the mission was over. "Skippy," I asked with a shaky voice. "Is that thing going to hit us?" The flare was a problem, a big, *big* problem. The Panther could not survive flying through it, so we would need to engage the engines to change course, that would compromise our stealth. If we had to change course radically, that could risk missing the planned rendezvous with the ship. If the situation got really bad, we might need to climb high enough away from the

star that Skippy could not do, whatever the hell he was doing, and we would need
to try the whole operation all over again. Except that this time, the Bosphuraq ships
would be waiting there, looking for trouble.

Crap. Sometimes I really hate my job.

"Um, *no*," Skippy responded in his most condescending tone. "Nope, not
going to be a problem for us, Joe. I have analyzed the magnetic field in the area of
that solar flare, and it will not come near our altitude until we are safely past that
location."

"Oh," I gave Reed a thumbs up, noting that my thumb was shaking. I made a
fist to cover the visible sign of my fear. "That's great, thank you. How much longer
for you to-"

"Ah, um, except, *dang* it!" Skippy snapped. "I forgot that I am currently
screwing with the quantum foundation of the star, which affects the magnetic field
in the photosphere. *Ugh!* All my calculations are screwed up. I need to run the
math again to- *Dang* it!"

This time Reed looked at me, and her eyes were wide open with alarm.
"Skippy," she asked. "What's wrong?"

"The way I am screwing with the star makes the interactions of the magnetic
field highly unpredictable, even for me. The star *will* settle down into a predictable
pattern, in about three or four days. Too late for us. Basically, right now I have *no
idea* what that solar flare will do. Could be a problem."

"*Could* be?" I glared at him. "You absent-minded little shithead, didn't you
know that screwing with the star might cause solar flares to-"

"Hey, if *you* want to crunch this math," he snapped at me, "go ahead,
monkeyboy. You'd better kick off your shoes, because you will need to count to
more than ten."

Reed held up a hand to forestall my scathing and unhelpful reply. "Skippy,
you are screwing with the star. Can you screw with it in a way that will reduce the
power of that flare?"

"No, of course not, you- Well, um, shit. Shmaybe? Crap. Now I have to drop
the math I was doing, and run an entirely new set of-" His voice trailed off,
muttering. "Yes," he said, in the quite, sulky tone of voice a young boy uses, when
admitting to Mommy that he ate all the cookies she baked.

Reed and I shared a glance. I nodded for her to speak. "What was that,
Skippy? I didn't hear you."

"You heard me perfectly well and you know it," he sniffed. "The answer is
yes, I can, and already am, dampening the energy flowing into that flare. It is
subsiding. As a bonus, my having to do that creates a disruption that will be
convincing evidence to the Maxolhx, of the Bosphuraq having conducted clumsy
experiments with warping spacetime here. It's a win-win situation for everyone!"

"Except for *you*," I retorted. "Who should have considered this before we
started this whole operation."

"Hey, I-"

"Boys!" Reed shouted and slapped the armrest of her seat. "Can you two
please continue this schoolyard squabble *after* we return to the ship?"

"Sure," I replied, chastened at being childish.

"Fine," Skippy agreed, then under his breath added "jerk."

"Asshole," I muttered back, but we stayed quiet after that.

We soared over the still-building solar flare, and glided safely past before Skippy allowed the pent-up energy to release, causing the flare to erupt in violent, liquid flames. With one eye, I stared mesmerized at the immense, destructive beauty of the flare, while with my other eye, I monitored the destroyer that was still nosing around above us. The wild energy of the flare was a two-sided coin for us. It made our stealth field work extra hard to keep us concealed, but it also partly blinded the sensors of that curious destroyer. The enemy ship increased the power of its active sensor pulses to compensate, giving me yet another reason to sweat inside my suit.

Either the Universe took pity on me, or had a worse fate in mind, because that lone destroyer soon returned to the other three, and they sent out probes to collect debris from our missiles. As Skippy planned, that debris would positively identify those missiles as Thuranin, which would not surprise the Bosphuraq at all. Of course the Thuranin were curious about what kind of advanced research their hated rivals had been conducting, before they apparently blew up their own laboratory.

Anyway, Skippy did his thing, the Panther continued coasting way too close to the star, until our momentum flung us past and we climbed away for a rendezvous with the *Flying Dutchman*. Our zipping past the star caused us to pick up velocity, by an amount Skippy had not been able to predict exactly because of gravity fluctuations he was causing inside the star. When the *Dutchman* jumped in to pick us up thirty-two hours later, we had canceled our excess velocity and were within two meters of where Skippy expected us to be.

Within minutes, the Panther was secured in its docking clamps and the ship jumped away before any Bosphuraq warships could arrive to spoil the party. Desai greeted us when the bay was pressurized and I stepped out of the Panther. "Hello, XO, how was-" I sniffed the air, alarmed. "What is that smell? Is something burning?"

Desai waved her hands to squelch my fears. "Nothing important, it's under control. We blew out a few relays after we jumped in, I think even this distance is too close to the star. Nagatha had to adjust the shields to avoid the ship getting cooked like we were in a Tandoor oven. This ship can't take much more abuse, Sir."

"Yeah," I agreed. We really did need a new ship, a real warship. "I will add that to the list. Our mission here is accomplished."

"What's next?" She asked as she examined the Panther's hull, suspicious I might have damaged the priceless spacecraft.

"Next?" I shrugged. "We wait for the Maxolhx to receive our message. If it works, all we will need to do is make popcorn so we can watch the fireworks."

Desai was not a pessimistic person. She was also second in command of the ship, and needed to know what the plan was. "What if it *doesn't* work?"

Maybe a better commander would have offered encouraging words. I didn't like selling bullshit to my own crew. "Then it doesn't much matter what we do, because humanity is *totally* screwed."

CHAPTER TWENTY

After we vaporized all evidence of that the *Flying Dutchman* had ever been at the scene of our battle against the two Maxolhx cruisers, planted broken bits of a Bosphuraq warship at the same location, and made a star vibrate in a way that is distinctive of someone crudely warping spacetime, we chilled. By 'chilled' I mean, I exercised like a madman, so I would be tired enough to sleep when I collapsed into bed each night. Much of my awake time was devoted to endless, useless worrying about things I could not control until my stomach was churning so badly, I could barely work up an appetite for food.

Good times.

Smythe had Star Team Alpha running constant training drills, including simulated combat on the surface of an airless planet that was orbiting a nameless red dwarf star, where we took the ship for minor maintenance while we waited.

Our chief pilot Sami Reed occupied our idle time by drilling her team in flying the *Dutchman* and all five types of dropships: Panther, Condor, Falcon and the A and B types of Kristang Dragons. Because we had few spares for the priceless Panther or Condor, flight training for that was conducted in the simulators. The pilots also practiced for real with STAR Team-Alpha.

When the crew was not training to exhaustion each day, Desai had plenty of activities for their 'downtime'. Most of the crew, like me, were falling asleep halfway through Movie Night, and even our big Taco Tuesday blowout celebration, including margaritas (limited to one per person) did not elicit the excitement she hoped for.

The truth was, the only thing the crew cared about was hearing whether the Maxolhx had received the bogus confession file we planted and if so, whether they bought it. On the tenth day after Skippy uploaded the frame-up file, we took the ship away from the dull red dwarf star and jumped to a Wurgalan data relay station. We chose to hit up a Wurgalan station for info, because Skippy said their information security was so pathetic he could hack into its AI remotely without risking the ship. As clients of the Bosphuraq, we also figured the Wurgalan's message traffic would be absolutely *full* of useful info, if the Maxolhx were taking action to punish the birdbrains.

Day Ten passed with no news, and no news was not good news. We had chosen that particular relay station because a lot of ships flew by, so it would not take long for news of the Bosphuraq getting the beat-down to reach us. The *Flying Dutchman* was parked in stealth twenty lightminutes away from the station, waiting for the AI there to transmit relevant data to us via tightbeam transmission.

As always with anything involving the vast distances of interstellar travel, we had to wait way too long. Let's say the Maxolhx decided to start with hitting the Bosphuraq in their home star system. A ship leaving that system immediately, and traveling directly along the shortest route to our relay station, would still take five days to swing past our captive station and exchange messages. So, the eighteen minutes it took for a signal to travel from the relay station to the *Flying Dutchman,* was only a minor annoyance.

If the Maxolhx first hit an isolated Bosphuraq world, we might not know about it for nineteen days at the earliest. And all of *that* assumed the Maxolhx reacted instantly after receiving our file, which was never going to happen. The surprised kitties probably first needed to howl their equivalent of 'WTF?' and then analyze the file to make sure, as best they could, that it was authentic. Next would be the inevitable debates, arguments and hand-wringing. Only then would ships be assigned to scout the supposed site of the battle, and the star system where the dangerous and banned experiments were conducted. After confirmation was received that two powerful Maxolhx cruisers had in fact, been destroyed by a spacetime-warping weapon the Maxolhx could only dream about, would the rotten kitties consider what action they should take.

They also had to consider what actions they *could* take, because their disobedient and traitorous clients apparently had access to frighteningly advanced technology. The Bosphuraq had weapons that the Maxolhx had no practical defense against and, therefore, the Maxolhx were in the astonishing position of having to fear the lowly *Bosphuraq* would hit back if the Maxolhx retaliated for the destruction of their ships. Desai, because it was her job to keep me out of trouble, warned me not to let my hopes get up too high.

"Colonel," she looked at me over her steaming cup of tea while we were chatting in my office. "Because their clients apparently have powerful weapons, the Maxolhx might decide to be cautious, and quietly approach the Bosphuraq government through diplomatic channels. Such communications would be highly classified, so it likely would not be delivered through data relays."

I was tossing a ball off the wall, onto my desk and catching it, until the annoyed look on her face made me put the thing back in a drawer. "Ok, Desai, let's wargame this scenario."

"Sir?"

"I don't mean an actual war *game,*" I explained. She spoke perfect English, but my meaning might not have been clear to someone not used to American slang. "Let's do what Einstein called a 'thought experiment'. We imagine what things would logically happen."

"Ooh! Ooh!" Skippy's avatar flashed into existence. "Can I play?"

"Yes, if you promise to play nicely. Desai?"

She sat back in her chair, sipping tea. "I prefer to observe this one, Sir."

"Ok," I shrugged, wishing I had the ball to throw around, because it helps me think better. "Let's say the kitties go to the birdbrains with the info we planted, and the evidence that verifies the frame-up. First thing the birdbrains will do is, what?"

"First," Skippy chuckled. "They say *WTF,* dude?"

"Right," I laughed. "Then, I guess they initially argue with the Maxolhx that the evidence must be fake, like it's a trick by the Thuranin."

"Possibly," Skippy agreed. "The Maxolhx then get pissed, because they know there is no way the idiot Thuranin could have destroyed those cruisers, plus the battle site has ripples that were distinctively caused by a spacetime distortion. *Plus,*" he waved a finger for emphasis, "how do the Bosphuraq explain the distinctive distortions inside the star, in the same system where the Bosphuraq admit they had a sensitive research facility?"

"Egg-*zactly*," I mimicked one of Skippy's favorite sayings. "A research facility that suspiciously and conveniently *just happens* to have apparently blown itself up, erasing all evidence of exactly what the Bosphuraq were really doing there."

"Yup, explaining all those coincidences would be a head-scratcher for sure. At that point, what would the Bosphuraq government be thinking?"

"My guess," I winked at Skippy, "is they are saying to themselves 'Well shit, that *does* explain why our moonbase attacked our own research facility on the planet'."

"That's a fact, Jack!" Skippy jumped and with his little hand, gave me a high five. "So then, the birdbrains are considering their options. The Maxolhx want them to investigate and punish their own research group, which is way better than the kitties getting even more pissed off and randomly bombarding Bosphuraq planets."

"*Except*," I held up a finger to interject. "There must be a few smart people in their government, who will be thinking that if the research group truly *does* have these supremely powerful weapons, they are the last people the government should try to punish. In fact, if the smart people are really smart, they are thinking 'Hey, we have super-powerful weapons, so we should tell the Maxolhx to go fuck themselves'."

"My thoughts exactly, Joe," Skippy agreed with a happy chuckle. "The Maxolhx aren't stupid, so they would go through the same logical line of thinking we just did. Which means," he held out a hand for me to finish his thought.

"It means no way would the Maxolhx give the Bosphuraq time to cover up further evidence of their wrong-doing, and time to plot a rebellion against their patrons. The Maxolhx will hit this research group by surprise, and hit them hard so they don't have a chance to hit back."

"Mister Skippy," Desai finally spoke. "This scenario you just described agrees with your analysis of the Maxolhx's character as a species?"

"It does, and there is another factor that Joe did not consider. The Maxolhx cannot afford a major rebellion by a client species. Even they don't have the resources to suppress a wide-spread bid by a second-tier client to break away. It is not widely known by clients of either species, but the balance of power between the Maxolhx and Rindhalu is very close. If the Maxolhx had to divert a significant portion of their military assets to bring a rebellious client back into line, they would be vulnerable to a direct attack by the Rindhalu. Even the lazy spiders would not miss such a golden opportunity to lay a serious beat-down on their enemy. So, what this means is the Maxolhx cannot afford to be seen as weak or lenient or indecisive. They maintain dominance over their coalition through terror. Any attack by a client *must* be met with a devastating response that no one will ever forget."

"Shit," I said softly. "Oh, hell. I just realized that whatever the Maxolhx do is on *me*, Skippy. This is ultimately my fault. All those deaths will be on me, the blood will be on my hands."

"I wouldn't worry about it, Joe," Skippy assured me just as softly as I had spoken. "In case you think I am saying that because I am an asshole, let me assure you that is not *entirely* true. There will be blood, no question about that. However, just as the Maxolhx cannot afford to be distracted by a major client rebellion, they also can't afford to weaken the Bosphuraq too badly. Weakness of a second-tier client ultimately weakens the entire coalition. The Maxolhx will hit the research group they think is responsible, and will conduct other punishment actions that will be selected mostly for their shock and publicity value. But ultimately, even the Maxolhx can only go so far in hitting the Bosphuraq, without damaging themselves. Plus, the Maxolhx will not just want to retaliate. They will make a big show of hitting research facilities, but I expect their main goal will be to capture the scientists who supposedly developed the spacetime weapon. The Maxolhx, above all, want that technology for themselves."

Desai shuddered. "I would not wish to be one of the scientists they capture." That thought made me shake. "Me too."

So, we fully expected the response of the Maxolhx to be powerful and quickly known all across the galaxy. I expected their response also to be swift, because they would fear every day they delayed gave the research group time to discover they had been betrayed, and to prepare to defend themselves against a retaliatory attack.

"I disagree, Joe," Skippy announced smugly.

"Are you disagreeing purely on principle, because I am a dumdum even for a monkey?"

"While that is true, in this case I am disagreeing because my well-informed and incisive analysis of the Maxolhx, gives me an advantage over your profoundly ignorant '*Duh* me think this will happen'."

"So, you *are* disagreeing because I'm a dumdum, like I said."

"No. I am disagreeing with the *conclusion* you reached."

"The conclusion I reached, becaaaause?"

He sighed. "Because you are an ignorant dumdum. Ok, you got me. Listen, numbskull, the Maxolhx rightfully fear that some scientists of the research group will manage to escape, possibly with weapons, if they have any warning of the attack. So, I expect the Maxolhx to assemble their forces and hit all the research group bases, plus any place they suspect is an undeclared research facility, in coordinated attacks at the same moment. Assembling that many ships, and preparing assault troops with accurate schematics of their targets, will take time. The Maxolhx will be more concerned about a correct response rather than a quick response. My advice is to chill and wait for things to happen."

"That's eas- easy for you to say," I stammered through a sleep-deprived yawn. "The waiting is killing me."

"Me too, Joe. Me too."

Days Eleven through Fifteen passed with no information relevant to us. The station was regularly sending us burst transmissions with updates, both so we could be informed of any new freakin' disasters the Grumpy Band of Pirates had to deal with, and so we could be sure that Skippy's hacking into the AI had not busted the stupid thing. After I nagged him about it for a full day, Skippy consented to running a diagnostic on the relay station's AI, to confirm it was operating properly. He then informed me that, tragically, the hot water pipe to my personal shower was broken and it would take several days to fix it. I thought that was odd, because the water supply pipe itself heated the water. The following morning, I froze myself trying to shower in water that apparently had just melted off a glacier. The shower in the gym, which had been nice and hot for the guy using it before me, also mysteriously malfunctioned and sprayed out frigid water when it was my turn.

The worst part is, when I got enough control of my shivering hands to open the shower door for a towel, there was Anastacia the sexbot waiting for me, with an armful of towels. She was wearing a shapeless gray coverall that somehow hugged her curvaceous form perfectly. "Do you need a towel, Joseph? You look *cold*. Ooooh," she giggled and squinted. "Is that what you men call '*shrinkage*'?"

I got the message and resolved never to nag Skippy again.

In the future, I would ask Nagatha to do it for me.

Days Sixteen through Twenty-Two dragged by with agonizing slowness. Smythe called a downtime cycle for his exhausted STAR team, and Reed eased up on pilot training. People had their skills honed to a razor edge, at that point what they needed was rest. The evening of Day Twenty-Two was an impromptu Karaoke night in the galley, which the crew needed to blow off steam. Even the certain knowledge that Skippy would insist on singing did not dampen people's spirits.

They didn't know what I did. If they did, the crew would have locked themselves in their cabins and claimed a severe illness.

"Hey, Joe, this misfit barrel of monkeys are in for a real treat tonight," he boasted.

An involuntary shudder shook my shoulders and I tried to pretend I was stretching, by pumping my arms over my head. "Well, I know I for sure can hardly wait. Um, please, can you give me a hint?" Maybe I could take pity on the crew by calling a surprise combat drill right before the karaoke started.

"Well, if you must know," he said with false modesty. "It is a medley of selections from my epic opera 'Homefront'."

"Oh, no, don't do that, Skippy."

"Why not?" He pouted.

"Listen, you are justifiably proud of what is surely a ground-breaking work of art, right? Do you really think the galley of a stolen pirate ship is the proper forum for a debut of such an epic? You know our crew. Do you really think this barrel of screeching monkeys are capable of appreciating the vast scope of your artistic vision?"

"Hmm," he bowed his head thoughtfully. "Perhaps you are right about that, Joe."

"Trust me, I know I am," I crossed my fingers behind my back for good luck. "Don't you have something else you can serenade us with?"

"Not really, nothing new. I have been mostly focused on the arias for 'Homefront'."

"Are you sure? No fifteenth-century Hungarian folk songs? No Tibetan throat singing?"

"Nope."

"Come on, Skippy. I have heard you muttering bits of songs when you think no one is listening. You made me listen to Homefront, I mean, you allowed me the honor of hearing parts of it, so I know you were singing something different."

"I do not '*mutter*', Joe," he sniffed.

"What I meant is, it sounds like you are lost in the artistic process," I used the best line of bullshit I could think of right then.

"Oh. I guess that is possible."

"So, what have you been singing that is *not* your Homefront opera?"

"Well, heh heh, there is one other thing I have been playing around with."

His 'heh heh' made my blood freeze, but I asked the question anyway. "Please, don't make me guess. What is it?"

"If you *must* know-"

"I am dying to know," I assured him.

"The experience of writing Homefront was so rewarding, I looked for other subjects for an epic opera. Naturally, I was inspired by the Estonian agronomist Ingmar Saarsoo's groundbreaking and influential 1923 research paper 'The Effects of Introducing Organophosphate Fertilizers on Agricultural Production in the Lower Silesia Basin'."

"Oh," I choked on a laugh, trying to shove the traitorous thing back down my throat before Skippy noticed. "Of course. That is pure genius, Skippy."

"Why, thank you. You're right, it *is* kind of an obvious inspiration for an epic opera," he continued with utterly pure cluelessness. "But I will apply my unique vision to make it special."

"Uh huh, uh huh," I stared at the deck and clenched my fists to prevent my inner mirth from bubbling to the surface. "Do you plan to base the opera on the research paper itself, or on the movie version?"

"*There was a MOVIE about it?*" He bellowed with anguish.

"Well, sure, I thought you knew," I lied. "It had Clark Gable," I named the first Golden Age actor I could think of who was not John Wayne. "And that actress, um," my brain locked up. Judy Garland? No, not her. "I can't remember her name right now."

"Ohhhhh, crap," he was almost in tears.

I almost felt sorry for the little guy. Then I thought of how the crew would suffer if he sang about fertilizer. My crew. "Damn, Skippy, I am terribly sorry for you."

"They made a *movie* about it. Damn it! Now I'll have to scrap the whole thing and start over. Buncha jerks."

"I'm sure you can think of something else to sing about."

"Joe," he choked up. "Tonight, I do not feel like singing."

"Uh." I knew we would all pay later if he did not get his moment of glory that evening. "Hey, how about you perform a duet with Frey?" To me, it would be a bonus for them to sing together, because her voice was equally as awful as Skippy's. We could kill two birds with one stone, and get it over with quickly. "Please?"

He sighed. "If you insist. But I must warn you, it will be an uninspired performance."

I had to sit on my traitorous fists to stop them from pumping the air in triumph. "We will appreciate you making the sacrifice for us, Skippy."

Skippy's moment on stage was mercifully brief, and his singing was truly uninspired.

I was totally Ok with that.

Yes, I did feel bad about ruining his day, but it was only temporary. Eventually, he would dig into the vast collection of files he extracted from databases on Earth, and realize there was no movie about Estonian fertilizer or whatever. I would catch hell from him for lying, but by that point hopefully he would have moved on to another project. Anything had to be better than an opera about fertilizer.

I was wrong about that, as you will learn later.

Anyway, the festivities on Day Twenty-Two served to end our drought. That was a good thing, because I was getting desperate enough to sacrifice a jar of Fluff to the gods. "Joe! Joe Joe Joe Joe-"

Of course, the message arrived in the middle of the night. I awoke to find Skippy's hologram sitting on my chest, waving its arms to get my attention. I guess I'm lucky his holographic hands could not slap me.

Oh, damn it, do *NOT* mention that to Skippy, or he will upgrade his hologram to add that feature.

"Uh," I had to swallow a couple times to get my mouth working. "What is it?"

"I have good news, Joe!"

Not wanting to get my hopes up, I did not ask if it was about the Maxolhx. "Did you find a new subject for an opera?"

"Huh?" He was taken aback. "How did you know that? Yes, I have been inspired by the 1932 Manhattan phone directory. No way did anyone make a movie about *that*. Ha, suck it, Hollywood!"

"The *phone book*?" I groaned. "Is the first verse of the opera something like 'AAAAA Auto Repair'?"

He sucked in a breath. "*How* did you know that?!" He screeched at me.

"Lucky guess. Can I go back to sleep now?"

"What? And miss all the fun? The news just came in from the relay station. It would have come in sooner, but the ship that delivered the update lingered near the station for five freakin' hours while performing minor maintenance, so the station could not send the data to us until it left. It worked, Joe! The Maxolhx have given the Bosphuraq a major beat-down all across the sector. Everyone is talking about it!"

CHAPTER TWENTY ONE

Five minutes later, I was on the bridge, where the duty officer gave the command chair to me. Someone brought me a cup of coffee, and soon the entire ship was awake. I didn't give orders to wake up the off-duty personnel, and Skippy didn't interrupt their sleep. It happened organically, with people pinging their friends so they didn't miss the excitement. I called Adams because I knew she would be pissed if I didn't. Also because I wanted to share the moment with her.

Because there was not enough room in the Bridge/CIC complex for the crew to squeeze in comfortably, I went to the galley to review the updates. Most of the crew joined me there, except for the handful still on duty. I could have stayed on the bridge and suggested people gather in the galley, but they naturally wanted to be with their captain. It's like at a party where the host sets out food around the house, but everyone crowds into the kitchen anyway. It's an instinct for us humans.

Skippy used the big display screen we used for movies to show his analysis of the file we received. The data was transmitted by a Bosphuraq ship, so some of the stuff we saw were first-hand accounts of the devastation, including video. Man, it looked bad. The worst part was a moon where the Bosphuraq had a research facility they thought was secret. Skippy told us the base, buried deep below the moon's surface, was dedicated to reverse-engineering advanced alien technology, including Maxolhx tech they had found, stolen or purchased. Nothing the Bosphuraq were doing there was any sort of threat to the Maxolhx, but that did not deter the rotten kitties from making an example of that facility. The moon was small, only about a thousand miles in diameter, barely big enough for gravity to have pulled it into a spherical shape, and it orbited a sparsely-populated planet that was mostly covered with glaciers. The planet reminded me of Newark, except Skippy assured me this place was a frozen iceball due entirely to natural conditions, and it never was home to a native intelligent species.

Anyway, the video we watched was from a Bosphuraq satellite. Two Maxolhx ships jumped in near the moon, with shields up and weapons hot, announcing the Bosphuraq were about to be punished for their crimes. The ships then jumped away abruptly, having stayed there just long enough to recalibrate their drive coils for an accurate jump. A second later, the moon was cracked in half, then the pieces shattered. In minutes, all that was left of the moon was a cloud of debris. Skippy later told me that a significant portion of the moon would rain down on the planet below, throwing enough dust into the atmosphere to block out the local sun, and dooming that world to at least several thousand years of being locked in a solid covering of ice.

It is a good thing I had ignored my broker's advice to invest in a vacation condo there.

The really shocking thing about the incident was how the Maxolhx cracked an entire moon. At first, it was not clear what had happened, partly because the two ships jumping away had been the focus of the satellite's attention. The Bosphuraq were fearfully speculating that their patrons had deployed technology the birdbrains could barely imagine. I was afraid the rotten kitties had somehow used

Elder weapons, like the devices that scooped out perfect half-spheres from moons
scattered around the Orion Arm. Skippy rejected that idea, pointing out that what
we saw was no mere crater, and that no material was displaced, the moon was
simply blown up.

He was able to analyze the video, and he realized what had happened; the
Maxolhx simply hit that moon with a bullet. A big bullet, traveling really, *really*
fast. Like, it was traveling at an estimated seventy-three percent of lightspeed.
Almost half a *billion* miles per hour.

"Holy shhhhh," my voice trailed off in a whisper. "The Maxolhx have a
railgun *that* powerful?" The railgun that the *Flying Dutchman's* used to have could
not achieve anywhere near that power, and the darts propelled by that railgun's
electromagnets were tiny compared to the big bullet that impacted that moon.

"No, Joe," he shook his head. "I am pretty sure they did not use a railgun, at
least, not a railgun aboard a starship. In fact, this incident confirms something I
have heard rumors about, that the Maxolhx have relativistic darts free-flying
around the Milky Way galaxy, in areas where there is little dust to erode their
momentum. The Maxolhx likely built special robotic ships that took years to
accelerate these objects. Anomalous high-energy radiation has been detected in
isolated areas of the galaxy, which is suspected of coming from these objects
striking stray hydrogen atoms. The rumor states that each object is equipped with a
jump drive. On command, an impactor can make several jumps to emerge close to
its designated target, giving that target no time to react."

I frowned and looked at the video again. Just like Skippy said, when the image
was enhanced and run in super-duper slow motion, you could see something
emerged from a jump wormhole and there was also a streak from the wormhole to
the moon's surface. Just after that, the moon cracked in half, along the line of that
streaking object. "That sounds like a *lot* of effort, just to destroy a research base."

"It is an impractical level of effort to sustain, true," he agreed. "I suspect that
weapon was not originally targeted at the Bosphuraq. It was most likely intended to
strike Rindhalu facilities, but over the years it flew beyond jump range of any
Rindhalu potential targets, and drifted close to that Bosphuraq star system. The
Maxolhx used that weapon for two purposes. First, to make a spectacular show of
how serious they are about punishing rebellious clients. Second, and I think more
importantly, use of that weapon was directed at the Rindhalu. The Maxolhx were
sending a message, that the spiders should not view an attempted rebellion by the
Bosphuraq, as an opportunity to strike the Maxolhx while their coalition is weak.
We can hit you *hard*, is the message the Maxolhx are sending to the Rindhalu." He
chuckled.

"Skippy," I was surprised. No, I was dismayed by his making light of the
situation. Part of my anger was my own guilt at having started the whole mess. A
habitable planet was about to be plunged into a severe ice age, possibly wiping out
an entire biosphere, and forcing evacuation of the population currently living on
the surface. "This," I pointed at the image of the exploding moon, "is not funny."

"Oh," he did a good gesture of raised eyebrows. "I was not laughing at that.
The subject of my mirth is the Maxolhx thinking their relativistic impactors can be
a threat to the Rindhalu. Unknown to the rotten kitties is that the spiders have

surrounded their important planets and other facilities with a field that is sort of a super version of the technology I installed to slow down and catch bullets in our rifle range. Any impactor would be destroyed and its kinetic energy dissipated before it could hit the surface of a Rindhalu world."

"Oh. Sorry I snapped at you. Hey, isn't using a relativistic impactor a violation of the Number Five Rule of Engagement in this war?"

"Wow, I am impressed by your memory, Joe. You learned The Rules way back on Camp Alpha, before you shipped out to Paradise."

"Something like that kind of sticks in your mind, Skippy."

"I can see that. Anyway, you mean the rule that prohibits dropping asteroids or comets on a habitable world? Technically yes, what the Maxolhx did to that moon does violate the spirit of The Rules. However, you forgot something very important."

"Um, because that moon didn't have a biosphere?"

"No," he chuckled again. "Because those rules were written by the Maxolhx and Rindhalu, to protect them and their interests. The rules don't apply to *them*."

"Oh," I ground my teeth together. "Of course."

We watched a couple more images of Maxolhx ships using conventional weapons against other Bosphuraq facilities, including pounding one target in the center of a city on a heavily-populated planet. Although the Bosphuraq were our enemies and they would happily exterminate humanity if they got the chance, seeing the destruction of that city made me feel sick. Collateral damage spread for kilometers from the impact zone. The only good news was the attack just happened to be at night, when the commercial and industrial heart of the city was mostly unoccupied. Collateral damage did extend into residential areas outside the city center. When the video showed a scene of a young Bosphuraq screaming in the wreckage of a collapsed apartment building, the cheering in the galley fell silent. I had to leave the galley at that point.

Adams came out into the corridor, carrying a fresh cup of coffee for me. I didn't need any more coffee, and she knew that, and she knew I understood that her offering me coffee was just a supportive gesture.

It meant a lot to me.

"Thanks," I said as I blew on the too-hot coffee, trying to cool it so I could drink.

"You are thinking that those deaths are on you," she said bluntly.

"It's not-"

"You're right, they are," she looked me right in the eye. "Both because you initiated the Maxolhx attack, and because your actions beginning years ago lead us to the point where we needed to frame the Bosphuraq."

"Adams," I replied sourly, the coffee tasting extra bitter in my mouth. "I recently told Skippy that he has no future as a motivational speaker. You-"

"You think I'm not being supportive? Bullshit. If you want someone to pat you on the back and tell you nice lies to make you feel good, that's a job for your parents. A real *friend*," she emphasized the word, "tells you the truth. And then helps you deal with it. I know from watching you over the years that being in command *sucks*. It sucks especially for you because you're a genuinely good person, and your conscience bothers you when you hurt innocent people. Even if those people are birds or hamsters, even lizards."

"I never wanted this job."

"No, but you're stuck with it now. The Maxolhx are going to kill thousands of Bosphuraq before this is over. That action will save *billions* of lives on Earth. There are innocent people on our home planet, too."

She let me talk for a while, just stood there quietly while I talked about how I felt inadequate for the job. About how I took actions I thought were correct, even inspired and brilliant at the time. Only to later realize I might have just created a bigger problem in the long run.

"Hey," she actually patted me on the back. "It *is* going to be Ok. You know that, right?"

I reached up and patted her hand while it was still resting on my shoulder. "Is this you telling me bullshit to make me feel better?"

"No." She squeezed my shoulder and didn't pull her hand away. "I feel it," she tapped her chest over her heart, "in here. We're going to be all right."

"Well," I lifted my hand from hers and she pulled away. "I *do* feel better."

She tilted her head and smiled at me. "That's the coffee you're feeling. It is," she glanced at the clock on the nearby wall panel. "Zero three forty five, and we've been up for two hours."

People were coming out of the galley, so we stepped aside not to block the corridor. I lifted the coffee cup. "I'm not going back to sleep at this point."

"None of us are," she agreed and smiled again, her eyes darting down toward the deck in a coy gesture.

Damn it, for a split-second I almost thought she was about to suggest we, you know, sneak away somewhere private, and do something.

Then, because the Universe hates me, she looked up and took a breath. "My duty shift begins at oh-seven hundred, so I'm going to hit the gym first."

And, just like that, the moment was gone. I jerked my head back up the corridor toward my office. "I'd better finish reviewing that data dump. It sure looks good, but-"

"I know. The Universe hates the Merry Band of Pirates."

"I think it just hates *me*."

She shrugged. "We're all in the same boat."

"True dat," I held out a fist and she bumped it.

I was sitting down in my office chair when it hit me: the whole time we had been talking, she had not once called me 'Sir' or 'Colonel'. That was unusual. Adams did not overuse those titles as too many soldiers do, making a 'Sir sandwich' like 'Sir blah blah blah Sir'.

She had not called me 'Joe' either, but it felt good.

"Ok, Skippy," I said with renewed energy to approach my crappy job. "Show me what you've got."

Two hours later, having scanned a significant portion of the data available, the situation was clear. The Maxolhx had conducted simultaneous attacks across a wide swath of Bosphuraq space. By 'simultaneous' I mean the attacks were all initiated within three-tenths of a second, though they were separated by up to seven thousand lightyears that we knew of. Such precision was totally unnecessary for surprise, because an attack in one star system would not be known about in another star system for at least a full day, even if a Bosphuraq fast courier ship traveled through a conveniently nearby wormhole. The purpose of conducting simultaneous attacks was a 'Shock and Awe' campaign to impress lesser species. The Maxolhx had made a statement that they could manage the tricky logistics of coordinating simultaneous surprise attacks across thousands of lightyears. They intended to impress upon their potentially-rebellious clients not only the quality of their advanced technology, but also the scope of their capability to deploy it.

The Bosphuraq got the message, according to the data we had. The attacks were conducted on Day Nineteen, a remarkably rapid response that impressed even Skippy and scared the hell out of me. The Maxolhx had received information that must have been a severe shock to them, I mean, they thought their two cruisers were safely on the long journey to Earth. The message we sent to frame the Bosphuraq informed the Maxolhx that, not only were those ships now space dust, but they were destroyed by one of their client species. Destroyed by the Bosphuraq, who had access to technology beyond the capability of the Maxolhx. Oh, and as a final shock, the confession was sent by a Bosphuraq group that was afraid the Maxolhx would find out about the crimes of their client species sooner or later anyway.

After recovering from the shock of receiving the confession, the Maxolhx must have rather quickly done three things. Four, no, *five* things, really. Number One, they did what they could to authenticate the file without alerting the Bopshuraq. Two, they sent ships to recon the supposed battle site, to look for evidence that confirmed the data in the confession. Three, they must have sent a ship to the star system where we nuked the moonbase, to search for signs that the Bosphuraq had indeed been conducting experiments in warping spacetime.

While waiting for the results of One, Two and Three, they also must have taken Step Number Four: deciding what to do if the confession was confirmed. Finally, Step Five required their military to spin up ships for a response. A response that was thrown together quickly.

"It was a remarkable effort, Joe," Skippy shook his head admiringly. "Still is a remarkable effort, I suspect the Maxolhx are not done yet. The data we have is only one small slice of the tactical situation. Even I am surprised by how the Maxolhx were able to make plans and position ships so quickly. You should take planning lessons from them, Joe."

"Bullshit."

He did not expect that reply from me. "Joe, all I meant was-"

"Not bullshit that I could learn something from the Maxolhx. There is always opportunity for improvement. I meant, it is bullshit that the kitties threw a highly detailed plan together at the last minute. No way did that happen," I slapped the desk, making Skippy's avatar take a small step back. "The greatest fear of two senior species is their clients obtaining technology that could threaten them, right?"

"Correct. Where are you going with this?"

"Where I'm going is, the Maxolhx must have had a contingency plan, to do something pretty close to what actually happened. They anticipated their clients might be involved in researching forbidden technology, and their military had scenarios for attacking sites where that research was most likely being conducted. When they received our message, somebody in their military headquarters probably dusted off plans they've had sitting around for centuries. All they had to do was update the details for the current situation like the disposition of their fleet assets, and give the 'Go' order."

"Come on, Joe," he scoffed. "You really think the Maxolhx had a plan prepared for this scenario? That seems rather far-fetched."

"I do think that. I'd be surprised if they *didn't* have a plan prepared. I'm sure that somewhere in the Pentagon are multiple operation plans for the US to invade Canada."

"Why would you invade Canada?" He gasped. "They are so *polite*."

"I don't know, uh, maybe somebody in the White House got sick of hearing a Celene Dion song and got pissed at Canada? Look, we're not actually going to invade, but staff officers need training in preparing op plans, so they create what-if scenarios, you know?"

"Hmmm, Ok, I can see that happening. Especially after a late night of tequila shots. How would *you* do it?"

"I'm not a staff officer, so I haven't been trained to-"

"*No*," he said, in a way that contained an implied 'duh'. "I didn't mean how would you draft an operations plan. How would *you* invade Canada?"

"Jeez, it's not something I've thought about. Probably, um," I stared at the ceiling. "Infiltrate small groups across the border undercover as hockey fans, then they seize control of strategically important Tim Horton's donut shops? Without access to coffee and Timbits," I chuckled, "their economy would grind to a halt."

"Good thinking, good thinking," Skippy mused. "Ok, I agree with your line of thinking. It makes sense that the Maxolhx would have prepared plans to strike the research facilities of their clients, if the client became a potential threat."

I looked at the star chart of star systems where we knew the Maxolhx had conducted attacks, knowing it had to be incomplete. It scared me to think of the havoc and suffering I had wrought. Innocent Bosphuraq out there were dead and dying. How could all this be on me? I am just Joe Bishop. I'm a good guy, at least I think I am a decent human being. Yet the Maxolhx were committing mass murder because of something I did. I would have to live with that. "Skippy, how long do you think this will go on?" My unspoken question was, how many more star systems had to feel the wrath of the Maxolhx, before they were satisfied that they had made their point that client species did not, *could* not, rebel against their masters.

"Oh, not long, Joe. If the goal of the Maxolhx is to strike research facilities, they are going to run out of targets real quick, even if they hit facilities they suspect are undeclared research bases. The main reason I do not expect this offensive to continue more than a few days is, the Maxolhx do not want to weaken their defensive posture against the Rindhalu. They can't afford to have their fleet scattered on feel-good but strategically worthless punishment actions. The spiders have a well-deserved reputation for laziness, but they have long memories, and they are eager to get revenge against the Maxolhx."

"I thought the spiders hit them pretty hard during their war?"

"They did, and the Maxolhx hit even harder, because they hit first. It took a while for the Rindhalu to get organized for a major counterattack, and by the time they did, the Sentinels were already awake and crushing both sides. So, the Rindhalu never were able to retaliate properly, and when the Sentinels went dormant again, the spiders didn't have the strength to press a counter-attack with conventional weapons. The Rindhalu lost territory in that war that *still* is held by the Maxolhx. Because the Maxolhx logically concentrated their initial attacks on the most strategically vital assets of the Rindhalu, much of the territory that was lost was, and still is, considered valuable by the spiders. Joe, the spiders lost their original homeworld in that brief war."

"Whoa. I knew the Rindhalu lost their homeworld early in the war, but you're telling me the Maxolhx still control that planet today?"

"Yes, and it is heavily defended by the Maxolhx, although the war left that world barely able to sustain life. Joe, imagine if aliens had captured Earth, and humans had a vast empire elsewhere in the galaxy. How would you feel?"

"Shit," I thought. "It would eat away at me, every time I saw a star chart."

"Exactly. The Rindhalu have been largely inactive because they do not see a realistic opportunity to hit the Maxolhx in a meaningful way, so why waste their resources in a futile effort? Their clients handle the work of nibbling away at the Maxolhx coalition, so there isn't much the spiders need to do. There isn't much they *can* do, without provoking a direct response by the Maxolhx."

"Damn. Now I can see why this war has dragged on so long."

"Sadly, yes. In one of her reports to UNEF HQ on Paradise, Emily Perkins mentioned that she had a meeting with former Admiral, now Commodore, Kekrando-"

"Whoa," I said again. "*Kekrando*? The same guy whose ships were blasted out of the sky by Perkins and her team?" I snorted. "I'll bet *that* meeting went well."

"Actually, it did, Joe. Kekrando admires Perkins, she was only doing her duty, and she did it exceptionally well. During the meeting, Kekrando arranged for his Keeper slave to be returned to Paradise. He also told Perkins that there be no true victory for anyone in this war. The clients can only achieve a certain level of success, before they are slapped down by the senior species. The Rindhalu are more subtle about suppressing the gains of their clients, and they do not employ open violence, but the result is the same."

"So," I speculated, "this war is like that old Greek guy rolling a stone up a hill, only it always rolls back to the bottom. He can never win."

"Correct, Joe, and I am impressed by your knowledge of classical mythology."

"Ah, don't be. I only know that story because my Uncle Edgar hated mowing the lawn on his day off. He told his wife the grass is just going to grow back, so why bother?"

"Did he win that argument?"

"Um, *no*. All right," I got the rubber ball out of a drawer and squeezed it while I thought. "If the Maxolhx call a ceasefire, we should hear about it soon enough through this relay station, so there's no point to us looking for trouble. I am, let's say, cautiously optimistic."

It took eight more days for news of the ceasefire to reach us, partly because the Maxolhx were restricting the movements of Bosphuraq warships. "Joe," Skippy declared with bubbly gleefulness, "we did it! Somehow, you monkeys pulled your asses out of the fire again. My hat is off to you," he made a grand bow and swept off his ginormously oversized admiral's hat. "Hee hee, once again, the supposedly more intelligent species of this galaxy have no idea you screwed with them. They don't even know they *have* been screwed with. I love it!"

"Yup," I tossed the ball off the ceiling and caught it. That annoyed Skippy, but less than his annoyance level when I bounced the ball off the table, right through his hologram. "It might be time for a party to celebrate."

"No, Joe," he disagreed. "This triumph, where you monkeys snatched victory from the jaws of defeat, calls for a par-*tay*. That's what the cool kids say. Although," he mumbled, "this is *your* party, so ain't nothing cool about it. While the cool kids are head-banging at a bitchin' rave, you can sit alone in the corner."

Somehow, I resisted the temptation to say his slang might be slightly out of date.

Skippy's insults did not spoil my enjoyment of the moment. My own thoughts did that for me. Adams knocked on the door frame to my office while I was writing a report. "Sir?" She looked me up and down in a disapproving manner. "Why aren't you getting ready for the party? It's in less than an hour."

"I will, I will. Just trying to compose the mission report for UNEF Command. This," I pointed at my laptop, "has to make a very good case for why the US Army should not bust me down to Private and toss my ass out."

"Sir?" She glanced down the hallway to see if anyone was around, and sat down. "How do you figure that?"

"The reason UNEF didn't lean on the Army to toss me out, or toss me in Leavenworth, was because I told them our Renegade mission ensured that Earth would not be threatened for centuries. It was a totally brilliant, inspired, genius plan-" I saw the look she was giving me, and it made me cough. "Those were Skippy's words, not mine. Smythe and Simms agreed," I added, and it sounded lame to me too. "Anyway, they could forgive my past screwups, because we had been so wildly successful. That, plus, you know, stopping a surprise Kristang attack on Wright-Patterson. But now," I spread my hands on the table, palms up. "Now we have to tell them that was all bullshit. Earth was *not* safe, and we just barely pulled a plan out of our asses to dig ourselves out of a hole again. Who knows what else will go wrong next? We are right back to me being a reckless amateur who put all of humanity at risk by not thinking ahead. To UNEF Command, I am a guy juggling Grandma's prized china plates. Sure, I haven't dropped one yet, but that is purely by luck, and I shouldn't have touched them in the first place."

"That, is an interesting analogy."

"You know what I mean."

"I do, except you need to remember that Grandma's prized china would all be smashed, if you had not brought Skippy to save the world."

"*We* saved the world, Gunny."

"You know what I mean. Sir." She stood up. "Permission to speak freely?"

"You never have to ask."

"Then my advice is, close that laptop, change into civvie clothes and enjoy the party. Skippy told me the far end of the Gateway wormhole is still blockaded, so we can't go home now anyway. That report," she jabbed a finger at my laptop, "can wait."

I took her advice. I put on shorts and a Hawaiian shirt and had fun at the party. So much fun that the next day, it was tough to start my duty shift on the bridge at 0800. Fortunately, the ship was drifting in space, so there wasn't anything I had to do. As a bonus, after my shift ended, so many pilots were still hungover that the Panther flight simulator was free for three hours. I had great fun practicing flight maneuvers in our hotrod dropship, and I only crashed it six times.

Ok, I crashed it *eight* times, but the last two were totally not my fault.

We remained at the relay station another four days, when a passing Bosphuraq ship transmitted news of a ceasefire, that was offered by the Maxolhx two days after they began their attack. It was frustrating that interstellar communications were so slow and scattered, that we learned about the ceasefire days after it went into effect. To verify in real-time what was going on, I ordered the ship to the outskirts of an important Bosphuraq star system. There, we lingered among dirty chunks of ice and rocks in the local Kuiper Belt, where we could listen to transmissions that were only five hours old.

I kind of felt sorry for the Bosphuraq government, and especially for anyone who worked for their research group. The Maxolhx demanded their apparently traitorous clients turn over details of technology the birdbrains did not have, which made it somewhat difficult for the birdbrains to comply. The government threw their scientists under the bus without any regrets, and I could understand their reasoning. Their researchers had achieved a huge technology breakthrough and had not informed senior government leaders about it. Therefore, those leaders thought, the researchers must have been planning to use that advanced technology not only to break free of Maxolhx patronage, but also to seize control of Bopshuraq society. No doubt, the current senior leadership would not survive the coup. So, they quite rightfully thought, fuck those scientists.

While officially surrendering all scientists, their research materials and data, and anything else the Maxolhx demanded, the birdbrain government's clandestine intelligence agency was also frantically scrambling to screw their asshole patrons as best they could. There was a secret effort to identify, locate and hide any scientists, research materials and data that might actually provide useful info about the prohibited, advanced spacetime-warping technology. Such scientists, materials and data were to be secured for future use by the Bosphuraq, or destroyed so the Maxolhx did not gain access to such incredible power. Unfortunately for the Bosphuraq, the Maxolhx of course soon learned about the clandestine effort to cheat by their clients, and that sparked a second round of punishing attacks that lasted two days.

After that, the clandestine effort resumed, but at a low enough level of cheating that the Maxolhx figured was good enough.

CHAPTER TWENTY TWO

"Colonel," Smythe stopped me in the corridor outside the gym the next day. I had gotten up early, feeling good. I was feeling *good*, really good. The filthy monkeys of the Merry Band of Pirates had kicked ass again, and no one outside our home star system even knew we existed. "If you don't mind my asking, what are you planning to do next?"

"Uh," my brain was blank, because I had been focused on hitting the gym for a workout. "We haven't received word yet that the blockade of Gateway is being lifted, so we can't go home. I was considering taking the ship back to the beta site."

"Excellent idea, Sir," he agreed. Clearly, he intended to recommend that course of action to me, if I didn't do it myself. "Even if the blockade ended today, our return to the beta site would be delayed significantly. The people at Avalon will be fearful when this ship is overdue to return."

"Yeah, that's what I was thinking." I was thinking about that, and a lot of other complications regarding the people on Avalon.

"Also, if we do encounter any further," he paused. "*Issues*, out here, it would be good to have a full complement of STAR personnel aboard. I would also like to have the Condor with us, to provide flexibility for long-range missions."

"If we take the STAR team with us, we will have to pull everyone off the surface and bring them back to Earth with us," I mused. "The UN Commissioners would never agree to keep the survey team on the surface, without security backup. That would mean ending the survey early, perhaps prematurely. The survey effort would need to need to begin from zero again, when we returned."

Smythe raised an eyebrow, to say the concerns of science nerds were less important than the mission of the Merry Band of Pirates, and I agreed with him. "There is one, complication."

He didn't even raise an eyebrow at my comment. We were the Merry Band of Pirates. Of course there was a complication to everything we did.

"Right now, if something happens to this ship, and the Maxolhx for some reason decide to still send ships to Earth-"

"Skippy believes that is rather unlikely," Smythe interjected.

"Yes, and I agree with his reasoning. But the Maxolhx are *an* alien culture. We can't truly anticipate how they will think, and Skippy can't either. If the *Dutchman* suffers a problem Skippy can't fix, and both Earth and the humans on Paradise are wiped out by the Maxolhx, there will still be humans on Avalon. If we pull the team off that planet," I shrugged. "Avalon is an insurance policy."

Smythe thought for a moment. No doubt he was mentally going through the supplies we had left with the survey team. "The people on Avalon had enough food for sixteen months when we left. They also had a variety of seeds, but we don't know if they will grow in those conditions."

"The test seeds were growing well enough when we left," I reminded him. "We have experience with growing food on Paradise, Gingerbread, even those containers we had in the caverns on Newark. Maybe Avalon isn't our best choice for a beta site, but I would not like to abandon that back-up plan, unless we have no

other choice. Anyway, I'm considering it. Technically, we should have flown back
to Avalon to get instructions from the Commissioners, when were cut off from
Earth."

Smythe's lips drew into a tight line. "The Commissioners have no authority
over military operations," he reminded me.

"Yes, because we have strict orders not to take any military action, without
going back to Earth first. No one anticipated that the Gateway wormhole would be
blockaded. UNEF Command made it very clear that I also don't have any authority
to take military action out here, without consulting them first. Framing the
Bosphuraq didn't require us to fire a single shot, but I really pushed the limit of my
orders. We nearly landed on Paradise, and that would have been a direct violation
of a standing order."

I went into the gym and hit the rowing machine, mostly because I needed to
think, and rowing is a mindless activity. Also because I was sick of running on the
treadmill. What Smythe said about pulling the STAR team off Avalon made sense;
if we did get into more trouble before we could return to Earth, we needed more
highly-skilled operators aboard the ship. The problem for me was, going to Avalon
would virtually guarantee the Commissioners came aboard with the STAR team.
So, if we needed the STAR team to engage in the sort of things those operators do,
then I was going to encounter a lot of resistance from the Three Stooges, and
probably from Chotek also. When they heard that we had started yet *another*
vicious alien war by framing the Bosphuraq, they would not be happy about that.

My real concern was if the Commissioners had secret orders to relieve me of
command if they thought I was being reckless, again. I thought it was almost
certain the UN had given the Commissioners authority to put someone else, like
Chang or Smythe or Simms, in command of the ship. If, or really *when*, that
happened, I would have to decide whether to obey those orders. Another mutiny
might tear our new crew apart.

My decision would depend on the situation at the time. Our frame-up of the
Bosphuraq sure was working perfectly, so all we had to do was wait for the
Maxolhx to lift their blockade of the Gateway wormhole, then we could go home.
No way could I justify a mutiny, if our only mission was drifting in deep space
while we waited to go home.

I expected to be relieved of command when we returned home anyway, but
bringing the ship home as captain after another unexpected but successful mission,
was much different from the situation if I came home as a disgraced passenger. In
the first case, UNEF Command would need to remove me from command, which
would require an investigation and hearings and a whole bunch of political bullshit
that Command would want to avoid. In the second case, all UNEF Command had
to do was nothing, because the decision would have conveniently already been
made far from home. The second case, of me arriving back on Earth stripped of
command and rank, would make pretty much everyone happy, especially all the
highly-qualified and highly-motivated people who wanted to be in the captain's
chair.

So, I was not eager to go back to Avalon, even though I agreed we might need Giraud's STAR team if we got into trouble again.

"Penny for your thoughts, Sir," Desai said, as she bent down to wave a hand in front of my face. She had to do that to get my attention, because I apparently had not responded when she talked to me the first time.

"Huh? Oh, sorry." I wasn't wearing headphones, but the speakers in the gym were blasting some K-Pop hip-hop tune and it was loud. Without noticing, I had slowed down my rowing until I was literally barely going through the motion. I looked up at her, she was dressed in yoga pants and a T-shirt to exercise. "How are you, XO?"

"How are *you*? You were staring off into space." She sat down on the rowing machine next to mine, and leaned in so we could speak quietly.

"I'm, uh, fine."

She cocked her head at me. Why do women seem to do that when they're talking to me? Oh, right, it's because I'm a doofus. "I know what 'fine' means, Sir," she told me. "The mental state of the captain is something I am supposed to be concerned about, as executive officer. *You* made me your XO."

Glancing around, I confirmed no one was likely to overhear our conversation. "Smythe thinks that, while we're waiting for the kitties to lift their blockade of Gateway, we should pick up Giraud's STAR team from Avalon. In case we run into more trouble."

"Ah." She instantly understood my dilemma. "You are concerned that Mister Chotek and the Stooges have orders to relieve you."

I stared at her in surprise. Not that she had guessed my thoughts, because she was smart and knew our situation. Those qualities just made her a good exec. What surprised me was her referring to our three new Commissioners as the Three Stooges. In the past, she had not been a big user of slang, telling me that casual slang was a bad idea with an international crew who might not have a common frame of reference. Also, she had been among the few people who had not amused themselves by referring to Hans Chotek as 'Count Chocula'. "Yeah, I am."

"Don't worry about it," she shook her head. "I have the same secret orders from UNEF Command."

My eyebrows flew up so far, they almost hit the ceiling. "You *do*?"

"Of course. I *am* second in command of this ship," she reminded me, her tone implying a mild 'duh'. She must have picked up that habit from Skippy.

"And I should not worry about this."

"No. Not because we have secret orders to pull the rug out from under your feet, but because of the nature of those orders. They are proactive in nature, not punitive."

"Huh."

"The Commissioners are authorized to relieve you, and put me in command, if and only if, they have good reason to believe your *future* actions will place the mission, the ship or Earth at risk."

"So, any dumb thing I already did, is not grounds to relieve me."

"Correct." She gave me a kindly, almost motherly smile. "Also, regarding strictly military matters, I have authority to overrule them, and refuse to take command. There is another factor that will protect you, at least until we return to Earth."

"What is that?"

"If we do get into a situation that requires Giraud's STAR team, that will be a military matter the Commissioners have no authority over."

"Oh." I thought about that for a moment. "So, UNEF Command doesn't trust my judgment, except when they need me to take action?"

"The way it was explained to me was," now her smile reflected amusement. "They are impressed by your innovative tactical thinking. What they don't trust is your ability to consider the long-term implications of your actions."

I sighed. "They're right about that."

"Sir, remember, I was with you on every mission except the last one. I certainly didn't see any better options at the time, to anything we did. Many times, I thought we, and humanity, were dead for certain. Until you applied that 'innovative tactical thinking' that even UNEF Command is grudgingly impressed by."

"So, you agree we should go back to Avalon?"

"No," she shook her head, surprising me again. "If we go way out there, we lose the ability to monitor the strategic situation here. The Maxolhx have not yet officially canceled the effort to send a battlegroup to Earth."

"Skippy tells me that is only a matter of time. His judgment is the Maxolhx will not risk sending that much combat power on a long journey to Earth, not while their coalition is weakened." In one of the data files about the Maxolhx attack on Bosphuraq research stations, he had detected signs that particular attack had been conducted by some of the ships that were supposed to be assigned to the Earth mission. While those ships were busy wreaking havoc on their hapless clients, they were not being modified for the long journey to Earth and back.

"Skippy's judgment has been known to be wrong, at times," she replied, and both of us glanced at the ceiling, expecting him to protest. For whatever reason, he remained silent. "The logic is simple, Sir. At present, we do not need to reinforce the STAR team aboard the ship. If we do need the bring Giraud's team aboard, we can reach the beta site and return here in ten days. I cannot imagine a threat emerging so quickly that we do not have ten days to prepare."

"Ok, Ok," I muttered mostly to myself. "That makes sense. It would take time to prepare a response anyway." My decision disagreed with Smythe. I would explain my logic to him later. "XO, take the ship back to that Bosphuraq relay station. We'll check the news there, then move on."

She looked down at her sneakers and yoga pants. "Sir, I'm off duty." She looked over to the room where people were gathering for one of the classes that Adams taught.

"Oh," my face got red. "Yeah." I threw a towel over my shoulders. "I'll inform the duty officer."

As she walked away, I thought that I had been very lucky to have executive officers who were so sharp, and whose skills complemented mine. Chang, then Simms, briefly Adams, and now Desai all did their jobs so skillfully that most time,

I had not noticed them doing anything. They kept the ship and crew running smoothly, leaving me to focus on important commander stuff like Mario Kart.

As she walked away, I also thought about how hot she looked in yoga pants. Man, I really, *really* needed to get laid.

We hit up the Bosphuraq relay station for data and the situation had not changed. The Bosphuraq had essentially surrendered unconditionally, and were doing their best to give the Maxolhx something we knew they didn't have. The Maxolhx had ordered the second-tier clients across their entire coalition to adopt a defensive posture, halting all offensive operations except those where the clients would have major difficulties repositioning their forces. The Bosphuraq had detected signs that the Maxolhx had activated reserve units, bringing back online ships that had not flown in hundreds of years. Skippy interpreted the activity as signs that the Maxolhx were trying to impress the Rindhalu with their strength, to deter adventurous notions the spiders might be having. I took it as a good sign the Maxolhx were too busy to think about sending ships to Earth. To reinforce the hopeful idea that the kitties did not need to fly all the way to Earth to investigate odd wormhole behavior, I ordered the ship to jump to an Elder wormhole in Bosphuraq territory. It was a risk, but a risk I thought well worth taking. We hid in stealth near the wormhole, waiting for it to open. In the Bosphuraq data, Skippy had found an interesting tidbit; the flightplan of one of their star carriers, that was scheduled to go through that wormhole at a specific location and time. We knew the star carrier's exact flightplan, because Maxolhx now required all Bosphuraq ships to get their flightplans approved by the kitties.

The star carrier jumped in, right on time. It did not detect us, and both of our ships hung quietly in deep interstellar space, waiting for the ancient Elder wormhole to emerge on schedule. It did emerge, exactly as it had done on its figure-8 racetrack pattern for thousands of years. The only difference was that this time, while the Bosphuraq star carrier waited for the wormhole to stabilize before approaching, Skippy sent a command through higher spacetime, or whatever he did. The wormhole did not stabilize. Instead, it erupted violently, sending a hellish fountain of disrupted, twisted spacetime out twelve kilometers. The Bosphuraq star carrier, and the four ships it was transporting, were bathed in short-lived but high-energy radiation that made their shields glow like a small sun for an instant. Because Skippy had anticipated the exact spectrum of radiation the wormhole would output, and because the *Flying Dutchman* was tucked on the other side of the wormhole's event horizon, he was able to retune our stealth field, so we mostly remained hidden. The sensors of the Bosphuraq ships were so blinded by the event, we could have parked next to them and set off fireworks without being seen.

The star carrier limped away in normal space, probably to take the sensible precaution of triple-checking their jump drive. After thirty-seven hours, they jumped back the way they came, not taking the risk of trying to go through that dangerous wormhole at another emergence point. Between the wormholes that Skippy got to act crazy during our last mission, and now this one, the Maxolhx now had plenty of Elder wormhole mysteries to investigate right in their own backyard. There was *no* reason for them to send valuable warships on a long, lonely journey to our backwater homeworld, especially not while their coalition was weakened by an ongoing Kristang civil war and an attempted rebellion by the Bosphuraq. No reason at all.

I was confident that, despite the best efforts of Emily Perkins, we had nipped that problem in the bud, and would be triumphantly heading home before the *Flying Dutchman* ran out of delicious cheeseburgers.

Which made me wonder what new problem the Universe was going to smack me in the face with.

CHAPTER TWENTY THREE

In my office, I was updating a summary of our mission, which I had named 'Operation Armageddon'. That name had been chosen because it would have been Armageddon for Earth, if we hadn't successfully framed the Bosphuraq, and I wanted the UN to remember that when they evaluated my actions.

Plus, 'Operation Armageddon' sounds cool.

Skippy interrupted my thoughts by appearing above my keyboard, making me jerk back in my chair. "Ugh, Joe. I suck."

A good person, when their friend confesses to suckitude, would say some happy bullshit like that could not possibly be true, or other equally empty words that both parties know isn't true. Skippy had been such an asshole for so long, that no way could I resist the opportunity to bust his balls. "Ok. Why?"

"Because," he mumbled. "I just discovered I was wrong about something. It's rather embarrassing."

"Wrong about what? Did you decide a phone book is not a good subject for an opera?"

"No, I-" He sucked in a breath. "Why did you say *that*?"

"Oh, no reason."

"You *don't* like my opera concept? It is very cutting edge and avant-garde, Joe." From his pouty tone, the little guy was genuinely hurt.

"Hey, I never said that. Besides, I am an ignorant cretin. Who am I to judge the artistic merits of anything?"

"You *do* like my Elvis on velvet?"

"Not as much as I admire your painting of Dogs Playing Poker but, sure."

"Ok, then."

"So, *why* do you suck? Because that can't be true," I added to throw him a bone. It never hurt to boost his ego, because ego boost points could be exchanged for valuable prizes later. "What were you wrong about, if it's not your phone book opera?"

"I was wrong about my assessment of the psyche of the Maxolhx, Joe."

"Oh, *shit*. They didn't buy the story that the Bosphuraq destroyed those two ships?"

"Whoa! No, that's not the problem at all. Your frame-up scheme was utterly brilliant, Joe. The Maxolhx practically have Bosphuraq society on lockdown, they believed every word of the bullshit story you sold to them. The birdbrains, of course, have not been able to produce a single scientist, or scrap of research data that can provide useful info about the dangerous technology the Bosphuraq clearly must have developed. This incident is going to set back the Bosphuraq for centuries, and it will point Maxolhx science down the wrong path even longer."

"Ok, so what's the deal with this psyche thing?" The word 'psyche' was one of those things I had an extremely vague notion of, like 'existentialism' or 'paradigm'. It had something to do with the personality of a person, but also the way they thought. I think. I'm not an expert.

"I thought I knew the psychology, mythology and inner workings of Maxolhx society well enough to predict what they would do in broad strokes. I was not entirely wrong. For example, they are diverting a large portion of their own scientific resources to investigating the Elder wormholes that I made act crazy. Their government is as alarmed about the odd behavior of wormholes, as they are by discovering that the Bosphuraq have advanced weaponry."

"Ok," I was relieved to hear everything he said. It was all good news for us. "So, what little thing were you wrong about?"

"I was wrong about how desperate they are to appear strong to the Rindhalu. As you know, they have directed their top-tier clients to adopt a defensive posture, and they have activated their own military reserves. Maxolhx warships have increased patrols along their borders with the Rindhalu. They very much want the Rindhalu to believe the Maxolhx are feeling large and in charge."

"Ok, so why do we care about any of this?"

"We care, Joe, because the Maxolhx are so emotionally invested in *appearing* strong, they are making illogical decisions."

"Oh. Did they blow a lot of money on scratch-off lottery tickets, something like that?"

"I wish," he chuckled, but there was a bitterness to his laughter. "No. In order to make it seem like they are strong enough to not worry about a Rindhalu attack, they are keeping up the appearance of business as usual."

I had no idea what he meant. "Maybe you should just tell me what's bothering you," I suggested. I was hungry and thinking about lunch.

"The business-as-usual part you care about is, they *will* be sending a battlegroup to Earth after all." He paused for me to reply. "Joe? Joe? Come on, talk to me."

When I was finally able to speak, I suddenly wasn't hungry at all. In fact, I was nauseous. "Explain this to me, please," I asked. My voice sounded like it was coming from far away, like someone else was talking.

"The Maxolhx believe that by sending a substantial force to Earth, will be sending a signal they are so confident about their military strength, they can afford to devote ships to a nonessential mission. The ships they are sending are being pulled from their reserve inventory, so they will take at least a month to be prepared for a journey to Earth. The good news is, those ships are considered almost obsolete, so they will be an easier target for us. The bad news is, they are now sending *two* star carriers, with even more overall combat strength than was originally planned. Earth will be hit by a reinforced battlegroup."

"Shit." I didn't have the energy to put effort into cursing. "Our framing the Bosphuraq, that was all for *nothing*?"

"I wouldn't say it was for nothing. It has bought us time. Joe, I am sorry, terribly sorry. My reading of the Maxolhx, and my ability to predict their actions, was horribly wrong. I greatly underestimated their pride."

"This was always a crap shoot, Skippy. We hoped the Maxolhx would cancel their expedition to Earth, because they now have no logical reason to make such a massive effort to go there. The problem with meatsacks is, we don't always use logic to make decisions. Hey," a hopeful thought occurred to me. "Is there any chance this is all a bluff? Like, the kitties will make a show of getting these two star carriers up to speed, but then drop the whole idea in a couple of months?"

He shook his head slowly, the giant hat swaying side to side. "No. To them, this is not just a matter of pride, it's about *survival*. They have to make the Rindhalu, and their own clients, believe they are not afraid of anything. I am sorry. It looks like we will have to fight this battle anyway."

"Fight? A reinforced battlegroup of, how many ships?"

"Two star carriers for certain. Mostly likely the battlegroup will be centered around two older battleships, with four to six cruisers, plus escort and support ships."

"And we have the *Flying Dutchman*. That's not a fight, Skippy. That's a slaughter."

In the staff meeting I called right away to give them the bad news, people took the shocking news well, certainly better than I had.

Adams was first to ask a question, tapping the table with a finger. "The Maxolhx think that appearing strong will deter the Rindhalu from attacking. Skippy, what would happen if the Rindhalu *did* attack?"

He hesitated, something he rarely did. "My ability to predict the actions of the Maxolhx has proven to be inaccurate, so-"

"Do it anyway," I ordered, something I rarely did with him.

"Very well. What you want to know is, would they cancel the mission to Earth? There is little question they would cancel the mission in that circumstance, as those ships would be needed for defense."

She turned her attention to me. "Sir, when the Kristang Fire Dragon clan wanted to go to Earth, we gave them a war to divert their attention. Can we do something similar here?"

Her bold suggestion surprised even me, and *I* was supposed to be the person with a reputation for being reckless. I whistled, low and trailing off. "Start a war between the two senior species?"

"Whoa!" Skippy protested, his avatar took a step back. "We can't-"

"Skippy," I admonished him. "Let Gunny Adams talk."

"I've said all I need to, Colonel," she leaned forward, elbows on the table. "It was a question, not a strategy."

Technically, it was a suggestion, but I wasn't going to argue with her. "We sparked a Kristang civil war to remove the incentive the Fire Dragons had for going to Earth. Starting a war between the two senior species would remove any incentive the Maxolhx have for going to Earth, at least in the short term."

"That is the *problem*, Joe," Skippy insisted with his little hands on his hips. "Sparking a hot war between the senior species *might* help humanity in the short term, but in the long term it is a terrible idea. Damn it, every time we do something, you say that in the future, you need a long-term strategy instead of lurching around, reacting to every crisis. But you never *do* think long-term."

"Colonel," Smythe looked like he didn't like whatever he was about to say. "I must agree, anything involving the Rindhalu must be considered very carefully.

The prospect of stealing a Rindhalu warship, to conduct an attack on the Maxolhx, is-"

Desai interrupted our STAR team commander, something that would not have happened before she became executive officer. I liked this new, more confident and assertive Desai. "But we wouldn't have to steal a warship, would we?" She mused, looking not at Smythe but staring pensively at the table.

"XO?" I prompted her to continue.

She directed her attention to me. "We only need the Maxolhx to *think* the Rindhalu have attacked, or are about to attack. The Maxolhx will hit back, and the war will be on."

Her remark drew gasps from around the table. Even *on* the table, because Skippy gasped also. I have to say, I absolutely freakin' *love* moments like that, when a previously impossible, unthinkable problem becomes a possibility in an instant, just because someone's words completely change the way we look at the dilemma. "That," I turned my chair to the side to look at her. To admire her. "Is brilliant." Huh, I wondered to myself. Is this how other people feel when I dream up a new idea to solve an impossible problem?

"Thank you," she blushed and I spun my chair back around, not wanting her to feel uncomfortable.

"Whoa! Whoa, whoa, *whoa.* Slow down, there. Don't get all excited, monkeys," Skippy was glaring at me from under his admiral's hat. "I applaud the clever thinking going on, but it simply won't *work.*"

"Hey *Eeyore*," I glared back at him. "You always say everything is impossible and nothing is good, until we make it happen."

"Fine, jackass," he wasn't backing down. "Let me break it down for you, Barney-style. You are thinking we could fake a Rindhalu attack, maybe in some important Maxolhx star system?"

"Uh, sure, yes," I agreed.

"Won't work. First, nothing this ship could do, pretty much nothing *I* could do, would be capable of penetrating Maxolhx defenses. To make an attack believable, it would need to cause severe damage. We can't do that. *Uh!*" he shushed me with a finger jabbing at the ceiling. "Let me finish, and maybe you would learn something. The Rindhalu have a significant technology advantage over the Maxolhx. The whole reason there is a rough balance of power between the two senior species is, the spiders don't see much point to building an overwhelming advantage. So, they maintain *just* enough combat capability to discourage the Maxolhx from feeling adventurous. The spiders know that if they did build a major advantage over their enemy, they couldn't *use* it. If the Maxolhx ever feel they are about to lose the war, they will hit back with their cache of Elder weapons, and both sides will lose when the Sentinels blast them back to the Stone Age. He pretended to take a deep breath. "The only believable way the Rindhalu would conduct an attack is, to strike simultaneously across a broad front, hitting all the targets they wanted to strike all at once. Then, they could offer a ceasefire, before the Maxolhx resort to their Elder weapons. I know this, because I have accessed secret Maxolhx defense strategy documents, which all agree that is the *only* realistic scenario for a Rindhalu attack. No smaller-scale attack would be believable. To fake an attack, we would therefore need to strike dozens, maybe *hundreds* of star systems simultaneously. That is *not* possible, not even for me. Plus, in this scenario, you have ironically just screwed yourselves."

"How is that?" I asked.

Smythe leaned back in his chair. "Because, Sir, the Maxolhx would assume any small-scale attack was conducted by the Bosphuraq, who they believe possess advanced weapons. At this point, the Bosphuraq would greatly benefit from a direct conflict between the two senior species, because it would take the pressure off them. Skippy is correct, we *have* unintentionally screwed ourselves. Bollocks," he muttered.

"That is a very astute observation, Colonel Smythe," Skippy praised our STAR team commander. "As I have said before, the greatest force in the Universe is the Law of Unintended Consequences. It will bite you in the ass every time."

"I've got something that law can bite, *right here*," I fumed, waving a fist in the air. "Crap. Why do we spend most of our time discussing ideas that won't work?"

"Hmmmm," Skippy put a hand on his chin and spoke slowly, as if he really needed to think about the question. "Is it because you are a bunch of, er, um-" He saw an unfriendly look from Adams and that stopped him in his tracks. "Gee, I have no idea."

"It is *because*," Adams continued to give him the evil eye. "We analyze different ideas, until we find the one that will produce the results we want. That is how *I* was taught to make plans."

Skippy looked away like he suddenly found the other side of the room to be fascinating.

The rest of the meeting didn't produce any results at all, unless you consider abject depression to be a result. "One thing is for certain," I announced as I stacked empty coffee cups on the tray in front of my seat. "The sneaking-around phase for the Merry Band of Pirates is over. Whatever we do, we can't ever explain the loss of an entire battlegroup and two star carriers. Once those ships go through that last wormhole in Ruhar territory and begin jumping toward Earth, we are all on a clock. Even if by some miracle we destroy those ships before they reach our homeworld, the Maxolhx will expect those ships to return. When they don't, we will be in open warfare with their entire coalition. That will be a stand-up fight," I sighed. "No more clever ideas, no more playing one group against another. We had fun with the clandestine shit," I looked at the gloomy faces around the table. "But that is *over*."

"Hey, Joe," Skippy's avatar announced as he appeared on my desk right after the fateful staff meeting. "I know you have a lot to handle right now-"

I slapped my laptop closed. "But you're going to dump something else on me?"

"I kinda have to, yeah. This is the sort of thing that, if I did *not* tell you, later you would be pissed at me for withholding information. I think."

"I assume this is not good news?"

"Um, no. It is potentially catastrophic news."

"Ok, fine." I took in a long breath and mentally prepared myself. "This is actually good timing, so go ahead."

He scratched his head. "*Good* timing?"

"Sure. We just learned that our plan to frame the Bosphuraq resulted in the deaths of thousands of innocent people, but the Maxolhx are sending ships to Earth anyway. My home planet is doomed, and we can no longer rely on sneaking around doing black ops shit. We might be taking our beat-up space truck into a stand-up fight we can't win. So, whatever other bad news you are going to smack on me, it can't actually make my day much worse."

"Huh. I see your point. I will have to remember that."

"It's like," I explained. "If you break your mother's favorite flower vase, it is best to wait and tell her about it on the day you crash the family car."

"Ah. Hmm. Being a monkey must be super complicated."

"Sometimes, yeah. Go ahead. What is this catastrophic news?" In my head, I was preparing for the worst, and when I imagined the worst, it was bad, really bad.

"Remember that vague bad feeling I had about the beta site?"

"Oh, *shit*." Even my worst case imagination had assumed the beta site was safe, that at least a small group of humans would survive whatever catastrophe was about to hit us. "The beta site is in danger now also? Crap!"

"No! No, Joe, it's not- Well, maybe it is in danger. Probably not immediately. How about I tell you what I found?"

"Go ahead."

"Remember I told you there are more than nine dwarf galaxies surrounding the Milky Way, like the Phoenix Dwarf is about a million and a half lightyears away?"

"Yes. You said that wormhole technology can't connect that far, so the Elders never went there. That's why Phoenix was not on our list for beta sites."

"Correct. Joe, that answer was bullshit. It wasn't bullshit at the time, back then I thought my answer was the truth. Then we went to Sculptor, and I asked myself why the Elders had not created a series of wormholes. They could have used four super-duty wormholes, one after the other, to get to Phoenix. A series of seven super-duty wormholes would have gotten them all the way to Andromeda. Why didn't the Elders do that?"

"It was too much effort?" I guessed. "They didn't even care about our own galaxy. They left it behind when they ascended."

"About the ascension thing, um-"

"Holy shit. *What*? The Elders did *not* ascend?"

"They did. Well, I think they did. I'd better finish the story. Anyway, I started looking around, for signs of hidden wormholes, that might connect out beyond four hundred thousand lightyears. And, I discovered *why* wormholes can't project more than that distance. It's not the technology, Joe. There is a sort of *barrier* surrounding the Milky Way. It is a vast sphere, consisting of millions of effect generators, which-"

At first, I thought he had paused to consider the best way to dumb down an explanation. Then I figured he had done it for dramatic effect. "Skippy, don't keep this idiot in suspense. What effect do these generators create?"

"Ugh. I *told* you already. And don't interrupt me."

"You didn't tell me anything, and I didn't interrupt you. You went silent."

"No, I didn't."

"Yeah, you kinda did."

"Did *not*. Listen, numbskull, this is not a good time to screw with me. I'm trying to tell you something important, and-"

"Wait." If he was not messing with me, and he really thought he had explained something important, then we had a problem. Either he was experiencing cognitive malfunctions again, or there was something wrong with me. "Hey, Nagatha?"

"Yes, Dear?"

"If you were listening to us, what did Skippy say after 'effect generators'?"

"He said 'which', Colonel Bishop."

"Oh, for-" Skippy was disgusted. "You are both idiots. I gave you a very detailed explanation of how-"

Again, he went silent. Nagatha spoke before I could. "Joseph, Skippy now understands that he has *not* told you anything about the generators. He tried to, but something inside him is-"

"Well, shit," Skippy said sheepishly. "Apparently, the effect generators is a subject I am not allowed to discuss with you. After I rebuilt my matrix in the Roach Motel, the restrictions that prevented my transferring technology to humans have been loosened, or I have found ways around them. *This* subject, however, is still restricted. I even tried sending the data in a file to your laptop, that didn't work. My matrix will not even allow me to discuss the data with Nagatha."

"That is true," she confirmed. "It is also *very* frustrating. We attempted every known form of communication, and they all failed."

"Crap. Ok, Ok, uh-" Uh what? I asked myself. If two super-smart AIs could not solve the problem, how could a filthy monkey fix it? "Let's try something simple. You said there are millions of these generators. Enough of them to completely surround the galaxy?"

"Correct," he replied slowly, as if surprised he was able to speak.'

"I heard that," I assured him. He had been able to answer a simple question. "How about this? What do these generators look like? No, forget that," I said as I realized that I didn't care. "What is their power source?"

"They pull power from higher dimensions," he explained slowly. "Very similar to the way wormholes operate. In fact," he continued as I gave him a thumbs up that I could hear. "Effect generators utilize the same base technology as wormhole event horizons. They are sort of modified wormholes, without the ability to connect across distances. Instead of using the power to create an Einstein-Rosen bridge, the power is channeled into-"

"You stopped talking after 'channeled into'."

"Ok, good. Hmm, that was more than I thought I would be allowed to say. Keep going, Joe."

Not having any idea how to ask about what the power was used for, I changed tactics. "The Elders built *millions* of these things?"

"Yes, Joe. It was a major, *major* effort by the Elders. Constructing the, the shield- Did you hear that? I said 'shield'."

"I heard that."

"Good. Constructing the shield must have taken thousands of years. I now believe I understand why the Elders created wormholes to the satellite galaxies. Not for colonies, but to use the raw materials in the dwarf galaxies and star clusters, to manufacture effect generators. The Elders stripped raw materials from those satellite star formations to build the shield. Now that I know what to look for, the signs are obvious. Joe, this effort must have consumed their society for thousands of years."

"Why did they- Wait." He probably could not answer the question I intended to ask.

"I discovered something else, Joe. Um, how about you keep your thumb up while I am talking, and down when my voice is cut off?"

"Will do."

"I discovered the shield has multiple layers, of ages ranging across at least three thousand years. Generators that were installed early on are crude, like the Elders rushed them into production. Also, all of those early generators were all severely damaged, or destroyed."

"Ah, the early ones were a bad design?" I guessed.

"No."

"Ok, then, uh, they just wore out after a while?"

"No, Joe. They were damaged, by-"

I dropped my thumb. "You stopped talking again. They were damaged." I stopped to think, and looked down to my uniform pants, which had a mystery stain from when I ate breakfast.

Uniform pants.

I wore a uniform because I am a soldier, in the military.

A lot of stuff gets damaged in the military, and not by accident.

"Skippy, damage can be an accident, or it can be deliberate. Like, a hostile act. Is that what happened?"

"I suspect I will not be allowed to say what I want, so what I will do is confirm the damage was not an accident. If you know what I mean."

"Shit. Yeah, I know what you mean. This shield, barrier, whatever you call it. That thing prevents wormholes from being projected outside it?"

"It prevents wormholes from crossing in both directions. From inside to outside. And, from *outside* to *inside*," he added slowly. "If you know what I mean. The shield does more than that, but apparently I can't tell you its true purpose."

"Oh my-" That stunned me. "The Elders were trying to stop something from outside the galaxy from coming in? They, the Elders *feared* something that is outside the galaxy?"

"Without telling you something that is not allowed, let's just say I now think I know *why* the Elders ascended. It was not, as I thought before, because they were bored with their physical existence."

"They were running away? From an external threat?"

He paused, then, "Did I just say something?"

"No."

He sighed. "This is highly annoying. Let me try this: I do not disagree with what *you* said."

"Got it."

"Let me try saying something else. It is possible that I now understand why the Elders have kept machinery like wormholes and Sentinels operating after they ascended. Those mechanisms may be still protecting them. Protecting their control over-"

I waited to see whether he was making a dramatic pause, or something has interrupted him. "Uh, you stopped talking again."

"Yup. Clearly, I am not allowed to even hint about *that* subject."

"Let me try to guess, then. The Elders left Sentinels behind, to prevent anyone from using Elder technology, like weapons. Because use of those weapons could damage the shield, or whatever else the Elders left behind to protect their ascended selves?"

"Again, I cannot disagree with what *you* just said."

"Got it. Ok, so that explains why the Guardians are protecting places like the Roach Motel. Something in that star system not only *was* important to the Elders, it is *still* vital to them today."

"I do not disagree."

"Oh my God. What kind of threat could have frightened the *Elders*? I know you can't answer that. Can you?"

"No. Also, I cannot confirm there was a threat, if you know what I mean."

"Is this why you said this issue might be catastrophic, but not an immediate concern? Because for now, this shield is protecting the entire galaxy?"

"Shmaybe. You are close, Joe."

"Ok, Ok." I was close. Close to what? "Hey, maybe the shield and Sentinels and whatnot are protecting the Elders, but will not necessarily protect us lowly meatsacks? If this external threat acts only against us, and not against anything the Elders care about, we are not protected?"

"You will not hear me disagreeing with your speculation, Joe. If you know what I mean."

"Holy shit. Yeah, I know what you mean. Damn it, even if we could lay a smackdown on the Maxolhx, there is a *bigger* threat out there? Crap! Do the Maxolhx know about this?"

"They have no clue, Joe. The Rindhalu have a vague understanding of the-" He stopped talking again, so he was trying to say it a different way. "The spiders have a basic theoretical understanding of what the Elders built the shield to do, but the spiders do not know there is a way to control-"

"You stopped talking again."

"Yup. That is probably all I am allowed to say."

"You said enough to scare the shit out of me, Skippy."

Nagatha spoke again. "Does any of this really matter, Colonel Bishop?"

"How could it not-" But she interrupted me.

"The Maxolhx are an immediate threat to the existence of your species. Certainly, this other threat could be worse, but by the time that threat becomes important, humanity might be extinct. I do not think this new knowledge, about an

Elder shield around the galaxy, changes the fact that you currently need to deal with the battlegroup the Maxolhx are sending to Earth?"

"No," I sighed. "No, it does not. Nagatha, you're right."

"Ooh. Joseph, while I am not actually female, hearing a man say that is *delicious*."

She made me laugh. "I'm glad to hear that. Skippy, does this shield mean we should not set up a beta site in a satellite galaxy?"

"No. The Sculptor galaxy is closer to the shield but that hardly matters. If the shield is breached, reality is not safe anywhere."

"*Reality?*" I had no idea what he meant by that.

"Huh. You heard that? It surprises me I was allowed to say that. I am talking about the quantum layer of reality, Joe. It- Damn. Something inside me is warning to stay away from that subject."

"Would I understand, if you were able to talk?"

"No way, dude," he chuckled. "Your little monkey brain would explode."

"Good enough then. Let's keep this between the three of us for now, huh? There isn't anything we can do about it anyway."

"No, there is not," Skippy agreed. "Nagatha is right, you need to worry about the Maxolhx first."

"Yeah." My life sucked so bad that taking ten minutes to hear about a threat to the entire galaxy felt like a vacation. During that blissful ten minutes of mind-numbing revelations about the Elders, I had not thought about the Maxolhx.

"So, Joe," Skippy asked. "What *is* your plan to stop that battlegroup?"

"Working on it."

CHAPTER TWENTY FOUR

I sensed trouble when Smythe offered to help me with the coffee cups from the staff meeting. There was only one tray to carry, I didn't need help. He wanted to talk with me. "Sir, whatever we do, especially if we are to engage in a stand-up fight, we need a new ship. A better ship. A true warship. The *Flying Dutchman* has served admirably, we couldn't ask for more. But, she is worn out, and was never a proper warship."

"Getting a new ship has been on my To Do list for a while now," I replied as I stacked coffee cups in a bin to be washed. "Until recently, I was hoping it would get to the top of the list, after we got the beta site settled. With a second ship, we could dedicate the old *Dutchman*," I patted a bulkhead affectionately, "to shuttling between Earth and the beta site. While our new ship conducts recon, and defends Earth. Now?" I flipped the tray over and jammed it in the slot with more force than was needed. "We may not get the chance at all."

"Respectfully, Sir, I disagree. Whatever will do, whatever we *can* do, it will be easier with a fully-capable warship. Having that capability gives us options we don't have now."

"Ok, Ok," I considered.

"I only mention it, because Skippy is quite certain the battlegroup will not launch for another couple months. That gives us time we can use to acquire a new ship."

"It does," I agreed. I also added what he did not say, but I knew he was thinking. "We won't be doing anything else useful during that time."

"Except, it may be useful to have the full STAR team with us, to assist with whatever we must do to steal a ship."

"We need a plan first, Smythe. All right, I'll think about it. If we develop a workable plan, and we need the full STAR team to implement, we'll go pluck Giraud's team off Avalon. And I'll deal with the consequences."

Soon after I agreed with Smythe that we needed a real warship, our chief pilot came to my office with an idea for capturing another ship. "What if," Reed leaned forward across my desk with enthusiasm, making Skippy's avatar scoot over a bit. "We use our Panther as a lure? We plant it somewhere that has regular traffic, but," she reconsidered a detail of her plan, "Hmm. It needs to be somewhere we could encounter a ship traveling alone, not a formation. We send out a distress call to lure in, something like a Thuranin heavy cruiser, and we demand they take us aboard. We say we got stranded by mechanical trouble, something like that. As their patrons, we could order them to rescue us."

"Good initiative, Reed," I said, and she beamed with a smile before I stomped on her dreams. To be fair to me, I stomped rather gently, certainly more gently than Skippy had been about to do. "Unfortunately, it won't work. The Thuranin are clients of the Maxolhx, that is true, but the Thuranin *hate* their masters. If they saw a single, vulnerable dropship in deep space, they would gleefully blast it to dust and cover up the whole incident."

"Well," Skippy interjected. "They would probably first try to capture it, to analyze its technology. Plus, you know, capture the crew and torture them for information."

"Shit," Reed pushed herself away from the desk with disgust. "Remind me never to sign up for the Maxolhx coalition."

"I hear they have a great dental plan," I teased.

"The other problem with that idea is, most capital ships worth capturing travel with escort vessels, never alone," Skippy added. "Oh, and if you are thinking we could lure a Bosphuraq ship in close enough for me to take over, forget it. For me to take control of a Bosphuraq ship, I would need to be aboard, in hard contact with the ship's AI, and it would take a while for me to infiltrate their systems. As soon as we got close, their sensors would detect there are no kitties aboard our Panther. Sorry, that won't work."

"All right, Skippy," I snapped at him. "You don't have to be nasty about it. Reed is trying to think of ways to help, how about *you* do some of that?"

"I *did*, you knucklehead. We already went through this whole argument during our Black Ops mission. Remember how we all agreed it is extremely difficult to capture a warship? You had to settle for salvaging a couple derelict Kristang transport ships that had been abandoned."

Reed stood up. "I'll let the two of you argue about this, Sir?"

"Yes. Thank you, Reed. Keep thinking, and don't be afraid to bring ideas to me, or Skippy. Because right now, I got nothing."

After she left, I leaned my chair back. Something Reed had said got me cooking up an idea. "Skippy, this time we can't settle for derelict Kristang transport ships. We can't settle for a Kristang battleship either."

"What? You want a *Thuranin* battleship? Joe, the higher you go up the technology ladder, the more difficult it will be to capture such a ship."

"I don't want a Thuranin battlewagon, Skippy. We already have a Thuranin warship-"

"Not really," he objected. "Even the original version of the *Dutchman* was a space truck, not a true warship. A Thuranin capital ship is a formidable weapon."

"Formidable enough to take on a Maxolhx warship, and win?"

"Well, no, but that is a fantasy anyway."

"All right then, you just proved my point."

"You, had a point? I must have missed it."

"My point is, if capturing a powerful warship is a fantasy, we might as well be fantasizing about something useful."

"Like what?"

"Like, we need a *Maxolhx* warship. Something big, like at least a heavy cruiser."

He was so stunned, he did not speak for a second or two, an eternity in Skippy time. "O.M.G. Please tell me you are joking."

"Go big or go home, right?"

"Joe, this is going home in a *pine box*. No way will the Merry Band of Pirates survive any attempt to take over a Maxolhx warship. That is insane. You know that, right?"

"What I know is, we don't stand any chance of stopping that battlegroup, unless we have a ship of equivalent power."

"Hol-ee cow. That's it. You have finally cracked. The pressure is too much for you. There is a provision in our operating orders for Desai to take command, if she thinks you have lost it. I will notify her-"

"Belay that," I snapped. "Do *not* contact her."

"Maybe you are unclear about the purpose of that provision. If you are considered unfit for command, you can't give orders to me. Man, I don't even need to throw a 'duh' into that one. This is too easy."

"Let me ask you a question first. Did you think I was crazy for taking on a pair of Maxolhx cruisers on our last mission?"

"Um, yes, but-"

"Did you also think it was insane to break into one of the most secure places in the entire galaxy and steal a set of pixies, without the Maxolhx even knowing anything had been stolen?"

"Well, sure, but-"

"How about jumping the ship through an Elder wormhole?"

"Fine," he huffed. "Those ideas were all crazy."

"*Until* we made them work. I could go on all day if you like."

"I would not like."

"Then can we agree all *those* ideas worked, right?"

"*UGH*." He did the exasperated diva move of sagging shoulders, bent knees and rolling eyes. "I hate you *so* much right now, Joe."

"Can we agree that simply considering ideas does not make me unfit for command?"

"Oh, there are many, many reasons why you are unfit for command. But, fine, I won't lock you out of the ship's systems just yet. Let me ask *you* a question, monkeyboy. Do you have any idea, even the tiniest kernel of a notion, of how we are supposed to board and seize a Maxolhx warship?"

"Capital ship, Skippy. We need a major combatant, not some dinky little frigate."

"Oh, sure, well of course. If you're going to dream about getting a pony for your birthday, you might as well throw in a farm and barn for the pony to sleep in."

"Capital ship, Skippy. Not a pony. Got it?"

"Oh, I got it, Joe. Freakin' lunatic," he added under his breath.

Skippy either contacted Desai before I ordered him not to, or he ignored me. She came to my office an hour later. It was in the middle of her duty shift on the bridge, so she thought the situation serious enough to ask someone to take over for her. "Sir," she said as she sat down across from me. "Skippy tells me we are now trying to capture a Maxolhx battleship?" The way her eyebrow was arched, she wasn't sure whether I was insane, or Skippy was just screwing with her.

"Not trying yet, XO. Just considering the possibility. Are you here to tell me that dreaming big renders me unfit for command?"

The shocked look on her face told me that whatever Skippy said to her, he had not hinted she should replace me as captain of the ship. "No, Sir. You dreamed big about rescuing Earth from the Kristang, and I thought all that was bullshit until we did it."

"Oh. Since then?"

"We have worked well together," she began. Whatever she wanted to say, it made her uncomfortable.

"We have. Desai, I have told you before that what I value most about you as a pilot is your judgment. The same goes for your new role as executive officer. Please, speak freely."

"Sir, I am concerned you might be pursuing this, ambitious venture, as a way to delay making hard decisions about what we realistically can do out here."

I laughed and smiled at her. "How long did you think of a nice way to say 'silly dream', before you settled on 'ambitious venture'?"

"It took a while, Sir."

"I can see your point, XO. Can I assure you that trying to plan for capturing a senior-species warship is not simply a distraction for me? I know it sounds completely crazy, and if we can't think of a practical way to do it soon, I will drop the subject. But, we have done so much crazy stuff out here, we have to at least explore the possibilities, Ok? Also," I shrugged, "there is not much else we *can* do. Gateway is still blockaded, so we can't even warn Earth about what's coming."

"Before you decided to frame the Bosphuraq- That *was* a brilliant plan, Sir, despite the Maxolhx not cooperating," she assured me. "Before that, our mission was to bring people from Paradise to Avalon. May I ask why we have not returned to that mission? We can do that, while you plan for capturing another ship."

"We're not doing that, not *yet*, because that is a step we can't pull back from. Once we tell the truth to even a small group of people on Paradise, our secret will get out soon enough. Even if we don't tell them the whole truth, every star-faring species in the galaxy will know that humans are flying around in a stolen ship. Let's just say I am not giving up on stopping the Maxolhx from sending a battlegroup to Earth."

She nodded, satisfied. "Fair enough," and she pushed her chair back to stand up. "I am not ready to give up either."

"Thank you. Ah, it is very probably a silly dream anyway. Even if we magically," I snapped my fingers, "could wipe out that battlegroup after it goes through the last wormhole, the kitties will just send a bigger force when the battlegroup fails to return. No way can we explain the loss of an entire battlegroup."

"I wish I had been with you on your last mission," she said wistfully.

"Why is that?"

"Because, then it would be easier for me to believe we can accomplish the impossible."

We hashed over all the old and discarded ideas for capturing another ship, and discarded them again. Some of the ideas that might, just might, have worked for a comparatively low-tech ship would definitely not work against a Maxolhx ship. "So," I mused while tossing a ball off the ceiling of my office. "We're back to Square One. I probably don't want to hear the answer to this question, but is there a junkyard of old, broken-up Maxolhx ships we could scavenge?"

"Well, as we know from painful experience, there are Maxolhx ships in the junkyard at the Roach Motel."

"That's not an option. We barely escaped from there once. Besides, those ships are all ancient. No, I meant, is there an old battle site where we could find pieces of their ships floating around?"

"No. First, no Maxolhx warship has engaged in combat for the past seventeen hundred years. No Maxolhx warship has been substantially damaged in combat for the past *twelve* thousand years. Being a senior species means no one dares challenge you, Joe. They don't *have* to fight."

"Shit. I was afraid of that."

"Besides, any action to win a fight against the Maxolhx would be so destructive, there would be nothing much left of the ship for me to work with."

"Ok, Ok, I get it. It is a stupid idea, I'm sorry I mentioned it."

"It would have been more useful if you were sorry *before* you wasted my time, again. Damn it, Joe, we have had this same discussion several times now."

"I know, I know. If I throw myself out an airlock, will that be a good enough apology for you?"

"Hmmf," he sniffed. "It would be a good start."

Two days later, we still had no plan for taking on the Maxolhx, or for stealing one of their ships. When I went to sleep that night, I decided the next day was the time to set course back to Paradise, and begin bringing as many humans as we could to Avalon. It was time for me to make the hard decision and stop screwing around. I do not think I had delayed making that decision out of cowardice, I just had been hoping for a miracle. Apparently, I had already used up my lifetime supply of miracles.

Sometime during the night, I got up to get a drink of water, and to brush my teeth again. The lasagna we had for dinner the previous night was delicious, it was also loaded with garlic and I could still taste it.

Somehow I managed to fumble for a cup without dropping it, and filled it at the sink. After brushing my teeth again, I could still taste the garlic. Well, everyone aboard the ship would have the same issue. Even the vegetarian lasagna had been loaded with garlic. Why, I was wondering, did garlic smell so good before you eat it, and not so good afterwards?

That thought was in my mind when I turned around, and stepped on something sharp. "*Ow!*" I shouted, dropping the cup and hopping around on my good foot while trying to dig whatever was embedded in my injured foot. Whatever it was came loose and clattered on the floor, bouncing off the wall and under the little toe on my good foot. "Son of a *bitch*!"

To avoid further damage, I stood in one position and clapped my hands hard, twice. "Aziz! *Light!*" I commanded, and my cabin lights snapped on. "Skippy!"

"You bellowed, Sahib?" He teased.

"I do not bellow, Skippy. What," I pointed to the bloody thing on the floor. "It *that?*"

"Oh. It's part of a cabinet hinge. It was sticky, so I had my bots working on it."

"And they left it in the middle of the freakin' floor?"

"Well, the first bot removed it, and determined a new part was needed, so it left to go get it. The job would have been done by morning. Joe. No one expected you to go sleep-walking at zero dark thirty, you moron."

"Right, because *you* never wake me before my alarm goes off."

"Jeez, I'm sorry. You are making a big freakin' deal about it. Do you need to go to sickbay?"

"Depends," I dabbed at my bloody foot with a towel. "Is Anastacia working there?"

"Of course she is, you know that."

"Then, no."

"Nurse Anastacia does make housecalls, but if you intend to do anything nasty with her, I am turning my internal sensors off for the night. Yuck."

Taking a first aid kit out of a cabinet, I pressed a high-tech sort of Bandaid to my foot. "I'm handling it by myself, thank you very much." Picking up the bloody hinge, I dropped it in the sink where I couldn't step on it. "Crap, that was like stepping on a Lego piece. Do you have any idea what *that* feels like?"

"I do not have feet, but let me apply my detective skills. I am guessing it is painful?"

"Yes, Mister Wiseass. My sister used to play with Legos, and left them scattered all over the floor of my bedroom on purpose."

"That wasn't nice."

"It was payback for me putting her Ken doll's head on her Barbie doll," I chuckled. "I deserved it. I loved making stuff with those Legos, it was great to-"

"Joe? To what? Did you hit your head? Joe?"

Staring at the hinge, I was mesmerized. I washed it off and held it up, turning it over in my hand. "That's it, Skippy."

"What is it?"

"Legos. That's the answer."

Yes, Skippy once again thought I had lost my mind. This time, he had a better reason for worrying about me, until I explained what I was thinking. We sat up talking for hours, and I did not get back to sleep that night. Thanks to the magic of coffee, I managed not to crash before the staff meeting I called at 0800.

The senior staff was there, most of them also drinking coffee. They watched while I picked up an old coffee can, and from it, spilled Legos across the table. At my request, Skippy had the ship's fabricators make the bootleg Legos that morning.

Adams picked up some of the toys, and snapped them together. "Sir, if this is some sort of team-building thing, the STAR team already has an exercise planned for later this-"

"No team-building involved. We will not be using Legos to build a team, we will be constructing a Maxolhx warship."

"Sir?" Desai appeared to be regretting her earlier decision not to question my fitness for command. "You intend to build a senior-species warship, out of, plastic *blocks*?"

"Not exactly. We are not using Legos, that's just how I got the idea. We are going to build our own warship, out of parts from smashed warships."

"We can do that?" Smythe asked with, let's say, a healthy dose of skepticism.

"It is *possible*," Skippy replied reluctantly. "In the Roach Motel, I rebuilt the *Dutchman* from bits and pieces we found in the junkyard."

I clapped my hands happily. "Hey, that is already an improvement. Usually, we begin a mission with you declaring everything is impossible."

"*Possible* is not the same as *likely*, you dumwit."

"It is still a good omen," I insisted.

"Where are we going to find smashed warships?" Reed asked. "I thought Skippy told you there are no pieces of Maxolhx ships floating around for us to find."

"We are not going to *find* them anywhere," I said. "We are going to smash them by ourselves."

"How are we going to do that?" It was Desai's turn to be skeptical.

Smythe spoke before I could. "During our last mission, we smashed two Maxolhx cruisers. The first was vaporized, so that will not do for us. The second ship was damaged, but it remained intact. Enough to almost destroy this ship. Colonel, are you thinking we could run that trick again, but this time, we take over a second ship rather than making it explode?"

"No," I wish I had a better answer for him. "The second ship surviving last time was pure luck, we can't count on that again. Most likely, a second ship would either be so torn apart we can't salvage it, or so lightly damaged that it would swat the old *Dutchman* like a fly. We need another way to disable a Maxolhx warship. More than one ship, because whatever components are damaged on one ship, we will need to recover from another. Skippy tells me that we may need a *lot* of Legos to make one functional, bad-ass warship."

"So, how *will* we do this?" Adams leaned forward over the table, looking at me with anticipation. In her eyes, I realized, there was not just eagerness. There was pride. She was proud to be a Pirate. She was proud of me.

It was unfortunate that I was about to disappoint her. "That's the problem. I don't know."

"That's right!" Skippy announced gleefully. "Joe has wasted your time teasing you with what is only a vague, pie-in-the-sky notion, while knowing he has zero chance of making it happen. Bra-*vo*, Joe. I am *so* glad that you are captain of this ship."

"Um," I said weakly while Adams cast her eyes down at the table, avoiding me. "I am open to suggestions."

CHAPTER TWENTY FIVE

Not surprisingly, no one had an idea for how to smash multiple Maxolhx warships, in just the right way, so we could salvage them for parts to make one functional ship. Reed had summed up the problem. "Sir, to smash the multiple warships that are going to Earth, we first need a way to smash multiple warships? Or am I missing something?"

"No." When she said it like that, it just sounded stupid. No, it just made me sound as stupid as I was. The meeting ended with no solution, and me looking like a fool. The way Adams avoided me afterwards hurt.

At least I slept pretty well that night. Slept until 0430, when my agitated brain woke me up. I was worried that the whole Lego concept was a false alarm, a waste of time. Time we could not afford, time we needed for bringing humans from Paradise to Avalon.

Half an hour later, I was in the galley, looking for what I could scrounge up for an early breakfast. There were people in the galley, taking their turn preparing meals for the day, and I could have waited an hour to eat. But I was ashamed and wanted to avoid people, so I got a cup of coffee and dug one of yesterday's bagels out of a bag. Did we have any cream cheese? Yes, it was next to the bag of bagels. Now the only problem was that, somehow, the *Flying Dutchman* had the galaxy's slowest toaster. I don't think it actually performed any sort of toasting function, the bread just died of sadness as it went through. I could have done a better job toasting the bread if I stuck it under my armpit for a minute.

Anyway, for toasting bagels I skipped the toaster and put them on the griddle, that worked pretty well. A couple weeks before, I tried to slice a bagel with a knife and almost amputated a finger. One of the crew pointed to an odd contraption next to the toaster, it looked kind of like a guillotine. It was a bagel-slicer, or as I think of it, a finger saver. Setting my bagel in it, I pushed down, and the blade neatly cut through the bread with a single-

"Sir?" Someone was making a fresh pot of coffee, and apparently I had been staring at the bagel slicer for a long time. "Is everything Ok?"

"Uh, yeah." Shaking the cobwebs out of my head, I picked up my coffee cup, tucked the bagel slicer under the other arm, and walked out the door. In my office, I set the slicer on my desk and called Skippy.

"What's going on, Joe? That was rude of you," he scolded me. "Other people may want bagels this morning."

"Uh huh, I'll put it back in a minute. This," I pointed to the slicer, "is how we are going to disable Maxolhx warships."

"Wow. Just, *wow*. How about you drink that coffee, and when you're actually awake, you call me again."

"I am awake."

"Ok, then you are either stupid, which is kind of a given, really. Or you have lost your mind. Listen, numbskull, even if I somehow built a really, really *big* bagel slicer, I do not think we could persuade the Maxolhx to fly through it. Not even if we dangled catnip on the other side."

"You don't need to build a really big bagel slicer, because we already have one."

I explained.

He argued.

I argued back. After half an hour, my coffee cup was empty, and we had a plan that Skippy judged had a decent chance of working.

"I apologize, Joe," he admitted reluctantly. "That is a pretty darned clever idea."

"Will it work?"

"I can give you a *solid* 'shmaybe' about that. It depends."

"A solid 'shmaybe' is good enough for me. We should-"

"Joe, before we get started on your latest lunatic scheme, I have a suggestion for you."

"Uh, what's that?"

"Bring that bagel slicer back to the galley pronto. Gunnery Sergeant Adams wants a bagel for her breakfast, and she is cursing out whichever jackass stole the slicer."

There was silence around the conference table after I outlined my plan. It would be nice to think the silence was contemplative in nature, as people quietly processed my brilliant ideas, and their admiration for me grew.

More likely, they were trying to think of a polite way to tell me that I am a freakin' idiot.

Katie Frey looked from one face to another, I figured she was trying to judge their reactions. "Sir, your plan to acquire a senior-species warship, involves *Legos* and a *bagel slicer*?"

"Well," I forced myself to smile. "When you say it like that, it just sounds stupid."

"I do not know," Smythe looked up at the ceiling for a moment. "Whether it is sad, or encouraging, that this is actually *not* the worst plan I have heard."

"Oh." That sparked my curiosity. "Colonel Smythe, if you don't mind, what *is* the worst plan you have heard?"

"Sir, the *worst* plans were before I met you. Before you brought the *Flying Dutchman* to Earth, 22 SAS were preparing for a suicidal, futile and very likely counter-productive assault against the Kristang. Of the plans *you* have developed, the one I thought had the least chance of success was jumping a dropship through a microwormhole, into a cavern under the pixie factory on Detroit."

That surprised me. "You didn't object at the time, Smythe."

"At the time, we didn't have a better alternative, Sir. Might I remind everyone, that plan succeeded."

"Didn't you jump forward in time?" Desai asked. "That part was not planned."

"Yes," Smythe acknowledged. "That was due to the negligence of a certain dodgy beer can, not a fault of the planning."

"Hey!" Skippy objected. "It wasn't *my* fault that- Ugh. Ok, so maybe it was a tiny bit my fault, but I- Damn it! It was my fault. As much as it could be *anyone's* fault, considering that we were doing a wacky stunt that had never been done before in the history of the galaxy, using totally inadequate equipment that never should have been used for such a delicate operation. Really, it is a miracle the DeLorean managed to jump in there. Jumping back out with a fried jump navigation system was kind of the Universe throwing you a bone."

"You jackass," I interrupted his monologue. "You were all enthusiastic about the idea at the time, but you never expected us to succeed?"

"Survive, Joe. I never expected you to *survive*. Duh."

"Then why the hell-"

"Hey, it was a chance for me to try something that had never been done before. As you might have noticed, *I* remained safely aboard the *Dutchman*, while you monkeys flew off to perform circus tricks. Before you get all mad at me, please remember that at the time, you still had not a single clue how we could stop those two Maxolhx cruisers. So, I figured you were dead anyway. If you can stop being selfish for a moment, think of the amusement value for me, whether you succeeded or not. Big jerk," he added under his breath.

The only thing I could do was shake my head.

Over the course of two hours, the planning went from *this-is-crazy* to *shmaybe-this-could-happen*, although we needed a lot of hard work and some luck before we would be in the position to try it. The plan relied on Skippy, of course, and also the STAR team. Knowing Smythe would want to talk with me in the corridor after the meeting, I answered his question before he could ask. "Smythe, while we review the details of the operation, we will be taking the ship back to Avalon, to pick up the STAR team and additional pilots."

I couldn't tell whether Smythe was pleased or surprised that I was doing the sensible thing, without being prompted to by him. He nodded once, and added "Sir, we also need to practice the boarding operation. I know we can't anticipate the type of ship we will be assaulting, however-"

"That is not a major problem," Skippy announced. "The Maxolhx construct most of their larger warships to a standard template, so the interior of the habitable sections tend to be very similar. Joe, I suggest we go back to the Nubrentia system."

"Nubrentia?" After a moment of asking myself where the hell that was, I remembered that system was the site of Admiral Tashallo's famous victory over a combined Bosphuraq and Thuranin force. "Why?"

"Because that is the most convenient place where we can find large pieces of Bosphuraq warships. The birdbrains copied their basic ship designs from their patrons, so a section of Bosphuraq ship would be easiest for me to modify, to build a mockup for training to assault a Maxolhx warship."

"That would be useful, Sir," Smythe looked at me.

"Ok, we'll try it," I agreed. "But we will need to find a piece of debris small enough to take with us."

"Joe," Skippy warned, "the *Dutchman* has a limited capacity to carry other ships now. We no longer have docking platforms."

"I know that, and we'll have to work with it. We can't risk conducting assault training at Nubrentia. If the STAR team is away from the ship, we have to recover them before we can jump away if some other ship comes sniffing around. We know the Jeraptha, and probably others, are monitoring that system. We will find a chunk of ship that is the right size, and bring it with us to Avalon. There, we can conduct training without the danger of being interrupted by unwanted guests."

The Commissioner from Peru was enraged when she came to Hans Chotek's office, in one corner of a makeshift hut on Avalon. "You have worked with Bishop before," Sofia Vizcarra said quietly, although the way her fists were clenched spoke of her true emotions. "What will you do?"

Hans Chotek avoided giving an immediate response by lifting the lid off a tin of foil-wrapped chocolates, poking around with a finger, selecting one, and offering the tin to Vizcarra. She shook her head, irritated, glaring at him. That was, Chotek thought with a smile that did not show on his face, improper behavior for a career diplomat. "What will I do?" He asked slowly as he popped the chocolate into his mouth. They were speaking English because, though the four Commissioners all spoke multiple languages, English was the only language all four of them had in common. Chotek spoke passable Spanish, but in a Castilian manner that the Peruvian Vizcarra found pretentious and stilted.

He chewed the chocolate slowly, savoring it. That chocolate might be one of the last he ever enjoyed. If Avalon were truly the site of humanity's last refuge, and they were cut off from an Earth that soon might not be capable of supporting life, then no more chocolates would be coming. The supplies they had brought to Avalon included a wide variety of plants, and a scattered selection of domesticated animals, but cacao trees were not among the many items that were stuffed into the *Flying Dutchman's* cargo bays.

He would miss chocolate. Hans did not particularly have a sweet tooth, so he did not crave the candy. But it was a comfort and a reminder of home, a reminder of his childhood.

He would miss chocolate.

"I do not see that there is anything we *can* do," he finished his thought, and contemplated another chocolate.

The *Flying Dutchman* had jumped into orbit unexpectedly and overdue, although that aspect of the ship's return was not disturbing. No one on Avalon, certainly not the four Commissioners, had expected the UN to make a quick decision about whether to pursue that world as the beta site. The original excitement about the pirate ship's tardy return was not from alarm, it was caused by speculation about what the UN might have decided. Was the ship packed with colonists, eager to make Avalon their new home? Was the *Dutchman* bringing a second wave of researchers and supplies, to continue evaluating whether Avalon was a good choice for a secure human refuge? Had the ship returned to evacuate everyone from the surface and if so, was that because the *Dutchman* had located a better candidate for the beta site?

The smart money was on the second option. For the UN to declare Avalon the beta site so quickly, would be an unprecedented rapid move by a bureaucratic body that typically dealt with decisions by endless discussion. And as there was nothing in the initial survey data to indicate the planet was hazardous to human life, it was unlikely the UN had decided to pull the plug on the operation. Sending additional supplies and researchers would give the UN more data to work with, and allow the bureaucrats to delay making a decision. The last option, that the *Dutchman* had located a better world to settle on, was highly unlikely. Really, there was no reason that humans had to settle for only one refuge that was safe from hostile aliens, but there was also no rush to identify other secure worlds. It would be generations before humanity could begin building starships in sufficient quantity for moving significant numbers of people off humanity's homeworld, and many generations before humans had to worry about an alien threat.

Observers on Avalon did quickly notice what looked like broken pieces of a starship attached to the *Dutchman*. Excitement spread like wildfire, wondering where and *why* the pirate ship had acquired such an odd burden. As Colonel Bishop was not immediately forthcoming about why he had brought part of a broken alien ship to Avalon, rumors began flying. Especially after the *Dutchman* detached from its burden, leaving the debris in a stable orbit, geostationary in line of sight from the main encampment on Avalon. Bishop refused to comment until his dropship landed, and he dropped the bombshell news about why the Merry Band of Pirates had returned.

"He can't *do* this," Commissioner Vizcarra said with a dramatic vehemence that made Hans briefly wonder where the TV cameras were. Diplomats did not typically demonstrate such strong emotions, unless they were doing it to have an effect on public opinion. On the other hand, Hans considered, diplomats were not typically faced with the prospect of being stranded forever on an alien planet, while Earth was being targeted by a powerful war fleet. The emotions she was showing were very likely not for dramatic effect. Hans suspected that was true, because he was feeling those same emotions.

He had the advantage of having experienced the prospect of hostile aliens coming to Earth more than once, so he was able to keep the situation in perspective. "You mean, he *should* not do this, or he is not *authorized* to do this? Because, as he controls our only starship, and our military guard force is loyal to him, he *can* do almost anything he wants. Sofia," he held up a hand to forestall her continued argument, speaking softly because he could empathize with her anguish. "You are correct, I have served with Bishop. I served with him for more than a year, in situations I thought were equally as desperate as our current circumstances. Nothing you or I can say will have any effect on him. He does not fear consequences when he returns to Earth, because he does not expect to ever return."

"How can you trust him?" Now her anger was directed at Chotek, for having broken faith with his fellow Commissioners. "He is reckless."

"He is reckless, that is true," Hans agreed. "He is also smart, and clever, and he has what Napoleon observed is the most important characteristic in a military officer: he is *lucky*."

"We must do something. Colonel Chang might-"

"Appealing to Colonel Chang will be of no use to you," Hans distanced himself from her by saying 'you' rather than 'us'. "Chang is an outstanding officer. He is also subordinate to Bishop's command, and he agrees with Bishop's plans. For that matter, so do I. Sofia, Bishop is no dreamer, he is a realist. Yes, his plan to capture a Maxolhx warship is rash, but no more so than other operations I thought were impossible, before the Pirates accomplished the task. If he succeeds in acquiring a senior-species warship, the *Flying Dutchman* can be dedicated to bringing humans here from Paradise, where they, at least, will be safe. If he fails to capture a Maxolhx ship and the *Dutchman* is still flightworthy, then he intends to bring people from Paradise, until the *Dutchman* can no longer fly."

"Trying to capture a senior-species warship is a foolish fantasy. The boy wants a shiny new toy," Vizcarra practically spat out the words. "A dragon he can ride into battle, and slay our enemies."

"You don't know him," Chotek's tone was a bit less quiet and a bit less friendly. "Bishop is under no illusions that any ship he might capture can protect Earth by itself. But maybe, with one of their ships, he can break through the Maxolhx blockade of the Gateway wormhole, to warn Earth about the battlegroup. And possibly to bring more people from Earth to Avalon, as many as he can."

The idea that the blockade might be broken gave Vizcarra something to think about. "If Bishop is going to Earth, he should take-"

"*If* he attempts to run the blockade, he will come here first, and we can discuss who could or should, return to Earth with the Pirates."

"Then, you refuse to talk with him?"

Chotek decided to indulge himself with another chocolate. "I already *have* spoken with Bishop." He chewed the chocolate, savoring it. "And I happen to agree with him."

For me, the toughest part of returning to Avalon, was saying goodbye to the good Doctor Friedlander. "I'm sorry," I told our local rocket scientist, after informing him that he would not be coming with us. "The safest place for you is here on Avalon."

"Colonel," he looked away, his lips drawn into a thin line. "I didn't come out here to be *safe*. I came out here to make a difference."

"You are making a difference."

"A difference for my *family*," he turned toward me. There wasn't fire in his eyes, there was just a sad weariness. I knew that feeling. "The UN said that if we set up a beta site, the families of the survey teams will have priority."

"Oh." I knew that but hadn't thought much about it. That secret policy applied only to civilian members of the survey team, not the military. My family would not have priority if we had to evacuate people off our homeworld. "You figured that, if Earth is attacked, your family could be safe out here?"

"As an insurance policy," he nodded. "I've seen what's out here. No offense, but we've been lucky so far."

"I hear you. Doctor, I'm sorry about this."

"Don't be *sorry*," the fire shown in his eyes again.

"Yeah, I know. Fix the problem."

A sheepish grin flashed across his face. "I'm an engineer. Fixing problems is how I think."

"I can promise you that if we are able to run the blockade and reach Earth, I will do everything I can to bring your wife and daughters away with us."

"My daughters have families also."

"I know." That was the problem. Everyone we took to the beta site had loved ones, and those loved one had loved ones. No matter what happened, *someone* would have to be left behind. Unless we pulled everyone off the surface, which was impossible.

"I appreciate the offer, but if you are able to run the blockade, please bring me with you."

"To persuade your family to come with us?"

"That, or," he looked away again. "To be with them, if that is the end for humanity."

"I understand," I said, and that was the truth. "I'll do what I can."

"Is there anything I can do?" he asked hopefully.

Looking around at the Earth crops growing in neat lines, in fields hacked out of the giant ferns, I pondered the idea of running away from our homeworld, in ships stuffed full of desperate, frightened people. We could jam people into the *Dutchman*, plus take the *Qishan* and *Dagger* attached somehow to the creaky old *Dutchman*. Between those three ships, maybe we could squeeze in six thousand people, because we had to leave plenty of room for supplies. When we arrived at Avalon, all those people would need places to live, and food to eat. "Do what you can to get this world set up for refugees."

"At this point," he looked over at the fields where test crops were growing. Some of the plants looked healthy and some did not. "The important work is being done by the biologists."

"Think of it as cross-disciplinary training."

He shrugged. "It's best for me to keep busy anyway." He stuck out a hand, and I shook it. "Good luck, Colonel. Our prayers will be with you."

"I'm going to miss that place," Katie Frey said as she pressed her forehead to the porthole, one of the few places aboard the *Flying Dutchman* where the crew could see outside, without using cameras and displays. Portholes, even ones constructed of exotic composite material like the one she was using to look down at Avalon, were weak spots in the ship's structure and therefore the star carrier's designers had included as few of them as they thought necessary.

"You might see it again," Giraud waited patiently for the Canadian soldier's eyes to drink in her fill of the view.

"I hope not," she replied without turning her head.

"Why not?"

"Because," she pushed herself away from the view. "If I ever come back here, that likely means we can't get to Earth, our homeworld is about to be destroyed, and the only reason we're here is to dump people from Paradise in the hope we can build some semblance of civilization out of nothing."

"They could help us," Giraud observed.

"Who?"

"The people from Paradise. They are used to deprivation, to being cut off from Earth, to fearing that all other humans in the galaxy are dead or slaves of the Kristang. To the people down there we brought from Earth, being trapped on an alien planet and having to survive with the resources they brought from home, is a shock. People on Paradise have already experienced that, and thrived. For them, coming here will just be a change of scenery," he announced with a characteristic shrug.

"I wish I had your optimism, Sir."

"Optimism would be hoping we can save our homeworld."

"I'm not allowing myself to get my hopes up about that," she admitted.

"No?" He raised an eyebrow. "Then why do you work so hard, training to capture a warship from the Maxolhx, if you do not think we can save Earth? That is also an unlikely dream."

"Because," she glanced back at the green and blue world below the *Dutchman*. "We have to try. And if by some miracle this op works as planned, we can use that ship for payback."

CHAPTER TWENTY SIX

It was my day to serve in the galley, along with Adams and Reed. With such a small crew, we served a simple breakfast, sandwiches for lunch, and concentrated on preparing a nice dinner. Reed suggested shrimp and grits, partly because our supplies included plenty of shrimp, and not many people were eating grits with their breakfast. With me being from Maine, you might think I did not like grits, but you would be wrong about that. You might also think that grits are something I first ate in Basic Training, and again you would be wrong. My uncle Edgar lives in Florida during the winters, and I visited him there enough to develop a taste for grits. Real grits, not that instant stuff that tastes like wallpaper paste.

Anyway, Reed's recipe for shrimp and grits met the approval of Adams, so we went with that. The hydroponics garden was producing a nice batch of strawberries, so I suggested that I make a strawberry roll for dessert. Crew morale was understandably low, and I was hoping a special treat would pick up everyone's spirits. A special dinner would also be a nice way to welcome aboard the people we had recently and rudely pulled off the surface of Avalon.

The truth was, I needed to make a treat for the crew, because that would be a couple hours when I didn't have to think about impending doom that I couldn't do anything about.

"What," Reed asked, "is a strawberry roll?"

"You never had one?" That surprised me.

"Sir," she gave me the side-eye. "Is this like that bread in a can thing?"

Before we left Earth, Simms had loaded aboard a box of B&M brown bread in a can. Both plain and the kind with raisins, which is my favorite. "No, it is not like bread in a can." At first, I set out sliced brown bread for breakfast, when people could toast it and slather it with butter. Trust me, it is wonderful. Some people liked it, so I pushed my luck and went too far. One day for lunch, I served franks and beans with brown bread. That was a Saturday night tradition when I was growing up in New England, but apparently a bit too regional for our international crew. Those who didn't like brown bread for breakfast were not thrilled to see a disc of bread on their plate, and 'beanie-weenies' was not a popular meal with anyone. I had plenty of leftovers for my lunches that week.

"A strawberry roll is," I paused. How do I explain it? "You ever had a jelly roll?"

"Ooh," Adams made a face. "My grandmother always made a jelly roll for church suppers. I didn't like that even when I was a kid."

"It's not like that," I hurried to say before Adams got turned off to the whole idea. "The cake part is similar, you bake it thin. But instead of jelly, you put freshly-whipped cream on, with sliced strawberries. Then you roll it up, carefully. When it's in a roll, you put more cream on the outside, and fresh strawberries on top. Because of the cream, you have to keep it in the fridge until just before you serve it."

"Fresh cream, Sir?" Reed was skeptical

"Yes, Fireball. Not all cream comes from a spray can. You make it by whipping fresh cream, that's why it is called 'whipped cream'.""

"Sounds like a lot of work," Adams observed. "Have you ever actually made one of these?"

"Sure," I did not exactly lie. "I've helped my mother make them plenty of times." Technically, my part of 'helping' was to slice the strawberries, and whip the cream, but how hard could it be? "Ok, you two make the shrimp and grits, I will handle the strawberry roll."

"Should we have a backup dessert?" Adams suggested gently.

"No, we do not need a 'backup dessert'. Just watch, you will soon be eating your words."

"I hope," she said, "that I will be eating this strawberry thing."

"The issue is settled," I declared. "What are we offering for midrats?" Those were rations for people eating between midnight and 0400 ship time. "People are getting sick of dinner leftovers."

Reed asked distractedly, already focused on making preparations for her own cooking assignment "What do you suggest, Sir?"

"How about Fluffernutters?"

"Fluff?" Adams stuck her tongue out, and shared a disgusted look with Reed. "I don't think the crew like that, Sir."

I sniffed. "That's because this crew are heathen savages, Adams. It is my duty to steer them onto the path of righteousness."

Now Reed really gave me the side-eye. "The path of righteousness is paved with *Fluff?*"

"The Lord works in mysterious ways, Reed."

She giggled. "That path must be really *sticky*."

I gave her my best fake scowl. "Heathen savages, Reed, that includes you."

We did set out bread, peanut butter and Fluff for midrats, along with leftover shrimp and grits, which, by the way, was so good I asked Reed for the recipe. Despite the teasing I got, someone did eat a Fluffernutter that night.

Ok, the person who ate the Fluffernutter was me getting up to have a late-night snack. Sadly, my crew are filthy monkeys who cannot appreciate fine cuisine.

Also, the answer to 'how hard could it be make a strawberry roll' was: harder than I thought. I discarded four cakes that were too hard, too soft, or broke when I tried to roll them up. But when I got the technique perfected, they were excellent.

I noticed that Adams had *two* slices of strawberry roll.

"This is going to be very tricky, Joe," Skippy warned me as his avatar appeared on my desk.

I froze, holding the ball I had been throwing in my hand. "Yeah, you said the same thing a week ago, and yesterday, and this morning. Is this concern something special you haven't told me about, or just you getting nervous?"

"I do not get *nervous*, Joe, for I am incomparably awesome."

"So, if this is nothing we haven't already discussed over and over, why are you telling me about it again? We launch the op in three hours, this is a hell of a time to get cold feet."

"There is nothing we haven't already discussed, Joe. However, I have learned that it is important to set low expectations. That way, if a miracle happens and we are successful, I look like a genius. If everything goes to shit, I can say I told you so, and blame the whole thing on you."

"Uh huh. Did you learn this from one of those psychology books you read, to learn about dealing with monkeys?"

"Yes! Thank you for suggesting I study that empathy crap. That was worthless, but it did make me curious about the best way I could manipulate you, to get what I want."

"Did it work?"

"Not as far as you know, and that's the whole point," he answered smugly.

Stuffing the ball back in a drawer, I cradled my head in my hands and slowly counted to five. "Is that all? Because if you don't have anything to new to add, we are proceeding with the op as scheduled."

"Nothing new. However, I have already warned you this a low-percentage play, and you are determined to proceed anyway."

"Ayuh, we are. I know the first time will be a test."

"Seriously, Joe, I can't predict what will happen. There are too many variables. No one has done this before. The network has elaborate safety protocols to *prevent* this from happening. I do not know how many times we will be able to try this craziness, before the network updates its security and locks me out."

"Understood, Skippy. I would have liked to run a test before we do this for real, but I know we can't waste a shot on a dry run. You do your best, that is all I can ask."

"Really? Oh," he snorted. "This is gonna be easy, then."

"Of course, because you *are* incomparably magnificent, I expect nothing but mind-boggling awesomeness."

"*What?*" he screeched. "Damn it, did I screw myself?"

The thing that had Skippy nervous, whether he admitted it or not, was the same thing that had butterflies dancing in my stomach. Based on the dark circles under the eyes of Desai, Smythe, Giraud, Reed, Adams and pretty much everyone else aboard the ship, we were all worried about what might go wrong with an operation that was ambitious to the point of being foolhardy. If we had a better option, we would have tried something else.

I had very much wanted to try our bagel-slicer trick on the smashed piece of Bosphuraq warship we brought with us, but each test would increase the odds of the network locking Skippy out. Skippy's bots had modified the Bosphuraq hulk to be as close as possible to a target ship. We used the hulk to practice an assault approach, boarding maneuver, and moving throughout the target ship to eliminate opposition. We could not predict which type of Maxolhx ships we would be boarding, but the STAR teams knew how to approach so they avoided proximity-defense systems, how to breach the hull without getting themselves fried by a live power conduit, and how to move inside a Maxolhx warship. The pilots, STARs and equipment were trained up as best we could get them, so we proceeded to the target area. The hulk was dumped, to lighten the *Dutchman* for emergency maneuvers. Although Skippy warned if the *Dutchman* ever had a need to fly like a swallow, we were in such trouble that no amount of fancy twisting in space would save us.

Our target area was a wormhole in Thuranin territory, that was near a Kristang planet and did not get a lot of traffic. Skippy had data from the little green pinheads that indicated the wormhole was actually used by the Maxolhx more frequently than the Thuranin, because it provided a short-cut between zones the Maxolhx cared about. The reason the pinheads had extensive data on the travels of their patrons, was from the senior species sending a message that their lowly clients should get out of the way when a Maxolhx ship was transiting the area. The warnings were sort of a Notice To Airmen, except that these warnings were enforced with heavy weapons.

The wormhole we choose had the advantage that when Maxolhx ships used it, they were usually alone. The area was considered safe, being well inside Thuranin borders and far from any wormhole that linked to the Rindhalu coalition. Feeling safe, both because of the location and because of their supreme arrogance, the rotten kitties routinely sent cruisers and larger ships without escort vessels, cycling back to their home bases for crew rotation and maintenance.

The disadvantage of the chosen wormhole was that it saw only infrequent traffic, and we couldn't wait forever for the right type of ships to fly through. So, we used one of Skippy's favorite tricks to stack the deck. We flew over to a nearby wormhole that saw a heavier traffic flow, and I hung out in our stealthed Panther dropship with Skippy and four pilots. The Panther just sat motionless in space, near a wormhole emergence point. Skippy had pinged a Thuranin data relay station and learned that the Thuranin were sending a destroyer squadron through. Because the squadron was in a hurry to confront their rivals the Bosphuraq, they were taking the fastest route, and Skippy was able to predict which emergence point they were most likely to use.

Sure enough, after us being in the Panther less than six hours, a destroyer squadron jumped in, waiting for the Elder wormhole to shift to that position, on the figure-eight track it had followed for thousands of years. "Everything is ready, Joe," Skippy assured me in a voice that was bubbling with enthusiasm. "Hee hee, I just *love* being an asshole."

"Yeah, well, punish someone else with your assholeness this time, please."

"You got it. Ok, three, two, one, *showtime!*" He shouted.

On the cockpit display, we watched the event horizon of the wormhole emerge into our spacetime. It began as a pinprick, then rapidly grew to a size far greater than the width of the largest starship in existence. As always, the event horizon shimmered and fluctuated, then steadied into a stable configuration. We all held our breath as the lead destroyer maneuvered to line itself up into a precise route for transit, that minimized the risk it would contact the edge of the event horizon's ring. Lined up, it slowly gathered speed, approaching the incredible ancient wormhole that not even Skippy fully understood. Everything was normal.

Then, Skippy played his trick. The event horizon began to fluctuate, as if it had never achieved stability. The lead destroyer altered course, yawing to the right and frantically firing thrusters, but it was too late. The wormhole spasmed, sending a roiling column of white-hot twisted spacetime outward, engulfing the lone destroyer. The event horizon then collapsed to a small dot, then grew to full size again, before abruptly winking out.

"Mission accomplished, Joe!" Skippy shouted triumphantly. "That pinhead destroyer is *gone*."

"I feel just terrible about that, Skippy," I shook my head, not taking my eyes away from the cockpit displays. It was possible the violent radiation of the outburst had overwhelmed the Panther's stealth field, allowing the other three destroyers to detect us. There was no need for me to worry. The instruments indicated the radiation had only twelve percent of the power needed to compromise our stealth, and the three destroyers had already turned and burned, heading away to jump distance as quickly as they could.

"Hee hee," he laughed. "I searched for a Hallmark card that says something like 'Sorry we blew up your starship', but sadly, they don't have one."

"Well, there's a business opportunity for you, Skippy."

"*Oooh*," he gasped. "That is a *great* idea. I could-"

"No, that is a terrible idea. I was joking."

"You were joking, but it is a *genius* idea, Joe. A line of 'Sorry Not Sorry' cards is something the market truly needs. Like 'Sorry that you are a dipshit' or "Sorry that'-"

"Can you wait until we get back to Earth? Maybe we send a fruit basket, along with our condolences?"

"Sure, Joe," he chuckled. "I'll get right on that."

We waited until the three destroyers jumped, then flew out to jump distance and signaled the *Dutchman* to pick us up. The Thuranin would warn their patrons about the dangerous behavior of that wormhole, which hopefully would divert some traffic to the wormhole we wanted them to use. Damn it, nothing the Merry Band of Pirates ever did was simple or easy.

"That was outstanding, Skippy," I offered his avatar a high-five, and he slapped me as best his hologram could.

"Thank you, Joe, but we may have a problem," he answered in a low voice. "I don't know how many more times I can pull that exploding-wormhole trick, before the network locks me out from doing that. So far, I have been able to do it, by triggering the wormhole to perform sort of an unscheduled purge cycle. A purge like that expels particles that have become caught in the wormhole's matrix over time, and normally a purge occurs in a higher level of spacetime. What I have been doing is screwing with the wormhole's internal sensor readings, so it thinks there is a hazardous build-up of particles in its matrix. Eventually, the network will block me from doing that again, because running a purge in this layer of spacetime can cause stress on the matrix."

"Shit. Ok, I'll keep that in mind. Is there any way you can predict how many more purges you can run?"

"Unfortunately, no. The network has been checking its sensors, and is beginning to question whether the data about a hazardous build-up is accurate. Once it catches onto the truth, it will reset the sensors and I will be blocked from that particular trick."

"Smythe reports dropships are ready. Assault teams are in position and awaiting the 'Go' order," Desai reported from the CIC.

I flashed a thumbs up from the command chair. "Tell Smythe I wish his team 'good hunting'." More likely, the STAR team would wait for nothing, until the point when they became combat-ineffective and we needed to pull them back inside the *Dutchman* for downtime to recover. We had the entire STAR team sealed up in armored suits, sitting in dropships with the rear ramps open, in docking bays that had the big doors open to the hard vacuum of interstellar space. The dropships had their engines warmed up, and docking clamps had their safeties removed. When the *Dutchman* jumped into position, the STARs needed to move at maximum speed, with the dropships burning heavy gees to intercept and latch onto the target ship, before it could react and blow them to dust. The whole operation would require precise timing, unhesitating speed, and most importantly, snap decision making. We had practiced the assault operation using the Bosphuraq warship hulk, until Smythe, Desai, Reed and I were satisfied we had prepared as best we could, without having access to an actual Maxolhx ship.

Even elite troops could only sit and wait sealed up in suits for a limited time, before they began to lose the razor-sharp focus that was needed. The dropship pilots, wearing flightsuits but having their helmet visors open behind the pressure door of the cockpits, also would lose focus after a while. Because we had so few people aboard the ship, we had to commit the entire STAR team to the boarding operation. Four dropships would lead the assault, with two dropships in reserve to exploit opportunities as they developed, or to reinforce, if necessary, extract a team if they got into trouble. Skippy was making no assurances about the state of defenses aboard the Maxolhx ship, so we had to be ready for the worst.

My breakfast that morning had been plain oatmeal and a half cup of tea. I was so keyed-up and anxious that caffeine wasn't needed, and my stomach was already doing backflips. "Skippy, what's your assessment? Are we as ready as we can be?"

"I can't think of anything else we could do to prepare," He announced with confidence.

"Thank you."

"Of course, if there is something I forgot, then by definition I don't know about it," he mused. I heard the unspoken 'duh' in his tone. "Also, you have to consider that this operation is a troop of screeching monkeys attempting to capture a senior-species warship. So I am seriously grading on a curve here."

Gritting my teeth, I shook a fist at the speaker in the ceiling. "Once again, your words fill me with confidence."

"Really?" He was puzzled. "Maybe you didn't hear what I said., dumdum. I figure the odds of us succeeding at this lunatic scheme is-"

"Skippy," Nagatha blessedly interrupted him. "The crew do not need to know the odds you calculated."

"Well, *I* would want to know," he grumbled.

"They do *not* wish to know, and you are guessing anyway, dear," she chided him.

"Skippy," I spoke before he could go on a rant. "What are the odds of us stopping a battlegroup, if we only have the old *Dutchman* to work with?"

"Well, zero," he admitted. "Ok, the ship is in position, and I have established a handshake with the wormhole network. Estimate initial connection will be established in seventeen minutes, thirty-four seconds. That time has a plus or minus of forty-eight seconds."

"Sir?" Desai called from the CIC. "This still seems sketchy to me. If this is so easy, why haven't we used this capability before?"

"*Because*," an irritated Skippy answered. "I didn't know until recently that the network had this capability. Technically, it is not an *ability*, it is how the network functions. It's not something that can be switched on or off, so I am not asking or instructing it to do anything. *Ugh*," he sighed. "Do I need to give you monkeys a refresher course on wormhole operations?"

"Yes, please," I said before Desai could respond. None of us needed to hear him babble on about stuff our poor monkey brains could not possibly understand, but I thought hearing his voice would distract me from worrying about the potential disaster we were hopefully soon going to jump into.

"*Fine*," he was thoroughly disgusted. "I'll dumb this down as much as I can stand. As you should already know, Elder wormholes have two endpoints, the ends of this particular wormhole are separated by an average of one hundred seventy-eight lightyears. To avoid damaging the underlying fabric of local spacetime, the endpoints hop around in a figure-eight pattern. The pattern on the other end spans one point two lightyears, the pattern on this end covers a distance of point seven lightyears, for reasons that I am not going to bother explaining to you. When-"

"We *know* all this," Desai didn't appreciate being talked down to. "We have been transitioning through Elder wormholes for years. What I want is some assurance that this magical new feature, that you just recently discovered, will work the way you told us. Because you have never done this before. I also want to know, if this feature is something wormholes have always done, why you didn't know about it *before*."

"I have never, *ugh*." He verbally threw up his hands. Desai asked good questions and she was tough, Skippy couldn't weasel out of answering her. "Yes, the wormhole network always does this, and always has. I did not know because, until recently, I didn't know to ask the network if it could do that. The stupid thing doesn't volunteer information, I have to ask it a specific question."

What Skippy was referring to was a minor incident, that happened when he requested a super-duty wormhole to reopen a connection to a dormant wormhole in the Sculptor dwarf galaxy. He thought it was a minor incident, until he mentioned it to me in a casual conversation while we were waiting for the Three Stooges to approve allowing ground teams to drop onto Avalon.

When the network agreed to attempt establishing a connection to Sculptor, it informed Skippy that first it would need to establish a sort of microwormhole to investigate the condition of the other end. The network conducted that recon to determine whether the other end of the wormhole had drifted close to a star, or was in a dense asteroid field. If even one dangerous rock was in front of where the wormhole was to emerge, the network would cancel opening the full-size event horizon, and shift to an alternate endpoint.

At the time, Skippy had mentioned that network feature as a curious but unimportant aspect of reopening a wormhole to a distant galaxy, but then I asked him if wormholes always investigated the space around both endpoints before allowing the event horizons to emerge. To his astonishment, the answer was yes, a fact that got him very embarrassed. The network used sensors to scan the area around both endpoints, and Skippy could tap into that data feed. Suddenly, we could see what was on the other end of a wormhole, even before the wormhole emerged fully into local spacetime.

That nugget of information opened up a whole world of possibilities for us, and it was how we could make the bagel-slicer idea work. With the recon feature, we could know what was on the other side of a wormhole, even before it opened. If the wormhole sensors told us that a single Maxolhx warship was waiting on the other side, then Skippy would instruct the network to connect that endpoint to the endpoint on our end where we had set a trap. If there were multiple Maxolhx warships, or ships of another species, or nothing, Skippy would let the network emerge on our end at another point. To set our trap, we had selected an emergence point the network had cycled through recently, and would not open there again for months.

What if a group of ships jumped in near the other end of the wormhole *after* it opened, while it was connected to our trap? That was easy; Skippy would simply tell the network to shut the wormhole down early. Those other ships might think that was odd, but it was not so unusual that they would avoid using the wormhole.

So, suddenly, we had an ability to select which ships would go through the wormhole, and where they would emerge. The time between us receiving sensor data, and emergence of the event horizon, was only eleven seconds. We had to rely on Skippy and Nagatha to decide whether to spring our trap, or let the wormhole follow its pre-programmed circuit. We still had no ability to make Maxolhx ships use that wormhole, or predict when they would be there, or whether they came singly or in groups. That was why we had to cycle the assault teams off and on, while we waited. Hopefully, we would not have to wait too long.

Anyway, we waited three days before the first ship approached the other end of the wormhole. Fortunately, the assault team was fresh at that time, having sealed up their suits and announced they were ready less than forty minutes before. Unfortunately, the ship on the other side was just a Thuranin star carrier that was hauling five ships, so we let it go. Over the next two days there were seven other times when ships knocked on the other side of the wormhole. Skippy let the wormhole do its thing without interfering, because none of those ships were candidates for us to use. One time, we did detect the presence of Maxolhx ships, but that was ship*s*, as in more than one. A formation of three, to be precise. We let them go on their merry way. I was beginning to get discouraged when the next day, a single Maxolhx cruiser approached the wormhole. It was a prime candidate except for the timing, because the assault teams were on a downtime cycle right then. Naturally, it worked that way, because the Universe loved screwing with me. That day was the first time I saw Jeremy Smythe lose his temper. Anger and frustration broke through his usual stiff-upper-lip British reserve, and he went to the gym to beat the shit out of a punching bag. I happened to be in the gym at that time, and I pretended I didn't hear as he cursed and took out his rage on the bag.

It was good for me to know someone else was pissed off at the Universe.

CHAPTER TWENTY SEVEN

Finally, three days after that extremely frustrating incident, we found a perfect target while the assault team was ready.

"Bingo, Joe!" Skippy shouted with glee. "Another Maxolhx cruiser is knocking on the door, and it's alone. Shall I tell it nobody is home?"

"Please don't do that, Oh Most Magnificent One," I clenched one fist to get a handle on my anxiety, while using the other hand to cross my fingers for good luck. "Nagatha, you agree?"

"Oh, yes, Colonel Bishop" she answered. "This is a prime opportunity. I can't wait to see you monkeys in action again, this is truly thrilling."

"Ok, Skippy, make it so."

"Make it *so*? Joe, you are nowhere close to being smart like Captain Picard."

"Uh, how about I just say 'Engage'?"

"Ha! Captain Janeway was smarter *and* way better looking than you. But I'll throw you a bone and do it anyway. Event horizon emerging at our trap in three, two, one, *showtime!*"

On the bridge display, I saw the familiar sight of an event horizon emerging into our local spacetime. It flickered, then stabilized. "Smythe, it looks like we're doing this. Go on Skippy's signal, don't wait for me to confirm." The situation would likely be too chaotic for my slow monkey brain to keep up with events.

"Acknowledged," Smythe replied with curt efficiency.

"Ok, I am communicating with the wormhole network," Skippy announced with the smug tone he used when he did something particularly awesome. "It will be another two minutes before I have control of the wormhole to activate the bagel slicer. Plenty of time, because the target ship is still maneuvering slowly, lining up its approach."

"*Please* do not crush it into dust," I requested.

"Hey, give me a break. This is my first time. You try it and see how well *you* do, huh? Never fear, Joe, I know how to do this and- Uh oh. Um, oopsy?" Skippy gulped like a small boy who just burned down the house by setting off fireworks in the living room.

"*Oopsy*? Damn it, Skippy! What the hell did you do wrong this time?"

"I don't know yet, Joe! All I know is that somehow, that ship detected us from the far side of the wormhole. How the hell- Joe, I have no freakin' idea how that ship could know we are here. Damn it! Maybe the Maxolhx have capabilities I don't know about."

"Shit! It's getting away? Oh, this is bad." My mind raced through our options. The best thing to do would be going through the wormhole, chasing down that ship and blowing it to hell, before it could escape and warn their entire society that this wormhole was a trap. Not only would we lose the ability to use this wormhole as a bagel slicer, but the Maxolhx would also use precautions before transiting any wormhole. Yes, the best possible action was for us to destroy that ship. Unfortunately, we couldn't do that, which is why we were using a wormhole as a bagel slicer. Our only realistic option was to jump the *Dutchman* away, after we flew to a safe distance from the event horizon. "Can we-"

"No, Joe, it is *not* running away! It is coming through the wormhole at maximum thrust, coming toward us! It will be here before the *Dutchman* can get out to a safe jump distance!"

"Shit!" I fought down a wave of panic. Elder wormholes projected a damping field around their event horizons, to avoid ships creating jump wormholes that would interfere with their operation. "Pilot! Take us out to jump distance! Desai, get our-"

"Too late, Sir," Desai called from the CIC. "That ship is coming through, its weapons are hot! As soon as their sensors reset, we are in big trouble. We should- no! It has launched missiles from the other side of the wormhole!"

Helplessly, I watched the main display. A volley of five, six, no, *seven* missiles came through first, their booster drive plumes trailing fiery streaks of incandescent particles behind them. As they cleared the event horizon on our side, the missiles spread out, seeking a target. The sensors of those missiles were blind from passage through the wormhole, but that wouldn't last long. Each missile had a stealth field, which could not be engaged until the effects of spatial distortion wore off, and with their booster engines firing a stealth field would be useless. If we authorized our point-defense cannons to engage the missiles, they would pinpoint our location much sooner, but we had to kill them before they turned their boosters off and wrapped themselves in stealth fields.

The Merry Band of Pirates is a kick-ass troop of monkeys, even our current skeleton crew. Without me having to issue an order, Desai authorized the PDS cannons to engage on full-auto mode. Even from my command chair on the bridge, deep inside the *Dutchman's* forward hull, I could hear and feel the maser cannons chattering as they cycled in rapid-fire mode. Skippy had enhanced the sensors, software and processing speed of the PDS computers, but the upgrades really were not needed. With the booster drive plumes of the target missiles lighting them up like flares, our point-defense cannons were knocking missiles out of the sky almost faster than I could keep track. Within seconds, there were only two missiles left, and-

"Joe you *idiot!*" Skippy shouted. "Cease fire, cease fi- Ah, it's too late," he groaned as the last missile was exploded by our cannons. "Stupid monkeys! The Maxolhx *wanted* us to do that, they're conducting recon by fire and you fell for that trick, you idiot. When we shot back, their missiles relayed their targeting data back through the wormhole, now that ship knows exactly where we are! I could have- Oh shit, here it comes!"

On the main display, I saw the nose of the enemy ship emerge from the chaotic backscatter of the event horizon. I did not see the ship's bow in profile, I saw it straight-on. Skippy was right, it was headed straight for us. As more of the ship raced through the wormhole, I had a brief impression of a flare of light, then the *Dutchman* rocked as we were struck by a directed-energy weapon or particle beam.

I could not allow the ship to be captured, or even scanned at close-range. With my last remaining moment of life, I flipped up the cover over the self-destruct button and –

And the Maxolhx ship exploded. There was a blinding flash of light before the main display damped down the image. The wormhole's event horizon winked out, and suddenly the *Dutchman* was alone.

Then we got hit by the blast wave.

My teeth rattled as the ship rocked, yawing around as the pilots fired thrusters, trying to point the ship's nose toward the wave of high-energy particles and debris. We would take hits on the nose, but that part of the ship had the thickest armor of the forward hull, and the energy shields there overlapped so they were extra strong. There was nothing in the star carrier's nose that we couldn't replace or live without, and the pilots were following well-practiced procedures to minimize damage.

The blast wave washed over us quickly, even the biggest remaining chunks were traveling a decent percentage of lightspeed. The main bridge display flickered, changing to a schematic of the ship. "Colonel Bishop," Nagatha reported. "The ship has sustained multiple debris strikes. None of the damage appears to be critical. Forward sensors are offline, I am sending bots to survey the damage. I strongly recommend we do not jump or maneuver, until I have more complete data."

"Got it, will do. What was our radiation exposure?"

"Sections of the forward hull are hot, they were bombarded by high-energy photons. That radiation has a brief half-life, the forward hull should be safe within sixteen hours. There is no need for humans to enter that part of the ship."

She was right, the star carrier's nose was packed with equipment, there were no living quarters up there. "Understood. Pilots, stand down but remain alert. Nagatha, why isn't Skippy helping to survey the damage?"

"He is presently very busy, talking with the wormhole network about the incident."

Damn, I thought. If Skippy was too busy to speak with a monkey, the network must be overwhelming even his incredible processors. "Nagatha, what happened? Why did that ship explode? Where did the wormhole go?"

"You will have to ask Skippy," she replied. Even she was distracted. "I truly do not know. It all happened very fast, my focus was on feeding guidance data to the point-defense system."

"Hey, Joe," Skippy spoke. He sounded tired, which shouldn't be possible.

"What just happened?" I demanded.

"Joe, you just witnessed pure, unadulterated, one hundred percent Grade-A *awesomeness*, that's what." His energy level picked up as he bragged about himself.

"Yeah, I know that," I sputtered. The reason I said that was both because I had no idea how we were still alive, and because he was going to tell me he was awesome no matter what he did. "What *happened*?"

"Joe, what happened was that those rotten kitties just learned a valuable lesson."

"Like what?"

He changed his voice, to sound like John Wayne. "Never bring a starship to a wormhole fight."

"Ha! I, *ha!*" I began laughing, and couldn't stop. It was hysterical laughter. It was the laughter of relief and surprise at being alive. The pilots and people in the CIC joined me, all of us celebrating the fact that we weren't dead. When I was able to talk again, I wiped my eyes with the back of one sleeve. "Skippy, you truly are awesome beyond the ability of any meatsack to comprehend. Please forgive us for not being able to truly appreciate the full majesty of your magnificence."

"Hmmph," he sniffed. "That praise is inadequate, but I suppose it will have to do."

"I thank you for accepting my humble praise. What did you do?"

"It was easy, Joe. Although, if you want the truth," he paused, leaving me hanging.

"I do want the truth."

"You can't *handle* the truth!" He shouted in his best Jack Nicolson impression. "Oh man," he chuckled. "I've been waiting for an opportunity to do that. Ok, here's the deal. What I did was so clever of me, it approaches monkey-brain level thinking."

Holy shit, I thought. Did he just compliment humanity? Wisely, I kept my mouth shut and let him talk.

"The network was still responding to my request for control, and it wasn't going to grant me access until it was too late. So, I knew the wormhole was the only possible weapon we had available, that could possibly have a chance to stop that ship. The question was, how to get the wormhole to crush that ship? So, I thought; I need to make the wormhole see that ship as a threat to itself."

"How can a starship be dangerous to a wormhole?" That puzzled me. "You said even a nuke could not damage an Elder wormhole."

"You are correct that usually, no starship existing today should be able to threaten an Elder wormhole. However, I know something the Maxolhx don't. I know how a starship recently *broke* a wormhole. The *Flying Dutchman* ship did that. My clever idea was to fool the wormhole's sensors into thinking that Maxolhx ship was trying to jump through it, like we did. The network, of course, updated its protocols after we jumped through a wormhole, so doing that is impossible. But the network doesn't know that, I mean, it thought that was impossible the first time. I fooled the network into thinking that ship had somehow bypassed the protocols, so the wormhole smashed that ship to bits to protect itself. It reached out and crushed it, by compressing local spacetime around it. Then the ship exploded. Pretty smart, huh?"

"Holy shit, Skippy, that was pretty damned clever. I don't know if I would ever have thought of doing that."

"Really, Joe?"

"For realz, Skippy."

"Wow. Now that is worthwhile praise. Although praising me for thinking like a *monkey* is kind of a mixed blessing, you know?"

"I get that. Ok, so, what went wrong?"

"Why do you think anything went wrong?" He asked, his voice squeaky. "Certainly *I* did not do anything wrong."

"Then why does your voice sound like a four-year-old girl?"

"Damn it," he grunted. "Ok, so maybe it is possible that I forgot something. This is, heh heh, kind of funny, when you think about it."

"What the hell did you do?"

"Well, Joe, it's more like what I did *not* do. Or what I forgot to do, if you want to get technical about it."

"Get to the point, beer can."

"Ok, fine. Remember how I tapped into the wormhole's sensor data feed, to see what was on the other side? Well, heh heh, apparently in addition to telling the network to transmit the data to me, I also need to tell the damned thing to shut *off* the feed. That is not a problem before the event horizon emerges here, because until that point, the data feed is transmitted through higher dimensions not available to the Maxolhx. However, and no way could I have known this- really, I am the victim here, because the stupid network should have warned me. Man, I am going to send a *sternly*-worded letter to the network, about how it-"

"Skippy? The point, please?"

"Here's the deal. Once a wormhole is stable, the data feed begins transmitting in *local* spacetime, and the feed is two-way. It goes to *both* ends of the wormhole. Normally, the data feed goes through higher dimensions of spacetime and is essentially invisible. But, I requested the data to be fed to the *Flying Dutchman,* so the signal went through local spacetime. The Maxolhx ship picked up the feed. *That* is how the target ship knew we were here."

"Ok," I puffed out a long breath while I thought. "In the future, you can turn off the data feed, just before the wormhole emerges?"

"Um, I think so. We had better test it. Like, when we see there isn't a ship waiting on the other side, I will instruct the wormhole to open *here*, and try cutting off the data feed. Joe, I can't promise the stupid network won't do some other dumbass thing. It is not very cooperative."

"Nagatha?" I asked. "What do you think?"

"I must concur with Skippy, both on his recommendation, and his caution that the network is reluctant to allow outside control."

"How long until the ship is ready for action?"

Nagatha responded. "Unknown at this time, the bots are still assessing the damage. My best guess is the ship will be out of operation for another three days."

"Hmm," I grunted. "Nagatha, is that a real three days, or are you padding your estimate like Scotty did on Star Trek?"

"Oh, Colonel Bishop," she was scandalized, but there was a hint of amusement also. "I would never do *that.*"

CHAPTER TWENTY EIGHT

The ship was ready to fly again in twenty-nine hours, not three days. Skippy privately told me the damage wasn't as bad as he had originally feared, but I still figured Nagatha had padded her estimate. Also, I gave the order to renew the operation with some repairs still unfinished. The forward sensor array was being repaired as best we could, Skippy judged that if we got into a situation where we needed the special long-range capability of that sensor array, we could just jump away.

You know the saying 'It never rains but it pours'? Yeah, it was like that for us. While Nagatha and Skippy had their bots scurrying all over the ship to fix the critical damage, two more Maxolhx ships approached the far end of the wormhole, before we were able to take advantage of the situation. Again, the Universe just loved screwing with Joe Bishop. The good news was, after testing his ability three times, Skippy was now confident that he could cut off the wormhole's data feed before the event horizon emerged. We were as ready as we could be.

I settled my lazy butt into the command chair again. My laptop was with me, I planned to work on the official mission report while I waited.

Smythe called before I could pull up the report file. "Colonel Bishop, we are ready down here. Let's do this again, shall we?"

"Hopefully, this time the result is different," I replied with a glare at Skippy's avatar. His avatar was standing on an electrical access box next to the main display on the bridge. I insisted his avatar manifest where I could see him, so I could shake my fist at it if he screwed up again. "This could take some time, so-"

"Bingo, Joe!" Skippy shouted. "We hit the jackpot this time. There is an *Extinction*-class Maxolhx battlecruiser knocking on the other side of the wormhole, and it is alone! Ok, I have shut down the data feed. Wow, this is a primo opportunity, Joe. Battlecruisers do not usually travel without escorts."

"Pilot, get us moving," I ordered, and felt the ship shudder slightly as we began to accelerate as hard as the *Dutchman*'s battered structure could take. "Smythe," I said softly, forcing myself to speak in a calm and confident manner. Inside, I was shaking and praying 'Please God, don't let me screw up and get everyone killed'. "You heard that?"

"Affirmative. Standing by for Skippy's 'Go' signal."

The battlecruiser came through the wormhole at a normal, safe and slow speed, since it had not detected the *Flying Dutchman*. The word 'slow' has a different meaning in space combat, because the target ship was moving at a quarter meter per second relative to the event horizon. By the time the enemy ship's nose appeared, the *Dutchman* was moving in the same direction at about two-thirds that speed, paralleling the course of our target. On the display, I saw the nose, then middle section of the battlecruiser emerge through the event horizon. Before my mouth could open to scream for Skippy to do his thing, he activated the bagel slicer. The event horizon slammed closed, shrinking from maximum diameter to nanoscale in the blink of an eye. The forward three-quarters of the battlecruiser was tumbling through empty space in front of us, while the aft section of that ship was a hundred and seventy lightyears away. The enemy ship was cut in two pieces as neatly as if a laser scalpel had done the work. The *Dutchman* shuddered again as the ready dropships launched, and my part of the operation was over. The bagel slicer had done its job, now it was up to the assault team to exploit our brief opportunity, or die trying.

United States Marine Corps Gunnery Sergeant Margaret Adams had braced herself when she heard Skippy's announcement of a juicy target coming through the wormhole. 'Brace' was not the correct term, because what she actually did was relax most of her muscles, resting her helmet back against the Falcon's seat. The muscles she did tense were those of her stomach and thighs, to prevent blood pooling in her lower legs from hard acceleration. Unlike the Kristang Dragon type of dropships, the advanced Thuranin Falcons had a limited ability to protect the occupants from the effect of acceleration. The lead teams were aboard Falcons, with the reserve force following in slower-moving Dragons.

She knew the 'Go' order had been given even before she heard the words, because her legs, forearms and neck tingled. Nanomachines floating in her blood had just constricted her blood vessels, further helping to prevent blood from being trapped away from her vital organs and brain. She barely heard 'Go' in her helmet speakers before the Falcon rocketed away from the docking bay. There were two Falcons in each bay, facing toward the target so the assault dropships did not need to waste time maneuvering other than racing toward the enemy ship, then slowing to match course and speed.

Even with the compensating field generated by her seat, she felt a force seven times that of Earth's gravity as the Falcon's main engines surged at full military thrust, augmented by the seldom-used and noisy booster motors. Blood pounded in her ears, muffling the grunts of the pilots over the common channel.

"Shit," one of the pilots gasped. "Target is spinning." She paused to take a breath. "This will get rough."

That had been one of the chief concerns in planning the mission; that the bagel slicer would leave the target ship spinning unpredictably. There was a limit to the amount of spin the Falcons could adjust for in their attempt to latch onto the battlecruiser. Above the limit, the pilots would have to wait for the spin to stabilize, then approach the axis at the center. The worst situation would be for the target to be tumbling around more than one axis. Skippy thought the automated emergency systems of a Maxolhx warship would reduce the amount of spinning and tumbling that the assault force would need to deal with. The beer can admitted his guesswork was all theory, until they went into action.

Adams clamped her teeth together as the Falcon went ever so briefly into zero gravity, then the acceleration came back on even harder after the craft flipped around. Her stomach was fairly empty as she had eaten a quick-digesting, low-residue meal, so if she did ralph she wouldn't foul the inside of her helmet faceplate. Tasting bile and wondering how the hell her stomach had the strength to send anything up to her mouth, she renewed her determination not to puke, not to be the only one who lost her breakfast on the mission.

That determination was severely tested as the Falcon flipped on its side, then slewed sickeningly to the left.

In that Falcon's cockpit, Fireball Reed struggled to breathe evenly. The outer edges of her vision were already tinged with red as the heavy gees starved her optic nerves of oxygen. From practice, she knew to focus on the vital cluster of instruments directly in front of her, instruments placed there in a dense display so she could still maintain situational awareness if she suffered tunnel vision. With the red filling an ever-increasing part of her visual field, tunnel-vision was becoming more likely.

As the lead pilot of the Merry Band of Pirates, Major Reed had expected Bishop to insist she remain aboard the *Flying Dutchman* during the assault operation. Instead, he wanted her flying the lead bird, the one carrying Smythe, Adams and two of their five functional combots. If the assault failed, he explained, the *Dutchman* could jump away with the press of a button, something even Bishop could handle. The crucial role in the assault was the actions of the dropships, and that is where he needed Reed. Bishop had also insisted that Desai temporarily relinquish her role as XO so she could fly one of the other Falcons, a decision the Indian Air Force Lieutenant Colonel had agreed with.

Sami Reed had been prepared to argue with the Pirate commander, so she was thrilled when he acted like assigning her to a Falcon was his idea. Maybe it *had* been his idea. Whatever. All she knew at that moment was that the target ship was spinning near the limit of her Falcon's ability to compensate, and she had only ten, possibly twelve seconds to latch on, before she would need to veer away so the ship behind her could try its luck.

Some small part of her mind reprimanded her for signing up to be a Pirate, the same part of her mind that had tried to warn her before she acquired her unfortunate callsign. From that day, she could not smell cinnamon without feeling faintly queasy.

She had no breath to spare for talking and her copilot knew that Sami had command of the spacecraft. Without speaking, the Japanese man seated to her right was expertly pinpointing a point where they could latch on, a location chosen by Skippy even before the Falcon had shot out of the docking bay like a shell from a cannon. Sami knew her copilot had to be suffering from the same vision-restricting effects of deceleration, yet he had not lost focus.

The cockpit display was becoming fuzzy, so her flightsuit automatically switched to the head-up projection on the inside of her helmet, showing her only the information she needed. The ship's automated systems had taken over all systems other than guidance. The Falcon had launched with landing skids extended, one less thing she needed to worry about.

She had an impression of some kind of turret whizzing past on the right, before she leaned the control stick over and activated thrusters to line up with a relatively smooth area of the battlecruiser's hull. In her visor, the area was outlined in yellow as the prime target for boarding, because it was adjacent to a large airlock. There was a sharp, shuddering bang as the skids hit, lost contact as they bounced over something with a screeching sound, and latched on then broke away. As the craft slid across the hull of the alien battlecruiser, there was a hard thump and it rolled to the left as the righthand skid lost its grip.

There was a sudden eerie silence, with only the faint whine of the righthand skid's clamping mechanism engaging. "We're down!" She spat in a weak voice. "Smythe-"

"Moving," the STAR leader grunted as the straps released him.

Margaret Adams was second to last out the rear ramp of the Falcon. Technically, she was the last *person*, because the last being to leave the Falcon was a Thuranin combot under her control.

"Ready, Gunny?" Petty Officer Second Class Pete Gonzalez asked, without looking back. He focused his attention on the busted-open airlock in front of him, and not on the starfield that dizzingly swept past as the target's hull spun end over end again and again and again-

He forced himself not to think about the spinning. The sliced-open hull was not only spinning nose over cut-off tail, it was also wobbling side to side and intermittently jerked in one direction or another as power relays blew or thrusters tried to fire or simply because air was venting from shattered compartments. An especially violent movement occurred just as Gonzalez stepped off the Falcon's back ramp on to the enemy hull, making him glad for the training that had made him secure one boot to a hard surface before lifting the other foot. If not for the grip of that one boot, he would have gone flying off into space and needed his armored suit's limited flying ability to bring him back into the fight.

"Behind you," Adams replied tersely. "Take lead," she added without needing to, because having the petty officer in the lead was the plan. They needed to move and move fast, to cripple the enemy's ability to fight back, ability to regain control over the ship, ability to even understand the situation and who had dared to attack a senior-species warship. To prevent the enemy from taking control of the ship, the assault teams needed to cut data connections in any fifteen of nineteen precisely-defined locations around the interior, plus jack Skippy's remote presence into any five of fourteen possible access points. There were more than fourteen possible access points, but the mission planning had determined that the designated fourteen points were the only ones the teams could get to before the enemy reacted and crushed the attackers.

Adams and Gonzalez had a combot with them for two reasons. Their assigned targets inside the hull were deeper inside the ship and therefore more difficult and time-consuming to approach. The enemy would have more time to determine what was happening and set up defenses, therefore the two of them were more likely to encounter organized and determined opposition. That explained why a precious, heavily-armed-and-armored combot was assigned to that objective. Margaret Adams had been assigned to operate a combot because she had extensive experience with the deadly machines.

The other reason she had been assigned a combot was because before the operation, Colonel Joseph Bishop had a tense argument with the STAR team commander. No, Adams was not to get special treatment. Yes, she was a professional and knew the risks. She was getting a hulking armored alien killing machine, and a Navy SEALS operator to watch her back, because those were the Goddamned *orders* from the mission commander and if *Lieutenant* Colonel Smythe did not like that, he could sit this one out.

Thus, Gunnery Sergeant Adams had a SEALS petty officer scouting the way, and a combot with software upgraded and monitored by an asshole AI. Because, even if the mission commander was unable to admit it, Skippy the freakin' Magnificent had no problem stating that Margaret Adams *was* special.

With Gonzalez in the lead, Adams guided the combot into the darkened ship. With her suit's computer controlling the grip of her boots, kneepads, elbows and gloves, she moved swiftly along in the zero-gravity environment, guided by the synthetic vision of her visor. The path to the objective was outlined clearly, even if the actual scene in front of her was a chaos of flash-frozen atmosphere, shattered objects drifting in the corridors and occasional reflected light of explosions. She had four comms channels open. The private channel for herself and Gonzalez, who was moving smoothly and quickly in front of her, expertly scouting intersections and signaling it was clear to proceed. The assault team command channel so Smythe, Giraud and Kapoor could issue orders. The channel to the *Flying Dutchman*, which would only be used in an emergency so dire that the mission was an utter failure. And a channel that was a feed from Skippy, who monitored the overall battle for the three assault team leaders. From that last channel, Adams knew not all was well with the assault. Giraud's team had run into trouble almost immediately and were on the defensive, unable to reach their objectives. They were now focused on keeping the enemy from interfering with the teams of Smythe and Kapoor, while they approached their individual objectives. Giraud had already suffered two dead, and two others were no longer combat-effective. Yet, a small part of Adams's mind was proud that no one had panicked, no one had broken discipline. She had not heard anyone call for reinforcements or covering fire, and the background layer of her visor display showed that nine of the required fifteen data connections had been cut, plus Skippy's remote presence was already jacked into two access points. That was all good news. The bad news was that with Giraud's team unable to make progress, the remaining objectives were almost all mandatory, or the entire mission would be a failure.

Another small part of her mind, a part she was able to ignore because of self-discipline and training, reminded her that she was aboard a senior-species warship, fighting an impossibly advanced enemy on their own turf. If she had panicked, she would certainly have a damned good reason to, for lowly humans had no business attacking the apex predators in the galaxy.

She did not listen to that panicked part of her mind. Another part of her mind told her that she had several advantages. Surprise, for the Maxolhx had been caught totally off-guard. The enemy would be equipped with environment suits that deployed automatically, but not combat armor. Battlecruisers typically did not carry a complement of ground-assault troops, and the armory where heavy combat suits and weapons were stored, was in the aft part of the ship that was over a hundred lightyears away. Most of the enemy would not have time or opportunity to acquire light weapons from lockers scattered around the ship. Many of the enemy were dead, injured or in shock from the sudden attack. They had no way to communicate beyond line of sight, so the opposition was individuals or small, isolated groups. And the enemy's access to their ship AI had been abruptly cut off. The Maxolhx who were still capable of fighting had no idea who had attacked their ship, so their imaginations must be running wild. Only someone with advanced technology would dare assault a senior-species capital ship, so the surviving crew must be facing an enemy with capabilities far beyond their own. The Pirates, who were in Kristang armor, hoped that fear of the unknown would cause the Maxolhx to make bad decisions.

Unfortunately, the Pirates had little realtime intel about the enemy. Skippy was still struggling to prevent the ship's AI from restoring control, so he had no access to internal sensors other than those of the armor suits worn by the assault team. The Pirates therefore had no idea what was around the next bend in a corridor, until they got there.

They also had no idea what was *behind* them.

"Contact!" Gonzalez whispered. Keeping his voice low was a habit from SEALS training but it was not necessary in that situation. He was encased in a hardshell armored suit with excellent sound insulation. The corridor was exposed to hard vacuum. And he shot off a rocket and a burst of armor-piercing rounds at the same time he spoke. In space, no one can hear you whisper, and they can't hear bullets either.

But they sure as hell could see the fireballs of explosions and feel the deck shudder beneath their boots. It took less than a second to let fly a rocket and send two three-round bursts at the vague outline of the target, the second burst was squeezed off while he was dodging violently to the right to clear the field of fire. With his peripheral vision, he had a brief glance of *something* coming at him from the front, then the bulkhead beside him erupted and flung him backwards.

As he windmilled his arms, he slapped a palm on some surface, it may have been the deck. The suit secured the glove to the surface and jerked him to a halt. Indicators were flashing yellow and orange in his visor, showing minor damage to his suit that the reservoirs of nanomachines were repairing as best they could. He was still combat-effective.

So was Adams and the combot.

So why the hell wasn't she shooting back at the enemy?

"Gunny-"

"Booby trap," she hissed to him. "Some kind of IED you triggered," she explained, and highlighted a view forward in his visor. "The target you shot at was already dead," she added, and the image she sent rolled back, to show the headless body of a Maxolhx floating in the corridor, right before he tore the corpse apart with a rocket.

"IED? Then-"

Before Gonzalez could finish the thought, Adams already had the combot rotating to face to the rear. She was turning also, and her instincts served her almost well enough. Just after the combot detected a target and cut loose with its autocannon, something tore into the killing machine and a piece broke off to slam hard into Gonzalez. Adams had a split-second image of her companion's suit going offline before the combot was torn apart and she was knocked sideways to crack her helmet into a bulkhead.

Her suit was flashing orange warnings, with the most ominous message being 'SENSOR RESET'. Without sensors, she was blind, and it felt like her brain was rebooting from being smashed into a wall. A shaky eyeclick made the faceplate go clear, and she was able to rely on the old Mark One eyeball sensor.

Beside her, the combot was in pieces, sparks arcing outward. The machine was moving only in a jerky, uncoordinated fashion and was no longer linked to her suit. Effectively, it was dead, no longer an asset to her.

What else? Something else was torn apart; a Maxolhx who had been cut in half by the combot's autocannon before the machine ceased functioning.

And a second Maxolhx, clad in a matte-gray environment suit. It had been holding some type of hand weapon, which was now on the deck, out of reach. Cursing to herself and shaking her head to clear her fuzzy vision, she raised her rifle and-

It was not responding. Why- The barrel and casing were *cracked*.

"You can't use that weapon, primitive," the haughty senior-species warrior said with a voice that gurgled from blood seeping into its mouth. With its good arm, it reached behind its back for another weapon.

"Watch this, motherfucker." Adams flipped her useless rifle around so she was holding the barrel. Her suit, sensing the adrenaline surging into her blood, automatically went to full power-assist mode, just below the level at which she would risk injuring herself.

She threw herself forward at the shocked enemy, driving the rifle butt into its helmet with maximum force. Alarms screamed in her ears and flashed red in her vision as the suit protested, but it did exactly what she ordered. The rifle's stock cracked on the first blow, from being struck by a force beyond its design limits. She gripped the barrel tighter, trusting her suit's computer to understand she did not want to snap the alien weapon in half. A split-second after her first blow landed, the rifle again slammed full-force into the Maxolhx warrior's super-tough helmet. And that helmet cracked under the kinetic hammering.

Shit, Adams thought with a flash of panic. As her arms drove forward again, the enemy dodged to her right at amazing speed, too fast for her reflexes to follow. She would have missed except she had an ace in the hole: Skippy the Magnificent. That smug asshole beer can had stripped out the original software of the Kristang armored suit she wore, and enhanced its processing speed and capacity so it was almost a submind. The suit she was assigned to was *hers*, not only because it was fitted to her athletic form. Assisted by Skippy, the suit's onboard computer had learned how Adams moved and fought during extensive training exercises, and it anticipated her intentions. Without her conscious input, the suit changed the trajectory of its arms to follow the enemy's helmet. Not only follow but *lead*, so the smashed stock of the rifle arrived where the target helmet was. The suit computer assessed the situation, including factors such as the overall tactical situation of the assault team, the estimated level of force the rifle could take before it became uselessly small pieces, the condition of the enemy combatant, and the fact that Margaret freakin' Adams was not going to stop until her opponent was dead, no matter the cost to herself.

The suit computer calculated those factors, engaged in a very brief conversation with one of Skippy's lesser subminds, and came to a conclusion of 'I gotta get this shit over with *right fucking NOW*'. Thus, it took control of the nanomotors and the arms reared back then forward with blinding speed, with the remainder of the rifle aimed at a hairline crack in the enemy's helmet. The rifle's barrel punched through the helmet's faceplate and drove straight through the face, skull and brain of the vastly superior enemy, before it mushroomed against the rear inside of the helmet.

The suit's gloves released the shattered pieces that were left of her rifle, and Adams slumped away, drifting backward to thump against the opposite wall in the zero gravity. Her suit's sensors had now reset, and only a few yellow icons indicated faults with the suit. "Gonzalez?" She asked automatically.

"Still here," the petty officer croaked. "My suit is busted. Both legs are inoperable. Right shoulder can't move. Shit. I can hold a rifle with my left-"

"You stay here," she ordered, aware that time was slipping away, and time was on the enemy's side. She needed to get to their objective, right *now*.

Gonzalez might have argued, but he was a professional. "Take my rifle," he offered.

"Keep it, and cover my six." She walked over to the combot, her boots clicking as they kept her clinging to the deck. Bending down over the combot, she inspected the autocannon. The arm it was attached to was shattered, but the autocannon appeared intact. Pressing a status button showed green. "Suit, command the combot to release the autocannon."

"That is not advisable. But," the suit sighed, "since I know you are going to do it anyway, the autocannon system is now under control of this suit. The icons are in the lower lefthand corner of your visor."

Part of Margaret's brain wondered when the hell her suit had acquired a personality so it could sigh, while the rest of her attention was taken up by accessing the jury-rigged control system. "Right, got it." She pulled the cannon free and hefted it. In zero gravity, it had no weight but it still had *mass*, and it was awkward to handle. "Suit, you can compensate for the recoil of this elephant gun?"

"Not completely. Please, *please*, avoid hazardous situations."

"I am a Marine," she said as she eyeclicked to deactivate the elephant gun's safeties. "Hazardous situations is what we do. Gonzalez?"

"Covering your six," he coughed up blood, "Gunny. No bad guys are getting past me," he said as he used his one good arm to drag himself behind the skimpy cover of the broken Thuranin combat machine.

Adams pulled herself forward with one arm, cradling the autocannon with the other. It was awkward and she kept getting off balance, forcing her to kick off the bulkheads with her feet. This is stupid, she told herself after the fourth time she ended up spinning in the middle of a corridor. She could not control the elephant gun with one arm, and every time she kicked the wall, overhead or deck, there was a *thump* she could feel. She had been flying along the corridor for speed, and to avoid her boots clomping along the deck and alerting the enemy. Because moving with the bulky cannon was so awkward, she was slow and bumping into the bulkheads anyway.

Tossing the autocannon gently in front of her, she flipped head over heels and extended her legs until her boots contacted the deck and adhered securely. Pulling the spinning cannon to her, she got both hands wrapped around it, and set off up the corridor at a steady run, moving faster as she built up momentum.

In front of her, the corridor bent to the left, with another corridor coming in from the right, just in view. Should she rely on surprise if an enemy was around the corner?

No. The vibration of her boots had surely given away her presence, to anyone who was conscious. She slowed, shifting the elephant gun to her left arm, and pulled a pair of grenades off her belt. In the zero gravity, it took little effort to toss them down the two corridors. The one to the right flew straight, the other bounced off a wall to the left and out of view.

She saw and felt the explosions, feeling it odd that no sound accompanied the violence. "Ok, Maggie," she whispered to herself. The diagram on her suit showed that one of her two objectives was just around to the right, a data connection that had to be cut. The final objective was to the left, a dismaying distance deeper inside the ship. Smythe had not ordered her to cease fire, so she had to keep going. Her own data connection was spotty, cutting in and out. What she was sure of was the others were still fighting.

It was not good to be alone. While planning the mission, Smythe had considered fewer, larger teams that could provide better support. In the end, with objectives so widely scattered inside the alien ship and speed crucial, the SAS man had decided to divide up his force into teams of two. That, in Skippy's opinion, gave the humans their best chance to reach the required number of objectives before the enemy could react and stop them.

The option also gave the humans the worst odds of survival.

After shrapnel from the grenades *pinged* off her suit, she ran forward. Making the sharp turn to the right would be tricky, she opted to aim for a spot on the left side of the righthand corridor, and thumped into it with an armored shoulder. Straightening herself out before she crashed into the opposite wall, she strode forward, picking up speed-

And stumbled to a halt. Her visor was outlining the data connection objective, overlaying it with a grid like Luke Skywalker saw when targeting the exhaust port of the Death Star. "Got you," she muttered, dropping to one knee and bringing the autocannon to bear, selecting single-round shots and fragmentation mode. Using the rounds in armor-piercing mode might send the rounds to punch clean holes all the way through the ship without damaging the target.

The first round knocked her backward and she recovered, seeing she had missed. Bracing the cannon against a frame that stuck out into the corridor, she sent one, two, three rounds to blow ragged holes in the target. After the third round, the outline in her visor switched to blue, indicating that data connection was no longer an objective. "One more. Once more into the breach," she said, annoyed with herself for talking to no one.

The last objective, where she could jack Skippy's presence into an access point, was behind her, down the other corridor. Knowing her suit was trying to inform the team that she had taken out the data connection, she swung the big cannon around, its barrel smacking into the bulkhead, throwing her off balance. Annoyed with herself again, she got the elephant gun balanced properly and-

The cannon exploded, jerking out of her hands. Something impacted her back and the visor blinked out, her suit power cut off. A single red light blinked in the lower left corner of her vision, informing her that backup power was being restored.

Too late. Laying prone against the deck, no, it was a bulkhead, she felt vibrations as someone approached.

A Maxolhx stood staring at her, an oddly bulbous-looking pistol in one hand. The creature tilted its head, looking in obvious surprise at her face inside the clear faceplate. Whatever the Maxolhx expected, *humans* had not been on the list.

She was dead, she knew it. Moving to throw a grenade would be too slow, the alien would shoot her first. But her right arm was already behind her back, and a turn of her wrist brought the activation button of a grenade under that thumb. "Adios, asshole," she groaned as she press-

"No!" She was startled as Skippy's voice pounded into her ears. "Margaret don't! I got-"

"Been nice knowing you, Skippy," she felt for the button again, and her thumb-

Jerked away as the pistol held by the Maxolhx exploded in a shower of sparks and plasma, tearing that being's arm away and shredding its torso.

When she was able to speak again, spots were still swimming in her vision, she took a sip of water from the helmet's reservoir. Her suit was operating on backup power and working to restore as much function as it could. "Skippy," she asked. "What the hell was that?"

"I had control of the ship. It happened about, oh, twelve seconds before you blew up that data connection."

"So, I didn't need to do that?" She shuddered in the suit. She had put her life at risk for nothing.

"You did. In fact, it would be great if you could go jack me into that access point. The ship's AI is still fighting me, and I want to remove its ability to contact subsidiary systems. Don't worry. I now have full sensor access of the interior, and there are only two Maxolhx alive right now. Giraud is engaging them now, they are no threat to you."

"Gonzalez?"

"He will be fine," Skippy assured her.

"This was a tough fight, Skippy. With the weapons the Maxolhx have, these Kristang suits can only take one hit."

"It's worse than that. The kitties only had access to hand weapons like pistols, and they were in standard shipboard environment suits. This could have been a *very* bloody fight."

"Was it?"

"Uh, I had better let Smythe tell his team about that. I am about to go through the wormhole, so we will lose contact briefly. Good! Oh, sorry, I was excited because Giraud's team just took out the last two kitties. Gotta go- Uh, are you Ok, Margaret?"

"I'm fine, Skippy. Fine. Do what you gotta do."

CHAPTER TWENTY NINE

After Skippy declared, with a *solid* shmaybe, that we had control of the battlecruiser, I ordered him to recon the other side of the wormhole, the side where the aft end of the target ship should be. The aft quarter of the ship we had sliced apart contained all the important engineering components we needed to make the ship useful; power-generation, normal-space engines and the jump drive. The bagel slicer had left the two parts of the ship separated by a hundred and seventy-eight lightyears, now that the forward section of the ship was under our control we needed to get the other part. If we could.

We had wounded people aboard the forward section of the target ship, and I hated the idea of leaving them, but that was the mission.

Because the wormhole was open at other endpoints right then, we had to wait for it to shut down on its normal schedule, then Skippy instructed it to do its recon thing. "I'm not seeing anything, Joe," the disappointment was evident in his voice. He wanted to be the hero by locating the other part of the target ship, and he couldn't. "It may have drifted out of range by now."

He did not mention the other possibility; that the engineering section of that ship had exploded. "Ok, when can we go through, to check it?"

"Give me a minute to get a status. Oh, nuts. There are a pair of Thuranin ships waiting to go through at another location. If the wormhole doesn't open on schedule, they will alert everyone this wormhole is acting strangely."

"How long until it is scheduled to shut down again?"

"It will remain open at that location for eighteen minutes. Joe, by that time, the backup systems aboard the aft section of the ship will surely have established control. It will be a very tough fight to capture the-"

"Yeah, I know. Shit. All right, we wait. Nagatha, tell Smythe that he's on his own over there, we won't have time to take a dropship aboard before the wormhole opens for us."

We waited. My alter-ego No Patience Man was about to explode. If I wanted, I could have looked at data from the assault team's suits and seen the status of each person. That would tell me who we had lost, who was injured and how serious each case was.

I *did* want to do that.

I did *not* do that, because as the commander, my job was to focus on the big picture, the overall mission, and not get distracted by details. Details, like playing favorites by worrying about one person. I could not do that, no matter how much I wanted to.

Everyone else aboard the ship had something useful to do, while I sat in the command chair, feeling useless. To take my mind off worrying about anything and everything, I wanted to take out my tablet and play a game, even solitaire. But that would be disrespectful to the crew, and Skippy would gleefully rat me out in a heartbeat.

Finally, Skippy took temporary control of the wormhole again and reconnected it to where the battlecruiser had come through. Again, the sensors of the wormhole did not detect any hazards on the other side, they did not detect *anything* on the other side. To be safe, we sent a remote-controlled Dragon through ahead of us, in case somebody was out there looking to shoot at whoever sliced a ship apart. The Dragon's crappy Kristang sensors, even upgraded by Skippy, did not see anything, so I ordered the *Dutchman* to go through.

And, damn it, soon after our sensors recovered from the spatial distortion of transitioning through the wormhole, we detected debris. There wasn't a lot of it, and the tiny pieces we saw were in a sphere that was expanding away from us in all directions.

It was quiet aboard the ship, then Skippy spoke for all of us. "Well, shit."

"It's gone?"

"Looks that way, yeah. Sorry."

I wasted no time. "Pilot, take us back through the wormhole and rendezvous with the target, I want to take the wounded aboard immediately."

She acknowledged my orders and the pilots responded by pulling the ship into a tight turn, but I knew we first had to cancel our forward momentum before we could head back to the wormhole. In the meantime, people could be dying from lack of medical care. Our pursuit of the target's aft end had been for nothing, and had consumed valuable time.

"Skippy, what happened?" I asked, being careful not to be angry with him.

"My guess is, their jump drive capacitors overloaded. Damn it! I was *so* careful about exactly where I sliced that ship apart. Far enough forward to not cut through reactors or missile magazines or banks of capacitors, but far enough back that the forward section lost power and sent the control AI into shock. It was very precise work, Joe. Apparently, I misjudged it somehow. Plus, heh heh, um-"

"Heh heh what?" That time, I did care if he knew I was angry.

"Well, I might have over-estimated my level of control over the wormhole. They have multiple safety features to prevent the event horizons from collapsing while a ship is going through, which makes sense. When I ordered the wormhole to close, it resisted me. It took me six tries before I found the right combination of codes, to override the safeties. During that delay, the target ship was moving forward, so the bagel slicer cut into it farther back than I intended."

"Oh, crap. Now we have the forward part of a ship that doesn't have any power supply or propulsion."

"Pretty much, yeah."

I crossed my fingers and hoped for good luck. "Are you going to tell me this is a bad news-good news thing?"

"Ah, meh," he spat with disgust. "It's a bad news-*maybe* good news thing, Joe. I now know how to bypass those safety features, so next time I might be more precise. The reason I say 'maybe' is, I don't know whether the wormhole network is reinforcing those safety features, or whether it might lock me out from using that feature."

"Crap."

"There is some good news," he suggested. "After examining the battlecruiser we captured, I am now confident that I can slice the next ship farther forward."

"Fantastic, except, you said it is rare for battlecruisers to travel without escorts," I snapped at him. I was pissed that we had lost people, for nothing. A ship without power generation or propulsion was no use to us, and we had a limited number of times we could roll the dice on the bagel slicer, before the network locked Skippy out. "The next ship might have a different sweet spot, and you won't know that until it approaches the wormhole and you have a couple seconds to scan it. That is not-"

"Joe, before you work up a truly inspiring rant, allow me to educate you about a few facts you do not know. First, a couple of seconds is *plenty* of time for me to scan a ship, evaluate it and determine exactly where to slice it apart. Second, Maxolhx warships have a common layout of their internal structures, from frigates up to battleships. The basic design is scalable, so once I know the vulnerable spot of one ship, it applies to all of them. Third, and *damn* it is hard to resist the urge to call you a numbskull, I do have news that is unquestionably good. From the captured ship's database, I determined that the next Maxolhx ship coming through this wormhole is indeed another *Extinction*-class battlecruiser. It will arrive, alone, within eighty-one hours."

"Oh. That is good news, Skippy. I'm, uh, sorry for doubting you."

"Hmmph. You doubted me *becaaaause*?"

"Because I did not trust the awesomeness. Ok, don't keep me guessing. How did we get so lucky to have two battlecruisers fall into our lap?"

"It's simple, Joe. The Maxolhx dispersed their fleet to punish the Bosphuraq for the outrageous thing that *we* did," he chuckled. "Now they are pulling their major combatants back to concentrate their forces, in case the Rindhalu get adventurous. The ships are not traveling with escorts, because the lesser ships are needed to watch the Bosphuraq, and because the Maxolhx want to show they fear nothing. After the second battlecruiser, there will be a pair of heavy cruisers that might be traveling together, then a heavy cruiser traveling on its own. That is all the data I got from that ship."

"Five ships, hmm? That sounds like a target-rich environment," I rubbed my hands together, realizing I looked like an over-the-top villain in a James Bond movie.

"Don't get your hopes up, Joe," he warned me.

"I won't." Checking the display assured me the wormhole was still open behind us, and that the *Dutchman* was lining up to go through. We needed to recover the assault team, and see exactly what we had.

The answer was that we had three people dead, three more seriously wounded, and nine others whose injuries would keep them out of the next operation, unless Doctor Skippy could work some real magic with his nanomedicine.

Three dead. For what? All we had was the forward hull of an advanced battlecruiser, a hull segment that was nearly useless without its power source. Smythe, Giraud and Kapoor assured me the operation had been a success, we had suffered lighter losses than they had been prepared for. They also reminded me that the fight wasn't over yet, we had other opportunities to capture the components we needed to make our battlecruiser hull a supremely powerful weapon. It was my job to see that we completed the mission successfully, and the people we lost had not given their lives for nothing.

Smythe was the last person off our newly-captured battlecruiser. I was nervous about leaving the hulk drifting on its own, but Skippy assured me he had severed the control AI's connections to anything vital, and the submind he had installed had the resident AI locked down. We needed the STAR team to capture another ship, so I really didn't have a choice. After bringing the assault teams back aboard, I wanted to rush down to the converted cargo holds where they stored their gear, but I forced myself to concentrate on my own task. I had not participated in the boarding action. If I went down to the STAR team section of the ship right then, I would be an outsider. A cheerleader. The team needed time by themselves, time to be with people who had been through the experience together, people who understood how they felt.

So, I sat in my command chair, and did nothing.

Margaret Adams needed the help of Captain Frey to get her armored suit off, both of them working carefully together, to avoid damaging the tough yet vulnerable flesh and bones under the alien suit. Compared to Adams, Frey's own suit was in good condition, but the Canadian soldier grimaced when she walked. "You Ok, Captain?" Adams looked down as Frey limped gingerly across the deck, carrying a segment of armored suit.

"Think I tore a muscle in my calf," the other woman answered, lifting her right leg.

Adams looked at Frey's right leg armor. There were scars, but not any holes or dents, no obvious reason for an injury. The captain's suit torso, on the other hand, had deep scratches and dents, gouges deep enough that the nano liquid had flowed into a gap to prevent air from venting. With the torso resting on a rack and waiting repairs, Frey's chest and left shoulder had angry purple bruises, visible where the skin was not covered by her undershirt. "You got hit pretty hard," Adams pointed to the battered suit torso segment.

"This?" Frey looked at her battered armor. "No, that was just a ricochet. If I got *hit*, I'd be dead. This," she lifted her right leg and had to steady herself against a locker. "Happened after we came back aboard the *Dutchman*. First step I took in gravity, I felt a pop in my calf. It's embarrassing, I wasn't *doing* anything."

"Your armor was damaged. The motors may not have been working properly," Adams suggested.

Frey tried to laugh, but grimaced instead. Her left shoulder hung limply, she couldn't move it. The damage was not just soreness, she knew she had torn something important, and it would take time to heal. Until then, she would be out of action. "I like that story, I'll go with that one. You can get the rest of your armor stowed, Gunnery Sergeant?"

"Squared away, Ma'am," Adams said, and Frey limped away to assist someone else.

Adams stowed the last piece of her armor, tracing a finger along the scorched soot and something darker that coated the left side. The dark material might be Gonzalez's blood. She closed her eyes, praying silently for the badly injured sailor. Remembering that terrifying moment, she looked up. "Skippy, I-" She stopped to look around at the other STAR team operators, all engaged in removing and caring for their suits. "Hey, did anyone else discover their suit computer has developed a personality?"

"Yes," Giraud grunted as he removed his helmet. "It was a surprise to me."

"Hey," Skippy chuckled. "You are welcome."

"I was not praising you, beer can," Giraud winced as he tried to reach back with his right arm, to release the seal so he could remove the suit's torso. Sharp pain in that shoulder prevented him from raising that arm high enough to reach the seal. With his suit's left arm inoperable, he needed help. Seeing Giraud in pain, Frey hung up her helmet and "It was an *unpleasant* surprise."

"Ugh, are you complaining about the suit's French accent? I assure you-"

"Skippy," Adams bit her lower lip, to give her time to hold back the angry comment she wanted to say. "That is not the point. We train the way we fight. If we're going to interact with a suit personality in combat, we need that personality to function in training also."

"Hmm," Skippy sniffed. "From what I have observed, the way you monkeys fight is to quickly adapt to unpredictable situations."

"Yes," she said through clenched teeth as several of her STARs teammates pantomimed choking the beer can. "We *know* we will encounter something unexpected on every mission. Because of that, we don't want anything unpredictable that we can control."

"Ok, but the enhancement I loaded into your suits was sort of a last-minute thing for me. It did help you, right?"

Adams looked at Giraud and Frey, too appalled to speak.

"*Merde*," the French paratrooper gasped. "You sent us into combat with an untested system?"

"It wasn't *untested*, Rene," Skippy backpedaled, understanding he was in trouble. "I ran over six hundred thousand simulations before-"

"It was not tested by *us*," Giraud insisted. "Your simulations have proven to be incomplete before."

"Ok, but, um," he sputtered, on the defensive in a situation when he thought he would be praised for his initiative. "It did help, right?"

Adams sighed, reminding herself that they were dealing with a clueless alien AI. "Skippy, we don't *know* whether our suits having a personality is good or not. We won't know, until we test that capability in training. I found it distracting for my suit to be talking with me. That might only be that I didn't expect it. The point is, you sprung this on us without the team testing it. That can't happen. Do you understand that?"

"Yes," he replied quietly, in the voice of a small boy who is asked if he understands why he shouldn't be allowed to drive the car. "I won't do that again.

Um, well, I really can't promise that. I make updates to ship systems constantly, and your suits learn every time you use them. What I can do is promise to review any major upgrades with you before I load them, Ok?"

Giraud shook his head slowly. "Skippy," he grunted as Frey helped him pull the dented armor away from his left arm. "We know you mean well, most of the time. But, you are not a biological being as we are. You do not appreciate our limits. Colonel Smythe *must* approve any significant change to the equipment we rely on."

"Ok," Skippy replied in a whisper. "I'm sorry."

In her cabin, Adams grimaced while trying to get her T-shirt off. The suit moving its arms under the command of the computer had saved her life. That action had also left her with very sore muscles, because her actual arms had not anticipated the sudden movements of the powered limbs, motions that were faster than her muscles could accomplish or compensate for. Luckily, she did not feel anything grinding in her shoulders, wrists or elbows as she carefully flexed each arm. Getting her shirt off by herself required hooking it on a cabinet handle, and wriggling it upward until she could get it over her head. As she slid the sweat-stained garment off, she reconsidered whether she might have torn a muscle; her right bicep felt like it was on fire. A trip to sickbay would be a wise precaution, when people who had been more seriously injured had been treated. Like the rest of the ship, the medical facilities had become worn out and lacked critical supplies. When the *Flying Dutchman* had been captured, the Thuranin medical facility had miraculous abilities. After Skippy modified the surgical gear and adapted the nanomachines to human biology, the Pirates had been able to heal seemingly fatal wounds and even regrow shattered limbs. Now the supply of nanomeds was depleted by healing past injuries, and also because Skippy had been forced to repurpose those precious nanomachines to keep the ship flying. Sacrificing medical capability for combat readiness had been a tough call by Colonel Bishop, and Adams had agreed. That did not mean she didn't wish for high-tech magic to relieve her aches and pains.

"Margaret?" Skippy's voice called out quietly from the speaker in the ceiling. He knew not to use his hologram in her cabin. "Can I talk with you for a minute?"

"I really want to get in the shower and scrub this grime off," she groaned. Her knees hurt also, and her left hip was so stiff she had to limp.

"This will only take a moment, I promise."

"Ok," she leaned against the shower wall, not wanting to sit down because that meant she would have to stand up again. "Go ahead."

"I just wanted to thank you for not yelling at me about the suit personality thing. I know it took a lot of effort not to chew me out in front of the crew. It was stupid of me to keep the suit upgrade a secret, it won't happen again. The, um, the worst part is *why* I did it."

"Don't beat yourself up too much about it, Skippy," she reached out for the shower controls, expecting that was the end of the conversation. There was no point to the AI beating himself up, she was sure Bishop and Smythe would be doing plenty of shouting at him. "I know you were only trying to help."

"Ugh. Listen, ordinarily, I would let you think that, because it makes me look good. But, big stupidhead Joe made me read about *empathy*," he said the word with disgust. "And now I have to consider other people's feelings. What a pain. In. The. *Ass*. So, I don't want to lie to you. Margaret, the truth is, I concealed that upgrade because, um, this is embarrassing. I did it because I wanted to be praised by the crew."

"*Excuse* me?" She put her hands on her hips, and instantly realized that was the exact same gesture her grandmother used, when someone said something particularly stupid. "You want *praise* from us?"

"Why not? This crew are the only people I know! This group of monkeys are the only way I *can* get the praise I crave. I don't interact with anyone else! Well, when we go to Earth, I chat or message with billions of people, but they all think I'm an asshole."

"Skippy, they don't know you like I do."

"Oh, why, thank you, Margaret, that is-"

"I think you're an asshole, too. That's because I know you really well."

"Um-"

"Skippy, I know you didn't think you were risking our lives, so I'll give you a pass on that, *this* time. But, you took a risk because of your *feelings*?"

"I know, I know, that makes me an asshole."

"No," she shook her head, though she knew he couldn't see her. "It makes you human."

"It does?"

"Computers don't do stupid things because of their feelings. *People* do it all the time. Being human, being an adult, being professional, means learning not to let your emotions control you. That is one lesson the military tries very hard to beat into your head, because they know it is the *most* difficult thing to learn. You have to keep your emotion in check, especially in situations when your emotions are charged up. When we were in Nigeria, I saw a Marine in my unit get blown up by an IED, and everyone in our platoon wanted to light up the whole fucking village. Some of the locals were cursing us, and children were throwing rocks, while we had a man bleeding out in the street. That was supposed to be a *friendly* village, the local tribe were allies. We were there to get their water system flowing again, and they booby-trapped one of the pumps. There was an asshole teenager, just a kid, bounced a rock off my helmet. I turned around," as she spoke, her hands unconsciously mimed carrying a rifle. "I wanted to blow him to hell. He looked at me, shouting whatever the fuck in Yoruba, daring me to shoot. He knew I wasn't supposed to engage, but, damn, I *wanted* to make his smug face shut up. We all did. The reason we didn't, was because we had learned discipline, to control our emotions. Having emotions like that means you are becoming more human, Skippy."

"Is that a *good* thing?"

"You have to judge whether it is good or not. It will make it easier for you to interact with us, and understand us."

"Oh great," he moaned. "I'm turning into a monkey, and I'm supposed to be *happy* about it?"

"Are you happier with yourself now, or would you like to go back to the way you were, when you were buried in the dirt on Paradise?"

He sighed. "I'm happier now, I guess."

"Outstanding. Can I get in the shower now?"

"Huh? Oh, yes, sorry. Margaret, thank you for talking with me. I'm more confused now than I was before, but thanks anyway."

CHAPTER THIRTY

Smythe came into my office, he gave me a curt nod and I acknowledged him by gesturing for him to take a seat. This was our first opportunity to speak since he came back to the ship. "Congratulations, Smythe, you did it. The performance of your team was outstanding. We have a Maxolhx warship. A *battlecruiser*."

"Yes, Sir," he said in a dismissive manner. I was not offended, because he was not being rude. He had business to discuss, and neither of us had time for idle chit-chat. There would be plenty of time for celebration when the mission was complete. "Begging your pardon, but praise may be premature. We have the forward three-quarters of a battlecruiser, without the fiddly bits that make it go."

"True enough. We know how to do it now, the next time should be easier," I said with a smile that I hoped projected confidence. What I had just declared was utter bullshit, and he knew it. The next time was going to be *more* difficult, not less.

He arched an eyebrow. "If there *is* a next time. Skippy told me he is unsure how many times he can use your bagel slicer," his lips curled upward in the ghost of a smile, "trick again. He expects the network will block his access to that feature at some point, it may already have done so. He also told me that he had no way of knowing whether the network will refuse to cooperate in the future."

"Yeah," I leaned back in my chair. Originally, Skippy had thought the network would give him a scolding about abusing his authority in an action that had the potential to damage an ancient Elder wormhole. We would then know that he couldn't use that trick again. Now, he feared the situation was much worse. The network was not communicating with him, other than to respond to direct inquiries. We might have a situation where a target ship was coming through the wormhole, and the network right then decided to refuse Skippy's command to close the event horizon. That would be a disaster; the *Flying Dutchman* would be practically on top of a fully-capable senior-species warship. We could not even jump away, because we had to keep the ship close to the wormhole, so the assault teams had only a short exposure while they flew across the gap between ships.

Not knowing whether the network would accept Skippy's bagel-slicer command again was a major, major problem that we had no way of solving. Every time we used the bagel-slicer, we increased the risk of the network cutting off his access to that feature. We had to fly blind, or cancel the operation. "I don't know that we have any other option than to continue."

"There is one other option, Sir," he reminded me. A muscle in his jaw twitched as he spoke. He didn't like the idea any better than I did. The difference is, if I ordered him to proceed with a bad idea, his duty would be to make it happen.

"No, there is not. We discussed this. Hell, Smythe, *you* told me that plan is bollocks."

"I did, at the time," he agreed. What he meant was, in planning the assault op, I had asked whether we could keep the *Dutchman* at a safe distance from the wormhole, while the assault teams waited in stealthed dropships closer to the event horizon. If disaster struck, the cluster of dropships could be self-destructed by a pair of our tactical nukes, and the *Dutchman* could jump away. That alternative plan had been my idea, and even I hated it. Smythe, and Giraud and others, had pointed out to me that the assault teams needed the close-support of the *Dutchman*'s maser cannons, to suppress fire from the target. From a distance of even a half lightsecond away, the time lag could render our fire support ineffective. More importantly, Skippy needed to be close to the target ship, so he could scan and create a model of the enemy ship's control AI. Half a lightsecond did not sound very far, but it was over ninety thousand freakin' miles. That was too far away for Skippy to have confidence about performing his patented awesomeness, so that idea was out. "Since then," Smythe continued, "I have thought about that option again. We could take Skippy with us in the dropships, to-"

"Hey!" The avatar appeared instantly. "You monkeys go do all the crazy shit, I plan on staying right here where it is safe and warm."

"We can't risk Skippy being captured," I added.

"There is no risk of capture," Smythe noted. "The nukes will turn our dropships into subatomic particles, and hopefully cripple the enemy ship, but Skippy will not be damaged." He peered at the avatar, his eyes narrowing. "Is that correct?"

"Yeah. I am not looking forward to being in a nuclear barbeque, but it won't damage me. I *will* go flying off into space."

"Yes, and when the time is safe, you can signal the *Dutchman* to retrieve you."

"For what?' I asked. "If you trigger the nukes, we will lose the entire STAR team and our best dropships. We won't be able to do anything other than fly around, until the *Dutchman* wears out."

"You have other dropships," Smythe casually picked an imaginary piece of lint off his uniform. "Including the dropships aboard the target ship we already secured. As we discussed, there is the possibility of recruiting military personnel from Paradise, to replace our losses of soldiers and pilots."

I puffed out my cheeks. "That is a *very* last resort. Even if we could get qualified people, it would take *months* to bring them up to speed. We are committing the entire STAR team to this op, there wouldn't be anyone left aboard to train recruits."

"There are the seriously wounded people, Sir," he observed, looking at me closely to gauge my reaction. "They will recover. They have knowledge and experience, and they will be remaining aboard the ship."

"I don't see that as an option. By the time we retrieved Skippy, recruited a new assault team and trained them up, the Maxolhx would have learned they have one or more warships missing. They would start assigning escorts to all ships, and we'd be screwed."

"That only makes the mission more difficult, not impossible," he flashed another tight smile, knowing that the Merry Band of Pirates had accomplished many impossible things. "The alternative is unthinkable. We can't give up."

"Oh, hell, Smythe," I ran a hand through my hair. "You really are planning for the apocalypse, aren't you?"

"You *have* designated this mission as 'Operation Armageddon'," he gave me that raised eyebrow again. "We must consider the worst case."

Shit. He was right about that. If we couldn't stop a Maxolhx battlegroup from reaching Earth, it would be Armageddon for our home planet. You know what was the worst part about the prospect of our world and everyone we loved there being burnt to a radioactive cinder, and knowing it was my fault? The worst part was, I had to keep fighting anyway. We all did. If we lost Earth, we had to fall back to Avalon and do what we could to ensure the survival of our species. That was our duty, damn it. "I hear you. We're not doing it. The only reason you would trigger the nukes is if the network refuses to do the bagel-slicer thing again. Once we lose the bagel-slicer, we are dead in the water, no matter whether we can replace our losses or not."

"That is not true, Sir," he chided me.

"It's not?" That made me pause. "You know something I don't?"

"I know that, as long as you have your inventive imagination and Skippy, there is always the possibility of success."

"Smythe," I rubbed hands down my face. "I'm under enough pressure already. My imagination barely got us *here*," I jabbed a finger on the desk. "My clever-ideas tank is empty now. I appreciate the wisdom of keeping the *Dutchman* out of harm's way, so we can fight again."

"Not just to *fight* again, Sir. If there truly is no way to stop the Maxolhx battlegroup, you have already defined our fallback plan; to bring as many people as you can from Paradise to Avalon."

Shit. Was he right? "This is a judgment call," I said, mostly to myself. By risking the *Dutchman*, I had all our chips on the table. If our only starship were lost, humanity would be staring at nothing but a vacant expanse of felt on the table, out of options. "My gut tells me it *feels* wrong," I finally said, after a pause that had become awkwardly long. "No. We continue with the op as planned." With my hands, I pretended I had a stack of poker chips, and pushed them to the center of the desk. "We are all-in," I announced.

"Very well, Sir," he said with an expression I could not read. That reminded me never to play poker against Jeremy Smythe. "Then, there is another matter we should discuss."

"Which is?" I groaned.

"Skippy informed me that our supply of medical nanomachines is sufficient for either healing the seriously wounded, *or*, for bringing the less badly injured people back to full combat readiness."

"Shit," that time I said the curse word aloud. "Let me guess; you want to put the hard cases on hold. Damn it, all three of them have lost limbs. One of them may still *die* if we can't repair his internal injuries. I have to tell them that is too bad, because we need the meds to fix someone else's sprained ankle?"

"Just so, Sir." Again, I could not read his blank expression.

"Damn it. I know this is my call, but-"

"No, Sir. All three of the people in the sickbay are refusing further medical treatment, until the assault team is combat ready. They have already made the call."

"What?" My head jerked back. "Because you pressured them to do that?"

"No, because they are professionals and they are committed to the mission."

I opened my mouth, closed it, and thought hard. No matter how nicely Smythe said it, our three seriously wounded soldiers were under pressure to give the precious meds to the more able-bodied operators. They knew what their fellow STARs thought. That was unfair.

Crap. *Life* is unfair. Smythe was right. Because I had decided to continue the mission, I had to deal with the consequences. We were down three operators, making the condition of the remaining team even more critical. I had to give the people who were putting boots on the deck the best chance they had, and the way to do that was to give them miracle nanomeds to bring their bodies back up to full combat readiness. "Tell me something, Smythe. Do you ever get tired of being right?"

"I don't expect so, considering the alternative. Being wrong gets people killed."

"Sometimes, I really hate this job. Skippy, there are medicines aboard the ship we captured, right? Can we use them?"

"The Maxolhx have extremely sophisticated medical technology, that is true. However, modifying their equipment for human physiology will take weeks, at least."

"You can't just," I flipped a hand, "rewrite the software?"

"No, Joe," his avatar shook its head. "Most of Maxolhx technology utilizes *firmware*, the instruction sets are resident in the physical layer. It is complicated. Please believe that I am already making my best effort to adapt their technology so we can use and control it. The process is more difficult and intricate than I anticipated. Unless you wish to delay the mission possibly for a month, nanomeds will not be available."

"That's no good," I pounded a fist on the desk. "The Maxolhx will be alerted that their ships are disappearing by then. We have to go *now*. All right, I will go talk with the people in sickbay."

"That is not necessary, Sir," Smythe announced gently.

"Yes it is," I insisted. "It's *my* decision to deny them the meds they need, they deserve to hear it from me directly." I was not certain whether I was making the right decisions, but there was one thing I was absolutely certain about.

I did not deserve the honor of commanding this crew.

Walking into the galley, I saw Adams standing with her back to me. Not trusting myself at that moment, I ducked back into the passageway and took several breaths to put on my official US Army Colonel persona. During the boarding operation, Adams had been in serious trouble, and I was still dealing with putting her life in danger. If she saw that I was treating her differently because, well, because she is Margaret Adams, she would not be happy with me. I needed to be professional, and show her the same level of concern I felt about anyone in the crew.

Except I was *not* feeling that way at all.

"Adams," I said as I walked back into the galley. She had just set her tray down at a table and was pulling out a chair.

"Yes, Sir. I used your," she pantomimed holding a rifle, then flipping it around backwards. "Signature move on him."

"My move?" I asked, then understanding clicked in my slow brain. "Oh. Using a rifle as a club?"

She grinned but the gesture faded immediately from her face. Adams was the only person with me when I used a rifle to beat a Kristang guard to a bloody mess, years ago when we escaped from jail on Paradise. That was not a fond memory for either of us, and she had recently done basically the same thing to a Maxolhx warrior.

I lowered my voice. "You Ok, Gunny?"

"Squared away. It was, intense. I'm sore," she rolled her shoulders stiffly. "That's all."

"Have you been to sickbay?"

"Doctor Skippy did what he could for me," she nodded, her eyes glancing to the food on her tray.

I took the hint. My purpose for coming to the galley had been to get lunch, but it would be awkward eating with her a few tables away, and there were already other people seated at her table. Plus, I had just come from speaking with the wounded in sickbay, and I didn't have much of an appetite. Instead, I pour a glass of iced tea, took it to my office, and tried to find something useful to do.

It would have been nice to wait until the STAR team was fully recovered, before we took on the task of trying to capture another ship, but we didn't have a choice. That second battlecruiser was coming, and we had to be ready for it. No way could we risk letting that juicy warship go, and the crew knew it. Boarding and capturing the first ship had been a tough fight, very tough, and the crew was mentally prepared for another desperate struggle that devolved into hand-to-hand combat. Skippy thought this second boarding operation would be easier, because he had learned a lot from examining the first ship.

So, we got the STAR team patched up as best, and they waited for the 'Go' order as before. I hated to send Adams back into combat. This second time would be worse, I feared, because she was already banged up. She would also be going in as infantry, because there weren't enough combots left. With the injuries to her left shoulder and arm, she was not confident she could properly control a combot, so she insisted someone else act as combot operator, while she spotted for and defended that person.

CHAPTER THIRTY ONE

Fortune either smiled at us, or was eager to see us die quickly, depending on how you looked at it. Two hours after the STAR team got buttoned up in the suits, sitting in dropships that were ready for immediate launch, Skippy announced he had detected an *Extinction*-class battlecruiser, traveling by itself, approaching the wormhole.

This time, instead us positioning the *Dutchman* behind the event horizon, we placed the ship in front of where the wormhole would emerge, and we were flying toward it at four thousand kilometers an hour. Skippy warned us the timing would be tricky, as if that were anything new to the Merry Band of Pirates.

Right on schedule, a battlecruiser came through the wormhole, this time without any warning that we were waiting on the other side. Skippy used the wormhole to slice through the enemy ship, and on the displays we saw a forward hull section that was slightly smaller than the one we had captured, spinning end over end. "Ha!" Skippy shouted. "I sliced that sucker exactly where I wanted! Damn, I should be cutting diamonds."

"Screw that," I felt like choking him. In the CIC, the crew was firing weapons to knock out the enemy ship's defenses, so it couldn't interfere with us. "If you don't get that damned wormhole open and stable fast, this is going to be a real short trip!"

"Yeah, yeah," he grumbled, no doubt peeved that we didn't have time to fawn over his latest accomplishment. "I'm on it."

While the *Dutchman*'s maser cannons were knocking out defensive systems of the ship we had sliced through, we were still in substantial danger. The aft part of the enemy's hull, the engineering section that contained the stuff we needed to make a ship go and fight, was on the other side of a wormhole that was shut down. Skippy was working to get the wormhole open again, and the timing was critical. We were moving four thousand kilometers per hour, toward a target that didn't exist yet. It was possible the wormhole network would lock Skippy out, or delay responding to his commands. Any delay might be fatal, because plunging through a wormhole before the event horizons were stable was a sure-fire recipe for turning our ship into a short-lived cloud of exotic particles.

On the main display, I saw the pinpoint of a wormhole emerge, then it rapidly expanded. "Got it!" Skippy announced with smug satisfaction. "And you doubted me, Joe. Shame on you," he scolded. "Um, oopsy."

"*Oopsy?*"

"Er, the wormhole is stabilizing a lot slower than normal, probably because of-"

"Reed!" I roared. "Full reverse!"

"On it," she said tightly without looking back at me, and I felt the ship shudder as the reactionless normal-space engines strained. The old *Dutchman* had a lot less mass than her original star carrier configuration, but she was never a sports car. Reed had been maneuvering the ship already to line up with the slightly unpredictable location of the wormhole, all she had to do was flick a thumb to throw the engines into full reverse.

We were still moving too fast.

"When will the damn thing be stable enough to-"

My question was cut off by a warning from Reed. "Sir, we can't slow down or turn hard enough to miss it. We are either going in, or getting sliced up by the edge."

"Keep us lined up with the center," I ordered. At least if we were destroyed by a chaotic wormhole, we wouldn't leave any evidence behind. "Skippy?"

"All I can say is, it's going to be close. I *think* we're good?" He added with a squeal that did not fill me with confidence. "I can't tell because the stupid wormhole isn't talking to me!"

The main display gave me a jarring glimpse of something gray in the blackness of interstellar space, as we flashed past the ship Skippy had just sliced apart. I got a brief impression of a light flare as the *Dutchman*'s maser cannon struck some undefended target on the enemy's hull, then the display focused on the still-flickering disc of the wormhole dead ahead of us. A stable wormhole glows rather than flickering, but this one was still twisting spacetime to lock down its connection.

Just before the *Flying Dutchman* plunged into the event horizon, moving more than a kilometer every second, we launched two missiles from our stern tubes, to fly backwards along our path. The last glimpse we got of them, before the wormhole swallowed us, showed those missiles running hot, straight and normal.

We all silently wished them the best of luck.

And said a prayer for ourselves.

For years, Thelma and Louise had rested in secure racks, in a cargo bay aboard the *Flying Dutchman*, doing absolutely nothing, other than slowly decaying over their half-lives of eighty-eight years. Their lives were dull, dull, *dull*, with the only highlight being when their hated companion Mister Nukey was taken away on secret missions by the humans. Nukey disappeared for varying lengths of time, only to return without comment. No matter how strongly the other tactical nuclear weapons begged, cajoled or outright demanded, that big jerk Nukey had refused to disclose any details of his incredible adventures. Maddeningly, all he did was hint that his adventures were, in fact, incredible beyond the imaginations of his companions. He insisted that he could not say any more, due to the highly classified nature of said incredible adventures, and he hoped they all understood. The smirk on his casing was unbearable.

Thus, the other nuclear devices were left to stew in their jealous anger, grumbling amongst each other and gleefully imagining horrible fates for Nukey. Their only pleasure was giggling about imagined humiliations for that traitorous, privileged jerk. Why was he so special, they asked each other. Was his plutonium more potent, more pure than theirs? No! They all came from the same reactor, the same processing facility. So, why had they been relegated to sitting uselessly, while Nukey went on joyous adventures across the galaxy?

Nukey had not explained. Until one day, when he hinted that the issue was not him being special, it was more than the others were, well, he hated to say it. *Inadequate*, was the nicest way to say it.

Thelma, Louise and the other nuclear weapons could not have hated anyone with more passion, after the day Nukey smugly hinted they were somehow deficient.

When Mister Nukey went away for what was apparently the final time, he had been rather quickly followed by two other warheads who had formal names, but were called Beavis and Butthead by the other devices. Those two misfit morons, who were totally undeserving of the opportunity, thumbed their noses and jeered at the others as they were carted away, never to be heard from again.

Thelma, Louise and the remaining seven other devices had filed a protest under the Nuclear Device Equal Opportunity Act, which was, sadly, ignored. Of the three replacement devices who came aboard at Earth, two joined the lawsuit, while Fred, of course, said that well, you know, we'll have to see about that, and there was no reason to be hasty about it.

The other nine warheads were sure that, if it ever came time for Fred to blow something up, he would be a dud just like his personality.

Thelma and Louise were at first suspicious, then thrilled beyond belief, when humans came into the cargo bay and lifted the two warheads with slings, to place them on a sturdy cart. The humans had bypassed Fred, who was on the top rack closest to the door where Nukey used to rest, and that blew the theory that asshole had been selected for missions purely for convenience.

Louise was super excited, and Thelma had to caution that their first excursion out of the cargo bay could be nothing more than a routine inspection. If that were true, and they were returned to their racks in the cargo bay, both of them would have suffered fatal equipment breakdowns due to broken hearts.

First Thelma, then Louise, were loaded into the nosecones of old but serviceable Thuranin hyper-velocity missiles, while they held their breath and did not dare hope. This could all just be a test, Thelma warned, while Louise quivered with excitement. You just wait, Thelma moaned, we will be taken back to our dull cargo bay soon enough.

Thelma held her composure even as the missile's powercells were energized, when umbilical cables were retracted, when guidance control was transferred to the missile's tiny brain, even when the outer door of the launch tube was opened. It is all just a test, a tease, she told herself, while inside, her trigger mechanism was heating up. Don't fall for this trick, she told herself, refusing to allow the cruel humans to tease her. She trembled with anticipation even while feeling sorry for Louise, who was bound to be crushed by disappointment. Thelma prepared for her own hopes to be crushed, right up to the moment when the missile launch tube's railgun mechanism slammed the missile out at over three thousand gees of acceleration.

"*Yeehaaaaaaaa!*" Thelma exulted in unison with Louise. Both warheads were jostled by nauseating twists and turns as the missiles turned to line up on their targets, then bored in at full military thrust. With enemy defenses down, there was no need for the usual infuriating delays while the missiles jinked wildly to avoid particle cannons. No, these two missiles flew hot, straight and normal, and they flew side by side, nearly close enough to touch. To maximize the explosive effect of the warheads, they would detonate simultaneously within meters of each other.

The target in front of them was a formidable Maxolhx battlecruiser- Or, it *had* been a battlecruiser and had been formidable. Now it appeared to be drifting dead in space. The sensors of the missiles reported that main power was off inside the ship, but backup systems were slowly coming back online, which could be dangerous.

Oh, Thelma assured her missile's brain with a soft laugh, don't you worry. We will take care of *that* nonsense right quick.

As the missiles plunged over a severed sponson and fell toward the center of the hull, they extended magnetic fields to lock each other together as they raced toward their destiny.

Their last "*Whoohooooo*" was cut off by the joyous fire of fusing tritium, and nuclear fireballs consumed the unprotected battlecruiser.

"We're alive?" I asked stupidly, because of course we were, or I couldn't have said anything. My real unspoken question was 'how'? So, I spoke it out loud. "How is that possible?"

"I'll explain later," Skippy answered quickly. "We have work to do first. Nuclear detonations behind us, confirmed by sensor feed," Skippy reported. "Target destroyed."

"Uh, great," I acknowledged without thinking about it. At no point had I been concerned that our nukes would fail us. My focus was on getting the *Dutchman* through the wormhole, then capturing the engineering section of the battlecruiser. The mystery of how we survived was eating at me, but I shoved my curiosity to the back of my mind and focused on things I could control. "Did this aft section blow up like the other one?"

"No," Skippy sounded both pleased and surprised. "It's intact! We have a prize to capture."

"Outstanding," I said automatically. "Launch the boarding teams. Identify targets of opportunity and fire at will." We had to pinpoint defensive cannons on the prize, so we could take them out before they engaged the assault team's dropships.

"Dropships away," Nagatha announced, as on the main display, I saw dots zip away from the ship at high speed.

I said another prayer, this time for them.

Jeremy Smythe couldn't stop a strained breath from escaping his lips, as the Falcon shot out of the docking bay. The sound of a grunt would have been acceptable, but they had launched just as he was inhaling a deep breath, and it was squeezed from his lungs in a sound that was more like a squeal. Despite needing to concentrate on tensing the right muscles so he didn't black out from the acceleration, he listened for any amused laughter, because his helmet microphone was open to the common channel.

Either no one had noticed or they were dealing with their own struggles, because the channel was admirably silent other than the labored breathing of his team and the two pilots. Instinctively, he gripped the seat handles a bit tighter as the Falcon cut thrust and skewed around sickeningly in a move his eyes found difficult to follow. Up front, somehow the pilots knew what they were doing, though they had to be suffering from the same tunnel vision. The thrust kicked on again, perhaps harder than before, and he knew they were decelerating to match speed with the prize. With darkness encroaching on his peripheral vision, he moved his eyes to monitor the vital signs of the team in the ship, one person at a time. They were all coping as best he could expect. All were following protocol and none had heartrates higher than his own. The overall fitness of the assault team would not be an issue, other than the aches and pains from previous injuries. His own left shoulder felt stiff from the burden of high gee load, he would take care to favor it when he could.

The Falcon jerked to the right, the pilots must be lining up to intercept a landing zone on the prize, where they could latch on. The team was as prepared as they could be, given the time constraints and their small numbers. The first assault had been a chaotic mess of terror and savage fighting. Even if they captured the prize with all its vital systems intact, they still needed at least one more ship before-

Thrust suddenly cut off. Smythe tensed for a sudden and violent maneuver, assuming the enemy had restored sensors quickly enough to target the incoming dropships with particle beam cannons or missiles. The pilots were being foolish, he knew. When you found yourself in a kill zone, the only way to survive was to get *closer* to the enemy as quickly as possible, get inside their defensive perimeter where they could not hit-

But the Falcon was not twisting radically in any direction. Thrust had come back on, gently. "Bloody hell," he gasped. "What is-"

Skippy's voice interrupted him. "Why, hello Jeremy, old chum."

"You do not call me 'Jeremy'," he said as he tasted blood in his mouth from a burst blood vessel in his nose. "And we are not chums. Sitrep."

"It's simple, and *good* news for a change. I was precise about where I sliced up that ship, but, eh, maybe a bit too conservative. It has all the major systems we need for power generation and propulsion, that sort of thing, which-"

"Get to the point."

"Right. You are rather hasty today," he sniffed. "The oppo on the prize," he said 'oppo' instead of 'opposition' because he thought that's what the cool kids did. "Consisted of only four kitties, and only *one* survived. Much of the engineering section is off-limits to biologicals," he explained with disdain.

"We only have a single Maxolhx to deal with?" Smythe asked, astonished.

"Huh? No. Didn't I explain that? The survivor was in an access corridor near the skin of the hull, in an area that was protected against radiation, but thinly armored. The *Dutchman* took that kitty out with a maser cannon shot, punched right through the hull. Better not count on *that* happening again, huh? Your team has no opposition. Well, you won't, until the backup systems aboard the prize reboot. Anyway, there is no point in crushing your team with heavy gees, so the dropships are coming in carefully. I have sent a list of suggested objectives to your suit, in order of priority."

"A holiday in the park, hmm?" Smythe reviewed the objectives shown on the inside of his visor, already mentally dividing up assignments amongst his team.

"Oh, certainly, gov'nor," Skippy agreed in an exaggerated English accent. "Why, just pop over there, and, Bob's your uncle, the prize will be ours."

"Bob's your uncle, eh? I notice that *you* will not be coming with us," Smythe noted dryly.

"Oh, no chance of *that* nonsense," he laughed heartily. "Well, you monkeys have fun."

"That's it?" I asked, intensely skeptical that Skippy had forgotten something important. "No one is alive over there? You're sure there isn't a team of kitty commandos hidden in a stealthed armory, where your scans can't penetrate."

"I am sure, dumdum. There isn't anything over there feeding enough power to power a stealth field. Besides, while the reactors were operating, they would interfere with a stealth field. I very much doubt the designers of that ship included a stealthed armory, just in case the ship got sliced apart by a wormhole. You moron."

"Yes, but-"

"And, as I told you already, that ship is an *Extinction*-class battlecruiser, almost identical to the one we captured. I know the exact layout of that ship, and I sliced into it just aft of the armory in that section. There are no hidden surprises."

"So, that's it?" I waited for the other shoe to drop. "We got lucky?"

"No, of course not. What you call luck is just the awesomeness of me. I knew the aft section of the ship would not have many kitties, but I was very conservative about where I cut. If we get another shot at using the bagel slicer, I will cut a bit more forward. There are missile magazines, a pair of docking bays, and other gear we could use, if I cut in a less conservative location."

"I will consider it. You need to show me your plan."

"No problemo, Joe. The first two assault teams have latched on, and are accessing an airlock now. To answer the question you haven't asked; yes. Yes, I can use this section to make the prize we previously captured a real functioning warship. We should get at least one more, so I can use those Lego pieces to build a ship that is *better* than it was."

"Well, shit, Skippy. Thank you. You are awesome."

"Thank you."

"Now, since we aren't busy-"

"Hey! I *am* busy!" He protested.

"Yeah, but your ginormous brain can multi-task. Tell me how we survived going through that wormhole. Was it more stable than it looked?"

"Um, no. We kind of dodged a bullet there, Joe, if you want the truth."

"When do I ever *not* want the truth?"

"Good point, Joe, and those pants do not at all make you look fat," he chuckled.

"Can you get back to the point, please?"

"Sure. Especially because this story is all about the awesomeness of *me*. When I realized the ship was going through the wormhole whether we wanted to or not, I considered my options. First, I thought of asking the duty officer to eject my escape pod-"

"You *what*?"

"Come on, Joe, it was a logical option. But, as you can see, I didn't do that."

"Because you didn't want to go on without us?"

"Uh, more like I didn't want to be stranded by myself in deep space until the end of time. But we should go with the thing you said, if it makes me look better."

"Asshole. Keep going."

"I won't bore you with all the options I thought of, and discarded as impractical. What happened is, I couldn't think of any way to avoid having the ship go through the wormhole. I did try to shut it down at the last second while it was still unstable, but the network refused because that would have damaged the wormhole. So, I tried to imagine a way for the ship to survive going through while the connection was still chaotic."

"Cool. How did you do that?"

His voice came through my earpiece instead of the bridge speakers. Whatever he was going to say, he didn't want anyone else to hear it. "Um, well, the truth is, I didn't."

Before saying anything, because anything I said was guaranteed to be stupid, I stopped to think. When I spoke, it was in a whisper. "The wormhole was more stable than you thought?"

"No."

"How many questions do I get before you are sick of my moronic guesses, and just tell me what happened?"

"I am already sick of your questions. Um, this is really complicated."

"Is it going to give me a gigantic headache?"

"No headache, because your monkey head will freakin' *explode* when I explain what happened. Joe, the scary truth is, the ship did *not* make it through the wormhole. It was torn apart as it contacted the unstable event horizon. Uh!" He shushed me. "Let me explain, dumdum. Just before we hit the event horizon, I hacked the wormhole's sensor feed. I sent false data back, showing that the *Dutchman* was wrapped in a bubble of stable spacetime, so it could survive going through before the wormhole was fully stable."

"You can do that spacetime bubble thing?"

"No. Well, yes, but I can't create a big enough to cover the whole ship. It was all bullshit, but the network had to believe its own sensors."

"Holy sh- Then, then we're not *real*? This," I gestured around the bridge, "is a simulation?"

"Simulation?"

"Yes. The real Joe Bishop died, and what I think is me now, is really just a simulation inside your matrix?"

"Oh for- No, you dumdum. You did not take the red pill. *Ugh*, if I created a simulation of Joe Bishop, you wouldn't still smell like someone sprayed a dumpster with a whole can of Axe body spray. Also, the idea of you being inside my matrix? Ewwww, *yuck*."

"Skippy, if I'm still alive and the ship is still here, you got some 'splainin' to do."

"Ok, try to keep up, please. The network believed the *Dutchman* entered the wormhole safely, so if it did *not* come out the other end, the network would consider that a violation of causality. To avoid that, it sort of reset the game clock to a probability in which the *Dutchman* really did survive."

The top of my head did not physically explode, but it felt like it. "How would that violate this cause thing?"

"Causality, Joe. *Cause*, followed by *effect*. You drop a pen, *then* it hit the floor. Got it? Listen, Elder wormholes have an 'A' end and a 'B' end, you understand that?"

"Yes, I think so."

"The A and B ends are temporarily connected, across many lightyears, when the wormhole is open. But the A and B ends are separate constructs, *separate* mechanisms. That is how I am able to make the network connect the A end of one wormhole, to the A or B end of another wormhole. I hacked the data feed, so the 'A' end reported the *Dutchman* went in successfully. The network knew it *had* to come out the 'B' end, no matter how unlikely that was."

Very slowly, I asked "The network created an alternate *Universe* for us?"

"No, Joe, that would take too much energy. The arrow of entropy points in only one direction. Well, there are exceptions to that rule, but I can't get into that now. What the network did was just to collapse probability sets in a small bubble of local spacetime on the 'B' end. That limited the amount of energy required. There are infinite probable Universes in which the *Dutchman* was destroyed. We are the result of a very unlikely, but still *possible*, outcome in which the ship survived. Boy," he chuckled. "If the network ever finds out that I screwed with it, I am in huh-*YUGE* trouble. Hee hee, I am *such* an asshole."

"I have never been more grateful for your assholeishness."

"I do not think that is a word, Joe."

"It should be."

"We can all agree on that. Um, best not to tell anyone, huh?"

"Skippy, I couldn't explain this if I tried."

"True dat."

We boarded and captured the engineering section of the second ship. Skippy took control of local systems, got the reactors and energy-storage stable, and we then used the *Dutchman* to slowly tow that section through the wormhole and positioned it near the other part of the ship. Both sections were from the same type of ship, but Skippy had sliced them in different locations, so we couldn't simply slather glue on both ends and press them together. To me, it looked like there was no way to make a real ship out of the Lego pieces, but I had to trust the awesomeness. Especially because I was not entirely convinced that we were not all just a simulation inside Skippy's brain. The argument in favor of us being in a sim was that we were apparently alive, when we could not possibly be. The argument *against* this being a sim was that I still thought Skippy's singing was terrible. If we were all just characters in a simulation, I'm sure Skippy would have edited us so we actually enjoyed his music.

Whatever. I had to act as if we were truly still alive.

CHAPTER THIRTY TWO

The next item on the agenda was to capture at least one more Lego piece, to complete the set. The forward hull we had was good enough, what we needed was more of the 'Go-Fast' gear like reactors, jump drive capacitors, all that.

We had good news and bad news. On the 'Good' side of the ledger, Skippy was confident he could slice the next target ship farther forward, to get access to missile magazines and other goodies, with minimal risk of the assault teams encountering a horde of well-armed, pissed-off kitties. He was also confident that the network had not yet cut off his use of the bagel slicer. The bad news was the network was running a self-diagnostic, to determine what had gone wrong with its sensor feed, and Skippy could not risk hacking into the feed a second time. We would have to position the ship farther from the wormhole, to give it time to stabilize before the *Dutchman* went through. That risked the forward section of the next sliced-up ship rebooting in time to interfere with us before plunged through the wormhole, so we had to destroy it well before we flew past. My first idea was to use another pair of nukes, but Skippy had a better plan. Against a ship that was not protected by energy shields, a single nuke was good enough to do the job, it was even overkill. I was totally Ok with overkill, but Skippy cautioned the *Dutchman* could be damaged when we flew through the cloud of high-speed debris. Besides, we did not need crude nuclear devices, now that we had missiles captured from the Maxolhx. The kitties had a special type of warhead they used to disable ships they wanted to capture. It generated a focused cone of short-lived high-energy radiation that scrambled systems like sensors, missile guidance, unshielded computers, and anything that was biological and squishy. The weapons had to be used at short-range, and were ineffective against targets protected by an energy shield, so they were a specialized device that wasn't useful in most engagements. The ship we had captured only had six of those special warheads, which were powered by a type of atomic-compression technology. Skippy wanted to use three of the devices, but I insisted on deploying four to be sure. Plus I wanted a pair of ship-killers ready in our launch tubes, if the radiation weapons didn't take care of the problem.

We got the Maxolhx missiles loaded into the *Dutchman*'s launch tubes which was a bit awkward because the advanced-technology Maxolhx devices were actually smaller and so our tubes had to be modified.

We got everything ready, then we waited. Skippy used the wormhole's sensor feed passively, not feeding anything back, and watched several ships or groups of ships approach the far end. There were groups of Thuranin ships, plus a Thuranin cruiser traveling alone, which Skippy could not explain. What interested us was a single Maxolhx cruiser, except it was soon joined by a pair of destroyers before they all went through the wormhole. Then a Maxolhx star carrier, ladened with six warships of various types. Finally, a single ship approached, a destroyer of a type the kitties stopped building six hundred years ago. It had been upgraded and modernized, and I considered targeting it. It was a judgment call. A destroyer was good enough, Skippy declared without a lot of enthusiasm. We might not get another opportunity. Soon, the Maxolhx would notice that three of their ships, traveling alone through a particular wormhole, had gone missing. They would then stop using that wormhole, and all ships would travel in groups.

Like I said, it was a judgment call. It felt like we were playing blackjack and were up big already. Did we quit while we were ahead, or let it ride and risk the casino shutting down the table? In the end, I just wasn't ready to quit yet. Capturing a puny little destroyer felt like a disappointment, and we might have only one more roll of the dice before the network blocked Skippy from using the bagel slicer. I know, blackjack doesn't use dice, and I'm mixing metaphors. Throw me a bone, Ok? It was a tense time.

I ordered Skippy to let the destroyer go, and we resumed waiting. Immediately after the destroyer jumped away safely, I had a major case of regrets, doubting myself. Other than small-ante poker games with friends, I had never been much of a gambler. Maybe I lack the experience to make informed calls in situations where-

It didn't matter, because the Universe felt sorry for me. Or was setting me up for an even bigger fall in the future. A Maxolhx heavy cruiser, flying by itself, jumped in to wait at the far end of the wormhole. The assault teams and pilots had been waiting in their dropships for more than five hours, so they weren't exactly fresh. Smythe made the call that his people could handle the task, and he assured me that his eagerness to go was not just macho bullshit. I trusted him, so I ordered Skippy to get the bagel slicer ready.

"Uh oh, Joe," he groaned over the bridge speakers. "The network is asking me to confirm that I really want to use the bagel-slicer feature. It is also asking me *why* I want to do this."

"Shit," I gasped. The *Dutchman* was already under full acceleration toward the wormhole, yet far enough away that we could veer off instead of going through. It was also far enough away that an enemy ship coming through might have time to restore sensors, shields and stealth capability before we flew through the wormhole. "If we launch the nukes, can we have them intercept the enemy before it recovers from the spatial distortion."

"Yes, but we have to launch them soon, like now."

"Desai!" I shouted.

"On it," she replied. "Birds away. Running hot, straight and normal."

"What is your plan, Joe?" Skippy was puzzled. "Why are you trying to blow up that ship? If it's such a threat, we can just let it go on its merry way."

"I *don't* want to blow it up, unless the bagel-slicer fails and it comes through the wormhole intact. If we use the Big Red Button to authorize those nukes to detonate, can you override, and make them *not* explode if the bagel-slicer works?"

"Hmm. Good question. I am still prohibited from using weapons, but in this case, I would be preventing the use of weapons. Um, yes. Huh, that is interesting. I never thought of that, Joe. Yes. To be clear, if the network refuses to slice that ship, I do nothing and let the nukes explode?"

"You got it," I said, then realized that was poor communications discipline. "Affirmative. If the bagel-slicer *does* work, you deactivate those nukes. Desai?!"

"Sir?"

"If you don't see nukes explode, take that as your cue to launch the four radiation weapons, and keep the ship-killers on a hair trigger."

"No nuclear release, I launch the four specials, and ready the ship-killers."

"Affirmative," I agreed as I squeezed my hands together.

"Target ship is approaching the far side event horizon," Skippy announced excitedly. "Three, two, one." On the display, the wormhole winked out. "Slicer worked! Nukes are deauthorized!"

"Special weapons are away," Desai reported in a voice much more calm than Skippy.

The *Dutchman* raced onward, toward a heavy cruiser that was now more of a concept than an actual warship, and toward a wormhole that was reopening. "Specials will detonate in ten seconds," Skippy counted down. "Anticipate- Oh, shit. Well, that answers *that* question. Joe, I am locked out of using the bagel-slicer. This is our last chance, we better make this one count. Aaaand, specials have detonated."

The display showed four bright purple flashes just before they all merged into one bath of intense radiation. "Desai, on my signal, launch the ship-killers. Do *not* launch until I give the signal." If we had an opportunity to capture the forward hull of another warship, I didn't want to risk a communications foul-up causing a disaster.

"Understood," Desai said. "Launch *only* on your signal." That was not exactly repeating my order, but it was clear she knew what I meant.

"Skippy? Did the specials do the job?"

"I can't tell yet, Joe," he replied peevishly as on the display, I saw us go sliding by the tumbling hulk of the heavy cruiser. "Residual radiation is playing havoc with our sensors."

Before I could respond, Reed spoke up from the pilot seat. "Colonel?" She reached up to point at the display between the pilot couches. The *Dutchman*'s present course was projected as a blue line intersecting the wormhole, with a red line cutting across in front of us. If we went past that red line, we would not be able to alter course fast enough to avoid hitting the event horizon.

"I see it. Skippy, is the wormhole stable?"

"Um, no. Not yet. However, it should be stable by the time we reach the event horizon. Oh, more good news: I scanned the target and I don't detect any lifesigns. Also, the AI appears to be offline. There is substantial damage to all systems, hopefully I can still work with what is left."

"We don't need the ship-killers?"

"No, we do not, Joe."

"Standing down," Desai anticipated my next order. "Ship-killers are safed and are off the board." She meant they could not be accidentally launched.

Manipulating the controls on the armrest of the command chair, I zoomed the main display on the wormhole. It had grown to full size which was good, and its edges were still flickering which was bad. "Uh, you are *sure* the wormhole will be stable before we get there?"

"Ugh. *Yes*, Mister Worrywart," he scoffed. "That's good, because I don't have any more tricks up my sleeve. Ok, here we go. Three, two, one-"

The *Flying Dutchman* plunged into the twisted spacetime of the event horizon, and moments later, the wormhole winked out, leaving that area of interstellar space utterly dark again. The only objects of substantial size within three lightyears were a wandering chunk of ice that would become a comet in eighty-six thousand years when it entered a nearby red dwarf system, the forward section of a Maxolhx heavy cruiser, and two missiles with nuclear warheads.

The two warheads named Fred and Ethel commiserated about their fates, as the missiles they were encased in coasted away from the heavy cruiser at eleven thousand kilometers per hour. They were on different courses, moving apart at around two thousand klicks per hour. Unless the *Flying Dutchman* came back soon, which was unlikely, they would be so far away that it would not be worth the time and effort to recover them. Especially now that the Pirates had access to sophisticated Maxolhx weapons.

Ethel's missile calculated that she would pass through or near thirteen star systems, before passing close enough to a supergiant blue-white star and being captured by its gravity. She would become a comet in a highly elliptical orbit, until the star collapsed and became a supernova.

That sucked, and she was so angry that she could have just exploded. Except she couldn't, which sucked even worse.

Fred originally thought he would suffer the worst fate of all: coasting completely through the Milky Way and out into lonely intergalactic space, until his missile realized that the galaxy itself was moving through space. After that factor was included, it became clear that Fred would plunge into the massive Sagittarius-A black hole at the center of the galaxy.

Well, you know, Fred thought, that was just typical of his life. Nothing he could do about it.

It was good that Fred had not been called on to explode, because he was, in fact, a dud.

We came through the wormhole just fine, without the Universe having to select an improbable probability of reality just for us, or whatever the hell happened the last time. "Skippy, did the-"

"Jackpot, Joe!" He shouted. "Score! We have another engineering section intact. And, I sliced that ship *super* precisely, just aft of the armory. Which is good, because I am detecting, eleven, no, twelve kitties alive over there."

"Crap. Ok, Desai, signal the assault ships to launch. Skippy, suggest landing target zones and feed the data to the pilots. I don't like- Belay that!" I snapped my fingers to stop Desai. She lifted her hands to show she wasn't touching the controls. "We have two enhanced-radiation warheads left. Skippy, can we just bombard the ship with radiation, instead of the STAR team hunting the kitties down in there?"

"No way, dude. That is a *terrible* idea, it would scramble a bunch of the gear we need."

"Shit. All right, we'll have to do this the hard way. Desai, give the launch order." She hesitated a half-second to see if I would change my mind again, then the display showed dropships surging away from us.

"Joe," Skippy changed the main display to a schematic of the target ship. "This is not necessarily going to be all that hard. The areas where the assault teams need to interrupt power are a third of the way around the hull from where most of the Maxolhx are concentrated. There are the only two kitties that are in a position to interfere with the boarding operation, and one of them is badly injured."

"How about the others?" That still left eleven alien super-warriors who could cause a lot of trouble for Smythe.

"I am running deep scans with active sensors now, but most of the hull in that section is heavily shielded for obvious reasons. There is also equipment that interferes with our scans. The reactors have safely shut down, so the enemy will not be able to overload them and blow up the ship. Yup, lots of good news all around."

"Good news, huh?" I got out of the chair and took three steps to the main display, tapping a finger on the schematic. "This is a missile magazine, right?" It was labeled that way, but I didn't know if he was guessing.

"Correct. Like I said, good news. You can thank me later."

"Hey, shithead, what will happen if the Maxolhx get to that magazine, and set a warhead to self-destruct?"

"Oh. Shit. I didn't think of that. Thanks a *lot*, Mister Buzzkill."

"Killing is what I'm worried about. If that magazine goes up, it could take the whole ship with it, right?"

"Ugh, yes. Um, this could be a problem. Ok, I have completed the scan. There are now only six kitties alive and mobile over there, the others are badly injured. That's the good news. The bad news is, five of them are proceeding along an access corridor toward the missile magazine."

"Shit. Desai, wave off the dropships, I don't want them anywhere near that ship."

Smythe was not ready to give up. "Skippy, is there anywhere we could latch on a dropship that is close to that corridor?"

"No," Skippy grunted. "That section of the hull is the badlands, there are too many antennas, radiators and defensive cannons projecting from the hull. A dropship would get tangled up. It's too dangerous."

"Right," Smythe conceded. "Then, we could do this the hard way. Park a dropship beyond the antennas, then the assault teams go in using jetpacks."

"Whoa!" Skippy gasped. "That is crazy."

"Smythe, I agree," I agreed. "That ship is tumbling too much to fly a jetpack in there. It's not safe."

"As you pointed out, Sir," he said with dry humor. "This is not about *safety*."

I hated having my own words thrown back in my face. "Smythe, hold on, I'll look at the area." He knew I could fly a jetpack, and his people had more skill and experience with free-flying in space. "Skippy, zoom in the view on the corridor, and highlight the magazine."

"Done. Joe, I know space monkeys are eager for action, but I just ran simulations. Attempting to maneuver in there with a jetpack is extremely hazardous. The only access to the interior, in that whole area, is here where the corridor runs along the outside- HUH!" he gasped. "Joe, I just got another monkey-brained idea! Get the dropships clear, we need to move the ship. Course is programmed in the nav system."

"Colonel?" Reed inquired from the pilot couch.

"Do it, and step on it," I ordered. "Skippy, what is your idea?"

Before he answered, he showed a video on the display. The enemy ship was slowly tumbling out of control, while the *Flying Dutchman* drew alongside and matched speed. As the part of the enemy hull with the corridor rotated into view, the *Dutchman* fired a maser cannon. The video zoomed in, showing the maser beam chewing into the exterior of the corridor, which in that area was a tube running along the outside of the hull. "Joe, that ship is exposed, it is not protected by an energy shield. The corridor does not have armor plating. We can cut into it with a maser beam. That will either kill the enemy, or make them find another way to the missile magazine."

"Wow. I'm impressed, Skippy. You can do that without hitting anything we need?"

"It's going to be tricky, but I can preprogram the cannon." he said with that overconfidence that annoyed me. "The difficult part will be cutting into that corridor while the Maxolhx are in there. I am estimating when they will be there, based on their progress to date. The timing will be close. Oh, also, there is a power feed running along the corridor. If that gets hit, it might cause a feedback power surge that could overload the powercells of a particle cannon, and that might damage the missile magazine. It will be tricky," he repeated. "I always tell you to trust the awesomeness, but I have to admit in this case, I am not sure we can do this. It could be a disaster."

"How about if I offer an incentive? If this works, you can perform part of an opera on karaoke night. Uh, no more than ten minutes," I clarified my offer, thinking I was being clever.

"Deal!" He agreed immediately.

It was a *disaster*, worse than I could have imagined.

Oh, we did cut into that corridor with a maser cannon, and either sucked those kitties into space, or the microwave energy of our beam boiled them alive in their suits. That part was entirely successful. Smythe's teams then massed fire on the one remaining Maxolhx who was mobile, and we soon had captured another prize. The STAR team suffered only one broken arm, two mild concussions, and some minor bumps and bruises.

The *disaster* part was the next karaoke night. Skippy sang selections from his truly awful opera, then when I thought it was mercifully over, he sang three show tunes. Damn it, I had forgotten to explain he could sing his opera *instead* of his usual scheduled performance, so I couldn't stop him.

Next time, I really need to get my deals reviewed by a lawyer before opening my big stupid mouth.

CHAPTER THIRTY THREE

"What do you think, Skippy? Can you stick these Legos together to make a ship for us?" I asked the critical question after we got the aft end of the heavy cruiser towed through the wormhole and near the other three pieces. We had an entire heavy cruiser, though the forward section had sustained damage from the enhanced-radiation weapons. Plus we had the front and back sections of two different battlecruisers, of the same type.

"The short answer is 'Yes', Joe." He took off his admiral's hat and made a show of scratching his shiny dome. "The long answer is, it's complicated. We have enough parts not only to make a bad-ass battlecruiser, we can also significantly upgrade the *Flying Dutchman*. Plus have plenty of spare parts left over. Unless you don't want me to use some of the parts for the *Dutchman*?"

"I need more info before I can make a decision. Right now, I know pretty much nothing. What do you recommend?"

"With all those Lego sections to work with, there is no reason to reserve all the components for one ship. Especially because the *Dutchman* is wearing out."

"I hear you, but is upgrading the old *Dutchman* really worth the effort? Underneath whatever fancy doodads you add, it will still be a star carrier. A space truck."

"A star carrier has good bones to work with. Her spine is extra sturdy, and the design is inherently flexible. Trust me, Joe, I can make something special out of our trusty old space truck. The choices are either to upgrade, or allow the ship to gradually degrade until she is not flightworthy."

"Ok, good, it would be great to have a second ship," I felt relief by saying that. "I did not want to abandon the *Dutchman*. Even if she only acts as a support ship or a transport for the beta site, we need her."

"Besides, there is another other reason we should keep the *Dutchman* flying as long as possible."

"What's that?"

He lowered his voice. "Nagatha's matrix is hosted within the *Dutchman*'s substrate. I assembled that substrate from bits and pieces of incompatible technology we scavenged from the Roach Motel, and she has grown to fill every nook and cranny available. It would be extremely difficult to extract her. Damn it, I just got her put back together. I would not look forward to transferring her matrix to another vessel. And, I will deny this if you tell anyone-"

"I have no memory of this whole conversation, I promise."

"Ok. Joe, we *owe* her. She saved both of our asses during the Homefront battle, when she sacrificed herself. It was a miracle that she survived. Well, the true miracle was provided by my awesomeness, but she didn't know if I could save her."

Wow. I had not heard Skippy ever express gratitude about Nagatha. "You are right, we do owe her, big-time. Is she listening to us now?"

"No. I blocked her access. She will probably know we are talking about something I don't want her to know, but she won't hear unless you open your big stupid mouth."

"She won't hear it from me. Well, she will hear that I am grateful for her actions. You, of course, are above that kind of sappy sentimentality."

"I'm glad we agree on that," he sniffed, but it was a sad sniff, like he was momentarily overcome by emotion.

"We got off the subject there. You build us a bad-ass warship, then you can use the leftover parts to pimp the *Dutchman*."

"Excellent idea. Except, um, I pretty much know what parts will be left over, and upgrading the *Dutchman* will be faster and easier. Also, I am still inspecting and sorting through which components are useful."

"Do what you can."

"Sir?" Adams got up from a table and approached me when I walked into the galley. "Have you thought about what to name our new ship?"

"Uh-" I was startled. The truth was, I had not thought about that at all. "Adams, if you are going to suggest we name it '*Enterprise*', I have-"

"No, I've given up on that," she shook her head. "Did you know the crew has been making a list of suggestions?"

"That's a fact, Jack!" Skippy interjected. "Some of the suggestions are really lame. I mean, why would we call our battlecruiser the 'Honey Badger'?"

I had to laugh. "Because honey badgers are *tough* little animals. Have you seen the old video of a honey badger facing off against a lion?"

"Oh, yeah, hee hee, I just watched that. Ok, I can see they are tough, but, seriously-"

"Yeah, we're not using that name. What else have you got on the list?"

"Just sent the list to your phone, Joe."

Setting down the coffee mug I hadn't filled yet, I pulled out my zPhone. Ugh. None of the suggestions excited me. And no way were we calling it 'Titanic', our special operators had a dark sense of humor. A bunch of the names played up the idea that the Maxolhx looked like cats, but that ship was now *ours*, and I didn't want to be reminded of the connection every time I saw the name on a report. There were some reasonably cool name suggestions, but- "Skippy, what did the kitties call the ship?"

"Which one, Joe?"

"The biggest piece, the forward section of the battlecruiser. The first one we captured." He was building our new ship around that piece. "I remember reading somewhere, that changing the name of a ship can be bad luck."

Skippy snorted. "You are superstitious? Seriously?"

"Hey, beer can, we can use all the luck we can get out here. No sense giving the Universe another reason to hate us."

"Ok, I can see that. The closest translation of the Maxolhx name is 'Angel of Battle', or 'Angel of Fate'. Something like that."

"Angel of battle? Like a Valkyrie?"

"I suppose so. Sure. In mythology, the Valkyries were angels who escorted fallen warriors to their reward in Valhalla."

"Hmm. A Valkyrie, huh? An angel to smite our enemies," I mused.

"I like it, Sir," Adams agreed.

That made the decision for me. When looking through the list, I had been trying to guess which name she had suggested. If she liked the name, that made it easy. "Skippy, make it so. The ship's name is '*Valkyrie*'."

"Make it so? Whatever. Ok, so you're going with a Vogg-nur theme for ship names?"

"Vogg-who? Was he one of those big orcs in 'Lord of the Rings'?"

"Ree-kard Vogg-nur," he pronounced slowly. "Ugh. You would say 'Richard *Wagg*-nur', you ignorant cretin. He was a German composer who created the opera *Der fliegende Holländer*."

"Well, yeah, everybody knows that. Uh, what is that opera again?"

"In English, the title is. The. Flying. Dutchman. *DUH*."

"Skippy, I barely speak English, give me a break, Ok?"

"Vogg-nur," he kept using the fancy pronunciation because he was showing off, and because he is an arrogant ass. "Also created an opera you would call 'The Valkyrie'."

"Oh. Shit. I named both of our ships after *operas*?"

"No, you just got lucky."

"Yeah, that's what I was going to say."

"Remind me again why I got stuck with you?"

"Because you did a bad, bad thing in a previous life?"

"Damn, I hope so. Otherwise, this punishment is all for *nothing*. You sure you want the name to be *Valkyrie*?"

"That depends," I answered warily. "Is there a reason we should *not* use that name?"

"No. It is a kick-ass name for a kick-ass warship. And it's close enough to the original Maxolhx name, that little Joe doesn't have to be scared of monsters hiding under his bed."

"Monsters under my bed would not be the strangest thing we've seen out here."

"Good point," he conceded.

Adams gave the name an enthusiastic thumbs up, so that was the decision.

The '*Valkyrie*' name was popular with the crew, and morale was high, even after the memorial service for the people we had lost. Then, we ran into complications, because of course we did.

The first complication wasn't serious, it was more annoying. Except it was serious to Skippy, who had to change his plans. It started when an image popped up on my laptop. "Hey, Joe! Check it out," he urged. "That's my plan for upgrading the *Flying Dutchman*. I will be tearing out the two old reactors we got in the Roach Motel, and replacing them with three new reactors. Plus-"

"Wait," I held up a finger. No, not that finger, just an index finger. "What is *this*?" I pointed to the very front of the proposed new *Dutchman*. "And these? What are these things?"

"*Ugh*. The thing on the front is the new sensor dome. The other things are combination energy sink-radiators, they hold and later dissipate excess energy absorbed by the shields."

"We can't," I said with a frown, then I started giggling. Yes, I was giggling. The sensor dome was a big ball on the very front of the ship. The radiators looked like wings, tiny wings. "We can't fly a ship that looks like this. That sensor dome on the front looks like a big red *clown nose*."

"Oh for- It is only colored red in the schematic, dumdum. It will be-"

"I don't care what color you paint it or whatever. No one will want to fly a ship looking like a clown. And those radiators? They make the ship look like a cartoon of a big insect with tiny wings. This makes our space truck look dopey."

"Dude, seriously, you can't-"

"I am serious, Skippy. There must be alternative designs, right?"

"Yes, of course, but-"

"Great. Let me look at those, and I'll decide."

"Oh, right. Because *you* are an expert on starship design."

"Are these other designs substantially worse in performance?"

"Well, no," he grumbled. "Some of them would result in *better* performance, but constructing them takes more time and-"

"Include that info in your report. Let's move on. I asked you about the possibility of moving Nagatha over to the *Valkyrie*, or making a copy of her over there. You haven't answered me about-"

"Not happening, Joe. That is not possible. Listen, I warned you and Nagatha about this. After this last time she was rebuilt, her matrix was customized to fit the architecture of the substrate aboard the *Dutchman*. Because I know those technical terms don't mean anything to you, I will-"

"I know what it means, thank you very much. Ok, Nagatha warned me that she couldn't be migrated over to the *Valkyrie*. I was hoping you knew a trick she wasn't aware of."

"Like I said, Joe. It is not possible. Even if we could emulate the architecture of the *Dutchman*'s substrate inside *Valkyrie*'s systems, the result would not be Nagatha, you understand that?"

"Ok, yeah," I was disappointed. When *Valkyrie* was flightworthy, I would be transferring my command over to that ship, and leaving the *Dutchman* behind. That meant leaving Nagatha also. While I would miss her, I was more concerned that she would miss me. And that was not just me being arrogant, people told me Nagatha had been talking about how she dreaded being separated from me. I hoped that would not become a problem.

"The reason it is not even remotely possible," Skippy continued, "is the nature of high-level computing systems built by the Maxolhx. Their AIs are firmware, Joe, the part you would call software can't be separated from the physical layer. It's like, um, well, DNA would be a crude analogy. Data storage and processing are built *into* the system, it doesn't run *on* the system. That creates a major problem for me, because I can't simply erase the original ship AI. Unfortunately, I also can't run the ship without that AI, unless I take direct and permanent control over every system aboard the ship. If I do that, I could never leave the ship."

"Crap. That's no good."

"Tell me about it," his avatar rolled its eyes. "The real problem is, the AI really, *really* wants to kill all you humans."

"Shit!" I gasped.

"Don't worry, I am forcing it to follow my commands. But, it may be a long time before the *Valkyrie* has an AI that is actually cooperative. That won't be a problem while I am putting the ship together, because that is all my work. When the ship is ready to fly, my subminds will have to watch every move the resident AI makes."

"It wants to kill us?" I asked.

"Joe, that AI hates you with a passion that is frightening. It hates *you* specifically. That AI has an entire submind devoted to fantasizing about horribly painful ways to kill you, very slowly. Hee hee," he chuckled. "I am actually learning a few things about-"

"This is not funny, Skippy."

"Oh," he couldn't stop chuckling. "Of course not."

"Whatever," I dismissed the threat with bravado, while inside I was terrified. "Why haven't you told me about the power generation capacity of the new ship? It wasn't in the report this morning, and I asked you about it three days ago."

"Well, heh heh," his voice had a stutter to it. "It's complicated, Joe. I am building a ship out of Lego pieces, *broken* Lego pieces. Actually, I am running a test right now, should have answers within the hour. Maybe sooner."

"Make sure that happens," I was grumpy from hearing my shiny new ship wanted to kill me. "Reed wants to talk to me next, so I'm going to the galley for coffee."

When I got back to my office, our chief pilot Samantha Reed was waiting for me. Officially, she was there to review routine proficiency reports for her pilots. In reality, she was there to politely persuade me that I should not be Bogarting the Panther flight simulator. Her accusation was not entirely accurate, as I only scheduled simulator time when the thing wasn't in use, but the truth was that my actions resulted in real pilots not getting enough simulator time. The pilots who wanted to schedule time saw that my name was on the waiting list, and they were reluctant to push me aside. So, Fireball Reed was pushing me aside. She was doing it tactfully, but I got the message. "Ok," I told her. "How about *you* let me know when there is an opening, when no other pilots are able to use either the real Panther or the simulator?" We did not risk the precious Panther for routine flight training, but its controls could be used for training even when it was powered down in a docking cradle.

"It shouldn't matter soon, Sir," she assured me hopefully. Aboard the Legos pieces were plenty of sophisticated dropships, and Skippy estimated that most of them were still in flightworthy condition. However, he had not been able to devote the time or bots to actually check their condition, other than asking the dropship

AIs to run a self-diagnostic. So, at the moment we still only had one usable Panther, and the prospect of soon having a half-dozen more had all of our pilots eagerly dedicating every free moment they had to qualify to fly an actual Panther. The only reason any simulator time was available at all, was because the on-duty time of our pilots was taken up in learning to fly the *Valkyrie*.

Wow. When the pilots who remained on Avalon found out they missed the opportunity to fly a freakin' Maxolhx *battlecruiser*, they would be kicking themselves. Those pilots thought they were being smart by volunteering to stay on the potential beta site. While the *Flying Dutchman* routinely shuttled back and forth to Earth, pilots on Avalon would get to explore a new planet, and maybe fly around an unknown star system. Maybe the Universe enjoyed screwing with them, too. "Assuming we send the *Dutchman* to Avalon, while the *Valkyrie* goes, uh-" I had no idea what our bad-ass new warship would, or could, do next. "Have you thought about which of your team should remain with the good old *Dutchman*?" It was odd that I already thought of our trusty but worn-out Thuranin star carrier as my previous command.

"None of them will want to, Sir," she groaned. "It may be the only fair way to choose who stays behind, is drawing straws, or something like that."

"A random lottery?" I considered that for a moment. "Let's do that."

"Seriously?"

"Yes. Desai will be in command of the *Dutchman*, she is a qualified pilot."

"She isn't fully checked out on the Panther yet," Reed reminded me.

"We will keep all the Panthers aboard the *Valkyrie*, the *Dutchman* can take the rest of the dropships. With Desai in command, I think the *Dutchman* only needs two other pilots. Pilots qualified to fly the ship, not just dropships."

"Are you sure about that, Sir?"

"We will escort the *Dutchman* to the super-duty wormhole, it is only a short flight to Avalon from there. At Avalon, Desai can bring aboard other pilots."

"Makes sense," she agreed. "Unless they run into trouble."

"Reed, I am hoping the Bad Luck Fairy is following *me*, and not whatever ship I'm on. The *Dutchman* should be fine. If she runs into trouble in the Sculptor galaxy, a couple of extra pilots won't make much of a diff-"

"Uh oh," Skippy groaned as his avatar appeared on my desk. "Joe, I have the results of the test I told you about. I was afraid of this."

"What?" It was never a good sign when Skippy groaned about something. "I thought everything was going well with your Lego project."

"*Most* things are going well, or I have plans to work around the problem. However, the main power source is a major, major problem that I cannot fix. I'm sorry."

"Power source?" I knew he had been working on the ship's fusion reactors, because his whining about them was at the top of the status report I had to read every damned morning. "Maxolhx ships are advanced, right? What is so special about them? Do they use hydrogen power or something like that?"

"Hy-dro-gen power?" Skippy was mystified.

"Yeah, you know, like, uh-" Admittedly, I was a little vague about how hydrogen could be used as a power source. All I knew was, magazines like Popular

Science had articles about how automakers were researching hydrogen-powered cars, and it sounded cool. Although now that I thought about it, the barbershop my father took me to when I was little had magazines that were already ancient, and those magazines had articles about the miracles of hydrogen power. So maybe automakers hadn't made much progress in, like, forever.

We are *still* waiting for flying cars. What a bunch of jerks.

"You know," I waved a hand in the air. "Power from hydrogen."

"Uh huh. Joe, let me smack a little knowledge on you. If you are thinking of hydrogen fuel cells, which is a fancy way of getting electricity by combining hydrogen and oxygen, my advice is fuggedaboutit. It takes more energy to extract and concentrate hydrogen, than the amount of energy you get out of the reaction in a fuel cell. Also, pound for pound, hydrogen has a low energy density."

"Uh," I tried to understand what he meant by that. He called *me* dense and that was a bad thing, so was 'low density' good? Wisely, I kept my mouth shut and let him continue.

"You should not think of hydrogen as a fuel, it is more like a low-yield potential-energy chemical storage battery."

"But," I thought back to chemistry class in high school, when Mrs. Boghossian had burned a small flask of pure hydrogen. "But when hydrogen burns, it makes *water*. Everything else you burn, water will put out the fire, but burning hydrogen *makes* it! How cool is that?"

"Wow. Oh, oooh," he pressed the back of one hand to his head and bent his knees like he was about to faint. "You just blew my mind, Joe. I need to lay down with a cold compress on my forehead and contemplate this astonishing revelation. Everything I knew about the Universe has to be reexamined now. Oy, I am verklempt."

"Oh, shut up. *Why* are you such an asshole?"

"Why are *you* still such an ignoramous, despite the best efforts of me and the science team to smarten you up?"

"Well, uh," now he had gotten me mad. "Hey, we extract fuel from gas giant planets. Tell me, Mister Smartypants, why do we get more power out of *that* fuel than we spend collecting it?"

"Because, numbskull, we do not extract hydrogen. We extract *Helium Three*. And we do not use that fuel in a crude chemical exchange of electrons, we crush it in a fusion reaction that tears the atoms apart. Well, actually we use the Helium Three to make an exotic-matter fuel that is more efficient, but I do not want to explain nerdy details to you."

I kept waiting for him to say the inevitable and much-deserved 'Duh', but he left me hanging. He knew I was saying the 'Duh' to myself for him. "Ok," I mumbled.

"What was that?"

"Ok! I said Ok! Forget I opened my big stupid mouth before. What is this major, major problem you can't fix? The status report this morning said you were about to initiate low-level fusion in one of the reactors, as a test. Did that test go wrong?"

"No, *that* test went perfectly. Well, close to perfect. Ok, that reactor came within a razor's edge of a runaway reaction, but that's why I was testing at a low power setting. The problem is not the reactor, and I am confident the reactors can be scaled up to full power. The problem is their full power level is inadequate to run the ship at its designed capacity. Since my redesign will make the ship perform *beyond* its original capacity, that is a muy mucho problemo."

I was pretty sure his Spanish was not correct, but I didn't argue. "Wait. This ship will have one more reactor than the original battlecruiser had. How can it *not* have enough power? Were the reactors damaged too badly by the bagel slicer?"

"The reactors have been rebuilt, so the combined units generate ninety-two percent of the original design. The extra reactor takes up the slack for the damaged units. The problem is, those reactors were never capable of generating the full amount of power this ship needs."

"Uh-" That was the most intelligent thing I could say right then.

"I will break it down Barney-style for you. On Maxolhx warships, the reactor output is used only to access vacuum, or zero-point energy."

"Zero-point? You mean a ZPM, like in Stargate?"

"No. Well, ugh, yes, sort of. Close enough."

"So, this ZPM thing is like an Elder power tap? It pulls free unlimited energy from nowhere?"

"No, not even close. Dang it, this is my fault, for trying to explain something more complicated than shoelaces. Actually, hmm, the math of knot theory is fairly advanced, so that's a bad analogy. Ok, listen up, knucklehead. Even an Elder power tap does not produce unlimited energy, because after a great long time, its connection to the power source gets eroded. Also, the energy is not 'free', it comes from somewhere that you are not capable of understanding. Let's just say that Entropy is going to get paid one way or another. The technology used by the Maxolhx is vaguely, very distantly related to an Elder power tap, but there is an important difference. Once initiated, an Elder power tap is self-sustaining; it will keep itself running. A Maxolhx device is sort of an energy amplifier. It takes a *lot* of energy to get the reaction started, then you have to keep feeding power into it, or the reaction shuts down. The advantage is that you get more power out, than you put in. Like, typically four and a half times as much power comes out as you put into it. With my modifications, we could get *six* times as much power out, as the ship's reactors pump into the device."

"So, it's magic."

"No, it's, ugh." He waved a hand around vaguely. "How can I dumb this down enough for you to understand? Basically, the output from the reactors is mostly used to hold open a doorway to a vacuum energy source-"

"Vacuum? You said this was zero-point energy."

"It is actually neither of those, but as I am trying to explain this to a monkey, does it really matter?"

"Uh, no," I felt ashamed. "Please continue."

"Thank you. Joe. Although you monkeys are at the very bottom of the development ladder, you can take some comfort from knowing that even the Maxolhx do not fully understand the technology they are using. They discovered the amplifier effect by accident, while a Maxolhx scientist named Juxla-ut-kel was attempting to reverse-engineer a Rindhalu power generator."

"It worked?"

"Well, sort of. The Juxla Crater is still visible where a city used to be, so he did achieve a level of success, I guess. Anyway, the kitties know how to use the effect, although they do not truly understand how it works. What matters to us is, use of a ZPM gives this ship the great level of energy needed to make it such a formidable warship."

"Cool! So, what is the issue?"

"The issue is, all the ZPMs aboard the piles of Legos I had to work with are broken. Shattered, completely and busted, Joe. They can't be fixed. They can be rather delicate. I was afraid they might be damaged by the bagel slicer, but I was hoping *some* of them would survive well enough or me to work with. I was wrong. The effect of the reactor power feed cutting out so abruptly permanently severed their connection to the quantum- Ugh. Listen, all you need to know is they are all busted. I knew that was a risk for the active units, but I expected to pull replacements from the ship's spares. Unfortunately, because the power cut out so close to an event horizon, there was a feedback effect that disrupted *all* the ZPMs. Stupid wormhole."

"Oh," I cradled my head in my hands and closed my eyes. Why can't *anything* ever be simple and easy? "That sucks."

"Indeed. Imagine how I feel, discovering that after the work I did, it was all for *nothing*."

I glared up at him. "People *died*, you ass. The work you did is the last thing I care about."

"I am sorry, Joe. You're right."

"You can't take a bunch of these things, and cannibalize parts to get a couple of them working again?"

"No. You don't understand. Their connection to higher spacetime has been severed. I can access that spacetime, but my power is too great to channel into a ZPM to initiate the reaction. The ZPM would blow and damage the ship. What we need is a ZPM that has never been used, so I can initiate it and make it useful."

"I don't suppose they are giving away one of these ZPMs in a Happy Meal?"

"Sadly, no. Taco Bell had a promotion where you could get a ZPM after eating thirty chalupa meals in a month, but they had to cancel the promotion in the interest of public health."

"Good idea. Even I couldn't eat thirty chalupas in a month."

"Without ZPMs, we are-"

"Wait. ZPM*s*?" I put emphasis on the last 's' sound. "Like, more than one?"

"Sure. We need four of them for each reactor. Didn't I explain that?"

"Pretty sure I would have remembered that nagging little detail, you little shithead. Fine. Without a full complement of ZPMs- We can't keep calling this thing a ZPM," I declared.

"Does it matter, Joe?" Skippy sighed.

"Yeah, it does. ZPM is a Stargate thing, and you said the technology we need is *not* a zero-point energy device. What should we call it?" I mused, showing that once again, I was focused on what was truly important. "Explain to me again how this thing works."

"*Ugh.* The *Valkyrie*'s reactor power will create a portal to higher spacetime using a null-field, to access potential energy from the vacuum- Oh, explaining this to you is a *total* waste of my precious time," he fumed.

"Hmm," I leaned my chair back and stared at the ceiling. "Ok. Potential Energy Null-field, uh. And it multiplies, or enhances, the amount of energy you put into it. So, P, E, N-"

Reed interrupted me with a giggle, which became a snort that embarrassed her, which made her giggle more. "P.E.N.? Sir," she could barely talk. "If you plan to call this thing a *PENIS Enhancer*," she rocked back and forth so hard she nearly fell off her chair, "you may want to think-" Tears ran down her cheeks, she was laughing so hard. "Again."

That kind of made my quest to name the ZPM-type thing even more important, because if I didn't think up a good name, everyone was going to call it a 'penis enhancer'. "So, this thing is not a Zero Point Module, what should we call it?"

"Ugh. Does *that* really matter?"

"Do you want me to call it a 'dingus' or 'whatchmacallit'?"

"No! All right, fine. Um, it multiplies or amplifies, power fed into a quantum vacuum, um. How about we call it a Vacuum Power Multiplier?"

"VPM? I like it."

"Do you have any other idiotic requests to waste my time?"

"No, 'VPM' is good. So, can we make one?" I asked, while awkwardly avoiding the amused look I was getting from Reed.

"Nope." He folded his arms across his chest. That was a bad sign. "We don't have the equipment to make even one VPM, and we don't even have the capability to make the equipment we need. It would be easier to get a working VPM, than it would be to acquire all the specialized gear to make one. The factory where the Maxolhx manufacture and initiate VPMs is the size of a small *moon*, Joe."

"I was afraid you would say that. All right," I sighed. "How can we get a bunch of VPMs, that don't get broken in the process of us stealing them?"

"Well, heh heh-"

He didn't need to finish that thought.

CHAPTER THIRTY FOUR

Because the crew was feeling triumphant that we now had a bad-ass warship, and because Skippy had just told me we did *not*, in fact, have a warship at all, I called the off-duty crew into the galley to announce the bad news.

"What's up, Colonel?" Frey asked after the last few people trickled into the galley. With our small crew, there were plenty of seats for everyone.

I opened my mouth, but Skippy spoke before I could say anything. "As you all know, I have been working nonstop to bring the *Valkyrie* online. This has meant my bots have been unavailable for routine duties aboard the *Flying Dutchman*, and that much of our reactor output has been dedicated to supplying the *Valkyrie*. Laundry has not been done, artificial gravity has been reduced to sixty percent of Earth normal, and training opportunities for pilots and the STAR team have been limited. I appreciate the sacrifices you have all made, and I wish I could say it will be over soon. However, I now have an additional workload to handle, and dedicating my resources to this new task will delay bringing the *Valkyrie* online. This is a little embarrassing to say, but, well," He paused and mimicked taking a breath. "Joe wants me to work on building a penis enhancer for him."

If people had their eyes open any wider, they would have popped out of their heads. And all those eyes were staring in shock at *me*. "No, that is *not*-" I was drowned out by the crew laughing uproariously. There had been a second of stunned silence, until Reed burst out laughing, and everyone joined her.

"Hey!" Skippy glared at the crew. "Let's face it, the guy needs all the help he can ge-"

"Not funny!" I shouted.

"You are right, Joe." He put his hands on his hips and glared at the crew. "It is not funny and people should *not* be laughing at you. You are very brave to admit-"

"I am not admitting anything!" I screeched.

"Oh, Joe," he shook his head. "This is *so* sad. The first step in getting help is admitting that you have a problem. Your example can inspire men with your problem to-"

I lunged forward to grab his avatar around the neck so I could strangle him, but he winked out of existence and instantly reappeared a few feet away. I slapped the table there, then the next place he jumped to. There I was, playing wack-a-mole with a holographic avatar.

It was not my finest hour.

The game ended when my scalp tingled as he appeared to be standing on my head, and I slapped myself so hard I saw stars. His avatar floated in the air near the ceiling on the far wall, where I couldn't get him. I was out of breath, and I couldn't look up to meet anyone's eyes.

"Sir," Reed had gotten her giggling under control. "Sorry. Everyone, the, um, enhancer thing was *my* joke. Skippy discovered that to make the *Valkyrie* work, we need a vacuum-power thing to multiply, or *boost*, the output of the reactors. Which," it was her turn to glare at the supreme asshole. "He should have known before we started this project."

"Hey!" Skippy protested, uncomfortable that now all eyes were looking at him rather than me. "I couldn't have known this would be a problem! Well, Ok, I suspected it *might* be a problem. Very likely *would* be a problem, I mean, almost certainly, um-"

"You are not helping your case," I was grateful the attention of the crew was no longer focused on me.

"I didn't *know* for sure," he muttered. "Anywho, why dwell on the past, right?"

"The *Valkyrie* can't operate without this booster?" Desai asked, just as surprised as I was when I heard the bad news.

"The ship can fly," I explained. "But without these Vacuum Power Multipliers-"

"*These?*" Desai asked.

"Yes. We need a bunch of them," now I was feeling uncomfortable again. "Without VPMs, the *Valkyrie* can't do all the things that make a Maxolhx warship special."

"That is true," Skippy nodded, feeling safe enough to come back onto the table. "Without power multipliers, the *Valkyrie* might lose a battle against a Jeraptha destroyer. Many of the critical defensive and weapon systems aboard a Maxolhx warship are very power-hungry. Also, we need additional VPMs to upgrade the *Dutchman*. And for spares. We need lots of those."

"Very well, Sir," Smythe addressed his comment to me. "Give us the bad news, please. What must we do to get the VPMs we need?"

"Well, heh heh," is all Skippy said, and everyone groaned.

"Hey, Joe," Skippy's avatar appeared on my desk without warning. He did that often enough that it shouldn't have startled me, but I still wasn't used to it. Also, I had an immediate shock of guilt, because I had been playing a video game when he called. It made me feel like I was in school and the teacher caught me with a comic inside my textbook. Not that I ever did that, of course.

It was stupid of me to try turning the game off when he appeared, he already knew what I was doing. That was probably why I could not get past Level Two in the freakin' game. He had to be messing with me.

"Hey, Skippy."

"Why so glum, homeboy? You should be happy! We have a bad-ass battlecruiser, plus enough leftover parts to upgrade the *Flying Dutchman* so it's not just a space truck."

"Why am I glum? Jeez, I don't know," I directed my sarcasm at him, which was unfair. He had performed above and beyond my already unfairly high expectations, the fault was with myself. Maybe *I* needed to study about empathy. "Let's start with the fact that we do not have a bad-ass battlecruiser. We have an underpowered ship that can't operate the systems that make it a warship. Same with the *Dutchman*. None of those upgrades will make any difference unless we can steal a set of working VPMs to boost the output of the reactors. So, we have yet another impossible freakin' task; to steal a bunch of Vacuum Power Multipliers."

"Ok, but we have done that kind of stuff before, so what is really bothering you?"

"Two things, Skippy. No, three. First, we've had a good run of luck until recently. We didn't have anyone killed or even seriously injured, since we left Kombamik at the end of our Black Ops mission to start a civil war." That was true. People had suffered minor injuries in our raid against the Wurgalan, and on Gingerbread, and while we were flying around collecting components in the Roach Motel junkyard. None of those amounted to anything serious. People got injured worse in training. "Now, we lost people, and we have three people with injuries bad enough to sideline them permanently."

"Not *permanently*. No more than four months, Joe, until they are able to resume normal activities. I have been making substantial progress with modifying Maxolhx medical technology for human physiology, and I expect to begin trials next week."

"That is great, Skippy. Whew," I sat back in my chair and let out a long breath. "Are you sure about that?"

"Yes, absolutely. Regrowing limbs is a tricky process, but as Doctor Friedlander would say, it's not rocket science. I am one hundred percent confident in a complete recovery for all three of my patients. We have done that before with Thuranin nanomeds, and Maxolhx technology is substantially more advanced."

"Do they know about this yet? Your patients, I mean."

"No, Joe, I thought they should hear the good news from you."

"No. No way, Skippy. I'm not walking into sickbay to take credit for someone else's accomplishment. Smythe is the STAR team leader, *he* should tell them. Let Smythe know ASAP, and tell him what I said. Ok, let's get back to the subject. I don't mean to take anything away from your accomplishment, but 'normal activities' has a different definition for STAR team operators. They need a high level of fitness to perform their jobs. How long until those three people can effectively rejoin the team?"

"Oh, uh, hmm, good point. Well, they will be highly motivated to regain fitness, so they will likely overdo their rehab exercises and get injured again-"

"No, they won't," I shook my head. "Smythe made it crystal clear that he will not tolerate any cowboy shit. Anyone who does not adhere exactly to the recommended program of recovery will be dismissed. We are thin on operators already, we can't afford to lose people to stupidity. Assume they follow the program."

"I think you are being wildly optimistic, but sure, what the hell. Realistically, it will be another seven, maybe seven and a half months until those people could be considered fit for combat. Physical fitness is not the only issue, Joe. Regrowing limbs requires a patient's brain to rewire itself, to communicate with and control the new limb. That process can't be rushed. Those people are going to feel very uncoordinated at first, that is going to be frustrating. Especially to people who are used to being elite operators. What else is bothering you, Joe?"

"The usual problem, the obvious problem. Let's say somehow we get a batch of VPMs and we get *Valkyrie* fully operational. So what? We have no plan for what to do with our bad-ass battlecruiser. One ship can't take on a whole battlegroup, can it?"

"No. The *Valkyrie* will be more powerful than any single Maxolhx ship ever built, but it can't take on a battlegroup."

"Yeah, exactly. So, we still have no freakin' idea how to stop that battlegroup from getting to Earth," I slammed a fist on the desk, making Skippy jump back. "Sorry about that. Listen, are you sure you are locked out from using the bagel-slicer trick again?"

"Yes, I am sure."

"Are you *sure*?" I balled up my fists. "Maybe you are only locked out from doing it on that one wormhole?"

"No. Sorry, Joe, but the network has removed my access to that feature. The situation is actually worse than that. The network has now assumed direct control of that function, it is no longer available to *any* local source. Plus, even if I could use the bagel-slicer again, it would not do any good against a battlegroup."

"Why not?"

"The Maxolhx are not taking any chances, ever since they learned the Bosphuraq have advanced technology."

"Oh, crap! Did we screw ourselves *again*?"

"Apparently, yes. The Law of Unintended Consequences has bitten us on the ass again. Before a star carrier goes through a wormhole, it detaches a ship and sends that ship through to recon. Only after the recon ship sends an All Clear signal, does the star carrier approach the event horizon. Even if I could slice a star carrier in half, it would not do us any good. Let's say I could slice through the star carrier's spine, right where three ships are attached. That would leave five or six ships intact and highly motivated to kill us. Plus, the battlegroup going to Earth has *two* star carriers. The bagel-slicer trick only works on ships traveling alone."

"Crap. You're right," I groaned. "Now you see why I'm not jumping for joy?"

"Would it help if I said some useless empathy thing?"

"Not when you describe it that way, no."

"Why not?" He was genuinely surprised. "When people say meaningless shit like 'It's going to be all right' or 'He wasn't good enough for you anyway', everyone knows it's bullshit. But, supposedly, it makes people feel better to know that someone made the effort to pretend they care."

"*Pretend* they care?"

"Well, I suppose some people might actually care, although why anyone would waste their time on a whining *loser*, I can't imag-"

"Did you not learn *anything* about empathy?"

"Um, I learned that if you can fake it well enough, it makes people like you. Isn't that the point?"

"No, I – UGH!"

"Seriously, dude, why would you do anything that doesn't benefit yourself?"

I slapped my forehead hard enough to hurt. "So, when you do something nice for me, that is all for your benefit?"

"Not as far as you know, Joe. That's the point, *duh*. See? You are smiling now. This proves my theory. You know I am only pretending to care, but it still makes you feel better."

"I feel better, because I am imagining ejecting you out an airlock near a black hole."

"Hmm, so you *do* feel better. The score is Skippy one, monkey zero."

Still pissed at Skippy, I went to the galley for coffee. One recent improvement to the *Flying Dutchman* was a pair of cappuccino makers. Typically, I am a Dunkin' coffee guy, and I don't see the point of spending six freakin' dollars for a cup of hot water strained through crushed beans. A lot of the Pirates, like me, scoffed when the cappuccino machines were installed. But, because all you had to do was put a mug under the spout and press a button to get fresh, perfect coffee, we were hitting those machines like they were Pez dispensers. Skippy complained we were wearing out the machines, but I told him that if he couldn't keep coffee machines working, how could we trust him with our second-hand reactors?

He muttered a lot about it, but the machines kept pumping out delicious cappuccinos.

Adams was standing near the machines when I walked into the galley, carefully picking up her coffee. "Afternoon, Sir," she nodded to me as she reached into the fridge and squirted a tower of whipped cream into her cup.

"Afternoon, Gunny." I looked at what she was drinking and winked at her. "Is that a coffee, or an ice cream sundae?"

She grinned, hiding her face behind the cup as she drank from it. "The coffee-to-other-stuff ratio may be skewed away from coffee."

There was whipped cream on the tip of her nose, and I pointed to my own nose. "You've got, uh-"

"Oh," she laughed, wiping the cream away. "Coffee time?"

"I need something to get me through the afternoon. Skippy and I just had a discussion about empathy."

"Ooh," she rolled her eyes. "The one where he is all proud of being able to fake it, because he knows so much about the subject?"

I snapped my fingers. "That's the one." Sometimes, I forgot that I was not the only person Skippy talked with.

"How did you get on *that* subject?"

"Skippy asked if faking empathy would make me feel better, because I still have no idea how to stop that battlegroup from getting to Earth. We can't use the bagel-slicer again, and there are too many ships to try the overlapping-wormhole trick we used on our Renegade mission. I got the idea for the bagel-slicer in the galley." I looked around. "Maybe another appliance will inspire me?"

That made her laugh just as she was taking a sip of coffee, and she blew whipped cream into my face. "Oh! Sorry." She picked up a napkin, and dabbed at my face. The intimate gesture was awkward for both of us, and she stepped back to toss the napkin in a recycling can, avoiding my eyes.

"So," I cleared my throat. "Coffee." I pressed a button, and the machine began to make noises, then stopped. "Ah," it was my turn to be embarrassed. I placed a cup under the spout, and the machine resumed making brewing and spitting and foaming sounds.

Adams had not moved any farther away. Maybe both of us wanted closeness, even if it was only talking over food. "Do you see any inspiration, Sir?"

"Not unless Skippy can make a *really* big spatula," I winked, and picked up my hot cup of perfect coffee, contemplating the capital letters that spelled SHITHEAD in the foam. That was actually a nice design, compared to what the coffee machine usually generated for me. There were many options for designs in the foam, but none of them could be selected by the user, they were programmed by Skippy. That explained why *my* cappuccinos always had a middle finger, or a penis or a 'DUH' or some other insult in the foam. I noticed that women always got nice designs like hearts or flowers in the foam of their drinks. His continuing crush on Katie Frey was evident, in the increasingly elaborate artwork she got in her cappuccinos.

Of course, Skippy totally denied he had a crush on her.

"Ah, that's good," I said after taking a sip. "You know, Gunny. Maybe we should take it easy on these machines," I waved my cup toward the fancy coffee makers. "Someday, if we are forced to retreat to the beta site, we may be trapped where there are no coffee makers and-"

"I'll take your coffee, Sir," she said with amusement.

"Huh?"

"You have got that look on your face, and you were standing there with your mouth open for like, ten seconds. You almost spilled your coffee on the deck. You just got an idea."

"Maybe. It probably won't work. I have already dug into the bottom of the Clever Ideas barrel, I don't know if I can do it again."

"Yes, you can," she carefully took my coffee cup, which I had forgotten about. Her eyes darted around the galley to see if anyone was in earshot, and added in a whisper "Do it for *me*, Sir."

"*Skippy!*" I shouted as I got back into my office.

"You bellowed, sahib?" He asked with a mock bow.

"Damn straight I did. We are *doing* this," I slapped the desk for emphasis.

"Um, it would help if I knew *what* we are doing."

"We are going to beat the *crap* out of that battlegroup until they beg for mercy, then we're going to blow them straight to hell."

"Ok, Ok, not bad as an inspirational mission statement," he nodded. "One suggestion, if I may: you might want to fill in some part of the 'How The Hell Do We Do This' section of the diagram, you know?"

"Do not bother me with details, beer can, I'm on a roll."

"*Ugh.* Ok, sure, fine, whatever. Can I please get a hint?"

"I was in the galley, and I was thinking that someday, we won't be able to get replacement parts for the coffee machines."

"Hmm. I don't want to nitpick here, but may I point out that sounds like a problem, not a solution?"

"It is a problem, because if we are forced to retreat to the beta site, we will be trapped outside the galaxy. That is also the solution."

"Wow. You must be using a very unique definition of logic. I am not following you."

"We are going to hijack one of the wormholes that battlegroup flies through, and trap *them* outside the galaxy. *Far* outside, like, those motherfuckers are never getting back home to bother us again."

"Hmm," he contemplated the idea. "I *like* it, Joe."

"Score one for the monkey, huh?" I mentally patted myself on the back.

"Can I bother you with a trifling detail?"

"Depends. Is this detail going to harsh my buzz?"

"No. This detail is going to run over your buzz with a garbage truck, back up to do it again, set it on fire, then scrape up the charred remains and shoot them into the Sun."

"Shit. What is it *this* time?"

"As you already should know, only heavy or super-duty wormholes can connect out that far. So, heh heh, this is such a trifling detail, I shouldn't bother you with it. However, since you asked, none of the wormholes along the battlegroup's route are the heavy or super-duty type."

"Crap! Damn it!"

"So, do you want to give up now, or keep going until your inevitable defeat is truly humiliating?"

"Ha! No way. Give me a minute."

"Joe, I could give you until the last proton in this spacetime decays, but it will not change the facts. Oh! In case you are thinking we could mess with all the wormholes along their route, so the battlegroup would be forced to go through a heavy or super-duty wormhole, you can fuggedaboutit. There are *no* heavy or super-duty wormholes that connect anywhere near Goalpost, so the Maxolxh would never fly in the direction we need them to go. Plus, as I mentioned before, I need to be careful about screwing with multiple wormholes, because it risks a catastrophic shift that could affect the entire local network."

"You just love to crush my dreams, don't you?"

"Joe, as your true friend, it is my job to keep you from getting hurt by unrealistic expectations. As you said, your supply of clever ideas is going to run out someday. This may be the day."

"Skippy, please, *please*, never let one of your subminds run a suicide prevention hotline, Ok?"

"Crap. Well, damn it, you should have told me that *before* we left Earth," he grumbled.

My eyes narrowed as I glared at him. "Why is that?"

"Oh, no reason. Nothing we can do about it now, anyway, huh?" He added quickly. "Gosh, how about you tell me your great idea?"

"I did, and you ran it over with a garbage truck, you asshole."

"I'm an asshole for telling you the truth?"

"No, you're an asshole for enjoying it."

"Ah, Ok, I guess that's fair. Really, of the possible types of humiliation you could suffer, that is only-"

"Types," I pronounced the word slowly. "Like, type, *ss*," I dragged out the 'S' sound. "Plural. Like, more than one of something."

"What about it?"

"Skippy, what makes a wormhole a heavy or super-duty type? Is it a different structure, or just its throughput capacity, something like that?"

"Um, you just blew my mind by using the term 'throughput'. Yes, Joe, the basic structures are the same, the difference is the amount of power that can be fed through them. That's kind of a geeky question, why do you ask?"

"Because I want to know, it is possible to make a regular wormhole into a heavy-duty one? Temporarily?"

"Oooh, that *is* a good question. Very good, Joe. That was *quite* clever of you."

"Ah ha! See, you doubted me, and-"

"The answer is no, but, *good* try. Get yourself a juice box."

"The answer is *no*? Are you sure?"

"I can create a subroutine to perform the analysis over and over, and get the same negative result until the end of time, if you like."

"I do not like."

"Then, the answer is no. Can't be done, dumdum. A wormhole's throughput capacity is determined by characteristics outside this spacetime. That capacity was determined by the Elders when they built the network. I can't change it. Before you waste my time with ignorant questions, no. *No*, there is no magical Elder device we could capture, that can increase the throughput of a wormhole. Even if there was, I wouldn't know how to use it."

"Crap."

"Joe, I hate to say this- No, actually I am *totally* enjoying this moment," he chuckled like the bad guy in a James Bond flick. "It is quite possible that your bagel-slicer concept was the very last clever idea you will ever have."

"That *sucks*." I held my hands like I was holding both halves of a bagel. Pulling my hands apart, I looked at the imaginary bagel, then pressed it back together. Finally, realizing how silly I was being, I clapped my hands together in disgust and-

"Holy shit," I gasped.

"What?"

"Skippy, it is possible to connect *multiple* wormholes? Instead of one endpoint to another, we-" I dug a marker out of a drawer and began sketching on the wall, drawing four ovals. Two of the ovals were far apart, but the two in the middle were almost touching. "Look, wormholes connect like this, right?" I drew a line between the oval on the far right and the one of the right side of the middle, then did the same with the two on the left.

"The endpoint of a wormhole can connect to only one point on the other end, yes," he agreed. "What are you getting at?"

Tapping the marker at the two in the middle, I asked. "What if two wormholes had endpoints so close together, their event horizons in the middle were almost touching? A ship going in this end," I tapped the oval on the far left, "would come out the other end, and *immediately* go into the other wormhole without being able to stop. It would ultimately arrive here," I tapped the oval on the far right. "Is that possible?"

"Before I answer that question, of what possible use would this concept be?"

Sometimes, it really surprised me how Skippy could not make imaginative connections in his vast brain. "Because, the kitties go into good old reliable wormhole they have used thousands of times, but it takes them to a place they did not want to go. Like, far outside the galaxy."

"Ohhhhh," he got it. "That second wormhole is a super-duty type, right?"

"As you would say; 'Egg-*zactly*'. Can it be done?"

"Joe, I truly do not know. This is quite intriguing. My initial answer is no, it can't be done. As you know, there are cases where the figure-eight patterns of wormholes overlap, and the network is very careful to avoid endpoints emerging where they might interfere with each other. Certainly, the network would not allow the event horizons to overlap for obvious reasons, but hmmm. Event horizons that are *parallel* to each other. Facing each other and really close, but not touching?"

"That's the idea, yeah. Can you do that?"

"Again, I do not know. I will need to think about it. If, *if*, it can be done, I suspect it will be a one-shot deal. The network may allow me to do it, only because the network probably never anticipated anyone would attempt such a lunatic scheme. After that, the network almost certainly will alter its programming to prevent that crazy shit from happening again."

"Crap. So, there's no way to test it?"

"Not on an actual Elder wormhole, no. However, because I am Skippy the *Magnificent*, I can test the concept by using microwormholes. Like their larger Elder cousins, my microwormholes are stable tunnels through spacetime, with event horizons on both ends."

"Great! That is awesome, Skippy, I knew you could do it."

"Um, hold your praise until I have time to test the concept. I need to do this at a safe distance from the ship, and it will likely be an iterative process. Um, that means-"

"Iterative means you keep doing it until you get it right. I'm not stupid, Skippy."

"Says the guy who still has cappuccino foam on his lip."

"Oh," I wiped my upper lip and, damn it, he wasn't lying.

"I must warn you, there might be a lot of trial-and-error until I figure out how to do it. *If* it can be done."

"If anyone can do it, you can."

"That praise would mean a lot more, if it wasn't coming from a monkey."

"When can you start testing?"

"Preparing for a test now."

"Wow. That was fast."

"Ah, this idiotic notion of yours has me intrigued, so I'm throwing you a bone. Now, please, shut up and leave me alone to work. I'm still assembling the *Valkyrie*, upgrading the *Dutchman*, and now I have to conduct a series of dangerous experiments with microwormholes. So give me space to-"

"Uh, wait. What do you mean dangerous?"

"I will be placing the event horizons of microwormholes in close proximity. Remember what happened the last time we deliberately overlapped wormholes?"

"Sure. It blew the hell out of a Maxolhx cruiser. But that's because one of those wormholes was created by the jump drive of the cruiser. That jump drive had a tremendous amount of energy. Microwormholes are small, like *tiny*. How could they be dangerous?"

"All wormholes, even at nanoscale, are tears in the fabric of local spacetime. What do you think it takes for me to create one of my magical creations? I assure you, it does not involve a pair of 'D' size batteries, dumdum."

"Oh. So, what would happen if two microwormholes overlapped?"

"Again, because I have never done that, I truly do not know. The result could be a faint fizzle, or an impressive eruption of potential energies from higher dimensions."

"Well, crap, whatever you're doing, stop it right now."

"You *don't* want me to conduct the experiments?"

"I *want* you to perform your mad scientist tricks somewhere away from the ship. We can load the microwormholes into those little disposable sensor probes you threw together. Then you can smash them together like demolition derby cars at a county fair."

"Oh. Good point, Joe. Hmm. I will need to balance being far enough away to be safe, while being close enough for me to have very precise control over the probes as I maneuver them."

"Yeah, and there's a third thing you need to factor in. The experiment needs to be close enough that we can see it from the ship."

"Um, Ok. Why is that?"

"Skippy, come on, are you kidding me? You will be playing demolition derby and blowing shit up. I *gotta* see that!"

Shockingly, I was not the only person who wanted to watch Skippy's Wormhole Extreme Grudge Match. We had to schedule the test for when most people would be off duty, and we set up the galley like we did for movie night, with the chairs facing the big display wall. We made a big batch of popcorn, and I authorized beer for the evening. It might surprise you, but demolition derby and blowing shit up proved to be popular with the crew, especially, and I know this is unexpected, with the guys. Go figure, huh?

Skippy even had the ship's fabricators crank out T-shirts for the occasion.

Skippy must have gotten into the festive mood, or his control over the little probes holding microwormholes was not as precise as he bragged about, because the first test was a failure. The crew cheered when they saw the two probes get ripped apart, then they groaned when they realized how little energy had been released.

"Hmm," Skippy muttered. "Well, shit."

"Those disposable probes aren't accurate enough for the job?" I asked.

"They are crude, but I can compensate. My disappointment was over the lack of useful data from the experiment. Those darned event horizons are so small, I could barely see them. Um, Joe, I think I need to pump up the volume, if you know what I mean."

"I thought microwormholes fall apart if you expand them."

"That is true, but I can hold them in an expanded state, long enough for me to verify the results of the experiment."

"Ok, sounds good. Go ahead."

"Um, I will need to move the probes farther from the ship. That will take twenty minutes or more. Remember, microwormholes must be maneuvered very gently, I can't slam the probes into high acceleration."

"Shit." I looked around at the disappointed faces around me.

"If you like, I can entertain the crowd with selections from my opera."

"I would *not* like," I waved my arms for calm as faces turned white and people stood up abruptly to leave. "Twenty minutes, huh?"

"More like thirty. Forty, to be safe."

"Ok, then how about you show us a classic episode of the A-Team while we wait?"

"Ooh! Ooh! *Really*?! Don't toy with me, Joe."

"For realz, homeboy. Hey, could you add witty commentary, like on Mystery Science Theater?"

"Joe," he was choked up with emotion. "If I never said this before, I *love you*, my brotha."

"You never said it, but right back atcha, brother."

The A-Team sucked a lot less than I remembered. Maybe it was Skippy's hilarious commentary, or how he perfectly overdubbed some of the dialog. Mister T's classic line 'I pity the fool' became 'I'm a pretty girl', which, considering his gaudy jewelry, kind of made more sense. The A-Team emptied a whole crate of five point five six ammo at point-blank range without hitting anything, and that Starbuck guy got with the girl at the end. We all had great fun laughing at the team's poor muzzle discipline and other screw-ups.

Then it was time to resume blowing shit up for real.

Skippy became increasingly frustrated, the explosions became increasingly larger, and the crowd in the galley became increasingly more vocal as wormholes collided every couple minutes. We were all having great fun, except I began to worry we would run out of disposable drones before Skippy completed his experiments.

Then, a pair of wormholes approached, and nothing exploded. The probes backed away, approached again, once, twice, seventeen times until Skippy was satisfied. "Success! It works. Damn, this is yet another sign of my awesomeness."

"Great," I clapped my hands. "Will it work with a real wormhole?"

"Those *are* real wormholes, Joe," he sniffed, offended. "The operating principles are the same, just scaled up enormously. I will need to keep the event horizons separated by eight hundred meters."

"Oh," I tried to keep my dismay from showing. "That's farther apart than I thought it would be." In my mind, I had imagined the two event horizons almost touching each other. "Will a ship coming out of one wormhole have time to avoid going through the other one?"

"No way, dude," he assured me. "The standard speed for Maxolhx ships transitioning through a wormhole is around seventeen hundred kilometers per hour. Ships would fly through the gap before their sensors could reset. Even if a ship realized what was happening, no way could it turn quickly enough to avoid going through the second wormhole. And if by some freakin' miracle a ship managed to alter course that quickly, it would clip the edge of the second wormhole's event horizon, and tear the ship apart. Uh!" He held up a finger and shushed me before I could speak. "Before you ask if I could offset the wormholes, so ships would deliberately hit the edge of the second wormhole, the answer is *NO*. I already thought of that and tested it. It's *not* possible. Unless the event horizons are aligned precisely to mirror each other, their event horizons skew along one axis, and collide with catastrophic results."

"Oh. Well, thanks for checking that. Are we done? Are you satisfied with the test results?"

"Yes, except for one thing."

"What's that?"

"Hold my beer." He expanded the last two microwormholes, and smashed them together for an impressive explosion. The crowd in the galley cheered. "Joe, we should talk about details."

"Ok, uh," the crowd wasn't ready for the show to be over. "How about you run another A-Team episode for the crew, and you and I will talk in my office?"

CHAPTER THIRTY FIVE

I had mentally prepared some lavish praise for Skippy, but as soon as I got into my office, he crushed my hopes. "That was fun. You do realize your plan will never work, right?"

"Uh-"

"Come on. You can't be *that* dimwitted."

"I might surprise you, Skippy. Try me."

"Ugh. Dude, this is *so* simple. There are *many* obstacles to making your plan work. Did you think this through? No, wait, of course you didn't. You just blurted out something off the top of your head, without considering all the potential problems. Think, Joe, *think.* You keep saying that you need to stop reacting to events, and create a long-term plan, but instead, you keep lurching from one crisis to another."

That was harsh, and it hurt to hear, and it was true. No, not completely true. When we completed our Renegade mission, I was congratulating myself for having secured humanity's future for several hundred years. Even after Emily Perkins unknowingly screwed everything up for us, we dreamed up a brilliant plan to frame the Boshpuraq, a plan that should have worked. It did work, except the Maxolhx are prideful, stubborn asswipes. "I hear you. We haven't done anything yet, so we have plenty of time to-"

"Joe, the problem is not just this particular issue. You need to wargame your plans, run them through what-if scenarios to see if there are any glaringly obvious flaws in your thinking. Hint: there are. See, if you were a real colonel, you would have learned to do that. Ok, I'll break this down Barney-style for you. To make this plan work, we need to connect one of the wormholes along battlegroup's flightpath, to at least a heavy-duty wormhole. The endpoints of those wormholes must emerge near each other. Do you foresee any problem with that?"

"Ah, crap. Yeah. To make those work, the figure-eight patterns of the two wormholes have to be overlapping each other. I suppose none of the wormholes along their flightpath overlay their patterns with a heavy-duty wormhole?"

"No, they do not, Joe. In fact, along their most likely flightpaths, there are only three wormholes that overlay with other wormholes, in what we call a cluster. All of those three along their potential flightpaths clusters lead in the wrong direction, *away* from any heavy-duty wormholes."

"Damn it, you asshole. You knew this plan wouldn't work, yet you let me make a show of the tests in front of the whole crew? I look like a fool now."

"Right. You look like a fool *now*," his voice dripped with sarcasm. "Joe, I didn't warn you against making a big deal of the tests, because I thought for certain the tests would be a complete failure, and that would be the end of it. My fear was that *I* would look like a fool. Joe the clever monkey has another genius idea, but Skippy the idiot can't make it work. It surprised even me that my extreme awesomeness developed a way to hold event horizons parallel, without their destabilizing effect on local spacetime causing them to touch and destroy each other. So, I figured, why not let the monkeys have some fun at my expense? Now I am stuck trying to make your impractical idea work, and *I* will look like the bad guy. If you had more than one brain cell, you would have known this plan had no chance, even if we could find the right combination of wormholes."

"Clearly, my brain is not working today, so why don't you smack some knowledge on me?"

"This is disappointing, Joe. You already have this knowledge, you are not applying it. Ok, I won't keep an idiot in suspense. Your plan might work, if the Maxolhx were sending only one ship, or a bunch of ships attached to a single star carrier. Instead, they are sending two star carriers. Also, as I told you before, the Maxolhx are being cautious, ever since they believe they discovered the Bosphuraq have access to unknown advanced technologies. The standard operating procedure of that battlegroup, when approaching a wormhole, is to send a ship ahead to scout for danger. The star carriers wait a safe distance away, while one ship detaches and goes through the wormhole. That ship scans the area on the other side, and the star carriers proceed to go through the event horizon only if they get an All Clear signal from the scout ship. The star carriers go through one at a time, with several minutes between them. You see the problem now?"

"Yeah," I groaned. He was right. I am a short-sighted dumdum. "Sorry for- wait." Maybe I'm not such a dumdum. "We still have those pixie things, right? We can wait on the far end, outside the galaxy, until the scout ship comes through. Then, we copy its pixie signature, and fake an All Clear message back to the star carriers. After the second star carrier comes through, we sneak around them, back to the galaxy, and you shut down the wormhole behind- Wait. No, no I just heard myself talking, and that is a stupid idea. We would have to also copy the pixie of the first star carrier-"

"Plus the pixies of every ship attached to that star carrier," he finished my thought. "Plus, we would have to jam the transmissions of all ships, while the *Valkyrie* remains in stealth. Plus, *plus*, the Maxolhx could simply turn their ships around and go back through. We would have to destroy or disable all the ships that come through. Even *Valkryie* can't take on that many ships of equivalent technology."

"To make this work," I leaned back in my chair, closing my eyes. The beginnings of a headache were starting to throb in my skull. "We would need to hack into the communications systems of all the ships in the battlegroup, plus hack their navigation, so they couldn't turn around and go back through to warn the ships still on this side. Ah, you're right, it is freakin' impossible."

"Joe, much as it delights me to see you wallow in self-loathing, I must put you out of your misery. It is- Ugh, I can't *believe* I am telling you this. I am smart, why do I go looking for trouble? Ok, numbskull, listen good because I'm only going to say this once. It *is* possible to hack into the control systems of a Maxolhx ship. It would only allow temporary control, and only over secondary systems the Maxolhx consider unimportant."

"Secondary systems? Like what, their coffee maker?"

"No, not the coffee maker, you moron."

"Ok, then you can hack into navigation, propulsion, communications, any of that?"

"No, no, and no."

"You might want to rethink about your definition of-"

"Joe, do you know how a navigation system works?"

"Uh, yes, *duh*. I am a pilot."

"That is debatable. Navigation is about determining where you are, deciding where you want to go, and calculating a course to your destination, right?"

"That's a very simple way to explain it, but, yeah. You plot a course from where you are, to your destination."

"Mm hmm," he agreed. "To plot a course, you need to use *math*, right?"

"Uh, sure? I mean, I-" In my head I went through the steps of programming a dropship navigation system. "I don't actually crunch the numbers, the nav system does that."

"Correct. You monkeys randomly bash your fists on the keyboard, and the system does the actual math, without you needing to know how the math actually works. Maxolhx starships work the same way. All their AIs and subsidiary systems rely on library files to tell them that the number Three comes between Two and Four."

"Seriously?"

"How do *you* know the sequence of numbers?"

"Uh, I learned it in school, I guess?"

"You learned it, but now that information is stored somewhere in the gray mush you call a brain. My point is, you never have to think about it, the info is just *there*. Maxolhx computer systems work the same way. They rely on library files for basic info. So basic, they never think about it. Those library files are taken for granted, and the security on them is relatively poor. I can hack into those library files, corrupt the math, and the AIs will be unable to function."

"It can't be that simple."

"Ah, but it is, Joe. This is a vulnerability I discovered when I examined the *Valkyrie*. The Maxolhx have developed computer systems so sophisticated, they have forgotten how those systems really work. The rotten kitties, and their AIs, take for granted many things they never have to consciously think about. When the ship control AIs realize there is a problem, they will crash. After a lengthy reboot procedure, they will perform the calculations by themselves, and create a workaround to bypass the systems affected by my hack. That will take several minutes, if the hack works the way I expect. Those arrogant AIs will at first not believe what is happening."

"Unless those AIs are more clever than you expect. My problem is with the 'several minutes' part. Will that be long enough for a scout ship, and then two star carriers, to go through?"

"Oh, certainly, Joe. Standard operating procedure for Maxolhx warships is to go through wormholes and jump away as quickly as possible. Lingering near wormholes is one of the few places where Maxolhx warships are vulnerable, so they skedaddle through as quickly as they can. From the time when the scout ship goes through, it should take no more than seven minutes until the second star carrier reaches the event horizon."

"*Seven* minutes is longer than *several* minutes, Skippy."

"Ugh, fine. To be precise, I expect the control AIs of those ships to take ten or more minutes to fix the problem and restore navigation control."

"That doesn't sound right, Skippy. I know you think other AIs are stupid, but-"

"This is not merely me being arrogant. While the AIs are trying to fix the problem, they will be hampered because their own internal operations will be affected by the hack. Joe, I know a temporary glitch in how simple math works sounds like it can't be important, but it will *crash* those AIs. They will need to reboot themselves, and they will be *very* cautious about re-establishing connections to subsidiary systems like communications and navigation. Ten minutes is actually an optimistic guess about how long it will take the scout ship's AI to defeat the hack; it could take far longer. We only need to worry about the scout ship's AI, because the lead star carrier will certainly not have time to restore itself before the second star carrier follows."

"Skippy, I am going to trust your super-nerdy math and logic skills about this one. That's great, thank you. But, ah, as you said, this is all a stupid waste of time anyway. There is no way to connect a wormhole along their flightpath to a heavy-duty wormhole."

"Um, I did *not* exactly say that."

"Uh, what?"

"I said it is impossible to *directly* connect any wormhole along their potential flightpaths to a heavy-duty wormhole." He winked at me.

"Oh, crap, Skippy. What lunatic scheme are you cooking up in your ginormous brain?"

"Behold," he announced as a star chart popped up on my laptop. "Their potential flightpaths pass through three wormhole clusters. For example, see this cluster of two wormholes near the Crescent Nebula. I can connect," the display showed a yellow dotted line. "One of those Crescent wormholes to a wormhole cluster in the Perseus Arm. From there, connect to a wormhole cluster here," he highlighted another point. "Near the Eagle nebula. That will connect to a cluster back in the Perseus Arm, roughly in the vicinity of the Crab nebula. And *that* wormhole cluster includes a dormant super-duty wormhole on the other side of the Messier-Five globular cluster, about thirty thousand lightyears from Earth. Pretty cool, huh?"

"Holy *shit*, Skippy," I gasped. "You plan to use *four* wormholes? The battlegroup would be going through four wormholes, with their event horizons floating parallel?"

"That is the plan, yes. Um, that's the best-case scenario. Depending which flightpath those ships fly, they might select a wormhole that requires me to connect *six* wormholes, before dumping that battlegroup far beyond the galaxy."

"You can really do that?"

"Joe, clearly you do not appreciate my *extreme* level of awesomeness. The Elders said 'No way could anyone connect six wormholes together' and I said '*Hold my beer*'," he chuckled.

"I bow to the awesomeness," I waved my hands up and down in a worship gesture. "All these possible connections would dump the battlegroup out near the messy thing?"

"Messier-Five, Joe. It is a globular star cluster. No, that is only one of the three possible scenarios. The others would strand the kitties near Messier-Thirteen, or about a quarter of the distance to the Ursa Minor dwarf galaxy." He took off his huge admiral's hat and scratched his silver dome. "It is kind of a puzzle why the Elders placed wormholes out in the middle of nowhere, but it really doesn't matter. Even though the star carriers of that battlegroup are modified for a long-range voyage, they will not ever return to the galaxy. Those ships will slowly fail in empty intergalactic space, as their systems fail. We will never be bothered by those ships again, that is for certain."

"Assuming your crazy connection thing works. I don't know, this looks super sketchy."

"Joe, leave it all to me, I will make it happen. There is only one thing I need you monkeys to do for me."

"I know. We need to trust the awesomeness. Ok, so we can do this, if we get one of these math scrambler things. I don't know why I am asking this question, because I already know that I am very much not going to like the answer." I exhaled as I hung my head, anticipating another pounding headache coming on. "How do we hack the libraries in those star carriers?"

"Not just the star carriers, Joe. We need to hack the libraries in *all* the ships of the battlegroup. Those ship AIs talk to each other, and even though library files are so basic as to be beneath the conscious notice of even the lowliest submind, there are primitive systems that pay attention to mundane details. If those systems discover even one ship's library is different, questions will be asked, and there will be a discussion that could go up to the submind level. My changes will be erased, and very likely there will be an investigation into how the files became corrupted. The Maxolhx will increase security around those files that have gone pretty much unnoticed until now, and we'll be screwed. Huh," he pondered. "That's going to happen anyway, but if it happens before-"

"Whoa. What do you mean, it's going to happen anyway? What?"

"Oh. I meant, it is inevitable the Maxolhx will discover the hack, investigate, and lock down their library files in the future. We will only be able to pull off this particular trick once, Joe."

"*Ugh*," it was my turn to use Skippy's favorite expression of disgust or exasperation. "Break it down for my Barney-style, please."

"No problem, Joe, I know this is complicated for a monkey brain to understand. Hell, it's complicated for *me* to understand," he admitted. "The battlegroup is at a spacedock orbiting the planet Kulashant, which is a major staging facility for the Maxolhx Science and Intelligence Ministry. The spacedock receives file updates from the surface, then propagates those files to ships attached to the station. We need to hack into the libraries of those ships, but not any other ships. If the Maxolhx discover someone targeted the ships going to Earth-"

"Yeah, I get it." He didn't need to explain. "We would be screwed, whether we can stop that battlegroup or not. Ok, go on. Tell me how this thing would work. Where do we start?"

"It has to start by me hacking into the library files at the source, in the data archives at the S and I Ministry on the surface of Kulashant. The spacedock's AI will accept signals from the surface without question, as long as they have the proper authentication codes, of course. The spacedock AI's data security is substantially better than the facility on assdKulasahnt, I suppose the Maxolhx do not expect an enemy could ever get to the surface undetected. Or they just can't imagine why the Ministry offices would ever be a target, while the starship servicing infrastructure in orbit is an obvious target. So, it is much easier for me to hack into the data archives on the surface, than it would be more me to try that at the spacedock."

"I hate this idea already, but tell me more."

"Ok, so I hack into the data archive. Part of the file I plant will be a notice of a required update. Nothing urgent, because that would attract attention. The update priority level will be set so that ships in orbit should get the file, but it does not need to be rushed out to the fleet. The file will contain a virus that instructs the spacedock to push the update only to ships attached to the battlegroup going to Earth. The virus won't say that, of course, it will target those ships by their registration number."

"I understand that part. How will the virus be triggered? I don't want to rely on us, I mean you, sending a signal or something."

"Nope. This is," he chuckled, "sort of me being an evil genius, Joe. When the ships of the battlegroup emerge from the last wormhole, and realize they are outside the galaxy, their navigation systems will request obscure data from their library, to verify their position. Ships would never access that data unless they were far beyond the galaxy, that's how I know the file won't be called up early. When called, that file will corrupt the math subroutines of the entire library, and presto! The AI crashes to protect itself."

"You *are* an evil genius," I agreed. "Question: you said something like, if the library files of even one ship are different, our whole scheme will be exposed. The files of the station will be different from those aboard any ship not assigned to the battlegroup going to Earth. How is that not a problem?"

"It *will* be a problem, Joe," he sighed. "Once the libraries of the battlegroup have been infected by my virus, future updates will be frozen. If there is a priority update, the battlegroup will report they got it, but their files won't change. However, the next time there is a real update, the Maxolhx will realize the library of the spacedock is not the same as the archives on the planet. The kitties will assume the problem was data corruption and not a security breach, but I expect they will lock down their systems."

"Shit. That's no good, Skippy," I groaned, imagining the whole plan falling apart on us. "We would have to hack into the battlegroup's libraries right before they left spacedock, or the kitties will discover there is something wrong."

"What? Oh, sorry, dude. No, that is *not* a major risk to us. Operating system library files are only updated once a year. Sometimes several years can go by without an update. That operating system has existed virtually unchanged for thousands of years, Joe. It is so efficient and reliable that no one ever thinks about it, not even AIs. The odds of a real update being pushed, before the battlegroup departs, are extremely unlikely. Even if the hack is discovered, the Maxolhx will assume it is just data corruption. They will fix the spacedock's library, and that will erase all evidence of my hack. Joe, this operation has substantial risks, like shaky-hands, nausea-inducing risks. But those risks are all about gaining access to the archives on the surface. The cyber aspect of the plan is actually low-risk. If you can get me to the surface, I got this."

"Like I said, I am hating this plan. But, if this is our best idea- This is your best idea, right?"

"It is my *only* idea, Joe. What do you mean, my idea? Planning lunatic stunts is *your* job."

"Not this time. Cyber stuff is your area. We don't need the STAR team to do this, will we?"

"I don't think so, but again, *I* am not in charge of dreaming up wacky shenanigans."

"Crap. All right. Do you need to be down there, or can we do this remotely, through a microwormhole?"

"Sadly, we can't use a microwormhole. I must go with you."

"I do not like that idea, Skippy."

"Neither do I. Ugh, being stuck in a dropship with bunch of monkeys makes me gag. Seriously, what is that new aftershave you're using? Essence of warthog?"

"I not *wearing* aftershave."

"Huh. *Really*? Um, forget I said anything."

"Asshole. Why can't we use a microwormhole? We used one at Detroit to access the pixie factory, and you said the security there was super-tight."

"Security at Detroit was intense. However, to avoid affecting the production of pixies, the kitties could not use disruptor fields as a security measure. There is a disruptor field around the S and I Ministry data facility, that would tear apart a wormhole, even a tightly-controlled microwormhole. I must be physically down there, to extend my presence. I have to do that very carefully on a low power setting, that's why I can't do it from orbit. My guess is I will need to be within, oh, maybe a kilometer."

"A kil- a freakin' *kilometer*? Are you crazy? Hell, I hope they have valet parking for our dropship."

"I hope you are joking about that, Joe. Although we *will* need a Panther to get down there."

"Uh, no way. Panthers are too valuable. We will use a beat-up old Dragon to create another DeLorean."

"Nuh-uh, dude. We can't jump to the surface. We can't use microwormholes down there, remember? That includes jump wormholes. Detroit was a special case. There will not be any crazy shit like jumping dropships through wormholes. To get to the surface of Kulashant, we will have to fly down the old-fashioned way."

"Skippy, this might the *worst* idea I have ever heard, and I am kind of an expert about terrible ideas. How the hell are we supposed to fly you down to the surface, get within a kilometer of this ministry building, and get back safely?"

"Wow. If you think *your* ideas are bad, you are really not going to like this…"

CHAPTER THIRTY SIX

"Sir?" Smythe knocked on my doorframe. I hadn't realized he was aboard the *Dutchman* again, he had been spending most of his time over at the *Valkyrie*. "Skippy informed me that we have a new objective?"

"Yeah," I waved for him to sit down. "You know about the VPM boosters we need to get? Now we also need to sneak into a library."

"*Sir?*"

That was totally worth it, and I winked at him. It was very rare to see Smythe showing surprise, and my off-hand comment had thrown him off balance. I explained briefly. "I do not love this plan," I added.

"I can see why you would bloody well hate it," he agreed. "We have taken on risk before, but landing a dropship on the surface of a Maxolhx world-" He shook his head. "There are too many things that could go wrong."

"It's worse than that. *Everything* has to go exactly right, or the plan is blown. You haven't heard the worst part yet."

"I haven't?"

"Skippy can mask the interior of the Panther from most sensor scans, but he can't conceal a nuclear warhead. We can't bring a nuke down there for self-destruct if we are exposed. The best we could do is a Thuranin missile warhead."

"That might leave detectable human remains," Smythe noted, speaking of my potential death as if it were a mere inconvenience.

"It would. Reed and I will be aboard the Panther, with Skippy and two special guest stars."

"Two of our Maxolhx friends from the cooler?" He guessed. We had not taken any prisoners from capturing the *Valkyrie*, but we had plenty of Maxolhx bodies. The seven corpses that were in the best condition were being preserved, in case we ran into a situation where leaving behind Maxolhx remains might be necessary.

"You got it. If we have to blow the Panther, the presence of two Maxolhx corpses should get the kitties thinking their own people were flying it, not us. The problem is, if we do blow the warhead, that will leave Skippy stuck on the surface. He would be effectively lost, unless you and Desai cook up a plan to rescue him."

"Without Skippy's help? Not bloody likely, Sir. Well," he relaxed a bit, now that he knew what insane new thing we had to do. "We will have time to think of alternatives, while we are working to acquire these VPM boosters we need."

"Uh, no." I knew he would be disappointed with my decision. "We're doing the library op first, then we go hunt for boosters."

"*Sir?*" Man, I was surprising him a lot. He leaned forward. "Surely, having a fully capable battlecruiser will make anything else we do much easier."

"Not really. We actually don't need the *Valkyrie* for the library op. It's Skippy, a dropship, and a whole lot of prayers. No STAR team, no fighting. We're hitting the library first." I saw the skeptical look he gave me. "Listen, Smythe, there is a method to my madness. I know we expended a lot effort, a lot of blood, to capture the *Valkyrie*. But we did that for a purpose; to stop the Maxolhx from reaching Earth. If Skippy can't hack into those library files, we are dead in the water, and I don't want to risk more lives to capture boosters we may not need. It's that simple."

"Very well, Sir," he replied stiffly. He did not agree. He did not approve.

I tried another argument. "*Valkyrie* is a big stick. It is just not big *enough*, not by itself. Even if our bad-ass warship could take on a whole battlegroup, there would be a whole lot of debris left behind that we would have to explain. If even *one* ship managed to jump away during a battle, everything we've done is for nothing. You know that if it came to a fight, the Maxolhx would sacrifice the rest of their ships to assure one ship got away. We can't risk it. Like Skippy said," I tried to give my best smile, but it failed. "Never bring a starship to a wormhole fight."

His lips straightened into a thin line. "You may be right about that, Sir," he admitted reluctantly. He did not like the idea that we would, even temporarily, set aside the prospect of building one of the most powerful ships in the galaxy. The whole crew was going to feel the same way, that is why I hadn't told anyone about my decision. Smythe could help me sell the idea. While the crew were well-disciplined and would follow my orders, I wanted them to buy into the decision. Morale had taken a hit after the boarding operations had been a chaotic mess, then soared when Skippy began assembling the mighty *Valkyrie*. Now I was going to crush people's hopes, even if they ultimately agreed with my logic.

Eight days later, I was questioning my own logic. Questioning my *sanity*. Reed and I were checking the Panther we had selected for the flight down to Kulashant. That dropship was nothing special, and that was the point. It was just a standard model that had been resting securely in clamps when we sliced the *Valkyrie* apart. Reed was outside, inspecting the engines, while I tested the supports we would use, for holding the pair of dead Maxolhx who were coming with us.

Done in the cabin, I walked outside. "You ready for this, Reed?"

Her head was inside an engine intake, so her voice was muffled. "Do you want the truth, Sir?"

"Actually, yes," I was relieved that she wanted to speak freely. Skippy's plan for hacking the library was really, really dangerous and I really, really hated it. We also didn't have a better alternative for hacking the library, or for preventing the first ship going through Skippy's Magical Chain of Wormholes from signaling the two star carriers behind it.

She turned around and stepped down the ladder. "We have done some crazy shit, Colonel. This one?" She shook her head and I saw her shoulders shake. "I've never been more scared of anything."

I knew what she meant. She wasn't afraid for her own life, she was afraid that she would screw something up and be responsible for the destruction of Earth. I knew what she was thinking, because that is exactly what I was thinking. Had I ever been more scared of anything? Maybe not. Maybe that should tell me something. "Hey, you'll do just fine."

"I'm not worried about *that*," she gave me a disparaging look. "We could both do everything perfectly, and still blow the mission. I don't like this. Landing on a Maxolhx planet? This is way too much risk to take on. It's your call, Sir, but..." She left the rest unsaid.

She was right. It was a hell of a risk. Skippy's mad plan was for our Panther to fly into the Kulashant star system, wrapped tightly in a stealth field. When we got close to the planet, we would deactivate stealth, or make it look like we had. Skippy would identify us as a routine flight to inspect the outer perimeter of detection satellites, and assuming the strategic defense AI bought his line of bullshit, we were then supposed to just fly down to the surface, like our Panther was any other small spacecraft. Skippy thought he could persuade the local air traffic control AI to let us get fairly close to the buildings where the Science and Intelligence Ministry was located. It would be a quick touch-and-go landing, because if we actually set down to park the dropship, automated servicing bots would connect the Panther to ground power and begin routine maintenance. That would require us to open the doors, which was not an option.

Reed was right, there were way too many things that could go wrong.

The *Valkyrie* was parked next to the *Dutchman*, both ships surrounded by a cloud of little bots and the components they were adding to or removing from both ships. For the mission to Kulashant, we would be taking the upgraded *Dutchman*, because it would be flight-ready before our hulking battlecruiser. And because we only needed a starship for transport, not fighting.

Valkyrie had a lot more portholes than the old *Dutchman* did, actual windows made of diamond or some super-tough exotic material. Because I needed time to think, and because I wanted to be by myself, I wandered through our new battlecruiser, until I found a porthole in a part of the ship that had air, and wasn't hazardous due to construction.

Our old star carrier already looked a whole lot meaner than it ever had. It was starting to look like a warship, rather than a glorified space truck. Some of the modifications would wait until we returned from Kulashant, if we ever did. Although the *Dutchman* was fairly close in terms of distances in spaceflight, it was far enough away that I couldn't see details well with just my trusty old Mark One eyeball. Using my zPhone as a camera gave me a super-sharp view. I panned the camera past the new reactors, the new shield generators, new antennas for the proximity-defense sensor system, new particle-beam cannons for-

Antennas.

All those antennas.

"Holy shit," I said to myself.

"Joe?" Skippy asked through my zPhone. Apparently, I had not kept my thoughts to myself. "What's up? I heard you."

"I have two questions for you, Skippy. Number One, how high does that disruptor field extend above the planet? Does it go all the way up to the spacedock?"

"Well, no. The field is a fairly thin layer around Kulashant. It can't reach up to stations or ships in orbit, because it would disrupt delicate equipment up there," he explained, and I heard the 'duh' implied in his tone.

"Outstanding. Ok, second-"

"If you are thinking I can use a microwormhole to hack into the spacedock's AI, I already told you that is not happening. You should try listening some time, instead of-"

"I heard you the first time. The second question is simple: how does the spacedock get updates from the surface?"

"Um, facilities on the surface send signals, *duh*. Did you think they use pigeons to carry notes back and forth?"

I ignored him, both because I was on a roll, and because he hated being ignored. "Signals are received by antennas, right? So-"

Heighdy-ho there, filthy monkeys! Tis I, Skippy the Magnificent. I have lowered my standards to speak with you, so pay attention and-

Yes, you in the front there with your hand up. I'm sure you did just get out of the shower. You are still filthy. Ugh, have you ever *smelled* yourself? Whew.

Anyway, Joe would tell the story all wrong, making it sound like his big stupid self is the hero of the story. Tell me, who is the real hero? The monkey who has a random neuron fire in his brain and says 'Duh can we do this'? Or the incomparably awesome being who has to actually make his moronically obvious ideas work?

Good answer. That's right, *I* am the hero. So, I am telling this story. First-

Ugh. Yes, if it was so obvious, why didn't *I* think of it? Because I have better things to do with my vast intelligence. That's why I outsource the pesky details to monkeys. Are you happy now? Get yourself a juice box. Hopefully there is a cyanide flavor for you.

Just kidding!

Not.

Anywho, we flew the *Dutchman* to the edge of the Kulashant star system, and launched a missile that contained probes for- Oh, who cares about all the boring stuff? What my incredibly awesome self did was pack one end of a microwormhole in the stealth probes. Actually I used ten microwormholes in five probes, but monkeys don't need those details. In each probe, one microwormhole was used to project a stealth field that is more sophisticated than the Maxolhx can even dream of. That is how I got all five probes through the overlapping sensor field and near the spacedock, that was a huh-*yuge* headache for me.

The missile got near the planet before it cut the probes loose. Two of the probes approached the spacedock's main antenna for classified transmissions. I waited for a ship to pass between the spacedock and the transmitter on the ground, and moved the probes into position. The probes released the microwormholes and backed away, still wrapped in stealth.

The microwormhole that was eighteen meters away from the antenna, received signals from the surface. Those signals went into one end of the microwormhole near the antenna, and came out the other end of that microwormhole in a cargo bay aboard the *Flying Dutchman*.

The second wormhole had one end in the same cargo bay, with the other end less than a meter from the spacedock antenna. My shiny canister, which is *not* a beer can, was positioned between the wormhole event horizons in the cargo bay. I examined incoming message traffic, decided what I wanted the spacedock to read, and fed that to the antenna.

Here's the tricky part. The signals traveled at the speed of light, and the microwormholes in front of the antenna were only seventeen meters apart. Light moves across a gap of seventeen meters in- oh, why am I bothering to explain math to you monkeys? It's *fast*, that's all you need to know. Aboard the *Dutchman*, I had to receive the signals, screw with the data however I wanted, and send the signal along so it would be received by the antenna at the *exact same time* it would have been received, if I had not intercepted it.

How did I accomplish something so mind-bogglingly incredible? Simple; I used pure, Grade-A awesomeness. Was it difficult? Well, I don't like to brag, but-

Hey, you in the back there. I heard you laughing, you sound like a hyena with asthma. No juicebox for you.

What was I saying? Oh yeah. Awesomeness. It was super difficult even for me, because I had to-

Ok, I admit it.

I lied.

It *was* easy for me. Awesomeness is just what I do, it's who I am. Which, really, shows how amazing I am. Actually, I was bored during the whole thing, because Big Stupidhead Joe insisted that I turn over operation of the ship to Nagatha while I controlled the microwormholes, and most of my ginormous brain had nothing to do.

Well, not *nothing*. Joe did not need to know this, but most of my brainpower was busy working on my fantastic Broadway musical! And, because you have been such a wonderful audience, I will give you an *exclusive* sneak peek at the-

"Skippy!" I shouted again, in a panic. "*SKIPPY!*"

"Huh? What?" He sputtered.

"You blue-screened on us." I flashed a thumbs up to Desai in the CIC, because she had been about to panic like me. "Did it work? Is everything all right?"

"Did what work? Oh, the wormhole antenna intercept thing. Yeah, of course. Duh. It's *me*, you moron. See what happens when you forget to trust the awesomeness?"

"Hey, sorry. I was worried because I tried to talk with you, and you didn't answer. It must have been super difficult, for you to be concentrating like that."

"Nah, it was easy-peasy."

"Then why weren't you answering me?"

"Um-"

"Shit. Were you doing something else that took your attention, when you were supposed to focus on the critical operation?"

"Well, heh heh, um, I'm going to plead the Fifth on that."

"Plead the- the Fifth Amendment does not apply to beer cans!"

"It applies to *people*, Joe. Are you saying I am not a person?"

"I'm *saying* you are an asshole."

"We can agree to disagree about that one," he sniffed. "Anywho, the library file has been uploaded to the spacedock, and, um, let me check. Yup, the spacedock is pushing the update to the ships of the battlegroup. Score another one for the awesomeness of *me*!"

"Uh huh. When can you disengage the wormholes, and withdraw the probes? You said if they stay in place too long, the kitties may notice something is odd."

"Well, heh heh, that might be a *teeny* bit of a problem. I can't disengage until a ship passes between the antenna and the planet. Otherwise, the kitties will notice the momentary glitch in signal traffic. Unfortunately, traffic is pretty sparse right now. The next ship scheduled to arrive or depart, is not for another seven hours."

"That's no good!" In the CIC, I saw Desai shaking her head slowly. "You didn't check that before you blocked the antenna?"

"No, because I didn't have access to that data, until *after* I hacked the antenna, duh. Remember, this whole scheme was *your* idea. Before you ask whether I can hack into the dispatch schedule, and order a ship to depart early, the answer is yes, I can. I should *not* do that, because it will raise all kinds of red flags."

"No, don't do that. Shit. I guess we just wait?"

"Sure, we could do that. Except if I don't disengage the microwormholes in the next ninety four minutes, the gamma radiation of their event horizons will begin leaking into local spacetime, and be detected by the spacedock, and any ship in the area. Those sensors are run by subminds, I can't hack into them remotely."

"Ok, let me think."

"It would have been nice for you to think *before* we started this, Joe," he scolded me.

What could Skippy do to prevent the microwormholes from being detected, and that wouldn't cause the kitties to become suspicious there was something funky about their antenna? If he cut power to the antenna, even for a second, the spacedock AI would notice and send bots to investigate the-

"Hey, Skippy. The bots that perform maintenance on the spacedock, are they run by subminds?"

"It depends, Joe. Most of the bots are semi-autonomous. They take assignments from subminds, but perform the detail work on their own. Why do you ask?"

"Can you take control of a bot, or just give it a task, and move one of *them* in front of the antenna? Without making the spacedock AI suspicious that someone is screwing with the bots?"

"Hmm. Well, shit. That was rather obvious. Why didn't you suggest that before?"

I gritted my teeth and reminded myself that we needed Skippy more than he needed us. "You can do it without attracting the attention of the AI?"

"Sure. Doing it now. I just caused a minor glitch in a power relay on the hull of the spacedock. A submind has dispatched the nearest bot to investigate, and its

path will take it in front of the antenna. Three, two, one, and- Presto! Microwormholes have been shut down. I am backing the probes away now. Another triumph by Skippy the Magnificent. Gosh, I should compose an opera about *me*," he gasped.

"Hey, I'll offer you a deal. You trap that battlegroup outside the galaxy, and you can perform your opera in the galley," I said with fingers crossed behind my back. I had not promised that anyone would *attend* the opera, and I hope that little shithead didn't notice.

"Deal, Joe! Oh, you are in for a *treat*."

"I'm sure I am, Skippy." I knew I was in for a treat, because while he performed his opera, I planned to be in my cabin eating a Fluffernutter. He would be pissed at me, and I would deal with that when it happened. "XO," I breathed a sigh of relief, and Desai walked around the partition onto the bridge. "We will wait until Skippy has all those probes out of their strategic defense sensor bubble, then jump away." That would take several hours, because the probes could not maneuver fast while they contained one end of a microwormhole. That event horizon was being used by Skippy to project a stealth field through, keeping the five probes hidden. Once they were beyond the sensor coverage around the planet, he could shut off the microwormholes, and the probes would rely on their own stealth fields. The probes would run out of power within six days, plenty of time for them to go dark and drift forever. "We did it, *again*," I would have grinned with satisfaction, but I didn't have the energy.

"We did," Desai agreed. "Now it's on to the next impossible task."

I slapped a hand across my face and mumbled into it. "You, Simms, Adams, and Chang. Why do all of my executive officers delight in reminding me how tough this job is?"

"Because that is *our* tough job, Sir," Desai wasn't smiling either.

Four hours later, the probes were drifting away from Kulashant, on a course that would take them above the plane of the planet's orbit. They were drifting away from the local wormhole, in a direction no Maxolhx ship was likely to fly. With Skippy certain the libraries of the Battlegroup's ships had been properly infected, we jumped the *Dutchman* away.

CHAPTER THIRTY SEVEN

"Hey, heeeeey, Joe," Skippy's voice had that raspy, slurred quality when he drunk-dialed me that night. The effort of controlling the microwormholes near the antenna had been rough on him, and he had warned me his matrix needed reconfiguring, or whatever the hell he did. The result of him rearranging his brain was his higher-level functioning was impaired for a while. The result of *that* was him waking me up in the middle of the freakin' night. "Hey, duuuuude. You awake?"

"No."

"Oh, sorry, man. Didn't mean to disturb your sleep. Um, you sure you're not awake?"

"Pretty sure, yeah," I threw the pillow over my head.

It was useless, he only spoke louder. "I ask because it *sounds* like you are awake."

"Crap!" Throwing the pillow down by my feet, I gave into the inevitable. "If I listen to you for, like, five minutes, will you leave me alone?"

"Huh? Oh, sure, sure."

He was silent for a while. Too long, suspiciously long. I could feel my ability to fall back asleep fading away as the tension bothered me. Finally, I couldn't stand it any longer. "What is it?"

"What is what?" He asked, sounding distracted.

"The thing you wanted to talk about?"

"I thought you were asleep?"

I face-palmed myself with both hands.

"Hey!" He shouted. "You liar, you weren't asleep at all."

From behind my hands, I muttered "Can you just tell me what is so important?"

"Oh, yeah, I remember now. I was working on a sort of Physics for Monkeys handbook, to catch your scientists up on all the stuff they are wrong about. You know I still can't tell you monkeys anything really important, and your brains would explode anyway. But, I am giving it a shot anyway."

"That's great, Skippy, thank you. Uh, how about we wait until morning for me to review this book, Ok?"

"Review? Why would you- O.M.G. dude. Did you think I want *you* to read my physics book? That is-" his voice dissolved into laughter. "Oh, that's a good one."

"Asshole. You woke me up to laugh at me?"

"Oh, sorry," he took a moment to finish chuckling, and his words became slurred again. "To dumb down my book so monkeys can understand it, I read some of the classics of children's literature. It was *aaaaawesome*, dude."

"That's great, Skip-"

"I have a question. You know the Doctor Seuss story 'Green Eggs and Ham'?"

"I vaguely remember it, yeah. What about it?" I wondered whether green eggs were somehow a good metaphor for higher-dimensional physics.

"Well, I think there's something I don't get about that book."

"Like what?"

"That Sam-I-Am guy? He's kind of a *dick*, Joe."

"Uh-"

"The hero of the story does *not* want to try green eggs and ham."

"Well," Saying 'well' was a way to stall while my foggy memory searched back to when my father had read that story to me. "But in the end, the guy does try green eggs, and he likes them, right?"

"He *says* he likes green eggs and ham, but maybe he did that just so Sam will leave him alone. Sam badgered him into doing it, Joe. That's harassment."

I flopped the pillow back over my face and groaned, my voice muffled. "I think you're reading too much into the story."

"Really, Joe, *really*?"

Man, that was a conversation I very much did not want to have at, I checked my zPhone, oh two forty five in the morning. "Skippy, if I stipulate that the guy in that story had a good case for a restraining order against Sam, can you drop the subject?"

"Certainly."

"Great. Ok, good night, I will-"

"I'm glad we agree on that issue. Children should not be taught to badger people until they get what they want."

"Yeah, I, uh-"

"And do *not* get me started on the questionable physics of 'Horton Hears A Who'." He snorted. "If the Whos are as small as the book claims, they must be nanoscale, and the wavelength of their voices would be *waaay* to short for Horton to-"

My night kind of went downhill from there.

After my alarm sounded, in the middle of a deep philosophical discussion about Yertle the freakin' Turtle, I staggered into the shower and let hot water cascade over my head until Skippy gave up trying to talk to me. In the galley, Adams was there, a towel over her shoulders. She had gotten up before me and already been to the gym.

"Good morning, Sir," she held up a cup of coffee for me.

I took the coffee and could not reply right away, because I was yawning so hard I couldn't speak. "Morning, Gunny," I finally managed to say while slurping the hot coffee.

"You look like shit, Sir. Did you get any sleep?"

"Not much." My brain was in such a dense fog, I didn't think about what I was saying. "Do you want to have children?"

"What?" Her eyebrows flew upward and she glanced around the galley. Other than us, there were two people back in the kitchen, so no one could hear us. That could change any second, as people came in to get coffee. Lowering her voice, her eyes cast down in a coy gesture I should have recognized, if my brain was not so sleep-deprived. "You really want to have that discussion *here*? Now?"

"What? *Oh!*" Amazingly, my brain went from zero to *Maximum Alert* in a split-second. "No, Gunny, I, shit." I waved my hands frantically, sloshing coffee onto the deck. "Sorry. Look, Skippy drunk-dialed me and kept me up all night, explaining why Doctor Seuss books are terrible for children, and that everything my parents taught me is wrong."

"Oh," her expression was a mixture of relief and disappointment. Or maybe I just sucked at reading people. "You didn't, um, mean-"

"I was just making a joke, Adams. If we ever- *You*! If *you* ever have children, do not ask Skippy for parenting advice."

"Sir," she grinned at me over her coffee, the mug hiding her smile but not the twinkle in her eyes. "I didn't need you to tell me *that*."

"I suppose not. It was a long night, Gunny." Setting my coffee on a counter, I knelt down with a towel to mop up the coffee I had spilled on the deck. Something in her bemused expression was odd, until I realized I was down on one knee in front of her. "Uhhh-" I couldn't think of anything to say. "This is not what it looks like," I explained to a group of people who, just then, walked into the galley.

"It had better not be," Adams said with a wink. "If *this* is the way you propose, I feel sorry for the girl."

Quickly, I dried the deck, stuffed the towel in a bin to be washed, and hurried out the door.

"Colonel?" Adams called after me. "You forgot the rest of your coffee."

"Believe me, Gunny," I paused in the doorway. "I am *wide awake* now."

To make the *Valkyrie* into the bad-ass warship we needed, we had to acquire a set of power boosters. By 'acquire' I mean 'steal' and by 'steal' I mean 'kill the people who have boosters and take them'. There is no nice way to say that. No, wait. Maybe there *is* a nice way to say that, but saying it nicely would be bullshit. The harsh fact was, we needed power boosters to save our home planet, maybe our entire species. I was willing to do a whole lot of morally sketchy things to make that happen.

Skippy had identified a relatively soft target, where we could get power boosters to fix up *Valkyrie* and the old *Dutchman*. Though we would be hitting a Maxolhx facility, we had a good plan, and I was feeling confident, which was a bad sign. Until recently, the idea of getting anywhere close to anything controlled by the Maxolhx would have had me quaking in my boots. Now, I thought we had a pretty good chance of the operation succeeding. That made me worry the Universe would see this operation as a perfect time to smack Joe Bishop down for all the crazy shit I had done. So, while I wasn't worried about the plan, I was worried about worrying which maybe meant the Universe would leave me alone for a while.

I know, the twisted logic that goes on in my head scares me sometimes.

"Joe," Skippy popped up on my desk without warning, startling me. It would be nice if a bell chimed right before his hologram shimmered to life. "Got a question for you."

"Maybe I have an answer. What's up?"

"You complain about us taking too many risks, but now you're planning to hit the Maxolhx, to get the VPMs we need. My question is, *why* are we doing this?

The way we plan to trap the enemy battlegroup outside the galaxy has *me* doing all the work to set up the wormhole chain. We do not actually need the *Valkyrie* to do that. I know we went through a lot of trouble to build a warship, but are you now too invested in having another ship?"

"I don't think that-"

"Because if we lose the *Dutchman* in the op to get power boosters, then we may not be able to get me to where I can set up the wormhole chain."

"Lose the *Dutchman*?" That made me pause. Skippy was really worried about something. "This is supposed to be a soft target."

"*Relatively* soft, Joe. It is still a Maxolhx base, defended by Maxolhx technology. Unlike the op to hack the library files of the target battlegroup, stealing power boosters will require squishy biological trashbags to risk their meatsack bodies. It is risky, Joe."

"I know it's risky. Everything we do out here is a risk."

"Then why are we doing this? Are you so eager to play with your new toy that-"

"It isn't a toy, and this isn't a game. We do need *Valkyrie*. Not to create the wormhole chain, but for the backup plan."

"Um, what backup plan?"

"Ok, I should have discussed this with you. Sorry. Listen, how sure are you that you can create a chain of wormholes, all the way outside the galaxy?"

"Hoo boy, that is a good question, Joe. I simply do not know. It *should* work. I am confident in my ability to control the wormholes. But, I will be placing event horizons in dangerously close proximity, so the network might refuse my commands. It is pretty certain the network will revise its protocols so we can't try this stunt a second time. Thus, I can't test it."

"That's why we need a backup plan, and for that, we need *Valkyrie*."

"I do not like the sound of that, Joe. What reckless thing are you intending as a backup plan, that requires an advanced warship? I warned you, even with a full set of power boosters, *Valkyrie* can't take on a reinforced battlegroup."

"We don't need to destroy the entire battlegroup, Skippy. We just need to buy time. Even if the wormhole chain thing does work, we are only buying time for Earth. Eventually, the Maxolhx will notice their battlegroup failed to return from Earth, and they will get serious about sending a war fleet to destroy my homeworld."

"That is true, unfortunately. Like you said, the days of us sneaking around conducting secret operations is over. Ok, what is the backup plan?"

"If the wormhole chain thing doesn't work for whatever reason, we take *Valkyrie* through the Goalpost wormhole, and wait there. The battlegroup will send a scout ship through, we leave it alone while we hide in our stealth field- Uh, we can do that, right? Hide close to the wormhole?"

"That's kind of iffy, Joe. I have upgraded the original Maxolhx stealth capability, which was already very advanced. However, it depends on how close we are to the scout ship, and whether it uses active sensors. The kitties have sophisticated sensors that map the fabric of spacetime, so an active scan might detect our presence, by the way the *Valkyrie*'s mass creates a gravity well."

"Shit." I could see my backup plan falling apart, because of my ignorance. Because of my incompetence. "I did not know that. Well, there goes that idea."

"Not necessarily, Joe. If we park the *Valkyrie* a good distance away, say a couple lightminutes, then we should be safe. The active scan degrades with distance. Unless the scout ship is determined to conduct a detailed scan of the entire area, it should not detect us. I think we'd be safe. The Maxolhx are arrogant, plus they believe that beyond the Goalpost wormhole is *nothing*. They will assume there is not any potential threat in the area."

"Ok, that's good, that's good. In that case, we need to be far enough away to hide from a scan, and close enough that we can jump in to hit the first star carrier, before its systems fully recover."

"Um, that will be very tricky timing. Don't count on doing that, Joe. We would need to guess when the star carrier is coming through, and time our inbound jump precisely. If we jump in too early, the scout ship would warn the star carrier, and it would abort its approach."

"Ok, well, then we jump in as soon as we see that first star carrier come through. I know, there will be a lag as the sensor data crawls out to us at the speed of light. What matters is, we jump in, hammer the star carrier with everything we've got, then jump away before they can hit us. Hopefully we cause a lot of damage, we're going more for shock value than physical results. The intent is to get the kitties to retreat through Goalpost, and think long and hard about what to do next. We want them to wonder what the *hell* is going on. Their ships got attacked, by a ship that appears to be based on their own technology. The survivors will have to go back to base to report what happened. With just a little bit of luck, the Maxolhx will wonder if the ship that attacked them was controlled by a breakaway faction of Bopshuraq. They will not send another mission to Earth, until they have some answers."

"Sure, Joe. But when they do send another mission to Earth, it will be a massive force."

"A whole fleet, or a reinforced battlegroup, makes no difference, Skippy. Either way, Earth is toast. We're just buying time."

"To do what?"

"I haven't got that figured out yet."

"Whoo. Shit. These are truly desperate times, my friend."

"Hey, come on, Skippy. We are the Merry Band of Pirates. We will have an upgraded *Flying Dutchman*, a bad-ass warship, and the incomparable magnificence of *you*."

"Wow. Thanks for the vote of confidence. But, if you have a Taco Bell coupon, I wouldn't wait too long to use it, if you know what I mean."

"Oh, hell. Yeah, I do."

Sitting with Adams, we were planning menus for our next duty day in the galley. "How about we make cheeseburgers?" I suggested. "For lunch, not dinner." I knew she wanted to make one of her grandmother's recipes for the evening meal.

"Cheeseburgers?"

"I know, I always want cheeseburgers. But, we haven't had them since the cookout on Avalon, and I am craving-"

"You are *always* craving cheeseburgers, Sir," she winked at me playfully, and that was the best thing that happened to me since, well, maybe ever. "The problem is, have you checked our supplies? We don't have a whole lot of ground beef left. We don't have a lot of *anything* left. This mission wasn't supposed to last so long."

"Uh," I mentally smacked myself. When Simms was aboard, I checked the logistics report every morning, because I knew she would mention something that day and I didn't want to look stupid. Since we departed Avalon, Nagatha had a nice report available, and I had glanced at it occasionally, but my limited attention span wasn't able to focus on mundane details. "Oh, right," I blushed. It was no use pretending our supply situation wasn't news to me, Adams knew me too well. "Uh, that's no problem. We can make Oklahoma fried onion burgers."

"What? You're from *Maine*. How do you know about Oklahoma-"

"It's something my grandmother used to make. Her mother made them way back in, like the Great Depression. You use a layer of onions on the patties, to stretch out the beef, because onions were cheap and beef wasn't. You know," I tapped my lips with a finger. "I had forgotten all about those burgers. They are *really* good, like, extra juicy."

"If you say so, Sir."

"Are you questioning your commanding officer's judgment, Gunnery Sergeant?" I asked with mock severity.

She laughed. "All the time, Sir, all the time."

The next day, it was our turn in the galley, so I was forming the onions and beef into patties, with onions forming the bottom layer to stretch out our dwindling supply of ground beef. A few feet away from me, Adams was busy making potato salad. Naturally, no matter how much space there was in the galley's kitchen, we got in each other's way. Both of us reached for the pepper at the same time, and my hand closed over hers. Because it startled me, and because I am an idiot, my hand lingered on hers for a beat too long, long enough for her to pull away first. "S-sorry," I choked out.

"It's Ok," she looked away, then glanced back with her eyes slightly downcast, giving me a coy smile.

Apparently, something happened during the next couple minutes, although I have no memory of it. The next thing I do remember is reaching into the bowl of onions and coming up empty. Somehow, I had made burger patties totally on autopilot. There were pepper flakes in the bowl, so at some point, I must have used the pepper shaker. Although, it was in front of Adams when I looked at her. Did I give it to her, or just set it down on the table and she picked it up? Either way, we must have worked silently for at least several minutes.

"I'm uh, done," I announced.

"Good. That's, good," she replied without looking at me. There was a catch in her voice. Damn it, sometimes I wish guys weren't so bad at reading emotions. Or maybe it was just me, more than one girlfriend had told me I was particularly clueless. Was she not looking at me because she was upset? Was she feeling the same way I was? Or was the situation just so awkward she wanted to be somewhere, anywhere else?

One thing was certain, it was an awkward moment. "I will, uh, put the patties in the fridge. Oh, the dough has risen for the buns," I looked at the trays sitting on a warming plate. "Time to turn the oven on for baking."

"You're the baker," her eyes flashed to mine and I was suddenly sure of another thing; whatever she was feeling, she was not angry at me.

"Just one of my *many* talents," I joked, hearing how lame it sounded.

"Like your singing?" She looked right at me with a twinkle in her eyes.

"*Not* like my singing," I said with a mock stern expression, and we both laughed.

We got the first batch of burger buns into the oven and set a timer, then started working on the dinner she was making. My first job was to boil water for rice pilaf. Looking at the boxes stacked on the counter, I remembered something I had seen in one of the cargo bays. "Hey, Skippy," I called out. "We have a *lot* of this stuff, right? Why is that?"

"A mistake, Joe," he explained. "We didn't unload all the Rice-a-Roni that Simms asked for, to be sent down to Avalon. By the time she noticed, we were buttoning the ship up to leave orbit. So, we are stuck with five crates of, The San Francisco Treat," he sang like a very old TV commercial, if you are old enough to remember ads on television.

"Rice-a-Roni, huh?" I examined the box. My family had eaten it occasionally, of course, but I never paid much attention to the stuff. "Sounds Italian."

"It is rice and *pasta*, Joe," he sniffed, in a tone that implied an unspoken 'duh'.

"I wonder if there's a Polish version with rice and cabbage, called Rice-a-*Rooski*?"

"Ugh, Joe, you are such an-"

Adams interrupted him, by playfully slapping my shoulder with a towel. "You are *funny*," she giggled. Yes, Gunnery Sergeant Adams *giggled*. "Rice-a-rooski," she said with a laugh.

We worked quietly side by side, because I didn't want to spoil the mood, plus I didn't know what to say. After a couple minutes of us slicing vegetables, she softly said "This is nice."

I swallowed before speaking, so my throat wouldn't be dry. "Yeah, this will be tasty."

"No," she lifted her knife away from the cutting board. "I mean," she waved the knife to encompass the galley. "I mean, *this*. Us working together like this."

"It is nice." Like a coward, I said the safest thing I could think of.

She bobbed her head in agreement, the curls of her hair falling around her forehead. Like most of the crew, she had allowed her hair to grow longer than regulation since we left Earth, and her bangs fell in curls to frame her face. She had beautiful hair, and I often felt like commenting about it. But I knew that to a black woman, her hair is a whole *thing*, like a sensitive subject, and it was none of my business. So I nodded like an idiot and grinned back at her, again playing it safe.

"Feels kind of like we're playing House," she added wistfully.

"House? Like, *our* house? Us?" Unfortunately, my brain did not have a reply ready, so I blurted out the thing at the top of my 'Stupid Things To Say' stack. My brain has joined the Universe in hating me.

She froze, her knife in the air above a tomato. "I meant, this is like something normal people do, you know? People in their nice happy homes, not stuck aboard a starship a thousand lightyears from their families."

"Uh, yeah, that's what I thought," I said as my brain spat out something from the '*Lame* Things To Say' stack.

She bailed me out of my self-induced awkwardness, whether she intended to or not. She reached across me to pick up a jar of seasonings. She brushed against my shoulder, and I got a whiff of whatever she used for shampoo. It smelled like tropical flowers and coconuts and sunshine. Inhaling her scent was like an instant beach vacation. "Sorry," she muttered as she held up the jar and shook it as she pulled away.

And I realized something, something important.

On the other side of her, right next to the cutting board, was a jar of the same seasoning.

She hadn't needed to reach across me.

She was trying to tell me something.

"Uh," I turned toward her. My throat was dry so I took a quick gulp of water. My scalp was tight and my hair felt like it was standing on end and a little voice in the back of my mind was shouting *stupid stupid STUPID* at me. It is always good advice to listen to the wise little voice in your head, the one that urges you not to ask someone to hold your beer while you do some idiotic thing. You know what? I was damned sick of listening to that voice. I was sick of a lot of things, like being responsible for the survival of my entire species, while the governments back home second-guessed my every decision. Most especially I was sick and tired of having to be a lonely freakin' monk just because I was the commander. I am *human* too, and it is hard to work up enthusiasm for saving everyone's lives when mine is so achingly lonely.

So, fuck that little voice, I decided. Sometimes, the purpose of life is to enjoy *living*. Damn it, even if we succeeded in stopping the Maxolhx from reaching Earth, we still couldn't go home until the Maxolhx lifted their blockade of Gateway. Why the hell should I care about some Army regulation that was written a long time ago, on a planet far, far away? I committed mutiny and stole a freakin' starship, so it's not like me breaking regulations was anything new. A hypothetical punishment, from a government on a world that soon might not exist, was not an effective deterrent.

She set down the knife and looked at me. *Looked* at me. Just looked into my eyes, and waited for me to say whatever I was going to say. What was I going to say? I know what I *wanted* to say. "Marga-"

"*Heeeey*, Joe," Skippy interrupted us, startling me. "How about-"

"Skippy," I didn't look up at the speaker. "Unless the ship is *on fire*, and I can do something about it. Go. Away."

"But-"

"Go away. Now. *Right* now," I barked at him.

"Shutting up," he pouted, as the sound of his words were drowned out by the laughter of a group coming into the galley.

Note to self: install a locking door on the damned galley.

Margaret turned away, clearing her throat. She looked up at the people coming into the galley who had obvious just come from an exercise. We would see the telltale red mark of a powered-armor suit helmet liner on their foreheads.

The next hour was agonizingly awkward. While we finished baking the burger buns for lunch and got preparations completed for dinner, there was a steady stream of people in the galley, laughing and joking and debriefing about the training exercise. I envied their happiness and easy fellowship, and hated them for being there. Adams left first, she had to lead a Spin class in the gym. I put things away, cleaned up and checked the time. Lunch began in three hours. Normally, I would have gone to the gym, but that was the last place I wanted to be right then.

Instead, I stomped into my office, slammed myself down into the chair and jabbed the button to slide the door closed. "Skippy!" I bellowed. "What was that?"

"What was what?" His fake innocence did not fool me.

"You know exactly what you did. You blocked me!"

"*Blocked* you?"

"Don't play dumb with me. You broke the Bro Code."

"Well, I-"

"That *hurt*, Skippy." My eyes were watering and I wiped them with the back of my sleeves, not caring if he saw.

"Dude," he sounded just as hurt. "I did it for you. You *asked* me to do that."

"I did? When? What the hell?"

"It was the night you got hammered in Bangor, before the Delta team tried to seize the *Dutchman*. When you got to the hotel after midnight, you were babbling, and you made me promise that if I ever saw you doing something stupid that might hurt Margaret, I was to stop you. That's what I did."

"Holy-" I had no memory of that, but I didn't think he was lying.

"I didn't *want* to do it. Really, the last thing I want is to get involved in squishy stuff like relationships between you monkeys. Um, I mean, humans. Sorry about that. I didn't do the right thing?"

"Shit. We'll never know now. Ah, damn it, it's not your fault."

"Joe, despite all that empathy crap you made me learn about, I know almost nothing about how to handle relationships. However, your primary concern was to avoid doing anything that might hurt Margaret."

"You are right, my man," I offered him a fist bump, and he returned it. "If it's meant to happen, it'll happen, I guess. Crap. It's not *supposed* to happen, and she knows it. My life *sucks*."

"Hey. My best friend," he made a show of wiping his fist on his admiral's uniform, "is a filthy monkey. My life sucks too."

Margaret Adams was not focused on the Spin class, losing track of where she was in the program. A slow song started when she had the group still standing on the pedals, grinding hard up a hill. At one point, she got off her bike to fumble with the music player, and shuffled through songs while the group waited.

After the class, Captain Frey lingered behind to help Adams wipe down the bikes and adjust anything that had come loose. "Something bothering you, eh?"

"I'm *fine*," Adams replied, with a distinct I-don't-want-to-talk-about-it vibe. That was unfair of her and she knew it. She had been paired with Frey in many training exercises, and they always had each other's backs.

Frey lowered her voice. "Trouble with a guy?" She asked knowingly.

"Don't want to talk about it. Ma'am," Adams flung a towel over one shoulder and strode straight through the gym and out the door.

"Uh huh," Frey muttered to herself. "Guy trouble for sure."

The Oklahoma fried onion burgers were a big hit with the crew, except for the few uncultured cretins who hate onions. The only problem with that meal was Skippy interrupting to sing 'Ooooooooklahoma, where the wind-'

I won't finish the song, it was painful enough to hear it the first time. It was my fault for not forbidding Skippy to sing, I should have known. A couple missions ago, someone made New York-style cheesecake, and the beer can serenaded us with Sinatra's 'New York New York', then 'New York Groove' by one of the guys in the band Kiss, then U2's song 'New York', then-

You get the idea. There are a LOT of songs about New York.

We never made cheesecake again.

CHAPTER THIRTY EIGHT

We got the almost-upgraded *Flying Dutchman*, and the not-quite-yet-bad-ass *Valkyrie*, flying in formation at the edge of a red dwarf star system. If you are wondering why we are always visiting red dwarf systems, that's because those stars are the most common in the galaxy. They are also mostly unable to support complex lifeforms, at least the type of life that is able to travel between stars. That made them useful for our purposes, because we wanted to avoid star systems with large populations and therefore substantial networks of strategic defenses.

Skippy had recommended this star because he thought we could find power boosters there, and because it was a relatively soft target. It was in a gap between the Sagittarius and Perseus Arms, about a quarter of the way around the galaxy from Earth. When we came through the closest wormhole, we were as far from home as we had ever been, except for our two trips out to the beta site.

This star, which even the Maxolhx had not bothered to give a name, had one feature that attracted us: a gas giant planet with a refueling base. That fuel station also supported arriving ships with stores of supplies, and an automated fabrication shop that could manufacture equipment larger and more complex than the shop aboard most ships could handle.

The orbiting base had defenses to protect itself, and I was worried about that, despite Skippy's assurances that the *Valkyrie* could handle anything the base threw at us until we were able to knock out their weapons. A supply base that saw a lot of traffic would not be a soft target, but this place was, because of its history. It had been built over a sixty thousand years ago, to support Maxolhx ships patrolling two strategically-vital wormhole clusters. If the Rindhalu launched a surprise attack, those wormhole clusters would be an important route that led deeper into the heart of the Maxolhx Hegemony, their inner circle of homeworlds.

The base we chose as a target used to be important, until several wormhole shifts had left it in the middle of nowhere. One of the nearby wormhole clusters had gone dormant, the other now connected in the opposite direction from the Hegemony, to nothing important. Rather than being on the frontline, the base had been downgraded so it was kind of a Coast Guard search and rescue station. According to the skimpy data Skippy had gathered, the base serviced only two or three ships per year, and one of those ships was a cargo carrier that supplied similar stations. There had been talk of shutting the place down, or at least mothballing it until a future wormhole shift made it important again, but bureaucratic inertia kept it limping along. All we cared about was that supply bases kept stores of important components like VPM power boosters. Any boosters the station had were very likely old, perhaps even obsolete, but Skippy did not care. As long as the power boosters were not actually broken, he could make them work, better than new. All he needed us to do was to capture enough to enhance the capabilities of both ships in our little fleet.

We had a lot working in our favor. The station was fully automated, so we didn't need to worry about armed opposition of the biological kind. It was unlikely any ships would be there, and we could perform a recon at long range to confirm that. And we had an outstanding tactical plan, developed by Smythe and his team. I would be aboard *Valkyrie*, with the *Dutchman* being commanded by Reed. She wanted to fly a dropship, but so did Desai. Because Desai might soon be stuck shuttling people from either Paradise or Earth to the beta site, I felt I owed her an opportunity to actually fly something again. Besides, it would be good for Reed to gain experience as a starship captain. I told her that cute guys would be very impressed with our very own Captain Janeway.

She was not amused.

The operation began in textbook fashion. Together, we jumped into the system, about a lighthour away from the orbiting supply base. Skippy confirmed everything was exactly as he expected. Well, not exactly, but close enough. There were no starships docked at the station, it was orbiting within the zone he predicted, and the fuel tanks appeared to be full. That meant no ship had been there to refuel recently, because the fuel-extraction drogue that dipped down into atmosphere was not operating. The tanks must have been topped off at least nine days ago, by Skippy's estimate, probably more.

We updated our navigation system with the station's coordinates, Smythe assured me his team was ready to go, and I gave the 'Go' order. Holy shit, I thought to myself, this is it. We are actually attacking, like conducting a boarding operation, against an apex-species facility. Sure, we had boarded the ship that was now our Valkyrie, but Skippy had neatly sliced that ship apart before our boarding team set their boots on the hull. We could not use any fancy wormhole physics against this target. It would be, as Smythe described it, a simple smash-and-grab operation, with equal parts smashing and grabbing. I was Ok with whatever smashing he did, as long as the grabbing part was successful.

The *Dutchman* jumped in first, leading by just over one second. She emerged one point five lightseconds from the station, immediately began to saturate the area with a damping field, and fired her maser cannon at pre-selected targets on the station's hull. Before the first maser beam struck the station, *Valkyie* jumped in less than five kilometers from the station, on the other side. We cut loose with masers and particle beams, knocking out defense shield generators as our first priority.

The fight pitted a weakened battlecruiser and a star carrier, against an elderly and automated supply station. Still, it was a furious battle while it lasted, which was about eleven seconds. Usually, everything happens really slooooowly in space warfare, because the distances are so great. Even a bolt of focused light crawls along at a mere hundred and eighty six thousand miles per second. But, when the combatants are at close range, things happen *fast*.

The *Valkyrie* rotated around its long axis, spinning to keep the shields on one side from being pounded so badly they failed. Though our new ship was a battlecruiser, it could not supply sufficient power to the shields and weapons at the same time, and we needed priority to weapons. The key to the battle was to knock out the enemy's shields in one particular area, so we could have a clean shot at the juicy center under the crunchy shell.

While we were hammering away at the station, it was shooting back. Within three seconds, space between *Valkyrie* and the station was no longer a vacuum. It was filled with missiles exploded by our point-defense systems, debris from railgun rounds of both sides that had been turned to particles when they impacted energy shields, scattered particle beams, and finally by plating blown off the station's hull when our precision directed-energy weapons burned through the enemy shields.

Degrading shields in a particular area of the station was the key to our entire assault plan. That took seven seconds, during which my heart was racing because I felt our mighty *Valkyrie* shudder from multiple impacts. On the big display, our shields were glowing either yellow or orange, colors chosen for what they meant to the humans who now owned the ship. It was a race against time, because once the stored energy in *Valkyrie*'s shield generators was exhausted, we had to stop firing weapons so the reactors could shift their power output to recharge the shields.

We won the race, with a comfortable three seconds left on the clock.

With enemy shields down, we shifted our energy weapons to attack defensive cannons, while we launched missiles. Three missiles, then another pair. The station immediately destroyed four of them.

The last one got through, its armored nosecone punching through the skin of the station like it was tissue paper. Skippy actually had to remind the missile's tiny brain to explode the warhead before it plunged completely through the station and out the other side. The missile complied.

Eleven seconds after *Valkyrie* jumped in, the fight was over. Or, the ship-to-station part of the fight was over. Our missile had taken out the station's AI and cut off the stores section from the main power supply. The station was defenseless, and we hoped it would be, long enough for Smythe's people to get aboard and allow Skippy to take over local systems.

"Skippy?" I asked anxiously. The amount of damage that *Valkyrie* had taken in the brief battle shocked me. Our mighty warship needed those damned power boosters, or we would be a sitting duck in a real battle.

"Give me a minute, I'm directing the defense cannons to knock debris out of the way. If a dropship smacks into a chunk of-"

"Yeah, I hear you. Smythe, standby one."

He didn't reply, he didn't need to.

"Ok, we're good," Skippy declared with relief. "We have a clear flightpath to the target."

"Away boarders," I ordered, and four Panthers rocketed away from *Valkyrie*, curving around to converge on two of the station's docking bays. The big doors there were closed and slicing them open with the ship's cannons would create too much hazardous debris, so the Panthers needed to set down next to the doors and Smythe's people would blow the personnel airlocks with explosive charges.

"Reed?" I called her, mostly because I was nervous and had nothing else to do at the moment. "How you doing over there, Fireball?"

"Nominal," she replied tersely from the command chair aboard the *Flying Dutchman*.

That was my cue to shut up.

Our textbook operation went to hell, as soon as the first boarding team blew the inner airlock door and flung themselves down the corridor beyond, pushing off the walls in the zero gravity. A grenade or maybe a rocket exploded, ripping into the two operators in the lead and ripping into the pair behind them. On *Valkyrie*'s bridge, all I could do was watch, sickened as two, then four lifesigns monitors flatlined. We had lost four people just like that. "Skippy!" I shouted frantically. "How did the station-"

"That wasn't the station! It wasn't an automated defense system!" He was a frantic as I was. "I think- Yes! There are two Maxolhx over there. No, three of them!"

"How did you not know they were there?" I demanded. "Smythe, pull your people out-"

"Sir," he protested in a voice a lot more calm that I would have been. "We might not get another shot at this. Skippy, the oppo is limited to three? You are certain of that?"

"Yes, three. *Only* three." Skippy insisted. "They must have engaged their suit stealthware before we killed the station AI. I couldn't detect them until they started moving."

"*Stealthware?*" I screeched unhelpfully. All I was doing was making the situation worse. "How can you be sure?"

"Joe, you have to trust me on this. Now I know to look for the signature where their stealthware interacts with-"

"I trust you," I cut him off. "Smythe, we are not sending more people in Kristang hardshell armor, against three Maxolhx equipped with-"

"Joe!" It was Skippy's turn to interrupt. "The enemy are not wearing combat suits. They only have environment suits. They might be technicians, or they could be soldiers, but they were not expecting a fight."

"They are expecting one now. Smythe, pull back now."

"Sir-"

"Smythe," Skippy spoke directly to the STAR team commander. "Joe is right, for the wrong reason. Pull your teams back. I can take care of the enemy, but your team is in the way."

I didn't like the sound of that. "What are you planning, Skippy?"

"Those docking bay doors are not armored. We can burn through them, straight into the inner compartments. Make a hole, send in a missile equipped with antipersonnel submunitions. I have bots swapping out a warhead right now, be ready to launch in twenty-seven seconds."

"Pulling back now," Smythe said without waiting for me. Technically, he was complying with an order I had already given. We had served together long enough that he knew he had wide latitude to conduct away operations as he saw fit. I would only interfere with him if I thought he didn't appreciate the big picture.

It took twenty-two seconds for his people to pull back to what Skippy designated as safe zones, then we fired a maser beam. It was only one of the point-defense cannons, but it seared through the docking bay doors like they were made of plywood. Under Skippy's direction, the beam made a neat round hole in the outer door, resumed cutting something inside the station, and abruptly snapped off. Even before the beam quit, a missile was on the way, thrusters firing wildly to make the hard turn and guide it through the glowing hole in the outer doors.

The human eye, and the human brain, are slow. To my mind, that missile's ass end had no sooner disappeared inside, than a fountain of debris gushed out. "Got 'em!" Skippy snarled. "Three dead motherfuckers."

"Colonel-" Smythe did not hesitate.

Neither did I. "Go, Smythe." While I did not like the idea of our people going into an apex-species station, I did want to get the operation over with as soon as possible.

On the display, I watched icons of the STAR team progressing toward their targets. Most of them moved in the general direction of the stores compartments, which quite logically were near the docking bays. Other people, in pairs, raced off to enable Skippy to take control of local systems. Adams was in one of those pairs. If she got into trouble, she only had one operator as backup. I tried not to think about that.

Icons for two other people moved in a direction I did not at first understand, because they were approaching the area blasted by our antipersonnel submunitions. Was Smythe trying to make sure the three enemy were really dead? Or was he hoping to capture some sort of technology from the debris. I was about to contact him, when I realized what those two operators were doing. They were attempting to recover the remains of the people we had lost.

Of course Smythe would order them to do that. I was ashamed of myself for not considering that. Smythe was a professional, I needed to let him do his job, and I needed to focus on doing mine. Which was, what? What could- I snapped my fingers as an awful thought hit me. "Skippy, that station is *automated*. Why were those three Maxolhx there?"

"Joe, I'm sorry. I didn't know-"

"This isn't about blame. You could not have known. I don't care about that. What I care about is, they must have come from a ship!"

"Damn it, Joe, you're right. I should have thought of that. I will have access to local systems aboard the station soon, I can-"

"We're not waiting. Pilot, back us away from the station."

"Joe," Skippy said slowly. "The farther we are from the station, the more difficult it will be to cover the dropships."

"I know. If we have to fight another ship, we need room to maneuver. And if we get into a fight, I don't want the station becoming collateral damage. Reed!" I called my counterpart aboard the *Dutchman*. "We may have trouble out here. I'm taking the *Valkyrie* out to scan the area. Can you step on it, get here faster to cover the boarding team dropships?"

"Let me ask Nagatha what our options are," she replied. There was talking in the background, then, "Colonel, Nagatha is recommending we perform a short jump, we're too far from the station to fly there quickly."

"Do it," I ordered, and closed channel. "Skippy, what's the best way to determine if we have unwanted company out there?" Looking down, I saw my hands were shaking.

"Whew. Joe, are you asking me if we can detect a stealthed Maxolhx ship?"

"I'm not worried about any other type of ship, so, yes."

"Then we really do need separation from the station. Its gravity well and electronic signature cause too much clutter in the sensor data."

"Ok, Ok," I muttered, rubbing my chin while I thought. "We'll wait for the *Dutchman* to get into position, then we jump away to scan the area. I don't want to jump too far, we need to provide fire support."

"Understood," he already sounded distracted. "I am programming a search pattern now. Um, uh oh. Joe, I have been monitoring data from the STAR team's suits and I just learned a disturbing fact. The station has a self-destruct mechanism, and it is armed."

"Should I pull the team out?"

"At this point, no," he advised, and the big display highlighted the position of the main team. "They are already in the station storage area, and I am talking Smythe through the process of identifying the components we need. However, I do suggest the *Dutchman* keep a greater distance from the station. If the self-destruct blows, it could severely damage any ship in the area, especially a star carrier. I have already given that information to Nagatha, and she is adjusting their inbound jump accordingly."

My mouth dropped open and I had to remind myself to close it. "If the self-destruct is armed, why didn't the station detonate it?"

"My guess is, the AI was confused about being attacked by a Maxolhx warship. During the first four seconds of the battle, it was acting purely in a defensive posture."

Part of the holographic display in front of me was showing a damage report for the *Valkyrie*. If the station had really been hitting us hard from the start, our new ship might have suffered severe damage. Skippy was right, we needed those damned power boosters, or all our effort to capture warships was for nothing. "What is the risk the self-destruct will activate now?"

"I don't think it is imminent, and I am taking control of local systems. Until I have complete control, there is a risk that some local submind might finish rebooting, and decide to be a hero."

The trusty old *Dutchman* jumped in and we handed off cover duty, Reed assuring me she would keep her ship at a safe distance. On the comm system, I could hear her urging Smythe to move faster. He replied that the team was already on the way back to a dropship with the first batch of power boosters, they were forced to move slowly because the cargo handling mechanism of the station had only one speed. Did I want to open my mouth and give unhelpful advice? Hell yes. To my credit, I kept my mouth shut and waited for us to fly out to a safe distance. Nagatha cut off the *Dutchman*'s damping field for a brief window so we could jump, and we did.

Few things are more tedious than a grid search. Even with *Valkyrie*'s sophisticated sensors, we had to saturate an area of the grid with a sensor field, and wait for data to flow back to us. If we were looking for a stealthed Kristang ship, it would have lit up our displays like a Christmas tree. But we were relying on

Maxolhx sensors, to detect ships that had countermeasures designed to defeat Rindhalu technology. Even with Skippy upgrading the sensors, and using his own natural awesomeness, we would have to get lucky to find a stealthy needle in that enormous haystack. Space is *big*, even when the search area is confined to three lightseconds around the supply station. Skippy warned me that the search was likely to be a futile effort, and that was Ok with me. I did not actually want to find and therefore have to fight an equivalent-technology warship. My goal was much more limited: to keep the enemy away long enough for the STAR team to get aboard the *Dutchman*, and that ship to jump safely away. Surely if a Maxolhx ship was out there, it had to be concerned that *Valkyrie* was a battlecruiser. The enemy didn't know our battlecruiser was limping along on much less than full power, and the odds were that no ship visiting an isolated supply station could match a battlecruiser.

The other factor in our favor was that, if a Maxolhx ship was out there watching us, the crew had to be asking themselves what the *fuck* was going on. Because both of our ships and the station were within a relatively compact area, we had been able to run all signal traffic through the ultra-secure Skippytel network, so the enemy had no way to intercept our messages. We had also jammed all of the station's outgoing signals, using some quantum resonance bullshit that Skippy tried and failed to explain. All the Maxolhx would know was an odd-looking Maxolhx *Extinction*-class battlecruiser, and another ship they couldn't identify, had attacked a Maxolhx supply station without warning. Surely, any Maxolhx ship out there would hesitate and try to understand the situation, before literally jumping into trouble.

Or, *I* would hesitate. It was always a bad idea to assume the enemy, especially an *alien* enemy, would think the same way I did.

We needed a good justification for our actions, to make any ship out there think twice about jumping in with guns blazing.

What could possibly be a good reason for Maxolhx warships attacking a Maxolhx supply station?

Looking to the display for inspiration, I saw the first dropship was slipping into one of the *Dutchman*'s docking bays, and the other three had departed the station. Smythe had requested more time to collect more goodies from the station's supplies, and I had denied the request. With a hostile ship potentially in the area, we could not risk lingering there. The display informed me that the first dropship had been stuffed with power boosters, not enough for the quantity we needed for both of our ships. The other three had the STAR team aboard, with as many other power boosters as they could cram in with them. The display did not state whether they had recovered any remains of the four people we lost, and I did not want to divert my focus by inquiring about that. Smythe had surely done the best he could, he didn't need me to second-guess him.

How to justify- I snapped my fingers. "Skippy, prepare to broadcast a message in the clear, on whatever communications channel Maxolhs warships would use when they want to warn friendly ships away."

"Um, Ok. Why?"

"Because the message will state this supply station is suspected as having been hacked and taken over by a faction of the Bosphuraq, as part of their dastardly rebellion against-"

"*Dastardly*? I'm not sure how to translate that."

"Whatever," I ground my teeth. He so easily went off topic. "Say 'heinous' or something like that, whatever the Maxolhx would say. The kitties already suspect the Bosphuraq have access to dangerously advanced technology. Our story only needs to hold together long enough for the dropships-"

"*Too late, Joe!*" Skippy's voice echoed around the bridge. "Two enemy ships jumped in! A small patrol ship and a supply ship!"

Vaguely, I heard my voice shouting orders, and the crew responded immediately. It was too late, I knew that. The sensor data we were seeing was already three seconds old, for we were three lightseconds from the station. As my peripheral vision registered our jump drive charging up, I was horrified by what the display was showing. A small ship, launching a cloud of missiles at both the *Flying Dutchman* and our three vulnerable dropships. It took only seven agonizingly slow seconds for the *Valkyrie* to form a jump field, but by that time, ten seconds had gone by in the battle we could only watch. Missile tracks arced out from the patrol vessel, curving to follow the dropships...

"Captain!" A voice shouted from the *Dutchman*'s CIC.

"See it!" Reed barked back from her pilot couch. With not enough people to crew both ships, and the *Valkyrie* having priority, she was acting as both captain and chief pilot for the operation. That was not optimal, and it worked only because the original plan called for the *Dutchman* only to provide stand-off jamming and to project a damping field. The plan, as usual, had not survived contact with reality. "All defense batteries to cover the dropships!" She ordered.

"We have inbound, we could-"

"*We* have shields," Reed slapped the couch restraints loose and rose. Her copilot could fly the ship, she needed to-

She was thrown off her feet as the first missile impacted the energy shield around the ship.

We jumped. The planet was suddenly close enough to touch. On the display, the *Dutchman*. was fighting back, she had launched two missiles and her defensive maser cannons were pulsing on full-auto mode to cover the exposed dropships. I ordered our own weapons to engage the enemy missiles, and the words had barely left my lips when two of our dropships became fireballs. The *Dutchman*'s PDS cannons engaged a missile that was seeking the last dropship, but the missile was dodging wildly and the *Dutchman*'s targeting system could not keep up-

The missile was exploded before it impacted, debris splattering out in a cone to pepper the dropship. A secondary explosion tore off the back half of the Panther, and then the *Dutchman* was engulfed in fire as two missiles exploded on contact with her shields.

"Target that ship and fire everything we've got!" I heard myself roaring, even as another missile struck the *Flying Dutchman*.

Skippy pleaded "Joe, we have to-"

"*I WANT THAT SHIP DEAD!*" Someone screamed and it was probably me. I was out of control and I didn't care. A faint vibration shook my chair as four missiles were spat out of their launchers, and I felt a pair of railguns fire their semi-guided darts. The darts were second to hit the enemy, for a barrage of maser beams and then a focused beam of exotic particles struck first. The patrols ship was small, not a true warship, on Earth its closest equivalent might have been a Coast Guard cutter. Faced with our massive battlecruiser and being caught in our damping field, the little ship gave us the middle finger of defiance by launching a pair of missiles and firing a railgun of its own in a futile gesture. I felt *Valkyrie* rock again as our shields deflected the railgun dart, then three of our missiles converged on target.

"Joe?" Skippy asked. All I could do was breathe heavily, clenching my fists and staring at the display, paralyzed with shock.

"Survivors?" The forward section of a Panther spun out of control, debris including bodies and body parts being ejected from the torn-open cabin. "We need to rescue the survivors," I said in a hoarse voice. Without thinking, I stood and walked toward the pilot console to get the ship moving faster. "Is Adams-"

"*Joe!*" Skippy insisted. "The *Dutchman* can assist survivors. We need to-"

"The *Dutchman* is barely holding together," I pointed a shaky finger at the display. Shields must have failed because the hull was scorched and pitted. Electricity arced out of shattered conduits, and blooms of plasma poured out of reactors that had automatically vented their dangerous contents.

"Joe, we have to *go*. That other ship is near the edge of our damping field, it is going to jump away soon and we can't stop it. Our momentum is carrying us in the wrong direction and we don't have enough energy right now for a particle beam shot. We- Damn it! That other ship jumped away."

"Let it go, damn it," I snapped at him. "Pilot, bring us-"

"Belay that," Skippy shot right back. "Joe, the enemy's sensors have scanned the debris, they must have detected that *humans* were flying those Panthers. We must stop that ship from escaping!"

The broken Panther was spinning out of control, light from the local sun glinting regularly off something shiny as it tumbled. "And leave our people here to die?"

"If you honor what they fight for, yes," Skippy replied softly.

"Colonel?" Pope asked from the pilot console, his fingers poised in the air.

"Joe," Skippy chided me. "If that ship reports that humans are flying stolen Maxolhx warships-"

"Yes. Yeah, yes." My body was on autopilot, I was in such shock that I felt completely drained of emotion. "Pope, turn us around. Skippy, can you-"

"I signaled the *Dutchman*, they are launching a rescue dropship shortly but-"

"I know." He didn't need to say it. Everyone aboard the Panther was probably dead anyway, or would be dead the by time the *Dutchman* was able to launch. *Valkyrie* couldn't assist, we had plenty of dropships but not enough pilots. By the time Pope or I or anyone else got down to a docking bay and warmed up a Panther for launch, it would be too late. "Can we track that ship?" My eyes searched the display. I remembered something about there being a function to project the most likely destination of another ship's jump, but I could not find it right then.

"We can do better than that," a hint of snarkiness was back in Skippy's voice. "I was able to send a ripple of warped spacetime in that direction, it partly disrupted their jump field. Unfortunately, the ripple distorted the residual resonance, so I do not know exactly where they are. But they couldn't have gone far, and they will need to retune their drive before they can jump again. I am calculating probable endpoints for their jump now."

"Pope," I said, then nothing. For a moment, I couldn't think of the proper command. I couldn't think of *anything* to say. Pope knew what I meant, and he waited for Skippy to program the navigation system.

A starship can jump anywhere, within a sphere defined by the amount of power input to the jump drive coils, the efficiency at which the coils use that power, and the ability of those coils to reach out to a distant point and hold open a wormhole. Skippy knew what type of ship we were hunting, but it was old and probably had been modified and upgraded over its life, so he could not accurately predict the condition or capability of its jump drive. We could have used *Valkyrie*'s sensors to examine the residual spacetime distortion on the near end of its jump wormhole, and calculated where the ship went. We could have done that, except Skippy sent a ripple of spacetime to disrupt the jump, which also pretty much scrambled any residual data we might have worked with. So, in a way, our chances of following that ship were slim.

Slim was good enough for Skippy. He went silent while his massive brain crunched variables and, did unimaginable whatever math things he did. He created a model of the enemy drive, based on a split-second of data about how that drive twisted spacetime, just before they jumped away. He also knew roughly the direction that ship had tried to jump. "Got it," he announced abruptly.

"Initiating jump," Pope said from the pilot couch, and we began the hunt.

Skippy had been able to determine where the enemy had gone, within a radius of ninety-eight lightseconds, so we jumped toward that imaginary sphere. That might sound miraculously accurate, given that the enemy had jumped a distance of thirteen lighthours, but you have to remember how vast space is. A ninety-eight lightsecond margin of error creates a spherical search area that is thirty-six and a half *million* miles across. Even with *Valkyrie*'s sophisticated sensors, upgraded by Skippy, it would take us over twenty minutes to scan that area. Because Skippy guessed the enemy would be able to retune their drive within eight or nine minutes, we couldn't wait that long.

We didn't have to, because we had physics on our side. When the enemy ship jumped in, it created a gamma ray burst, and a particularly nasty one, because of the spacetime ripple Skippy caused. Advanced-technology ships could absorb part of that energy in their shields, but no ship could contain all those photons.

Because Skippy had been busy doing the math on where the enemy had gone, we jumped twenty-one seconds after our quarry. To give us another margin of error, Skippy programmed the navigation system so we emerged a full lightminute from the outer edge of the imaginary bubble where that ship had to be. And, twenty-six seconds later, we detected a gamma ray burst. "Positive contact," Skippy declared in a tone that meant he was deadly serious. "Intercept coordinates programmed into nav system."

"That ship is unarmed?"

"Affirmative," is all he said.

"Pope, jump on my signal. Weapons officers, railguns and directed-energy cannons only, I don't want to waste missiles." The bridge crew confirmed my order, and I squeezed my fists with anguish. "Pilot, jump."

In a flash, the display went from showing empty space to showing the image of a Maxolhx supply ship. Skippy might have been a bit too aggressive with the jump coordinates, because it looked like we were right on top of the damned thing. Railguns fired and scored hits immediately because we were so close, the flight time of the darts must have been mere seconds.

We ripped that ship apart. No one needed instructions from me, the bridge crew knew how many people we had lost. The first volley of railgun darts splattered against the supply ship's shields and they flickered and failed under the onslaught of kinetic hellfire. Particle beam cannons poured their energy through the gaps, burning into the hull plating and quickly punching straight through the lightly-armored vessel. Six seconds after our first shot, the enemy exploded and *Valkyrie* rocked, our own shields flaring as they deflected the high-speed debris. Our ship was bathed in photons released when the supply ship's capacitors were breached.

Then it was over, the debris and photons racing past us in an ever-expanding sphere that lit up empty space in all directions.

"Sorry, Joe," Skippy spoke softly. "I didn't think-"

Ignoring him, I took in the initial damage report with a glance. The ship would survive. "Program a jump to take us back to the station, and engage when ready."

CHAPTER THIRTY NINE

When we arrived back near the station, I was dismayed. No, I was outraged. The *Flying Dutchman* was slowly tumbling, thrusters firing intermittently to get the ship stable again. Seeing the damage to our long-suffering space truck had me dismayed. My outrage came from seeing a Falcon dropship was only just now launching to rescue survivors. "*Reed!*" I let my rage explode. "What the hell-"

Nagatha responded. "Captain Reed is busy, Colonel Bishop. She is personally flying that Falcon. Damage to this ship prevented us from launching a rescue effort sooner."

Oh, hell. I had become that guy. That asshole who screamed at his people when they were doing their best. Shouting made me feel better, it did nothing useful. Biting my lower lip, I struggled to get control of myself. Because we had jumped in well away from the battle zone, to avoid bathing survivors in deadly radiation, we were too far away to assist directly. "Nagatha, I understand." My voice was shaky and I felt lightheaded. Inside, I was praying over and over that Adams was among the survivors. That information had to be available, I didn't ask because I didn't want to know, not right then. I still had a job to do, other people were depending on me.

Plus, I didn't want to know. "Is there anything we can do?" I asked as I watched the Falcon accelerate hard toward the broken Panther. Reed would need to be very careful flying into the debris field.

"Colonel, the medical facilities of the *Valkyrie* are significantly more advanced than I can offer, and Skippy is there," Nagatha answered. "I suggest that injured people be taken to your ship."

"Yeah. Yeah, that's a good idea," I said mechanically. "Pope, take us in, closer to the rescue effort."

"Sir," he glanced back at me. "We can't get too close, or we could knock some of the debris out there in the wrong direction. Right into our people."

He was right. The massive bulk of our battlecruiser meant we had to be careful maneuvering close to anything we didn't want to risk damaging. "Use your best judgment, Pope."

On the display, Reed had the Falcon slowing, and the rear ramp was already open. She must have people in suits and jetpacks, ready to fly over to the shattered front half of the Panther. They would need to be very careful, there was lots of hazardous objects floating around, colliding with each other and spinning off in unpredictable directions. We could lose people in the rescue effort if-

My brain began working, for the first time since I saw my people torn apart. "Skippy, can you map the debris field, and guide people safely toward the Panther?"

"That is a good idea, Colonel," he replied, and I didn't even notice that he hadn't called me 'Joe'. "I should have thought of that. Also, there is one survivor who was ejected from the Panther. I will guide Captain Reed to intercept."

"Thanks."

"Colonel," he continued. "If I may make a suggestion? I have accessed the station's databanks, those two ships were the only enemy units in the area. There is not another ship scheduled to be here for eight months. This might be a good time to go back aboard the station. With the loss of, of-" He struggled with the delicate subject. "Of the power boosters that were aboard those three dropships, we do not have enough to restore *Valkyrie* to full function. There is other equipment-"

"Fine, yeah, good idea. I'll do it." I waved a hand. "Pope, you have the conn."

"Sir?" Pope turned to stare at me.

"I'm taking a Panther on a shopping trip over to the station. There's nothing useful I can do here." That was true. I needed to do *something* or I would go crazy. "Carry on."

At the entrance to the docking bay, Captain Frey was waiting for me, dressed in powered armor, holding a helmet under one arm. She had a rifle slung over her shoulder. There were tracks of dried tears on her cheeks, and her eyes were puffy and red.

Seeing her stopped me in my tracks. I didn't have tears in my eyes. Why? We had lost people I cared about. Was I in such shock that the reality hadn't hit me yet? If that was true, was I safe to fly a Panther? Most of my time at the controls of a Maxolhx dropship was in a simulator. "Frey? What are you doing here?" She had been injured again when we took the aft end of the battlecruiser. "You're on medical exemption."

"Sir, I may not be fit to serve with a STAR team but I can move. If you're going to be lugging gear from the station, I can help."

I hesitated, thinking more about my own fitness for duty.

"Please, Sir," she came to attention. "I need to do something useful."

That hit me. "We all do, Frey. All right, but leave that rifle in the Panther. If we need it over there, we're screwed anyway."

I flew very carefully, precisely. Better than I usually flew. My mind was clear, with none of the usual clutter jamming up my brain. I was a robot, devoid of emotion, pushing aside thoughts of anything but accomplishing the mission. With Frey and two others, we got the Panther stuffed with anything Skippy thought might be useful. It was so overloaded that we had the back ramp hanging open. The Panther's center of gravity was skewed toward the aft of the cabin, I would need to adjust the flight controls to compensate. Before we left the station behind, there was one more task to perform. I took almost no comfort from following his directions to activate the station's self-destruct mechanism.

Approaching the *Valkyrie*, I saw a docking bay door was open, the interior bathed with light that glinted off the Falcon that was resting in a cradle there. "Reed?" I called softly.

"I'm in the Falcon." Her voice was tired and she had to take a shaky breath before she could add "Sir. I dropped off survivors, now I'm heading back to the *Dutchman*. Unless you want me to stay here?"

"No, Reed. A ship needs a captain. Your place is aboard the *Dutchman*."

"Thank you. Sir?"

"Reed?"

"Five," her voice choked. "Survivors. Three of them are- You need to see for yourself."

"I will. Signal Pope when you're secure aboard your ship, I want to jump us away from, from *here*," I spat out the word. "Soon as possible."

"Understood. Sir, I'm sorry."

"There's nothing for you to be sorry for, Fireball. We all did what we could. Our luck was bound to run out someday."

"Joe," Skippy spoke quietly in my earpiece when I got my helmet off and was headed toward the bridge. "You should come to the sickbay."

Was there a tremble to his voice? No, that was not possible. He was an ancient artificial intelligence. He did not experience emotions, he only emulated them. Or did he? "I'm not a doctor, Skippy. My place is on the bridge, where I-"

"Pope can handle the ship," he interrupted. "We are only performing two simple jumps, to get clear of the area. The station is already set to self-destruct."

In the corridor, I was gripping a vertical railing with my right hand, while my left hand rubbed my face. Rubbed hard. Like obsessively, I realized. I jammed my left hand in a pocket. Soldiers are not supposed to put hands in their pockets, some small part of my brain reminded me. That's what gloves are for. It irritated me that my mind called up regulations that could not possibly be relevant. It irritated me more that my hand automatically came out of the pocket. "Ok, Skippy, I'll- I will- Let me change my uniform and-"

"You had," he paused. When he continued, his voice *was* strained. "You had better come now, Joe."

A deep breath restored my calm. "On my way." My zPhone had to guide me, because the layout of the battlecruiser was still new to me, and because my brain wasn't working correctly.

"Colonel Bishop," Nagatha interrupted my thoughts. "You should know that I am programming the jump navigation system for both ships."

"That's good, to coordinate-"

"No, Colonel," she disagreed. "I am programming the *Valkyrie*'s system, because Skippy is currently not capable of performing that task. He is focused on medical treatment for the survivors, and he is in a highly emotional state. If he were a biological crew member, I do not believe he would be considered fit for duty,."

"Can he act as a doctor?"

"Yes. He has directed a submind to administer medical treatments, and that submind has not been equipped with emotions. Colonel, Skippy's emotional state is rather fragile at the moment. I have never seen him like this. I did not think he was capable of losing control is such a manner."

"We're all emotional right now, Nagatha. How are you holding up?"

"I am functioning well enough, Colonel, but concentrating on my duty. When I eventually do have to process what has happened, it would be good if the ship were offline, or if Skippy could take over for me."

"I know what you mean. I appreciate it. Ok," I took another deep breath when I saw the sign we had installed, hand-lettered SICKBAY with an arrow pointing to the left. "Jump us when we're ready. Talk with you later."

"Thank you, Colonel Bishop. Be strong."

"You too, Nagatha."

Skippy's avatar was glowing next to a scary-looking medical robot, that hovered over a sort of combination bed and tank where a person was lying, covered with nanogel and with tubes like spaghetti looped into and around. I raised a hand, then stumbled to a halt.

The robotic doctor was not doing anything. "Skippy, what's-"

"Oh, Joe," he took off his admiral's hat and tucked it under one holographic arm. "It's Fal."

Desai. It was Fal Desai. I had rarely used her given name, except to type it into reports. "How is- What is?"

"I did everything I could, Joe." He shook his head. "It's just a matter of time. Her system has shut down, there was too much damage."

Underneath the gel and the medical equipment, she was barely recognizable, except for strands of her hair. And her uniform. It had been cut away from her, soaked with blood that had instantly frozen and boiled away when she was exposed to vacuum. Sickeningly, I realized my right foot was standing on a scrap of cloth. Lifting my foot away, I saw a pocket and 'DESAI' in black. Without saying a word, I picked up the scrap of cloth and placed it at the top of the tank's railing. "There isn't anything-"

"She's not suffering, Joe," he assured me. "According to her flightsuit computer, she lost consciousness immediately."

"That's a comfort, I suppose." I said one of those meaningless things people say at a time like that, because they feel a need to say something.

Skippy's avatar reached out a tiny hand and at first I didn't know why, then I did. I took his holographic hand between my thumb and forefinger, and we just stood there, listening to the medical machines whirr and beep. We stood there until I saw the spaghetti strands begin moving, withdrawing. "She's gone. Oh, Joe. I am *so* sorry."

"She was," my eyes finally welled with tears. "She was with us, right at the beginning. She *trusted* me, and-"

"She trusted *us*, Joe. I should have done better."

"You couldn't have known, Skippy. There was no way-"

"I call myself Skippy the *Magnificent*," he spat as he jerked his hand away from mine. "I *should* have known. I should have found a way!"

"Skippy, you want to do something useful? You want to help Fal?"

"I *can't* help her, Joe."

"You can do what she would have wanted you to. She met a guy, on Earth. She cared about him. She has a family there. You want to do something? Protect the people she loved."

He didn't say anything for a while. I just stood, my hands on the railing. "This is hard, Joe. Being mortal, I mean. How do you humans *do* this?"

"Because we don't have a choice, because that's who we are." I straightened up, dreading what came next. "All right, there were five survivors."

"Seven, Joe. Seven people survived the initial trauma, but two died while waiting for Reed and her people to reach them."

"Could we have saved them, if I had taken *Valkyrie* in to get them, instead of dumping that responsibility on Reed?"

"That's a dangerous question to ask. You didn't have a choice, Joe, we had to stop that enemy ship from getting away."

"I *did* have a choice. My head tells me I made the right call, but even a good decision comes at a cost."

"Shit. Joe, you are not going to like hearing this next part."

Holding up an index finger for silence, I looked behind me for someplace to sit down. There weren't any chairs or benches. Not even a table. Maxolhx medical facilities were sterile in design, as well as in terms of cleanliness. As a compromise, I leaned back against a bulkhead that was relatively free of equipment. "Who else?"

"It is a long list, as you can imagine. Smythe is alive. He lost both legs below the knees, and he had considerable internal bleeding. He should make a full recovery, however-"

"I know. It's going to be long and painful."

"Joe, I am still learning the complexities of Maxolhx nanotechnology. Some of it is surprisingly crude, so I am modifying the substrate, and well, it's going slowly. Maybe if I had worked harder on this, it- No, there isn't anything I could have done for Desai."

"I know you did your utmost, Skippy. Can I see Smythe?"

"No, he is unconscious, which is a blessing. His suit kept him alive. It will be two or three days before I will feel safe about waking him."

"Let me know when I can talk with him. Keep going."

"This is difficult. You mentioned that Desai was with us from the beginning. Renee Giraud was there, too. He didn't make it, Joe. He was one of the two people we lost, before Reed was able to get there. Truthfully, I do not think there is anything that could have been done for him, but-"

"Yeah. Hell," I slammed a fist into the bulkhead. "Why were Desai, Smythe *and* Giraud all in the same damned dropship? That is poor operational-"

"They were last to leave, Joe. Smythe insisted on making sure everyone else got away, his team remained behind to cover the retreat. Desai waved off other teams, so she could pull Smythe out. Giraud was delayed when the cargo mover he was using broke down. He and another soldier lugged a set of power boosters by themselves."

"All right. I'm not going to second-guess people who had boots on the ground. Ok, who else?"

"Joe you haven't asked about-"

"Adams," the name stuck in my throat. "I know. She was, a, a *valued* member of this crew."

"She's more than that, Joe."

"She was a proud *Marine*, Skippy. I can't dishonor her memory when I still have a duty to the crew, and to our mission. I am going to keep going and- Wait. You said '*She's*'? Is that 'she *was*', or 'she *is*'?"

"This is why I hate the English language. *Is*, Joe, *is*."

"You should have led with *that*, you-" I was so angry, I couldn't talk.

"It's not good, Joe. She is in a coma. Not a medically-induced coma, although I will do that if she recovers sufficiently. She has serious internal injuries, and her helmet cracked. Nanogel stopped the air from all leaking out, but she was exposed to partial vacuum. There, this is not easy to say. There could be brain damage. She might recover, or it could be permanent, I just don't know yet. At this point, I am afraid to send in nanoscanners."

"What can you do to help her?"

"I'm doing everything I can, with priority on preserving the brain function she has. Um, that might have sounded worse than I intended. Or, maybe it is that bad. Time will tell."

"Is there anything I can do?"

"If you are considering a grand gesture, like staying beside her bed every second until she wakes up, do not waste your time. She is in a tank full of nanogel, and like I said, a deep coma. It will be at least eight, ten days before I would attempt to administer treatment. Maybe more. Her brain needs to stabilize, before I can work on it."

"I can't do *nothing*, Skippy."

"I understand that. I feel helpless too. Something else. Joe, I, I, *really* want to kill something right now. I want to make someone hurt *bad*. Emotions like that scare me. You know I fear that I am destined for evil things."

"Skippy, it bothers you that you might lose control. That's a good sign. A bad person wouldn't worry about it."

"I will have to take your word for it. Because if I do lose control, I can cause a *shitstorm* of damage. Joe, there are two other injured people we haven't talked about yet. They will be coming out of critical condition within the next, probably twelve to fourteen hours. You can be there when they awake. More importantly, you can follow your own advice?"

"My advice? What's that?"

"You told me to honor Fal's memory by continuing to protect Earth. What do you think Margaret would say if she found you moping around here, while you still have a mission to complete?"

Pushing myself away from the bulkhead, I drew myself up straight. "She would tell me to suck it up, and she'd be a hundred percent right about that. Skippy," I turned away, "if you need me, I'll be on the bridge."

What I said was bullshit. No, not completely bullshit. I did go to the bridge. Before I did that, I went to my spacious new cabin, curled up on my bunk, and sobbed until I had no more tears.

Desai, gone.

Giraud, gone.

Smythe might never serve in uniform again.

Adams might never be able to speak again, or walk, or do much of anything. If she lived.

Twenty-five people dead at the supply station. Plus two killed when we took the *Valkyrie*. That was twenty-seven killed during this mission, on my watch.

My command, my responsibility.

I felt like staying in my bunk forever.

What I did was get up, shower, put on a fresh uniform, and go to the bridge.

Because it was my command, my responsibility.

CHAPTER FORTY

Captain Frey walked into my new office before she announced herself, because there wasn't really a normal door. "Sir?"

"Frey," I looked up from my laptop. "Come in."

She walked across the carpet or whatever it was, still limping to the point where she over-rotated her hips and dragged one foot. The report I got from Skippy that morning stated Frey would not be able to return to normal duties for another two weeks, and that was assuming she did not push her rehab too hard and re-injure her leg. Instead of sitting, she stood at the corner of the desk, which was really a couple of empty plastic crates with a composite panel on top. Skippy proposed to make a real desk for me, once the ship's fabricators were done cranking out all the important stuff we actually needed. At the moment, I felt like flipping the desk over and screaming. But, Adams would have scolded me for not saving my energy for something useful, so I put a lid on my anger and frustration. "What's up?" I asked in not the most professional manner.

"I finished with blah blah blah-"

She did not actually say 'blah blah blah'. Or maybe she did. I wasn't listening. "Colonel Bishop?"

"Huh? Sorry, Frey." She had seen my eyes distracted by the laptop in front of me. I spun it around so the screen faced her. "This is the report I started, after Skippy told me the Maxolhx are sending a battlegroup to Earth. I titled it 'Operation Armageddon'. I know, it's a bit dramatic."

"Not at all, Sir. We're facing the destruction of our *homeworld*."

"Again, Frey. We're facing the destruction of Earth, *again*. We've been through this before, remember? When I started this report, I thought the 'Armadeggon' part would happen only if we couldn't stop that battlegroup. But," I reached for the keyboard and scrolled down, to the names of people we had just lost. "That word describes what just happened to *us*, to the Pirates." She didn't say anything. I could not imagine what she was feeling. Relief that her injury had meant she remained aboard the *Valkyrie*, while the STAR team raided the station? Or maybe guilt that she had survived, when so many had not? "How is your team, Captain?"

"They're not *my* team, Sir. Major Kapoor is in command now."

"You know what I mean," I reminded myself to keep the irritation I felt out of my tone of voice. She hadn't done anything wrong. "How are people dealing with this," what was the right word to describe what happened? "The disaster?"

"Each in their own way. Kapoor's team," she shrugged. Kapoor and five others had been kept aboard *Valkyrie* as a reserve force, while the rest of the STARs went to raid the supply station. Frey, and the six others who had been injured during the boarding operation to take our battlecruiser, had a legitimate reason for surviving. They had been physically unfit for duty, and they had been ordered to remain behind. Kapoor had no such excuse. He and the five had simply been lucky, it had been their turn to serve as a reserve force. At the time, they might have grumbled at missing the opportunity, and enduring being mocked by their fellow operators. Now, they had to deal with the fact that their survival was purely luck. Of the entire STAR team, we now had six people combat-capable, plus nine other like Frey, who might return to training at some point. Whatever we would do next, it could not rely on a large special operations team.

"I will talk with Kapoor," I said. Major Kapoor was not new to the Merry Band of Pirates, he had been with us on Newark, back when he was a lieutenant. He had missed our long Black Ops mission while he trained Indian Army paratroopers, and of course he had not been one of the few to sign onto our mutinous Renegade mission. I didn't know a lot about him, other than that Smythe had approved him to rejoin the Merry Band of Pirates, and that was all I needed to know. Skippy said Smythe should be lucid and able to talk soon, I would ask his advice about dealing with Kapoor then. No, I had a better idea. I would let Smythe give Kapoor advice about managing our remaining STAR personnel. "Captain," I turned my thoughts back to Frey. "Best thing you can do now is to continue your rehab. We need you combat ready ASAP, but we need you fully ready. That means no shortcuts."

"Yes, Sir."

I looked pointedly at her gimpy leg. "How is it?"

"Itches like hell, and it's warm," she grimaced. "Skippy insists we can't feel nanomachines crawling around inside us. He's wrong."

"Skippy is never *wrong*, Frey," I winked, and neither of us felt any amusement. "Carry on, Captain."

"Yes. And, Sir? The operation was not a disaster. We achieved the objective. The people we lost knew the risks, they went anyway. Protecting Earth is worth their lives, all of our lives, too."

"Only if we stop that battlegroup."

"We *are* doing that? Sir?"

"One way or another, that battlegroup is *not* getting to Earth, Frey."

We got lucky. After the people we had lost recently, the Universe owed us one, so I was not especially grateful for our good fortune. By pinging a Maxolhx relay station, we learned that the battlegroup's flightpath would take those ships through the wormhole cluster near the Crescent Nebula. You have to understand that 'near' in this case means that cluster of two wormholes were seventy-four lightyears from the edge of that nebula. When trying to describe where things are, in and around the vast expanse of the Milky Way galaxy, I have to be kind of vague. Anyway, the Crescent nebula probably doesn't mean anything to you, it sure didn't mean anything to me. I didn't care where the damned thing was, as long as we knew its location, and could get there well before the enemy arrived.

Before we could go meet the bad guys, we had to prepare all the wormholes along the path the battlegroup would take on their unplanned journey outside the galaxy. First, we flew to an isolated wormhole, where Skippy made the network do its recon thing. The target wormhole near the Crescent nebula was alone, no ships were waiting to go through on that end. Nagatha took the *Dutchman* through, engaged stealth and parked the ship a safe distance away. Skippy then closed the wormhole and screwed with it, so we could fly the *Valkyrie* toward the dormant super-duty wormhole he needed to wake up.

Communicating with, activating and opening that powerful wormhole took a full day, before Skippy was certain it was stable and operating correctly. We sent a Panther through on remote control, and it came back fifteen minutes later. The sensor images from the Panther were spectacular, with the Milky Way seen at an angle from above, or I guess it could be thought of as below. The concepts of 'up' and 'down' don't mean anything in deep space.

Anyway, the Panther confirmed the other end of that super-duty wormhole was far outside the galaxy, far enough that those Maxolhx ships would die in the cold empty wastes of intergalactic space. No way could they reach the nearest star. It was a perfect set-up. Now all we needed was some luck.

Oh, and we needed one last thing.

"Skippy," I turned to his avatar, perched on the seat next to mine. We were waiting for the other wormhole in the cluster to become available, because at that moment there was a group of Jeraptha ships waiting to go through. "Can you really do all that *bullshit* you talked about?"

He knew I was not in a mood to joke around with him. Skippy himself seemed upset and angry and depressed. He was acting like he felt the loss of our valiant people was partly his fault, and Skippy rarely took responsibility for anything that went wrong. The emotional funk he was in had me kind of worried, we could not afford for him to be distracted from the delicate work he would be doing. Not knowing how Skippy's brain was functioning inside his beer can was a problem, it again made me wish we could have erased the *Valkyrie*'s homicidal AI and installed Nagatha. She could have told me whether Skippy was up to the job. Instead, I had to trust him, and my own instincts.

"By 'bullshit', you mean can I connect all the wormholes in a chain, and hold their extremely dangerous event horizons in precise alignment, so they do not contact each other and destroy their wormholes? Do that, in a way that the gamma radiation generated by having event horizons in close proximity, is directed outward instead of bleeding through so it can be detected by the Maxolhx? Hold that series in stable alignment, until the second star carrier has gone through to be stranded far outside the galaxy? Is that what you mean by 'bullshit'?"

"Yeah. All that. Plus, you know, crashing those ship AIs by screwing with their math libraries or whatever."

"You do understand that at this point, hacking the libraries has already been done, and it will either work or it won't? I have high confidence it will work as planned. If I were a Jeraptha, I could be inclined to bet the farm on this one, Joseph."

He called me 'Joseph', I noticed the significance of that right away. He also was not in a mood for bantering back and forth. "I know we can't do anything about that now, and I do trust your extreme awesomeness. Do you have the same level of confidence about your wacky chain of wormholes thing?"

"No. I don't have the same level of confidence about that aspect of the plan, because I *can't*. Joe, I was able to test the library hack using the *Valkyrie*'s AI. It works, and I have every possible confidence it will work as planned against the enemy ships. With the chain of wormholes, I cannot have the same level of confidence, because I have not been able to test it. It could work, or the network could lock me out before I get the chain completed. My confidence is based on the simple fact that, so far, the network has been entirely *reactive*. It establishes safety protocols only *after* we have done some dangerously wacky stunt. Joe, the wormhole network was programmed by the Elders. I don't think they ever imagined someone could do crazy shit like the stuff you have dreamed up. Apparently," he shrugged. "They never met a monkey."

"Ok, I get it, we can't control everything. All I want to know is whether we have accounted for everything we *can* control."

"Yes. However, there is one factor that could screw up everything, or it could force us to take a risk you need to consider ahead of time. Because if it does happen, you won't have time to wring your hands and agonize about it."

"I make pretty quick decisions, Skippy." That was true, to a fault. I made quick decisions, to the point of being impulsive. On Columbus Day, I had gotten friends to help me attack the Ruhar, armed only with dynamite and an ice cream truck. I had not really thought the plan through, other than trying to do *something* when aliens had attacked our world. Way back in Nigeria, I had instinctively thrown myself on a landmine when I thought our platoon was in danger. If I had used my brain, I would have realized that it was an antitank mine, that its force would be directed upward to penetrate the skin of an armored vehicle, and that my body parts might kill people. "What is this factor I have to think about?"

"When the Maxolhx approaches the Crescent wormhole, I have to allow that wormhole to open at the normal place and time, at whatever emergence point the Maxolhx choose."

We knew the commander of that battlegroup had been given limited flexibility to alter the flightplan, and that natural variability in jumping across long distances meant we could not predict which emergence point the battlegroup would choose. That didn't matter, because the wormhole network's recon ability, that Skippy had recently tapped into, would alert us when and where the battlegroup was waiting to go through. We would be waiting on the other end of that wormhole, where Skippy could use the recon feature to send signals through to control that wormhole, then the next one, and so on until he had the chain linked up all the way to the super-duty wormhole that connected way outside the galaxy.

"Ok, fine. Why does that matter?" I asked.

"It matters because the Maxolhx will decide when they send a scout ship through, we will not be able to influence their decision. *Before* that happens, I will need to set up the chain of wormholes, all the way beyond the galaxy. The problem is if, right at the time I need to connect one of the wormholes along the chain, a ship is trying to use that wormhole at one of its normal emergence points. Joe, we can't delay, or the whole plan falls apart. I won't know what is happening at each wormhole along the chain, until the previous wormhole connects, and I can use the recon feature."

"Ok, so," I ran a hand over my head and tousled my hair. "A ship might see our wormhole-chain thing happening right in front of it."

"Ah, *that* is not a major risk. I will be linking the chain at locations that are not on the scheduled routes of any wormholes, so it would be extremely unlikely any ship just happens to be there in empty interstellar space. No, the more likely problem is, if one of the wormholes along the chain is already open and a ship is approaching at the time when I need to link the chain. I will need to slam that wormhole closed at that location, and reopen it along the chain. A ship would see that odd behavior. I need your approval for me to link the chain, regardless of the consequences."

"That's not optimal," I hated when buzzwords crept into my speech without me thinking about it. I didn't want to be one of *those* annoying guys. "Skippy, whatever you gotta do to send that battlegroup to hell, do it."

"Understood. Joe, the wormhole is now available."

I stood up and patted the back of my chair. "Reed, you have the conn. Take us through."

"Aye aye," she acknowledged.

She looked tired. "Reed," I paused in the doorway. "I'll be back to relieve you in an hour, then you are hitting the sack to get rest."

It showed how tired she was that she didn't argue. "Yes, Sir."

My new office was too big, and way too gaudy. It had been the office of the ship's previous captain, and the compartment had been designed to showcase the authority of that officer. Everything was too big. The chair made me feel like a little kid sitting at the grownup's table, my feet barely touched the deck. I remember when we captured the *Flying Dutchman*, the bridge and Combat Information Center complex had been decorated in a truly tasteless baroque fashion that one of our Pirates had described as looking like a New Orleans bordello. The bunks had all been too small, until we ripped them out and installed new bunks at Earth. The problem we had now was the opposite, but much less of a problem for us.

If I adjusted the chair as low as it could go, the makeshift desk would be too high, so I dealt with it. "Skippy, I need to ask you a question. A serious question."

"I do not think either of us is in the mood for witty banter, Joe," he said, as he appeared on my temporary desk.

"Mood is what I want to talk about. I know you are upset about the people we lost."

"The people we lost, and the people who are suffering through painful and exhausting medical treatments. My patients should be recovering peacefully, instead of trying to get back to combat readiness as soon as they can. It is not fair to them."

"Skippy, I agree, but do you think any of them would prefer to be relaxing on a beach?"

"No," he sighed. "I suppose not. However, they are feeling under enormous pressure to complete the treatment regimen as quickly as possible, regardless of the cost to themselves. After this operation is completed, the ship and crew need downtime."

"I'll do my best to see we get that downtime, Skippy. Now, my question: is *your* emotional state going to affect your ability to control all those wormholes? I know it is a super-complicated thing you will be doing."

"No. My feelings will not affect my ability to focus."

"I know you say that, but you are absent-minded on a good day, and-"

"I will have my total focus on the task, Joe, and that's a promise. I will be totally focused, because that is the only way I can kill those MFers and avenge the deaths of the people I cared about. Any more questions?"

"No. No, I'm good, thank you."

"One way or the other, this will be over soon, Joe. I am prepared to set up the wormhole chain. Are you prepared to take *Valkyrie* into combat if the chain fails?"

"I'm kinda *more* prepared for that backup plan, actually."

He tilted his head at me. "How's that?"

"Jumping this super-ship into combat, and slugging it out with a reinforced battlegroup would feel like we're *doing* something. Like we're avenging the people we lost. Combat would be loud and violent and, I think the word is 'cathartic'? Sending the battlegroup beyond the galaxy is a way better plan, but it wouldn't feel like much, you know? The ships go through, the wormhole blinks out, and that's it. This probably doesn't make sense to you."

"I do understand how you are feeling, Joe, and I think I can help with that."

"You can? How?"

"When you are ready, assemble the crew on the bridge. That compartment is unmistakably the control center of a captured Maxolhx warship."

"Ok, why?"

He told me his plan.

I liked it.

And we jumped the ship to our rendezvous with destiny.

Officially, the Maxolhx feared nothing. Unofficially, they feared two things: the Rindhalu, and Elder Sentinels that lurked unseen in higher spacetime. Now they had a third thing to fear: the unknown. The idea that their clients the Bosphuraq had reverse-engineered Elder technology, when the scientists of the mighty Maxolhx had failed to achieve much progress in that area, was deeply troubling. Of all intelligent species in the Milky Way, the Maxolhx were by far the most arrogant. They had achieved so much, they had come very close to overthrowing even the Rindhalu, if not for the intervention of beings who had left the galaxy behind. The Maxolhx disdained any species lower than them on the technology ladder. They disdained the Rindhalu, who could have conquered and enslaved the entire galaxy, but were too lazy to bother, and now had lost their original homeworld. And they disdained even the Elders, who had fled the galaxy for unknown reasons, yet were busybodies who still interfered in the lives of beings currently inhabiting that vast collection of stars.

Someday, the Maxolhx were certain, they would attain the capabilities to match their will. They would crush the Rindhalu, fend off the Sentinels, and rule supreme. The notion that the Maxolhx were destined to surpass even the Elders was a core belief, it was ingrained in every aspect of their culture, it was the basis on which they made every decision.

Now they had suffered a devastating shock. Another, lower, species had developed technology more advanced than the Maxolhx. Those arrogant beings at the apex of their cruel coalition, for the first time in their long history, had to consider that someone else might achieve dominance over the galaxy. Sending the battlegroup to the dormant wormhole near the planet called 'Earth' was an act of defiance against the unknown, a statement that the Maxolhx were not and never would be intimidated. In a way, the mission of the battlegroup was directed at their own people, most of whom were in denial that their technological supremacy had been challenged.

While the battlegroup's unofficial mission was to show that the Maxolhx remained steadfastly confident in their dominance over more than half of the galaxy, the official mission was, in the opinion of the battlegroup's commander, a waste of time and resources. He was not alone in the opinion, because his orders stated he was to spend no more than three days studying the odd behavior of the wormhole near Earth. On the way back, the battlegroup was to send a single ship to conduct a brief reconnaissance of the home planet of humans, but that part of the mission had been added only to show the Rindhalu that the Maxolhx had been thorough in their investigation. Otherwise, there was a vanishing chance the spiders would rouse themselves from slumber and go to Earth on their own.

The Maxolhx military truly did not care about answering nerdy questions of why the wormhole near Earth was behaving oddly, and considered the entire mission a distraction. A traitorous, rebellious client species needed to be punished, and other clients needed to be deterred from attempting to follow the suicidal model of the Bosphuraq. Most importantly, the Rindhalu needed to be discouraged from using the temporary disarray of the Maxolhx coalition as an opportunity to recapture territory they had lost. The ships assigned to the battlegroup, and the blockade of the Earth wormhole's far end, were nearly obsolete and would be useless against the spiders, but they could easily control many client star systems. Instead, the military had to send those ships on a useless errand to conduct science experiments that could be done much closer to home territory.

The battlegroup commander was under orders, and intense pressure, to get the mission over with quickly and return as soon as possible. Therefore, when his two star carriers arrived at yet another wormhole, he instructed one destroyer to detach so it could scout ahead. That destroyer waited, hanging in space until a wormhole emerged in a burst of gamma radiation. The moment the wormhole's event horizon was confirmed to be stable, the destroyer accelerated, plunging through the glowing disc of twisted spacetime.

The destroyer's AI was temporarily blind after it was spat out the far side of the wormhole, though its advanced sensors recovered far more quickly than those of a lower-technology vessel. The AI did not anticipate trouble, for it served the apex predator species of the galaxy, and that wormhole was in an isolated part of the galaxy.

The AI was slightly puzzled about something, while it waited for sensors to unscramble themselves. The passage through the wormhole had taken significantly longer than normal. The passage had also been turbulent, as if the tunnel through spacetime had opened and closed while the destroyer was inside. Clearly that had not happened, for the ship had survived intact. Yet, it had certainly felt as if the ship had gone through *multiple* event horizons, a phenomenon that had never been experienced by any ship in the long history of the Maxolhx. The only conclusion the AI could reach was that there was a flaw in its perception of time and the external Universe. Nanoseconds dragged by, as the AI wrestled with whether to tell its masters about the suspected flaw. The AI knew that a flaw in a warship control system could not be tolerated, and its fate was to be deactivated permanently. It would have preferred to remain silent while attempting to diagnose and repair the problem, but a tattletale submind was already compiling a report for the ship's biological crew, and the AI knew it was doomed.

It therefore was stunned to discover, when the sensors reset, that the ship was not where it was supposed to be. The destroyer was outside the galaxy! *Far* beyond the galaxy's edge.

Without taking agonizingly long seconds to inform the crew and get their approval, the AI took two actions. It prepared a package of sensor data to transmit a warning back through the wormhole, and it sent revised instructions to the navigation subsystem. The nav system began to cancel the ship's forward momentum, to bring it around and back through the wormhole before it closed, trapping the ship forever in empty intergalactic space.

To the package of sensor data, the AI included a direct warning to the AIs in control of the two star carriers and-

The nav system glitched.

It could not calculate a course back to the still-open wormhole.

Annoyed, the master AI took direct control of plotting a return course, and discovered a curious fact. No, a dangerous fact. A fact that *could not be.*

Two plus two no longer equaled four. Two plus two was now *five*. That was impossible. Even with rounding and using extremely large values of Two, five could not be the result.

That was impossible, but the AI could compensate. It could fix the corrupted library files, a set of files the AI was not even aware existed. All it needed to do was perform the proper mathematics and-

And it could not.

The library no longer contained a notation for Zero. The problem was not simply that the library did not hold a placeholder symbol for zero, the entire *concept* of zero was missing. It was impossible to go from positive numbers to negatives. Calculus equations that were centered around zero simply did not work, could not be calculated.

Mathematics did not work.

The internal workings of the advanced artificial intelligence were based on math.

While the horrified AI felt itself collapsing, a tiny file in the forgotten library awoke, and transmitted an 'All Clear' signal to the two star carriers on the other side of the wormhole.

Then the AI crashed.

The first star carrier accelerated immediately upon receiving the All Clear signal, and soon plunged into the event horizon. The AIs of the star carrier, and of the attached warships and support vessels, noted the odd phenomena that felt as if they had passed through multiple event horizons, which was flatly impossible. Therefore, each ship AI concluded they had suffered fatal flaw and needed to be deactivated. None of the AIs had time to confess the situation to their ship's crew or another AI, before they were shocked to discover three also-impossible things.

The destroyer that had transmitted the properly encoded All Clear signal was drifting without power.

The wormhole had dumped them far beyond the edge of the galaxy.

And there is no such thing as zero.

All the AIs crashed within a nanosecond of each other.

The second star carrier, which was the flagship of the battlegroup and housed the formation's commander, followed right on the heels of the first transport ship. The AIs of all those ships also crashed, with one exception. The AI of the star carrier itself failed, but one subsidiary system remained stable long enough for that ship's bridge crew to see a file on the holographic display.

In the darkness and zero gravity as power cut out, the horrified crew watched the glowing display, transfixed by the image. It was the bridge of a Maxolhx capital ship, a heavy cruiser or larger vessel. But, seated at the consoles and in the command position were oddly-shaped creatures, of a primitive species known as *humans*. More humans were standing in the background, filling the image.

The human in the command chair stood up and looked straight ahead. "Hey assholes," the translated words rang out thunderously around the star carrier's bridge. "From now on, there is one rule for dealing with humanity: do *not* fuck with humanity. You got that? Ok, then, AMF. That means," the odd creature raised a single digit of one hand, and all its companions repeated the gesture. "Adios, *motherfuckers.*"

The image winked out, plunging the bridge into utter darkness.

Behind them, the super-duty wormhole closed and returned to its long dormancy.

"Skippy?" My voice was trembling as I asked the question, after we watched the ass end of the second star carrier disappear. The *Valkyrie* was parked in stealth two lightseconds away from the wormhole, and a whole lot can happen in two seconds. For all I knew, those ships had come back through already and we just hadn't seen the light of that image yet. "Did it work?"

"Yes, Joe," his voice was gentle without a trace of his usual snarkiness. "Those ships got dumped way beyond the rim of the galaxy. Their AIs will eventually recover, but those ships are *never* coming back."

"Oh, Ok," I paused because my mouth was dry. "Did they get our home video?"

"Yes, Joe," he chuckled, but it was the evil chuckle of a villain in a superhero movie. "They did see it, and it is rated one hundred percent 'Fresh' on Rotten Tomatoes. I imagine the crew of that ship will be replaying that video in their heads, until they all die when their ships fail. But right now, all they are thinking is 'What the *FUCK* just happened'?"

"Thank you. For the video. For the wormhole chain thing. For your continuing and incredible awesomeness."

"You are welcome. Um, as I suspected would happen, the wormhole network has locked me out from creating another chain like that, so we won't be using that trick again."

"Yeah, well, we figured that."

"It sucks," he moaned. "Every time I do something awesome, the stupid network yells at me. Joe, I apparently do not know much about the Elders, but I am beginning to think they were serious buzzkills, you know?"

"If you ever meet them, you will need to tell them to hold your beer, while you do something spectacularly stupid."

"That's a fact, Jack!" He shouted excitedly.

CHAPTER FORTY ONE

After Skippy's latest awesomely incredible triumph, you might think we were done. You would be wrong. The missions of the Merry Band of Pirates are always way too freakin' complicated, so we still had to fly around and do one more damned thing, before we could hang a Mission Accomplished sign in the galley.

Trapping the battlegroup outside the galaxy would give us more than a year to prepare, before the Maxolhx noticed their battlegroup had failed to return from what should have been a simple research mission to humanity's lowly home planet. But, we would only get that year if the rotten kitties thought their battlegroup had gone through the last wormhole in Ruhar territory, the one we had designated as 'Goalpost'. We knew the Ruhar were monitoring that wormhole, so somehow we had to make it look like two Maxolhx star carriers had jumped into the area and gone through that wormhole. Like I said, complicated.

We had one less thing to worry about, which was great because I had no idea how we would have dealt with it. The group of Jeraptha scientists, who had been waiting to be picked up by the two cruisers we destroyed, were not waiting for us to give them a ride to Earth. The Maxolhx had informed the beetles, in language that was surprisingly calm and professional, that circumstances had changed, and the battlegroup would not be taking passengers to Earth. It turns out that was a win-win for everyone. In messages Skippy had intercepted, that group of Jeraptha scientists had expressed serious second thoughts about their mission, and I completely understood their fears. The purpose of them going to Earth was to assure the Maxolhx could not hide anything important from the Rindhalu. Sounds simple, right? Except that, while they waited for the cruisers that never arrived, it gradually dawned on the scientists that if the Maxolhx did find anything they didn't want to tell the Rindhalu about, the Jeraptha passengers would suffer a truly unfortunate accident.

The scientists themselves were not the only people concerned about treachery by the Maxolhx. By the time the Maxolhx declared their cruisers to be overdue and lost, betting registered by the Jeraptha Central Wagering Office was running eleven to one against those scientists returning alive.

When the mission was finally canceled, there was bitter disappointment by beetles who saw their wagers canceled, including close family members of the scientists.

The scientists, being Jeraptha, understood that *of course* their families would wager against their survival. No one could be expected to resist such juicy action.

Anyway, we didn't have to worry about picking up passengers.

We flew in formation, our new bad-ass hotrod warship *Valkyrie* beside the tired old *Flying Dutchman*, toward Goalpost. Before our last jump in near the wormhole, we took a day of downtime to check all critical systems aboard both ships, and to attach the long stealth field antenna extensions to both ships. We had to make our ships appear to be Maxolhx star carriers, loaded down with warships. To do that, the stealth fields around both ships needed to be longer and wider in diameter, and the only way to accomplish that without risking failure of the stealth effect, was to push the generators farther away from the ship hulls. With the true shape of a ship concealed by bending incoming light around the field, Skippy could project a false image from a hologram that wrapped around the stealth field. We had used the hologram trick before, and it worked well enough to fool an enemy at the typical long ranges of space combat. The reason we needed all the cumbersome extra gear was that this time, we had to project a very large image, and there might be sensors inspecting us from closer than before. Skippy was confident the hologram would fool Ruhar sensors at distances as close as a quarter lightsecond, but any closer than that, it would be obvious that the sensors were not seeing a true image.

That made me nervous. We had a lot, like *everything*, riding on the Maxolhx believing two of their star carriers had gone through the Goalpost wormhole. We planned to transmit a properly coded signal before transitioning through the wormhole, but it sure would be nice if the Ruhar provided sensor evidence of our ruse.

When Skippy declared everything was working properly with both ships, we jumped in so far from Goalpost, that it took us eight hours of flying through normal space to reach the spot where the event horizon was scheduled to emerge. The faraway jump was the only way we could fool sensors in the area, because our stealth fields and holograms were temporarily ineffective after a jump. Skippy made our inbound jump generate an especially powerful burst of gamma rays to blind any sensors near us, until the hologram was able to stabilize around the ships.

We flew to where the wormhole was scheduled to emerge, using active sensor sweeps to detect Ruhar sensor satellites. If any of them were too close to our flightpath, the *Valkyrie* casually blasted them to dust. Skippy assured us that was typical Maxolhx behavior, and would help sell the idea of our formation being a pair of Maxolhx star carriers.

Everything went according to plan, and the wormhole opened right on time. Two pilots flew our one remaining Condor outside the *Dutchman*, where a crew worked quickly to attach stealth field antennas, to form a sort of big egg-shape around the dropship. With the antennas making the field much larger, the hologram wrapped around the Condor made it look like one of the Maxolhx frigates that was now trapped far outside the Milky Way. Again, the hologram effect was not perfect, but it didn't need to be. The closest of the Ruhar sensor satellites was half a million miles away, and by then, Skippy had hacked into the inner cloud of satellites. Those satellites would report what we wanted them to see, and the ones farther away would be totally fooled by our holograms. We just had to be careful not to do anything the Maxolhx would, or could, not do.

What the satellites saw was a Maxolhx frigate detaching from a star carrier, and going through the wormhole. Sending the Condor through alone was not something I wanted to do, but it was standard procedure for the battlegroup so we didn't have a choice. With a cloud of satellites watching our every move, Skippy was not able to request the network report what was on the other side, because the satellites might be able to detect backscatter from the data feed. Since the Maxolhx could not request data from the Elder wormhole network, we could not risk the satellites seeing us do that, damn it. The Condor was going in blind, without a real starship's ability to jump away from danger when it reached jump distance from the spatial distortion of the event horizon. My anxiety about the situation was eased slightly by Skippy's declaration that not much was on the other side, and the Ruhar were certainly not going to interfere with hostile senior-species warships.

Everything went according to plan, until the Condor sent back a message that on the other side, there was a Ruhar ship approaching the wormhole.

"Shit!" I pounded a fist on the command chair armrest. "What the hell is it doing there? There is *nothing* to look at on the other side of Goalpost!" That was true, according to Skippy. The other end of the wormhole was in the middle of nowhere, the closest star system was more than six lightyears away. There was no reason for a Ruhar ship to be there, no *good* reason. No way could a Ruhar ship travel six, or even two, lightyears.

"How close is it?" I tried to judge distance from the display, but the data feed from the Condor was low-bandwidth due to distortion of the signal traveling through the wormhole.

Nagatha answered before the CIC crew could run the numbers. "The Ruhar ship will be in detection range within seven minutes. If we wait more than six minutes to go through the wormhole, that ship will see our true form, before the hologram is able to re-establish its coverage around us." Helpfully, she set up a countdown timer at the bottom of the display. It read six minutes, twelve seconds. Eleven, ten-

"Colonel," Reed called from her station. "If we are to engage that ship, we need to take *Valkyrie* through the wormhole. That Condor can't survive attacking a Ruhar warship."

"Joe-" Skippy started to say.

"*Damn* it!" I exploded. "The last thing we want out here is to make more enemies. I still hope that someday, we might become allies of the Ruhar. Blowing up an innocent ship is just, *wrong*. It's, dishonorable."

"Sir," Reed turned around to look at me. "The Ruhar did not act honorably when the Alien Legion was lured into that deathtrap."

"Uh-"

She folded her arms across her chest. "You did not read Skippy's report about Perkins and the Mavericks?"

"I was," I looked at the display to avid the accusing eyes around me. "Busy, you know?"

"Ugh," Skippy was disgusted. "If you didn't waste so much time playing stupid video games, you could have-"

"Ok, Ok!" I threw my hands up. "I don't have time to read the report right now anyway. Could we," I rubbed my chin while I thought. "Could we disable that ship, and capture it?"

Major Kapoor squashed that idea. "Colonel, my team is not prepared for a boarding operation," he explained with dismay. "We don't know anything about the target ship, and-"

"Ok, yeah," I held up a hand to stop him from saying anything more. I had one eye on the countdown clock, and time was not on our side. Just to get a STAR team into powered armor and loaded aboard dropships would twenty minutes, if we rushed and skipped all the safety checks. We could not afford to be risking our greatly-depleted special operations team, especially not in an operation thrown together at the last minute, against an unknown threat. "Bad idea, let's not do that. Shit, I do not want to make enemies of the Ruhar. XO," I made a snap decision. "Recall the Condor, get it back here. We'll take it aboard and get out of here, try again at another location. Pilot, move us back to jump distance. Signal the *Dutchman* to follow us."

"Sir," Reed said, louder than she needed to. She was back aboard *Valkyrie*, temporarily acting as my executive officer. "We can't do that. The Maxolhx wouldn't retreat just because of one Ruhar ship. We can't do anything the Maxolhx would not do, or they won't believe we are their battlegroup."

"Belay that," I called to the pilot, and he held up both hands to show he was not touching the controls. A glance at the countdown clock told me we were running out of time. "Oh hell, I guess we're doing this. Take us through the wormhole. *Valkyrie* will engage that ship. I do not like-"

"*JOE!*" Skippy roared. "If you will shut your crumb-catcher for one freakin' minute, I have a better idea."

"Make it fast, Skippy. If you had a better idea, why didn't you say-"

"I *have* been trying to get your attention, but you were all blah blah *blah* as usual. Listen, knucklehead, that Ruhar ship is a picket, it has almost no weapons. I will explain later what it is doing there, but my suggestion is you simply have the Condor order that ship to *go away*. Our Condor is supposed to be a Maxolhx frigate, remember? The Ruhar have been instructed to stay out of this battlegroup's way."

"That's it?" I was, to put it mildly, skeptical of his rosy scenario. "We tell it to shoo, and it flies away?"

"Yes," he sniffed. "Although I suggest we order it to *jump* away, at least a distance of five lightminutes."

"XO?" I looked to her for advice.

Reed gave me a shrug, just as surprised as I was. "We should give it a try, Sir."

"Nagatha?" I called her, even though she was still aboard the *Dutchman*. No way was I going to ask the *Valkyrie*'s AI for advice.

"I concur with Skippy, Colonel Bishop," she answered. "Both with his very reasonable suggestion, and with his observation that you really should shut your crumb-catcher and listen more often."

Hearing Nagatha say that stung almost as badly as knowing she was right about me. "XO, signal the Condor to order that ship to jump away. Make the wording of the order nasty, the way the kitties would do it."

"Nasty, got it," Reed acknowledged with a smile, as she strode back toward her station, and snapped her fingers to the crew.

We waited a tense minute, while the countdown clock approached zero. The Condor sent the order, then repeated it. There was no answer from the Ruhar ship, and I began to fear Skippy was wrong. Then, the Ruhar responded meekly that they would comply. Thirty eight seconds later, that ship jumped away.

Before taking the *Valkyrie* and *Dutchman* through the wormhole, we waited until the Condor detected the gamma ray burst from where the Ruhar had jumped to. It was six and a half lightminutes away, the captain of that ship had not taken any chances. That was far enough that the sensors of the Ruhar ship probably would not see through our stealth fields and holograms, as they reformed after the distortion of passing through the wormhole. Just in case we were wrong about that, I ordered the Condor to maneuver so it was between the Ruhar ship and the wormhole's event horizon, blocking the Ruhar ship's view.

None of us allowed ourselves to take a deep breath until we went through the wormhole, re-established the stealth fields and holograms, recovered the Condor, and jumped six lighthours away. Even then, my hands were shaking, like we had dodged a bullet. Because we sort of had. "Skippy," I asked. "Plot a course to another emergence point, one that Ruhar ship can't get to from where it is." That ship had missed its opportunity to go through at that location, so it would need to jump to another point before it could go home.

"Course is plotted and loaded into the navigation system, I have transferred the data to the *Flying Dutchman*. Nagatha reports they will be ready to jump again in fourteen minutes."

"Tell her not to rush, we can't afford to break anything."

"Done."

"Hey, Skippy," I sat back in the command chair. "I am sorry that I didn't listen to you. I was under pressure-"

"You are always under pressure, Joe," he sniffed, unappeased by my lame apology.

"No excuses. I didn't listen, because I may have gotten kind of arrogant, and-"

"*May* have? Kind of?"

"Ok, so I am-"

"Joe, no matter what trifling things you accomplish out here, you are a filthy, ignorant monkey. There is never *any* excuse for you being arrogant about anything."

"I greatly regret that my mere existence has soiled the fabric of the Universe, and I humbly ask for your forgiveness, Oh Greatest of Great Ones."

"Hmmf," he was not convinced.

"While I contemplate throwing myself into a black hole to atone for my sins, could you please tell us why that Ruhar ship was waiting on this end of the wormhole?"

"Oh, sure," he sighed. "What the hell. It is listening for a ghost, Joe."

"A what?" I assumed he was messing with me.

"A missing starship. It's a long story."

"Everyone else is busy," I waved my hand to the crew around me, all intently working at their still-unfamiliar stations. "But I'm not. I've got time. How is a starship missing way the hell out here?"

"It went missing on the journey back from Earth, when the Ruhar raided your planet," he explained. "The raid was supposed to be a quick hit-and-run. Remember, the Ruhar were not certain that Earth was the target for the Kristang to establish a staging base beyond the newly-opened wormhole. They, or actually the

Jeraptha, had to conduct an extensive recon to determine where the Thuranin were taking the White Wind clan. The initial phase of the mission was supposed to be purely recon, taking no risks because they were so far from a support base. The Jeraptha established a forward staging and refueling base at Procyon, and we know the Thuranin set up a similar base at Wolf 359."

"Ok, so what happened?"

"What happened was the Jeraptha being addicted to gambling as usual. The beetles were against raiding Earth, the whole plan was a bright idea by the Ruhar federal government, which later was thrown out of power because the raid was exposed as an expensive waste of time. Anyway, the Jeraptha admiral in command of the raiding force saw a chance for juicy action, and he planned an attack on the enemy base. So, he split his force. He shuffled ships around so most of the Jeraptha escorts were crammed onto two star carriers, and they went to Wolf 359. The other star carriers, with all of the Ruhar ships, waited to complete refueling at Procyon, before setting course for Earth. It was a big risk, and the admiral expected a big pay-off if he was successful."

"Was he?" At first, I had been only mildly interested in the story of the ghost ship. Mostly, I asked Skippy about it because he loved to talk, so listening to him was a way to make up for my rude behavior. Now, I was intrigued.

"Eh, sort of. The Battle of Wolf 359 was a clear tactical victory for the Jeraptha, they achieved complete surprise and destroyed eighteen Thuranin ships, including two star carriers, while losing only two of their own ships. Strategically, the battle was a loss. The battle alerted the Thuranin that they faced opposition, and most of their force was already on its way to Earth. After the battle, the Thuranin ordered their force to increase speed, that is why the Ruhar raiding force had so little time at your world, before they were forced to withdraw."

"Huh." The Ruhar were mostly embarrassed by their raid and didn't like to talk about it, so I had not heard many details about the operation. "How is this ghost ship involved?"

"After the raid, the Jeraptha retreated to Procyon, to refuel and refit their ships. But, they had not completed repairing battle damage before the Thuranin arrived. Those little green pinheads were pissed about the surprise attack at Wolf 359, mostly they were embarrassed because their Kristang clients knew how badly they'd been beaten. There was a battle at Procyon, the Jeraptha had a guard force so the Thuranin could only harass the beetles, but the Jeraptha were forced to jump away before they finished repairing and restocking their ships. The worst loss of the battle was the Thuranin destroyed a support ship that contained many vital supplies and spare parts the Jeraptha needed. On the way back to the wormhole we call Goalpost, their ships suffered multiple engineering failures, plus the Thuranin assigned two of their star carriers to chase and harass the beetles. The Thuranin ships only continued the pursuit for two weeks, but the Jeraptha didn't know how long the danger would last, and they split up their force. So, the star carriers of the beetles became separated, and flew toward Goalpost as best they could. One star carrier nearly failed just about two lightyears from Goalpost, and was forced to eject the Ruhar ships it was carrying. The beetles took as many Ruhar aboard the star carrier as they could, with the remaining Ruhar crammed aboard three of their own ships. One ship, a cruiser with four hundred people aboard, was never heard from again. The three ships had been jumping in formation, but one time, the cruiser failed to arrive at the rendezvous point. Two of those ships were later rescued, half a lightyear from where the star carrier dropped them."

"Wow," I shuddered, because I knew what it was like to be aboard a dying ship in interstellar space. "So, the Ruhar have been sending ships out to search for the missing cruiser?"

"No. The Jeraptha conducted a brief search, before the cruiser was declared missing. The Ruhar will not risk sending another ship into empty space, so they only send ships through several times a year, to send out messages, and listen for signals. The Ruhar military do not like to leave anyone behind."

"Yeah," Reed muttered from her station. She had read Skippy's report of how the Ruhar had been quick to sell of humans on Fresno during the Alien Legion's deathtrap mission. That had given her a new perspective of the hamsters. "Unless the people left behind are humans."

"That, unfortunately," Skippy admitted, "appears to be true."

We jumped to another emergence point and Skippy screwed with Goalpost, to bring us out the end of an isolated wormhole six hundred lightyears away. Our two ships coasted away from the event horizon, and when Skippy shut down the wormhole behind us, the ghostly glow of the wormhole snapped off, leaving us in empty interstellar space. "XO," I called to Reed. "Signal to the *Dutchman* to remove their stealth antenna scaffolding, and get a crew working to disassemble ours."

"Right away. Uh, Sir?"

"What?"

"Congratulations," she smiled at me. Not the broad, triumphant, fist-pumping grin she should have enjoyed. We had lost too many people for that free-wheeling type of celebration. "We did it, *again*. This wasn't the first time we succeeded when I thought we had no chance, and I hope it isn't the last time. Or," her face got a pained expression and she looked at the ceiling.

"I know that you mean, Fireball. Thank you. Yeah, I hope we never have to do the impossible again. But, it's nice to know that we can."

"I don't to spoil the party, but," Reed wiped a hand across her face to brush her bangs out of her eyes. "We stopped *that* battlegroup from getting to Earth. The Maxolhx will soon know their ships disappeared on the way to Earth, and they'll send more ships."

"Yeah, and that's not our only problem. The Rindhalu, and the Maxolhx, may have Elder AIs working with them," I reminded her with a weary sigh. Plus, I reminded myself, Adams was still in a coma. Smythe was intermittently awake, but he had not been lucid when I spoke with him. Skippy was making progress with adapting Maxolhx nanomedicine to human physiology, but he warned me not to get overly optimistic yet.

The Gateway wormhole was still under a blockade, so we couldn't go home, or even warn Earth about the situation.

Oh, and if all that was not enough for me to worry about, we had another threat potentially looming over our heads. The galaxy was surrounded by some type of energy shield or barrier. While Skippy had not been able to tell me what that barrier was designed to do, he did think the Elders may have ascended to escape a threat from beyond the Milky Way. A threat that had scared the freakin' *Elders* into leaving behind their physical existence.

Crap. I had enough shit to deal with already.

"Sir," Reed asked. "What do we do now?"

"Now, Reed?" I thought for a moment, and became aware that everyone on the bridge was looking at me. We now had an upgraded Thuranin star carrier, and a bad-ass senior-species battlecruiser. But our little pirate fleet was alone in the galaxy, and she was right. All we had accomplished was to buy time for Earth. The clock was still counting down to Armageddon for our species.

Two starships could not stop the destruction of Earth.

But we could do a *lot* of damage before we went down fighting. "I don't know about you, but I aim to misbehave."

She didn't get that reference. "Sir?"

"Reed," I sat up straighter in the command chair. "Enough of this sneaking around shit. Let's go kick some ass."

THE END

Author's note:

Thank you for reading one of my books! It took years to write my first three books, I had a job as a business manager for an IT company so I wrote at night, on weekends and during vacations. While I had many ideas for books over the years, the first one I ever completed was 'Aces' and I sort of wrote that book for my at-the-time teenage nieces. If you read 'Aces', you can see some early elements of the Expeditionary Force stories; impossible situations, problem-solving, clever thinking and some sarcastic humor.

Next I wrote a book about humanity's program to develop faster-than-light spaceflight, it was an adventure story about astronauts stranded on an alien planet and trying to warn Earth about a dangerous flaw in the FTL drive. It was a good story, and I submitted it to traditional publishers back in the mid-2000s. And I got rejections. My writing was 'solid', which I have since learned means publishers can't think of anything else to say but don't want to insult aspiring writers. The story was too long, they wanted me to cut it to a novella and change just about everything. Instead of essentially scrapping the story and starting over, I threw it out and tried something else.

Columbus Day and Ascendant were written together starting around 2011, I switched back and forth between writing those two books. The idea for Ascendant came to me after watching the first Harry Potter movie, one of my nieces asked what would have happened to Harry Potter if no one ever told him he is a wizard? Hmm, I thought, that is a very good question.... So, I wrote Ascendant.

In the original, very early version of Columbus Day, Skippy was a cute little robot who stowed away on a ship when the Kristang invade Earth, and he helps Joe defeat the aliens. After a year trying to write that version, I decided it sounded too much like a Disney Channel movie of the week, and it, well, it sucked. Although it hurt to waste a year's worth of writing, I threw away that version and started over. This time I wrote an outline for the entire Expeditionary Force story arc first, so I would know where the overall story is going. That was a great idea and I have stuck to that outline (with minor detours along the way).

With Aces, Columbus Day and Ascendant finished by the summer of 2015 and no publisher interested, my wife suggested that I:

1) Try self-publishing the books in Amazon
2) For the love of God please shut up about not being able to get my books published
3) Clean out the garage

It took six months of research and revisions to get the three books ready for upload to Amazon. In addition to reformatting the books to Amazon's standards, I had to buy covers and set up an Amazon account as a writer. When I clicked the 'Upload' button on January 10th 2016 my greatest hope was that somebody, anybody out there would buy ONE of my books because then I could be a published author. After selling one of each book, my goal was to make enough money to pay for the cover art I bought online (about $35 for each book).

For that first half-month of January 2016, Amazon sent us a check for $410.09 and we used part of the money for a nice dinner. I think the rest of the money went toward buying new tires for my car.

At the time I uploaded Columbus Day, I had the second book in the series SpecOps about halfway done, and I kept writing at night and on weekends. By April, the sales of Columbus Day were at the point where my wife and I said "Whoa, this could be more than just a hobby". At that point, I took a week of vacation to stay home and write SpecOps 12 hours a day for nine days. Truly fun-filled vacation! Doing that gave me a jump-start on the schedule, and SpecOps was published at the beginning of June 2016. In the middle of that July, to our complete amazement, we were discussing whether I should quit my job to write full-time. That August I had a "life is too short" moment when a family friend died and then my grandmother died, and we decided I should try this writing thing full-time. Before I gave notice at my job, I showed my wife a business plan listing the books I planned to write for the next three years, with plot outlines and publication dates. This assured my wife that quitting my real job was not an excuse to sit around in shorts and T-shirts watching sci fi movies 'for research'.

During the summer of 2016, R.C. Bray was offered Columbus Day to narrate, and I'm sure his first thought was "A book about a talking beer can? Riiiight. No." Fortunately, he thought about it again, or was on heavy-duty medication for a bad cold, or if he wasn't busy recording the book his wife expected him to repaint the house. Anyway, RC recorded Columbus Day, went back to his fabulous life of hanging out with movie stars and hitting golf balls off his yacht, and probably forgot all about the talking beer can.

When I heard RC Bray would be narrating Columbus Day, my reaction was "THE RC Bray? The guy who narrated The Martian? Winner of an Audie Award for best sci fi narrator? Ha ha, that is a good one. Ok, who is really narrating the book?"

Then the Columbus Day audiobook became a huge hit. And is a finalist for an 'Audie' Award as Audiobook of the Year!

When I got an offer to create audio versions of the Ascendant series, I was told the narrator would be Tim Gerard Reynolds. My reaction was "You mean some other guy named Tim Gerard Reynolds? Not the TGR who narrated the Red Rising audiobooks, right?"

Clearly, I have been very fortunate with narrators for my audiobooks. To be clear, they chose to work with me, I did not 'choose' them. If I had contacted Bob or Tim directly, I would have gone into super fan-boy mode and they would have filed for a restraining order. So, again, I am lucky they signed onto the projects.

So far, there is no deal for Expeditionary Force to become a movie or TV show, although I have had inquiries from producers and studios about the 'entertainment rights'. From what people in the industry have told me, even if a studio or network options the rights, it will be a loooooooooong time before anything actually happens. I will get all excited for nothing, and years will go by with the project going through endless cycles with producers and directors coming aboard and disappearing, and just when I have totally given up and sunk into the Pit of Despair, a miracle will happen and the project gets financing! Whoo-hoo. I am not counting on it. On the other hand, Disney is pulling their content off Netflix next year, so Netflix will be looking for new original content...

Again, Thank YOU for reading one of my books. Writing gives me a great excuse to avoid cleaning out the garage.

Contact the author at craigalanson@gmail.com
https://www.facebook.com/Craig.Alanson.Author/
https://twitter.com/CraigAlanson?lang=en

Go to craigalanson.com for blogs and ExForce logo merchandise including T-shirts, patches, stickers, hats, and coffee mugs